I0779141

The
Golf Mystic

Shifting the Paradigm

Gary Battersby

Published in the United States of America by Golf Mystic Publishers.

3909 Indian River Dr., Cocoa, Florida 32926

954-868-5545

www.golfmystic.net

ISBN 978-0-615-47829-6

Editor: Donna Dawson, CPE

Printed in USA

GB

To my parents,
who sacrificed their time and worked tirelessly to provide
six children opportunities that they never had.

Acknowledgments

Many thanks to all my friends who took the time to read the manuscript and make helpful suggestions, especially Kay Erlanson, who got me started; Kaysie Usher and Tristan Boyd, who took on the tedious task of transferring my handwritten notes to computer; Len Golub, who enlisted Nancy Popick in the first edit; Sari Mathes for her editing and insightful creative suggestions; Kim Martin for formatting the book; Harold Wine for his encouragement and support; Terry Miller for his candid observations, suggestions, and last push to finish the manuscript; and lastly my loving wife, Ali, for her unending support in this project and all areas of my life.

Foreword
by Bob Toski

When Gary asked me to write the foreword to *The Golf Mystic*, I readily agreed. Little did I know what a challenging task I had accepted. I had not yet read the work. As I began reading the manuscript and reached deeper into it, I soon realized I was hardly prepared to write it. However, after taking the time to absorb all the material Gary presents and some long thought, I felt that I could acknowledge the tremendous insight and philosophical thinking described in this book about golf, the golf swing, and life. Indeed, Gary is reaching out with a message about his ongoing journey in life through golf.

I know one cannot standardize the art of teaching the golf swing, but this book gives some serious thought on how to improve the teaching and learning of this great game. I hope and believe this work will create a much-needed paradigm shift in golf instruction. *The Golf Mystic* will captivate you. I found the conversations throughout the book wonderfully intriguing, as they related to golf and life. I consider this book an immense achievement. It is hard to imagine the time and effort it took to produce this unique work for both learning and reading pleasure.

For me, there are not enough words to describe the beauty of Gary's writing. One should read it more than once to grasp the depth of thought and insight. My thanks, congratulations, and sincere best wishes to Gary for writing *The Golf Mystic*.

3/17/2011

Contents

INTRODUCTION

This story had to be written. That belief is based on my experience of a life in golf. I began caddying at the age of eight, first at Grosse Isle Country Club in Michigan, then at the Sharon Golf Club in Ohio, and finally at Congressional CC in Potomac, Maryland. I caddied for the best players and observed as many talented golfers as I could.

As time passed, I began working at these courses in every capacity. I cleaned clubs, worked the range, and washed dishes for parties. I was on the golf maintenance crew, where I began working at the bottom rung of the ladder. With my brother Alan, I weeded flower beds, tees, and greens.

We had the good fortune at these clubs to have fine skilled leaders with integrity, leaders who had great patience with our lack of experience. As time went on Alan left golf, but I stayed. I learned to maintain machinery and grow healthy turf. At the same time I took advantage of the employee privileges that allowed me to practice my game.

Years later, with the help of several friends and my partner, Bob Toski, I developed the first Golf Learning Center in the United States at Broward College in Coconut Creek, Florida. We started from scratch and did almost everything ourselves. We had to clear the land; shape the tees, greens, and bunkers; dig irrigation; grow turf; and plant trees. All the while my mind was preoccupied with developing better ways to teach and communicate about the golf swing. I kept practicing and teaching. My teaching continues to evolve, but now taking center stage in my work are the many relationships that have developed because of this great game. I treasure these friendships beyond measure.

Over the years, there has hardly been a moment when golf was not on my mind and in my heart. This game, and the golf swing itself, has brought intrigue, wonder, sorrow, and joy to my life. In recent years, however, I have disagreed with the direction in which the game has been heading, especially golf swing instruction. I am skeptical about some of those who have been chosen to lead the game. I believe the majority of golfers deserve better than they are getting. Thus, the need to write this book.

Rather than writing a typical golf instruction book, I wanted to create something unique in style and content. Because I have witnessed such struggle and frustration at every level, I also wanted to provide the tools needed for golfers to improve. And I hope to entertain the reader a little along the way.

I would love everyone to know that within them they hold unique potential and that there is a way to draw it out without spending a fortune and a lifetime on the practice tee! The goal of this book is to encourage golfers to begin thinking usefully on their own and trusting their instincts so they can ultimately enjoy the game like never before. My method begins with developing enough awareness and confidence to feel safe and carefree with one's swing. It culminates when a golfer looks forward to getting out on the course and playing the game to their potential.

I believe golf mirrors life in the emotions, the learning, the sport of it, and the relationships it fosters. In keeping with those ideas, this narrative provides a window into the heart and mind of a golfer who has lost his way, both in his professional life and his personal relationships. During his journey, the golfer begins to transform, with the help of a seasoned mentor who had experienced similar struggles. He provides strategies that awaken and free our golfer from his self-created failure. But ultimately, deep and profound change is always a choice, and the decision is in the hands of the decider.

Freedom and peace of mind are probably two of the most sought-after quality of life goals. Golf has the potential to elicit great feelings of freedom. We play the game outdoors all over the world on beautiful natural terrain. This is one of the most appealing aspects of the game. Whether we're walking nine holes at the local 'muni' after work or playing for a national championship, golf has the potential to provide limitless feelings of freedom, achievement, sorrow, gratitude, struggle, and joy. Every emotion conceivable will manifest itself at one time or another if you play the game long enough.

Golf encompasses so much of what makes us human and so much of what makes life worthwhile. We must not lose this perspective, no matter why we play the game. I hope that in reading this story you catch a glimpse of yourself and learn something. If readers can smile, chuckle, or shake their heads in amusement, I have in some small way been successful.

PART ONE

1

REMINISCING

Curled under the blankets, trying to stay warm, I anxiously waited for the alarm to go off. I had given up trying to sleep hours before. Every ten minutes or so, my eyes would open and squint at the red numbers on the clock radio, willing them to tell me it was five AM I had an early flight to catch.

It had been bitter cold, the kind of brutal New England winter when your feet dread the morning floor and the shower can't steam up fast enough. I was happy to be getting away from the dark days and grimy slush for even a little while. I pushed myself out of bed. The smiling TV weatherwoman was forecasting a Nor'easter, but her sadistic grin held no power over me. I would soon be in the tropical land of Bermuda grass, sand, and sunshine. In no time, I was dressed, packed, and waiting by the front window for my ride. Before long, the cabbie pulled up and flashed his lights. I locked up and was on my way.

The cabbie was obviously an expatriate from an equatorial country: heat wafted through the partition as we headed for the airport. Fifteen minutes later, he handed over my bags and took my money with fingerless gloves, hustling back into his four-wheeled furnace before either of us could utter a thank you.

I checked my luggage and went through the usual security rigmarole. I grabbed a *Boston Herald* and stood on yet another line to board.

Eventually, I was on the plane and belted into my seat. But we sat for a good thirty minutes with no movement. A flight attendant finally explained that we were waiting for de-icing. I wondered if the plane was going to get off the ground before the storm hit. I turned to the sports section, but my attention wandered.

This journey was essential—it was when I would either realize my quest or abandon it. Claire had accused me of running away from her and from reality. I hadn't been able to make her understand that this trip wasn't about fleeing because I hadn't been able to make it clear to her, or myself, exactly what I was pursuing.

Could I find him? Would he agree to work with me? Would I be able to learn from him? Could he change my golf teaching philosophy and help me find my groove? Would my dream come true or was I in search of the Holy Golf Grail?

A family of four occupied the three seats directly in front of me. Nice, I thought, a winter vacation in sunny Florida, family-style. However, the two boys were chattering at high pitch, squawking for their parents' permission to order Cokes. I shuddered to think how they'd sound after a dose of caffeine. It was barely breakfast time and they were already marching their dirty little boots up the backs of the seats in front of them. It amazes me when parents think their little darlings are the entertainment crew and that when the kids are performing, the parents are off duty. Dad let his seatback down and cracked my kneecaps.

Beside me, in the aisle seat, was a middle-aged woman who seemed to think she owned the whole row, including the entire overhead compartment. One of her bulging carry-on bags wouldn't fit in the compartment, so she crammed it under the seat—in front of me. Patience was never my strong point. "This is the last time I fly," I muttered, not caring if my neighbors heard the irritation in my voice.

But I knew it probably wasn't being crammed, sardine-style, into the middle seat in coach, these people, or the tedious airline procedures that were the real sources of my frustration. Confusion and negativity had dominated my emotional weather for more than a season. God knows there was a lesson for me here. The few mortals who remained in my life had advised me that my state of mind needed adjusting. Besides my golf game being in the gutter, my relationship with Claire had just ended.

Claire. She was beautiful, clichés be damned, both inside and out. She was smart. No, she was wise. She had the kind of common wisdom that you'd expect from someone older, someone who had had a lot of experience riding life's roller coaster. She was a serious woman in every sense of the word. Wearing one of my old flannels, she could pass for a teenager, but in a dress, Claire defined 'woman.' Big hazel eyes, high cheekbones, golden skin, and hair the color of chestnuts in autumn. But gorgeous as she was, Claire didn't seem to know it.

Claire, my most difficult student. Serious and literal, she took her lack of golf skill in stride. Her lessons began as a Christmas gift from her fiancé, meant to convince her she wouldn't become a golf widow after the wedding. Jason accompanied her to her lessons, although his ability on the golf course was exceptional. He wanted immediate results, but Claire seemed hopeless. She'd roll her eyes and toss her bangs to the side with every missed shot, tension ricocheting between her and Jason.

I tried to make light of it, to break the tension, but Jason's interest in Claire diminished with her lack of progress. By Easter, there wasn't much to mask his derision and her disdain. At a Mothers' Day outing with Jason's parents, Claire handled herself with dignity when Jason's mother, a matronly golf queen, deadpanned that he shouldn't want her for a caddy, much less a wife. Jason apparently agreed. By Memorial Day, she was coming for her lessons alone.

It took a while, but when I finally got up the nerve to ask her out for coffee after a lesson, we followed up Starbuck's with burgers at a local dive. I took her to a comedy film festival for our first real date, and by Labor Day, we were an item.

Claire was a little older than me, but that only seemed to make her more fragile. Jason, among others, had eroded her trust. And she had seen things as a nurse, and later as a social worker, that had opened her eyes to the darker side of human nature. She wore a serious demeanor like battle armor. If my mission was to make her laugh, hers was to make an adult of me. She indulged my taste for the Three Stooges, Fletch, and Britcoms, while I humored her by sitting through *Gone with the Wind* and countless Cary Grant movies. We both loved romantic comedies, but saved them for the rain.

We learned to cook together and mastered the art of the perfect burger. That was at the beginning, when everything was perfect. Then, with my game spiraling downward, my golf practice consumed my time. She complained that I was emotionally unavailable, whatever that meant, and it caught me completely off guard. I got defensive. Didn't she understand that I was making a last-ditch effort to get my career on track? She couldn't seem to accept the time and commitment my career required, just as I was surprised to hear that our relationship needed more of those same things.

I thought she would be the one, but the timing was obviously off. She wanted serious commitment, while I was content to enjoy the pre-honeymoon of our getting to know each other better while I dealt with the really important stuff in my world, like my golf game. Yeah, I was head over heels for Claire, but I figured she should just know how I felt and trust we'd have a future together. Somehow it all fell apart before I could tell her.

Sitting there on the runway, reminiscing, I knew I needed to be more positive if I was going to get anything of value from the next few days. I felt broken and depressed about practically everything in my life, especially how things had ended with Claire. Somehow, contemplating how this trip had come together, I managed to lie back in my seat and close my eyes. I fell into a semi-conscious state.

My mind drifted over the whirlwind of events this past weekend—the golf summit in New Orleans, back to Boston for an overnight, catching this flight to Ft. Lauderdale, and all the little coincidences that had led me to this seat on this plane.

My teaching had provided me with a decent income. I was a popular instructor and many golfers sought me out. My reputation, built on a great eye for finding flaws in a golf swing, was something I prided myself on. It made me feel good, and I had made a career of it. But deep down I felt something was missing. Lately I had been dissatisfied with the direction my career was taking. The depth of my boredom was quite evident when I'd recently found myself watching the clock during lessons, wishing they would end. My teaching had become listless.

It was embarrassing for me, a teaching golf pro, to admit I really wasn't interested in my students' problems, at least not as much as my own. To be completely honest, I didn't believe I was good at teaching or at playing the game. I had pretended for a long time, concealing these sentiments, until I could no longer bear the feeling of being an imposter. I had to either get out of the game completely or change the course I was following.

What became painfully obvious, though, was that hard as I tried, I could not change on my own. I had tried all kinds of ways to get interested again, to bolster my confidence, but nothing seemed to last. Just when I'd think I was making progress, reality would set in and I'd be back at square one.

Then one day I was checking out the program for the National Golf Teachers Symposium, a sort of summit meeting of the so-called best golf teachers in America. This year it was in New Orleans. Though I had decided to boycott these events just a year earlier, this one was different: I had long before accepted an invitation to speak at the symposium. But there was a problem now. Me. I just wasn't into it. Sure, I could go through the motions of giving a presentation, but I was unlikely to get anything out of the other sessions.

On top of that, these meetings usually become major social events. I'm not a great socializer to begin with; after Claire, I was feeling pretty anti-social. Partying did not appeal to me. I would be better off not attending. I had more serious matters to tend to. I needed to break my golf roadblock. My instruction was stale and going nowhere fast, but I didn't know how to stop it.

But then something changed my mind. Just as I was about to pick up the phone and cancel my appearance, my eyes had fallen on the list of speakers. Just below my name was another that caught my eye—and piqued my curiosity: Joe Burlington.

Burlington had a sort of mystical allure in golf circles. If he were in politics, he would be considered a fringe element. He was deliberately and proudly different. He wasn't cast in the mainstream golf teacher mold. Some people derisively called him a rebel; others held him as a guru. I was surprised he was speaking at the summit at all. I knew Burlington's approach to teaching was radically different from mine and fundamentally different from everything popular in golf, from the traditional school to the currently accepted state of the art. But maybe a dose of Joe Burlington's far-fetched, off-the-wall philosophy was exactly what I needed.

I had heard bits of gossip about him over the years from other pros, but Burlington's name did not really come up very often. He had almost disappeared some ten years before; as far as I knew, he wasn't even teaching anymore. Despite his unorthodox style, I had heard some wonderful things about his teaching. I guess one could say Joe Burlington was a bit of a golfing legend. Talk was that he had a gift—he could always get the most from the least. Curious golf teachers from all over would come to watch him work. Some became fans, others critics.

Burlington's communication skills and ability to flight a golf ball were uncontested, but it was the way he used his various interests and hobbies to engage his students' learning that was controversial. Teachers who had worked with him praised him to the heavens. They said you had to experience Joe Burlington personally to have any idea of how special he was. "There isn't a teacher alive with more talent, awareness, and compassion than Joe Burlington," one of my golf teaching heroes told me. Burlington's critics found his offbeat persona entertaining fodder for jokes.

If I could arrange to meet him at the summit and discuss my problems with him, maybe he could give me a strategy that would extricate me from some of my problems. I figured his would at least be a different approach, and I needed *something* to shock me out of my inertia.

I was going to the symposium after all. I would take the opportunity to seek him out, with the hope that he could turn my game around, give me some magic. The sudden clarity of my decision surprised me. It was not a decision based on logic. It was born of desperation—in my mind, Burlington was my eleventh-hour effort before I threw in the golf towel for good. I would be totally honest with him and hold nothing back—no more masks, no more pretending. I'd just let it all hang out and see what came of it.

I had arrived in New Orleans the night before the summit and planned to attend Joe's talk, which was right after mine. I thought I'd introduce myself backstage and take it from there.

I had presented my session rather robotically, just going through the motions, and answered questions on autopilot. Nothing I said was new, but thankfully my talk seemed well received. I was distracted by my real reason for being there.

Anxious to get to a good seat for Burlington's session, I had hurried from the hall where I had given my talk. I made my way quickly around the oval building to the larger theater where Burlington was to speak. I arrived early—the doors hadn't opened yet. I took a seat outside and waited. The sign near the door read,

Speaker: Joe Burlington,
Topic: The Future of Golf Instruction

Interesting title, I thought. A few other pros were gathering around the entrance. When the locks turned and the doors creaked open, I raced inside to get a seat close to the stage. Within minutes, many people had filed into the hall.

The stage was set with only a solitary chair and a small table holding a glass of water. The simplicity contrasted with the atmosphere of most golf seminars. Normally stages were filled with chalkboards, props, electronic devices, and video screens. Presenters were essentially selling the latest gadgets—all the newest instruction accessories and devices. Burlington's setup seemed bare and incomplete.

I was psyched for Joe's arrival. The packed hall was noisy—everyone was chattering in anticipation of what the enigmatic golfer would have to say. The lights finally dimmed and the room fell silent. Onto the stage strode Joe Burlington. Tall and slender, but with a sinewy, muscular build, he had a crop of reddish-brown hair and a coppery tone to his face. The Florida sun had taken its toll. Burlington had distinctive features: high cheekbones, a prominent jaw, and deep lines across his forehead. His arms were long and well-defined, his hands massive. He wore a yellow knit shirt, khaki slacks, and moccasins with no socks. Joe Burlington definitely did not dress the part of a typical golf pro. He appeared confident. The audience began to applaud with what seemed a warm greeting. When the noise quieted, he had walked slowly to the front of the stage, looked into the audience, and begun.

"Thank you all for coming. I am delighted to have been invited to share with you tonight. I'm Joe Burlington, and it's been a long while since I've done anything like this." He paused, squinted up at the spotlights, and continued. "Well, let's get right to it. I'm here to talk about the future of golf instruction. The popularity of the game is flourishing throughout the world. Golfing has grown up." His voice boomed.

"Tonight I'd like to limit the discussion to how we approach instruction of swinging the club as it relates to the multitude of people who we now serve, our students. Secondly, it behooves us, as golf professionals, to examine the direction our teaching is headed, don't you think? I'd like to ask everyone to think about these questions for a minute."

Burlington paused and then fired his ammo. "Why did we all choose this profession? Are our instruction techniques really working? Are we making a positive impact or are we confusing our students? Are we actually moving in a better direction? Are we really serving our public well?"

He took a moment to let his audience absorb his buckshot questions. Immediately there seemed to be growing discomfort in the room. The air had changed. No one expected this stinging demand for self-examination. We were all used to feel-good, ego-stroking seminars that praised our efforts—pep rallies for the status quo. The pro sitting next to me had muttered, "Who does he think he is?"

But my God, we all should know these questions need to be asked. Agreeing with Joe Burlington appeared put me deep in the minority, though. The pros had been waiting for the jokes and small talk that usually warm up the audience; they weren't ready for Burlington's serious questions and obvious passion.

A pro near the front had raised his hand, and Joe sat down on the chair and gave him the floor. "Since we already seem to be getting deep into teaching philosophy, Mr. Burlington, what do you consider the most important aspect of learning a golf swing? What do you think is essential?" I had recognized this pro, but couldn't put a name to his face. He didn't look happy. I thought it was possible he was trying to trip Burlington up.

Burlington had been silent for a moment, then stood up. The whispering stopped; the hall was still. He had walked along the front of the stage, looking up to the lights again, and as he turned his eyes back downward, he stopped directly in front of the pro who had spoken and offered a pleasant smile. "A very good question. To really get down to the bare bones, the essentials, as you say, the only thing a golfer needs to do is create an environment of swing motion for release."

The pro had pursed his lips, but his eyes registered comprehension. He smiled back at Burlington with a nod of approval. Wow, I thought, Joe's answer immediately disarmed that pro. Whether the pro had meant to provoke an argument or not, Burlington had just described the essence of the whole golf swing in a single sentence. He had delivered, wrapped with a bow, what I considered the golf swing's Holy Grail.

But the pro hadn't finished with Burlington. "Could you clarify release?" He stressed each syllable of the last word as if they were separate words.

Without hesitation, Burlington had responded, "Release of the club's energy into the ball to the desired target."

"Then what do you mean by an environment of swing motion?"

"An environment of swing motion is a particular swing rhythm and path pattern that provides for the release. The key is that they are repeatable and, in my view, completely compatible with momentum and centrifugal force."

The front rows had remained quiet. Many of us had never heard such a complete, yet succinct, explanation of the essence of the swing. A few pros in the back, though, had begun to murmur among themselves. They didn't seem to want to be questioned.

"Any more questions before I continue?" Burlington had asked. No one moved. Then Burlington had asked another question. "Why is it that with all the advanced technology, instruction gadgets, video analysis, and special clubs, today's golfers, on average, are poorer players than they were years ago? Have any of you ever wondered?"

It was as if Burlington had bent down, put his hand upon my crown, screwed open my head, and snatched the thoughts right out of my mind. The audience had begun buzzing, but not from curiosity like I was. An undercurrent of displeasure and derision had become apparent in the whispers. Burlington waited and began again only after giving that part of the audience time to load and take aim.

"You see," he'd continued, "one problem is that we're losing creativity in our approach. We've signed on to one cookie-cutter way to impart our experience and it's in direct conflict with the way individuals learn. I believe we really must get on the wavelength of our students, meet them at the point where they are in their development, and then just nudge them in the best direction. As we teach, it's important to awaken students and show them how to use their tools of awareness."

Another pro in front had raised his hand. Joe graciously paused and acknowledged him. "Question?"

"I just wanted to know if your program gives students a roadmap to help them get where they're going."

Burlington had contemplated the question. Speaking in a low voice, almost to himself, he said, "How can I put this? Socrates said that our job as teachers is to help sharpen our students' sense of direction so that when they really get going and are on their own, they can travel without a map. Fellas," he'd said, "and ladies, the truth is that the most successful learning experience will leave the student confident and with no need for a coach anymore. Yes," he'd mused, "really, the goal for us as instructors is to become obsolete."

I could tell folks were really getting uncomfortable now. Over the rumbling, I had heard some comments. The consensus was that this philosophy would put us all out of work.

Burlington had continued. "From all I've heard recently, we're headed in the direction of trying to clone golfers, make them all the same, and teach them all the same. With the new technology and all, we have deluded ourselves into believing that there's no room for uniqueness." He had put his foot on the chair and leaned into the audience. "You see, I diametrically oppose that point of view. Each person is unique. It is our job to enter each student's own world and view it from their perspective. And then use all of a student's individual strengths to help him improve. I have found that if you approach instruction this way, it is likely that you will reduce inner and outer conflict. The student's mind and body will be more receptive. You will find that his or her potential will emerge and, more importantly, it will be sustainable.

"And just maybe, all these gadgets and theories are not really helping. Maybe they're just confusing the issue. I believe we need to completely revamp our approach."

A pro in the front row spoke up. "And what do you propose?"

Burlington hadn't answered immediately. He'd nodded slowly before speaking. "I believe we need a complete paradigm shift."

"What does that mean?" the pro had asked.

Burlington had walked back and forth across the front of the stage, pondering. Then he came to a dead stop and pivoted toward the audience. He smiled as though he had just had an a-ha moment. He spread his arms wide. "The whole creates the parts; in other words, the behavior of the parts of a swing comes from knowing the whole swing."[1] He brought his hands together, matching his words. "That's it. That's the paradigm shift." Judging by the satisfied look on his face, he seemed to think he was getting somewhere. Little did he know the agenda of the majority. I really hadn't understood his answer. A paradigm shift? How could the whole create the parts?

As Burlington took a sip of water, I had heard some snickering. To my surprise, I heard the doors at the back of the room open. More people started to stand up. The doors slammed shut, then opened again. The exodus had begun. To my right, one of the young teachers had looked at me and asked under his breath, "Who the hell is this guy?" I didn't respond. "What success has he had?" he mocked, louder. "If we're teaching for the right reasons, we should become obsolete? Paradigm shift—is he nuts?"

Burlington had heard the end of the pro's comment as he moved across the stage toward us. Playfully, he asked the guy to elaborate. Without hesitation, the pro reiterated his opinion. "Mr. Burlington, with all due respect, we don't need to be told how to teach or even be told to look at what the future might bring. We're already successful. We've gone from the caddy shack to five-star hotels and teaching on television."

Burlington had nodded in agreement about the change in status of golf pros over the past thirty years. But I knew that wasn't his point. Burlington went back and sat down, facing us, his elbows on the table. Waiting in silence, he sipped his water and peered first at the young pro and then into the remaining audience. As he'd scanned the room from back to front, he'd seemed to be taking in what was left of the audience. He'd seemed to be looking deeply into each of us with a look of sadness, but no trace of anger. He was clearly not intimidated.

He had answered the young pro quietly. "One should be careful how one defines success." His voice increased in volume as he continued. "Taking a hard, honest look forces us to examine and evaluate. It gives us an opportunity to improve our present condition. It's OK to disagree with me. When I'm finished, I will gladly answer any more questions you may have."

But then another pro had begun speaking without waiting to be called upon. Courtesy was no longer part of this gathering. "Can't you be more specific with this paradigm shift thing? I could never teach without my video camera!"

Burlington had fired away, describing three more major differences in his approach. "Since you're using video, I assume you believe in parts, position, and analysis." The pro had nodded. "When it comes to developing a swing, I believe in wholes, patterns, and feel. We are on opposite sides of the spectrum. That doesn't make me right and you wrong, we are just very different. So a discussion is in order, wouldn't you say?" The pro sat down and turned his face away. Negative emotions were running high.

Very few of us were still there to listen. Even Burlington's logic and conciliatory tone couldn't create a positive atmosphere. More of the remaining people had filed out. Burlington, to my surprise, had raised his hands as if to say, OK, I tried. I thought, no, don't stop now, but there was just too much resistance. The hall had gone from standing room only to being less than half full. I was sure he felt disrespected; it would be difficult to misinterpret the almost hostile energy.

He had started to apologize to those still sitting quietly. "Maybe some folks aren't ready for..." but his voice trailed off. Then he placed the glass of water back on the table and left the stage. The hall had emptied in seconds. I had heard the remarks of some of the younger fellows: "Who *is* this guy?" "What a waste of time!"

Even so, there were a few in the crowd who seemed to be thinking along my line. They had walked out more slowly. I shook my head. I thought I could really use some of Burlington's experience. I had gone into the game for something more than material gain, not just to raise my standard of living. I wanted to help others improve their game and I wanted to be an example of what he was talking about. I wanted to be able to *do* what I taught, too. I sat there stunned and disappointed. I already admired Joe Burlington. His message was clear and he was fearless in speaking his mind: Be creative, be different, be effective, and seek true success. I really needed to meet him. I urgently had to talk with him. Maybe this is *the* guy.

I couldn't believe what I had just witnessed. What was I to do? I couldn't just sit there and watch what seemed like my last hope vanish. I needed to make my move if I was ever going to meet Joe Burlington.

I had rushed backstage and asked a stagehand where Burlington had gone. He nodded toward an exit at the end of the hall. I was almost at a full run as I slammed the crossbar of the emergency exit with both hands. My heart was pounding. I felt like the walls of my chest couldn't contain the pressure building up within me.

Adrenaline surging through my arteries, I knew I could catch him, but which way to go? One thought kept cycling through my brain: This is your chance, there is no other chance; this is your chance, there is no other chance. I'd let my instincts take over and turned left down St. Louis Street, toward the hotel district of the French quarter.

There were people everywhere. As I'd moved steadily forward, weaving my way through the crowd, I'd scanned both sides of the street. There! Just half a block ahead of me I thought I caught sight of him. Tall; yellow shirt, khakis, moccasins. There couldn't be two of them. He was getting into a cab.

I'd screamed out his name but my voice was drowned out by the noise of the street. He did pause and look around, as though he had felt something, but then ducked into the cab and was gone. I'd tried to yell again but the air escaping my lungs arrived on my lips voiceless.

Relax, I commanded myself, take a deep breath, get ahold of yourself. He's gone, but he's not dead. I just need to get to South Florida. But I don't have my clubs and my flight back to Boston leaves in a couple of hours.

I'd figured I could get back to Boston, collect my stuff, and catch an early flight to Ft. Lauderdale. I could probably look Burlington up on the Internet, give him a call, and arrange a one-on-one. I knew he had taught at a driving range on a college campus at one time. How many of those could there be? All I really had to do was make sure I was on that plane in plenty of time. I walked back to my hotel, collected my stuff, and checked out. Soon I was on my way to the airport.

After checking in, I still had plenty of time before the flight, so I'd gotten out my laptop and tried Googling "Joe Burlington, South Florida." The search came up empty. I should have known—he's not on the Internet. He's from a completely different time and place and has a whole different way of thinking. Probably doesn't even own a computer. I'd have to try to reach him when I got there.

The flight to Boston had gone smoothly. Before I left the airport, I'd booked the first flight out to Ft. Lauderdale the next morning.

I still had some big problems: I had no appointment with Burlington and no place to stay. But my mind had gone into high gear. When I got home, I'd called my friends the Pedersens, who ran a little bed and breakfast on the beach in Pompano. Claire and I used to stay there whenever we visited South Florida. Mrs. Pedersen explained that they really weren't open for the season yet and wouldn't be there, but if I didn't mind self-service I was welcome. She cheerfully said she'd give us our usual room. She couldn't know Claire and I had broken up and it was too complicated to tell her now.

Plan B was working. I'd go down to Florida and ask around. Someone had to have heard of Joe Burlington at one of the local munis. Was this magical thinking? Had I lost touch with reality? Claire had accused me of impulsive, compulsive, and every other pulsive behavior they dissect in therapy. I would call her when I knew she would be out, leave a message about my plan, and that's that. I didn't want to be talked out of it. This was my chance; there was no other chance.

That thought became my mantra and volleyed back and forth in my mind with the doubts. What if he wouldn't see me or didn't have time? Could I pull this off? This is my chance; there is no other chance.

Just then a tap on my shoulder from the flight attendant awakened me from my daze: We would be landing in Ft. Lauderdale soon and could I please raise my seatback, etcetera. I couldn't believe I'd been in a semi-conscious dream-state of recollection through the whole flight.

The captain announced that it was sunny and fifty degrees warmer than the Boston winter I had left. I rented a car and made my way north on I-95.

The B&B was nice—a typical Florida two-story home from the sixties, white brick with yellow trim, a tile roof, and a wrap-around porch. It always amazed me how bright things were in Florida at this time of year. There is so much color and life, while up north, everything is gray and barren. I strode up the front walk and found the keys under the planter, just as Mrs. Pedersen had said, and let myself in. The front room opened up to a beautiful view of the dunes and the ocean just beyond. It was as blue as the sky, with hints of deeper turquoise. Visions of Claire and I on the beach washed through my mind, leaving me with an empty feeling in my gut and an ache in my chest. I couldn't accept that she wasn't in my life anymore.

I found a note on the kitchen table welcoming me and giving me a few details about the house. I took my bag up to my room and unpacked. I wanted to be ready to get going early in the morning. The room had two dormers overlooking the ocean.

I opened the windows and let the sea sounds lull me back to another time. I thought of calling Claire, but didn't know what to say. Memories intruded—us sharing this spot, walking the beach, swimming in the sea, and making love in between. The warm twilight breeze made me miss her.

Determined to block those thoughts, I lay down on the bed and went through a mental checklist of my plans for tomorrow. I decided to skip dinner and fell asleep early.

I got up later than I had intended, showered, got dressed and walked down to my favorite local diner. It was owned and operated by a guy named Lou, a former commercial fisherman turned sport fishing guide turned short-order cook.

Lou was a down-to-earth guy and I always enjoyed shooting the breeze with him. He had been through life's school of hard knocks, working most of his life on the water, and he looked it too. We had gotten to know each other fairly well with my annual visits and had become good friends. He always had hot coffee, great bacon, and fresh bread from the bakery next door.

I picked up a newspaper and headed inside. Lou wasn't here today—probably fishing, I guessed. I opened the paper to the sports page, where there were ads for golf courses. Pompano Beach Municipal was a short ride up Federal Highway.

At the course, I found the parking lot full. Must be a tournament today. I parked, got my clubs out of the trunk, and headed to the practice putting green. The first tee was full, with about ten golf carts lined up. There were several guys putting. The course was adjacent to Pompano Airport and I watched small planes practicing touch and goes. It was refreshing not to see houses or condos, just thirty-six holes and a clubhouse. Even though the condition looked a little rough, the course had character.

I put down my bag next to the green and got out my putter and three balls to get a feel for the Bermuda grass. At the far side of the green I noticed three guys having a match. I tried a few putts, waited till they finished, and went over to them. "Excuse me, I'm not from around here and I'm trying to locate a local pro. Was wondering if any of you knew of him."

"What's his name?"

"Joe Burlington."

They looked at me funny, and all three answered in unison. "Joe Burlington." The oldest-looking one took over for the group and offered, "He's already teed off. Probably on the third hole by now. Sometimes he plays in our weekly skins game. Usually wins too. If you wait around maybe you can catch him. Are you a golf pro?"

"Why, yes."

"We have room for one more. Do you want to play with us?" the spokesman asked.

"Well, I don't know. I've just arrived from Boston and haven't played since last fall. I'm not sure you would want me today."

"Come on, you can't hurt us. We'll even pick up your greens fee."

"No, really, I was just looking to speak to Mr. Burlington."

"Well, you can't speak to him now, so why not join us and I'll introduce you after the round. He'll be at the bar having a cold beer; you won't miss him."

I gave them a shrug and decided it was fated. "OK. When do we tee off?"

"In a couple minutes."

"I need to hit some practice balls."

"No time for that now, brogie. Just do like Joe; he never warms up. Besides, it's just skins. If you can make a few birdies or an eagle, we'll have a great day. And maybe take some of Joe's money."

I wasn't comfortable with this arrangement, but went to the side of the green to get my clubs and headed for the first tee. Tim, the spokesman, introduced me to Jake and Will. "Geoff," I replied, to introduce myself. Soon our turn came and they nodded me the honor; they were going to play from the regular tees; I had to play back. The first hole was a short par four so I drew my three wood from the bag, made a couple of practice swings, and slammed it down the middle. Not bad for not warming up.

The three older guys teed off, all with their own peculiar style, but nailed the balls a good distance down the middle. Everyone had a short iron to the green. They each, without hesitation, landed their shots on the green not too far from the hole. When I reached my ball, I needed only a short wedge. I hate these half shots. I took a couple practice swings and proceeded to fat the shot into the front bunker. My reaction was to slam the toe of the club into the ground in disgust. I pulled hard and got the club out of the turf and slammed it into my bag.

Great. Here we go again. I was angry and embarrassed. In front of three amateurs, with an easy shot like that I couldn't even hit the green. I called myself stupid and muttered my displeasure all the way to the greenside bunker. The three of them pretended not to watch out of standard golfer's courtesy. But I knew what they were thinking: What kind of pro is this? Having not lost my turn I took my wedge into the bunker. Great, a buried lie. I closed the face and took a wicked lash at it. The ball came out and scooted across the green. I was still away, took my putter and holed it from thirty feet.

The guys applauded, but I could hardly smile considering the way I had played the hole. What a lousy par. The embarrassing half wedge on the first hole lingered in my mind for several holes, taking its toll on my whole game.

We continued to play at a good pace through the first nine holes. Once a player was out of the hole, he would just pick up. As we made the turn my mind was getting cluttered. Which swing would I use to just get through the day and save face? I was inconsistent throughout that first nine, which was what frustrated me so about this game. I never knew what was going to happen. I tried to avoid my driver, too. After a couple of blocks sailed out of play to the right on the front nine, I knew my driver and I were definitely not friends today. I managed to scramble for a couple more pars on the front nine, but never scored a birdie. I knew these guys thought they'd wasted their money with me on their skins team but at least we weren't waiting on every shot. That would have been the last straw for me.

On the eleventh hole, Tim approached me. We were stalled by two groups waiting to play a long par three over water. He could tell I was frustrated. I had taken a seat on the bench next to the tee. "So you're here to see Joe Burlington?"

"Yes." I shook my head, looking down at my three iron. "Well, I don't actually have an appointment—I was hoping to get one. I came down here on a whim, just hoping to get some time with him. I saw him in New Orleans speaking at the teaching summit."

"Oh, we heard about that. Some spectacle, I understand."

"Yes—I've never seen anything quite like it." I paused and then asked, "How well do you know Joe Burlington?"

"Quite well, but mostly as an observer. I've watched him teach a lot over the years. His whole demeanor fascinates me, but that's just me."

"Have you ever had a lesson from Joe?"

"Well, yes."

"Do you still work with him?"

"No."

"Why not?" I asked, a little surprised by Tim's answer.

"Don't get me wrong: I don't take lessons from anyone anymore 'cause I don't need 'em."

"What do you mean?"

"I learned what I had to watching him give lessons to others and taking that one lesson myself. Joe doesn't believe in giving a person a lot of lessons. Once you know yourself and your swing, you just keep working on the principles he teaches."

"What did he do for you? Or for the people you've seen him give lessons to?"

"Let's see...how can I put this? He gets everyone to find the patterns of the club, and then has you identify how it feels, and then you are off on your own. He really gets you to know yourself. Knocks out all the conflict."

"How did he help you with your swing?"

"Before Joe, I had worked with a lot of teachers; they all thought I had a chronic problem not shifting my lower body in my swing."

"You didn't?"

"Well, I did, and I didn't."

"What do you mean?"

"I tried with all my other teachers to shift," Tim explained. "It was obvious that I needed to, and video showed it clearly. But every time I tried to shift, everything would go haywire. My swing would become completely discombobulated. I was at my wits' end, and even though I'd heard he was rather eccentric, I decided to give him a call."

"What did Joe do?"

"You might not believe it, but he really didn't do anything with my swing directly, except for teaching me his release trigger, which he calls 'the curl.'" I pretended like I'd heard of it and motioned for Tim to continue. "Well, he pulled out one of his foam Pathfinders, pieces of foam that could be bent any way to help a golfer see and adjust his swing path or any impact dynamic. The foam tubes replaced the old three-foot two-by-fours teachers used to use." I still used the wood and my students feared it—golfers could really wrench their hands if they hit the wood with a club as it approached impact.

Tim continued. "Joe explained that the foam provides a visual boundary so the golfer wouldn't swing the club outside the target line. He said when these flexible boundaries are set on the ground, the mind unconsciously takes care of the path and the golfer can singularly focus on the timing of the release, the angle of attack, and the curl, as Joe put it. I had never heard of the release referred to that way and was intrigued. So Joe set the Pathfinder up about twelve inches behind the ball and looped it up a couple inches above the ground. Then he had me place the club on the ground behind the foam instead of behind the ball. He asked me to make a swing from there but on the way down, I was to swing the club over the foam and let the club impact the ball. I was skeptical at first, and hesitated, but I did as he instructed. I missed the ball completely on my first attempt as the club passed over the foam and the ball, but I noticed that without trying I did the 'Gary Player walkthrough.' I mean, my feet and legs shifted well forward to get the club over the foam without me even trying!

"I waited for more direction, but Joe stood there silently nodding for me to swing again. I made another swing and barely contacted the ball, but I knew he was onto something because I shifted like never before. I looked back at him again as he waited without speaking. So I tried a third time. I swung the club over the foam and into the ball. To my amazement the club struck the ball solidly on the downward side of the arc. My feet, legs, and whole lower body had shifted to get the club over the foam again. I even took a divot in front of where the ball lay and I hadn't taken a proper divot in years. What impressed me most was that he never told me how to do it. It just happened naturally when the club swung over the foam.

"It took about five minutes, then he spent five more minutes on my release and I haven't seen him since, except here at the golf course. Geoff, the sophistication and elegance of his strategy is masked by its simplicity. He always asks me how I'm doing, and I can honestly say, once I got the picture of the club's pattern, I've never had a problem shifting again. Go figure."

Just then, Jake turned to me and said, "Geoff, you're up."

I was excited by Tim's story. It took me completely out of the self-created funk I'd experienced since the first hole. I walked up to the tee and launched my three iron ten yards over the green directly over the flag. It was the most solid shot I'd hit all day. New hope was liberating me, and my golf swing seemed to get easier with each successive shot. Exhilarated, I played the final eight holes in four under. The guys were impressed, but I knew that most of my success was the result of the optimism planted by the story of Tim's lesson with Joe.

After we finished the round, they invited me to play again later in the week. Jake even wanted a lesson from me after seeing my play on the back nine. I guess he figured I just needed a nine-hole warm up, never suspecting the real reason for my late-game success. Tim and I walked together to the bar outside the clubhouse, where we turned in our score card. I looked up at the skins board. So far Burlington had three skins but my four birdies on the back nine negated two of them. It made for an easy introduction to Joe.

Tim grabbed my arm and directed me to the far side of the bar, where Joe seemed to be admiring what was left of the head on his amber Labatt Blue. He was sprinkling salt in the glass and watching the granules descend to the bottom as bubbles ascended, giving life to the beer and more of a head on top—an old Irish trick. There were several golfers milling around chatting about their rounds and how close they'd come to getting a skin; after all, they were worth about $150 each. Typical of golfers—I'd done it many times myself—they were lamenting what could have been. Joe was just sitting there listening.

Burlington turned as he sensed our approach. Tim reached for Joe's extended hand and said, "Joe, this is Geoff Mallory. He's from Boston. He's just foiled two of your skins on the back nine, but he wanted to meet you, and I agreed to do the honors." Joe reached for my hand and smiled.

"Nice play, Geoff. Pleased to meet you. What brings you to South Florida?"

"You," I blurted out.

"Oh, really?"

"Yes." I stammered a little, then continued. "I was in New Orleans two days ago when you gave your presentation. I've been chasing you since you left the stage."

He looked at me somewhat perplexed. "Chasing me?"

"What you were saying really intrigued me." I hesitated, but he simply waited. "I was wondering if I could speak to you about working on my golf."

He sat still and silent for a moment. Had I caught him off guard? With the break in conversation, things seemed awkward. He repeated, "You were in New Orleans? Nice town."

I repeated my request and his expression signaled understanding. It was a strange moment. He looked over at the scoreboard. "Judging from the way you played on the back nine, it doesn't seem to me that I could be of help to you."

"You don't know the half of it. I'm a teaching pro too, and I know I could really use your help." That was as politely as I could put it without sounding desperate.

"Well, what kind of help do you need?"

I hesitated, not expecting the question. "I need any kind of help you can give me."

Burlington paused for a moment. "Let me think about what I have going on." He counted to himself on his fingers. Then he looked up at me and said, "You can come out tomorrow. How long are you in town for?"

"A few days."

"I could work with you on your game and if you like, you can observe some lessons I'll be giving this week." I didn't know how to thank him. He changed gears as he downed the rest of his beer. "Listen, I'd be happy to chat, but right now I have to run. There are a few things I need to do at the golf center, since I took most of the day off to play in our little skins game. You can get directions to my place from Tim. Meet me there tomorrow, nine AM sharp."

I couldn't believe it had really been that easy. Joe left, but Tim invited me to stay for a late lunch. I was hungry. We all ordered cheeseburgers and fries at the outdoor bar under the tent, where there was a charcoal grill. I picked up the tab with my winnings and listened to their stories about Joe Burlington.

Tim, Jake, and Will had all worked with the enigmatic pro, but Jake was the only one who couldn't seem to sign onto his approach. "He was just too strange for me," he said.

Tim interrupted, "You never gave him a chance, Jake, with your attitude and all your techniques." Apparently, Jake, besides taking a lot of lessons from a lot of pros, had tried all kinds of techniques that overpopulated the monthly magazines and the golf channel.

Before we left, I got the phone numbers of my newfound friends. I was feeling proud of the way I finished the round and they were serious about playing again later in the week. I felt a twinge of self-doubt at the invitation. What if I couldn't continue playing the way I'd left off on the back nine today? After playing well, I was already feeling insecure.

Would Burlington be able to help?

2

THE FIRST DAY:
JOE'S STORY

The morning came quickly. I hadn't slept soundly; I was too excited. I grabbed a quick breakfast and dashed off to the golf center. I didn't know what to expect.

As I got closer, I thought maybe I'd made a wrong turn, but was certain I'd followed Tim's directions exactly. This was clearly not the nicest part of town; I was more than a little surprised. Years earlier, I had attended a teaching summit at the palatial Boca Raton Hotel, dubbed the Pink Palace, just up the road. It was only a few miles away, but it seemed Burlington's Golf Center would be light years from the Palace—in appearance, at least.

The golf center seemed to be an afterthought, tacked onto a local college. It had no parking lot of its own, so I parked on the street. As I approached the long wooden ramp leading to the pro shop, memories of the caddy days of my youth hit me. The Burlington Golf Center building resembled an old caddy shack from where I grew up in Boston.

The shop attendant was a pleasant little guy in an old Yankees jersey. He paused in his work filling the club-cleaning buckets with fresh water when he saw me. "Good morning, I'm Jim. What can I do for you?"

"I'm here to see Joe Burlington. I have a 9 o'clock appointment."

Jim nodded. "He's down at the maintenance barn." I followed him into the pro shop. "I'll buzz him." He pushed the call button on the squawk box, but there was no answer. He tried again. "He never answers this thing," the Yankees fan muttered, shaking his head in frustration. "I don't even know why we have one. You'd better go down there yourself." He pointed toward a barn about 300 yards away. I grabbed my clubs and headed in that direction.

My mind was racing. I was having serious second thoughts. Was coming here a big mistake? This place wasn't what I'd expected at all. Claire was right: My impulsiveness had gotten the best of me again. Part of me wanted to turn around then and there, but something made me keep going.

Nearing the fence that surrounded the maintenance area, I came close to stepping on a big yellow dog that looked exactly like Marmaduke of comic book fame. The dog lay motionless, except for one eye, which he opened to take a good long look at me. He let out a big sigh and resumed his slumber. I guess he figured I was no threat.

I passed through the gates into a yard filled with all kinds of turf equipment and several vintage golf carts. I moved through the white pines that surrounded a wooden workshop of about twenty by thirty feet, its doors wide open. I stopped just inside the doors on a rather uneven concrete floor covered with pine needles blown in by the wind. I looked for Joe. Or any sign of life.

I scanned the room. One side contained a table saw, stone grinder, drill press, and air compressor. Several tables were loaded with various tools and golf course maintenance supplies. Looking up into the rafters, I saw old golf clubs, boxes of shafts and grips, a ladder, and what appeared to be green foam tubes with orange ends sticking out of boxes. On the other side of the room was a stackable washer/dryer, a microwave, and a small refrigerator. It looked like someone both worked and lived in here. Still, there was no sign of life inside.

My doubts were growing fast. My gaze fell to the floor toward the back of the building. There *was* somebody there. A utility vehicle was jacked up a few inches above the floor, and a pair of legs peeked out from under it.

I called out tentatively. "Joe?"

He slid out from under the machine. "Good morning. Geoff?" His hands were darkened by dirt and grease from the old machine he was working on.

"Yes. Jim tried to call you on the squawk box, but…."

"Yes, I know. I hate that thing," he chuckled, "especially when I'm in the middle of something. I was just about to adjust the rollers and sharpen the reels on the cutting units, but first we need to get them up on that table over there." I noticed he had included me in this task. He pointed across the room. "I figured Jim would send you down here. We use those reels for the main practice tee. They're beginning to tear the grass instead of giving it a clean cut. I need to balance them out, too. I figured I had some time before you arrived so I got started."

He got up off his roller, grabbed an old towel to wipe some of the dirt off his hands, and pointed at the reels on the floor. "These are heavy." I stood there, still somewhat dumbfounded, until he asked, "Would you mind putting down your clubs and giving me a hand with this reel? We need to get it up on the table so I can adjust it. It'll only take five minutes."

I felt it was a little presumptuous of him to ask, but I put down my bag and went over to help him. The reel was indeed heavy and awkward. We got it up on the table and he propped it up so the front roller was in the air. Then he picked up what was clearly a homemade tool and slid it back and forth along the rollers. It was tight on one end and slid too easily on the other. He quietly said, "There, you see? This is not even." Burlington began loosening bolts on each side of the rollers. He pried on the adjusters until the steel bar was equal in tension on both ends and the middle.

"Just one more thing and we can get started. Let's lift this reel down onto the floor." He skidded one of the reels along the floor to the triplex and angled it in place to reconnect to the mower. Then, grease gun in hand, he lubed the tee mower. There must have been a hundred grease fittings on that machine and he had to crawl on his knees on the concrete floor to get at some of them, but his overalls were already filthy. While he performed that task, he explained the importance of lubricating all the joints.

I was beginning to get impatient. It looked like Joe Burlington was more into golf course maintenance than golf instruction. Didn't he remember why I was here? I wasn't interested in this stuff. I was accustomed to being treated like a true pro and my ego was protesting. Maybe this *was* a big mistake. If things continued this way, there was no way I was going to spend a week of precious vacation time with a man who looked like a turf mechanic! But judging from his score yesterday, I knew he could play golf. Could he teach? But what could I do—tell him I had a new shirt on and I didn't want to get dirty? Burlington, in contrast, was filthy and sweating from his work but apparently didn't care how he appeared.

I stood there in his shop, looking down at him working under the mower. I argued with myself: Don't be so quick to judge; see what happens next. Take it easy for once in your life. I forced myself to shut down my initial judgments for the moment and declared a temporary ceasefire. I tried to convince myself to stick with this commitment. Claire had accused me of lack of commitment, not just with her, but even with the small stuff of life. Her exact words were that I couldn't even commit to a frozen dinner or an ice cream flavor. Looking over my current situation and how much I'd invested in it, I decided at least to go through with the first day as planned.

While I pondered, Burlington was putting another cutting unit back on the mower. As he called out for different wrenches, like a surgical nurse I automatically assisted him; I don't know why. I watched as he adjusted the cutting unit and turned a few nuts to secure the reel to the machine. His hands worked quickly and with ease, his experience obvious. I got some grease on my hands from handling the tools, but it wasn't much, and watching Burlington work was hypnotic. Burlington seemed very keen on preventive maintenance. He was smiling and humming and really seemed to enjoy this work. I was still a little miffed at the reception, but curious about what might come next.

"Well, that's it for now," he suddenly exclaimed, and got up from under the mower. He stood up, took off his cap, wiped the sweat from his brow, and walked to the sink outside the building. Soaping up, he bent and grabbed a fistful of loose sand from the ground to help scrub the grease off his hands. Drying with a shop towel, he said, "Now—let's begin again. Good morning!"

This time, looking me straight in the eyes, Joe Burlington shook my hand with a sure grip. As I looked at him, I could tell he had spent a lot of time outdoors—his skin was weathered and his hands were rough. He looked more in his element here; I noticed again his strong jaw, youthful eyes, and full head of auburn hair, streaked where the sun had bleached it.

As we shook hands, I could feel him studying me. I could sense something different. Joe Burlington radiated an energy—a force—one that I can only describe as an inner strength emanating outward, something I had never felt before. Powerful, yet peaceful and friendly, not intimidating at all. I sensed a strong compassion—so strong I could almost see it.

Our conversation began again benignly—small talk at first. We exchanged the pleasantries scripted for first lessons. As I shifted my focus away from my first impressions of the place and Burlington's maintenance work, I could tell he was decidedly different. He had a presence, something special, but I couldn't put my finger on it just yet. And I couldn't merge this new image with my first impressions. Had I reacted prematurely and with prejudice? I figured I would find out soon enough.

Burlington interrupted my second-guessing. "You can go on ahead, Geoff. I need to change into more comfortable clothes." He pointed me in the direction of his practice area just around the corner from the shop. "I'll join you in a few minutes." As I walked out, I heard him call after me, "You can warm up if you like."

Burlington came around the corner with "Marmaduke" (whose real name, I learned, was Otter) at his heels about ten minutes later. Just like the summit, he wore a plain yellow shirt, khaki trousers, and moccasins without socks. This guy didn't look like he was about to give a golf lesson. But it occurred to me that it might be refreshing to work with someone who wasn't from the celebrity golf pro mold. I had hit a few shots to warm up, but then decided it would be more productive if we could talk before I showed him my swing. He came up next to me and said, "Let's get started." We stood on a small square of closely cropped Bermuda grass. He motioned for the dog to join us. Otter yawned, reluctantly got up, and waddled over. He sniffed the spot on arrival, laid down right behind us, and closed his eyes. It seemed like only a few seconds passed before we could hear Otter's rhythmic snoring.

We sat down on the chairs that stood off to the side and Burlington said, "Well, you've come a long distance. I hope I can help you make it worth your while, eh?"

"I think you can from what I've heard about your reputation."

"I wouldn't put too much stock in someone else's say-so if I were you, Geoff." What did he mean by that? I had given him a compliment and he had volleyed it right back at me, not gingerly either, but spiking it over the net.

I intercepted. "I notice you have a Canadian accent of sorts. Do you come from Canada?"

"No, but my father was from Ontario and his family was from Ireland. I think that's where I got my love of links courses, from the Irish ancestors. Those courses are so naturally beautiful, they prove nature's elegance, don't they?" He looked at me and I nodded in agreement. "But to answer your question, I was born in Michigan. I'm a Midwesterner. My habit of saying 'eh' comes from years ago, when I taught in Canada. I adapt the language based on how I feel and what I need to say. Invariably, the meaning is clear, even if the words are incoherent. I believe communication is about meaning, not structure. Like golf swings—it's not form, it's function, eh?" He looking directly at me and lifted his brows. I could tell he was wondering if I'd picked up on his neatly packaged morsel of golf and life philosophy.

There was a long pause. Burlington didn't help to push it along much—he didn't seem like one to engage in trivial talk. Silence between sentences didn't seem to bother him, but I felt awkward and pressured to keep the conversation going. "Did you grow up in Michigan?" It was all I could think to ask.

"No, not really. We moved around a lot growing up. Dad always provided for us, but he lived simply, working daily and playing golf a couple afternoons a week during season. He started us playing golf. As I think back on it, he had a pretty good swing himself." Burlington smiled, enjoying the memory.

" 'Us'?" I questioned.

"There were six of us—a real handful for my mother—and we each have dramatically different personalities. My mother, well, she was whatever she needed to be—a homemaker, a hairstylist, sang on the radio. I think I got my diversity from her. She was not a golfer when she and my father met, but as soon as she touched a club you could tell she had a natural knack for it."

"Where did your mother come from?" I asked.

"Mom's family immigrated from Italy. She was Italian to the core. Family, family, family. Her whole focus was on raising us kids. She gave up all other activities in her life to concentrate on us not going astray." Burlington had no reservations about sharing his past.

I didn't want to pry, but I did want to know more about him, and I felt that these were perfectly normal questions. "Did you begin your golf career in Michigan?"

"Yes. Like many older golf professionals, I began as a caddy. But, because of my dad's work, we never lived in one place too long. It was hard once we got into high school. You make new friends and miss the old ones. We'd have to find new jobs and adjust to a new town just when the old one was becoming comfortable and familiar. But I really got into playing golf and teaching when we moved to the hills and horse country of Ohio, where my brothers and I worked at a club in Sharon Center. "

"How old were you?"

"I was just fourteen." This time he didn't crack a smile.

"You mean you began teaching at fourteen?" I asked, incredulous.

"Well, in a sense I did. Club members, and even the golf pros, would ask me my opinion about their swings and I would just tell them what I thought. The surprising thing was that I felt very comfortable doing this. They trusted me. I really don't know why, except they knew I was pretty good for my age and I practiced a whole lot. I was very consistent with my swing and my shots. They used to admire my balance." He laughed, remembering with delight.

"I was…diminutive for my age," Burlington went on animatedly, "so I was somewhat disadvantaged when I competed within my age group. I knew at a very young age that I wanted to work in golf and be outdoors. That is what really attracted me to the game. The golf swing itself just fascinated me, and it still does. I studied hard and watched all the best players on television. I did go to a few matches and tournaments in Akron. Yeah, I was fascinated by Hogan, Nelson, and Snead, but I was too young to go in person. Except for Snead; I saw him play up close." He added, "I did study film of them all practicing, though.

"We—my brothers and I—always worked at the golf course. As employees, our privileges and playing time were quite limited. We got into the habit of practicing our swings and that, as you know, can be a two-edged sword. We could practice however much we wanted. We were fortunate that there were two exceptional pros where we worked in our teens, and they encouraged us to work on our games as much as possible. These pros were highly skilled players and understood what it took to get good. I tried to emulate their examples—you know, pass it on to kids the way they did to my brothers and me. Anyway, I practiced a lot and loved it. I wanted badly to have the best swing and play the finest golf game I could."

"What happened to get you into golf full time? I asked. "Did you go into college on scholarship?"

"No, I did not have a scholarship," Burlington said. "They were hard to come by, but I did qualify as a walk-on at university—

only to be told that I couldn't play," he smiled wryly. "I didn't beat the scholarship players by enough strokes. C'est la vie! I got over it eventually and it was a good lesson in life for me: It's not always fair."

"You competed a lot?"

"Yes, and I had reasonable success as a junior golfer. But then things turned sour. I mean, my whole golf game turned inside out. I got steadily worse even though I knew what I wanted to achieve and had access to the best instruction."

"Did you take a lot of lessons?"

"No, Geoff, I don't believe in taking a lot of lessons. I had spent approximately eight days taking lessons from one man. I didn't need more than that. Since then, I have been working on mastering what he taught me forty years ago, and I will tell you that it can never be mastered. All you can do is keep moving in the right direction. I'll explain this in more detail when the right time comes. Despite the truths I'd learned, I was not getting better, so I had to do something. At my lowest point in golf, I realized I had to change drastically."

"But if you had the best mentoring, what had to change?" I felt I was missing something.

"Good question. I had to change my whole perspective and my complete personality when it came to golf. My belief system had derailed me with all the failure it absorbed. If you play badly for long enough, you will find it a chore to get out of bed in the morning. You will fear the golf course, the tournaments, the other competitors, everything. It's a terrible state to be in."

"There are some prominent players on tour going through that right now. Do you think you could help them?" I asked.

"It's hard to say, because it's always up to the individual. If they were open-minded I could probably lead them back to their natural potential. It's my experience that people can usually get back on track from there. For me, I had realized I had to do something and decided to take action on what had been, up until then, the lowest days of my career. I also knew no one could help me and I had to figure it out for myself. It took a lot of time, but eventually I came full circle. When the realization dawned on me that I wasn't alone in these sorts of problems, I decided to develop a program to help others get back on track, too."

I began to wonder how someone could be so honest about his own failures. I guess Joe Burlington was so secure in his experience that it didn't matter that he had, at one time, failed miserably. He wasn't ashamed of failing. He had no pretense about how good he was or how much he knew. He definitely wasn't trying to impress me: When Burlington spoke, he spoke with humility. I was used to teacher-student relationships that cast the teacher in a starring role and the student as a supporting player, as if the teacher's glory might rub off on the student with the proper attention.

But Joe Burlington spoke to me on the level, with no superiority, no condescension. Even with me probing for information, Burlington didn't seem bothered—he volunteered information genuinely and naturally once he'd gotten his motor started. He didn't seem to mind being bombarded him with questions.

"Anything else contribute to the change?" I probed.

"Well, things got real ugly, and I don't mean just my performance. I mean my attitude—especially on the course. One day, while we were playing in Texas, my brother told me, 'You know, Joe, you're no fun to be with on the course. No one wants to play with you. You're so miserable and you hit some of the worst drives I've ever seen. I don't think you'll ever get it.' He was partly right. I would never get it if I kept going about it the way I had been. I was playing scared from the very first tee and it didn't get any better.

"But I was very angry with him for saying that—I felt he had disrespected me. I had worked so hard to improve myself and help him as well. Anyway, I should have thanked him because he supplied my spark for change. What he said was true—and sometimes the truth hurts."

"What happened next?"

"I decided to go out the very next day with the attitude that no matter what happened, I was going to enjoy myself. Sounds stupid, but it was the first glimmer of hope I'd had in a long time. My brother's words gave me the energy to prove him wrong. So I drastically changed my way of doing things, first in my head and then in my body. That was the beginning of my transition and of seeing a smidgeon of my potential again.

"My first step was to find something to enjoy while I was on the course so I could relax a little. I had gotten so anxious about golfing that I needed to find a way to calm down. If it wasn't in the way I played, it would be in the birdsong, a cool breeze, or the way the light filtered through the trees. I had to take the focus away from my problems and myself and find something delightful in the moment. It is this attitude—which has nothing to do with golf and everything to do with my *performance* in golf—that allowed me to begin turning myself around."

"Well, then what happened?"

"That turned out to be my first glimmer of hope about what the solution could be. I played shots that day that were up to my potential, just a few, mind you, but it gave me hope. Though I didn't understand why on earth it worked, I decided to go further with this positive attitude. I designed a self-help program that might work for me—and for others, too."

"What did you do, specifically?"

"I'd repeat positive statements in my mind to obliterate negative thoughts. I would picture success in every shot and swing. I'd tell myself that this was easy and that I'd done it well a thousand times before. This program put attitude first and didn't allow a player to judge results."

"How can you improve your game without judging results?"

"Simple," he said. "By being aware of what's happening."

"That seems like the same thing."

"Oh no, Geoff, it's very different. You see, awareness has nothing to do with right and wrong or good and bad. It's just what is."

"Sounds interesting," I said, still puzzled. "Could you tell me more?"

"Not just yet," he replied.

3

THE LESSON BEGINS

Burlington suddenly switched gears. "Enough about me. Tell me about yourself, Geoff." In a flash, he had turned the table and now I was the one who needed to be brutally honest. Caught off-guard, I said nothing. He rephrased the question. "Tell me a little more about what happened to your golf and your teaching."

OK, I've come this far.... Jumping in with both feet, I recited the preamble I'd practiced in my head. "I feel I've run into a roadblock. Although I'm considered a successful teacher, I still don't think I'm very good."

"So you came here because you figure there's another way?"

"Well, yes; that's part of it."

"Well, what is it that you really want?"

"I really want to improve the way I teach and how I swing and play so that I don't feel like a fraud. If I can't do what I'm talking about, I feel like a phony."

Burlington nodded, taking in what I was saying, then challenged me again. "Tell me again: What do you want?"

"I want to feel authentic. I want to *be* authentic. I want to be able to perform consistently as a golfer what I teach my students and to be a complete coach to them. I'm hoping that the problems I've run into lie with my program and not with me."

"I see."

"For example, at the summit, I saw that as teachers, we're all going in the wrong direction and none of us seem to have an alternative approach. There is very little difference in our methods—although we all claim to be different. To me, we're six of one, half a dozen of the other. It's all about body positions, the core, and nothing else matters. In one camp, you have the big muscles controlling the swing, and in another, the small muscles. The whole thing has turned into a great debate, almost muscle by muscle and bone by bone, on the mechanics of the swing.

"Let me tell you, not only are the players in golf competing with each other, but now teachers show up at tour events and are competing for students. It's turned golf upside down. And these summits—" my voice was rising "—have turned into popularity contests. My talk was a typical uninspired session: I talked the talk. Maybe we are all doing the best we can with what we have, but we don't seem to be getting better!" I slapped the arm of my chair. A moment later I was a little sheepish. "I hadn't realized how strongly I felt until this moment."

"OK, so we need to get you organized. Let's begin with a simple history of your experience. You, Geoff, not those other pros. How do *you* view the true nature of golf and golf teaching?"

Wow! I've been waiting for that question all my life! Encouraged, I began. "I grew up learning that golf and the golf swing were inseparably tied to feel and the use of one's imagination. It wasn't so technical. The whole learning experience was supposed to be natural, not to mention a lot of fun. The way things are now, so complex and competitive, it seems that something has been lost. The mechanics and all the debate seduced me, too, though. But I just don't like the way I teach golf anymore."

Burlington raised his eyebrows. "I agree that things are out of balance, but complaining about what's wrong won't get them back in balance. You need to do something positive about it."

"That's why I came," I said, not hiding my irritation.

"I understand that," he said quietly, "yet you keep referring to approaches that don't sit well with you. By the way, they don't sit well with me either. But you need to let it go so you can open up to what is possible for you."

I noticed a different expression coming over Joe's face, as though he was thinking back and remembering. There was another long pause before he spoke. "I agree with you, Geoff. I, too, was deeply concerned about the direction golf instruction was going in some years ago. I chose to slip into the background, to drop out in a sense. I didn't want any part of what was happening. I had new trails to blaze and I'd never minded being different. But that's another story. Right now, we need to help you get your instruction going in the right direction. We need to get you to be authentic and confident so you can become as complete a coach as you've told me you want to be."

"I'd like that," I responded. "Can I ask you a question I've asked many other teachers, but not gotten what I consider a complete answer?"

"Fire away!"

"What do you consider to be the most important fundamental in teaching? Some people say it's the ability to teach someone to turn, others say rhythm, and still others talk about the total path of the club. What's your opinion?"

"I think some of those answers have their place, but they're certainly not at the top of my list. In my experience, there is one quality that is a must." There was another pause as he leaned in closer and looked me straight in the eyes as if to make an important point. "*Listening...*"

"That's right!" I interrupted, before he could finish, in total agreement, I thought. "I never thought of that, but you're right, Joe. My students constantly interrupt me. They don't listen. If I could ever get them to listen, we might make a lot more progress in a lesson."

"Well, no," Burlington chuckled good-naturedly, "I wasn't talking about you teaching your students to listen. I'm talking about you learning to listen."

I tried to pry my foot out of my mouth, face red.

"You see, nothing is more important in a teacher than the quality of being a good listener and an astute observer. The only way to get on the wavelength of a student is to listen to his or her story. You need to learn about the student—not vice versa. You need to draw from each student what's within them. It's an inside-out approach, rather than a cramming-it-in-from-the-outside method. A teacher must be an exceptional observer and listener, taking in what they're saying and how they present themselves. These are the only tools available to us to truly get onto our students' wavelength."

"Seems simple," I said.

"Yes, Geoff, it is a simple principle, but you would be surprised how much golf instruction either violates this principle or is completely unaware of it. If you listen between the lines of what your students are saying, they will give you a clear picture of the source of their problems. The answers are there in what the student says and in their body language. The students' eyes, their hands, their facial expressions, and their words are invaluable clues to help your students solve their own puzzles."

"But isn't solving their problems my job?"

"No. You need to allow them to do the work. It's like the old saying goes, 'Give a man a fish, he may enjoy one nice meal. But teach him to fish and he can eat for a lifetime!' The goal is that a student learns to trust in his own experience to become a solid and independent self-coach."

"So, in a sense, the teacher facilitates learning, but doesn't instruct?"

"That's right," he replied. "The art of it is that the student begins to believe he has always had the ability—which of course he has."

"Joe, I can understand an accomplished player accepting this approach, but what about a beginner?"

"Well, of course. With an accomplished player, you are essentially removing stumbling blocks that don't allow them to see clearly—in a sense, getting the player back to the potential they seem to have misplaced. Beginners absolutely have to gain experience with club in hand from the beginning of their natural swing, but we'll get into that later."

"So the most important ingredient in golf teaching has nothing to do with golf itself?"

"That's right," Burlington confirmed. "The universal quality of all teaching, whether it's sports, music, dance, whatever, is listening! And the student's words and actions must fall on unbiased ears and eyes. Being outwardly focused really takes practice—I've worked on it every day of my career. And when you're focusing on your student's words and actions, your life and your experience must fade into the background. You must, in a sense, detach yourself from yourself."

It never occurred to me that as a golf teacher I needed, first and foremost, to work on listening skills. This sounded like something Claire would say, something she worked on as a social worker. I bounced the idea around in my mind. "Kind of like a psycho-physical therapist." I said.

"Yes, Geoff. I'm glad you included the physical too because being involved in athletics, we need to have an in-depth knowledge of how the body learns its skills."

"Like, balance and motion?"

"Yes, that's part of it," he agreed. "As a golf teacher, you need to be well grounded in the physics of the club and the body's responses, but you shouldn't be teaching that to your students. Only you need to know it. You see, often teachers try to prove to their students what they know and how good they are, but this doesn't serve the student. The instructor really needs to concentrate on observing the student's learning process so that accurate adjustments can be made."

"Is that what you mean by 'awareness'?"

"Exactly. Awareness is just noticing the details and the nuances—waking up rather than being asleep. That's why you need to get your students to train their minds to practice self-inquiry. The onus of development is on them; you merely open the door and let them do the discovering. You help students discover their own ability. That's your only job. Your experience and knowledge are instruments to facilitate discovery. When your students discover for themselves, they can never be fooled or misled because it's their own experience that gave them the answers. And that's the kind of learning that's never forgotten. To discover your own best swing allows you to play with trust and confidence.

"And instructors must use diverse approaches to relate to all the different backgrounds of their students, their individual ways of understanding, perceiving, and interpreting. You must be able to relate to each one's individual nature. You can't pigeonhole them or conform them to your nature—you must teach them to embrace their own."

"OK, but after listening and observing, and letting the students discover, what next?"

"I believe in using a bare-bones approach so as not to confuse the student. While you must cover everything, you have to pare it down. You must only speak of essentials."

"Which are?"

"The essence of the golf swing is to create an environment of swing motion for the release of energy into the impact. And what is an environment of swing motion, you ask?" He seemed to read my mind. "It's a tempo and rhythm, a flow with a consistent path pattern," he explained.

"Yes, that's it!" I had a flashback to the seminar. That was the answer that really excited me. It had become my Holy Grail.

"Great golfers have all kinds of ways of swinging, Geoff, long and short, flat or upright, but what is essential? What is universal? They all have a rhythm and a path, and they release the energy into the impact consistently. We can get into some detail later, but that is as simple and complete as I can make it."

I absorbed this new idea while he paused. He was about to speak when I blurted out, "I've found that I get into ruts in my teaching, Joe. It doesn't make me happy, but I get stuck in routines and, even though one isn't working, I rarely seem to break free of it and then..."

This time he interrupted me. "Have you ever noticed that you seem to be teaching students the same things the same way, lesson after lesson?"

"Well, yes—all the time. I never questioned why. They all need to learn the same skills, don't they?"

"But the same way?"

"And why do my students need to learn the same things over and over?" I asked. "They keep coming back with the same problems. I know I have told them correctly what to do to improve."

"Because you told them what to do. It's that simple. You haven't gone through the lesson as a discovery process. You just gave them their adjustments from your treasure chest of knowledge. You did the work for them and they were very grateful. You were great; that is, until they fail again. It becomes a vicious cycle and you become the object of praise—or slander—depending on the outcome of their performances. I've said it many times: Never take credit for a student's success or the failure."

I raised my hand to plead for a pause. I needed him to slow down. There was so much meat here. I couldn't digest it all at once. I was processing his words, but still hadn't put all the pieces together.

Burlington took my cue and didn't give me the chance to ask another question. "Geoff, you can observe a few lessons, up close and personal; I think you'll begin to realize what's possible when things come together through this discovery process. You will have the opportunity to see new students and a couple of players that I've worked with before who wanted to come back. Hopefully, you will get the whole enchilada and, at some point, maybe it would be helpful if you experienced this type of lesson for yourself, as a learner. As you said, you want to improve your own game too! Anyway, you can decide later if that would be helpful for you."

"I'd like that!" I volunteered prematurely. I sat for a few minutes, absorbing it all, before I continued. "I was also wondering if you could clear up a few more questions about the common golf swing talk and the corrections that golfers and teachers make—you know, your take on the typical responses to a golfer's mishit or misdirection."

"Sure," he smiled, "fire away."

"Thanks. There are a lot of things said about a golf swing that are confusing. In fact, I have a whole list of them. For instance, one that I hear all the time is about keeping your left arm straight."

Burlington smiled. "I assume you're talking about a right-handed player? Naturally, that's based on observation and really has no ground in our fundamental program, and I'll tell you why. The first fundamental of motion is to be fluid-like, right?"

I nodded in agreement.

"Often, when a golfer concentrates on keeping the left arm rigid, it leads to rigidity throughout the body. It tends to destroy the very pacing control the golfer's looking to achieve because, physically, he has become somewhat numb. That's detrimental to control—not good at all."

"But let's say the player's left arm does collapse," I said.

Burlington swiftly refuted. "Then our golfer is lacking a good arc of the club in the swing; the problem has nothing to do with strength or a consciousness of rigidity. The key to having a good swinging lever is being able to picture the club's travel route or swing arc—and visualize the desired path. There is an arc to the handle, too, so you need to notice how it travels back. The answer is to free up the entire body so it can move to support the arc, and if you do, you'll never have a problem with an arm collapsing."

He caught his breath before continuing. "The arm actually stays relatively straight—simply by knowing the fundamental arc, or where you would like to swing, and the angle at which you would like the club to swing. Fact is, Geoff, the left arm is attached to the left shoulder and for arc momentum purposes, the lead hand and arm begin the swing back. The trailing arm will naturally bend to accommodate the circle of the swing and the limitations of standing in place while swinging in that direction. In other words, based on the swing, one side of the body folds and the other stretches. Therefore, knowing the arc, and seeing how we're put together anatomically, it would be virtually impossible to swing the club in an arc and collapse the arm."

Joe stood to demonstrate. "Notice how my right arm bends in the swing. Because the swing is progressing in the direction of my right arm, it must bend to accommodate the swing direction and arc, just as my left arm may stretch as the swing progresses away from its starting place at address. The left side of my body is being pulled by the momentum and direction of the swinging hand, arm, and club.

"Watch as my swing progresses. Notice how my torso moves naturally to accommodate the arc and path. It can all happen naturally to satisfy the club's dynamic needs." He winked. Was he being good natured or sarcastic about explaining the extension of the left arm? I could see that Joe Burlington could go toe to toe and beyond with any so-called golf intellectual. But he acted like their various philosophies were useless chatter.

"There are all kinds of degrees of arm straightness, Geoff. It really becomes personal; it's not fundamental. I have never suggested any learner try it, yet I don't have chronic arm collapses in my students' swings either," he said matter-of-factly.

I was beginning to feel somewhat irked with his simplistic responses to what I believed were complex questions, and I wanted to move on. "I've often heard that a golfer should begin his swing by turning his shoulders..."

The arc of the handle.

GB

"Yes," he interrupted, "I've also heard that lately and, again, I think it's very dangerous."

"Why?" I challenged. "It seems to work with some students."

"Well now," he scoffed, " 'seems' is the key word here. Geoff, it's first a question of intimacy."

"Intimacy?"

"Yes, intimacy. When the player's swing is controlled, or more aptly put, dominated by attempting to feel in the shoulders, then they're working with a part of the body that is not designed for that task. Also, that part of the body is not directly associated with the club or hand and handle's action. Golfers who go this route will eventually lose touch with the action of the club. To elevate awareness, golfers must have an uninterrupted intimate relationship with the club; it's their dance partner while swinging. A golfer who's no longer feeling what's going on with the club is headed for trouble, don't you think?"

Joe waited to let his question penetrate. "The golf swing has to be linked to your proprioceptive awareness," he explained.

"What?" I had to raise my hand at that one; I didn't understand the term. "What is proprioceptive awareness?"

Joe looked at me as though I hadn't done my homework in human physiology or something. But he indulged me. "Proprioception comes from the Latin word *proprius*. It means 'one's own' and of course, perception is one of the human senses. Proprioception is our sense of the orientation of our limbs in space. Without proprioception, we'd need to consciously watch our feet to make sure we stay upright while walking. Proprioception records fine muscle movements and sends the signals back to the brain.[2] That's why the fine muscles are concentrated in the hands and feet. The brain regards shoulder muscle movements as coarse. In other words, the torso is not linked to the brain in the same manner as your hands. Those parts of the body have not evolved to make the fine movements required in golf or music or dance. That's a major reason I believe so much in the hand control of a golf swing; there are no proprioceptors in your torso. Your torso relies on your inner ear for balance and center of gravity; it has absolutely nothing to do with the speed, place, or motion of your extremities.

"But of course the club is attached to an extremity! The club is an extension of our proprioceptive hand, which is perfectly designed to carry out the tasks of a golf swing. It makes no sense to try to redesign the mind-body complex in an attempt to gain awareness or consistency through the comparatively dull senses of the bulk of the body."

I felt I'd been given a heavy dose of understanding. But still Joe continued. "You cannot circumvent the most valuable feel network in the body. The hands have the tactile sense, the sense of touch and proprioception. I can't even believe there is a debate about this. You really need to get your colleagues up to speed on the sensory system." He shook his head in disbelief.

Joe got up, took a club from my bag, and made a few more swings as he spoke. I felt mesmerized by his ease and gracefulness. "In my opinion, exceptional proprioception is one of the main reasons some people have an outstanding feel for a swing right from the get go. The good news is, it can be learned and developed. My experience is that focusing on the torso can fool a player for maybe a few swings, particularly a player who tends to swing the club in a very narrow vertical pattern. However, that shoulder fix—and that's exactly what it is—is very short lived. Soon the swing becomes very horizontal or flat to the ground, and, as I've said, the player loses touch with the action of the club. Consequently, the club face rotates out of balance with the swing path, and that usually leads to an almost completely closed club face.

"Did you notice how easily my shoulders rotated when my hands and arms swung on a fundamental arc around and up behind me? Why would you want to place your attention on something that will occur naturally? Trying to rotate your shoulders, or to consciously turn them, is not a fundamental! It is a function of the action of the proprioceptive hands and arm swing. If you approach the golf swing this way, you will never sacrifice control or energy. Working with consciousness placed on your torso is a good way to dull your sense of feel."

"Then how do you get a vertical narrow swing, as you said, to become a better arc and path?"

"Geoff, there are several exercises you could teach to demonstrate it and never leave the handle-head relationship. In developing awareness, how much the player turns their shoulders, again, is unique to their body breadth, size, and flexibility. The answer is to swing the club and notice the action of the handle and head. This way, you'll never sacrifice club awareness."

"OK, Joe, I get it. Can we move on?"

He smiled and said, "Be my guest."

"How about this classic statement: When a golfer mishits the ball, he's told, 'you lifted your head' or 'you moved your head.' In a lot of cases, the player knows he didn't, yet he still missed the ball."

"They're not still saying that, are they?" Joe mocked, incredulous. Then his smile turned serious. "To focus solely on the ball is very dangerous because it really doesn't encourage club head awareness. It tends to restrict the free flow of the swing as it progresses to the finish, too. That statement, Geoff, more than any other, is one of the most destructive pieces of advice a golfer could get while learning to swing the club!" he said forcefully.

"Why?"

"Because it leads golfers directly away from developing club awareness. When golfers first learn to swing, the ball often distracts them from feeling the swing. After all, the ball is not moving. In fact, as you must have heard, I teach most of my students to swing with their eyes closed to develop the proprioception with club in hand. It helps them become aware of what's moving—the hands, the club—and the club's relationship to the ground, the target, and the ball.

"So never tell players to concentrate on the ball or to keep their head down or still. Those are natural consequences of fundamental club action."

"You've never held a club up to a golfer's head to help keep them still?"

"Absolutely not." Joe was emphatic. "That usually causes a golfer to freeze, just like keeping the left arm straight. I've never needed to do that; if their club is OK then their head is OK, right?

If the golfer swings on a sound swing arc, the center is a result of the orbit. The outer orbit creates the center."

I pushed the subject in another direction. "OK, Joe, I hear this one from just about everyone and it seems that no one is able to give me an answer that covers all the bases. Everyone seems to swing differently, especially the tour players. Yet they get similar results. Where does all that power come from?"

"That's a very good question. You need to realize that there are different ways to generate power or, more precisely, optimum club head speed at impact. You might add the glide path of the club head, which includes the square center contact on the face at a good strong angle, but let me just address this question of speed for now. As you've noticed, golfers do have differing techniques. To keep it simple, I'll tell you about the two differing approaches to generating club head speed. The first, which you hear about so often today, is power generated from a completely synchronized system of torque and resistance of the upper and lower torso. Of course just based on what we've discussed regarding feel, I question the prudence of teaching this technique. Really fine athletes, with outstanding body flexibility and superb body awareness, can generate tremendous speed this way. They will still never have high energy in the impact without the timing for release, which is centered in the action of the hands and wrists. Anyway, to me, it is a very unstable approach, particularly for the club-level player. And it lacks intimacy, as I mentioned. The risk is not worth the reward, because the chance of mistiming such a volatile system reduces a golfer's consistency greatly, not to mention the physical and mental strain it places on him."

He stopped long enough to make sure I was following him. "The other way to generate power or club head speed is through timing; that is, through momentum and centrifugal force. This type of energy reduces stress on the body and really poses no physical or mental risk to anybody. Basically, one just knows the direction and speed of the flow and allows the rest of the body to respond. The beauty of this approach is that it's like riding a bike. Once you feel the synchronization and energy of these forces, you will always know them and have no need to manipulate your swing. It is really the only way for the club-level player to learn to swing. And it never sacrifices the intimacy or feel for the club," he added with a wink.

I agreed that it would be difficult to teach a golfer to swing by torque in the upper torso and resisting with the lower torso while at the same time asking him to feel the speed and direction of the club. "It would be real overload, and yet I know it to be one of the most popular approaches out there."

"Yes," he nodded, "I know, but for me, the whole body's flexibility, suppleness, and elasticity are where I get my club head energy, and I teach it that way too. Geoff, it's as though your muscles and joints become warm like soft taffy on a hot summer day; as you swing, your muscles and joints need to stretch, rotate, bend, and flex. I rely totally on the synchronization of my whole body's movement during the swing in conjunction with the club's pattern. That's what I rely on for generating power. Most of my students are very consistent—even though they don't have to practice much once they get the principles." I nodded my agreement.

He continued. "You also always need to remember that they will be on their own when the lesson's over, which means you really need to keep it simple! And, as I said, you're not compromising power, you're just making it available more often—differently, more simply, and certainly with less strain on the mind and body." This time his pause seemed to indicate that he was finished making his point.

"One last question, if you don't mind, and this is a big one." Maybe I was getting ahead of myself, but Joe looked at me expectantly. This particular problem was one I'd considered monumental—with emphasis on the 'mental.' This aspect of the game has baffled golfers since the beginning. I tried to think of a way to articulate it elegantly, but gave up. It all boiled down to this: "How does one get confidence? I mean, how can you regularly feel confident? I know it's easy to spot confidence in a player, just as easy as it is to see the lack of it. But how does one get it?"

As he slowly nodded, his brows lifted. The muscles spanning his forehead formed deep, curved lines. Was my question out of line?

"Yes," he responded, but not to my unvoiced thoughts. "Really, it is an easy question. And it has an easy answer. However, it has been made out to be complex and mysterious. Many teachers simply believe that some people have it and some don't, but I don't agree. The good news is you can get it and it doesn't need to be a difficult process. Yes, you can nurture it within yourself. Over time, your confidence will be sustainable and when it wanes, you can build it up again."

His answer surprised me. He paused in his usual manner then began to explain the source and truth of confidence. "You must simply learn to deliver the club: Know the release."

"That's it?"

"Know it by feel, know it by awareness, and learn to trigger it. Yep, it all boils down to that. It just so happens I've learned how to teach each and every golfer this release so that they'll be able to get it time and again. If a golfer learns how to do this, confidence is a natural result of it. Of course, you need to believe in it too, but I've found that any player willing to practice both the physical and mental triggers will ultimately practice and play with solid and genuine self-confidence."

The simplicity of his answer surprised me again. He made it sound so easy. I said it to myself in my head: Know the release and believe in it.

He continued. "Confidence is the positive feeling that things will go well. For example, when a golfer sets up to hit a shot, the instant before he swings is when he knows whether he's confident or not. He gets a feeling about the swing and the anticipated impact and can fairly accurately determine the chances of pulling it off. That feeling is the golfer's confidence level. The way to feel positive is to have a keen awareness and be present to the feeling of the release of energy into the impact. And there you have it! We've circled right back to 'an environment of swing motion for release.' The psyche and the physical swing are unified under the umbrella of knowing how and believing in your ability to impact the ball."

"And what are you present to?" I asked.

"You are present to the feeling throughout your whole body, Geoff. Ultimately the sense of release must be centered in the hands, those parts of the body holding the club, right? You notice as soon as a player picks up a club whether or not he is confident; you really can't hide that. The hands connect the body to the club and the mind and it's that connection that's a conduit to your whole system. It's like electricity, like plugging a light into wall socket. When you grip a club, the light can turn on and now there's current flowing through the whole system. It's like a current traveling from your brain to your hands and from your hands to your brain. Your grip on the club is the most accurate communication system for golf swing development."

"I know you explained about the differing roles the muscles and joints play in a golf swing; just tell me again so I can get it once and for all," I asked. I needed to reinforce his system in my brain. He seemed a little frustrated at my questions, but I wanted to have all his ideas, all the proof, and all the different ways to express this beautiful philosophy about what is real control and power in a golf swing.

"It's like this. Relative to your hands, your torso muscles are dull. Physiologically, in terms of the network of nerves and the sixth sense that operates on a subconscious level—proprioception—the hands are the only part of your anatomy capable of giving you accurate fine-muscle feedback on the speed and direction of the club. They are also uniquely designed for the task of making any necessary adjustments."

"Often I hear golf teachers speak as though the hands are unreliable and dangerous," I challenged.

"Hogwash," he said matter-of-factly. "Of course, they need to be trained, but no other part of your body can replace their role in a golf swing."

"But then why do so many golf teachers and skilled players say the larger muscles control the swing?"

"Do you want the truth?"

"Of course!"

"Fear. Fear coming from a lack of understanding. They have no knowledge of how the mind and body communicate; I mean the circuitry and design. After all, most of the golf swing takes place out of sight, but it doesn't need to take place out of mind. The proprioceptors take care of that for us. A basic lack of understanding is why these folks cannot fathom controlling the fast action of the swing through the true source of the swing. They hope and pray that the hands will behave, if they don't mess with them. Really, that's a very defensive way to go about swinging a club, and anyone who does it is setting themselves up for a fall, because you can't play any sport well in defensive mode.

You've got to be proactive and aware and present to what you want; don't expect good things to happen without sound training. Your hands cannot be eliminated or glossed over in your training program. They are a rich, dense, fertile sensory garden."

These seemed like solid opinions backed up by science. Obviously Joe felt strongly about these conflicts in learning that golfers had had to endure in the past few years. But it was exactly what I needed to hear.

He had more to say, though. "I'll tell you another reason folks miss out on the truth: The hands and wrists move so fast during the release that it's hard to see what's going on. You asked about power and you and others have equated golf swing power with size. Sports are heading dangerously in that direction, but there is no direct correlation. We need to re-evaluate how we observe the body during the golf swing. What are we looking at? It's easy to see the larger slower-moving parts of the swing—the shoulders—and assume they're in control and provide the power. But that's not the source of the swing at all. Your torso moves a relatively short distance during the swing, and it moves slowly, so there's no way it can conduct the other parts of the body through greater distances, changing angles, and huge speed."

"Then what is the role of the torso?" I asked.

"The torso simply supports the swing pattern—the speed and direction—of the hands, arms, and club. Like a swing set, the frame allows the seat and chains to swing and supports them because it's anchored to the ground, like the torso is through the legs. The beauty of this system is that if you know the action of the hands and the club, then your mind-body system can respond in kind."

"You know, Joe, I tried to work with the hands years ago, but I found that most golfers' swings became narrow, weak, vertical in swing pattern, and extremely unstable in the wrist action. So naturally, I tried something else, because I couldn't get a student to develop any sense of club control that way."

Shaking his head, Joe responded, "You simply didn't do it with enough understanding of how the hands needed to be placed on the grip and how they function throughout the swing. You know, the hands are capable of deft control, and of course, if not taught with proper care and understanding, their action could create disastrous results. What you really needed to do was try to understand how they're supposed to work, not leave them to fend for themselves in developing a swing. To assume, when you concentrate on hand action, that the swing would become too 'wristy' is to really not use the hands in a fundamental way.

"For example, the beginning of the swing of hand action is to feel the arc of the handle that combines the lead hand and arm in a unified swing action." He demonstrated again how the handle has an arc. "That's certainly not too wristy, is it? The lead arm moves naturally in conjunction with the lead hand to create a swing arc that's useful." His hand and left arm swung back and his torso moved in kind. It was silky smooth. I could not tell what controlled what.

"Notice how my whole body responded to this arc. This is how one puts together a swing through the proper use of the hands—without sacrificing club head awareness. This way you gain total control of it." He demonstrated again. "You notice I have a swing arc that has great potential. Would you agree?" I nodded. His backswing was classic and potent. "However, my swing has no potential without a sound release, has it? One still needs to know how to deliver the club."

"So is this arc and a smooth swing the environment for it? Wow," I said, "that sounds great, but how do I do it?"

"We'll get into the release triggers in due time," he said. "Anything else?"

"I do have more questions, but maybe we should take a break."

Just then, the dog, who had been snoring steadily throughout our discussion, let out a sound that could only be described as a sighing yawn. He had obviously heard this discussion before and seemed glad it was over! Otter stretched his long legs and blinked at Joe. Joe gave him a pat and looked at his watch, excused himself and said he had to put some more lapping compound on the reels he was sharpening and would be back shortly.

My mind was ricocheting all over the place as I processed what I had learned. My negative vibes about Joe Burlington and this place had dissolved. There was a lot he could teach me—maybe it would get me out of my rut and take my mind off the break-up with Claire. It all felt good. It felt proactive for my game. Besides, my alternative was a bitter winter in New England, indoors, golfless, watching movies without anyone to share my popcorn.

4
AWARENESS: FEEL OR ANALYSIS

Burlington returned ten minutes later with two bottles of grapefruit juice and a few triangles of buttered breakfast bread. We sat down in the shade of some large trees near the building, and I thanked him for arranging for me to observe some lessons. "I know you don't teach much anymore, so I really appreciate it."

"It's not that I don't still love teaching," he said, "but many do not want to take the time to process and integrate the changes I suggest. It takes some real stick-to-it-iveness—if that's a word—and faith! In most cases, they'd rather be spoon-fed information and fixed and adjusted than acquire changes through their own practice. Spoon-feeding students is very empty, very boring to me. Desires are being served, but not true needs. That approach doesn't breed confidence and self-trust. Students who want that look at a teacher as a wizard performing magic on their minds and bodies. To me, though, that's sacrilege—when instructors take credit for talent that students already have. Big egos are being fed at the expense of the student!"

Burlington took a breather to eat his snack. My guilty conscience wondered if Burlington had lumped mine in with those other oversized pro egos and if his silence was to emphasize his point. The pause hung in the air, and except for a soft breeze from the east, we were a still life painting. These conversational gaps were uncomfortable for me, but Joe seemed to need and enjoy them. I picked up another piece of bread to keep my mouth busy before he began again.

"Golf is meant to be fun. It's played all over the world in the most beautiful settings. Yet so many players seem so frustrated most of the time, especially the ones who spend a lot of time practicing. The perception is that if you didn't learn it as a child, then forget about learning it now. That's misleading, and it's very limiting. Naturally, learning when you're young is a great advantage, but golf can be learned by anyone willing to take a good look and apply some principles of awareness." I nodded my agreement, still chewing on the bread.

"The golf swing needs to be learned," Joe explained, "through development of a personal physical feel, and relationships between the club, the ground, the ball, and the target. It's like developing an extra sense that combines all physical and emotional feelings—balanced to optimal potential. If you take golf analysis, it's like therapy, isn't it, Geoff? Fixing the golfer's physiology to conform to a standard. But that aside, the analytical approach, even though it's so universally accepted and praised by adult golfers, is of very little value and likely sends learners down the wrong road. An instructor needs to enlighten the student to the fact that figuring out every posture and move involved for each situation is of little value, especially if it means changing their nature. Analysis is too slow and awkward. It's unnatural! A great performance never relies on such a slow and clumsy tool. If a golfer is relying on intellect, trouble is lurking for sure."

I caught his wink, but I was still chewing. He took a swig of juice and continued. "Once you have imprinted an engram, a pattern, you can become accurate yet work subconsciously. Then you can begin trusting your own senses and experience. How it feels to you is all that's of value when you play golf, or any game for that matter. That's once the club is OK, right? I call it 'learning feel.' It is where your focus should always be when you teach and practice."

"But how can a golfer learn to feel? How do you show someone to rely on instinct when each learner's makeup is different? I'm sorry, but I don't understand your theory, Joe."

"It's not a theory, Geoff, it's natural and the best way a human can learn. You can learn just by paying attention to the action of the club and then asking yourself what it is to you, at that moment. In most cases you need to begin very gently and slowly so that accurate coordination is developed—like Tai Chi swings! At this speed, muscle overflow or 'trying hard' with muscle tension won't likely occur and your students will begin to get a sense of ease and timing from the get-go. Some teachers prefer to begin with shorter clubs and swings, but I prefer the longer whippy clubs and full swings at extremely slow speeds. It's a matter of preference, really, and it depends on the student. I like to begin right from the start cutting and grooving those neuropathways with the whole swing pattern. And practically anyone can do it at Tai Chi speed. The key is to make it a total quality exercise so the coordination is learned immediately.

"Through your suggestions of swing patterns, they'll start to get an imprint of the swing. It will take a conscious effort at first, but with enough repetition the proprioceptors will learn the swing and create such familiarity that conscious practice will give way to unconscious trust of the new pattern. Just like riding a bike or skiing down a slope: At first you may fall, but in due time, with repetition, your body will learn the balance and almost never fall again. It's muscle memory."

Questions popped into my head but I didn't want to interrupt him.

"Anyway, because feel is flux, it can be confusing to a student. They'll ask why they can't do it every time. Remind them it's like each day of their life: Every day is different, so they need to be ready to adjust based on their starting point. That's why you must teach them the fundamental action of the club—that's constant. They will learn to trust in a swing without consciously trying hard. The more opportunities you give them to discover on their own, the greater the likelihood they will be able to sustain their improvement. Simple as that.

"Ultimately, when they possess this confidence, they need to learn to simply observe, to not be part of making a swing. Their consciousness becomes an audience to their unconscious swing. They must trust it and let it perform. That's high-altitude confidence."

I finished my juice and put the cap back on the bottle. "Where can I throw this—do you have a recycling bin?" Burlington took the bottle and tossed it in the direction of an uncovered dark-blue bin outside the shed, a good twenty feet away. He scored an effortless three-pointer. "Good shot!" I exclaimed. "How long did you practice that one?"

"Geoff, that's exactly what I've been talking about! I knew it before I threw it, based on past experience. I never would have made that shot had I analyzed how to position myself and choreographed every move. You need to trust and rely on feelings when you practice, same as when you're teaching. I know people say you can't teach someone to use their feelings without analyzing the mechanics of their swing, but that's just not true. Once you go through the learning process you can let go of 'trying to do it.'"

Burlington smiled. He knew he'd gotten my attention. I returned the grin, and told him, "You know, Joe, you're making perfect sense to me and I realize that youngsters will be able to follow your feel technique, but I doubt I could convince most adults. I just don't believe that adults will accept your discovery learning approach, employing those proprioceptors and swinging with their eyes closed. I don't know if I could teach that way. Adults seem to want to fix their problems with mechanical adjustments and analysis. They want more obvious solutions than trusting their senses. Besides, they love to relate to positions and parts of a golf swing. They want something more concrete for their bucks!"

"That's true, but it's really your job, as the instructor, to do whatever it takes to help change this attitude."

"That's easy to say, but how do you go about doing it?"

"How do you change someone who's used to achieving success if they just follow directions by reading the recipe, memorizing the map, or mimicking a pro in a video? Most leisure golfers don't have the time to learn to feel. They want to purchase the answer key. That's why they hire a pro, no?

"Sometimes it's difficult, but I've found all kinds of ways to teach students to feel. My best example is that I used to be that way myself. In fact, I doubt if anyone was a more frustrated golfer than I. You wanna talk about mechanical issues? I had in my brain more swing analyses and recommended positions to integrate and sequence during my swing than there are grains of sand in that sand trap over there. I had been traveling in the wrong direction for so long I really didn't know where I'd gone wrong. It was my own miserable failures that made me take a good look and notice what was happening. I got to the point of having such self-doubt that I wondered where I ever got the idea that I could play and teach this game for a living."

Burlington's words mirrored my own recent thoughts. Were his pauses deliberate punctuations, allowing me to fill in the blanks with my own realizations? I stayed quiet and he began again. "I had lost all the things that had made me successful as a junior golfer. By the time I figured it out, I was miles from my best athletic self. You see, Geoff, I kept trying to perfect my swing. No matter how good I was, I wanted better. My preoccupation with perfection had a reverse effect. All the scrutiny and self-criticism diminished my swing's effectiveness.

"I had nothing to lose. The first thing I did, as I said, was change my attitude. I decided that no matter what happened on the golf course, I wasn't going to let it bother me. I made a commitment that I would just go on. I stuck to it. That was the beginning. Then I had to get rid of all mechanical thoughts—no more manipulation. I had to become techniqueless. Think about that," he ordered, giving me enough silent time to absorb his words.

"I imagine that's how the very first golf swing was taken anyhow, Geoff. It was probably a mighty lash that knocked that first Scotsman right off his feet. Just think what joy he must have felt when he shared his discovery of the game with his friends! Those first swings, those feelings and attitudes, need to be experienced again today. When I realized that I had left that approach in the rear view mirror long ago, it was a step forward for me.

"The people who brought us this game were earthy and natural. They were shepherds, farmers, blacksmiths. They never studied it. They were definitely not intellectuals. There was no technique in those days, Geoff. People played instinctually. There was no mechanical analysis. The ones who developed the most feel and trusted their own instincts won the game. That principle holds true today."

I visualized those earliest golfers. Golf with play! Playing golf! I couldn't remember when golf had lost its sense of play for me.

"Those first golfers were beautiful in their simplicity. They were in touch, Geoff, and to me it is this connection—this sensory approach—that I needed to return to also." I nodded with true understanding "Geoff, just think about it. The first golfers had no teachers. Their swings ranged from the rhythmic to the mighty. They were shot-makers and they had fun! They relied totally on their senses and intuition. That's exactly what we all need to get back to. So I agree with you: Things have gotten out of hand. Rigorously defining 'proper form' and using so-called mechanics excessively," he continued, "constrains your students. The result will bear little resemblance to an athletic performance."[3]

At the risk of frustrating him, I asked again, "But how does a golfer learn totally by feel?"

"How does a teacher teach totally by feel?" he countered. "You have to be creative. After all, you know the absolute fundamentals, the physics of the club for the shot desired. Help your students develop the swing qualities necessary for them to sustain positive growth within those dynamics," he explained.

"But there's so much to know," I protested. "The fundamentals, I mean."

"I beg to differ. There are only a few things to know very well." I asked him to explain. He looked at me a little puzzled, as if this were elementary. He took a sip of juice and continued. "All you need to teach a student is the speed and direction that the club head needs to be traveling through impact, then the shapes and speeds of the swing that make that action more possible more frequently. Each student needs to satisfy the physics component to the best of their mental and physical ability, realizing their own potential. Once the physics are satisfied, just ask them how it feels. All your questions will drive at their awareness of what is happening with the club.

"You need to ask a lot of 'feel' questions to get them to tap into their senses: What does it feel like physically to swing over there? Ask them what different speeds feel like, etcetera. Get it?" He smiled encouragingly. "But again, Geoff, they will ask you how to do it. And, if you're tuned in, you can make a guess at what they're feeling, and while you're observing, you'll find out how close to reality they are. Remember, it's your job to just wake them up, not rebirth them. They must view you as a coach, not a wizard or guru. Otherwise they will become dependent on you, which, in teaching, can only mean failure."

"But there must be some mechanics."

"Anything you want to categorize as mechanics can be covered under Feeling the Physics 101," he laughed. "After God, everything is physics."

"I wonder, Joe, if you could show me how you practice teaching feeling, becoming aware of it."

"Glad to," Burlington responded. He got up and pulled out his one iron. That was a surprise. I'd never heard of beginning a practice session with a one iron. He made a few practice swings in slow motion right there, as though he was feeling every muscle in his body. He began to swing, again very slowly at first, like Tai Chi exercises. Then he closed his eyes and continued to swing. His action was super fluid. Its shape seemed perfect and I wondered when he would begin hitting shots. Suddenly he stopped, took a mighty swing, and brought with it a divot of turf almost a foot long just below the surface of the grass. Then he placed a ball into the middle of the divot, took the one iron, looked once at the target, and took a swing. He hit it thin directly toward his target. At first, I wasn't impressed, but then in another instant he was into his next swing. He struck that shot a little heavy, but again toward the target. In another instant, Burlington placed the ball in the middle of the divot and swung again. This time it was solid, but a little to the right. He was into the next swing, no hesitation—wham! There was another crisp shot, only this time it split the pin. Another swing again—hit solid, right at his target.

The next few minutes were a display of one-iron shots off hardpan like I had never witnessed before. Burlington finished most of the bucket without saying a word and there was a definite groove to his play. What he did next really took me by surprise. He bent down and picked up the divot that he had slashed from the earth and replaced it. You could hardly tell he'd practiced there.

Impressed and excited, I thought here was a guy whose actions matched his words. I hadn't seen that very often. I thought back to some of the tour players I'd worked with. They can hit it, for sure, but when they try to explain how you can do it, they're at a complete loss. They relate only to themselves; they haven't a clue about your perspective, and therein lies the problem. And then there are teachers who can describe in detail how to go about it and yet can't hit it. But Burlington could practice what he was preaching. How he hit those shots so quickly and accurately was a puzzle to me, especially since he didn't even seem to look at the target. Yet the balls went directly toward it almost every time.

Next, Burlington pulled out his driver. Skepticism crept back in; this I wanted to see. At Tai Chi speed, Joe teed up six balls in a line and, one after the other, he hit them with barely a second between shots. The first ball flew about a hundred yards a little off-line; then he hit a little to the left and not quite solid. Then a little right, more solid, and then just right. Then to the left again. He finished the first set, and just as before, you could see he'd reached his groove. In the next set, each ball landed almost on top of the one before. Only now the speed was increasing. The balls were flying long. Burlington still didn't say anything. He kept swinging and the balls kept flying. As the display of shot and swing control continued, it became a marvel to observe. Burlington hit about thirty drives. After the first six, the accuracy was so good, you could have put a blanket over the balls.

Then he took his wedge, picked a target, and shot balls toward the base of the flag. I was astonished. He began to change the trajectories of shots and alter the spin. Some hit the flag, while others bounced just beyond it. There was clearly a ton of creativity and control in his shots. He could only be doing this by feeling and trusting in his swing. What also struck me was that this is exactly how everyone should be playing! That truth had been obscured by my own dismal past.

Silent as he performed, Joe Burlington smiled from time to time, emerging from the game he was obviously playing in his head. I desperately wanted to get in on it. This was the real deal. He took one last swing. "That's it," he said. He put his wedge back into the bag and sat down.

"How did you do that?" I asked.

"Do what?" he teased.

"You know, make all those swings and hardly take a breath."

"Oh," he replied, "you mean how fast I practice?"

"Yes, and why in the world would you begin with a one iron? What are you thinking from shot to shot?"

"Hold on there, Geoff; one question at a time. The one iron lets me challenge myself right from the start. It's one of my favorite clubs, but you know it requires a high level of awareness. I've learned that it tells me the most about my swing, so I begin with it to find out my baseline for the day. It helps me notice my patterns and my timing for the impact."

"But what about all the other contributing factors, like setup, grip, and plane?"

He lowered his voice. "Those things are rote," he whispered like he was embarrassed to have to clue in a big boy like me. "We learned those things a long time ago. There's no need to concentrate on them now. Besides, there's too much to feel in the impact zone to be distracted by things that we learned as children. Right, Geoff?"

"I begin slowly," he continued, "so as to wake my feelings and senses up, but once I get what I'm looking for, I just begin repeating. If I get something I don't want, I just cancel it out in my mind. I don't verbalize anything as I practice because I never want to engage the left brain in a session. Again, it's a discipline that keeps my mind in the right place—asking the right questions so that my senses, intuition, and body awareness can discover the feel of a sound swing for that day, based on the physics. I'm playing a mental game, a mind game, if you will, the whole time. I figure if I can time a one iron, a driver, and a wedge, that covers the whole ball of wax. Don't you think?"

Holding in a chuckle, I shook my head with amusement.

"What's wrong?" he asked

"I just find it very amusing," I replied. "Practically everything you do is contrary to how I learned to practice golf."

"Thank you," he responded with a smile. "I will take that as a compliment. But let me tell you in more detail what's going through my mind as I practice, Geoff. The questions I ask myself are fundamental. The fact that I begin with a one iron is just a challenge and fun to me; I wouldn't recommend it to most golfers."

"Oh, you don't have to worry about that," I quipped. "No one would take me seriously about that anyway."

"Good," he said.

"One other thing came to mind as I was watching—the speed at which you practice the routine for developing feel. I've always wanted to develop a clutter-free way of swinging and playing, and..."

"You're pretty sure you were just watching it?" he asked.

"Well, yes, I think you could say that," I said humbly.

"You'll get your chance to see how to teach and swing that way. Some of the students will be filled with ideas that are, as you put it, cluttered. We will definitely address 'monkey-mind syndrome' when the time comes. I agree that being uncluttered is a real good place to be, both physically and with one's psyche. Of course, the psyche always comes first."

"But back to what was going through your mind when you first struck those balls not so solid and off line."

"Actually," he said. "I don't remember them. I forget them right away. I chalk them up to being unaware in that moment of swinging the club. Really, I just say 'cancel' to myself and go to the next one. I do notice what they are and adjust according to my awareness, but that's all I use them for. They help me get in balance. I don't waste a second on what went wrong. They don't mean anything in terms of how I might play."

"It would have disturbed me a lot if I'd started that way."

"Really?" Burlington's eyebrows raised and he feigned surprise. "Those warm-up shots give me an accurate assessment of where I am at that moment—feeling-wise; it's like tuning in to my inner frequency. Missed shots are stepping stones, not stumbling blocks. Just because those shots weren't what I wanted doesn't mean they're wasted.

"Let me ask you this, Geoff: When you get up in the morning, does everything happen perfectly from the moment you leave your bed?"

"I guess not," I answered.

"Do you fret about it or do you just go on?" Joe asked.

"I usually don't pay it any mind. It's just part of the day."

"Right. There's nothing you can do about it, so your only option is to go on. The ball is always in your court when it comes to choosing how you're going to react to anything. You can either dwell on what didn't work or you can choose otherwise and move on." He turned his palms up, weighing the choices. "You'll probably see exactly what I'm talking about in a student this week. Looking in from the outside will make it easy for you to see clearly which choice was the best one. The same thing needs to happen in your own golf, Geoff, whether it's on the course or on the practice tee. I've found it to be a healthy way to handle learning and playing golf, and for that matter, handling life itself."

He laid down another one of his long pauses. I was starting to get used to them. Then abruptly, he stood up. "Excuse me, but I need to take care of a few things; you can stay here and practice if you like. I'll be back in a while."

5

JUST FLY THE PLANE

I sat there, trying to absorb what Burlington had told me and shown me. I didn't need to hit shots; I needed to think about what he had said and done. He had hooked me with his maverick attitude and his unorthodox, yet simple, technique. He was definitely unconventional, but his eccentricity was not the issue; I'd been accused of that myself. And it was obvious that as an athlete, Joe Burlington could do with a golf club exactly what he was talking about.

My own practice sessions were the antithesis of Joe's. I'd spend an hour hitting the same bucket of balls Burlington had hit in a few minutes. I'd developed a sort of slow ritual of checkpoints. I would always begin with a wedge or other short club. I would begin going down my checklist—first my alignment, then my setup, then my takeaway, ending with my top-of-the-swing position. When I think about it, I hardly ever got to feeling and knowing what I wanted at impact. I had always assumed that you needed all the other things to come first. Yet Joe claimed he never left impact with his awareness presence. I could never get to the one iron or the driver. Compared with Burlington's, my approach seemed backwards. To top it off, I would have been exhausted—and that would have shaved off confidence rather than building it. Joe was fresh. The whole time he'd been practicing, he was improving his feel and his confidence. Wasn't that what it was all about?

I had been digging myself into a deep hole, analyzing each swing and what was wrong with it, and then trying to extricate myself from that hole. My practice never seemed to have an end, either. There was always something else for me to do; I never felt ready to put it into action on the course. If I had a good day of practice, the doubt would cast a shadow over the next day. Would my swing be there tomorrow? How many years would I have to practice to ever feel ready?

This rush of honesty pivoted my mind to Claire. I was crazy about her and would do just about anything to make her happy. But my social life had always come second to golf. When Claire had shown up for her lessons after Jason dumped her, I was angry that he hadn't recognized what a prize he'd won in Claire. I only wanted to make her laugh again. And when she finally let me know that I could do more than make her laugh, I'd felt like I'd won the lottery. Yet I'd kept telling her I wasn't ready. "Life happens, whether you're ready or not, Geoff. All we have is the moment. Sometimes waiting for 'ready' is not an option," she'd told me before saying goodbye. I could have agreed with her, if she'd waited for a response.

Joe Burlington was right. I'd let too many meaningless things bother me—like the way things went when I first picked up a club, or how I'd feel if my swing deteriorated as a session progressed into the second hour. It stopped being fun when I didn't feel ready. My students complained about that, too. At times they would begin on a good note, but after a few minutes, things would take a turn for the worse. Sometimes no matter what they tried, and despite everything they knew, nothing worked. That's when it stopped being fun.

I hadn't thought about it before, but most golfers don't know how to practice to get better, me included. Oh, we know how to complicate the game and end up worse off for the effort. I remembered students—I'd done it myself—taking a hiatus from golf, and then doing pretty well for a while after resuming the game. But very quickly, the same patterns would emerge and things would go downhill. I kept thinking of how much time I'd wasted. I wished I'd met Joe Burlington years ago.

Before I had time to let my thoughts drift to other parts of my life that needed fixing, Joe returned with Otter, two containers of coffee, and a brown bag. It was closer to lunch than breakfast and Joe must have anticipated my stomach grumbling. As he sat, he proffered the bag with one hand and a napkin with the other. "Sorry it took me so long. I needed to check a few things in the shop."

And I had needed the break to process what I'd learned. Maybe it *could* get me out of my rut. I took a cookie from the bag.

Burlington sipped his coffee and relaxed in the chair next to me. Otter sat down at his feet, lowering himself slowly, leg by leg. He let out a deep groan. Joe broke off a piece of cookie and Otter made it disappear without blinking. Joe continued to share his cookie with the dog, balancing his coffee on his knee.

After a bit of small talk, I took the opportunity to regurgitate my ponderings. "You know, Joe, since I watched your practice session, I've been thinking about the differences between your routine and mine. When I was very young, I guess I learned your type of practice, but I wasn't aware of the process—or how my senses and 'feel' figured into it. Now that I think about it, as I got older and developed my analytical thinking, I abandoned my natural and intuitive self—and for the sake of trying to improve! You've made it clear that that's exactly how I lost my confidence. I became very unsure of myself and that snowballed. My skills plateaued when I began to get mechanical, and it all went south after that. Oddly, I had confidence in most parts of my life, except in what I wanted most—to be a really fine golfer!" As I said that I felt like I was sharing a great golf epiphany.

"I can relate to that," Joe said. "Your practice strategy was a stumbling block instead of being a stepping stone to your progress, Geoff. As your confidence eroded, so went your swing."

"Yes," I concurred sadly. "I understand now. When I reached the point where I had no place to go, the only strategy I had was to learn more and practice harder. I couldn't seem to get going in a positive direction." I really wanted to hear more about how Joe had gotten himself back on track and to hear in more detail about the changes he had made during the transition. I wanted a roadmap. I asked him, "What exactly did you find out about how to develop your confidence and how to get rid of your insecurity in golf?"

"Geoff, my mistakes were similar to yours—and to almost everyone who picks up a club to learn to swing better! You see, I also thought knowing more about the mechanics of how to play and how to swing would give me confidence. Boy, was I wrong! It's very difficult for people to understand, but knowledge is the opposite of trust and self-confidence. The more I thought about my golf swing and really knew how it worked, the worse I performed. Knowledge of how things worked, in fact, increased my self-doubt."

"How could that be?

"I guess as I learned the intricate mechanical details, I began to micro-manage everything about my swing. Now I knew how many things could go wrong. But knowing all the mechanical minutia would never provide me with the trust I needed. Remember, Geoff, I'm Irish. Murphy's Law, a given for anyone Irish, was at work!"

He laughed heartily and took a sip of his coffee, then tossed the last piece of cookie in Otter's direction. The dog snapped it down in one swallow that went straight to a yawn. Joe patted Otter's head and put down his cup. "Let me tell you a story about trust that illustrates what I mean. It comes from eastern philosophy."

Otter let out another yawn, but Joe continued anyway. "A master would frequently assert to his disciples that holiness was less a matter of what one actually did than what one allowed to happen. To demonstrate, he told the following story." Joe lowered his voice to a dramatic whisper.

"There once was a one-legged dragon, who said to a centipede, 'How do you manage all those legs? It is all I can do to manage just one.' 'To tell you the truth,' said the centipede, 'I don't manage them at all'."[4] Joe chugged down his coffee as I nodded a dim understanding.

"In the case of a golf swing, a lot is happening, and it's a matter of trust that we allow it to happen. So often, we think we need to be in charge of everything—as if that would really give us total control! But that control is an illusion, Geoff, and the odd thing is, we keep doing it and it keeps serving us poorly. We have to pause, examine, and change the way we do things.

"You see, trust and knowledge don't necessarily work together. It's not logical, but neither is any belief system. It's harbored in our unconscious, complex and often illogical. When one is learning, one is not necessarily getting more confident. That was hard for me to understand because I believed that the more I worked and the more I knew, the more successful I would be. You must develop your confidence, your trust in yourself, at the same time that you are becoming more aware. Many people fail to accept this principle."

He hesitated for a moment. "It's like spirituality. Have you ever asked anyone to really explain their faith? To a believer, that faith makes perfect sense. But to a non-believer.... Because if you have faith, you don't need an explanation, and if you don't, then no explanation will ever satisfy your intellect. If you don't have it—that instinct or feel or faith—you can't get it through knowledge or logic!"

During the pause that followed, my cell phone rang. I turned it off, embarrassed, and apologized. Joe dismissed it with a wave and a single nod and continued to speak. "So we cannot get trust through intellect. It's a matter of belief. You need to become a bit of a mystic, Geoff. Get to the point where no explanation is necessary. Have you ever noticed an athlete's response to either a great play or an unusually poor performance? Most often, they can't explain how it happened."

"So then what can one do to get better?"

"You build up your awareness, your in-the-moment ability to feel, and you believe in that. You don't need to know why or how, conceptually or intellectually. The trust component is vital when it comes to improving and needs to be developed while improving one's swing and playing the game. It's like when we learned to walk. We had to keep trying and, at some point, believe that we wouldn't fall down. After a while, it was automatic because we were designed to walk. We just don't realize how we learned to do it or how we developed our belief that we could. And now we don't question our ability to walk or run. The same thing can happen with your golf swing, but you need a program that covers all the physics and, at the same time, enables a golfer to become confident. Because as humans, we were designed to play golf, right?" He smiled.

I nodded, but really didn't know what I was agreeing with. "Physics. I have another question. When my students take lessons, they usually do fine with me. But when they get on the course, or if they practice alone, things don't work as well."

"Yes," he responded, "that used to happen to me all the time. If they're in balance with their swing, you could point directly at their trying too hard, which is, again, a trust problem. But if they're not trying too hard, and they *are* trusting, but it's just not working? What's happening usually relates to an imbalance of focus."

"Huh?"

"OK, I'm going to explain using an old physics theory from the 1930s." Otter sighed loudly. He had, no doubt, heard Joe tell this story before. Joe scratched Otter between the ears. "This story may be useful when your students are puzzled by their practice and play. You see, Geoff, focus is a two-edged sword! It may get you to change something for the better, but it may also disrupt something that was good before you zeroed in on it. Micro-focusing, compartmentalizing, often does not allow you to see the forest for the trees. Performance suffers because of this incomplete awareness, and then you get confused about the value of your changes. You may end up believing you went down the wrong road.

"Do you know the first thing pilots are trained to think when they have an in-flight emergency? Fly the plane. Don't get so into the emergency that you crash, having fixed the problem. In golf that translates into 'swing the club.' Don't get so into improving some aspect of your action that you don't swing the club well!

"Anyway, back to physics. Have you heard of Heisenberg? The guy who turned the physics world upside down with his uncertainty principle back in the thirties?"

"Uh, no, not really."

"Well, Werner Heisenberg came along when there was a great debate about light, classical physics, and the new quantum physics. The question was, 'is light a particle or a wave?' It caused great consternation among that branch of science. In one camp, you had the wavers and in the other, the quanta or particle fans. Heisenberg disputed both when he said that light can be both—it has a dual nature, and what it seems to be depends on how one looks at it. That principle kind of goes with everything we look at, doesn't it? Essentially, Heisenberg said that you cannot determine the momentum of light and the position of it at the same time, so when you look at light one way, it is a particle in a small space, but from another perspective, it can be a wave covering a very large area."

I wondered how this fit into our discussion of the golf swing. My puzzled look prompted Joe to say, "Bear with me, Geoff; there is a point to this story." I nodded politely and tried to look less confused. "The wave camp pooh-poohed Heisenberg's idea and, of course, so did the particle camp, but he was right."

I couldn't restrain myself. "How does this relate to golf?"

"Well," Joe said, "it relates to how we look at everything. Let's say you looked under a microscope at two words."

He took out a pen and wrote on the paper bag, very large, *momentum* and below it, in very small letters, *position.*

"If you focus the microscope on the word *position*, the smaller of the two, *momentum* goes out of focus, right? Heisenberg to the tee! The same thing happens to golfers, Geoff! In teaching, all you need to figure out is what's more valuable to your students. I'm sure you know where I stand on this. Momentum relates to a whole motion and of course position relates to static parts. To me, learning a golf swing through feeling motion and the sequence is the key.

"Anyway, back to Heisenberg. When we focus on one area, the others get fuzzy. If you only care about your flow in a golf swing, if you focus on it long enough, it's likely you'll become unaware of your path! If you concentrate on path, it's likely you'll become unaware of your timing. Now regarding practice, it's the concentrated way you look at things that can throw off the other fundamentals. That's why it's best to spend a few minutes on each discrete area in order for the whole works to stay in balance. When your students are not trying hard and they seem not to be making progress, it's usually a question of focus."

"What do you do then?"

"You give them a simple balanced program. Ten minutes of flow, ten minutes of path, and ten minutes of timing—and maybe ten minutes of nothing to do except swing to see how things blend."

"It seems that after the setup your program is all motion. I learned to swing in a totally different way."

"How so?"

"By getting my body and club into about eight distinct positions to create a fundamental swing action."

"That surely is popular, Geoff, but just like Heisenberg, you have to include the point of view of the observer, the student. Then ask the question. What POV gives them the most complete picture and the possibility of a sound swing action? Remember, your students are going to be on their own and need a way to go about it when they're alone on the course too."

"You seem to have a real aversion to teaching the golf swing in the separate parts that most instruction adheres to these days."

"You're exactly right, Geoff—this is a very important aspect of my paradigm shift. Have you ever noticed how much you can tell about a swing from a distance? I mean, it's easy to see the flow and path patterns from 200 yards away."

"Yes, I have noticed that I can tell who's on our practice tee from a distance."

"And that's a view of the whole, not the parts. Coming from this perspective allows you to help a student develop a swing from a totally different point of view. Teaching from a position development standpoint tends to shut down the mind-body sensory system because it lends itself to analysis. Feel comes to a grinding halt. On the other hand, the whole swing motion development, momentum, which the mind-body system relates to instantly, gives feel feedback continuously. Avoid the minutia and wake up the sensory system.

"Granted, for a teacher, it's a far more challenging way to go and requires a lot of experience and creativity, but in the final analysis (no pun intended) it is superior and longer lasting. Your students will be very well served.

"I'll give you an example. I had a student, Tony, who'd been playing for a few years and loved it. He played OK but felt he could do better, so he came to see me. I questioned him about his game and what programs he'd tried. And I asked him about his swing thoughts—what was on his mind while he practiced and played.

"He said he had many different swing thoughts for all occasions. He described it as putting out fires. For instance, he said when he wanted to hit it far, he used to load up on his right side—you know, increase his shoulder turn. But most of the time he'd get mishits—until a friend told him some magic way to hit it far and never to the right. He had all kinds of different adjustments friends and teachers had recommended.

"So I asked him to just show me his swing. This was almost an alien concept to him. He asked me what he should think about and how I wanted him to approach it. He had a lot of trouble with the idea of just being 'mindless' and hitting a few shots. He'd never made a swing before without a litany of things to think about.

"So I tried another approach. I asked him to show me his routine, and to swing, and tell me everything that went through his mind from beginning to end; from before he made the swing to when he executed the shot."

"So what did he think about?" I asked.

"It was quite something. First he lined up the club from behind the ball, then he walked to the side and begin working on his posture, bending his knees and sticking out his butt and kind of wiggling into position. You could tell his lower back had tensed up and he wasn't comfortable. Then he took hold of the club with what he described as 'good pressure.' He said if he wanted to hit it far, he made as big a shoulder turn as possible."

"Anything else?"

"Oh yes. He said then he had to really concentrate on coiling his body, keeping his head down on the ball for as long as he could and on trying to keep his left arm as straight as possible, and keeping his wrists stiff. And lastly, he prayed. Which is not a bad idea.

"And remember, Geoff: One manipulation begets another."

"What do you mean?"

"If Tony had to think of a step one movement, then he would have to deal with step two, three, four, and on and on. It never ends. He'd tied himself to a series of simultaneous manipulations. I watched him go through his whole routine, and he made solid contact. His swing looked like it took a lot of work, but you could tell he was pleased with the results. But after a few more swings, he was very erratic. His excellent start disintegrated into a hodgepodge. He would hit the ball solidly toward the target every fourth shot and chastise himself for every mishit.

"I asked him to swing with a longer club—a four iron. With that, his contact became seriously unpredictable. I remember he practically stuck the club into the ground, then hit it way left, way right, and also very thin. As he swung, his upper body coiled. The downswing seemed like springs in a motor wound as tightly as possible. The club flailed recklessly at the mercy of his unharnessed force. He was about one for ten using the longer club. He had no way of controlling the club's direction. His club face was really shut, too. That's a common result of a dominating torso torque in the backswing.

"So what did you do?"

"I told him he didn't have to think a thought at all."

"How did he take that?"

"He said it would be strange, and that his thinking it through was what allowed him to play well. 'I beg to differ,' I said, and told him it was exactly why his swing and shots were so erratic. I asked him how many of his swing thoughts dealt with the club."

"And?"

"None. So I told him that it was totally unnecessary for him to think about the things he was thinking about and that it was actually a detriment to his natural athletic ability. I mean, all he had to do was swing the club! That's the first order of business. Just like pilots need to first concentrate on flying the plane. Tony was so micro-focused on all these details that the big picture went out of focus.

"I explained to Tony how he could get back to a natural swing. For the swing to be repeatable, it needs to have a quality of fluid motion for consistency. In Tony's case, I suggested he begin to lighten his hold on the club and allow the club swinging to dominate his muscles and joints. He needed to see how supple he could feel throughout his body."

"At first he was concerned that if he held the club lightly, he wouldn't gain control over it or that it would fly out of his hands, but I told him that a golf swing needs to be graceful. Look at the best swings throughout golf's history.

"I got him to try a few practice swings and he began to loosen up and swing the club as though it were not so heavy. Then I had him tee up about six balls, six inches apart, and swing consecutively from the first ball to the last without stopping. Tony went right through the six balls and made solid contact with four of them. He teed up some more and went through four sets that way. He struck the balls solidly, for the most part."

"Because he stopped trying to focus on all those adjustments?"

"Yes. And he also discovered a nice bonus. He said that before, using his routine, he would have been tired and sore if he'd made that many swings, but he wasn't. I pointed out that this was because his body was very smart when it was swinging the club with such a rhythmic, fluid motion. There's just no need to be forceful. I then asked him what he had been thinking about while he swung through those four sets of balls."

"And?"

"He said, 'Nothing'. Just swing the club."

I heard a car and looked. A green pickup truck was coming down the dead-end road bordering the golf center. It pulled into the back entrance of the maintenance area. Joe followed my gaze. "Oh, that's my friend Bob. He's gonna be annoyed at me for not having prepared the loader for repair. We planned on replacing the seals on the lift arms. They've been leaking oil. I hate to end our session now, but it's a two-man job, and I need to help."

As he got up, Joe said, "You can practice here if you like; we can meet tomorrow, nine AM sharp." His mind had switched to his next task. I thanked him and we shook hands. I pulled out my money clip, but he waved me off. He had spent several hours with me and he didn't mention a fee. And he invited me to come back tomorrow. I thought surely I needed to pay him. But he was already on his way to his tractor. I guess we could do business later.

It was still early but I didn't feel like practicing. I got my stuff together and made my way to the car. I mapped out a plan for the afternoon. First, get some groceries for the week. At around four in the afternoon I would head to the golf course to try my technique-free swing. Nothing to do but swing.

I went to Publix and picked up cold cuts, rotisserie chicken, potato salad and rolls, filling my basket with my favorite foods, plus some wine and beer.

Back at the B&B, I sat down at the kitchen table overlooking the ocean, made a sandwich and had a cold beer to wash it down. After a short nap, I headed to Pompano, ready to try out a little Burlington philosophy on the course. I could play there anonymously.

After checking in, I went directly to the first tee. No one was around. This time of year the sun goes down around five-something. There was only an hour of daylight left, so I had clear sailing for at least nine holes; that's all I had time for anyway. I decided to improvise on Burlington's idea of all feel, no technique. I would go full Technicolor and pretend I was in Scotland with the original golfers; the craftsmen, herders, and fisherman. Here it goes: the beginning of my new golf game.

I pulled out my driver, walked to the championship markers, and teed up a brand-new Titleist. As I looked down at the ball, a swing thought leaped into my mind, but just as Joe advised, I shouted 'cancel' to myself. The thought dissolved. Amazing. That little shout from within shut down my misbehaving mind and allowed me to focus on this mental game of feel and imagining. Part of me felt uncomfortable not thinking about a position in my swing, but another part felt relief. I was determined to stick with it no matter how uncomfortable I got. What did I have to lose?

As I looked down the fairway, I pictured Scotland. It wasn't hard, because Pompano resembled a links course. It was rough, there were just a few trees, and sand dunes lined the fairways. Of course being near the Atlantic, the wind was gusting at a good 20 knots, too. After one more look at my target I proceeded to nail it down the middle of the fairway. Wow! It worked, technique-free! I had a half wedge again, rehearsed the feeling of the swing. This time, I put the ball just under the hole—almost exactly where I pictured it. This could be fun, instead of a struggle. I played the next several holes well, hitting each fairway and green and canceling swing thoughts as they entered my mind. That's how it's supposed to be done.

I couldn't believe it: I was getting good at this already. This must be the 'let-go' mode Joe had been talking about. I was two under through seven—not bad. Darkness was approaching. The eighth hole was a long par four dogleg right; the wind was blowing left to right. It was the most difficult of winds for me to make a swing. I couldn't help but try to keep the ball from flying too far to the right so I told myself, don't go right and just like that, I hit a wicked block out of bounds to the right! I couldn't believe I lacked the confidence to hit it somewhere down the fairway. But when I thought about it, that's exactly what should happen when you try too hard.

I needed to keep trusting, but I felt I just couldn't be techniqueless in this situation. My history in this wind had taken over and I had performed my 'trying hard' swing perfectly. I shook my head; that's exactly what Joe was talking about. Insecurity was written all over this swing.

I teed up another ball and said to myself, just swing. I did, and struck it solid and square. The wind barely touched it. It ended up far down the right side of the fairway. OK, good lesson. It was getting dark now. I drove to my ball on the right side of the fairway, leaned over to my left and snatched it off the turf without slowing down. I wanted to return the golf cart so the cart guys could go home. I could remember when I used to work the carts what it was like waiting for the last one to be returned.

I felt like I had found my first strategy to get out of my funk as a player. It was all mental, too. Maybe I was finally on the right track. But it was still too early to say. At least I'd seen that being techniqueless could work. And I knew Burlington's ideas of proprioception were right, too. Without any technique I could feel the action of the club through my hands, from driving to putting. It was total feel. I couldn't believe the difference in how I felt about things after only one day.

Optimism was becoming my mantra. I drove home elated. I nuked my chicken in the microwave and pulled the potato salad and a beer from the fridge. I was feeling pretty good, except for one thing. I was alone. I had come home to no one. It was now exceedingly clear to me that I needed a companion, a partner, an intimate partner. I thought about calling Claire, but it was still too early in this odyssey for that.

6

A NEW DAY

I arrived at the golf center, eager for more. Joe's whole approach really appealed to me now. I went directly down to the barn. Joe was ready for me, sipping hot coffee with Otter at his feet. As he sipped he occasionally tossed a morsel of his muffin to the dog. Otter concentrated on Joe until the last bite was gone.

Joe had set up another stool. I sat, gratefully accepting the coffee he handed me. I felt much more comfortable with him today. My impression was that Burlington was never uncomfortable with anyone.

"Let me ask you a question," he asked quickly.

"Sure!" I said, eager to begin.

"Since we're discussing fundamental learning, what atmosphere do you think we need to cultivate to really get the most out of our time with our students?"

"Atmosphere?"

"Yes. What do you think is most important to everyone in this world?" He hesitated a moment, then continued. "What I mean, Geoff, is what do you think is the best condition to be in, to grow, the most desired feeling in the world?" He looked around the shop as he waited for my answer. His question took me by surprise; I hadn't a clue where he was coming from.

Then Burlington said, "Everyone is seeking more freedom, aren't they?" I nodded. I guess that seems right, but I was fuzzy on it. He recognized my uncertainty but continued. "The more you understand the truth of this principle, the more you will understand what I'm doing as I share my experiences with you. If you make freedom part of every aspect of your interactions with others and never attempt to control them, you will always be assured of doing something good." He paused dramatically and took a long slug of coffee while searching my eyes. I was silent, not wanting to interrupt, waiting for his point to crystallize without silly interruptions from me. "In other words, if you don't limit the freedom of others, and if everyone else respects that too, the world is a better place. So it goes in life or in golf. When you are free, you are fearless. Defensiveness is eliminated because there's no need for it. And when you're fearless, you own both trust and confidence. In teaching, once you elevate trust, the student loosens up. You free the spirit, the swing loosens and they become, as you say, clutter-free. Ask yourself how straitjacketed you felt when you were struggling with your various swing techniques."

His voice dropped and he put his finger to his lips as if getting ready to tell me a sacred secret. "I hope you'll see it happen this week in the lessons you observe. Maybe you'll even experience it in yourself. You see, Geoff, when you understand this and experience it, you can relate it to practically everyone and everything in life."

"I'm looking forward to it," I responded sincerely. But I realized I was a little disappointed that he still hadn't spoken much about the fundamentals of the golf swing, except in very general terms. Even though I had experienced some success being techniqueless, I realized I was still somewhat attached to the angles, torque, and position adjustments of the body during the swing. Yesterday afternoon, on the first tee, I had fallen back on those elements. It was hard to let go of them, even though I realized that a comfort zone can be detrimental. Conditioning is a weird thing: Even when it doesn't serve us, we cling to it because it's familiar.

I had lived my life this way for too long. Claire had tried to enlighten me to this principle, but somehow I couldn't let go of old patterns. I knew it was time to change and that required commitment.

Joe awakened me from my thoughts. "I know you'd like to get into the physics more..." The way Burlington seemed to respond to questions before they left my lips was beginning to freak me out. "...the fundamentals of the swing and how they need to be taught, but it's important to reinforce our underlying purpose. You need to set up the conditions that give you a peek into a golfer's authentic swing." His hands framed the word *authentic*. "Otherwise you end up observing their trying-hard, heavy-effort swing. Really, there's no use attempting to work on adjusting that, right?"

That question didn't really require an answer, but Joe waited. I nodded.

"So a condition of ease and lightness needs to be woven into a lesson from beginning to end, with no pressure to perform. At this stage, we want only to discover. So, before we get to the swing, we must have a clear understanding of that."

"OK, I understand, Joe. It makes sense. Let's talk about the students," I prompted. "Where are they coming from?"

"Hold your horses. First, I have a story I think you'll find interesting. Learning is a process, Geoff. Everyone processes at a different speed. As a teacher, you must give the process time and not interfere with it. Do you have any experience in drawing?" *What?* He continued without waiting for my response. "I once read a book by an art teacher, Betty Edwards.[5] She studied the learning process intensively and from a neuroscience perspective. The brain is governed by its property of plasticity. Ongoing discoveries have proven that, though we know the brain does have specific areas of expertise, designated for particular tasks. The brain is all connected, but for our purposes we will separate the parts to determine the tools best suited for the task at hand. I can elaborate later. Betty Edwards claimed that she could help anybody learn to draw better in only a few minutes. You know how some people say they can't draw? Well, Betty was determined to obliterate that belief. She believed everyone had the ability—if you could write your name, you could draw."

I was still trying to catch up and asked, "How did she do it?"

"It's mostly a matter of perspective. She figured there was something going on in the brain that caused people to either be able to draw well naturally—or not. Light enters your eyes and the brain interprets and processes information. For our purposes, let's combine the brain and eyes and call it seeing! When we see, we automatically perceive. Our life experience typifies our responses and gives them a frame of reference— what we are familiar with is always a factor. The brain has an amazing capacity to fill in the blanks based on experience."

Burlington paused before continuing his lecture. "The brain can learn to see, and it can continue to learn to see better and more clearly throughout your life. In golf, it can then interpret things more accurately, know where to go, anticipate obstacles, or see openings, and will always be able to make good decisions based on seeing better. Betty Edwards caught an inkling of this nature of seeing. She identified left-brain judgments as interference: We don't have a vision handicap, we have an interpretive one! It's in the brain! She designed exercises that turned on the right part of the brain so it could not be interfered with.

"How did she do it?"

"There's a well-known example you've probably seen—the vase-profile exercise. She got students to turn a drawing of the outline of a vase upside down. When they did that, the brain didn't label it a vase anymore. Edwards obscured the brain's interpretation of the picture so that the picture was just a couple of curvy lines. That's when the magic takes place. Without a label, without being familiar with the form, and without preconceptions of what it is and how to draw it, the students began to examine the relationship between the lines. When they drew it, they drew two faces in profile. They learned to see things for what they are exactly in terms of the picture—one line's relationship to another. When the vase is no longer a vase, the brain's—the left brain's—interference is eliminated—it just sees the lines.

"What this proves to me is that when we have problems, our interpretations, the perceptions on which we base our understanding, are flawed. It's using this basic strategy of labeling and mind jumping that throws us off."

"I get it." I said. "They couldn't see the faces when it was right side up, because they saw a drawing of a complete object instead of the relationships between the lines."

"Right. It's all in the interpretation. They bypassed the line relationships and skipped right to the fact that it was a vase or a tree or a person. It happens so fast—the eye-brain interpreting process—that we're not conscious of it, and then we can't understand why we can't accurately do something seemingly so easy."

I was on the verge of an a-ha moment, but he continued his lecture. "Sound familiar from golf, Geoff? You see, players also interpret instead of just looking. For example, they make a swing, the ball curves and they call it a slice, a negative label. They rarely see it nonjudgmentally as a relationship between the club's path, face, angle, and target. If they did, they would adjust and the slice would be gone. But then golf is a little different than drawing; golfers also have to deal with another conundrum. They have an unconscious belief about the dynamics that create the flight of the ball that's skewed. You can tell by the change from their practice swing to their actual swing.

"Of course, golf teachers explain where the path of the club must be, but as soon as students attempt to strike a ball they return to the old familiar swing. So just knowing the better path is not the solution. Even though they know the path and face angle necessary for positive change, you have to let the belief system believe in positive change. It can occur in seconds with a dose of the right medicine, so to speak, but I will tell you more about that later. All I am saying, Geoff, is that in golf or in life, we miss a lot based on fear of the result or faulty mental judgments. We have to learn to see differently, to see the true nature of things. And that takes training. The beauty of it is, we have a way to go about it."

He clasped his hands behind his head and squinted at the sky. He could see I was taking in every word, but then he stopped abruptly. "Let's continue this later, maybe over dinner at some point. We had better get into the actual swing dynamics. Give me a few minutes to do some work in the shop, then we can get into it."

He left, and I sat there once again trying to understand this whole aspect of golf I hadn't ever entertained. But it made so much sense now that I'd had it explained to me—though in my mind, I still questioned the statement that someone's slice could be dissolved in a few minutes. I felt as if we were really getting somewhere now. I was beginning to like Joe Burlington, with his out-of-the-ordinary manner and way of relating to others. But I knew I was unable to communicate golf with words the way Joe could.

7

THE PHYSICS—
AND THE FEELING

J oe returned from the maintenance shed with ice cold bottles of water and a Publix bag. He took a few lemons out, rinsed them with a squirt from one of the bottles, cut them neatly in quarters, and then put them into tall cups he'd pulled from the bag. He then spooned some instant tea into the cups and filled them with bottled water. The resulting drink was icy and refreshing and hit the spot—especially since it was unusually warm for a winter morning, even by Florida standards. Once the tea was made, he began again, and we got right into the swing, but not like I anticipated.

"Where were we?"

"You referred to golf swing dynamics."

"Oh, yes." He picked up right where we had left off without skipping a beat. "As a golf teacher, you'll see the relationships of the club—that is, the relationship of the face, path, speed, and the player's way of handling it. As a golf physics expert, you need to know the probability patterns. You need to know the path/speed boundaries, so to speak."

"How do you mean?"

"Well, there are boundaries between the club, the ground, the target line, and the wielder, as I like to call the golfer. There are probability patterns of path and another probability pattern for success based on speed. And there are points of no return."

I looked at him quizzically, not comprehending. "What do you mean by probability patterns?"

Joe took a deep breath and more than a moment to figure how he could impart this concept to me. "When it comes to the physical aspects of the golf swing, what I mean is as soon as a student places their hands on the club and aims, an experienced teacher knows instantly the probability pattern of the swing path and face relationships quite accurately."

"You mean as soon as your students place their hands on the club and aim, you know what the swing will be like before they swing?"

"Yes, pretty close to what it will be like. I observe the student's way of handling the club and how they move it as they approach the ball. I can pretty well tell how the club will behave in terms of face, path, and angle of the swing just by the student's grip and aim."

I shook my head in disbelief, but asked him to continue.

"We can therefore know the probability of a golfer achieving the results—the ball flight—they prepared for, based on these relationships. So we're ahead of the game before they've even struck the first ball. I'm not always right, but I like to play a game in my head and see how close I come, and my observations rarely fail me. Anyway, that's why it's important to get a student going in the right direction fast.

"When you know the probability patterns of the speeds and directions of the handle and club face relationships, it's easy to suggest an adjustment for each pattern. Aim this way, hold the club in this manner, posture yourself this way, swing on this path or feel the face angle like this. It really is easy; the challenge is to get the students to picture, know, feel, and believe!"

"You know, Joe, I find most of my students are stuck on aiming their feet and bodies square to the target line. How do you posture your students?"

"It depends, but an important principle is that the foot alignment or body position has to be connected to the path pattern desired, not just square to the target. You could think of it this way: The club face is for target, but the body is for path. That's why I so often close the stance and body so my students can easily swing in a curve rather than a straight line."

"How does that work?" I asked, still puzzled.

"You see, Geoff, the student has come to you because he or she doesn't know or is not aware of these relationships as they're swinging. The students are simply not present. When students are unaware, you help them become aware so that when they become conscious of the imbalance, they can adjust. All the while, you're attempting to get them to feel the relationships—not as though it is right or wrong, just what it is. Everything points to the action of the club. With a golf club, there is right and left, up and down, fast and slow, wide and narrow, and all things descriptive of its physics. It's your job to create a strategy to get students to balance the club's relationships to those boundaries for their shots. Once the students are there, their swings will be a function of them seeing with this different perspective.

"With this approach to the golf swing, we can identify the true relationships between the physics of the club and the shots we're trying to create. You see, students are discovering and becoming self-coaches and, all the while, they're gaining confidence in themselves and their performances. I love it when they begin saying that it's not so hard. They've really learned, rather than just being fixed."

"That sounds great! When do we begin?" I asked, my excitement filled with new understanding.

"We can begin tomorrow, as I have a lot of things to do with the irrigation pump motor. I have a friend coming over to help me and I need to assist him."

"Anything I can do to help?" I couldn't believe I'd asked that.

"No," he said, "we can handle it, but thanks anyway. You can practice your golf right here, if you like. But while you're practicing, Geoff, begin to notice. Notice how you feel. Begin by asking a good discovery question, like are you in balance throughout your swing? Can you sense the pace changes during your swing? Does it feel effortless and powerful? Those are all good awareness questions to begin with. See if you can come up with your own questions. Let's meet tomorrow morning, bright and early."

Again, I was disappointed that our session had ended so abruptly, just as I felt we were getting into the golf swing now. But I knew he had a lot to do—the machines, the grass, the grounds, the whole business. Now I really understood how little time he had. I still wondered how he could do so many different things and still be such an excellent teacher.

I took Burlington's suggestion and began to practice what we'd spoken about. As I was swinging, I began to realize that I had never really practiced naturally—as Burlington termed it, discovering feel. I'd always had an agenda in my swing. My practice never dealt with feeling where I was, but rather where I wanted to get to mechanically. I wanted to give Joe's approach a shot.

I began with one of his eyes-closed exercises to feel my whole swing, the shape and the rhythm of it. I closed my eyes, swung and really felt the pace. For the first time, I felt my rhythm. I was not distracted by the results since I couldn't see them to judge. I just felt, and to my amazement, I didn't feel a need to fix anything.

I just grooved on feeling it. I was present with my golf swing and I was enjoying the process.

As I continued, with no fixing and no intent to change, my pacing improved. It was hard to believe, but it felt wonderful. Maybe Joe Burlington was right. Change was a matter of course when we're aware and impossible when we're not aware, no matter how hard we try. In fact, maybe it's the trying that gets in the way of awareness and change. This was the first time I'd thought this way. Was I truly discovering? I felt like I was. My mind was alert in a new way. I was discovering my swing, not interfering with it as I usually did.

My shots gained consistency. What a high! It felt like I'd only been practicing about twenty minutes. I looked at my watch, surprised to see that two hours had passed. I wasn't even tired, although my grumbling stomach reminded me that I was starving.

It had been the most satisfying time I'd ever spent practicing my swing. I absorbed the feelings like a sponge. I knew I had to get home and get something to eat, but before I left, I stood for a moment and took it all in, felt every sensation, just being. It was so different from being on the go, programmed and performing! I couldn't wait to tell Burlington about it.

I went back to the B&B with positivity swirling inside me. I felt the need to share it. I parked in the driveway and sat in the car looking out at the ocean. I dialed Claire's cell. It went straight to voice mail, so I left a message. "Hi, how are you? I really want to chat with you. It's just that something new is happening to me. I can't fully describe it yet, but I wanted to share it with you. Anyway, you don't have to call me back, I understand. Be well... I love you." That last sentence came out of my mouth just as the recorder beeped. I hadn't meant to say it, hadn't thought it, it just fell out. I didn't know whether to hope the machine had cut me off or not.

8

IF THE CLUB IS OK, THE SWING IS OK!

I awakened before dawn with excitement brewing inside me. The prospect of finally moving forward in my golf didn't allow for a deep sleep. I didn't feel like making my own breakfast, so it was a perfect day to visit Lou at his diner. I set out down the street and hoped he would be there this time since I hadn't caught up to him yet on this trip. I was looking forward to his freshly ground coffee as I made the short walk.

When I arrived, Lou was standing with his back to the counter, cooking bacon on the flat top. Hearing the jingle as the door opened, without turning around he said, "I'll be with you in a minute." The smells livened my appetite, bringing back Sunday morning memories of my youth, when my dad used to brew fresh coffee and fry up bacon long before the rest of the house got moving. The aroma became our Sunday morning wake-up call.

I had picked up a paper outside, and planted myself on a stool at the counter. Lou turned and registered surprise. "Geoff! When did you get in?"

"A couple days ago, Lou." Lou grasped my hand in a firm grip developed from years on his shrimp boat.

"So how's it going?" Lou put down his bacon fork, turned around to grab a pot of coffee, and poured me a cup. "Claire still sleeping?"

"Ah, no Lou… she, ah, didn't make the trip."

He paused for a moment, standing still, looking straight at me, still holding the coffee pot. "Remember, Geoff, you're talkin' to me. What's up?"

I had to tell him. After all, he knew us as a couple. "We broke up."

Lou just stood there for a few seconds and then said, "I'm so sorry to hear that. She is such a special lady. What happened?"

"Let's just say the timing was off."

"Really? I always thought that of the women you brought down to Florida over the years, she was the class of the field."

I nodded. "She was."

"And you let her get away? You know a girl like that doesn't come along too often in a lifetime."

"I just wasn't ready, Lou. I had too many problems; you know, with my golf and all."

Lou shook his head. "Your golf? What does that have to do with it?"

"I felt that I didn't want to commit to anyone before I got my own house in order."

"Geoff, you know me long enough to know I'm a straight shooter, right?"

"Yeah, of course."

"Let me give you a little advice, or better yet, tell you a little story." I nodded, since I knew I was going to hear it anyway. "It happened to me a long time ago." Lou's voice lowered; he got a serious look on his face. "I once had a special gal, and I let her get away." He shook his head regretfully. "And she loved me, if you can believe that. I've had my ups and downs, Geoff, but one regret I still harbor was letting her slip away. Sure, I've had a decent life, and I really can't complain, but I believe it would have been a wondrous journey if I'd taken just a little different road.

"At the time, I was livin' on my boat. I was shrimpin' off the coast of Charleston. During the season of course, I'm working seven days a week, on the water maybe fourteen, fifteen hours a day, sometimes with not much to show for it. I was new in the business then. I could only afford one mate; I needed three. After a catch, in the evenings, we would make the deliveries to the local markets and restaurants.

"Getting a foothold in the business was tough. I had to lower my prices to get any business at all. After paying for fuel, my mate, and the mortgage on the boat, I was practically working for nothing. Anyway, you get the picture."

"Yeah, Lou, I get it."

"Anyway, one day while making a restaurant delivery, I met this girl." Lou's face took on a peaceful look and a smile came over it. "She was good looking and intelligent. She had the most carefree attitude. Being younger than me didn't seem to bother her. Soon we began to date a little. Our first date was a picnic at the old park near the water. She was creative that way. We never went out to dinner at a restaurant; we couldn't afford it. We were a good match, though; both of us worked hard. She spent her days in school at the College of Charleston and most evenings waitressing at her stepmom's restaurant; me on the water. The little free time we had, we spent together. I got to know everything about her and found out that life at home was not rosy. Her mom had died suddenly when she was very young, and her dad took care of her by himself until he remarried several years before I met her. Anyway, her stepmom was tough. Jenny couldn't do anything right. No matter how hard she tried, her stepmother made things very difficult for her.

"But we enjoyed each other's company. She even began to work with me on her days off; it was a calm respite from being home, I guess. Geoff, no work on board was beneath her. She would do anything that needed doin' on that boat. As time passed, I guess you could say we were fallin' in love. Our friendship had become a love affair. Anyway, things got real bad at home, and she realized she needed to get out. Naturally, she wanted to come stay with me."

"What did you do?"

"I did just like you did. Fear got the best of me, and I just couldn't let her come. I got cold feet. I wanted to keep seeing her, but I wasn't ready for a live-in. Being on the water all my life, I figured I couldn't afford to be tied down with a wife. I was afraid of commitment."

"So what happened?"

"Like I said, she had to escape the situation at home, so she ended up quitting school and moving away to live with a cousin. I felt terrible about it. By the time I realized what a horrible mistake I'd made, it was too late. I've been living solo ever since. I never had a companion like that again. For me, it's too late, but you still have time. If you're really in love with her, and she loves you, find a way to make it happen."

"But," I stammered, "how can I be sure, how can you know?"

"Geoff, I just gave you the best advice I can give. What are you lookin' for, a guarantee?" He rolled his eyes like I was being ridiculous. I could tell he was a little annoyed with me. Then he perked up again. "Actually, Yeats said it better."

"Yeats?"

"As in, William Butler. In his poem 'Brown Penny.'[6] Google it, you might learn somethin'," he said with minor disdain.

I wanted out of this conversation, so I agreed to look it up. He sighed with a look of regret. "I wish someone had told it to me when I had my chance. But that's life." He left to help some other customers. Lou's story was sobering. He knew Claire and me well enough to give me that advice. I knew I had to fix that part of my life; I just didn't know how.

In a few minutes Lou returned with my breakfast, and I tried to enjoy it, but his words reverberated inside my brain. As he set down my plate, he asked, "What are you doin' down here anyway, practicing for the winter tournament series?"

"Actually, I came down to work with a golf pro."

"Who?"

Lou wasn't a golfer. "You probably never heard of him. Joe Burlington."

Lou stopped short and turned to me with a wry smile on his face. "Never heard of him? I used to fly fish with the guy in tournaments. What an angler! He can find fish where nobody else can. My friends used to have me invite him because he had some kind of extra sense when it came to fishing."

"It's not just in fishing."

"He can cast a line pert near 75 yards. We knew he was a golf pro, and had a driving range near Pompano, but he never really said anything about it."

"Typical," I muttered.

"So he's teaching you golf. Interesting! How's it going so far?"

"At first, I was skeptical, but he's opened my eyes to a whole new way of swinging a club and playing the game. It's simple and beautiful. I think that by week's end, I'll be far enough along to begin working on those other parts of my life."

"That would be good; I want to see you two back together." Lou was an exceptional guy. He had said as much as I needed to hear. He'd made me believe that somehow, I was going to find a way to win Claire back. I finished my breakfast, said goodbye to Lou, and walked briskly back to my place, emotions churning, then headed for the golf center.

I arrived earlier than I had yesterday. The dew was still on the grass and I saw tire tracks spaced about twenty feet apart in a grid across the whole property. I guessed that Burlington was on the tractor early that morning fertilizing. He seemed to take great pride in the condition of his turf, though it didn't look very plush to me.

Unlike yesterday, it was a bit chilly for Florida, but I figured the fog would burn off when the sun got a little higher in the sky. I looked down toward the maintenance barn and could barely make out the form of someone swinging a golf club. The first swing looked great, very fluid, like a professional golfer. But the next swing looked like a first-day player without much talent. Then it was super fluid, and then erratic again. I couldn't see well from so far away so I figured Burlington must be teaching a beginner and demonstrating rhythm. As I got closer, I saw Joe standing nearby, so realized it wasn't him swinging. His student made another swing. It was a thing of beauty, as though every movement was blended and all his muscles were moving in cooperation with each other. It was flawless. By the time I approached, the student was packing up and saying goodbye to Joe.

I was feeling pretty good about what I had learned from the day before. I blurted out, "That looked great, but what was up with that terrible swing before? It must be a real challenge to teach someone like that." Burlington ignored me, so I repeated the question.

He looked me in the eye and said, "I heard you the first time, Geoff, and, at first, I wasn't going to address your assumption. You remind me of some other students who watch novices taking lessons, with eyes totally focused on results. They will rarely recognize talent or what it looks like when a student is making the first step in awareness."

Uh-oh; looked like I was going to have to extract foot from mouth again.

Joe was as close to annoyed as I'd seen him, yet he remained calm. "But it is a good lesson for you. That was actually my student's attempt to be totally out of balance and then totally in balance."

"Could you please explain?" I asked, humbled once again.

"Sure." He got serious. "Do you realize what you just did?"

"No," I replied innocently.

"You broke a cardinal rule of teaching." I braced myself for a reprimand, but thinking a little humor would soften the blow, I said, "I thought listening was the cardinal rule."

"OK, this is cardinal rule number two," he said with a grin. "When you observe a lesson, you must not assume what its purpose is."

"What do you mean?"

"You assumed my student's erratic swing was a failed attempt at his best swing rhythm—to the point that you thought it was a terrible failure, indicating lack of talent." He waited for me to consider this and I nodded for him to go on, contrite. "But you see, Geoff, you didn't know his purpose. You presumed you knew what was going on and judged it based on your own criteria of a good swing versus a bad swing. Remember me saying that there is no right or wrong in awareness learning?"

"Of course, but I really didn't understand it entirely," I admitted self-consciously.

"Well, just then, I asked my student to produce an erratic swing. That was the purpose. It's just an exercise in awareness. If he identifies what feels erratic and what super fluid feels like, then he has the parameters or boundaries down. He can discover perfect balance and fluid motion from an exercise like that."

"OK, I think I'm getting it. You've defined the two ends of the spectrum between super fluid and erratic."

"That's right. It's like getting a note in tune if you're playing a piece of music. When the fiddles had trouble with a note, our conductor used to have us play flat or sharp intentionally so we could distinguish what was in tune. When we were conscious of the tones and could hear the flatness or sharpness of them, we could find the note we wanted. We rarely made the same mistakes twice."

"Your conductor?" I asked, wondering how many hats Burlington wore.

"Yes. For years I played fiddle in a local orchestra."

"Wow," I exclaimed. "That's really different from golf."

"Oh, but it's not. Playing music, more than anything else in my experience, takes exactly the same qualities that one needs in golf. Mostly, Geoff, you must be present to the task at hand. A measure of music takes a period of time and, especially when you play in a group, everyone must move along together. You can't stop to fix something or take a break to analyze what went 'wrong.' A golf swing also takes a certain period of time. I like to set up a tempo for students to get the idea that no matter what, their swings take this much time."

"I'm not really sure I get it."

"I like a three-beat tempo: Da, Daaa, Daa. Each beat takes a slightly different amount of time to reflect the distance and speed the swing travels from the beginning, to the change of directions, and finally to the end, but the total time is always the same."

"You mean a putt takes the same time as drive?"

"That's right. They have different ranges of motion and speed, but the amount of time in each direction is the same. Tempo is time. Of course you want to have a smooth pace in between the Da's, but the amount of time in the swing, for all the great golfers, from putting to driving, is the same."

"How does this tempo exercise work?"

He obliged me. "The first beat, you just get ready. On the second beat, you swing back, and on the third you swing through. Da, Daaa, Daa."

<table>
<tr><td>Da</td><td>Daaa</td><td>Daa</td></tr>
</table>

GB

"Knowing you're going to take this finite amount of time for each swing direction reduces the urgency in the swing," he explained. "It's a great tool for discovering your rhythm and pace. When you have a student making his or her first swings, you need to wake them up to the tempo, because the swing is nothing more than a synchronized sequence of motions in a finite time and space. An awareness of tempo needs to be imprinted right from the start. Consistency depends on being aware of the feeling of time and the pacing of the whole system, Geoff. Very often, if you focus on a part of the system, it's likely to disrupt the whole. I don't want to get too technical," he emphasized, "but knowing the whole pattern of speed and direction of the club can create the desired behavior of the parts of the body."

He added one caveat: "If you let it. The focus and picture must be panoramic, not microscopic. Let's get back to purpose in learning. You were surprised that a fundamental sequence of learning could be taught and defined in a few short sentences."

"State of mind is something I recognized as important before, but not that critical," I admitted. "Being present, as you call it, was not in my vocabulary. Until I practiced yesterday afternoon, I had never experienced it. I had a real epiphany yesterday during my practice session," I told him proudly. "I've actually begun liking my swing. I mean, the image I now have is much more positive."

"I was hoping that would happen. What surprised you the most?"

"I didn't try to be or do anything except feel my rhythm and I was able to do it! My swing changed for the better, just as you said it would, once I allowed myself to become aware of it."

"I'm glad you experienced that feeling. There's no really good way for me to explain it that would come close to you experiencing it on your own. It's like you could read a book about swimming and study what others have said it feels like in the water, you could know everything about it through words and thoughts, but not until you hit the water could you ever really know what buoyancy means." I could relate to that. Words are really clumsy tools when it comes to feeling.

"But I'm an experienced player," I said, hedging a bit. "I still find it hard to believe a novice could learn that way. I just can't see someone learning all those fundamentals. There are so many to learn, aren't there?"

"Well no, once someone gets to holding the club in a good zone and sets up to be athletic and ready to swing, there are only three, as far as I am concerned. You just build a 'swing house' out of this simple triangle of awareness. Begin wherever the player happens to be—which is at his or her athletic baseline. Once hands and alignment are in good order to begin the motion, there are only three fundamentals…"

"But…" I tried to interrupt, but he wasn't letting me in.

"The foundation of the motion is flow or rhythm. The frame is path. And the roof is timing the impact. That's the swing house."

"So flow, path, and timing cover the whole swing. And you're supposed to learn it totally by feel?"

"Yes. Think about it. None of us could ever get too good at our rhythm in a swing, or have too good a path pattern, or time the impact too well, could we? That makes these fundamentals universal in my book. My students cycle through those fundamentals. They first develop a fluid quality of motion—motion that seems effortless and very well-blended so you can't tell what causes what. There's an imperceptible change of force. Once that becomes a constant, we need to determine the direction this fluid energy is going in—the path pattern from beginning to end. Lastly, once the energy is traveling in a consistent pattern, a golfer needs to time the club face's direction and angle of delivery for the ball flight. That's the physics of it all. It's simply the action of the club. It's the club's dynamics."

"That sounds simple enough," I said, "but what do you mean exactly by timing?"

"I'll explain that later, Geoff, if you don't mind."

"OK." But I felt a little stung by his putting off answering. "But if the swing is so simple, then what's all the hoopla about body positions and planes and all that jazz? And all the mechanics I see the tour players fixing all the time during tournaments? What's that about?"

"Let's not go through that again."

"I promise this is the last time."

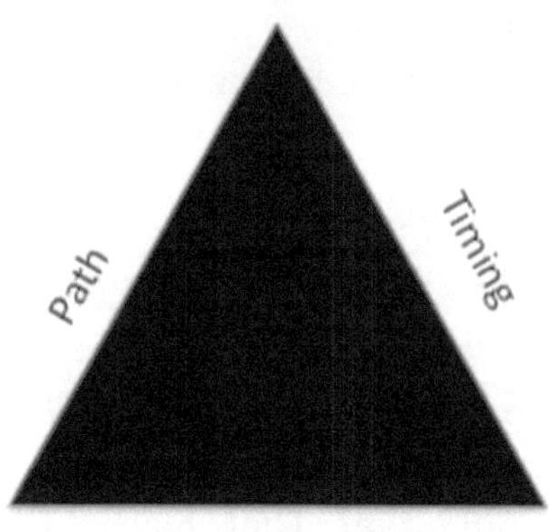

"OK, I know, one could really get messed up that way. Even superior players end up believing they can't play well anymore because they have bought into that approach. They're up against a mental wall. Following this block, there is a typical scenario. They hit the panic button and begin to follow a convoluted litany of fixes prescribed by the latest greatest wizard, so they no longer tap into their natural athleticism. Getting that technical erodes their confidence. They're using an approach so foreign to their natural talent that they probably *can't* play well anymore. Having thoughts like that streaming through their minds challenges their natural abilities."

I could see that my question had stirred something in Burlington. "Geoff, golf instruction has gotten so far away from making things easier that there needs to be a paradigm shift." There was that phrase again; this time I would get clarity.

"What do you mean?"

"I mean we need to completely shift out of a paradigm that breaks a golf swing down into minute individual pieces and then fails miserably when it attempts to put the puzzle back together. We must discard this Humpty Dumpty sort of thing, shift away from this Cartesian approach. The athletic mind doesn't process that way. The evidence is clear that it doesn't work for the vast majority of golfers. In fact, it's exactly why golfers end up frustrated and quit the game. They never give themselves a chance at seeing their potential."

"Cartesian?"

"Yes, the so-called scientific approach. Descartes was one of the fathers of breaking things up to discover their fundamental building blocks. But it just doesn't work in golf!"

"What approach must we use, then?"

"Basically, we need to teach the complete opposite. In other words, that the *whole* swing creates the behavior of the parts."

"How exactly do you do that?"

"It's like when you take a trip in your car. Mentally, you know where you want to end up, you know the route, and then you unconsciously drive the car to get there. You make the turns, you stop and go, based on where you want to end up. It can be similar in golf: Begin teaching the whole swing and watch as the golfer's body parts learn based on the whole swing pattern.

"Of course, you must set up the boundaries. My Pathfinder helps with that. Other than that, have your students pay attention to the flow of the swing without any care about anything else. Develop the complete path by showing the two endpoints and where the club must pass through the Pathfinder in the impact zone, and then learn the impact trigger. You don't have to reassemble the machine from scratch—your students arrive with an already well-oiled machine. You need to show them what they need in golf, where they want to go.

"The old paradigm reminds me of a situation involving one of the greatest golfers of all time. I once heard of Jack Nicklaus describing in an interview what it had been like working with Jack Grout. Toward the end of Nicklaus's playing career, he was having a devil of a time with his swing. One summer, just after the British Open, he had experienced one of his worst performances as a professional. He seemed dejected and probably wondered how he had arrived at such low a point." Joe paused to sip from his water bottle.

"Apparently," he continued, "golf teachers were flooding Nicklaus with input about how to fix his game and get out of his funk. Jack Grout had passed on at least ten years before. These self-proclaimed gurus were trying to get Nicklaus to change his swing to what they thought would be more effective. Apparently it was a complicated change, foreign, and difficult to perform in competition, especially at this stage of his career.

"Reflecting on his time with Grout, Nicklaus realized Grout had spent very little time talking about the golf swing, just the fundamentals, and of course there aren't many of those. Nicklaus seemed to be longing for one last conversation with his friend that would liberate him from his problem.

"As Nicklaus told it, Jack Grout had been plain spoken. He would have spoken first about the day, maybe the weather, family—a normal everyday conversation with a friend. But then he might interject a suggestion or ask a question for Nicklaus to contemplate, like, 'How's your aim today, Jack?' Or, 'How does your rhythm feel?' Grout said so few things to Nicklaus that every comment was essential, and they were easy to remember. He never wasted any words.

"You know, Grout helped Hogan too! Those original teachers were very well-rounded, and most of them could really play, too. Heck, Tommy Armour played the fiddle."

"Like you."

"Something like that. Anyway, as the interview went on, Nicklaus spoke about really missing his old friend and his approach to golf and life, so fundamental and simple, yet complete. It was very enlightening to me and, at the same time, a little sad to see Nicklaus so dejected. I believe he felt a little duped by this episode in his career. I had watched Nicklaus play as a younger golfer when his talent and ability bore no interference. His complete talent was something to marvel at; his work ethic, composure, concentration. Jack Nicklaus really had very few weaknesses, if any, and back then he seemed invincible. And contrary to what some teachers have said, he did have marvelous swing action. His swing exemplified what we have been talking about all along—freedom!

"For Nicklaus to be listening to these self-proclaimed gurus puzzled me. It isn't rocket science, Geoff. Yes, there seems to be an inordinate number of fine champions who, as they say, seem to have lost their touch in the past twenty-odd years. You know golfers used to be taught to get on the tour, but now with the technical complexities and all, there have been several champions taught off the tour! Many get confused. But they really haven't lost anything— they've just misplaced it. You could say it's lost within them."

I felt like one of those pathetic lost golfers and nodded in total understanding.

"It can be recaptured, Geoff. The problem, your problem, is you keep looking outside yourself to find solutions. Redeveloping awareness is always an inside job! The route to one's potential can never be found outside oneself. People believe their problems are complex and require complex solutions. Really and truly, most problems are actually simple. As teachers, we cannot afford to miss the boat when it comes to simplicity and awareness." He stopped speaking and looked me in the eyes and let his words sink in. "Simplicity is the ultimate sophistication. You know, sometimes I think it's better to be a little unorthodox."

"You mean like Trevino or Palmer?"

"That's right. They have decided on a way to play, and they don't mess with it, and nobody messes with them. Sure, they don't swing classically, but they are effective and never confused. That was probably their greatest asset. They didn't try to perfect their swings according to some model, they perfected their shot-making and knew how to produce it for themselves."

"What have you done to make it simple?"

"One strategy I use is to reverse the way we learn. The principle being, if the club is OK, then you are OK."

"Could you illustrate?"

"Sure. Usually it blows my students' minds. Let me ask you, Geoff: Where do you begin teaching a golf swing once the setup is in good order?"

"With the backswing, of course," I told him, as though it were obvious.

"Well, that's the opposite of where I begin. Did you know that starting from the finish can create the perfect backswing through momentum? Or with a more experienced player, that knowing the downswing approach of the club into the impact zone could create the backswing?"

"How can that be? The backswing happens before the downswing."

"Yes, that much I do know," he grinned mischievously. "But the backswing can be like taking that trip in your car. In fact, the beginning of a trip or a swing can begin at the end both physically and mentally. All the while, in the back of your mind, you're picturing where you're going. And because you know the club needs to strike the ball, it's on the route too."

"That seems right," I conceded, "but to work from the finish or the downswing first still seems backwards to me."

" 'Seems' is the key word," he told me. "It's the fastest and most effective way I know for the student to develop a feel for the shape and effortlessness of the swing. There's no need to exert force or use tension and strength to create the swing. And at the same time you awaken their feel for momentum and centrifugal force. You see, you're so bogged down in the new technical approach. There are umpteen steps and the belief that says, if you have step one, the setup, and you move on to step two, the take-away, and then three, a good top-of-swing position, it's likely the downswing will happen. Right, Geoff?"

"Well, yes; that is how I teach it."

"It's hogwash! I will tell you this: I have seen a lot of good backswings with inconsistent and erratic impacts. Besides, clogging your mind with too many things to do will surely send you down the road of confusion. On the other hand, when I see a consistent impact, I don't much care about the backswing."

"So you never teach the backswing?"

"I didn't say that. It's the way you teach it that will dictate whether or not your students will change for the better and sustain it. Instead of a multitude of steps and body positions, I help a golfer to change by suggesting better patterns of the club. If there is anything in the way of this, it is usually tension and the fear of being out of control, but they usually discover that control is letting go, both mentally and physically. They come to me thinking there are a lot of rules to swinging a club well. When they feel safe with me taking all the responsibility for the results, the freedom in their swings is quite remarkable."

Joe shook his head with a look of bewilderment, seemingly wondering how golfers could accept the complex 'rules' dominating golf teaching today, especially regarding the backswing. "Now let's talk about your backswing. You can get it by knowing where you're going—that picture and feeling can give you a direct route that includes your backswing. And it takes into consideration the uniqueness of every golfer." He picked up a club and swung it forward, first toward a target, then continued into a backswing through the air from there; the orbital pattern looked perfect. As he swung forward the club brushed the grass where a ball would be and then it continued around and up to where he began. This seemed like a lot of motion to control; would a beginner be able to do it?

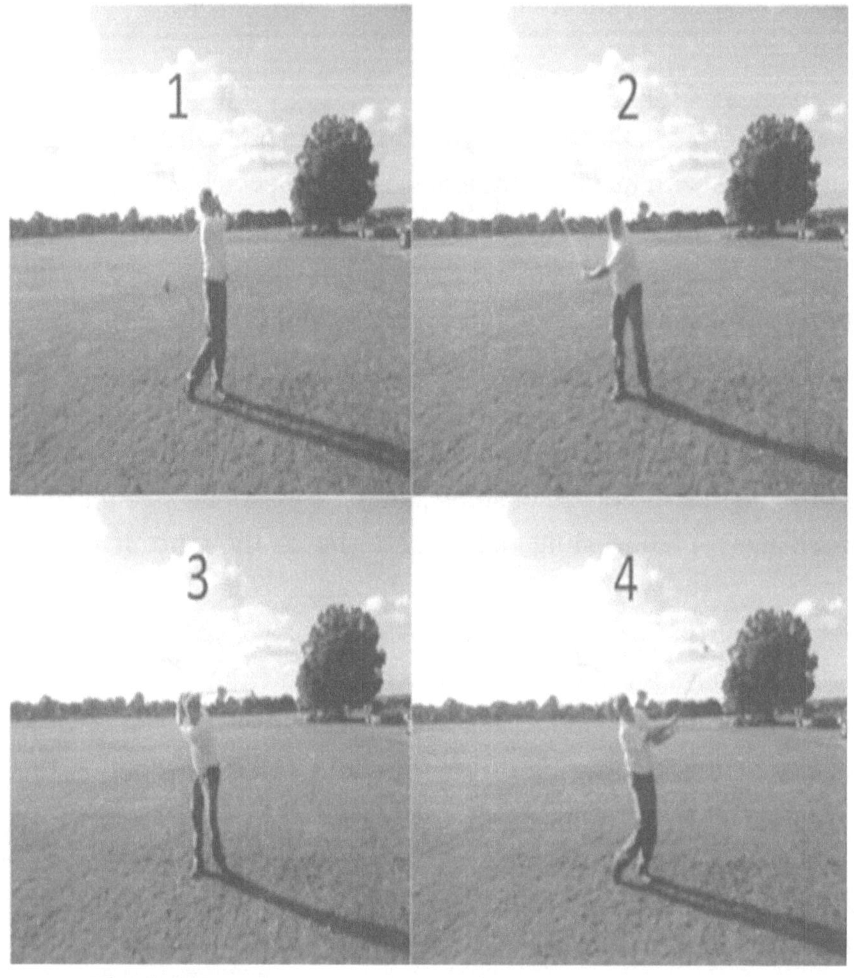

The front end.

GB

"This is a way to get your students to pay attention to the swing rather than being distracted by trying to impact the ball. Have them notice the club action only, where it's going, with your two endpoints as references. You could call them A and B. That's the beginning of getting the mind in the best place. The pattern will begin to take shape and smooth out as their bodies begin to learn. Of course all students will vary to some degree."

"Right—I mean, you wouldn't argue the fact that all the tour players' swings are different, would you? Of course they all take a different route to the impact, don't they?"

"Of course. They all look different and yet they achieve similar results. You see, Geoff, all their bodies are different in size, strength, flexibility, and suppleness, not to mention their unique psychological and emotional makeup. Most of the swings you see on tour are dramatically different. To me, that means there's no right or wrong in a backswing.

"On the downswing, there's effective and ineffective, and if a player's on tour, they must be effective. In your teaching, you must allow for the diversity of each student's physical, psychological, and emotional levels. So then really, the only close similarity from player to player is the club's physics near impact. That is, the speed, angle, path, loft, and so on. In short, if the club is OK, then the swing is OK. That means that the club has satisfied its physics at impact to produce the shot. I will tell you more about that later," he promised as we sat down for a moment. He pulled two bottles of lemonade from a small cooler and we refreshed ourselves with a few sips.

Soon we saw a man walking across the grass toward us. Joe turned to me with a smile and said, "Geoff, let me show you a good example of the simplicity of my approach."

Joe got up and tossed a golf ball toward the approaching man. The fellow reacted—he leaped like a cat, and he was no spring chicken. He caught the ball and seemed as proud of his athleticism as the littlest of little leaguers. "Come on, Joe," the guy said, a little out of breath. "Don't keep doing that to me every time I come to say hello."

Joe looked like Peck's Bad Boy, with a sheepish grin. "Just proving a point, George, and hello back." George continued on his way, shaking his head.

"I think I get it," I said.

"Go stand over there." Now my athleticism would be tested, I guessed. Joe picked up another ball and tossed it just out of reach. I leaped, stretching, and caught it, relieved I could show him I was athletic, too. "You might be surprised at all the things that go on to enable you to make a catch like that, Geoff. Actions you weren't conscious of happened automatically. If you analyzed how you caught that ball—if we broke down everything that happened in a split second to catch the ball, you'd realize it was pretty amazing. Just having a goal and trusting in your experience initiates the action without you even considering it. Think about it: All you really had to know is where your hand needed to be, and you had a shot at it.

"You can learn and teach golf in a similar fashion, taking all this unconscious athleticism and letting it work for you and your students." I felt my understanding growing. "In the golf swing, the club mirrors the hand action throughout. The club is nothing more than an extension of a golfer's hands. The back of the lead hand mirrors the action of the club face. There's a direct correlation there unlike any other part of the body." I watched closely as Burlington swung his hand and arm back, around and up, and then down again, his wrist flexed as I had not seen before as he went through the motion. "When the hands travel, they're the outer orbiting component of the body's swing. And they travel the farthest and the fastest. If they're functioning OK, then the club is OK. And if the club is OK, then the swing is OK.

"In other words, any action of the club is a reflection of the action of your hands, of what's holding the club—of what truly controls the club. It's an intimate relationship that must be nurtured!"

There was that point about intimacy again.

Concentric arcs.

GB

I must have looked like I was making progress because my hands gripped an imaginary club, as if to confirm what Joe was saying. I noticed him observing me as he paused to chug down the last of his lemonade. "I mean, all the core issues you hear about—shoulder turn, hip turn, etcetera, etcetera—it's really not necessary to be conscious of them; they can literally be placed on autopilot." Burlington had made his point.

As I thought back to catching the ball, I realized my whole body had reacted to place my hand in the space of the ball's anticipated position as it flew toward me, without me being conscious of my preparation. Everything happened without me consciously directing anything. I tried to understand and dissect everything that went on mentally and physically with that simple action. I saw the ball and just wanted to catch it, so my feet, legs, and lower body all pivoted to go in the direction of its flight. Then, through my shoes, I felt my toes grab the ground, my knees and ankles flexed downward, and I pushed off to jump. My left arm stretched out and up and my fingers opened to touch the ball. My right arm extended the other way so I could keep my balance—all without any conscious effort, except the mental goal: Catch the ball. "And the whole golf swing can be learned this way?"

"Of course, Geoff! Your mind and body learned this a long time ago. What I'm trying to get at is that our golf swings are already very much predetermined by our past athletic development. From an athletic standpoint, why should anyone begin from scratch when, for the most part, he or she already has what it takes to swing a club? We don't have to be conscious of every move. Why not make it simple?" There was that word again. Simple. "Just know where the club needs to get to with whatever speed and then allow the whole body to support that action. Again, the club is just an extension of our orbiting hands, or at least it swings in an arc in direct ratio to their movement. If they're OK, then the swing is OK."

My body knew exactly how to catch the ball and just did what it had to do to achieve that goal. If I were to try to break down the physical action that had just occurred and apply that approach to learning the golf swing, I would be completely confused. The golf swing is a lot more complex than catching a ball. But maybe that was all the more reason to simplify and not complicate.

I realized in a flash that complicating was exactly what I had been doing in my playing and teaching. No wonder I had trouble; who wouldn't? "So I don't need to know all about the rest of my body when I am swinging a club?" I questioned, emerging from my introspection.

"That's right," Burlington replied. "You can learn it, and then teach a person to swing clutter-free just by getting them to know, feel, and picture what the club must do, especially at impact. The rest of the body's action supports in leading or following or anticipating where the club needs to go."

"So the rest of the body is involved, of course," I confirmed. "I mean, it's all connected. But you don't need to get bogged down in all the inner workings that have been worked out for you since you were a toddler learning to run, catch, and throw. Just because you're swinging a golf club doesn't mean you need to reconnect your body. It's actually a waste of time and a distraction to really becoming aware. The golf swing can really be learned like that? It has so many moving parts." I sounded stupid, repeating the same question, but I couldn't stop myself.

"It's little more complex, but that pretty much covers it. There are ratios involved, but the mind-body system balances them beautifully, providing nothing interferes. Suffice it to say, if you know what you want the club head to do, and you use your hands as the sensory feedback center, everything else will support it. It really becomes easy. Just allow the rest of your body to move to support the energy and direction of the orbiting club. You just need to know the outer arcs or circles. Your hands represent the second-last outer orbit and the club head represents the farthest orbit from the swing center. The feet and legs, the support system, are moving to support the direction and momentum of the outer orbits, just like when you caught the ball. The torso is in the inner orbit, the center."

"OK, I can see that."

"When you caught the ball, your feet, hands, arms, legs, and torso—they all knew what to do, based on your entire lifetime of athletic experience. You didn't need to direct each muscle group consciously..."

"Yes, but—really, golf, this way...?" I tried to grasp what he was showing me.

"Of course," he smiled, "you do need to know the club's physics; otherwise, you'll surely get lost and confused, and so will your students. You see, Geoff, you don't need to know what's happening with all the circles, just the outer ones. The inner ones will respond in perfect balance."

"You just put the others on automatic pilot?"

"That's right.

"What about the swing center?"

"Autopilot!"

"Pivot?"

"Autopilot."

"Shift?"

"Auto. I'm telling you, man, if the club is OK, it's all OK! Leave it alone. Everything will naturally respond in leading or supporting the energy or force of the other circles, so that all the action of the core of the swing is a function of the outer orbiting club head and hands. The key is to get number one and two arcs, the outer arcs, going at a good rate of speed and path pattern. Arcs three and four, the center of rotation, are a function of one and two."

"That eliminates so much extraneous thinking."

"Thank the Lord," he said. "And that's the luxury of this approach. You have a complete method that's easy to learn and perform and, I might add, connected to touch. It's really that simple. It's exactly the same way you've learned every other action since you were a child! I could never understand why the so-called modern big-muscle, mechanical golf technique claims that we, as golfers, should not use this built-in awareness. It's an awareness we've been using daily since we came out of the womb!"

"That makes lots of sense, Joe."

Burlington continued his passionate lecture. "This is why children do so well when they learn golf. They don't have to be cerebral! They trust in a task by seeing it or feeling it! And children communicate totally by feel—they have no inhibitions and so they can go with their gut. Keep in mind, Geoff, learning to trust comes from early childhood; it's not something out of the intellect!"

I pondered it all. "It's hard to believe it's that simple."

"Oh, but it is, Geoff. You have got to stop trying to complicate things." Where had I heard those exact words before?

"But what about the fact that the lower body, the feet, legs, and hips, lead the way in the downswing?" I pleaded for clarity. Or maybe I didn't want to give up my investment in being right. After all, I had invested years believing the party line.

"Of course they do, but do your students have to be conscious of them? Depending on the athlete, you have to make choices on how much you tell them. It's very easy to ruin something good. In most cases you allow the feet and legs to move in response to knowing what you want the club to do on the forward swing."

"How do you do that?"

"Let's say you want to hit a knockdown shot that really bores the ball low into the wind. With that goal in mind, your body responds to the changes necessary in the club to get to that goal. I guarantee your feet and legs will shift and drive downward and more forward and squeeze the ball into the turf naturally. You see, your mind controls everything and if you tell it that you want the ball to fly low, your body will respond in kind.

"Someone once asked Sam Snead how he faded the ball. His answer: 'I see fade.' Asked about a draw, he said, 'I see draw.' Snead let himself perform totally non-technically! He was the epitome of non-interference. That's how I'm proposing we teach! Say the least and get the most by asking the best awareness questions."

"But you have to admit there was only one Sam Snead." I countered.

"Yes, and we should pay homage to his extraordinary awareness! Snead never interfered with his natural ability and he trusted his swing probably more than anyone. All we need to do with our students is show them how to learn this way. How far they get is uniquely personal. But I do guarantee that if they stick with it, they will learn to swing and play better than their wildest dreams!"

"Do you teach all your students this way?"

"As I said, students are diverse in their backgrounds and, as such, you need to find out where each one is coming from and get a feel for their unique histories. But the physics approach and awareness development is a constant. I just go deeper into the awareness as they progress. It's always about the club's physics and the feel and the action emanating from that. You need to facilitate this process for each student personally."

Joe wiped his brow with a handkerchief—the day had warmed considerably. Florida weather was still preferable to what I'd left behind up north, though. I adjusted my visor.

"You can't organize all the parts and hope the club is on autopilot and will be OK. You must be aware of the club and put the body on autopilot. You know," Joe concluded, "all sports are played well this way. Simply."

9

THE GRIP

"**Y**ou've mentioned the hands; what about the grip? How do you teach that?" I asked.

"Good question! There is no greater physical influence over the action of the club and the outcome of a shot. Getting a person's grip placement and pressure points optimum for them is key."

"I've heard so much about the importance of grip and yet there seem to be so many ways to hold the club. How do you go about teaching it?"

"There again, it depends on the situation. Are we talking about a beginning golfer or an experienced one?"

"What's the difference when it comes to the fundamentals?"

"There's a big difference. If a golfer is effective with the position of their hands on the club, and they're conditioned to hold the club in a manner that imbalances the face or path during the swing but still consistently impacts the ball solidly in the direction they want it to go, then why change the grip position? Just to accommodate some teacher's impression of what's orthodox? You could destroy a golfer's confidence and effectiveness in one fell swoop! The only time to adjust would be if the hands are poorly placed on the club and not being effective."

"But that's what I'm getting at, Joe. What do you change the placement to, and how do you change it?"

"Another good question. I really take into account a person's hand dimensions—their palm and finger ratios, long or short. I notice whether their fingers are meaty or lean, thick or thin. Then I do tests, experiment a little. I notice path and face relationships as they swing. I adjust their hands to fit and balance out those relationships, and of course the grip size plays a role in all of this too."

"I don't mean to sound obtuse," I said, feeling very much that way, "but do you think you could show me what you're talking about?"

"Sure. The hands, wrists, and arms have limits to their degree of rotation, and of course, flexing potential is limited once one's hands are fixed on the club. There are tendencies that you really need to know. You see, if the face of the club lies square to the target—I mean looking directly at it while addressing the ball—and the person has never held a club before, I place their hands on the grip with good leverage for lead hand control and a neutral look." He picked up a club and walked a few feet away from me.

"Like this," he said as he demonstrated. "Here is the leverage; notice where the club lies in the hand and its angle in relation to the fingers. From this position you can control the club without excessive pressure. This position of the club in the hand is for control and the lighter pressure is for speed. So often golfers think that heavy pressure is for control; it's not!

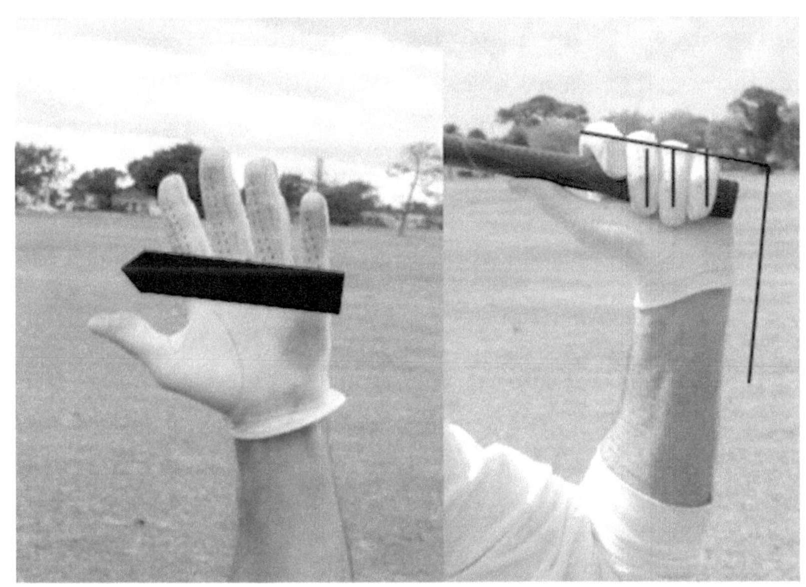

Proper angle in hand.

GB

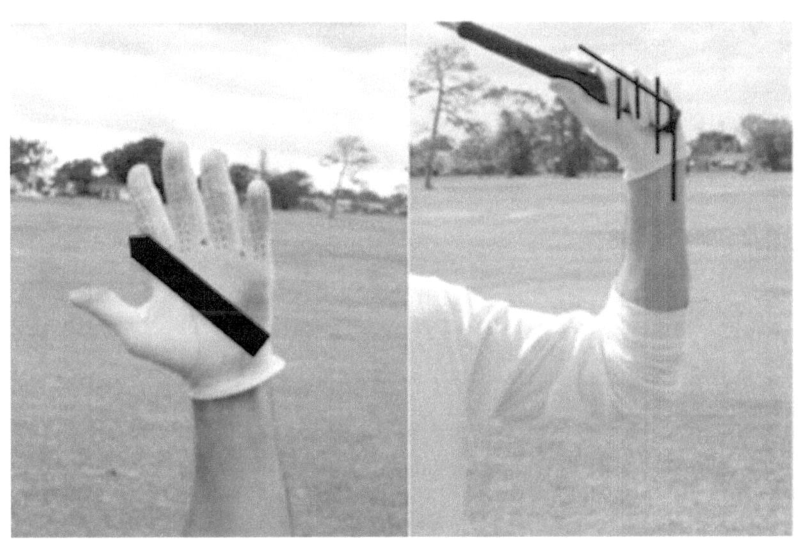

Improper angle in hand.

GB

"Now look at this grip," he commanded as he moved his hands. "Here, there's no leverage over the club. Notice the angle of the shaft in relation to the fingers and palm. Usually a player with this hand position cannot generate enough club speed because the hinging is compromised and they need excessive pressure to retain control of the club in hand."

Neutral grip. Square face

GB

Burlington changed position. "Having a neutral hand position almost always simplifies the path-face relationship throughout the swing. Neutral, in this case, means there's a close directional relationship between the back of the lead/left hand and the face of the club. They are at a similar angle to the target and can be used as a reference for face direction.

"Now look here: This is what is often called a weak grip. The hands can rotate excessively from this position. Generally, the face of the club will over-rotate open as the swing progresses away from the ball and then under-rotate swinging through to add loft and curve the ball to the right. Also, the arc of the swing is often narrowed and the swing tends to become too vertical from this grip; it reduces the potential for high energy."

Weak grip.   Open face.

GB

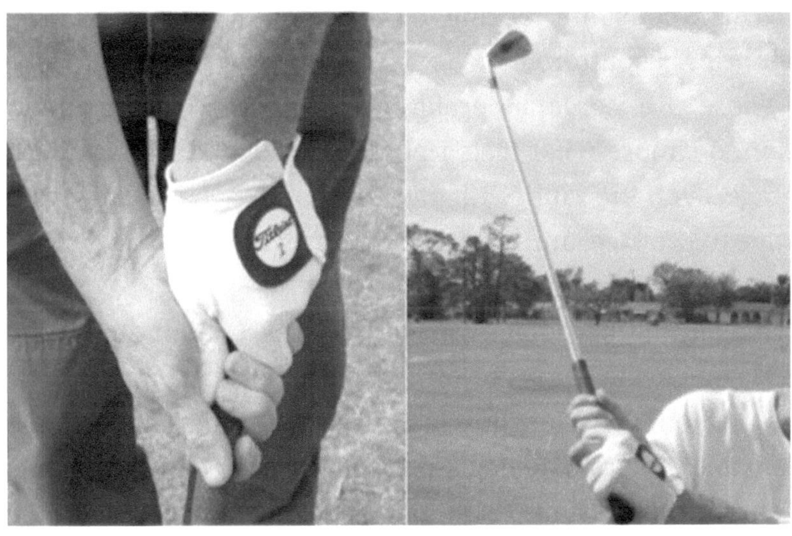

Strong Grip   Shut Face

GB

He changed again. "Here's what used to be called a strong grip. I just call it another imbalanced grip. Look what happens to the club in this position." He showed me what I knew to be a strong grip. "The hand is pre-rotated on the club relative to the face and usually it will not rotate as the swing progresses. The hands, being fixed at this angle to the face, have almost reached the limit of their rotation—the joints and muscles can't turn any more than they already have, so the club face doesn't rotate with the path and it produces what we call a closed club face. This grip also often produces a path that lays off the club shaft, a dreadful pattern to say the least. Usually on the return, barring a recovery or compensation, the club face will arrive closed and often produce a wicked hook or left curve for a right-handed player.

"Your hands really do influence the club directly and the rest of your swing absorbs the balance, or the imbalance, in which they function. These are all tendencies an instructor needs to be aware of. It will make your lessons a lot easier."

"What about interlocking, or the Vardon overlap, or the all-finger grip?" I sputtered.

"Those are personal preferences and we have to allow a person to choose what feels right," he explained. "The key is the leverage over the club with the top hand, a balanced position relative to the face, and pressure that provides the speed and the feel of what's happening at the club head."

The shifting paradigm was getting clearer to me now. But it was so much the opposite of how I'd been teaching. Just then, Otter let out one of his famous yawn-sighs, revealing his formidable molars. The dog stretched. By now I knew this meant the end of the session. I still had many questions, but time had run out for today. I thanked Burlington and decided to return to the B&B to reflect on all that had transpired.

10
DEFINING MOMENTS

Golf was a simple game and learning the golf swing should be simple. I'd learned that it could be learned without complex thinking and analyzing. Less really was more. I left the golf center with those thoughts streaming through my brain.

I didn't feel like cooking so I ordered takeout from a nearby chicken joint. I devoured my meal with a hunger I hadn't been aware of until the aroma of the food hit me in the car.

There was nothing of interest on television and I wasn't sleepy, so I pulled a book off the shelf in my room. It was the kind of book I would never have taken time to read otherwise. But I enjoyed the story of a father and son and a wily brown trout. It was heartwarming and it almost put me to sleep before thoughts of Claire intruded. There was still no message from her and I wondered if she had even heard my fumbling 'whatever—I love you' message. And if she had, did she hear my inadvertent confession? I didn't know if I was ready for her to hear it.

I did love Claire—that was never the issue. I just kept thinking I had too much going on in my life, my career, and the time wasn't right. When I had told her I wasn't ready to make us more official and tried to make light of it, she hadn't laughed. In fact, she'd become dead serious. She told me she wasn't going to waste any more of her time; life is too short. I hadn't thought us a waste of time. We'd had fun together, we cooked, we hiked, we complemented each other's personalities.

Claire was a few years older than I was, and in no uncertain terms, she had told me to grow up right before she walked out. "Oh yeah," I had brusquely retorted, "and be old before my time and serious and no fun, like you?" I hadn't expected the hurt on her face to assault me as badly as the door slamming behind her assaulted my ears.

Lou was right. I needed to mend things soon or forget it. I rewound my mental videotape to sweeter moments and drifted off.

After a deep and satisfying sleep, I awoke to my alarm, right away thinking about my golf lessons. I had come to some pleasing conclusions. I realized now that it didn't matter if Joe ever saw me swing again. I was learning principles that would always be available to me. I just needed to apply them. I also realized more than ever that I didn't want to lose Claire. The same mantra that helped me find Burlington was rolling through my mind about Claire: she is the one, there is no other one. I would figure it out, and hope I wasn't too late.

With Burlington, I was getting much more than I'd hoped for. That thought caused me to wonder briefly what kind of price he put on his time. After all, we still hadn't discussed his fee.

I dashed over to the golf center, arriving early and hoping to try out the 'if the club is OK, the swing is OK' approach. Joe was already there and Otter was wide awake. Miraculous! The dog was barking incessantly at the ducks on the shore of the pond, showing more signs of life than I'd thought him capable of. As I approached, I noticed Burlington had set up for us to begin. He was wearing a fresh outfit but almost identical to yesterday's khakis, yellow sport shirt, and moccasins, minus socks. No surprise in the wardrobe department; that aspect of him was already predictable.

"Good morning, Geoff. I set up early so we could finish early. I have a little running around to do this afternoon," he explained.

We took our seats, including Otter. "I really think your whole approach is beginning to sink in." Otter briefly diverted his gaze from Joe, who was munching a muffin, to sniff out my sincerity. Joe tossed a morsel to the dog and the muffin won back his focus. "But how do you begin a lesson with your by-discovery approach versus the traditional way?"

Joe took a moment to think. "I begin by getting to know my students. I delve into their background, I really want to know their own version of their history. I try to learn about their experiences so I can begin to understand how they interpret and perceive things.

"For instance, are they self-critical? Do they assume things based on hearsay? Are they really aware? Do they judge harshly? That kind of thing." He squinted into the sun and pulled his sunglasses from a pocket. "That's what I use for the basis of my strategy to get to a higher awareness. Without their cooperation, the lesson is doomed. Their success, as I said, has nothing to do with me."

"Have you always taught this way?"

"No, of course not! I'm always learning. I'm evolving as we speak," he said with a grin. "I've had my share of guinea pigs and I'm sure I've screwed up a few people in my time, Geoff, but I was always looking to improve my approach. Over time, it's gotten better."

I wanted that attitude. Burlington seemed to possess equally large quantities of confidence and humility, without a trace of arrogance. I asked him, "Do you remember your first experience of teaching through discovery and awareness?"

"Ah, my first experience," he sighed. "You mean, when I knew something different was happening?" Burlington's expression changed. He looked joyful and a contented almost trance-like smile came over his face. He snapped back to reality. "Forgive me, Geoff. I just had the clearest picture of a lesson I gave a long time ago. It was very different from a normal day at work. I guess you could say that for me it was a defining moment in my golf instruction."

I was on the edge of my seat.

"I was living here in South Florida when I received a call from a lady in Rhode Island. She and her husband were good golfers. They had a son about to enter college on a golf scholarship. He was a having a very bad time with his golf. Their son's teacher was a nationally recognized pro who, sadly, had recently died in a plane crash and the young man was left in the hands of the pro's assistants. Anyway, the kid had developed some serious imbalances in his swing that were obvious to anyone watching him. Instructors were able to identify the problems, but no one seemed to be able to resolve them. In fact, the harder he tried, the worse they got.

"Everyone had an opinion. They first contacted my friend Bob, who was a colleague of the kid's late instructor. Bob referred him to me. It was Thanksgiving weekend, and though I had planned a trip out of town with my family, I was in no position to turn down a series of golf lessons over a four-day weekend—I was having some financial difficulties at the time, even though I was already working four jobs." It surprised me to hear that Joe Burlington had ever seen lean years. I nodded in understanding and waited for him to go on.

"Anyway, this young man's mother seemed desperate. I changed my plans and decided to stay in South Florida and work with him. Mr. C, the boy's father was a well-known practitioner of the golf swing and was well-schooled in techniques and all the modern terminology. The young man's mother also warned me that Arthur, her son, would test me. He didn't just accept canned ideas and statements, so I had better be able to back up anything I said. Interesting situation, eh?" He winked.

"When the day came for our first lesson, I drove to their very upscale golf and country club in my old green Chevy Nova. The young man's parents had arranged for me to teach there instead of at my public driving range around the corner. I pulled up to the security gate. The guard looked me over good. I guess I looked like I'd made a wrong turn. After he checked a couple of lists, he let me through. I was a little out of my element. I was accustomed to the public courses and driving ranges. Back then, golfers like me were called trunk slammers. We never went into a locker room to change shoes. We always went from the car directly to the first tee." Burlington chuckled at this memory and it made him seem younger, like he had become the young pro of his story.

"Anyway, this fine-looking woman pulled up next to my Chevy in a Rolls Royce golf cart and introduced herself. She waited while I changed my shoes in the parking lot. I think she was surprised I was so young. She told me Arthur was already practicing on the driving range and she would take me directly to him. As I looked around and took a deep breath of the fresh, crisp morning air, I realized how fortunate I was to be working in this game of golf under these amazing conditions. It was a beautiful morning and this was a stunningly natural setting. The country club had perfectly manicured Bermuda turf, colorful flower beds, and lush shrubbery. Next thing I knew, we were off to the end of the driving range where Arthur had been warming up.

"It was a very private place, with tall Australian pines lining the fairways. We pulled up to meet young Arthur's father and a few friends of the family. I was introduced, and they scrutinized me pretty closely." Joe smiled at the memory. "As I was about to begin the lesson, a great blue heron sailed gracefully across the range just a few yards in front of us. I remarked on how graceful it was. Then behind us, I noticed an osprey in a tree munching on a sunfish. There was a mockingbird singing about ten different songs. I just couldn't stand there and not notice these creatures and the intense beauty of the blue sky and this setting. It was a glorious moment! Are you getting the picture?" He waited for me to nod. "This Mr. C. was a real go-getter, though, and was already getting impatient.

"His son, my student, was a handsome young man, slender with a thick crop of dark wavy hair. As we began chatting, I remembered his mother's warning, but Arthur didn't seem to be testing me yet. At least he wasn't trying to impress me, which I appreciated, considering I was out of my league socially. He and his father knew all about golf swing mechanics. Arthur had gotten great professional instruction early on. But I wasn't concerned about being challenged about golf. After all, I had studied for many years myself.

"Growing up, I had devoured the old Scottish classics in golf and anything else golf-related I could get my hands on. But as I matured, I began to find my own way. I had come to believe that while these books were interesting, they were filled with empty facts. I realized that without the feel and trust to perform, a golfer couldn't place much value in volumes of minutia about picking out positions at some arbitrary point in the swing—that sort of stuff.

"Anyway, I got into a conversation with young Arthur and he seemed to be enjoying it, too. Yet there was definitely some tension building behind us between the parents. Years later, his father told me how he had doubted me from the beginning of the lesson but how he was won over by the end. So, Arthur's father was impatient with me. There I was, for at least ten minutes, just taking in nature all around me. Then I started in on music. Arthur had told me he played the violin. We talked about that for a few minutes while Mr. C. paced behind us. He must have thought the golf lesson would never begin. He sighed and cleared his throat again and again, which I took to be early warning signals of his mounting impatience. After all, he was paying me by the hour!" Burlington chuckled.

"Of course, the lesson as he knew it would never begin! But I knew we were well into helping Arthur before he even picked up a club. I wanted to establish a rapport. I wanted to get to know him—in a sense, to enter his mind and his experiences in order for us to find some commonality. I continued to probe, asking questions to try to really understand how he had gotten to this point. I refused to even glance at his parents because by now his father was fuming. He told me later he was wondering where his wife had found this guy, and did we have to pay him? Did we have to listen to him talk for the next four days?"

I had some understanding of Mr. C.'s impatience. My first encounters with Burlington had me anxious for him to get to the point. His stories circled around and around. Although I enjoyed the way he colored in a story, I was accustomed to a more linear approach. But there was nothing linear about Burlington. In any case, it was turning me into a good listener, as I found myself wanting him to keep talking.

"Mr. C. knew Arthur had serious swing problems even with the so-called superlative instruction he had procured for the boy. The experts had exhausted their possibilities with little success and I was a last resort; that was apparent. Except for Dad's obvious displeasure, I was under the impression that things were off to a great start. So after our conversation, I asked Arthur to take a few swings. I heard his father let out a big sigh of relief."

"What was his swing like?" I asked, prompting Burlington to get to the meat of it.

"Arthur pulled out an iron and asked me which swing I would like to see. I thought, oh boy, this kid is really loaded down with things to do. So I told him, 'just make a swing toward that tree and don't think about it.' I told him our technique was to be techniqueless." Joe laughed. " 'You mean, just swing?' Arthur asked me, incredulous. 'That's right,' I told him. He swung and I was amazed at all the different angles his club swung through. And he missed the target by a football field. He was really messed up. All the lessons he had taken and all the analysis had obviously buried his natural talent, and that's a nasty trap to free yourself from. I knew Arthur needed something different from just verifying that the club was laid off and shut—that was obvious. The question was why. Arthur felt helpless, he later told me. The answer to the dilemma lay in the experts' approach to solving the problem."

"So what did you do?"

"I decided to start from scratch. As he continued swinging, I hummed a little of a Mendelssohn violin concerto. Arthur stopped mid-swing to say he loved that piece. I heard another sigh from behind, so I figured we'd better stick with his golf swing. We could talk about music later. Back to the problem of teaching him to swing. None of Arthur's family, friends, or teachers, no one, had ever experienced learning from a discovery and awareness process. They only identified problems and assumed that if they knew what a problem was, they could solve it. Easy to change, right? Over time, they realized it was not that simple.

"So Arthur's present swing was probably a conglomeration of all his teachers' approaches to solving his swing imbalance. It got so he could only produce his 'trying-hard' swing. The natural swing had been buried long ago. But it wasn't dead! It was still in there breathing! If we could get back to Arthur's natural swing, he would improve immeasurably. I asked him to hit a few shots and I observed that he swung the club in a manner that required a lot of recovery to strike the ball consistently solid." Joe paused to demonstrate, as deftly as a mime, Arthur's failed delivery.

Left: Club face is shut and laid off—not desirable.
Right: Club head is crossing the line open, *a la* Bobby Locke.

EW

"The club was shut and laid off, but every pro knew that, especially his father."

"As soon as someone tried to help fix the problem, it got worse. That was what was puzzling them all. I decided to find out just how much feel this kid had. So I asked Arthur to hold the club as lightly as possible to give him an opportunity to feel it as a sensitive instrument and to hit me a cut shot. As you know, that's very difficult with a laid off club shaft and shut face. At first, he just blocked the ball to the right. I pointed out to him that it was not a cut, even though it curved to the right. I told him that the cut must start to the left. Anyway, Arthur tried a few more times and the path of his downswing began to take on a different shape and direction. His path began to swing to the left of the target before impact, which was just what I wanted," Burlington explained cryptically.

"I was getting hopeful, but I still just went about the next step without even remarking about the swing path change that had already begun to take shape. The golf shot was still not exactly what he wanted, so those watching never noticed the improvement in Arthur's swing. You see, sometimes when you make a positive change, the results don't show up until later. There's a lag between the change in habit and the change in the results. The mind-body system is now processing something foreign and needs to be allowed to let that occur naturally, to let the athletic timing re-evolve.

"Most golfers are only result-oriented, not process-oriented, Geoff, and they miss out on what really takes place. It's a shame, too." Again, Burlington's eyes locked with mine, as if he knew how close he came to reading me. "A few more swings and Arthur's natural athleticism began to emerge from its long hibernation. It must have been a very long time since he had allowed his natural swing to surface.

"Anyway, Arthur's shots began to come too: one at first, then two, and then three in a row. Now things were quiet in the background. I asked him to see if he could hit it higher. Naturally, the face began to open more and more on his backswing— another improvement without thinking about how to execute it. Arthur just reacted to my request to fly the ball higher, and his mind-body system, not cluttered with things to do, responded. After a few more swings, the club face began to match the path. It was getting less and less shut, as Arthur practiced the cut shot." Burlington mimicked Arthur's improvement with his imaginary club and continued speaking.

"Now I needed his path to get more in line with striking the ball straight. I reversed the shot. I asked him to hit a high hook. He gave me a puzzled look, as did everyone else. I guess they thought I was going to confuse him, and his swing, but I was just working on the redevelopment of his feel and balance with the club. Arthur's feel for his golf swing was really beginning to activate and he seemed right at home with the approach. I think he was starting to have fun, something he probably hadn't experienced in golf for a long time. The shaft began to cross the line and the face was still open." Joe pretended he was Arthur again and demonstrated.

"What did you do then?"

"I thought, great, we have a nice orbit to this path and the face was getting in balance. After a few more tries, Arthur hit a high draw. His swing had been completely revamped in about fifteen minutes and yet I hadn't told him anything in particular about his swing. I had only asked him to feel, to notice, differently shaped shots. Then his athleticism made the adjustment! I could hear some remarks in the group of observers—they were getting excited! I still get goosebumps telling you this now, Geoff, and that was twenty-five years ago!

"The group had by now gathered in closer. They actually started applauding after each swing as the ball soared high from right to left into the target, an ever-so-slight draw. I don't think anyone noticed the swing changes, but everyone sure noticed the ball flight. People thought it was a minor miracle because they knew what Arthur's shots had looked like a few minutes earlier. But they hadn't heard me speak to him about his swing at all. They missed the process. It was a quick one, I'll grant you that, but it was still a process occurring in Arthur's swing. No one could figure out how it happened. He was getting where he needed to go, totally by his feel for the shots."

Burlington's story mesmerized me. The pieces of my golf puzzle were gradually clicking into place. I prompted him to keep going.

"Understand, Geoff, he already possessed the ability, but had buried it by over-thinking and analyzing everything he was doing. Arthur's God-given talent and all his athleticism were replaced by some experts' concepts of how to swing." Burlington paused to let that statement sink in and to take a sip of water.

Balanced path and face.

EW

"Arthur's father was looking interested, but still had his arms folded in front of him. I could feel him leaning over my shoulder; I turned and whispered, 'Club face isn't shut or laid off anymore, is it Mr. C?' A huge grin came over his face as he realized I had known what the matter was all along."

"Did he apologize for doubting you?"

"He didn't need to; his smile said it all. Later he told me that this lesson was so far removed from anything he'd seen or experienced before that he was put off at first. By the end he realized it was much more advanced than his own approach, light-years ahead of his way of adjusting the golf swing. He appreciated that it was sophisticated in its simplicity. He told me, 'You hadn't missed Arthur's grave swing imbalances, as I'd originally thought. I had you pegged as an imposter for the first ten minutes of the lesson. I wondered how Bob could have recommended you. I just didn't understand. But you knew a different route to get Arthur on track and it seemed effortless and easy. And it worked! You obscured your strategy by never mentioning the problems.'

"Mr. C. admitted that by paying such close attention to the golf shots and by feeling so annoyed at my seeming casualness toward the problems, he'd missed the swing transformation completely. More than that, he said he'd realized that it was obvious that Arthur had the ability to change all along; how else could he have gotten it so fast? 'We just didn't know how to go about it,' Mr. C acknowledged.

"You see, none of those folks had any experience in awareness learning. Arthur already had the ability to swing exactly the way he wanted to, but his system rejected it, and those try-hard, fix-it approaches as well." Burlington threw me his famous unreadable smile. "It ended up that Mr. C. paid me double what I had requested for my time; they have sent me many students over the years and we still have a close relationship even though we rarely see each other."

"So what happened to Arthur?" I inquired.

"He went back to school and qualified easily. It was quite a moment for me, Geoff; I just kind of looked skyward and said thank you. The wind-up is that that day changed my teaching forever. And Arthur has never forgotten how to retrieve his feel again. I understand from his father that he still plays very well today, even without much practice."

11
BEGINNING PLAYERS: AIMING

The story about Arthur lingered with me. I could see that Joe's approach was the best way to get an experienced player back on track quickly. I wondered about teaching a beginner or even an average player, though.

But Joe explained, "You can use the same technique even though a novice hasn't developed any depth of feel yet. It might take a little more time because of their lack of experience, but you must begin exactly at the beginning, wherever the player is."

"How do you mean?" I asked.

"You mustn't gloss over the precision of handling the club, the grip. It can be painstakingly tedious, but you have to do it. It will save mountains of time and frustration for you and the student in the long run. Take the time to organize the pressure points and position of the hands right from the start. Often the rest of the swing will fall into place as a result."

"So how do you actually begin a lesson with a beginner?"

"I do exactly what I just told you," he said with a little irritation. "You'd be surprised how many golf professionals teaching the swing don't really understand this fundamental. Once the golfer's hands are well placed and their pressure and tension levels are optimized, you might just ask them to feel for a simple swing quality, like the pace of a short pitch, or the path pattern on a full driver swing at Tai Chi speed. I usually get right on the club with my hands covering theirs; then I can literally feel the tension and pressure points they exert on the club.

"And ask awareness questions about their hands and wrists. Or maybe have them make a full swing, allowing the club to dominate their joints so they bend and respond to the weight at the end of the stick. Any of these options accomplishes the same thing—it's just that your starting point is different. You need to help them find their feel. Discovery and awareness is still the route. As a coach you just need to determine where to begin."

"How?"

"You do awareness and discovery testing," Joe replied. "Find out how in touch your students are with their bodies. Notice how they respond to the club in hand. You need to find out how they interpret and process things, what their perception is, so you can help them to use their mind and body together as a team. That is their reality. See how they respond physically when you ask a question, then you can tell. Start with something elementary and let their awareness determine where to begin. The speed of learning is very personal and cannot be rushed."

This was a recurring theme in all Joe had said: Find out how students interpret. "What exactly do you mean by using the mind and body as a team?"

"You give a student a clear task, so he has that task in mind and needs to inquire of his body. The mind asks and the body responds. You watch how close he comes to achieving that goal. There is a dialogue going on between the mind and body that can elevate awareness, or of course go the other way. When you watch students, you can tell whether they have accurate perception—of rhythm, for instance. Now when you ask them to perform a task, you're communicating with them exactly how they need to do it on their own. A student can just copy the discovery questions you're asking. That is the beginning of coaching between you and the student. Your job is to get students to learn how to communicate with themselves."

"So what do you actually say in a conversation like that?"

"Ask the student to aim at a particular target. He sees the target, aims the club, and focuses his eyes. Standing behind him, maybe you know he's ten yards right of the actual target. His perception is off. Therefore, you need to go through a process of aiming exercises that bring him into reality and get him accurately aimed at the target. You know, Geoff, I find that almost all my students think they're on line and they are actually not aiming accurately at all. Unlike other sports, when a golfer swings, they're not looking at or even facing in the direction of the target. Their view as they swing is not directly from behind and toward the target, and their body is aligned to the side of the target line too. Your students simply need to develop an accurate sense of target from an angle."

"Yes, I know," I replied, "but could you explain why?"

"You're viewing the target from an angle. When we view the target from one side of the target line a parallax is created. That means the actual position of the target seems altered based on our point of view. The physical eye often misperceives because of this. Anyone can aim the face from behind the ball on the target line with binocular vision. But as they set up from the side to try and aim the club face, invariably they misaim. Even accomplished players do this."

I knew that most of my right-handed students misaligned the club face to the right of the target.

The golfer's eyes naturally see the target to
the right of the authentic target.

GB

Joe continued. "Over time, I developed a method to train the physical eye to see accurately from the side. Some players can naturally compensate for the angle, but most have great difficulty. This way of aiming helps a student learn to aim accurately so the parallax doesn't interfere."

He drew a diagram. "You go way out to a very wide angle from the target line and begin training. Then when you go right near the target line, like in a normal setup, it's easier to see accurately. I get my students to pick a spot on the target line from this wide angle and usually they're surprised how far off they are, but it doesn't take long to get accurate." He pointed with his pen at the drawing. "Next I have them come back to the ball without looking at the target."

Taking a look from the wide angle.

EW

"Without looking at the target?"

"Yes. As they approach the ball and set up, I subtract the physical eye from the equation completely. They're forced to use their built-in homing device as they look only downward toward the ball and make a guess for aiming based on the original sight from the wide angle off to the side. It's amazing how they begin to use their real sense of direction rather than physically looking and being inaccurate. They are now truly using their mind's eye. Some students get so good at it that they don't want to look at the target anymore and they're aiming right at it.

"But let's say they come back to the ball and are way off. Then you go through a middle-of-the-road exercise without letting them look at the target. It works like a charm! I've never seen it fail. But you need to go through each fundamental to determine each student's needs. "

"A couple more questions about your teaching style, Joe, if you don't mind."

"Go ahead," he said. "Ask away."

"You talk about a light grip pressure and less tension throughout the body. Is that what you do?"

"Absolutely. Naturally all golfers hold the club with differing degrees of pressure and pressure points, but the grip is the absolute starting point of any physical instruction. As I've been saying all along, the golf club is an instrument and the golfer's hands are the feedback center for the action of the instrument. The only way to feel it accurately is to have them well placed, and for the pressure to be light enough, to give this feedback."

"I was hoping you could help me to teach the swing well without the litany of do's and don'ts that I've used in the past. How do you, in a positive sort of way—yes, through awareness," I stammered, "get someone to change their swing path?"

"Remember what I said about artists and drawing, Geoff?"

"Yeah."

"Well, as a teacher, you need to know the arcs and angles, and the source of the energy being exerted during the swing. You need to know the patterns thoroughly. You achieve this by asking the right question for the change you would like to occur. You could also suggest pictures or get your students to use their imaginations."

"Could you give me an example? I want to get this right."

"Sure. Let's say the swing looks stiff or rigid. It violates the fundamental of fluid motion, which is often the result of 'trying hard.' You may ask them to picture a graceful dance. Ask them what it feels like to be super fluid. You need to get them to let go inside. They need to discover real control, so they can be released from trying hard on the outside. We have a number of exercises to do this. You know, so often in golf, we teachers ask too much at one time. That causes a golfer to try too hard. Eyes closed is great for letting go of trying."

I changed the subject. "What about concentration?"

"That's a good question. I marvel at the ability of great players to stay focused, but I think it's a very misunderstood concept."

"How so?"

"Well, when we think of concentration, we often think of it as a grind. We focus singularly. I don't think that serves us well. You see, for concentration we need a panoramic view—being aware and at the same time, letting it happen."

"That sounds confusing," I blurted, bewildered.

"Let me give you a simple formula. We could describe concentration both physically and psychologically. The beginning of concentration is having a clear purpose. One needs to set up a goal. It could be a numerical score, a swing quality such as rhythm, or a ball flight, anything like that. The best way to get to that goal is feel—sensing it. Your body's response based on your experience rather than any figuring or analyzing. Then you must trust in your feel.

"Purpose, feel, and trust. To me, those are the three fundamentals of concentration. You can take that formula and achieve anything you want in golf! If you're missing any of the three, the performance is sure to suffer."

"Huh?"

He drew another diagram.

Concentration

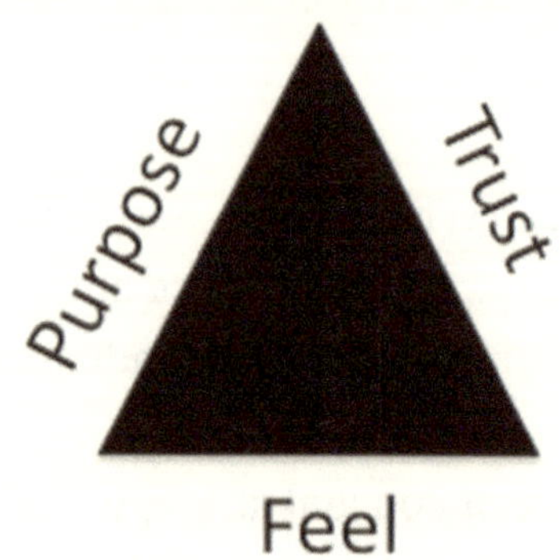

"*Purpose* is what you want. *Feel* is the vehicle to reach your goal, and *trust* means trusting in your feel. There are many strategies to develop each of these fundamentals of concentration. Remember what I told you about the physics of the swing? That, plus concentration, equals your best performance." He wrote the formula:

Flow, Path, and Timing + Purpose, Feel, and Trust = Performance

"I've never heard of a formula for performance. It's so different; I don't know," I protested.

It was beginning to sprinkle a little, a rare winter shower for these parts. We gathered our things and made our way back to the shop. There were two chairs and a small round wooden table already set up in his shop. Did he know it was going to rain?

12

TRUE FUNDAMENTALS

"But what are the fundamentals?" I asked when we got settled.

"The fundamentals comprise the club, ball, target, and ground relationships, along with you yourself. You see, to fly the ball a certain way, the club must arrive from a particular direction—angle to the ground, loft, face direction, and of course, the energy..." He began to use his hands to demonstrate. I must have looked puzzled because he said, "I see, Geoff, you're getting confused."

"Yes, how could you tell?" I still wasn't sure whether Joe Burlington was mocking me or whether he could read my mind. I went with the latter.

"Well, that's too much to think about. I never teach my students these things this way. What they need to know is the process of developing feel; *you* need to know the physics, the dynamic patterns of the club. Learn to avoid explaining it. You'll just put them off."

"How do you suggest I do this?"

"By asking the right questions. Let's say a student's club needs to be swinging in a more descending angle off a tight lie, making contact well before the bottom of the delivery arc. You could ask them what it feels like for the club to brush the ground more in front of the ball. Then you may notice the student's body moving to support a club head that bottoms out beyond the ball. You might notice a shift in their feet and legs; again, that's a function of the purpose of getting the club to do something different."

"Oh, I get it!" A new sense of understanding was dawning on me. "Your student wasn't shifting before, so the club had no angle to descend through impact and instead of talking about the shift, you reversed it by asking the question about the bottom of the club head's arc. Or asking in what part of the arc they'd like the club to contact the ball—descending or ascending portion?"

"You're getting it, Geoff. The shift isn't the problem, really. It's the club, the club, the club. I can show you how it works easily with my Pathfinder; it isn't only a Pathfinder, it's an angle finder too!"

He was referring to the foam tubes that could be bent to any shape needed to match a club's action in the impact zone. "In many cases the shift doesn't have to be discussed, and it happens. This approach allows the whole body to naturally blend the change rather than becoming disjointed."

I realized I would have discussed the shift, talked about the feet, the knees, the ankles, and hips, essentially each muscle and joint in the lower body, plus the left and right of it too. And most of the time my students would get totally discombobulated and the club would end up way out of whack. Burlington had pared it down so beautifully. Improve the club's action and the body will respond in kind. "I think I get it, Joe." I nodded with new understanding.

"We never want to interfere with the natural swing."

"But is there ever a time when you do discuss shifting?"

"Of course—when the student is locked up, or possesses exceptional body control; but again, by freeing them up and demonstrating the angle of the club's action, they usually begin to shift naturally."

"What else could you do to get them to know the angle of delivery?"

He answered without hesitation, but with finality. "I put them on a down slope and let momentum do the talking." He smiled mischievously.

It seemed our time was up. He gave no notice that the lesson was over for the day, but I got the hint. He lifted himself slowly out of his chair and began to clean up his shop. He picked up tools and put them away in the large red rolling tool box and placed extra seals and bolts into a wooden box labeled 'pump parts.' Finally, he picked up a wide straw broom that had definitely seen its best days, the ends frayed and worn. He swept the concrete floor slowly, with deliberate strokes, collecting the dirt tracked in from the yard. The broom seemed to be moving with the rhythm and pattern of a swinging golf club. I moved the chairs around so he could get under the table and emptied the garbage pail outside by the fence. When he finished sweeping, he suggested we take it up again tomorrow and wished me a good evening. I'd have offered to take him to dinner if he'd only keep talking. I made my way to the parking lot.

As I drove toward the ocean, I thought about all the things Burlington spoke about. I always knew that there must be a better way to teach golf, but before now I hadn't seen what it could be. Joe had thought long and hard about how to impart his understanding to any other golfer. I used to recognize improvement in my own play mostly when I didn't care about the results, or when I had taken a break, wondering why I was having trouble. But I just figured that was the way things were and accepted it. Now I believed I had really found a teacher who could help me, not only with my way of teaching, but with my game too.

Joe Burlington was different—and special. He was refreshing, wise, and sincere.

The drizzle continued outside, so going to Pompano for a few holes was out of the question. I stopped at Starbucks, ordered a grande latte, and started reading the paper I had saved from this morning. I opened it to the sports page and knew instantly how I would spend my evening. The Bruins were playing the Panthers at 8:00. I could go home, shower and save my appetite for the arena. I decided to phone Tim to see if he would like to go to the game. I wanted to thank him for hooking me up with Joe.

I got home, stripped out of my damp clothes, took a hot shower and dressed. I drove a little south and picked Tim up at 6:30 in plenty of time to get to the game, get decent seats, and find something to eat. To me it was always a treat to watch hockey. I've always thought the best athletes in the world were hockey players. I had worked with many of them in golf. Once I had their hands well placed and got them to open the face as they swung back, it was Katie bar the door. They all seemed extremely talented at delivering the club. But hockey players have great hands. It's weird how sometimes we need someone to point out the obvious.

Tim was good company, a good conversationalist and listener. He wanted to know all about my lessons with Joe. I told him we hadn't done much swing work yet; we had to get the groundwork done first—meaning, Joe's principal philosophy of the golf swing, which of course spilled over into life itself, or maybe it was the other way around. I was glad to have some company, someone to talk to, even if we weren't paying close attention to the hockey game. I discovered that Tim was a machinist by trade and had his own business.

"Has Joe shown you his release technique yet? You know, the curl?" Tim asked.

"No, not yet."

His brows lifted. "Well when he does, you will understand why your hockey player friends play such great golf. Watch how they hit slap shots. It's almost identical to Joe's revolutionary release in a golf swing! I'm sure when the time is right, he'll show you. And man, you think you hit it long and straight now. You won't believe how reliable the curl release is. I added about forty yards to my tee shots, and my swing tempo is like Freddie Couples'. Now that's timing, eh? I'm sure it's in the plan. Be patient with Joe; he works on Chiros time."

"Meaning?"

"God's time; he never knows how long things take because everything he does flows. He's so absorbed and immersed in his activities. You know how everything he does he claims takes five minutes?" I chuckled at the observation. "Two hours later he's satisfied and can't believe what time it is. He believes time is meaningless. Just a human invention for ordering events. Pretty far out, eh? The only thing predictable about him is his unpredictability."

"I'll second that."

I began to watch more closely how the players hit the puck, especially the long shots. It happened so fast their action was hard to discern. We had a good time and good food, and the Bruins won, although it was a hard-fought defensive contest. I took Tim home. We made plans to meet at Pompano some afternoon later in the week to play a few holes. With a twinkle in his eye, Tim told me he wanted to see if what I was learning with Joe was paying off. I was glad I'd invited him.

I reached home a few minutes later and it hit me how tired I was! I knew that even with the excitement of my next session dancing in my mind, I would sleep soundly tonight.

13
DITCH DIGGING

I got up late. The rain drumming steadily on the roof all night made for a deeper and longer sleep. It looked destined to be a stormy day too and it was quite chilly when I arrived at the golf center. With the rain continuing, I wondered where we would be today.

I walked down to the barn and found Burlington brewing some Irish breakfast tea. I gratefully accepted a cup of the hot brew. The kettle, pale green ceramic, was definitely from Ireland. He had set it up on a Bunsen burner that, judging by what was scattered around it, also served as a melt for adding lead to clubs that swung too light. Joe had peeled and sliced a banana, and had even stuck toothpicks in the slices. He also had some Italian anisette cookies with the bananas on a paper plate. There were two places set at the little table. I found this very thoughtful, especially since I hadn't had breakfast this morning. Joe's offering was a nice substitute for the instant oatmeal I would have had to settle for had I gotten up earlier.

Otter lay flat as a pancake on the cold concrete floor. With his eyes wide open and body alert, he reminded me of an alligator lying in wait—in this case, for a morsel to fall so he could vacuum it up. We sat down. I took a sip of my tea, almost burning my tongue. The squawk box let out a ring and the shop attendant came on. "Joe, did you know we have a leak out in the field?" the voice crackled.

Burlington walked over to speak into the box. "Yes," he said, "I saw it this morning."

"I can't water the green like you wanted—no pressure," the attendant snapped back.

"Yes, I know, but the slow soaking of this drizzle should be OK. Don't worry about it. We're going to get to it soon," Joe responded.

We didn't say much as we ate our bananas and cookies and washed them down with tea. "I don't like to rush like this, but we do need to get that leak fixed, despite the rain."

"No problem, Joe. What do you need me to do?"

"Just help me get these shovels and things into the Kubota. This will only take a few minutes." I smiled to myself as I thought of Tim's explanation of Joe's adherence to Chiros time. But I was happy to help and set my empty mug down.

"Except for these last two days, we're in the middle of a drought. The water table is still very low. During the dry season we need to keep the irrigation in good working order." We walked around the corner of the barn, where there were two pairs of boots, two shovels, and a small portable pump, I assumed to dry out the hole we'd dig to repair the pipe. We hopped onto the carryall and drove across the middle of the fairway. Only a few people were practicing, but I was still a little concerned that a shot from the main tee might drill us. It didn't seem to bother Burlington.

As we approached, I could see that the pressure of the water had blown a deep, wide hole in the turf. We got out of the vehicle and slipped on our boots. Burlington handed me a shovel, and then he hooked up the pump to the battery. The pump would empty the hole, and then we could dig out the sand that covered the pipe and repair the joint.

The chill in the air felt good, especially when the breeze picked up. The rain had slowed to a gentle drizzle. Even though it was cool and wet, we broke a good sweat digging out the area to expose about three feet of pipe on all sides of the broken T-joint. I figured a little conversation couldn't hurt. "How did you learn all these things, Joe, like taking care of the turf and the machines?"

"Well, Geoff, I've had a lot of help from many friends along the way."

So there we were, essentially digging a ditch, me on one side of the hole and Burlington on the other. Otter wandered over to inspect the hole, but would have nothing to do with the digging. I guess he figured we had it under control. Joe seemed to be enjoying the exercise. I wanted to get back to talking golf. I really didn't fancy working up a sweat in this hole—especially with my nice golf clothes on.

Burlington's attitude was the same as ever. He chatted about how cool it was and what really nice weather we had for digging. Thank God it wasn't summertime or we'd really be sweating like pigs. But it was muddy, wet work. After a few minutes, my enthusiasm for helping had all but disappeared. This really wasn't what I'd signed on for.

Burlington seemed oblivious to my discomfort. He told me he appreciated the fact that he still had the physical ability and health to do this kind of work and wanted to take advantage of it. I marveled at his perspective. This guy was enjoying the act of digging and sweating it up in a ditch fixing a pipe simply because he could. He seemed so at peace. "You know, Geoff, you can learn a lot about patience doing things like this." His expression changed. I could tell he was recalling something from the past. I expected him to say something, but he didn't. Maybe later.

I could see his plan was to mend the T-joint from all three sides with slip joints. He examined it and made a mental measurement of the sides. He wasn't much for writing things down. Burlington motioned for me to give him the PVC saw and began to cut the pipe. It was like a knife going through soft butter. There seemed to be no resistance from the pipe. He performed the work faster than seemed possible. He measured the pipe just by looking at it and cut it to the right length. I was impressed; I had never seen anyone do that.

I realized that everything I had observed him do he had done with ease. He didn't seem to waste any energy. He didn't rush things; everything was casual, as though he had all the time in the world. At the same time, he somehow did things swiftly. He was consistent—he cut the pipe just as he swung a club and struck a ball, fluid and square.

I asked him if I could make the last cut. He consented but he didn't tell me what to do. As I got into the pipe, the saw began to catch. The pipe was pinching the saw and I could no longer get through it. I increased the pressure and changed my grip. I held the saw with both hands now, and with all my might, tried to cut the pipe. The saw came to a screeching halt and stalled between the two edges of the cut. After a few seconds of standing still watching me, Burlington said, "Would you like some help?" Embarrassed, I gave him the saw and watched him carefully. The saw went right through, as though the pipe were already split.

There must be a trick to it. "How did you do that?"

"Lots of practice," he said modestly. "Oh, it's just like a sound golf swing, you know. You get experience with the angle of attack as it cuts right through. This saw is an instrument and, to be effective, you must use it as it was intended. The teeth are effective only if there is some speed balanced with the friction and angle against the pipe. Did you notice that when you had trouble, you instinctively applied more pressure rather than allowing the teeth to do the work or adjusting the angle of the saw to continue cutting? Did you ever observe that in your students? When they have trouble getting distance, they give up everything that gives the ball flight distance—unknowingly, of course, because the club is no longer used as it was designed!"

"What exactly do you mean?" I asked, puzzled.

"Well, we know that angle, loft, speed, and center squareness are the elements of distance. Most people apply more pressure, which negates speed and usually reduces awareness. So when the angle, loft, and squareness are compromised, the result is an ineffective impact." He grinned at me as if it were elementary-school stuff. "You did the same thing with the saw, Geoff. Success comes with experiencing fundamental awareness of the instrument you're using.

"You know, Geoff, everything is connected. If you realize the true meaning of that, you will have found the secret of being in the here and now. Then you can really teach golf as it was meant to be taught." It was hard to believe that there was a direct connection between how I had tried to cut a pipe and how my students tried to swing golf clubs, but there Joe was, drawing lines between the dots. And he was right. When we have difficulty, we generally apply more pressure and then tension becomes the significant force rather than the motion being fluid and natural. I saw it all the time and yet I did exactly that when I had trouble with the pipe. Sometimes I couldn't understand how my students could swing with all that force and no sense of direction or balance, but now I understood. The golf club is just like that saw was to me—a foreign object—and I needed, as their teacher, to guide them through awareness to let the club work as it was designed to.

What Joe Burlington had, I wanted, and I realized all these sidetracks were not really sidetracks at all. I could learn from every experience—indeed, be present at every moment—but it was up to me, no one else. If I chose, I could be there. Or I could go through life waiting to be where I thought I should be and miss out on the lessons and enjoyment of the moment. I imagined what it must be like to be Joe Burlington and find something of value in every moment, or at least to be there wholly. If I could find that, it would be the end of my chronic complaining and my criticism of people who didn't see things my way—the final chapter of my belief that I was the director of my own personal universe. The act of being present was the trick that allowed him to do things so effortlessly, almost casually, so that he didn't even break a sweat.

We repacked the soil around the repaired pipe. The dog got up and pawed the ground, then went back and lay down. I asked if we shouldn't check it under a little pressure before we covered up, but he winked at me. "No need; it's fixed. If Otter approves, it's good enough for me."

It was already lunchtime and I had worked up an appetite. Time had run away, so we must have been having fun! But more than that, I was understanding Joe Burlington better and at the same time coming to understand myself better and seeing that the real source of my malaise had been me. My attitude was my problem. Burlington had shown me by example; that was the beauty of it. I didn't feel judged by him, nor did I feel criticized or unnoticed. I just felt more aware of myself, simply by observing him. I realized that if I took a good honest look, the answers were inside me.

Burlington was right: The clues to helping others come from within. The key to helping myself was coming from a reflection I was beginning to see more clearly the more we were together. I was beginning to figure out his trick: There was no trick! I badly wanted his attitude. It allowed him to be totally aware and free. I figured that if someone practiced that attitude for a while, well, imagine how free they might become, and really good at what they did, no matter what it was. They might even become good at love.

Back at the barn, Joe went to the washer-dryer and signaled me to cup my hands together to catch the drops of liquid laundry detergent he poured. With his free hand, he wiped the spill drips from the side of the container and used that to wash his own hands. I was staring, my hands sticky with detergent, so he remarked that he loved the smell of it and how well it cleaned his hands. We washed up and rinsed at the basin outside the pump house. He took off his boots and reached up and took down some fresh blue jeans and a T-shirt that were hanging from the electrical conduit. He put them on and said, "I'm hungry. Let's get some lunch. You earned it this morning." I finished washing the dirt from my nails and fingers with his brush and I dried quickly. I hadn't brought a change of clothes, so all I could do was brush the dirt off mine.

We left the compound and jumped into his pickup truck and took a short drive down the road to a little diner at the local farmer's market.

I thought about how I was beginning to get the picture about attitude. Maybe now we could get more into the action of the swing. I understood the ratios of the circles and what they represented, but how did Joe get his students to swing based on that? I wanted to know how he taught the physics of the swing. I needed to color in some of the outlines. But during the ten minutes it took to get to the diner, my stomach was the only one talking.

The aroma of home cooking hit us in the parking lot and made my mouth water. The hostess showed us to a corner booth and the waitress came over and recited the specials. They all sounded good. After some enthusiastic eating and two drink refills, I questioned Joe.

"You talk about the physics of the club, Joe. When it comes to the motion, how does one get started?"

"OK," he said, "I will tell you the beginning of the physics of the golf swing and self-awareness, but it will have to wait until tomorrow. Better yet, I'll let you experience it for yourself. Meet me at the golf center at five AM and bring a bag lunch. Wear a hat, sunglasses, shorts, and a T-shirt. We'll begin the physics of the motion at seven AM sharp."

"I thought you said five."

"I said to be here at five. It's about a two-hour drive to Flamingo, where you're going to learn the true rhythm of all things." I didn't ask any more questions. Joe signaled to the waitress for coffee for both of us. I passed on dessert, but he opted for coconut cream pie. We finished our lunch and headed back to the golf center. Though it was clearing, the rainy weather dictated a short day so we shook hands and parted. I felt a little cheated with the time, but again, I trusted there was a good reason for it. Maybe he wanted me to absorb the lessons on my own. I began to anticipate tomorrow morning and what was in store for me.

I drove back to the B&B and changed into a T-shirt and cutoffs. The dreary weather had passed and it was becoming a beautiful day; I was thinking maybe a swim and then there'd be just enough time to play a few holes at Pompano.

I went through the dunes to the shoreline. The ocean was calm and inviting. I swam briefly, but wanted to sit and think about all I had experienced in the past couple of days. I stretched out under a row of palms. The diner coffee had no effect on me; I soon fell asleep.

I woke up well before dusk and made my way back to the house to get ready to play a few holes. I was well-rested and slightly red from the sun that had emerged from its half-day respite. As I freshened up, I tried to picture where Joe and I were going with this learning and how he would begin teaching me more swing physics and awareness. I couldn't guess what he had in mind, but I was willing to go along with it. I was still a little disappointed that today had ended so abruptly. But I would try the attitude shift at Pompano; playing alone should make it easy.

I figured the course would be empty at this time of day. I signed in, got my golf cart and went directly to the first tee. As I looked down the fairway, I thought of what Joe had said: The ball is in your court; how do you want to proceed? You choose the attitude. I felt powerful for the first time in a long time, mentally strong, as though nothing was going to deter me from being positive. I set the goal of appreciating every moment on the course.

I teed up the ball with the intention of not being technical. As I peered down at the ball, a thought about my backswing entered my mind. I thought, 'Cancel!' Just set up and hit it! I hesitated again and another swing thought entered my mind. I caught it, and inwardly yelled 'cancel' again. Now I felt clear. I made two waggles, looked down the fairway again and swung. This time I did it before another technique could enter my mind. I hit the first drive solid but a little right, just off the fairway. OK, this is good. Techniquelessness is working. I drove down to the ball. I hit the green with my second and two-putted for par.

The wind was strong coming from the airport just west of the course. It was playing havoc with the light airplanes coming in for landing. The second hole was a medium-length par three, 165 yards uphill and guarded by three huge bunkers, front, left, and center. The pin was tucked to the left side of the pie-shaped green, all the way back. I dropped my ball onto the deck between the markers and took my six iron out to play the shot. I rehearsed a low punch shot to escape the wind pushing hard from my backside. This used to be my toughest shot. With no hesitation I punched the shot low into the wind. It turned slightly left against the wind and landed hole high. Two rounds in a row, having fun. This was cool.

But this time I knew somehow I could keep it going. This attitude made golfing easy. I really had a good swing; many people had told me as much. But why had I had such problems? Joe figured it out without even seeing me play. It was my attitude, my mental state, and my practice strategy. If things didn't go well, it always bothered me. Now, if I gave it my best shot and it didn't work out, I would just go on. What a simple solution!

I played the next few holes carefree. I missed a few shots, but I just let them go in my mind and moved on. As I approached the ninth, a long par four back into a crosswind coming from the right, I aimed down the right side of the fairway and lashed the drive a good 300 yards. The ball sailed and curved slightly to the left into the middle of the fairway. Problem was, one of those Scottish bunkers lay smack in the middle and my ball had landed right in it. I chuckled to myself. I just didn't care about the result. I struck the ball just like I had felt and pictured it in my practice swing.

Familiar thoughts pushed into my mind. This was great, but I was playing alone. What about with others or in a tournament; could I be carefree then? Was I ever going to rid myself of that kind of doubt?

Just then, a voice came from behind the tee. "Nice swing laddie, but a little local knowledge would have been useful, eh?

You could have avoided the bunker!" It was Tim. He had walked a few holes and had to cut over to the ninth to get in before dark.

"Hey Tim, I didn't see you. Where did you come from?"

"Oh, I finished work earlier than I thought and since the rain stopped, I decided to come out and walk a few holes. The air is so fresh in the afternoon after a rain shower. And I get so much more out of walking than riding. I like to feel the earth through my feet when I play golf."

"I know what you mean. I took a cart because it was so late and it's the only way I could get in a few holes." He asked if he could join me for the last hole. "Of course, my pleasure; fire away." Tim walked up to the middle markers, set his ball up and took out his driver. He waggled twice and looked down the fairway. He had that Sam Snead kick start. He made a silky swing and hit a beautiful low shot down the middle. He smiled at me, picked his tee out of the ground and retrieved his Sunday bag. I went to my cart and caught up with him. I pulled up alongside him and drove his pace so we could talk as we went to our tee shots.

"How's it going with Joe Burlington?"

I had to think about it for a second. "To be honest, Tim, as you know, at first I was very skeptical. The place, his maintenance duties and all; he does things so differently from what I'm used to. He has expressed his swing philosophy to me with great clarity. It's refreshing, and there's no way I could have gotten what he's given me anywhere else. The lessons so far have been mostly about attitude and the general motion, besides the grip. Actually, now when I think about it, he has given me a lot of insight about the golf swing. It just didn't seem like a lot. I could practically repeat it all in about three minutes. I keep thinking there must be more to it than he's letting on. Don't get me wrong, it's far more than I expected and every day I get more surprises."

"Oh, he'll surprise you all right. What do you find to be the most interesting so far?"

"I don't know, really. He's just so unusual that it's hard to pinpoint one characteristic, but if I were to choose one I guess it would be his perseverance—you know, his attitude. No matter what, he keeps right on going, whether it's a golf lesson, an irrigation problem, a motor needing repair, or anything else that comes up. Nothing seems too big for him and yet he's so gentle when he's interacting with any creature. His compassion for everything is contagious. He's so appreciative of every moment, too. I guess you could say more than anyone I've ever known he appreciates the fact that he can breathe, see, speak, hear, communicate, and be outdoors doing it all day. I don't know.... Then you add in his golf swing, his music, his interest in science, and his love of life itself; it's beyond measure."

"You are getting a good dose of him, aren't you?"

"I guess you could say that."

We reached Tim's ball, and he pulled out a fairway wood and without hesitation lashed it onto the front of the green. He smiled and said, "Now that's what I wanted." I was ahead of him a good twenty yards. I got out a four iron, walked into the bunker, and proceeded to hook it into another bunker on the left side of the green, but I cracked a smile. It didn't matter to me; I had hit it solid. Tim looked at me and said "Why, that's a little different from the other day. Now get it up and down and we'll have a beer to celebrate your emancipation." I wondered how he knew that. I took my old rusty wedge, got down in the bunker and lofted it near the hole. Tim hit a beautiful putt that finished within inches of the cup. He walked up to the balls, picked them up, and said, "good good."

Tim set his clubs out on the rack outside, and the cart attendant cleaned mine up and placed them next to his. I tipped her and she smiled and ran back to wait for the remaining golfers to return. We went inside and found a booth. The place was set up like a British pub. They had all kinds of brew on tap. We ordered two Yuenglings and some fried calamari. "So you're getting a good dose of Joe Burlington. It shows."

"What do you mean?"

"For starters, when you hooked that ball into the greenside bunker, you didn't slam your iron into the turf."

"I know. I don't know how I got into such a habit. But I do know that Burlington wouldn't put up with it, and I just don't feel like acting like that anymore. I just can't be that serious and reactive after watching Joe practice. I'm committed to adopting his attitude."

I sensed that Tim was really relating to what I'd described when he asked, "I was wondering if you'd be able to spend some time with Jake. He was really taken by the way you played the back nine the other day."

"Sure. Tell him to come out any day around four PM; that's when I can usually get here. Would you like to come along?"

"Absolutely."

"OK, we have a date." We finished off the calamari and downed the rest of our beers. "See you tomorrow." Tim had to get home. He wanted to split the bill, but I told him to forget it. It felt good that Jake wanted to work with me. I believed I could impart some of the things I'd learned. He was by far the best golfer in the threesome. I left the pub, picked my clubs off the rack, and headed home.

When I got home I took another shower and hit the rack. I was exhausted. Meeting Joe at five AM meant a very early start for me. I still had a lot to digest about teaching and how to control a golf swing by just being aware of the club, but it definitely beat the lonely winter up north.

14
FISHING

I opened my eyes in darkness, showered, got dressed, then drove over to the golf center to meet Joe. On the way, I picked up my favorite breakfast—Dunkin' Donuts and coffee—bringing along enough varieties for Joe and his dog. It was still dark when I arrived at five AM sharp. With curiosity and anticipation, I wondered what was in store for today. I knew it must be something special for us to be getting up so early and planning to spend an entire day working. Burlington was already there and was just finishing hooking up his flats boat trailer to his truck. I parked my car and he motioned me over. I jumped into the cab with my bag of donuts. I served up the coffee and we began our trip.

The truck was roomy and comfortable, but the diesel engine clanked noisily, dugga-dugga-dugga, in perfect rhythm. Burlington filled me in on where we were headed. We were going down to Flamingo Point in Everglades National Wildlife Reserve, at the very southern tip of the Florida mainland. We were going to fish for tarpon, redfish, snook, or anything else we could get into with a fly. Joe had heard there were some good schools running and thought we could kill two birds with one stone. I knew from Lou that Burlington was an avid fisherman, but I hadn't figured I'd be going down near the Keys to fish and simultaneously learn about golf physics. I knew there was no use asking Joe why.

"I really like getting going early in the morning, before anyone is up. You can get in some good thinking, Geoff." I nodded in agreement, but this really wasn't my favorite hour to start the day. But the road was empty; we didn't see another car for miles. It seemed like we had a calm day ahead.

We drove down the highway, sipping our coffee without saying very much, which was OK with me. I was barely conscious at this time of day anyway. I had offered Otter his choice of donut, cream or old-fashioned. The dog sniffed both and chose the old-fashioned. I wrapped the cream one in a napkin and put it aside for later.

The coffee eventually started working its magic on me, but Burlington still hadn't said very much, so I decided to break the silence. "You really move to the beat of your own drum, don't you?"

"I guess you could say that," he said. "Don't you think we all should?"

"I guess so, but you are really different. How does golf physics fit into this trip?"

"You'll see soon enough."

"And you said I would be learning about awareness and rhythm."

"Yes, I did, and you will."

"I just don't see the connection. Why go through all this trouble to drive two hours in the middle of the night?"

"I'm sorry about the hour, Geoff, but we have to time the water. The fish will be coming in with the tide and it's no use starting at low tide going out, so we have to go early. You can go right back to sleep—just like Otter back there," he laughed. The dog had gulped down his donut and was now unconscious. I closed my eyes too, and remarkably did not open them until we arrived in Flamingo.

It was a rather rude awakening when it came: a sharp slap on my thigh and "Wake up, Sleeping Beauty! We're here!" I checked my watch. We had been driving about an hour and a half.

Flamingo really was the last stop on mainland U.S. All one could see south was the water, and it was beautiful. The sun was just climbing above the horizon. My eyes were beginning to adjust to the light reflecting off the water. I stretched and yawned along with Otter, who had popped up like a piece of toast when we parked.

We were going to go to the outer rim, where we could see the sand on the flats beneath the water. The sand was white as freshly fallen snow, just like you see in the high mountain country in winter—pure white! The water was about three feet deep and you could see forever.

To the right of the boat ramp was an old motel in disrepair. It had definitely seen better days decades ago. I guessed it served as a place to rest your head overnight, nothing more, nothing less. The setting was rustic and Burlington fit right in.

It's no wonder he was something of an anomaly in the golf industry. Everything that was important in American professional golf was meaningless to Burlington. He seemed more like what I imagined the old Scottish pros in the Hebrides must have been like. The attire, the props, and the overly polite greetings to members and media—all the cosmetic elements of the golf business—were just not his style. He seemed to reject the choreographed political correctness so prevalent among his peers. His golf center and this rustic place were typical of him— no bells and whistles, just the essentials. It occurred to me that maybe this principle and his way of doing things were exactly why Burlington was successful as a teacher.

We backed the trailer up to the ramp. There were already two boats getting ready to launch. Two of the men came over to greet Joe as if they were old acquaintances. "Bring a new friend?" one asked. "Good fisherman?"

"Yeah, he can do it all. Push pole, spot, cast, you name it." Joe said with a smile. I had no idea what they were talking about, so I just nodded hello and played along.

After backing the boat into the water, Joe tied up beside the floating ramp and pulled the truck back up into the parking area amidst long rows of enormous royal palms. There were so many of them that they actually provided shade. We got out and Burlington tied Otter up to the trailer hitch with about twenty feet of leash and set out a huge bowl of water. Otter went right under the truck with that big goofy dog smile on his face. "Aren't we taking him in the boat with us?"

"Oh no, he hates the water. Ever since a gator at the golf center nipped him, I can't get him to go in a puddle, let alone a boat in the ocean. He'll be happy right here in the shade until we return."

"Then why did you bring him with us?"

"Oh, he loves the ride down and now he's very grateful that he doesn't have to go in the boat." Otter watched as we headed toward the vessel. I just shook my head.

There were still a few things we had to do to get ready. Joe had to rig up the fly rods and put on the tippet and flies so he would be ready if we spotted one right off. It took about fifteen minutes, as he meticulously put everything in the boat and checked all our equipment. I just did whatever he told me to do. I saw that Burlington had a disciplined way of doing things—it wasn't haphazard. Lots of preparation. I noticed he had several rods and reels. He had thought of everything.

After putting on our vests, we slowly motored out of the dock area into the canal and around the bend; he found a channel that hugged the shore. There were old cypress trees overhanging the shoreline. Once we got out a ways, he killed the motor and got up on the platform mounted above the motor and began push poling—moving the boat with a long pole so as to move silently as we neared the fish.

He stopped the boat for a moment. Everything was quiet, no wind, the water glassy. The wildlife around us overwhelmed my senses, and it seemed as though it had all just awakened when we arrived. I figured I wasn't going to do any casting. Burlington put down the pole and reached for a rod. He made a few casts in the direction of the trees under the mangrove branches that hung out over the water. He made it look so easy. I thought, if I could cast like that, I could probably catch a fish; how exciting that would be!

Nothing was happening here, so Joe poled out between two small islands about 200 yards farther out onto the flats. He had tied a glades minnow onto the tip of his line. It was about two inches long, chartreuse and white, with a red eye on each side of its head. This fly was supposed to fool a fish?

"Just keep your eyes peeled for fish. We're looking for permit, bonefish, redfish, trout, or tarpon. We won't be picky." I acted as though I knew what they looked like and kept my eyes glued to the water, scanning across the bow. Joe was up on the platform looking out across the water and had a much better view.

Once I gave up my preconceived notion of what we should be doing, I had to admit this place was beautiful. The water was light green and the bottom starkly white. A soft breeze blew. I had to put on my sunglasses because the reflection of the sun off the water was blinding. I felt myself relaxing and forgot all about the golf swing and physics.

I was beginning to melt into the environment around us when Burlington spotted the dorsal fin of a tarpon meandering near some rock outcropping about fifty feet off the front of the boat. His voice became a whisper as though the fish could hear us. He cautioned me to be still. "Do you see him?" he asked. "Over there." He pointed toward a dark spot in the water. "You see the dorsal fin just breaking the surface." I was surprised to feel my heart beating faster in excitement.

Burlington lifted his rod gently. In an instant the line was running through the guides out in the direction of the tarpon feeding on the bottom. The line shot out about ten feet above the water and with each back cast, the line moved faster. The motion seemed almost poetic: Joe would shoot the line and roll it gracefully out in front of us. Then with his rod lifting in rhythm, he pulled it back and looped the line behind as though suspended in midair. A pause, and then he shot it over his head and out again.

The fly line flew out above the water and then, in rhythm, with his left hand Burlington pulled the rod up and back to about twelve o'clock, vertical, never further. There was definitely a particular pacing to keep it going. The pause was noticeable when the line straightened behind him and then cast forward again. As he did this, with the line running through the fingers of his right hand he would synchronize the pull of the line to increase its speed. He did this on both the backward and forward cast. On about the third false cast—when the line hovered over the water without being dropped into it—he shot it out beyond the fish.

It looked choreographed—like a ballet. I thought how sweet it would be to be able to cast like that. Burlington didn't look as though he was working hard, either. Then I noticed the rhythm of it. This is why he had brought me here—to notice the rhythm!

And not just the rhythm of his cast! He was showing me the rhythm of nature and how we fit into it.

Finally, he let the fly drop ever so gently onto the water. He didn't move it for a few seconds to let it sink, and then began to strip the line in slowly on a retrieve. His concentration was keen, his eyes were laser focused, still and calm, oblivious that I was even there. The tarpon hit the fly. Burlington pulled hard on the line with a swift lift of his rod, a tail swirled, and the fish was gone. The rod flexed back straight and the line instantly went limp. He relaxed and just looked at me with his wry smile. "Lost him," he shrugged. "Nice start, eh? Looks like a very promising day, Geoff." We ventured farther along, searching the surface of the water for signs of life below.

He knew all the spots, and told me conspiratorially. "There are always a few good fish in this little channel between the islands."

"Over there." I pointed, spotting the tip of a dorsal fin, another tarpon. Or was it a small shark? I pointed again, as it was hard for me to tell. Joe cautioned me to be quiet and still. He maneuvered us around with the pole so we were casting directly into the sun. With the sun in front of us, he could obscure the shadow of the line, the rod, and his motion from the fish.

Burlington focused intently; I just waited. He got his rod in hand and began casting again. His action was smooth as silk and the line just lengthened toward the fish, which seemed to be casually searching the area for food. Joe let the fly drop softly to one side of the fish and then began retrieving it in a short staccato rhythm this time, sort of darting it toward us like a live minnow. We could see the fish turn. It began to show interest and engage.

"It's coming toward the fly."

He shushed me. The water was perfectly clear and we could see everything, but, apparently, the fish didn't see us.

Bang! The fish hit it! Joe lifted the rod with a powerful stroke to set the hook. The tarpon broke the surface and there was a huge splash as it rose and fishtailed back down. It made a ferocious effort to dislodge the fly from its lip, but it was hooked solidly. Still it wasn't coming toward us voluntarily. It was swimming rapidly in the opposite direction and Joe's reel was buzzing, first the line and then to the backing. He yelled, "Grab the pole and push hard toward it! He could snap the line!"

I lunged frantically to the back of the boat, picked up the pole, and jumped onto the platform. I stabbed the pole into the sand and pushed as hard and fast as I could. With each push I picked up momentum, but we were still losing ground and the fish had lots of room to run. It headed toward the brush that grew along the shore of the island. "If it gets in there, it'll snap me off and that'll be the end of our relationship, plain and simple." I looked up, puzzled. "I meant with the fish," he said.

Then the tarpon broke the surface again, as though it was trying to get a good look at who had done this nasty deed. It had slowed a little and seemed to be spending its energy. Then it took off again, this time toward us. It was moving fast and Joe was retrieving.

"Wow, it must be four feet long! A monster!"

"Just keep pushing," Joe yelled. As I pushed, Joe retrieved a few feet at a time. After a few more minutes, the fish was beginning to tire and we were gaining on it. It was only a few more yards to the shoreline.

"We got him now," I said.

"Don't be so sure. He's likely just taking a break." I was already tired from pushing, but Joe held tight. He got the line to about thirty feet. As the tarpon slowly circled the boat, Joe turned around with it, coaxing it toward us. The fish gave one last tail swirl, then Joe reeled it in completely; we had it to the boat. Joe leaned over the side and lifted the tarpon up gently, part way out of the water, and removed the fly.

We both just marveled at this beautiful creature. Its body shimmered silvery in the sunlight. I knew this would be an experience I didn't forget. Finally, Burlington let the big fish down and coaxed it back to life, pulling it back and forth to get water moving through its gills, and then released his hold. The tarpon swam slowly back to its feeding ground, giving us the side eye, probably wondering what that had all been about—just as I was. But the whole episode was exhilarating. No longer feeling tired by it, I could feel my veins and muscles popping as my adrenaline crested.

"OK, Geoff, it's your turn."

"Oh no, I can't do this," I stammered.

"Of course you can. Just feel it! Feel what allows you to cast with accuracy and distance. I'll help you. With a little practice, you'll get it. It's just a matter of time." This didn't appear negotiable so I picked up the rod reluctantly and began casting, if you can call it that, awkward and tight. "What are you feeling, Geoff? What does the rod handle feel like in your hand? Hold the rod as lightly as possible, like a golf club. That'll allow you to really feel what's going on at the other end."

I was too nervous and tense and couldn't feel the action. "I'm not feeling anything."

Joe disagreed. "Oh, but you are, Geoff, you just may not like it. Are you feeling tight and forceful?"

"Now that you mention it, yes, I am."

"What would it be like to feel smooth?" Joe questioned me with serious intent, probably just like a golf lesson.

"I don't know, Joe. You know I have no experience fishing."

"It doesn't take fishing experience; just be aware."

"Well, it does feel like I'm forcing it."

"What would it be like to hold the rod softly in your hands and just cast the line a few yards?"

"But that won't do," I griped, "the fish are way out there."

"Yes, but a thousand-mile trip begins with the first step. Now think back to your golf instruction. Does this situation seem familiar to you?"

Yikes; I sounded just like my students—the bottom-liners who just aren't interested in the process. How do I get started? How did he get started? How did he begin his lessons...the hands, the motion, rhythm, flow; that's it. I paused my thinking for a moment and replayed the movie of his lessons, including this trip.

I thought about his rhythm. I pictured each exercise and all the things he had done. He never seemed to be in a hurry with his golf swing or his casting, or push poling the skiff, cutting a pipe, or digging a hole. He slid into tasks with ease and an economy of motion, as if he were part of the machinery. Burlington even drank a cup of coffee in a slow, measured manner, savoring each sip with more pleasure than the brew deserved. His rhythm was almost exactly like that of the great blue heron I'd seen sail down onto the water earlier, or the osprey now soaring above us. They all fit perfectly into what they were doing in the here and now. I seemed to be the only one feeling out of place and missing something. All I really wanted to know was how to get into the right places at the right time—the here and now—and find my own rhythm.

"Are you gonna make another cast?" I shook my head sharply to clear my head as Joe broke me from my trance.

"Joe, how do you get into the here and now? How does one get into the rhythm of nature and life? I still don't know how to dedicate myself to each moment."

"It's kind of an unconscious thing, Geoff. You simply don't try, you just be. As my wife puts it, be a human being rather than a human doing! Just be yourself, and then you can appreciate every moment."

"Can you really enjoy every moment?" I questioned with a hint of skepticism.

"Well, that depends. I might appreciate every moment, but not necessarily enjoy them all, because some of the lessons can be a bit trying—yet still necessary. Growth is sometimes painful, even grueling. And it often seems illogical when we're in the middle of it. Most of us have to make mistakes to learn. That's part of life, don't you think?" He paused to take a deep breath. "Usually after some time passes, we look back and clearly see there was a good reason for the growing pains; if nothing else, we gain appreciation for what it takes to reach our potential.

"When young tour players find themselves in contention for a major championship win, it is rare not to stumble on the first try. But if they learn and persevere, their performance will eventually match their talent. Or how about your beginning students who lack experience? They try to do things that are really outside the realm of achievability and they get deeper and deeper into trouble. It's important to know your current state of awareness and choose goals that fall within that state. You've got to get to know yourself, Geoff."

Just then, we watched an eagle swoop down into the everglades and clasp his talons around a nice fish. "Boy, that was easy."

"Good observation," he concurred. "How does that relate to us?" (I'd noticed he always included himself when he spoke of things I needed to learn and do to be more aware, as if he were going through the learning process alongside me.) "Anyway," he continued, "when you teach and play golf, it's important to be yourself all the time. Look at Otter. He's a dog and he spends his whole day being a dog. He eats, sleeps, and walks dog. Every moment he is a dog. That eagle, and the fish we fooled today? The fish, the bird, the dog, nature, never run into the problems we humans do. The fish just swims, the bird just flies, but we humans so often try to be something we aren't. We waste so much time acting with a mask on. We spend our lives not heading toward a better place. This is how we lose our way, by playing the wrong game of pretend. It really gets in the way of being at our best and putting our focus on what needs work."

"But what does all that have to do with learning rhythm?" I asked, feeling a bit lost.

"Until you be yourself and know yourself, can you ever find your own pace? There's rhythm in everything. All these creatures have it because they never spend time pretending to be other than they are. Learn your unique tempo. You be the judge of what's best for you. Make progress at whatever speed is right for you, in your swing rhythm, or just learning to get your students to discover their best rhythms and not forcing yours on them.

"And right now, you can copy how I cast or you can develop your own way based on how the rod feels in your hands and how the wind feels at your back. The point is, as you practice lifting the line from the water, you will begin to notice the pace that's most effective for you, just like a golf club. With a fly rod and reel, you find out quickly what's an effective rhythm and what's not when trying to get the line to shoot. As you begin to feel it, picture the line straightening out behind you and you accelerating the rod just right. In fly casting, you're using the weight and aerodynamics of the line and the flex properties of the rod to shoot the line. If you try too hard to force the line out without rhythm or timing, you will end up with the line slapping the water in a tangled mess right in front of you. It's easy to know if you're doing it rhythmically or not, Geoff. Granted, we could have cast the line at the golf center, but isn't it more fun to catch a tarpon or a bonefish?" He didn't wait for me to answer. "Here, we can get into how far we need to cast and how to present the fly softly onto the water so as not to give the fish reason to doubt the authenticity of the food you're serving."

With that, he pointed to a shadow swimming not far from us. "You see, we need to blend into its environment, to let the line land on the water gently, or it will be gone as quickly as you can say 'whatever.' And for that to happen, the fly needs to be presented in a way that requires a smooth rhythm. We need to use the rod and line as if they were a fine instrument, like a Stradivarius. A Strad in the hands of an untrained artist doesn't sound like a Strad at all. It's the player, not the instrument, who makes the first difference. You know, Geoff, I once heard that Schweitzer used to play Bach on an old rickety upright piano while he was doing missionary work in Africa."

Burlington was about to head off somewhere, but I didn't mind. It was fun to hear these tidbits of history and unusual anecdotes, which all seemed to point in the same direction: Get the most out of what you have and be authentic.

He continued on the Schweitzer tangent. "When Schweitzer was caring for the sick, several of his friends would periodically make short visits to bring medical supplies in from Europe. They said that almost every evening, even after a long day, Schweitzer would play the piano in the main room of his residence. The piano was so out of tune that almost every note he struck was off. But it didn't seem to matter. Why?" He didn't wait for my answer. "It was the love, intelligence, and talent Schweitzer brought to everything he did that was evident in his piano playing, not the quality of the instrument. Infectious disease was rampant where he was working, there were no antibiotics, and yet Schweitzer was the instrument that helped cure many of his patients when everyone else gave up on them. And the cure was love! This love pervaded all his activities, and Schweitzer got more out of that rickety old instrument than anyone could imagine." He mimicked tickling a keyboard as we floated amidst a panorama that had never heard one.

"The self-love that allows a person to truly care for others shows he has a spirit that can't be broken. They live each moment with such a deep faith that they solve seemingly unsolvable problems. They always find a way. That's the attitude we need to adopt every day, Geoff. Never give up. Never! Just keep plodding with an optimism that opens you up to whatever is possible, always moving forward." Joe Burlington's enthusiasm was contagious. I felt a new, serene sort of optimism just listening to him.

"As you move forward you must be open to possibilities. That is exactly what allows you to discover every day, just as we have out here on the water today. Every moment is an opportunity to see and experience, so we need to stay alert to what's happening. I brought you here so you could witness the rhythms in nature—in our casting, as in everything we do, there is a rhythm, and we need to find our own brand of it. We need our actions to co-mingle naturally, without being forced. That means being at the right place at the right time, and in the here and now. No stopping in the past or jumping ahead to the future. You need to tune in to your own here and now or you'll lose your rhythm and miss your chances."

A flashback to the seminar in New Orleans interrupted my reverie. And how did I happen to meet Tim at the golf course the next day? Was it by chance, or was it fate that ultimately led to me being here on this boat with Joe Burlington and finally beginning to see the big picture and how I fit into it? Was there a plan, and all I needed to do was go along?

I needed to let this play out and to stay on my journey with him—that much I knew. It was fascinating, though puzzling at the same time. "Joe, I think I'm beginning to understand your philosophy, but I just needed to experience what you're talking about, and coming out here has opened my eyes and my mind."

"Good, Geoff—that was my purpose in making this trip."

"I have been dedicated and worked hard all my life to improve."

He nodded in understanding. "You just needed a little direction."

"I appreciate that it's you who's providing it."

"A person can have all the energy and dedication in the world, but if.... Let me just say, zeal without awareness is like a runaway horse." That last statement sure rang true. I had worked hard for many years; probably as hard as anyone in golf, but without awareness, what did it get me?

We had a wonderful day on the water. Burlington kept me practicing casting for hours, but we switched when he saw me tiring. He also caught a bonefish and a permit, which with the tarpon, he dubbed the Triple Crown. Not often did that happen, he told me. I couldn't believe I could cast so well with one short lesson and a day of practice. And it was genuinely fun.

The day's true lesson was invaluable. I finally felt I was really getting it. I could go on from here and really, in a sense, begin my golf life again. It was a rebirth and, although it was strange, it was exactly the start I had needed.

When we got back to the dock, Otter was still under the truck, content, but ready to go. We put everything away and secured the boat onto the trailer. Burlington gave the dog some food and fresh water, then we were off. It was getting dark now and the drive back was quiet. We were both exhausted from the day, but it was a good tiredness.

By the time we arrived at the golf center, it was late and everyone had gone. I jumped into my car and headed back to the B&B. I devoured my leftovers ravenously and went to bed. Joe and I had planned to meet at ten the next morning, so I could sleep in a little.

Claire still hadn't called me back.

15

WHY GOLFERS SLICE

I arrived at the golf center and made my way to the maintenance area. Joe was seated at the table in the barn.

"Good morning," we greeted each other simultaneously as I entered. Hot tea and warm breakfast bread awaited me: everything to begin a conversation. I sat down and thought about how I wanted to begin today's inquiry.

Feeling more comfortable now, I had some questions about chronic problems and general tendencies that so many golfers encounter, so I got right down to business. "Why do so many players slice the ball? I've heard some people say it's because the golf swing is like nothing else we do in our lives, so that we have never formed the right habits athletically. There are a host of theories, for that matter."

Burlington smiled and then shifted to a more serious look. "I think it goes deeper than athletic habits or actions that students never practice otherwise. It's a combination of factors that afflict the greater golfing population, factors that inhibit them from sustaining positive change and getting out of the dreaded slice. If teachers had hit on the real cause, players wouldn't continue to have chronic problems with slicing."

"What do you mean?"

"Well, anyone who's tried to stop slicing and has accurately identified what's physically causing it—by that I mean the path-face relationships at impact—should be able to rid themselves of the problem, right? And of course there is a psychological component to it too. Yet somehow most golfers never seem to get out of the problem and execute the solution. They feel helpless and hopeless. So when a large percentage of golfers feel this way, more than likely we have not yet arrived at the source of the problem, wouldn't you agree?"

"That makes sense, but how do you know you've hit on the real cause?"

"Because none of my students are chronic slicers after we work it out. Mind you, I had a hell of a time figuring it out myself, but once it came to me, the most difficult part was imparting a strategy in a manner that allowed students to believe in it."

"So what is the problem?"

"First, there is the overriding psychological challenge of fearing that the ball will fly off to the right when the golf club is on a sound path from here." He demonstrated the club coming from an inside path. "This needs to be addressed first. After that, often centrifugal force contributes to the problem—assuming aiming is in order."

"What? How so? I thought centrifugal force was a good thing."

"Only when it occurs at a certain time during the swing. At the wrong time it can actually create the swing path of the slice. In a sound golf swing, the whole downswing needs to oppose C-force until it's triggered in the release fairly late in the downswing." He looked up toward the sky and continued. I sensed that this last bit was a peek into his deep understanding, although he spoke as though it were an afterthought. But I was on the edge of my seat again. I knew so many people who wanted this question answered—I had asked the question many times myself, yet had not found one adequate answer. I was hoping for a definitive one from Joe.

Otter was sitting up as though he wanted to know the answer too. His ears were alert. He had been delicately licking a rawhide chew that sat between his huge paws, but he stopped even that, seemingly for this pivotal revelation. "As I said, at the heart of the problem is the psychological anticipation of the results relative to the target. There is conflict both physically and psychologically."

"What do you mean?"

"Look, the target is forward, isn't it? But the release needs to be backward and downward. Almost every instinct a golfer uses to get the ball to fly toward the target is exactly what flies the ball away from it."

"How so?"

He didn't bother to answer my question. "The target for these golfers has become the obstacle. Let me tell you a little history of my discovering the truth about it."

"The *target* is the problem?" I wanted to be sure I had heard him right.

"Yes, the target." Now we were into the meat. "It was frustration that got me going. I could fairly easily get a golfer to become rhythmic and get them on a pretty good path pattern. Remember our equation. However, as soon as we progressed in the lesson to learning to square the face to consistently fly the ball toward the target, all those good swing qualities would dissolve. It would blow my mind. Their rhythm would deteriorate and their swing path would return to the dreaded out-to-in pattern. It was difficult to accept.

"On top of that, even when a golfer would improve with me, they would invariably go out onto the course and return to their old way of handling the club, and the slice would return. For years I was frustrated with these temporary results. What irritated me was that I knew it wasn't the students, it was my lack of understanding of how people respond and perceive, much of it on an subconscious level. I dissected my own brain trying to figure it out.

"Then one day it came to me. The culprit was the target and the effect it had on the player. It was the students' subconscious response to the target that dissolved the good swing qualities we had worked on."

"What did you do?"

"I simply changed the target. I asked my students, after aiming, to mentally let go of the target out in the field."

"That seems strange to me."

"Of course it does and that's exactly why the answer has eluded most of us for so long, but if you don't change the target for a chronic slicer, it's doubtful they'll ever get rid of their problem." What he was describing rang true in my lessons too. I have always been confused about the fact that a student can make the perfect practice swing, but when you add a ball and target to the equation, all the old bad habits make a return visit.

Joe continued. "Of course they consciously know the path and face they want through impact but when they place the ball in front of them with a target out in the field, the subconscious mind takes over and changes the swing back to its skewed pattern. The only way I've found to overcome this is to change the target. I knew my students needed something radical that could overcome this unconscious effect, but it had to be worked out with the physics of C-force during a swing too!" His voice demonstrated his enthusiasm for his discovery.

"And you did this."

"That's right. It all boils down to one point of reference. If a golfer is willing, it surely works, and he or she will consistently deliver the club with high energy and directional control of the ball flight."

"What did you change the target to?" He got a piece of paper and a pen and drew a diagram showing a golfer's swing pattern when he or she focused on the ball's target. He drew another that showed a golfer's delivery into impact when they focused on the new hand target. "I kind of understand that, but how do you get them out of their old belief?"

"Geoff, when someone is deep into this problem you must get them to change the habit and then the belief will change with sound physical exercises, just as a matter of course."

"But how do you get them to change the habit and the belief?"

"Therein lies another problem. The action of the hands and arms to create the improved action is totally counterintuitive. That's why teachers and golfers alike rarely touch on it." I sat there with my mouth open, waiting for him to continue, finding it all hard to grasp. "Be patient, Geoff. As I said, I simply change the target. It is no longer out in the distance, forward near the flag on the green. It's now in the area where the golfer is standing and backward. Give them a back hand target near the impact zone that relates to the face angle. The beauty of this target is it comprises all three dynamics. They'll all be in order: path, face, and angle. I've found it to be the most effective way to get golfers to sustain the change. When the brain registers— actually sees—the downward delofting closing face angle, it completely rejects the old habit of an out-to-in path pattern."

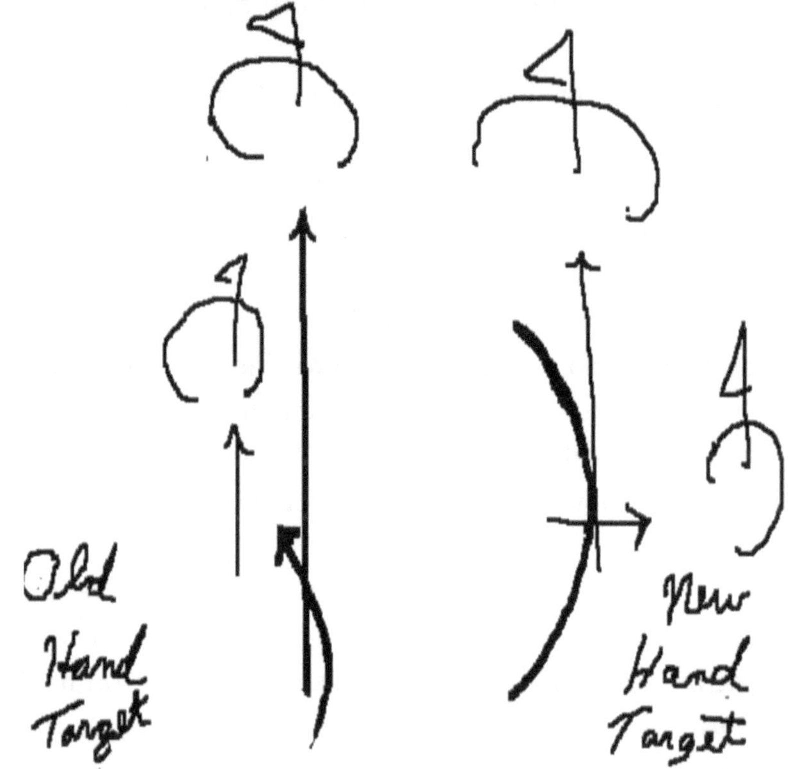

"That's the level we need to get to for the change to be sustained. When the brain sees the face angle of this release trigger, it totally rejects the old pattern of path. And then, when you get to the point of hitting a shot to a target, the subconscious brain doesn't switch the swing path back. It was a real epiphany for me, and I no longer get frustrated by people who arrive with a slice; it can be dissolved forever in short order."

"So when they have path and face problems, you work on the face first?" I asked.

"That's right. If they can't fix the path by working on it, then their subconscious may be driving the imbalance and has a false impression of how to flight the ball to the flag. You see, Geoff, that's the trick of it all. When you work on adjusting the face angle to improve their swing pattern with this back hand/face target, it produces an improved path. The brain can then trust in the new path with the new hand and wrist action that flexes inward and backward to produce this face. Essentially, what I've done is change the picture and hand action of the timing. Get the face first with this crazy-looking hand target, and then it's likely their brains will *not* reject the improved path.

"The inside path becomes not just a desire but a need, mentally! The brain, on every level, will never accept an outside path with this hand and wrist action. So you've not only solved the physical swing problem, but also the psychological problem the golfer has about the inside path, too."

"So to improve the path and swing, you must first develop trust in the hand/face action?"

"Exactly. When the sound path has not been sustained, you have to take a different tack to address the golfer's subconscious disbelief. You must get them to commit to this change, the inward/backward hand and wrist action, in the delivery zone or near impact. After a little while, it's very likely that their brain, subconsciously and consciously, will process an acceptance and trust of an improved path, especially once the brain knows the golf ball has no chance of flying to the right."

"Can you show me?"

"Sure. Turn the face downward, like this...." He got up to demonstrate. Here's the new target; it's a hand target. I call it a curl. You literally back the club into the impact with the action of your lead hand, wrist and arm. Like this." He showed me. Just as Tim had said, it looked like a hockey player swinging at a puck. It was strange the way Joe's wrist flexed and hand faced, because the direction of the action was not toward the target. I could certainly understand how it would be difficult to believe.

"Of course, the face could close a lot too, if not done in balance," he told me. "Give your students this impression of the delivery and they'll be making progress very soon. Let me show you." He took two clubs and had me help him form a triangle between the face of the club, the ball, and the direction of the back of his left hand. "This is basically what it looks like at this point in the downswing. This reference more than any other practically guarantees a solid impact toward the actual target. As I said, it combines all three dynamics of a sound delivery: face, path, and angle. This discovery enabled me to combine those three dynamics in one point!"

Path, face, and angle.

GB

"Can your hands and wrists really do this in the swing?" I asked.

"If you begin slowly and relax the muscles you can begin to get it. When I curl way down I'm exaggerating a bit, but if you try to achieve it, just coming close, you will improve and become consistent. The C-force during the swing will probably not allow you to get this much curl, but just get the impression and I guarantee you'll improve. As I've been saying all along, your hands and wrists are the most influential part of your body when it comes to club control. This method maximizes control over their action and therefore the club. The impact and wrist action is very stable when you use them this way.

"Too often, when the hands are mentioned in golf instruction, it's assumed that they're inherently unstable. When I speak about the hands I'm not talking about being slap happy with them! There's a duality to the process too. The swing action is fluid to make the impact solid. Fluid and solid are not mutually exclusive."

He winked at me and continued explaining how to gain maximum energy and control over the impact. "Mind you, as you learn, you may have to modify where, when, and how much you do this. At first, learn it to the extreme and teach it to the extreme, especially when a golfer has the so-called incurable slice. Remember, nothing in golf is really incurable. The average golfer really needs to learn the release this way, and once they get it, frankly, they hardly need golf lessons. When they see this closing and de-lofting face, they get a clear picture of the ball flight going straight or curving to the left. Then and only then do they trust in the path coming from what's commonly called inside. In fact, their brains will refuse to let them strike the impact from an outward swing path. And now you have the brain on your side. A great advantage, wouldn't you agree?"

"I was under the impression that the action of the hands and wrists had little to do with squaring the face to the target physically."

He looked at me incredulously. "How did you plan on getting your students to strike the ball squarely?"

"I thought it would happen naturally, if everything else was in order."

"Well, did it?" He didn't wait for me to say no. "Really, I won't delve into what you call 'everything else.'"

So here we are playing a target game and the way to get the ball to the target is to *not* concentrate on it. It still seemed crazy. I was still puzzled. Then I mimicked with my own hand and wrist the angle he prescribed. The back of my left hand was facing downward slightly to the right of the ball when my hand passed in front of my right thigh. It was a good 90 to 110 degrees away from the actual target. "If you're going to do this with your hand and wrist, why not just leave it that way all the time?" I asked.

I could tell he had heard this question before; he responded without hesitation. "This question highlights one of the reasons I teach the whole swing first before dynamically adjusting the delivery. As the club orbits, it's building up energy based on its design, mass, speed, and pattern of movement. Too often, golf teachers—and club makers—attempt to design a swing and club without appreciating the dynamics of the swing and how the mind works in conjunction with it! They assume a lot and try to preset what they ultimately want at impact. It simply can't be done that way.

"The swing itself is inherently dynamic. It's alive, always going somewhere. The club face, the path, and the angles in a swing are patterns of energy that depend on each other; they cannot be achieved statically. You cannot superimpose a static position onto that energy and be accurate and successful in balancing it. To find balance in an energy system you must recognize the Yin and Yang of it. You must account for this dynamic energy when adjusting how the delivery is created. There is a sequence and pace to it, too.

"Geoff, the square contact is achieved dynamically. All we can really do is pass through square. You've got to take the chance. The club is flying, whirling through the impact zone. There are no guarantees. You can't aim the club for square as you swing. The curling just provides a great opportunity for square and solid contact."

"That seems confusing."

Joe seemed to be trying to put himself in my shoes and patiently continued. "Well, Geoff, the club is traveling way out here, on a much greater orbit" He got up again and demonstrated the arc of the club head and how much larger it was than the handle arc, and then the difference in the speed and distance between the handle and the head as the downswing progressed. He then pointed to the action of the club head when he triggered the release with his curl. "This action is just a trigger, so the natural forces of momentum and C-force finish off the release so that the club face is looking toward the target through impact. The C- force can now be an advantage, instead of ruining your swing path and impact into the ball."

"You let it go from there?"

"Most of the time; sometimes I turn it more, and the more I let it go from there the higher I fly it," he said with a smile. "There are a couple of rules that must be adhered too, though."

It all seemed weird to me, but I was willing to listen because I had yet to find a release reliable under pressure. Maybe that's why I got so anxious when I played. I knew deep down that I didn't know how to feel or create the impact reliably. "Tell me," I said, "what those rules are."

"Well, first, it must be done by the lead hand, wrist, and forearm so that the hinge is supported when the change occurs, and, of course, there is a guaranteed positive effect on path when it has been done with the lead hand this way."

"That sounds like you're manipulating the club, which is unnatural, isn't it?"

"I guess you could call it manipulation, but it's a very valuable manipulation that's necessary in developing the release, especially when someone's hand action is that out of balance. What's natural at this point is not serving them well, but so many good things can happen when you do it this way.

"I recall a lesson some time ago with a fellow from Austria." He looked skyward, trying to remember his name. "Ah: Fischer," he said, pleased that his memory hadn't failed him. "Fischer was a fine student, extremely focused. He had learned the golf swing mostly by position and complex analysis, rather than dynamics and feel. He had a good swing and he was a good player, but intuitively had come to the conclusion that where he was would be as far as his approach could take him. Like many golfers, his game had hit a plateau. He came to me because he knew analysis was not getting him to his full potential.

"I was impressed with his perseverance but concerned about his seriousness. I thought that if he could couple his work ethic in feel with a lightness of mind, it would be a truly successful combination. I chuckle when I think of him, because he so enjoyed my simple approach. That is, the first two days of it. Our lessons up till then were only dealing with flow and path—you know, Da, Daaa, Daa—and then we worked with the Pathfinder for his orbit. It made perfect sense to him."

"What happened then?"

"I introduced the 'curl' timing, and an alarm went off in his head. His first reaction was to protest that it was too technical and ask what happened to simplicity. I told him that I was sorry that I couldn't make it more basic. I really believed we were at the bare bones, Geoff. You can only make it as simple as it is, and if your students are going to really see their potential, they need to learn timing. The wind-up is, Fischer trusted me and soon accepted my timing trigger and learned it well. He returned to Europe with the whole enchilada, and I believe he should be able to coach himself extremely well for the rest of his life. Sorry for the…" He apologized for getting away from my question.

I waved him off. "No, it's great."

"Where were we?"

"Back to the path?" I reminded him.

"Yes, the path has a much better chance of being fundamentally maintained from the lead side."

"How do you mean?"

"Well, picture this. It's like with a wagon. You can't control where a wagon is going if you push the handle. It won't steer well because there's no directional control. That's what pushing to get the delivery from the trailing hand during the delivery would be like. The link, the front of the wrist, collapses or flexes backward when pressure is applied from behind and the sound path is destroyed. That's why so often in golf past champions call the swing a left-side dominant swing—because the only way to control the hinge is by not applying pressure from behind."

"If you don't use your right hand, wouldn't you lose power?"

"Absolutely not. You don't add speed by pushing on the hinge; that only reduces energy."

"Are you saying that all these current great golfers are wrong about unloading the right side or hitting the ball with the right hand dominating the delivery?"

"I'm just saying it's neither pressure nor force from the right hand that they're really feeling. It's the flex-reflex action resulting from the club head weight and velocity orbiting, rotating, and accelerating. In other words, it's a result of allowing centrifugal force to take place in the delivery. That's where centrifugal force is useful! What those experts say they're feeling is what they're feeling, but I don't think it's the physics of it. Is it possible that they feel the right hand because they're right handed and that the hands and wrists are really flexed, a contracted position when entering the release zone?

"Let me put it simply because this is getting way too complicated. The feeling of the trailing hand releasing in the delivery is really the effect of the centrifugal force of the club head. It's an effect. I know from experience that if you describe the release from the trailing hand, you're in for a heap of trouble, confusing your students and making it more complicated than it needs to be.

"We also need to be careful about confusing golfers when we're talking about feelings versus fundamentals. Again, 'feel' statements in teaching can be very misleading, for several reasons. Mainly, golfers so often confuse a personal feeling with the physics and fundamentals of the club. I repeat myself at the risk of being pedantic: If the physical properties of the club are OK, then what you feel is OK. It's this interchange of personal feel with fundamentals that's confusing to many." Burlington was upping the velocity of his lecture with an infusion of passion.

"If someone feels that they deliver the club with the force of the right hand or side, that's their business, Geoff, but to misinform a golfer trying to apply true fundamentals makes it an unfortunate and misleading approach. You can't increase the centrifugal force of the delivery by pushing on the handle end from the trailing hand. Centrifugal force is an outward-pulling force. It's this misrepresentation of fundamentals that has set the average person's game back too far for too long. People end up feeling they have no talent or ability. It robs them of the pleasure they could be getting from golf. We as teachers need to improve far more than our students."

I saw Joe take a deep look at me—probably seeing that I was getting close to over-load territory—and he said, "Let's have a snack break."

Burlington went inside to get us something to eat. Otter was asleep, his snout resting on the rawhide. Burlington came back with a tray bearing grapes, a box of muffins, lemonade, paper cups and plates, and napkins. He broke the bunch of grapes and gave us each some. I poured the lemonade and opened the muffin box. We were quiet for a few minutes, just enjoying the ambiance before continuing our discussion.

"Joe, I'm kind of getting the picture of the release you're describing. What can you tell me about drawing the ball or curving the ball from right to left for a right-handed player?"

"I'll give you the dynamic formula for a consistent draw, and I would bet it's the opposite of what you think. Tell me, what do you imagine needs to happen in the delivery for the ball to curve right to left?"

I thought about it for just a second and described today's golf teacher's common assessment of why a golfer's club face is open at impact. "I believe the club head is stuck behind the golfer at impact and that causes the face to be open."

"Really?"

"That's what I hear players on the tour say all the time, especially when they hit a drive way to the right."

Joe began to shake his head. I hoped he wasn't going to dispute the great tour golfers; surely they must understand what's happening with the club when they lose control? Joe began, "Obviously, they're some of the most talented golfers in the world. But I believe they too have fallen prey to misinformation. I'll make this simple. The reason tour players mishit it to the right has nothing to do with the club being stuck behind them. If that were the case, and the other dynamics were in order, they should only strike the shot lower, not to the right! You do not draw or strike the ball straight and solid by slinging the club head forward during the delivery."

"Why do they constantly refer to the hand action as something negative?"

"I have a theory about that too," he said with a grin. "I believe one reason they so often ignore timing is because they always had an unconscious sense of it. I mean, it functioned well without them having to go through the process that most people have to go through to develop it. Most golfers are fairly incompetent with their timing at first, but through proper hand and wrist exercises they can become proficient consciously, and that leads them to an unconscious competence. That's where you want to end up, like signing your name or riding a bike.

"But these fine golfers haven't had to go through the process. I believe that's one reason they get all confused when they try to learn about their swing once on tour. It's easy for them to get lost because they're great athletes with great feel, but no program."

"So, how do you work on timing?"

"As I said earlier about the curl, you simply turn it downward while the club head is still behind, exactly as I showed you a few minutes ago. You curl it back there."

"You mean you want the club behind you?"

"Absolutely." He pointed to a spot well to the right of the golf ball during the downswing.

I raised my hand to interrupt politely. "It looks as though the ball would be smothered with that action."

Another head shake. "You don't continue to turn it down, you just trigger it downward and let it fly forward toward the ball from there."

"But the ball is on a tee. Wouldn't the club strike too downward a blow when you turn it down that way?"

I saw the first hint of Joe getting seriously impatient. He took my driver out of my bag and swung back and around behind him and then downward and forward to the point in his downswing when his left hand was near his right hip. Then he curled it down and stopped. It was revolutionary to me. I had never heard the release described as a curl.

He continued. "Now with a driver, from here you let the club head fly forward to impact the ball." He walked into the ball on the tee, made a curl and stopped, in slow motion so I could see it, then swung back up again and this time curled it down and let it fly at full speed. It sailed high, long, and straight, and he remarked, "That's how you drive it. When you time it here, you have no urgency to square the face near impact either. This delivery is very easy on the mind too." Again in slow motion, he curled it downward and then let the club head swing forward as his hands passed in front of him. The angle had leveled off and was now ascending into the impact. The release trigger had done its job and would surely launch the ball as high as he wanted.

"I thought it would be popped up or smothered to the left when you turn it over like that."

"Geoff, I never said turn it over." I was surprised by his look, his eyes squinted and his nose crinkled up as though disapproving of my description of his release trigger. "I said turn it down, not turn it over. I showed you."

"What's the difference?"

"There's a big difference." He seemed exasperated. "When you curl it down you maintain path, whereas when a golfer is told to turn it over, the path circles about to the far side of the ball. That's why I showed you the reference with the curling. Curling is turning it downward, not over. The point I showed you is critical to the timing."

"So I won't duck hook it if I turn the driver down like this?" I pointed my left hand downward as it approached my right thigh in my downswing. The club head was way behind me.

Joe's patience returned. "If you let it fly from there, you'll launch it, and if you're concerned about hooking it, after curling it downward try to launch it as high as you can. It all depends on when you do it. If done at the proper time, when the club head arrives, it will be a perfect launch angle and square. I once heard a great golfer describing his swing while playing well. I knew he was in for trouble because of his belief about timing. He seemed to believe that timing was some sort of recovery, not a fundamental, that it's unreliable and unstable. In my opinion that couldn't be farther from the truth. This timing trigger creates total stability of the hand and wrist action. You can't get it by eliminating the hand action from the swing; you must develop it and learn to trust it."

Joe had just taken the mystery out of what so many golfers are afraid of: the delivery. When I thought about it, I knew that's why we lacked confidence. Why should we all be afraid of the hand action? Maybe only because we hadn't worked it out. I tried to pretend my hands didn't exist and hoped they would behave.

Joe was shaking his head again. "Moe Norman once gave a friend of mine some of the best advice I've ever heard: When it comes to swinging a golf club, whatever you decide, stick with it! These great golfers should take a page from Roger Federer's tennis playbook. He travels the world solo, with his game, never doubting his technique. He knows it's within him because he developed it when he was very young. He has settled on how he plays and sticks with it. I'm sure he doesn't reinvent his technique every three or four years. He just elevates his awareness and sharpens his strategy. You know the paradigm shift isn't just 'the whole creates the parts;' it also encompasses the elimination of the unhealthy dependence golfers have on their coaches and teachers."

I was mesmerized by his assessment of the modern tour players. I wished everyone could hear his perspective. On the other hand, I was glad to be his private audience. We sat silently for a few moments before he continued.

"The issue, in my opinion, is that these great golfers are looking in the wrong places to regain their awareness. It's like fishing. My friend Lowell once told me of the time he met a fisherman on Big Laurel Creek in the mountains in North Carolina. This fisherman was not familiar with the stream but Lowell knew it like the back of his hand—he knew where every fish lay. Of course the fish lie where food is passing by and where they don't have to expend a lot of energy resisting the current. Lowell stopped to watch for a while as the fisherman cast time and again. No hits; the fisherman looked perplexed. He said he'd been working this section of the creek all afternoon without a single hit, though he was casting the fly perfectly and it dropped softly on the riffle in the stream.

"Lowell said to him, 'you'll never catch a fish here.' The fisherman asked him why not. 'Because there are no fish there. You can tie the best fly in the world, make the most beautiful cast, but you'll never catch one. You need to cast where there are fish. Throw your fly above that rock over there. Let it float down and around that swirl and let's see what happens.' No sooner had the fisherman cast where instructed than wham! A trout hit his fly like there was nothing to it.

"But there was something to it! You must look in a place that provides possibility. I know the story seems obvious, but all golfers, no matter what skill level, are often looking in the wrong places for the answers to their problems. No one is exempt. The answer to awareness is in the action of the club, which lies in the hands, right? These golfers need to identify the accurate swing keys, go there, and work on them. If they're looking in the wrong place, then they'll have to just wait for their talent to overcome their lack of awareness. Sometimes it never comes back."

I decided to continue my inquiry about novice golfers. "Why do so many people have trouble getting the ball airborne?"

"Precisely because they're trying to get it airborne! But it isn't hard to teach. The average golfer has the impression that one needs to get under the ball to get it airborne. They can do this when the ball is sitting on a tee above the ground. As soon as the ball lies on the ground, it's another story. They end up trying all kinds of ways to get it airborne, most of which are exactly what keeps it on the ground."

"The classic approach is trying hard not to lift their heads!" I interjected. "Can you believe some teachers actually teach that as a technique? And they tell students to concentrate on the ball."

Joe was shaking his head again. "Golfers need to concentrate on the club and its relationship in terms of angle of descent through the delivery, or where on the arc they want to impact the ball. That dynamic really has the greatest effect for getting the ball airborne. If I had my druthers, once a golfer has a swinging orbit of the club, I'd have them practice with a lofted club off a downhill lie or in front of a divot, not on grass. In a downhill lie the primary cause of flight is angle, not loft. Golfers would learn very fast that the angle of descent down the hill is the way to get the ball in the air."

"You mean you'd put a beginner on a downhill lie without a tee and expect them to get it airborne?"

"It may take some time, but they'd never get the wrong impression of what consistently gets a ball in the air. They wouldn't be making the error of trying to get the ball up from underneath. Did you ever wonder why novice golfers love an uphill lie? Well, there you have it—the upslope is appealing to the eye, and they're comfortable! They can see and feel loft from the slope. On the other hand, more experienced players will always favor a tight level or slightly downhill lie to one that's uphill and grassy, because they control the ball better and use the ground to their advantage with their angle of descent, not to mention the added head speed.

"If the novice golfer can get it airborne from the downhill, the level lie will never pose a problem. If they only get it to fly off the tee, we've set them up for a real negative shock when the ball is on the ground, and trying hard will most likely get in the way of everything. Golfers have been under the false impression that they could get the ball up from loft and a lifting angle, not from a descending one. So, when you put someone on a slight downslope, he learns naturally without trying hard to get the ball airborne.

"The bonus is that the slope acts like a magnet, especially for their legs. They can feel their lower body move down the slope in a sort of shift to support the angle of the delivery, so they'll really be getting the right impression in their whole body. They'll naturally learn to impact the ball at the best part of the club's arc, at the end of the downward section."

"Would you place the ball farther back in their stance, too?"

"In normal conditions, yes, but for learning purposes, leave the ball as though they're still on a level lie and that will make them move down the hill to strike the ball on the downward side of the arc. This is a good time to make it more challenging, like me using my one iron."

"I never imagined teaching someone to play off a downhill lie. I always thought it was so much harder that way."

"Well, yes, it seems so at first, but after a few minutes, they usually get the hang of it. Their mind-body system processes what it needs to do naturally, if you let it. They are well served by never again having the chronic problem of trying to get the ball airborne by lift."

"Do you believe in sticking with the short irons to learn the swing and then gradually lengthening to the woods?"

"In most cases, no. I'll tell you why: Especially with people who lack club head speed, the longer club provides more swing potential, not to mention the fact that the swing lends itself to improved timing. One cannot get away with being forceful. I often like to have my students begin with a three wood or driver. The key is to get them to swing at Tai Chi speed first, very slowly. Get them feeling a swinging force that comes from something other than their own strength. Have them swing about one-quarter speed with a full range of motion."

He looked at me and smiled. "Grab your clubs, Geoff. Let's have a look."

"Now?" I asked with surprise.

"Yes. I thought it would be a good idea to check out your swing."

I could feel an expression of shock spreading over my face and noted his grin in response. I knew this was an invitation I couldn't refuse.

16

MY SWING— AND MY BRAIN

Joe smiled his quiet smile as he said, "I'd like to give you a lesson so you can have the perspective of a student again. It's good to appreciate how your students learn and what they feel like while they're learning. It's especially good to try something new that you've never done before. If you let the process take place and don't interfere with judgments (yours or theirs) the transformation is usually quick and easy. I mean, how awkward does a beginner feel when he first picks up a club? We tend to forget because it's so natural to us, but the novice can feel so out of sorts, as though parts of his body won't take direction or aren't part of him. Do you know what I mean?"

"I think so," I said cautiously.

"Go fetch your clubs."

I went back to the rental car and got my clubs. I had had no idea Joe was going to work with my swing today. I could feel my blood pressure rising. I didn't know why I was nervous. I'd gotten very comfortable with Joe Burlington, so why didn't I feel easy now? I guess I still lacked confidence.

At his direction, I took out a wedge and hit some shots. Burlington relaxed in his chair. Otter, nearby in the shade, was again sound asleep, snoring in the background. There was just a whisper of a breeze, and it was a little chilly. The cloud cover indicated rain would be coming by afternoon.

Burlington didn't say anything while I swung with my wedge. I wondered what he thought about my swing. The doubt was rising and with it my insecurity. After a few shots, he asked, "So what would you like to work on, Geoff?" I told him that when I played, I often had difficulty getting the distance accurate, especially with a less-than-full wedge shot, just like the first wedge shot I'd played with Tim and the guys at Pompano. He nodded. "OK. Is there anything else?"

"Well, yes. I've had a lot of trouble driving the ball with good accuracy and distance. If we could deal with that, I think that with my other observations this week, I'll be OK. I'm sure it could really improve my scoring."

"OK then; let's begin." His face looked very intent—a little more serious than usual. "May I ask you, before you play the partial wedge shot, are you surprised at the result? Or is your play something entirely different from the practice?"

"Most of the time, when I play the shot, I think it's perfect, but then it invariably ends up short."

"OK, let's try this. We can do a simple exercise to determine whether you have a concentration problem or an awareness problem."

"I don't understand the difference." I responded, puzzled.

"A concentration problem means you have the awareness or the feel to produce the shot maybe in practice, but when you do it for real, something else happens. Awareness, on the other hand, means that you practice a certain swing—in this case, one for the energy of a three-quarter wedge—and you play it exactly as you practice, but then it ends up short and is not accurate. Let's find out which problem we're dealing with. What is going through your mind before you hit the shot, Geoff? How do you prepare?"

"I make a few practice swings, trying to determine the distance."

"Do you try to determine the distance with the length of your swing?"

"Yes, I try to visualize the length of swing for the length of the shot."

"OK, let's begin there. Are you aware that that may not be a good way to go?"

"What do you mean? I've always heard that it's a good criterion for gauging distance."

"But Geoff, what you're doing isn't working, is it? In my experience, there isn't necessarily a correlation between length of swing and energy of impact. You could have a short swing with a lot of speed at impact or a long swing with very little speed. The way to go is to feel the energy of impact to determine the length of the shot and then let the length of swing be a function of the energy. You also need to feel for, or take into consideration, the dynamic loft at impact, so you can picture and feel the flight pattern and the ball's response when it lands.

"I would suggest you use the Three Bears approach: the middle-of-the-road exercise."

"Three Bears? How does that work?"

"First pick a target, then make a swing feeling the energy for going too far. Make another swing for too short, and then make another one just right. Just like Goldilocks, remember?"

I nodded, rolling my eyes. "Yes, that much I remember."

He continued. "If you need to, just guess! Picture the flight pattern, high or low, etcetera, depending on what you're feeling with the particular club in hand. Make your actual swing and see what happens. If your actual swing matches your practice swing, and if it's not the right distance, then you have an awareness problem. If you don't play the practice swing, then you have a concentration or a confidence problem. There's a formula for this: *performance equals your potential minus your interference!*[7]

"Playing an instrument in an ensemble is a good analogy," Joe explained. "Let's say all the instruments—like the muscle groups of your body—are playing together nicely, and then someone gets out of synch. But no one stops playing. They just keep going. Honestly, no one cares that you made a mistake. If you're to be present, you need to continue playing or you'll miss what's happening in the next phrase. The process doesn't stop for you to correct yourself. Conversely, if a difficult passage is coming up and you start anticipating the mechanics of it in an effort to get it right, you rob yourself of the moment you're in. It's a state of mind thing, but it can be learned.

"If there's something bothering you, concern over the result usually, your potential is what you felt and saw in your practice swing, and the interference is what you felt and saw in your actual swing. If this is the case, then you don't have a swing or awareness problem. You then must work on developing your confidence and trust and you must do it on fundamental ground. Develop confidence in your ability to feel the impact energy. If things don't work out, just say 'cancel' to yourself. Do not, I repeat, do not spend a moment on what didn't work. To figure out on each occasion what went wrong is a total waste of time."

"But if I don't figure out what went wrong with my swing, then how can I avoid it in the future?"

"Your swing did not misfire before your brain did, Geoff, it did it after! But because you're so preoccupied with feeling in a physical way, you don't realize that you misfired in an emotional and psychological way. Your approach needs to address that aspect first."

"What do you mean? What does my brain have to do with it?"

"Sit down. Let me define it in a little more detail. Only part of your brain interferes, the doubting and logical part. Brain science, like quantum physics, is constantly changing, but there are some basics we can rely on. Your brain has two sides, or lobes, each designated for particular tasks and functions. We can personify the left brain and the right brain as though they were two different people in one body, which is exactly how they act a lot of the time.

"Now if we agree that the golf swing is a task best performed in the environment of the sensory system—feeling, and the imagination—that is, when it comes to instantaneous performance, then the right brain is the natural leader. The right brain can synthesize things and put them together quickly. It can do things in a complete fashion and it's intuitive. The left brain is inadequate for rapid complex synthesis, which is what's needed for athletics and such. The left brain is simply not designed for these types of tasks; it's just not the proper tool. The left brain is good at intellectual work, slow methodical analysis, categorizing, ordering, and breaking things down into pieces. If the sides of the brain could talk, and they do communicate in their own language, the right side would volunteer that it's dying to do the task. But the left brain attempts to block it, if given half an opportunity. There is a competition going on between them, going all the way back to when you were a child."

"Uh-huh."

"Before you could speak, Geoff, you were a total sensor. All your body's movements were based on how they felt—balance, speed, and so on—totally right-brain oriented. However, when you went off to school to get 'educated,' the left brain began exercising heavily, working out at the brain gym they call school. You got graded according to how well you understood or memorized material analytically, intellectually. You rarely got an

A because you were intuitive about something, right? That's because in general, Western education doesn't seem to value intuitiveness. That's why more and more, our school systems are eliminating music, art, and athletics. The powers that be seem to only believe in math and science, even though modern science proves the value of—and pleads for more—art, music, and sports. The brain needs those developmental exercises to blossom fully and function to its potential. The fact is, students who exercise their brains in music or art are more likely to be able to cope creatively within our complex society later on. Anyway, that's a topic for a whole other time.

"The left brain likes to sort things out, get them down on paper, and plan for the near future. So the left brain has been active and the right brain has for all intents and purposes been on a long vacation."

He took a long swallow of lemonade and broke off a wedge of muffin top. I refreshed both our glasses before taking a slug. I had worked up a thirst, swinging and listening, and we finished off the gallon container and four muffins before he resumed speaking. "Did you ever wonder why intellectuals have such difficulty getting better at golf or other athletic endeavors, Geoff? Or why the golfer who practices a lot often gets worse? It happens so often you'd think we'd have figured it out by now! The golf swing certainly is not so complex that it can't be known. We were meant to *play* it, not comprehend it! So I think, no pun intended, it's of no value to comprehend the golf swing; however, it's of great value to feel and trust the golf swing—which the right brain is just dying to do anyway.

"So the trick is," he said, "don't give the left brain an opening. Do things in a manner in which the left brain will simply surrender and allow the intuitive self to operate freely."

"Is there a method to doing this? Are there steps to get me to that point?"

"There are many strategies. A typical response to a golf task from the left brain is slow, as if you had a lifetime, and then it will give you the impression that you have a lot of figuring to do before you try to play this shot. It will try to list all the do's and don'ts about the swing and the shot. It could give you a detailed list of problems lurking. You can imagine the trouble this will create.

"The right brain, on the other hand, is like a kid at the front of a classroom with his hand in the air: 'Give it to me, I can do it now!' The right brain really believes. Your imagination and your feel are in right-brain central, which never questions the outcome and just takes chances. It has an optimistic bias, which is a good thing even when it's unrealistic. It will take a giant leap based on this optimism. That's the let-go mode, which great performers so often call being in the zone. They're in a zone, all right—the right-brain zone that allows all their potential to come out.

"We need to get our students started this way on day one, and get them into the habit of relying on feel. And we need to develop practice habits that turn it on rather than shut it down."

I conjured up visions of times when I had been in the zone and tried to recall how I'd gotten there. I couldn't tie my zone moments to any period when I had been taking instruction or trying on one of the new-and-improved methodologies.

"Don't be impressed with golfers who can recite great volumes on the so called mechanics of the swing, Geoff." He had read my mind again. I wanted him to elaborate, but he continued on his own track. "Take concentration; what is it? All you need to do is be aware of the space you're in and what's happening in that space. Avoid attempting to control things in other spaces."

I smiled, aware I was gaining another nugget of wisdom. "I'd like to learn more about the left-brain/right-brain relationship in golf." Although I was getting a sense of the connection, I needed it articulated more.

"Sure," he said. "How *does* it pertain to golf? OK, I'll give you a little scenario of what happens in your head between the brain's two halves when you knock a ball into trouble. It's a good example of the right brain winning the competition over the left brain.

"Knowing that the left brain is analytical and the right brain is about feeling sensing will help you understand the conflict that can cause trouble when they have to work things out. Take a typical golf shot from out of the trees. Let's say there's a very narrow opening and the ball has to fly through the hole and then curve to the right to get onto the green 150 yards away. The left brain will say, 'I can't do this. This shot is impossible.' At the same time, the right brain is dying to get involved. The left brain's got an attitude like a spoiled child because it knows it can't do such complex tasks expediently. It needs time to figure out how to program the action. If you give it a job that it doesn't accept for one reason or another, or if it gets lost while analyzing all the variables, it cedes to the right brain, and the 'feel' side takes over."

"Which is what you want, right?"

"Yes, but it happened here by accident. You need to learn to do this intentionally. There are many exercises you could do, and I'll show you some as we work with my students. If you looked to apply this idea to any other sport, it's easier, because most are very reactive, full of fast action, and, of course, the ball is always moving. Those performers are naturally in an athletic frame of mind—meaning, naturally trusting their feeling and employing their right brains.

"Golf, on the other hand, is such a slow sport, so it lends itself to interference from the analytical left brain. When you miss a shot and you're walking down the fairway trying to figure out what happened, you're just programming in another problem. Analysis of why things don't work is not conducive to good golfing." He took out a pack of gum and offered me a stick. I declined and he continued. "The subconscious mind does not know the don'ts. We need, as teachers, to create tasks that get our students to be into the feeling, tasks that are so sensory and intuitive that they cause analysis to shut down. When you do that, students have no choice but to trust their experience and their intuition."

"So you need to create tasks that cause the left brain to shut down?"

"That's right. Or at least, it has to shift out of the way."

"Does it shift because of the time frame you have to complete the task?" I asked.

"Exactly!" He clapped his hands. "That's one strategy I've found to be very reliable. I suggest you be creative and teach your students different things to keep their sense of feel awake and operational so they don't fall asleep—especially while playing. The analytical brain will, by its very nature, try to take over the tasks as if it were the best tool for performance. It has a greedy attitude toward tasks, so you have to keep it in check as much as possible. In putting, the left brain is especially obvious. That's generally where the most interference occurs.

"The real precision tool is the right brain, the sensor. Any athlete, even those with limited experience, will tell you analysis is the wrong tool for making instant adjustments. But your right brain is well suited to the task. It's specially designed for the delicate tactile action of a golf swing—it pares things down to their essentials. While doing the exercises, you can actually feel this brain shift from left to right if you pay attention.

"The right brain believes in itself, so to speak, so you must be creative when you teach a student to nurture it. You'll need to be able to demonstrate your own feel as an example of what you're teaching. There is nothing like a little live-action demonstration to make a believer out of a skeptic."

"You make this sound so simple. Can you give me an example of how you go about convincing a student to trust that feel is the only way to go?"

"Give them minimal time for preparation and have them hit shots through little openings in trees. Or have them swing five shots in succession without stopping to think about alignment, setup, or anything else. Then make them swing five shots in eight seconds. As they're doing this, ask them to pay attention to their rhythm. You can even ask them to swing with their eyes closed, which is a quick way to wake up feel. Ask them to be super precise with a shot—let's say, a nine iron shot flying through a three-foot hole between branches of a tree, with only a few seconds of preparation. I guarantee their analytical brain will shut down and the brain shift will create some amazing results."

This was solid information I could use. Just then, an errant range ball came flying and bounced between us, forcing us to pick up our chairs and clubs and move to a more secluded area, with Otter trailing behind. When we got settled in our new spot, guarded by a large pine against any more wayward shots, Burlington continued. "Geoff, what I'm talking about is keeping your focus on the task at hand, disciplining your mind, and not allowing yourself to transfer your thoughts outside the place or task at hand. It's simply a matter of being present..."

"Huh?"

"You, as a golfer and a teacher of golf, need to be in this mode too—it's not just for students. Create strategies so your students will naturally change their minds. The changes must occur without force because they need to surrender their way of going about it! Demonstrate your awareness by executing golf shots that require super-awareness, like flying shots through little openings in trees." Burlington picked up a four iron and demonstrated just that. The shot flew through a narrow opening in the pine tree in front of us. There was obviously no time to figure it out.

He continued without missing a beat. "Show them you possess the skills to perform with super-awareness. There's no time to waste on swing debates and resistance. Everyone who's learning to swing needs to get into habits that shut down the interference of the left brain. It's a real test to learn how to do that, Geoff. I call the right brain the 'let-go present mode' and the left brain the 'try-hard mode,' which operates in the past and future. To be primarily right-brain functioning, you need to be present in the golf task at hand, especially because the right brain trusts itself. It does not question, so it fits neatly into our program of concentration, doesn't it? It's the perfect tool for performing because it has confidence in its ability to get the job done."

"Isn't what you're saying contrary to what we hear today about being methodical and deliberate?"

"Yes, it is. I think being methodical to the point of stalling is extremely counter-productive. It causes tension to rise and that's dangerous to any sensory performance like a golf swing—it basically opens a Pandora's Box of doubt. Slow and steady lends itself to switching on the left brain. I'm not saying you can split your brain and function totally right brained. The lateral connection between the brain lobes keeps each side communicating and behaving as a whole.

"But just like in school, almost all golfers who practice increase the use of their left brain rather than their right brain because golf instruction has become scholastic, very complex and analytical. Don't you hear all the time, 'the harder I practice, the worse I get'? The left brain is the primary reason. Golfers simply don't know how to practice. They end up training with the wrong strategy often not only from the physical side, but the psychological side too. They never improve their golf self-image either. And that negative image will limit their success substantially."

"Wait, what do you mean?"

"Let me explain that later." I relented and he continued.

"Then they go out on the golf course with great expectations, but with only one ball and a few seconds. What happens next? Paralysis! That's followed by the next mistake, which is the one that befuddles me most: They go back to the practice tee to analyze more and dig themselves an even deeper hole.

"No wonder the average practicing golfer is frustrated. I would be too—and I have been! But this is where modern technical instruction has led us. The increase in analysis is inversely proportional to confidence. But we can talk more about this later. Let's take a look at that driver swing you mentioned."

17
SWING STYLES

"**B**efore I begin, Joe, I was wondering, is there a difference in swings from the driver to the irons? I've always been a superior iron player, but at best, I'm average with my tee shots. And I often have students who say they can hit the woods and not the irons and vice versa."

"Yes, I know. I've seen that a lot."

"Are the swings the same, though?" I repeated.

"They are and they aren't."

"What do you mean?" He seemed to enjoy confusing me.

"Well, Geoff, just as you said, some people hit irons well and others are better with the woods. In most cases, their natural swing is connected to one of the releases. I basically teach three releases of energy into the impact. One is more passive, with centrifugal force. We talked about it earlier. That approach lends itself better to the tee shots. If you really become aware, you can actually feel the handle slow down to let the club head accelerate and act on your hands and arms. The centrifugal force of the head pulls on the handle and, given that the path is still intact, the face rotates and accelerates from this action. You must get the ratios of speed and distance right for it to occur.

"Now let's talk about your driver swing."

"I remember when I first started having trouble with the driver. One summer I began working on retaining the angle, like this." I showed him what I meant.

Joe shook his head, as if he'd heard this many times. "That fad of trying hard to retain angle became popular years ago when golfers became aware of the tremendous left wrist angle that Ben Hogan had late into his downswing. Unfortunately, these golfers made a grave assumption, and it destroyed many good golfers' swings."

"What did they assume?"

"They didn't realize that Hogan's wrist angle was a natural function of the synchronization of the club and his body's action during his swing—not to mention the extraordinary degree of flexibility he possessed. Too many golfers tried to isolate that strong angle by holding it with pressure and tension. But angle must be a natural result of sequence, direction and the desired shot pattern. Trying to artificially retain it will inevitably disrupt the release of the club into impact. I can tell you more later, but for now, just avoid that approach."

Like a kid, I still wanted to tell him what had happened to me. He listened patiently. "I could retain the angle when the ball wasn't there. I took videos and people observed me. But my angle with a driver or longer iron would always dissipate when the ball was there. The pictures show that in the practice swing without a ball, the angle was great. The odd thing is I knew what I wanted, but when I saw pictures of my downswing, they showed I had lost angle prematurely, even though it was in my mind to retain it. The result was that I lost club head speed and distance."

Joe understood. "Yes, I know what you mean. There was obviously something going on in your head that caused you to lose angle when the ball was in front of you, ready to be put into play. It happens to a lot of golfers. What happened the first time you worked on retaining the angle, Geoff?"

"With the driver, I hit the ball way to the right."

"Did that happen when you played?"

"Yes. I had a chronic block or push slice. The swing after that would be this weak hook as I tried to adjust. I got to the point that I would drive with a three wood, which worked for a while, then I had to go to the one iron. Again, I was OK for a time, but then it got so bad I hated to play any hole except a par three. Even that got bad! It was as if whenever I was on the tee, I had zero confidence and my swing would prove it."

"I see. When you say 'chronic,' how long did it go on?"

"It has gone on for years now, and I've given up trying to get more energy from angle. I drive the ball OK, but very short for my size, strength, and flexibility. I know it was the mental side affecting the physical, but it was like this negative obsession was controlling me, the image deep inside, as you say, and I just couldn't seem to get out of my funk."

Burlington considered, then said, "I understand. I've been there and there is a way out. Let's first deal with the physics problem, if indeed there is one. Let me see you make a few swings with your driver."

I took a couple of practice swings and they felt like I had very good angle. Then I went to hit the tee shot and wham—way right.

"Go ahead," he said calmly. "Another swing." The ball flew off to the right, but not as far. "Did you feel as though you had good angle? Is this a typical result when you work on getting a strong angle of attack?"

"Yes, it is."

"And you did achieve the angle you desired?"

"Yes."

"When you try to increase your angle in the tee shot, you lose control over the recovery of the face to square. When you try to get the face square, you lose speed and angle, resulting in a weak shot to the left."

"I would say that's an accurate assessment."

"OK, Geoff. This is very simple." There he goes with that 'simple' again. "There are two ways to solve the imbalance. If this takes more than five minutes, I'll be surprised." As Tim had said, for Joe, everything took five minutes. He continued. "Your problem begins in your head and you support it with an imbalance in the delivery. May I make an educated guess about what's going on in your head on a subconscious level? Deep down, you have a negative self-image. You believe your swing is weak and the ball is going to fly way right if you have angle and so unconsciously your mind-body system gives up the angle to strike the ball squarer toward the target."

I considered his answer. "That makes sense, Joe, but how do I adjust?"

"Very easily. The physics in the swing that you relate to is the shape, or position—the geometry only. The problem with that is you end up missing the synchronization or the dynamic properties of the action from the good angle. It's part of timing, or the speeds and distances that things travel—more precisely, the speed and distance ratios of the handle and the club head needed to deliver it squarely from the strong angle that you want."

"What exactly do you mean?"

"Well, if you want that much angle, you must consider the speed and distance the handle is traveling in the delivery zone so that the club face has a chance to balance out for square contact. When the club travels in the pattern of an oblique ellipse (plane and path) the face will likely rotate to square with the speed/distance ratios balanced."

"That sounds good, I guess, but this is really getting confusing."

"I know. Let me tell you the first strategy I would share with most of my students who want to let the club square by centrifugal force alone—the ones who aren't yet ready to trigger the release physically with the curl." I wondered if he figured I was too dense or untalented to try the advanced release. I could feel my insecurity rising triumphantly.

Joe continued. "As your swing progresses toward the impact zone and you feel that strong angle in the wrists—just before the impact, imagine the handle slowing down—it's commonly felt in your lead arm speed; feel it in your lead hand and lower arm. And attempt to stay in the phone boot too, after impact!" I looked at him out of the corner of my eye and saw his smile but I didn't bother to address 'phone boot.'

"That way," he continued, "the club head can recover its rotation and travel the necessary distance for a square impact. Major centrifugal force at the right time is imperative for this swing timing to work consistently. Take the club again and swing like this." Burlington demonstrated a strong angle, but when his hands got down near his right leg, he slowed the handle down and the club head flew by. It must have rotated, because the ball launched off the club face squarely and flew a long way. "Here, take the club," he offered. "Now this time, get your strong angle by your swing sequence and as your hands and arms approach the impact zone, purposely slow down the forward speed of the handle."

I couldn't believe what he was saying. "Slow down?" I repeated.

"That's right."

"I've always heard you must accelerate through the ball to the finish and extend!"

"Yes, I know, Geoff, but just do the opposite this time and you may be surprised at what begins to accelerate." He pointed to the club head and smiled. I tried a practice swing while Burlington advised. "Slow down the handle." He got up, grabbed my driver, and demonstrated again. "Like this," he said. Then he took a full swing and swung down faster. During the second half of his downswing, he exaggerated the slowdown and the handle almost came to a stop and literally reversed directions near impact. The club head went right by the handle, fast, and rotated. The handle was pointing backwards.

I didn't realize that was the balance in timing. "Wow, just like that?" I admired.

"That's right. You can get the face rotation when you're on a good path, but you need to time the speed and distance of the handle-head relationship. That's essential in timing."

"But again, it seems so manipulative," I protested.

"I know, Geoff, but you may need to consciously develop the hand and arm action to change the dynamics of your delivery for the better."

"But everything is happening so fast, how can I do something that late and get it done?"

"Good point; you'll probably have to swing Tai Chi speed at first. On the other hand, if you rely on feeling the action, you can achieve precise tactile action beyond your wildest dreams at incredible speeds late into your downswing. Your mind-body awareness is quite capable of that." Then he added, "But not your intellect! Once you can do this rote, I'll show you other possibilities in timing too. For now, I suggest you spend time experimenting with the speeds, purposely slowing the handle and then maybe accelerating it and then balancing it out. You have to go through the process to get a balance and develop your confidence. I think it's exactly what you need for your mind to accept a strong angle into the impact with a driver. Otherwise, I don't believe you'll ever sustain a strong angle for a high energy at impact."

"Let me try again."

He gave me back my driver. I teed up about six balls and swung trying to slow the handle. The first few swings were consistently drop-kicked as I slowed the handle with my left hand and arm—not a very good feeling. I looked back at Joe, who was smiling, unfazed by my apparent mistakes. "Can you show me the other way to get it to square?"

"Not yet; you're just beginning. Be patient; keep going. Just stay with the speed-distance ratios."

I wondered what he was getting at. Could I begin curling the driver release? My mind began jumping in and out of old swing thoughts, but I was able to quiet it down even though I felt lost now. Neither my old way nor this new way seemed to be working. I was frustrated but had no choice except to surrender and follow Joe's direction.

Left: The hands traveling faster in the downswing. Right: The hands traveling slower in the downswing.

GB

He reassured me. "I will be responsible for the results; you just attempt to feel."

I relaxed a bit. I realized I was still concerned about the results and how my swing might look to others. But if I didn't need to care about the results, I could begin feeling more accurately. I began to swing again, this time carefree. I drop-kicked a few more and ducked several balls to the left.

"Good," he said.

I looked back with half a grin and said, "It's your fault!"

"I know," he said. "Keep going."

And then, just like that, something happened. I could actually feel the action of the club, its speed and rotation, and the slowing lead arm as it rotated and folded right against my left side. That must be the 'phone boot,' my left arm against my left side, and the forward swing feeling abbreviated, but now the results were there. It didn't seem right, but it worked! I began to get the hang of it. It felt like I wasn't even swinging. I mean, there was no resistance, no effort, yet I struck the ball with a lot of energy. I really could believe in a strong angle and hit it square now.

"Wow, I don't think I've felt that impact since I was a kid!" I was beginning to see how much my focus on outcome had been interfering with the changes Joe had proposed.

"It's a wonderful feeling, isn't it?" he agreed.

I teed up six more balls and experimented with this newfound idea of release. The balls began to fly straighter and farther. I could feel the energy and its release as though the club head had a life of its own. I stopped for a moment to catch my breath. I hadn't hit tees shots like that in years. "This is amazing, Joe. You really think that's all I had to do to get on track?"

"It's a start. We can go deeper into the release, like really backing it in with your lead hand, slowing it down and curling, but this is a beginning." Again he left me dangling like a participle. There was more to it, but he wasn't going into it now. "Let's just discuss this problem for now. You see, Geoff, you weren't allowing your mind-body system to function fundamentally, because you failed to realize the synchronization of the whole system and your negative self-image contributed too, but I will discuss that later. While you were trying to gain angle and energy through tension and accelerating the handle, you were sapping energy from the head, which is the type of release that feels like a drag. It probably felt like a heavy log, very sluggish, and the harder you tried the less impact energy you had. This approach is, again, very oriented toward shape and parts." Joe emphasized his disdain for golf teachers positioning the body parts of their students during the swing as though they were not already connected and ready to work as a team.

I made another swing during his dissertation. "Good! That's it!" he said. It did seem slow to me, but the energy felt great! But was it slower? Certainly not the club head! Lacking timing made me feel weak and I knew I was stronger than most of the guys I played against.

I blurted out, "I just felt weak at impact because of this imbalance."

"Precisely!"

Burlington was right. It took about five minutes. For years I had been thinking that I just didn't have it, or that I'd lost it. I immediately felt confident again. We had truly solved one of my problems. Now I believed I could repeat it forever.

18

THE CURL AGAIN

"Is there anything else you'd like to work on, Geoff?"

"Well, since you mention it, Joe, there is. In my iron play, I've been having difficulty gauging distance."

"Go on," he said, encouraging me.

"Is the release the same as with a driver?"

"No, not at all. Because of the angle you'd like the club to strike and the length of the club, the release is more active and aggressive. Some call it an offensive release. You achieve that with lead arm and hand action. Remember the curl. You can learn it by hitting punch shots. You can develop a keen sense of trajectory and distance with all your irons, and, of course, you will spin the heck out of it. Watch me; I'll show you the release just like before."

He picked up a club and began to swing in slow motion. "Allow your swing to take its natural course until here," his hands followed the natural shift of his feet and legs down and forward. "Now make your swing in slow-mo and stop right here." His hand stopped in front of his left thigh. "It's a general reference for triggering this release. With your left hand, your lead hand, curl downward in this direction." I didn't move. "Your left hand and wrist," he repeated.

I didn't realize my hands were so accustomed to being firm and that this stiffened my wrists. There was no way I could get that flex with all that pressure. Before I could think, he said, "You need to lighten up first!" His voice was slightly elevated and I think he was surprised at how tightly I was holding the club. "Your wrist flexes inward like this when your hand gets to this point."

He showed me. His left hand was in front of his left thigh and the back of his left hand was pointing downward, which created a flex in his left wrist: the curl. As he demonstrated, his right hand came off the club with just the ends of his fingers still on the grip. Just then he stopped to place a golf tee into a small grommet he had placed in the Velcro flap of his glove for this purpose. "Here's your reference." The tee was pointing downward, indicating the direction and angle of his hand and therefore his club.

"That seems so radical," I said.

"Yes, it seems that way at first, but it's the only way to combine all the delivery dynamics into one."

"What do you mean?"

"This action will give you the best path, face, and delivery angle for consistent ball striking, and once you begin swinging rhythmically in an orbit, this can become your singular goal for consistency. This is the release trigger I've developed to cover all bases of impact. It affords golfers the ability to deliver the club as a tour player, and on top of that, I've discovered that practically anyone can learn it."

I questioned this in my mind; what a claim! "It seems so weird, though," I commented weakly. "I've never seen anything like it. Why point in this direction when the target is over there?" I wanted him to confirm this point of reference, this angle. I pointed down the fairway to the flag where I was aiming.

"Good question, Geoff, but you're making the same mistake most people do. You relate to the club as though it's not moving and as though you were physically attached to the club head. You are at the *handle* end. The weight and action at the other end is another story. Often when golfers try to square the face toward the ball's target like that, both the path and the delivery are seriously compromised. What seems a logical way for golfers to strike the ball to the target won't work. The target is forward, but the release needs to be backward, so to speak. You have to balance your physical action with the club's energy. You see, by this point in the swing, the club has built up a potential to rotate and the angle is compressed and wants to expand.

"As the club head travels on its orbit there's an energy that has to be accounted for in the delivery. So the physical action has to be congruent with this potential energy to strike the ball to the target. This is why the hand and wrist angle has to be in this direction—so that it's congruent with the energy built up in the club head, ready to be released into impact. Mentally, you need to let go of the target out there." He pointed to the flag in the distance. "To get to it, point the back of your left hand down toward *this* target," he pointed at his spot about 110 degrees away from the actual target. "This is exactly why golfers have such difficulty: They never let go of the target off in the distance. If you're having trouble, this is the best and fastest way to get the ball to fly to the target—by first releasing the ball's target from your mind."

"But it still seems way too complicated and strange."

"It's not, it's just different. All golfers are capable of this release as long as they aren't bogged down with the minutia of typical modern golf swing techniques."

I looked closely at the curled wrist angle again. "The club seems like it will arrive closed."

"It could, but if you commit to this angle you'll adjust what comes after naturally. This release takes all the urgency out of trying to impact the ball squarely, because it sets up a beautiful centrifugally released square contact. And the added value of this release technique allows your mind to trust in the inside path. That's the heart of it. When you commit to this face-downward trigger, your brain will want to swing the club from the inside all the time, and from this comes a sustainable fundamentally sound swing.

"This is exactly how your students will believe in the improved path and ultimately get the results they're looking for. This is what's missing when a golfer's best swing dissolves as he goes to play a shot. This is the basis for growing confidence."

I had never heard such an explanation of the release, but it made sense, even though it looked weird. How would I remember all this? Joe seemed to see that I really needed to know, so he explained how he arrived at such a radical approach to building a swing that flights the ball toward the target with incredible consistency. "Let me give you a bit of the history of my teaching this aspect of the golf swing. In the past, I was generally able, through swing exercises, to get a student to become more rhythmic. I could also help students improve their path—mind you, this was while they weren't caring about the ball flight. As soon as I asked them to feel the club face square at impact, the path would typically dissolve into an outward orbit that destroyed the energy and ball flight toward the target. In other words, if a golfer tried to feel the face rotation toward the target, the swing path would be off again.

"I've thought long and hard about this problem, Geoff. Surely they knew what swing path they wanted, but something changed once the target was added to the equation. You know most golfers suffer with the dreaded pull slice. The question is, why? I realized that a golfer could not trust in that swing path and, at the same time, try to get the ball to fly toward the target. That was the conflict. The very way a golfer typically tries to square the face toward the target destroys the path. A paradox, eh?"

I thought there wasn't much I didn't know about golf, but I had never heard things explained this way.

"The ball's target is the 800 pound gorilla in the way of their success. So I had to come up with a way for the average golfer to get the release into impact without losing the path and angle of delivery. I had to bring them around to a whole different way of knowing and believing. The target out in the field became insignificant. The target on the ground in front of them that they could see clearly as they swung was most important. The crazy-looking angle for the back of the left hand and wrist in motion achieves exactly the angle for the club face for the target in the field. The curl achieves this." He took out his pencil and drew a top view of how a golfer had to picture and feel the hand and wrist action to achieve a consistent square impact from a sound swing path.

"But I don't see the tour players doing this."

"Oh, but they do. In most cases it's blended in so well that you can't distinguish it from what you thought you saw. And it's not really apparent to golfers because these parts of your body are small and moving very fast. It's hard to see, unless you're looking for it."

Left: (Top) Backhand/face target. Right: Downswing: backhand/clubface target during the delivery.

GB

"Other parts of your body are much easier to see, but they don't mean anything to the fundamentals of impact. Of course you must adjust according to your unique physical abilities and reactions, but that's basically it.

"Let's go back to your earlier question about different releases. They are similar but are not the same for all the clubs. You see, you have different-length clubs that have a smidgeon of difference in releases, based on the angle you desire for the impact and the club in your hand. I'm not going to confuse you with the formula, because you can work it out by feel." My nature was to be more precise. I would have loved to see his formula, but thought it better not to ask.

"When you trigger the release," Joe explained, "how much you activate the curl, the degree, and the time all change according to the club and shot you desire."

"Could you give me some parameters for the different clubs?"

"Sure. The driver is the earliest and least curl, while the wedge is the latest, with the most curl. However, in most cases, golfers adjust naturally to the different clubs and shots. Essentially this is a universal release."

He showed me again. "All you do is swing the club downward and curl your lead hand and wrist, like so. Here's your target for your hand." He demonstrated with the tee in his glove pointing again. Placing a ball about six inches before the impact of the ball and a few inches to the far side of it, he said, "Now with the momentum of the downward force and the curl in this direction, you've set up or triggered the centrifugal release of the club head into the ball and toward the target. You then simply let it go." I watched as he demonstrated.

View of back/hand and club
face targets during delivery.

GB

"The beauty of this method is that you'll never lose the path pattern relative to the target. In the past, we had to qualify our instruction by saying that if you worked on the path, you could lose the timing, or vice versa—if you worked on the face you'd probably lose the path. No more; the curl combines the two.

"With a driver, you do everything the same, except let the club practically fly out of your hands. It's amazing. Now the target isn't a barrier to your ability to swing the way you'd like!"

I was awed. "So I don't have to worry about the real target down the fairway as I swing? Wow!" I exclaimed. "Does it really work?"

"You can try it and see."

"Are there any problems associated with this action?"

"Golfers can always get off track when trying anything. The only two problems I have found is that the golfer often begins to pressure the grip too much and gets tight working with their hands and wrists. The other tendency is for golfers to begin curling on the way back, unconsciously. Of course that would make it impossible to curl on the way down and at the same time strike the ball squarely, so I remind them that it's an opening and closing club face action that creates the balance. Other than that, it works incredibly well."

I couldn't resist. I picked up a club and began to swing, going through the sequence step by step. Swing down, curl, and let go—release! I was getting it with just a short pitch and executing it in pieces. I couldn't believe my control. Then Burlington showed me how to do an exercise without a club in hand. "Open your fingers, Geoff, and follow me."

He set up with his left fingers a little forward and down, then swung his left hand and arm back and said, "Sky." Then he swung downward and said, "Thigh." He used his fingertips as pointers and his fingers and wrist flexed forward as he whispered, "Fly."

"Sky, thigh, fly," Burlington repeated, "That's it. Do it a thousand times and you won't believe the control you'll gain. I know this is an exaggeration, but it's a great way to feel the hand and wrist action throughout the swing."

I followed his example a couple of times, then asked, "But what about the differences you just mentioned, like for various clubs or angles of attack?"

Top left: Begin with fingers pointing down and forward at address. Top right: During the backswing, fingertips are toward the sky. Bottom left: Fingertips are toward the right thigh during curling. Bottom right: Fingertips forward in the fly zone.

GB

"You may need to adjust the ball position for angle, but all you need to know is at what portion of the let-go arc you want to impact the ball." I must have looked confused. "Here's the arc of the let-go." Burlington let the club swing freely back and forth in two fingers. The club swung down and forward and then up and forward. "Now you must determine at what point of the arc you'd like the club to make contact. For an iron on the ground, I'd guess a little bit on the downward side of the arc. And with a driver when the ball is on a tee, you want it level or a little bit on the upward side," he explained. "However, you still curl and let go—

just adjust at what point you want to make contact relative to the let-go arc."

I started to do as Burlington said, even though it seemed weird and contrary. But it began to work and I was pleasantly surprised at the results.

"Release is a very misunderstood idea in the golf swing," Burlington commented. "Obviously in the timing fundamental of my program, it varies."

"Tell me more about how you teach it. You said there were three variations of the release of energy from the handle to the head and into the ball."

"I've already talked about the centrifugal force release in the driver and longer clubs. If the student is advanced enough, I'll teach the curling release. Sometimes with the centrifugal force, we add in a little 'double-secret probation rotation' with the lead hand and forearm. We'll skip explaining that for now, Geoff. It really requires a little more awareness, so you have to be judicious about whom you teach it to. Once a student is very good at pacing, and the path of his or her swing is sound, it's the last progression in my awareness program.

"So the swings are definitely different when it comes to timing and release. The general tempo and shape are similar, but the release is different, especially in terms of angle of attack in the timing. The picture most golfers have of the swing path is the same back and through. But actually, there are definite arc and angle changes. They don't have this vision. Therefore, it's difficult for them to deliver with this timed energy that I just showed you."

19
ARCS AND SWING LENGTH

"Could you show me the arcs you've been talking about?" Joe sketched them out for me. I reacted to his drawings with puzzlement.

He noticed my expression and nodded, saying, "Yes, this illustration may look different because in the past, the arc was over-simplified to be identical for the downswing and the backswing. Remember those big PVC circles that were so popular few years back? They gave the wrong picture."

"Is that why some golfers are better with the irons and others better with the woods?" I asked.

"That's exactly what I am talking about. All psychological aspects aside, often players with more hand and arm strength are generally better with the iron shots, and weaker-handed players are more centrifugally oriented and play tee shots better."

"What about swing length? I so often hear that too long a swing is where you lose control."

"Length is a very misunderstood aspect of the swing. It's not a fundamental, you know."

"What about extension through the ball? I hear all the time you must extend."

"Another fallacy," he said with disdain.

"How so?"

"The expansion of the swing arc through the impact zone, or extension as you say, is an effect of centrifugal force. If you attempt to manufacture it, you'll likely slow the club down and wreck the path too. It must be a natural consequence of letting go, the 'fly' aspect of the timing fundamental." His statement surprised me, but he continued without a blink. "Back to swing length. It's a very personal thing. Once you've checked out that the hand control over the grip and the swing arc are fundamentally sound, the range of motion really depends on the unique attributes of the golfer's physique and their internal rhythms. In most cases, if you start fooling around with a golfer's swing length without first checking the hands on the grip and the arc, you're on the wrong track and you'll likely destroy the golfer's natural rhythm and timing, which would not be a good thing, would it? The length is arbitrary, not fundamental."

The different arcs from the backswing to the downswing.

FT

He changed gears. "But first let me see you hit a few more wedges, working on the middle-of-the-road exercise for distance, and then we can combine what you need to say to yourself—your personal mind talk—and what you need to ask of yourself in terms of the impact action."

We practiced for about forty-five minutes and I was really beginning to get the feeling of my wedge shots. Making swings, imagining them flying too far, then too short, and then just right, I was surprised how accurate I was getting. My feel was definitely improving. I tried the curl at the same time and began to get some real control over direction and angle, too. As Joe had told me, I just needed a strategy that gave me fundamental awakening to my feel. How much time I had wasted, obsessing about the golf swing and the mechanics, rather than just feeling it!

Our lesson was over for the day. Burlington had to chip some of the dead branches and a huge pile of palm fronds he had picked up after the most recent storm. He told me he didn't need any help and left me there so I could continue to practice. Again I tried to pay him, but he waved me off, telling me in no uncertain terms that the time and experience he was sharing with me was not for money. He seemed uncomfortable with money, so I decided I would get him a special parting gift instead.

I really felt confident. I had never been able to figure out why I couldn't combine what I wanted in my swing with my driver. It made so much sense now. I could believe the club was going to square now that I had adjusted the delivery speed of my hands swinging forward through the impact. In the back of my mind I wondered if I would be able to curl a driver release too. When I used to think 'accelerate,' all I had moving fast was the handle. It had created so much resistance in my hands and wrists at impact and it always felt heavy and forceful.

Now I had a way to be energized and effortless. This was an absolute golf epiphany for me. I realized that I never really understood the physics of an effortlessly powerful swing. Burlington had three adjustable releases of the energy, and all centered on the action of his lead hand, wrist, and forearm. If I was going to be somewhere in my swing mentally, that was the place to be. What a luxury it was, having one place to put my mind!

I practiced for about an hour longer without tiring. Very pleased with myself, I felt I could now understand and teach this centrifugal release to my students. But the curl might be another story. I could wait on that for now; it was certainly something to look forward to.

My confidence in teaching was growing. More than that, my confidence in myself was growing. My image of myself was transforming too. I was beginning to see myself as strong and my swing formidable. I loved the track I was on. I knew I could continue and help myself, just as Joe Burlington had said. I was ready to go forward and see where this new road took me. I hoped somehow it would even take me back to Claire.

I drove back to the B&B. It had been a momentous day and very encouraging. My doubts about Joe's style had evaporated. There was concrete reasoning and a history to his method. The fact that he had helped me with my driver was a miracle to me. I'd taken countless lessons on it with no success. I was thrilled that it had finally happened.

I needed to call Claire, but again I had to be content with the machine. If she could only see what was happening to me now! How I looked at things was really changing. I knew that if we got back together, I surely would be a better partner. I was ready for it, for her. Just one more opportunity, that's all I needed. We had been like Harry and Sally, two good people with lousy timing. I felt like now we could get on the same page at the same time. Really, I'd just needed to be able to see myself as I truly was; surely she could understand that. She'd told me the same thing, but somehow I'd needed to learn it for myself.

This evening's message was two short words of optimism: "It's happening!" I was hoping that would pique her curiosity.

PART TWO

20
LARRY FINDS HIS PATH AND WALT FEELS THE ENERGY

When I arrived at the golf center the next morning, we set up again behind the barn. "Today is going to be different," Joe told me. "It's important for you to see how the method works with a variety of students, from beginner to advanced. I've scheduled the next two days with clients."

I'd been waiting for this! Observing a full day of teaching would be great. I wondered how Joe's approach for each student would differ from my lessons. I was grateful to be just an observer again. Out of the spotlight, I could get a better perspective.

Larry's smile arrived several seconds before the rest of him. He was tall, about six foot two. He looked fit and had a full head of curly blond hair. He also had enormous feet. I couldn't help but think how difficult it must have been for him to find the very expensive and obviously brand new golf shoes he was sporting at this, his first session with Joe. He set up his clubs on the bag stand and we all shook hands and introduced ourselves. "You found the place OK?"

"Yes," Larry replied, "it was very easy, although at first I thought I was going wrong. But I followed your directions and here I am." I recalled exactly the second-guessing Larry was talking about and smiled inwardly.

"Good, I love a student who can follow directions," Joe said with a wink. Then he got right down to business. "So, do you play much?"

"Yes," Larry said, "I love to play the game. But I think I could be a lot better. I can play to a twelve handicap on a course with a 128 slope rating and I've only been playing for three years."

Joe's face puzzled. Maybe he didn't know the new way of rating courses by slope, but suffice it to say, a 128 slope was a challenging course. "Well, do you have a story for me?" he prompted. It was now Larry's turn to look puzzled. "I mean, could you give me a brief history of your golf game?"

Larry repeated himself. "Oh yes, sure. I've been playing for just three years and, as I said, I carry a twelve handicap."

"Very impressive." Joe nodded in approval and waited for Larry to continue.

"I really enjoy playing, but I've run into problems with my path. When I get really bad, I take a lesson and it seems to straighten me out for the short run. But after a while, the same problems seem to crop up again."

"Have you come to any conclusions about your lessons or your corrections?"

"Well, yes, I have an analogy. I feel like it's putting a piece of duct tape on a leak. Eventually, it begins to leak again, since it really wasn't fixed properly."

"Oh, I like that," Joe told him. "So you're looking for a fix for the leaks in your game and you're willing to refit the plumbing, so to speak?"

"Yes. Why else would I have come?"

"Oh, you'd be surprised. I once read a story from eastern philosophy. To a distressed person who came to him for help, a

Master said, 'Do you really want a cure?' And the patient said, 'If I did not, would I bother to come to you?' 'Oh, yes,' the Master sighed. 'Many people do.' 'What for?' asked the puzzled visitor. 'Not for a cure. That's too painful,' said the Master. 'For relief. But,' the Master explained, 'people who want a cure without any pain are like those who favor progress without change.'[8]

"You can substitute the word *process* for pain in the story. A lot of the time," Joe explained, "we're unwilling to persevere through what's necessary to sustain a positive change. It takes time to process a change, to refit the plumbing the right way. Learning this program is a process," he emphasized. "It is not an event, a quick fix." Larry looked at me, trying to read my reaction. I ignored him, trying to appear nonchalant, if not invisible.

"OK," Joe said, relieving Larry's awkwardness. "Why don't you hit a few so I can see your swing."

Larry lined up a few balls and sent them off the tee.

"Now see what it feels like to swing as though the ball was going to fly to the right."

"Over there?" Larry asked, pointed some thirty yards right of the intended target.

"Yes," Joe nodded. He then stepped back toward me and whispered, "Now watch his swing path change."

"Why would I want to do that?" Larry interrupted.

"Just trust me," said Joe.

"OK," Larry hesitantly agreed. He swung what he thought was to the right, but the ball flew right at the target. Larry looked back at us and grinned. Then, a bit perplexed, he asked, "How did that happen?"

"Just keep feeling like you're going to hit the ball to the right, and do it until it flies way right," Joe answered. "You want the swing path of the club to feel like it's going to the right of the target line before contact and you want to get the path consistently from the inside during the delivery into the ball."

"Why are we doing this?" Larry asked.

"Well," Joe said patiently, obviously unfazed that Larry couldn't just trust him, "We are attempting to develop a constant on the club's approach to the ball relative to the target. If the club can come from the same angle or path, then your mind-body system can begin to settle in on a particular delivery of the face angle for square, if that's your goal. This is just one strategy. The path constant then becomes part of the timing for golf shots. On the other hand, if the path is a variable, then the mind-body system gives a variety of signals for what to do differently with the club face to get to the target. In other words, Larry, there is a need for a recovery based on the path variable. So if you get a path constant, it's likely that you'll develop a timing constant for impact."

Larry attempted to process this information. "But why don't I just try to hit the ball toward the target?"

"Simply because your baseline path—the path you arrived with—is not what you think it is. You came here trying to hit the ball toward the target with a path that you thought was directed toward the target, but most of the time the club was traveling unknowingly to the left of the target well before impact, right?"

Larry nodded in agreement. Burlington demonstrated to Larry the difference between his perceptions and his reality. His first shot nailed Larry's desired swing path. Burlington then showed him what the reality was. There was a disparity of about thirty degrees. "Oh. I get it," Larry said with assurance. "What I thought I was doing was not what I was doing at all."

"That's right. I just want you to realize where you want to go, so you can be in reality—and that reality is what will give you your best performance. To be perfectly honest, Larry, we could have chosen another strategy, but I think this one is best for you at this moment." Joe offered Larry's club back to him, but Larry's face still registered doubt. Burlington continued, "I don't want to confuse you so I'll explain as succinctly as I can. You have had a major path imbalance and the habits you've formed don't serve you, so we need to go through this process. I have no doubt that you will hit shots that will be beyond your wildest dreams, if you stick with it. Trust me, you will see." He coaxed the man to take some shots, again holding the club out to him.

Larry took the club and got started. The balls began to fly to the right. Then, all the way to the right. Larry was nervous.

"Just keep swinging, Larry," Joe encouraged him.

"B-but...it'll be OK, right?" Larry stammered.

"Trust me, Lare," Burlington told him. Then he whispered to me that Larry was almost ready to add in the timing component. I was taking it all in, fascinated, only regretting that this wasn't being videotaped.

"OK, Larry, now this time, see if you can notice when the club head flies by the handle."

"What do you mean?" Larry didn't appear to be nearly as fascinated as I was.

Joe took the club from him and began from his finish. "Notice the relationship between the club head and the handle when they reverse relative to the target. When do they convert from forward to backward, relative to the target?" He handed Larry back the club and stood back while Larry started the experiment. The man swung once. "Can you feel it?" Joe asked.

"Yes, I can."

"Now notice when they convert."

"OK."

"Keep swinging and noticing, Larry."

"I think I have it," Larry mumbled tentatively minutes later, more to himself than to Burlington. He took a few more practice shots.

"Good, OK. Now, see if it changes the same way back as forward."

Larry almost closed his eyes on the last two swings. I could see he was in a totally different zone than when he'd arrived. "OK, yes, about the same place. Yes!"

"This is the beginning of sensing and knowing the timing ratio in your impact, Larry. Now let's make some more swings. I want you to notice the club and handle relationship to see if you can feel the face rotation as the handle and head convert."

"Yes, I feel it."

"Good. Where do you feel it?"

"In my hands."

"Great, now let's add golf balls. Walk right through them, no pauses between shots," Joe instructed.

Larry began to walk and the balls began to fly long and straight. His smile had returned and he told us excitedly, "I've never hit four irons like this before."

Burlington whispered to me, "Geoff, this is a bit oversimplified, but we need to go this way because of Larry's level of awareness. Down the road, I'm sure, you'll see another one of my strategies for club face and path control." I wondered what he meant, but returned to being an unobtrusive observer as I watched Larry continue the exercise.

Burlington turned to Larry. "Now here's the kicker, Larry. We have been here about twenty minutes and your golf swing is in good balance. So if you didn't already possess that ability or talent or whatever you want to call it, do you think I could have given it to you in twenty minutes?" He paused to let Larry consider this, but didn't let him respond. "Of course not. It was always in you, fellow, and you just needed a program to draw it out. I just showed you how to access it. You just needed to focus on what would serve you better. Now isn't that a confidence builder? So make a few more swings now and keep noticing."

Larry's smile dominated his face. He continued and hit most of his shots well. When his path returned to its old direction, his awareness kicked in and he made the adjustment readily. Larry was clearly enjoying his success.

I was so impressed with Burlington. He'd made it especially clear what the basis for Larry's newfound awareness and subsequent success was—Larry's own talent. Burlington had only helped him to notice it.

While Larry was practicing, Joe explained to me that for Larry to leave here on solid ground, he'd need to use the exercises he'd learned. But he'd also need to ask good questions that would allow his talent to emerge. I could see now how an ego-driven instructor could sabotage a student. I realized what Joe meant about not taking credit for the success or failure of his students. He said that he only gave them a nudge in the right direction.

Larry's satisfaction seemed to be leveling. "This is fine for off the tee, but what about off the ground?"

"That requires more awareness of timing." Joe gave me a look as if to say 'there's the other strategy,' but answered Larry directly. "Just let yourself digest what we've done so far today. No overload. You go ahead and practice just as we have done here. That's really enough to keep you busy. Next time I'll go deeper into the release to address control over the angle off the ground." Joe seemed to have a feel for what a student could handle at one time. We all want more, I thought, and most of the time it probably isn't good for us. The dosage of a cure is critical.

So Larry shook hands and said goodbye. I thanked Joe and told him I'd be back in time for his next lesson, then made my way to the campus cafeteria across the street from the golf center. The time had flown and I was hungry for lunch. The cafeteria was full of college kids, all doing their own important thing. I picked out a chicken salad sandwich, found a seat and slowly ate my lunch. I tried to review what I had witnessed in Larry's lesson, how Joe had asked the questions. I needed to remember things as they were said, exactly.

So many things Joe had said and done were beginning to make sense to me. Yet I was unsure of my ability to impart what seemed to be such a passive method to my own students. I wasn't confident in my ability to ask the right questions at the right time. I needed to work on this a lot; that much I knew. What became clear to me was that Burlington believed in a student-teacher relationship that didn't try to fit square pegs into round holes, but rather seemed to find the right hole for each individual student. He really didn't say very much, but what he did say was so simple and made so much sense. I wondered why the answers seem so out of reach when we try to find them ourselves.

I had a lot to learn in not much time. I'd been through so many teachers and different theories that had fallen short over the years, but I felt I was inching closer to the right path, though I was still a little skeptical about which fork to take. After all, I had been gung-ho before. And I had been let down before. It took a little time for the honeymoon to end and for me to see the wrinkles in a new approach. Despite the fact that I had just seen amazing success, I decided to check my excitement so I wouldn't be disappointed yet again.

I did realize, as I sat surrounded by students, that my teaching had been all about me. I noticed that Joe Burlington never spoke about himself during a lesson. In contrast, I had spent lesson time on self-promotion; convincing students that I was the right teacher for them—and something of a golf wizard—was my primary goal. As perceptive as he was, Burlington probably knew where I was coming from, and knew that *he* was exactly where *I* wanted to be, but he was too polite to point this out.

Today with Larry, Burlington proved that the best teacher was actually within oneself. An instructor's job was to draw that master teacher out of every student and to make them aware of the gifts they possessed. A teacher really can't give them anything except a push in the right direction, which was all the job should be—that's what I'd gotten from watching Joe with Larry. Coaching is really just guiding students, getting them to wake up and do the work themselves so that, in the end, they became confident and enjoyed playing. Students need to be coached about what is deep within to recover qualities that have been misplaced, drowned or buried by the very instruction that was supposed to bring those qualities to the surface.

Over the years, I'd had some experience with this type of teaching, usually when I taught children. I'd always taught them differently from adults. Less instructing, more standing back and observing, looking for strengths to focus on. As Joe did, I just guided them, pointing out their abilities and offering very little remediation. It felt right with kids and it had worked. They learned so naturally, I didn't need to say much.

I don't know why it never occurred to me to try it with adults; I guess I just didn't think they would accept this approach. Adults wanted meat, I'd assumed. They needed to hear their name-brand teacher tell them things—not to ask what it feels like and then expect them to figure it out for themselves. Burlington had turned the dynamics of an adult lesson upside down for me, inverting the student-teacher relationship. Children didn't care about my credentials or want to copy my style. They were in it for the fun. It was a great joy for me to teach children. The realization of how I taught children and adults differently was enlightening. I had a lot to think about.

I awakened from my mesmerized state; I had been in the cafeteria for over an hour. I cleared my table and raced back to Joe's teaching area. He hadn't arrived yet so I took a seat and waited.

Joe soon came around the corner of the maintenance building. We fell into talking about students and I told him I would love to see him give a lesson to the type of student who always seems to get in their own way, the kind who keeps recycling the same problems and can't get out of the web. I asked Burlington, "What happens when you teach a person the awareness method yet they still can't seem to sustain an improved swing?"

"You mean they don't get it?"

"That's right," I said.

Just then, an older man ambled around the corner. "Well, you're in luck, Geoff. Here's a perfect example of what you're talking about. I don't think Walt would mind if you watch his lesson." Joe introduced me as a golf pro from up north and asked Walt's permission for me to observe his lesson. Walt was OK with it and set his clubs down on the turf so he could stretch his muscles before the lesson.

I was high with anticipation, and curious about how Joe would proceed. Walt told us that he'd been up late watching the basketball game and hadn't got much sleep. He was sniffling as well and said his sinuses were bothering him. Joe just listened. Then Walt pulled out a piece of paper. "I have a few questions before we begin, Joe. Joe nodded for Walt to proceed.

"First, I don't know if I should take the club back straight, or inside, like this." Walt demonstrated with his wedge. Joe just nodded. "Well, which is it?" Walt asked.

"That's personal, Walt."

"I knew you were going to say that. How can it be personal?"

"Well, it really doesn't matter because whatever will satisfy what you want to do on the downswing creates the backswing, and there are a lot of different routes to get there."

"You mean it really doesn't matter?"

"That's right."

"OK, but what about my weight shift?"

Joe asked Walt to come nearer and said, "Seems fine to me."

"I mean, when I swing." Walt said, seeming flustered.

"I know, Walt. I was joking."

"Last question," Walt said. "Shouldn't the club square itself without any manipulation from my hands?"

"Good question. It depends."

"You never have a definite answer, do you, Joe Burlington?" Walt teased back.

"I think so, but your questions seem to be more personal than fundamental."

"Well, what *is* fundamental?"

I was wondering the same thing myself when Joe answered, "Fundamental is anything to do with the club at impact. Everything else deals with margins. It's like statistics. There are no definite answers when it comes to style. It's quantum—the uncertainty principle. It depends on how you look at it." Now I was getting his point about the physics. "That's why there are so many different swings. All your questions deal with dynamic patterns of energy and nothing in this realm is set in stone. These patterns form according to the unique attributes of the wielder. Each swing is unique until the point of no return—that is, the impact zone—but I agree there are margins that increase your possibility of achieving a more consistent fundamental impact. Margins of speed, shape and timing..."

"Flow, path, and timing. I know, Joe."

"I would be glad to help you find a strategy to get what you want. It only takes a few minutes. I'll show you a couple of exercises to make it very simple." Good—I was finally going to see something. But Joe just let Walt go.

Walt took out a club and began to swing, and then he began to hit some shots. He was a little stiff to begin with, as if he were a robot with differing angles of swing. He definitely manipulated the club as he tried to swing it. It was the opposite of smooth. Obviously, in his mind, he had a lot to do in one swing.

Joe gave Walt some time to warm up, but Walt was getting less effective as he practiced. Balls were flying in every direction and I was wondering when Joe would intervene. I was sure I would have done something by now.

Just then, Joe asked Walt for his club. Joe began to swing from his finish. His swing was super fluid. It had a natural orbit and there seemed to be no effort in it. His whole body seemed to be in harmony and the orbit formed a perfect path for his club head. Joe and the club looked like partners who had danced together for a long, long time.

Then his swing began to pick up speed. Burlington seemed so relaxed as the club squared beautifully to his target through the impact zone. This went on until the last swing, when he let the club lower to the ball's level and *wham*! It flew straight, high, and long,

Walt stood there and smiled. "I'll never be able to do that."

"Yes you will, Walt. One day soon, in your own way, you will." Joe gave the club back to Walt and asked him to mimic what he had just seen as best he could.

Walt set up and swung the club forward from in front. His body complied, but his head was shaking no. He looked uncomfortable and remarked that he had no control over that much motion. Joe reassured him, "Just trust me."

Walt might have trusted Joe, but he didn't trust the exercise. "I have to tell you, Joe, this feels pretty awkward to me. There's just too much movement for me to control." He swung anyway.

Joe ignored the statement. "Oh, that's good, Walt." Walt shook his head a few more times in disagreement as he continued to swing.

As far as I could see, Walt's swing shape, coming from the finish and back, created the most beautiful blend of actions, and his tight manipulation of his swing was dissolving. He looked coordinated and fluid. Then Joe said, "The most important thing is to know where you want to go and use the momentum and centrifugal force of the swinging club to get you there. All you need to do is cooperate with these forces. This exercise will help you develop a repeating swing path—with no concern for the beginning of your backswing."

Walt stopped swinging and whined, "But I can't do that with a ball there."

"Of course you can. I heard that Jack Nicklaus practices with this very exercise. He's a master of flow and sequence. I believe it would be a great benefit to you too." Joe set him up to do the exercise again, this time without a ball. Walt began to swing and Joe coached him to allow his body to be free to support wherever the club wanted to go. "Just go with it," he urged him.

Walt was getting the hang of it. Burlington continued to coach. "That's right, Walt, just let it swing and allow your body to do whatever it wants to support the speed and direction of the swing. Then allow the swing to finish the forward motion, like so." Joe showed him the relationship between the grip end of the club and the target. Walt kept swinging and redirecting his finish.

Joe tried a new approach. "We'll call this home base, Walt. Always go to home."

"OK." Walt was beginning to trust in his motion and swinging the club naturally. The form of his swing seemed to shape automatically, without positioning him in the step-by-step method I was so accustomed to. Walt's body just seemed to move in perfect harmony with the club now. It was a beautiful orbit and path. "Is that a good backswing?" Joe didn't answer the question. He just asked Walt what it felt like. "It feels good to me."

"Then it is." And it was. Walt's body was cooperating with the swinging force.

"What a great lesson!" I exclaimed quietly.

"The lesson is just beginning, Geoff. We need to get Walt in tune with the feeling now. Walt, what picture does your swing remind you of right now? What does the feeling tell you?"

"It feels like a circle."

"Good. Notice how the circle relates to the ground and the target?"

"Yes, I see what you're talking about."

"The circle is at an angle; good. Can you feel the path the club takes as it passes over the impact zone?"

"Yes, it feels like a pathway moving around toward me, then up into the air again."

"Good, now notice how your whole body responds to knowing where you want to go with the club." Burlington had placed two small pieces of his Pathfinder foam on the ground that formed a corridor for the club to pass through on line with the target. Walt was still swinging. "See if you can get the club to brush the grass as it passes through the corridor going forward." Walt performed it with ease. "Now Walt, notice all the feeling in your body. Pay particular attention to how your hands and arms feel." Joe slipped a ball inside the corridor on the ground, but

Walt didn't seem to notice. On his next downswing, *wham!*—the ball flew into the air and straight toward the target. "OK, now stop."

Walt was out of breath. I guessed he was in his late seventies, but I was impressed with his stamina. "Wow, that felt like I wasn't even swinging," Walt exclaimed. "The ball felt weightless."

"Walt, that to me is swinging. I think what you meant to say is you didn't feel any resistance as you swung."

"That's it—no resistance! It felt effortless," Walt confirmed as joy lit up his face.

"I had one more question for you. Every time I take a lesson with you, I feel like I'm hitting the shot with my right hand. It feels great, but I know you always talk about the lead hand, so I'm a little confused."

"That's a good question. Many of my students have asked about this. Let me explain." Burlington turned to me, smiled, and said, "You knew we'd revisit centrifugal force, didn't you?" To Walt he said, "The feeling of the right hand releasing is only the centrifugal force of the club head in disguise. I will leave it at that." I was fascinated by his explanation. Essentially he had told us the right hand had nothing to do with the release. I would have liked a more detailed answer, but Burlington stopped short.

Walt moved on. "I've never been able to figure out why so many golfers, myself included, feel a need to be so forceful with the swing—to rip the cover off the ball with so much effort, even though it's counterproductive most of the time. You know, making the perfect rhythmic practice swing and then when the ball is there, swinging recklessly and completely different from the practice. What causes that?"

"Well, it's fairly obvious something is going on inside, right?" Joe pointed to his head to confirm. "But let's begin with those golfers who swing recklessly both in practice and on actual swings with the ball. They just don't understand that timing is power. The golf club is an instrument that needs to be handled with a deft touch and coordination. You see, gentlemen," Burlington addressed us both, "those golfers equate might with power and don't realize precision is an integral part of power. They try to muscle the ball with the force of their weight and the strength of the massive parts of their body. If I were you, I'd do a lot of hand and wrist exercises with the club and practice your swing exercises, with the bulk of your weight and body quiet during the swing. You can still hit it very far and toward your target. You know, feet together shots, etcetera."

"OK," Walt said, "I understand that, but what about the times my swing seems to change completely from one second to the next, from the practice swing to the actual."

"I'm getting to that." I had a couple of theories about this, too. Of course I, like a lot of my students, had experienced overworking the swing to get more energy at impact, only to find that it rarely worked. I wanted to hear what Burlington had to say about this. He cleared his throat. "The main problem is that golfers are insecure about their swing's strength—the power of the club into the impact. They aren't necessarily weak, but their swings feel that way to them. Something deep down inside, on a subconscious level—their self-image—believes the impact is going to be weak. Many golfers also think they're not going to get the ball to the target through timing.

"Let's say it's a long par four into the wind, which is the classic situation when this occurs."

"Exactly," Walt agreed.

"Our mind-body reaction becomes forceful—you know, 'heave-ho.' Of course, we get the opposite result. The more forceful we become, the less speed we generate and so the ball flies weakly and inaccurately. This compounds the problem, because as hard as we try, the results confirm our belief in our swing's weakness."

"Looks like we're back to the belief system again, aren't we?"

"Yes. We have to begin believing, deep down, that power and speed are not functions of brute strength. We need to learn how to generate speed through the shape, synchronization, and timing of our swing and to really have faith in it. We need to feel powerful and energetic without being forceful. Again, you can begin with the mind talk and visualization and then support it with exercises of timing, which generate club head speed, rather than forcing it, which diminishes club head speed."

"So then, it's this insecurity that causes the change from smooth to out of balance and forceful?"

"Yep."

I offered up my two cents' worth. "That makes sense. How else could a swing change so dramatically in a second or two? On a conscious level, we know what we want and feel, but subconsciously something else is operating."

"I see, I see," mumbled Walt. "What else can I do to get rid of the insecurity?"

"You need to do the mind talk and feel what real power is, Walt. Practice into a gale and try the different timing exercises I've shown you. Don't allow the wind to influence your timing. Get those angles and speeds organized and, after a while, you'll see the potential. But you need to do the mind talk and concentrate fully on the timing. Most people need to make an effort to feel a slower swing to get the club head to accelerate."

"That doesn't make a whole lot of sense to me," said Walt. "I have never seen anyone teach club head acceleration by slowing down."

"What I mean is to get in balance and usually this means for students to get less forceful. You see, Walt, you need a little lesson in centrifugal force generation in your swing, too. And allow it to occur at the right time during your downswing. Most golfers don't understand centrifugal force. They only relate to their own force and centrifugal force is the opposite of them working near impact. In a sense, you need to accelerate to a slowdown to get optimum centrifugal force in the swing, which is the most reliable timing force in the golf swing. It's a function of the sequence and direction of the swing, and it occurs when your hands are below your waist in the downswing. That's as much of a hint as I'm going to give you today, Walt."

I interjected. "Is that why, when I made my best swings, everyone said I didn't even swing?"

"That's right. Most golfers describe an effortless swing as not swinging. I'm always amused at those remarks, as it's obvious they don't know what a real swing feels like when it's effortless. What they mean is that it's a swing without resistance and to me, that is effortless. Let me try something that may make a stronger impression for you."

Joe's friend George and another friend, Billy, were sitting a ways off. Joe went over and enlisted them to help him create a human model of C-force. Billy, the largest of the three, gave Joe his hand, as did George. It was obvious that Billy and George had done this before. Joe explained that Billy was the golfer and the grip, Joe was the shaft and George, the smallest, was the club head. Billy took a couple of steps and began to make a turn. Joe was pulled along behind him and George followed. The three of them looked like a train going around a bend, simulating the path of the downswing.

Then Billy pulled a little more and made a quick turn to the left; he was now going in the opposite direction. There seemed to be a rippling and whirling effect. Joe's arms were stretching. George, the caboose, was picking up speed as he swung wide.

About halfway through the turn, Billy let go of Joe and then Joe let go of George. And off George went, flying away. They had just cracked the whip. It was a perfect human model of centrifugal force.

"Get it?" Burlington asked.

"Yes," I said, "I get it." Just like he'd said, Billy had slowed down and gone in the other direction, exactly like the grip end after impact. Joe was the middle link and he let George (the club head) fly past both of them. Smiling, George remarked how fast he'd run without trying to run; he was accelerated by Joe and Billy's action. "It wasn't coming from me. What an awesome feeling!"

I looked at Walt and saw that the demonstration had hit home for him, too. Walt smiled with appreciation and said, "I finally understand the release. That's why when I really swing, I feel as though I didn't do anything. What I actually did was finally swing!" Billy and George went back to their bench in the shade.

Joe was pleased with Walt's epiphany. "OK, Walt, that's it for today. Keep practicing the front-end exercise and you'll really feel the power of the swinging club." I was impressed. Burlington had solidified his point with this last demonstration.

As Walt packed up, Joe said, "Listen, I see the UPS guy delivering a spreader I ordered. I need to go show him where to drop it off. Practice, if you wish. I'll be back in ten minutes." He started to walk away, but turned to me and winked. "Kind of neat, eh?"

21

JUDY: A NEW GOLFER GETS A GRIP

Burlington returned a little later with two bottles of spring water and a plastic bag filled with cold, cut-up vegetables. He offered me a bottle and held the bag out to me. I took a couple of carrots and savored the cool crunchiness. My senses were awakened by the euphoria of understanding. Walt had just left with a spring in his step, his confidence buoyed by his lesson. Soon after Walt's car had pulled away, a young woman walked toward to us from the parking lot.

"OK, Geoff. I thought that since you haven't seen me work with a raw beginner, it might be useful for you to observe a lesson with someone who has never swung a club or taken a lesson before. Earlier this month, we had a raffle and only beginners could participate. The winner got a lesson with me. Some grand prize, eh?" He joked. "Anyway, this young lady, Judy, won the draw."

As the winner approached, I thought that Joe's method would be really difficult for a beginner, since there were no real concrete rules a person could sink their teeth into. Judy was in her mid-twenties and obviously athletic. She arrived with a look of optimism; she was bubbly, pleasant, and wholesome. She didn't have golf clubs, but knowing she was a beginner, Burlington had brought a few out. We introduced ourselves and the lesson began.

Joe started by asking Judy what she would like to happen in the time they spent together. Did she have any goals? Had she ever thought about the golf swing? She sheepishly told us, "I've only made a few swings before at a driving range. I quickly concluded that my boyfriend couldn't help me. That's when I decided to enter your raffle. I thought maybe I would get lucky, and here I am!" She went on to explain that she had become interested in golf watching it on television with her boyfriend, who was an avid golfer and played to a scratch handicap. "On TV it looks so easy and fun, yet my friends tell me it's very hard to play. I'd like to see if I can do it."

"OK, Judy, then let's begin," Burlington matched her enthusiasm with renewed energy. "Take hold of the club any way that seems natural to you." Judy took the club he offered and placed her hands with the club against her wrist and across her palm. This is going to be difficult, I thought. Judy had the club positioned diagonally across her palm and up toward her wrist. The pressure she applied looked like a white-knuckled death grip. Her grip position would make for a rigid swing with little or no wrist or hand action. This would be interesting to watch.

"OK," Joe said, "now go ahead and make a swing." Judy began to almost carry the club back and up into the air. Then her move took on a curve, sideways, with the club face terribly closed. She went back and forth like this a few times. She stopped and asked Joe, "Should I try to hit one?" She placed a ball on a tee and got ready to swing. Again the swing took on a sort of slow carry as though the club weighed five pounds, and she pushed the club downward and whiffed it. She looked up at Joe and he said, "Very good; let's begin."

I know I'd have said something like, 'we have a lot of work to do and it may take a while.' Burlington's response was the antithesis of that. He just asked her to take her right hand off the club and look at the grip in her left. Then he took hold of the club down the shaft and positioned the grip of the club in her left hand so her hold on the grip was down toward her finger channel, as he called it. He placed her thumb on top of the shaft, applying pressure to her thumb tip, thumb pad, and the heel of her left hand. The grip looked perpendicular to her fingers and the pressure points were now in order.

"There now," Burlington said, "you have leverage on the club. Can you feel it?"

She nodded and smiled at him. "That's what the position of the lead hand is for," he instructed, "control for the angle of swing and feel for the club face. Good! Now notice how the back of your left hand relates to the club face." He placed a tee in her glove between the Velcro strap and the leather backhand portion. It pointed basically at the target in the same direction as the club face.

He paused so she could see that. "OK. Now lift the club up and down with your left hand, letting your left wrist flex and allowing the weight of the club head to act on your wrist." Judy looked at him tentatively, so he demonstrated what he wanted her to do. "Now, Judy, with this newfound leverage in your left hand, you don't need so much pressure. In fact, the left hand position is for leverage and face control. Pressure is for generating speed. If you think about it, if there's a lot of pressure or tension placed on the grip, then what possibility is there to generate speed? I suggest much less pressure without letting go," he advised her. "Have you heard about timing?" Burlington asked.

"No," she said.

He gave her a reassuring smile and explained, "It's necessary to have it to swing with effortless power and consistency. Timing depends on flexibility and flow. We need to hold lighter." He included himself in her swing; now they were a team working together. What a great tactic! She seemed confident with his support.

Judy told him, "Before, I couldn't hold lightly; I had to hold on for dear life so I wouldn't lose the club out of my hand!"

"That's exactly right: When there's no leverage over the grip you would naturally pressure it heavily to feel secure," Joe confirmed. "Now let's get your right hand on the grip. Bring your right hand below the left and against the 'life line,' like this. Now close the fingertips around the shaft and allow the life line of your right hand to lie against your left thumb."

"So the club is really in the fingers of my right hand, but it feels like I have no control of the club with my right hand."

"Exactly. The club lies like this in your right fingers." He demonstrated the right-hand grip position. The club lay way down in his fingertips, straight across the ends of his fingers and far away from his palm. The life line down the center of his right palm was against his left thumb and his right thumb was lying over the other side of the shaft and it seemed to not even be touching the grip. His right thumb and first finger covered his left thumb on top of the shaft. His right palm was also facing his left palm, basically in the same direction as the club face.

He continued to show Judy. "Now cover your left thumb with your right thumb and first finger like a crab claw." He had the meat of his thumb together with the first finger and they did look like a crab claw. She followed his lead exactly. Her right hand was now pacified on the club, instead of dominant.

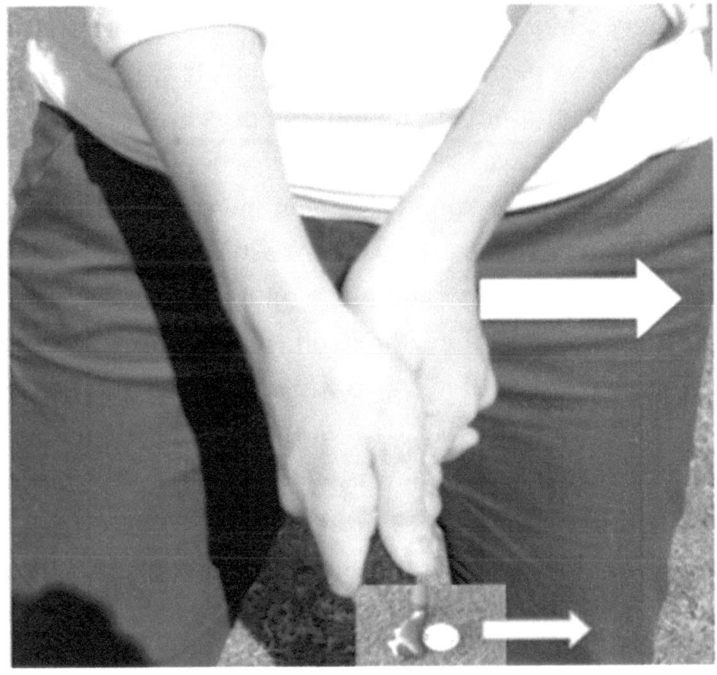

Neutral grip matching the direction
of the clubface.

JW

"I have to say," Judy said, "it feels weird to me—my right hand can't really do much. But now it feels like I have control over the club with my left hand and I can still feel the weight of the head at the other end. I couldn't have light pressure and control without this position, could I?" She seemed surprised.

"Right" Burlington said. "If you lightened the pressure without a sound position of leverage over the club, it would be difficult to control and it would be swimming in your hand! You would get a lot of slippage. How does it feel now?"

"I'm feeling pretty confident that I can lighten the pressure and not lose control."

"Good. Let's begin swinging again," he said.

I had never heard the grip position detailed so thoroughly. Her hands looked perfect on the club now. It was often difficult for me to get my students to lighten the pressure over the grip of the club. Burlington was right on target when he said that when you have leverage over something, you have control without the need for pressure. It was pretty clear to me now. Even if I got my students to grip it well, I would move on to the bigger parts of the swing and let the grip fend for itself. Burlington was obviously not moving forward until her grip was optimized and I suspected that if she had changed it back, he would begin again. I knew how important the grip position was, yet I wasn't this much of a stickler about it.

"This time," Joe said, "let me show you how to start the swing from the finish." There was no effort in her motion this time. The starting place made it that easy. Gravity and momentum were put into play from the beginning with this exercise from the front end. Judy's attention naturally shifted from hitting the ball to swinging the club. This technique of starting from the finish seemed to be the perfect beginning for swing motion, perhaps because there really is no effort involved in beginning the motion from the finish. Gravity and momentum are at work rather than physical exertion through one's muscle.

With the new grip position and pressure and new starting place, the shape and flow of Judy's swing began to emerge like magic. Burlington turned to me, smiled, and said, "Pretty cool, eh Geoff?" Then he turned back to Judy. "Now let's try the grip again, this time with your eyes closed, and I'd like to place it for you." He took the club and lifted it into the air so her grip was low and the club head was high. The grip went right into her finger channel. "Now, can you feel the leverage you have on the club again?"

"Yes, I feel it better with my eyes closed." Now he held her club horizontal and supported it for her while she gripped it. Still with her eyes closed, he asked her to turn the face of the club toward the ground. "How do I do that?" she asked him.

"Make a guess," he replied. She turned her hand, and the face of the club went right toward the ground. "Now turn the face toward the sky," he instructed. This time, no question. She just did it. She still had her eyes closed, but she had felt and already pictured what the club face did when her hand moved in each direction. He took out a ball. "Keep your eyes closed. First, turn the face toward the sky." After she did this, Burlington began to bounce the ball off the club face. He asked her, "Which direction did the ball bounce?"

She said, "Up."

He lowered the club head to the ground. "Keep your eyes closed. Do you remember where the flag is?"

"Yes."

"Now turn the face toward the target," he instructed. She did. He bounced the ball again and she responded, "I felt it bounce toward the target."

"What tells you that?" he asked.

"My hand. I can feel it in my left hand."

"Good," he said. Burlington turned to me. "You see, Geoff, the first step is to familiarize your student with the feel of the club. Get them to feel that the face of the club and the club head itself is just an extension of their hands. Judy can now feel where the ball may fly, based on the feeling in her hands."

This all took only a few minutes, and yet I knew Judy was more in touch with the club than even my students who had taken many lessons. "Let's take a break, Judy." When she opened her eyes, she was smiling. She had just had her first success experience. Joe found his drink and took a long swallow. Judy went over to his table and grabbed a water, too. They rested for a few minutes.

"Now, Judy, do you think you can find your new grip again?"

"I think so," she said.

"OK, swing the club as though you were going to let it strike a ball toward that target." He pointed in the direction of a flag about fifteen yards out. Judy took hold of the club again, placed it behind the ball, this time with her new levered grip. She made a swing that again did not remotely resemble a good swing as I knew it. I wondered what Burlington would do.

Judy had begun her swing from the ground again and that starting place returned her to the swing pattern she had arrived with. The club went up into the air immediately and she seemed to be carrying it again instead of letting it swing. Then, as she lifted the club back and up, it began to circle very low around behind her. The face was very shut. As she moved it forward, it whirled around the ball way to the left and she almost lost her balance. Judy had completely missed the ball. Her smile and look of optimism vanished. However, Burlington just smiled and said, "That's OK, Judy. Are you ready to begin again?"

"I guess," she said softly. "But how could that have been OK?" she asked, at the same moment I'd thought it.

"Well," Burlington said, "it's good because number one, we don't care about the results. During this lesson, I'm responsible for the outcome. You're responsible only for sensing and feeling. Anyway, I have seen where you are and, with your cooperation, I believe I can coach you to get where you need to be—in just a few minutes—if you just trust me." Looking much less burdened, Judy answered, "I like the sound of that. I'm all yours."

I had to see this happen—and in 'just a few minutes.' Yeah, right! I did notice one thing right away, though: In the lessons I had observed so far, Burlington had put people at ease. He exuded the feeling that he was in complete control and wherever their feel would take them, it was OK with him. Nothing to be concerned about! It was as if he were on the journey with them, an experienced guide helping them get where they wanted to go. Cooperate with him and he'd take you there. Nothing fazed him, either—not whiffing or shanking; none of the initial clumsiness a new golfer might exhibit seemed to give him pause. It was simply a matter of feeling the physics and, since he knew the physics inside and out, everyone could relax. Problems were not problems, just awareness challenges with Burlington. I couldn't wait to see more of his strategy with this first-time player. If Judy's awareness could make that quantum leap in only a few minutes, then I'd be a total believer too.

"OK, let's begin again," he said. He brought out a club that had the flex of a fishing rod. He called it a whippy. "Here, let's use this club." Judy looked at him with a baffled expression. Everything going through her mind at each moment was inscribed on her face just as soon as she felt it.

"What's this?" she asked. "It was hard enough with the other one."

Again, Burlington said, "Just trust me, Judy. Hold the club in the air in front of your face with your new grip. Notice the pressure with which you're holding it. Between one and ten, attempt to be about a five. Flex and unflex your wrists so the club head moves up and down. Can you feel it?" When she nodded, he said, "Now be a one. Got it?"

"Yes," she responded. "The club is almost loose in my hand."

"Good. Now be a ten. Can you feel it?"

"Yes, that's the pressure I used in my first swing."

"OK. Now when you're a ten, what part of the club do you feel?"

"Only the grip."

"Not any weight at the head end?" he queried.

"No."

"Now slowly reduce the pressure. What are you feeling now?"

"The weight at the other end."

"Good. Now find a pressure where you can still feel the weight at the other end."

She experimented. "It seems comfortable at about a five."

"Good. Let me help you. We're going to begin this swing with the club in the air over here again." It was similar to Walt's exercise, from the finish; Joe called it point B. Burlington positioned the club over Judy's left shoulder with the grip end pointing toward the target. "Now," he said, "begin swinging by letting the club pick up speed. As it swings back, down, and around through the air, allow your whole body to respond to the swinging club. Now here behind you is point A." Burlington pointed to a lamppost behind us at the end of the practice area. "You can watch the club as you swing, so you know that you're swinging in this pattern. Simply swing the club around you in a circular pattern from point B to point A."

Judy made a few swings this time, very vertical like a Ferris wheel. Joe told her it was good. He instructed her to continue swinging while he stepped away to set up his Pathfinder so the pattern of path could be improved. He set up his virtual wall and the curved path through the delivery zone, just as he had with Walt; no ball yet. He instructed Judy to swing from point B to the far side of the virtual wall; this gave her a flatter swing around on the way back to point A, and then through the center of the corridor of the two pieces of foam while brushing the grass on her way back to point B.

"You mean I don't have to concentrate on the ball?" Interesting question, considering there was no ball there yet. I guess she imagined one.

"Just the club."

"OK. It seems like a loop."

"Yes, it is. A good loop." Judy was puzzled but complied, and her eyes followed the club from B down and around the foam to point A and then back downward and through the corridor on her way back to B. It was amazing to watch her body learn as she concentrated on swinging her club through the corridor to the two endpoints. Like magic, her swing was morphing into a classic shape.

"Let all your muscles and joints give way to the swinging club, as though they were not strong enough to support it." Judy's arms were no longer rigid and her wrist action began to occur naturally. The club face was rotating too. The fundamental dynamics were coming alive right before my eyes. "Allow your whole body to be free to support the swinging club," Joe urged. Judy's feet and legs began to move in harmony with her arms swinging, and her torso began to pivot naturally as the club head's path took on a beautiful curve.

I noticed all this action, while Judy was only aware of the club. It was all happening just as Joe said it would—as a function of the club being OK. Judy's swing was smooth and natural. "She has a swing!" I exclaimed.

He gently, quietly corrected me. "She always had a swing. If she didn't, do you think we could have accomplished this in five minutes?"

Next Joe stopped Judy and asked, "Hey Jude, how does that feel?"

Judy was vibrant and said resoundingly, "Like a golf swing!"

"OK, take a break," he said. She was exuberant and clearly proud, but winded.

"That's real aerobics, isn't it?"

"Yes—and they say golf isn't exercise!"

I was almost a believer, but I wanted to see her swing with a ball in place.

"Let's begin again, Judy; you ready? As before, start your swing from in front, pointing at point A. On the way back, let the club swing on the far side of the foam and on the way through, brush the grass between the foam without touching the foam. Can you feel the flex, feel the pressure against your left thumb when your wrists flex near point A?" he quizzed her as the club changed directions. "Are you feeling a freedom in the motion? Let it swing," he coaxed her. All his discovery questions described a balanced hand and wrist action and a sound swing path.

Swinging from B to A and back to B.

KT

Judy responded, and her swing took on that perfect form again through the super-fluid quality of the motion. "Now this time," Burlington said, "I'm going to put a tee on the ground between the foam boundaries. Just knock it out of the ground as the club passes through." She did so with ease. "OK, are you ready now?"

"Yes," she said eagerly.

"This time let the club pass through and, on the way, notice the brush of the grass." Again, he knelt down near the foam but slipped a ball onto the tee as she was swinging, just as he had with Walt. It seemed to be a fun thing he challenged himself to do, getting his hand out of the way before he got nicked by a club. *Wham!* The club struck the ball up into the air and it flew about fifty yards. Judy was amazed, as was I—both of us inspired by Burlington's magic. But he just smiled and said, "Lucky again?"

All Joe had done was get Judy to focus on the right things without interference. Fifteen minutes into her first lesson, she had developed a beautiful swing! The ball flew toward her target and she was ecstatic. She had not gotten a ball in the air before and yet this time, she was exclaiming about how easy it seemed.

I was much closer to drinking Burlington's lemonade, but I still wasn't sure how he did it. Maybe Judy was just uncommonly talented. But remembering her first carries of the club, I didn't think that was the case. It would have taken me ten lessons to get what he got out of Judy in minutes. It was miraculous. I didn't need to see more; I was a believer!

Burlington had more lessons in store for me and I was determined to learn all I could through observation. Besides his experience in golf swing physics and his mindset about learning and performing, Joe had a knack, a gift. He obviously loved to see students grow and was willing to take responsibility for all the poor results to get his students to relax. I realized it was also his way of getting them to let go psychologically. When students could give up responsibility for the results, all their 'trying hard' dissolved. And then they could really see results. Sometimes he seemed more like a psychologist than a golf pro—he knew those boundaries he talked about.

The physics and his sensory questions shaped the swing and synchronized it perfectly, if the learner was at all in touch with his or her body. I could see from my own experience what he drove at with his questions, but I noticed he didn't explain much to his students. He never answered them directly about why he asked certain questions. He shaped their swings without much explanation. Students' swings changed naturally according to his questions. I was beginning to get the method and his style, but I knew it took talent, experience—the complete package. No one could synthesize all that overnight.

Joe Burlington was more than the sum of his experience and talent. It struck me how easy it was to be blinded by someone's talent but miss small, but equally important, things: Joe had compassion. He really cared about his students and he wanted success for them as much as they did for themselves. The difference was in what he considered success. His view of success was a student being able to stand on solid ground and grow confidently on their own. It wasn't about hitting one good shot, it was about helping themselves. In my case, I believed I could take his message and improve my game. He'd already started to transform me—all of me.

Judy was well on her way to improving her swing and he had left her alone to practice. She stayed with the program. I watched her club start at point B, swing down and around to point A, and then through the corridor to B again. She was enthusiastic about her new beginning and very thankful.

"You keep doing that exercise," he told her. Joe and Judy hugged, and she waltzed away with a bounce in her step as though the ground were flexible.

"Only two more left for today. Can you handle that?" I thought he was talking to me, but he had addressed Otter. The dog wagged his tail, as if giving his consent.

22
WALLY: SLIMMING DOWN THE FAT SHOT

Joe looked toward a couple approaching from about 200 yards away. "You will enjoy Wally and Kay, Geoff. They really suit each other, but they are very different. Wally has been Indianwood club champion more than once. I always work with him on letting go of his seriousness. It's not because I want him to be in la-la land, but because his seriousness gets in the way of his improvement. It leads to a demand for results. At the same time, what matters to him is his shot quality. He isn't so into his score, although he would not accept shooting in the eighties. I can relate to him very well because I was just that serious when I was learning. I also used to let poor shots get me down a lot." The man and woman drew closer.

"Anyway, Wally and I have been friends for many years and I enjoy working with him. We used to play a lot and I like to see him play well. Lately, I've worked on him getting more energy at impact and improving his angle of attack when the ball is in a tight lie, especially with a fairway wood or long iron. Since we've known each other so long we've developed a kind of lingo all our own.

"Kay's a fairly new golfer. She's demanding of herself and competitive, but seems more patient with the learning process than Wally is, although I've heard she can get pretty frustrated when she practices. But we're just working with Wally today."

Burlington gestured for the couple to come over. He gave them both bear hugs. After we were all introduced, Kay installed herself, her book and her latte in a lawn chair, and Joe and Wally got right into what was bugging Wally about his swing. He complained of hitting shots fat and drop-kicking his long irons and fairway woods again. He asked Burlington why that was happening.

"Beats me," said Joe. Wally just smiled. He knew Joe could tell him why it was occurring from a physics standpoint, but Joe said, "All those impacts need to be placed under the umbrella of non-awareness while you're trying to pull off the shot."

"What do you mean, Joe?" Wally questioned.

"Well, who knows what was firing through your mind at the moment you swung? You may have been thinking of what a tight lie it was. You may have been insecure about it and overreacted. We can't begin to really know the source of the imbalance. All we really see are the symptoms. The only place to put your mind, then, is on your goal. I have another idea. Get out your fairway wood."

"How about I warm up with some wedges first?"

"No, just get the spoon. Oh, and show me that fat shot you mentioned."

"What?" Wally asked, incredulous.

"I want you to attempt to fat the shot. Hit the shot you despise, purposely."

Wally took the club and made a swing. Attempting to hit it fat, he caught the ball just right, not fat at all. How does that work? Joe just smiled. He obviously knew Wally didn't just have a swing problem independent of a psychological one with the longer clubs. "Wally, have you noticed your pace change when you have a longer club in your hands?"

"Yeah, you know my swing becomes Flash von Rash. I get totally discombobulated with a long club—very little loft, and a tight lie." Joe turned to smile at me. "But Joe, tell me why I would practice what I want to get rid of?"

"Simply because as you play the shot you're trying to rid yourself of, you are becoming present mentally. If you really feel it, you may have a shot at getting rid of it. When you have difficulty hitting shots fat, one strategy is to intentionally hit the shot you're trying to eliminate. Identify it. Then, at least it's not happening because you're trying hard to prevent it.

"Very often, from a psychological standpoint, the problem persists precisely because you're trying hard to avoid it. You know, 'don't go right,' and you hit the ball to the right, or on a putt, 'don't be short' and of course you're short. The subconscious can't isolate the 'don't.' Once you can perform an imbalance on purpose, it's likely you'll know what to do to reverse the pattern. At least then you're aware of it!

"Here's another strategy. Place the ball way forward in your stance, and see how your mind and body respond to that," Joe suggested.

"But I'm making contact way back here; won't it be even fatter?" Wally asked as he pointed to a spot well before the ball.

"Just put it forward and see what happens."

I was curious too.

"Just give it a try, Wall. You may make a shift McRift. Just be aware of your tempo when you attempt a swing to get to this ball."

Wally was becoming frustrated. "How do you come up with this stuff?"

Joe smiled his enigmatic smile. "I don't know. I just think about it, and the answer comes to me. But really, besides the insecurity, it comes down to the action of your hand, wrist, and forearm. They are the most volatile parts of a golf swing and we can't expect them to become balanced without getting involved. Your wrists and hands must be fluid-like and stable at the same time. They can provide great consistency or total inconsistency based on your adeptness. To get this you must be proactive in the delivery, but I will show you later what I mean. For now just see if you can identify the release angle of the club for the shot at hand. Let's just set up a purpose that opposes your imbalance. In this case, we set up for the timing of the delivery in terms of angle. We can adjust this in about five minutes."

Joe continued. "First, let's get a picture of the swing arcs that will likely produce the angle you want." Joe took the club and demonstrated. Then he pulled a scratch pad from his pocket and began drawing. I couldn't clearly see what he was drawing but it looked like two intertwined circles. Joe explained, "Wally, all you need to do is know where on the arc relative to the ground you want to impact the ball. Here, I can show you a way to do it with the Pathfinder." He seemed to be able to make any impact adjustment using his device. His students seemed to get the picture and feeling immediately with this thing.

"But just a second, Joe." Wally looked puzzled. "You mean the arc in the backswing is different from the arc in the downswing?"

"Absolutely. The bottom of the arc on the backswing is naturally behind the ball and the bottom of the arc on the downswing for impacting the ball on the ground is in front of the ball." Joe pointed with his club some four inches in front of the ball.

Wally looked intrigued. "How can I achieve that?"

"First you have to know about it and then practice your swing and allow your body to get the club to go there. Beyond that I'll show you how to use the Pathfinder to achieve what you want." He had used it earlier with Walt and Judy, but this time he set it up in an L shape at the back along the ground and then bent it up to form a virtual wall for Wally's path to be maintained on the downswing. So going back, Wally would have to start the swing above the ground to get past the foam as the club swung back and around. I smiled. Wally's lesson was just like Tim had told me his lesson with Joe had been.

Then Joe asked him to swing the club well above the foam, swinging downward through the impact zone. "Now place the club here as though there were a ball and make a few swings. Can you feel the differences in the two arcs?" Wally caught on right away and realized it was impossible to hit the shot fat or drop-kick the ball when he swung over the foam into impact. "Is this the path and angle I want?" he asked.

It's pretty close, Wally, though a little extreme. The action I'm describing is really just an impression, but if you get near that angle of attack with the club in the impact zone, you'll never have chronically fat or drop-kicked shots." Wally seemed pleased. Joe continued, "Most golfers don't realize the difference in arc and angle between the backswing and the downswing. They've been led to believe that they are the same paths, but they need to be very different. Isn't your picture of them different now?"

"Very." Wally made a few more swings and noticed how far his lower body shifted to get the club over the foam coming down and to get the club head to the ball. It was way out in front of his left foot. "I feel like I'm shifting a lot."

"That's right! Your mind-body system has the built-in intelligence to automatically make a shift because it knows the

club has got to get over the foam to reach to the ball far ahead of
your previous impact zone."

The backswing under the foam, then the downswing
over the foam.

TC2

"I haven't felt a shift like that in a long time. And I did it without thinking; I just knew where I wanted to get to with the club."

Joe looked back at me and smiled. His expression said, 'if the club is OK, the shift is OK.' It was a real lesson in natural learning, and not just for Wally.

"Just remember the purpose: Get the club to swing in good patterns. In this case, relative to the angle—though you must be wary. This strategy tends to elongate the forward arc of the handle too much and get out of balance on the other side of impact. So you must stay in the phone boot. Attempt to swing within the boot and play the flute with your grip pressure."

"OK Joe, I like the phone boot." Wally seemed to know what Joe was talking about. Joe's silly side helped everyone around him lighten up and relax, including himself. I was really enjoying this lesson.

"Now take a few balls out front of the tee and hit some shots, Wall," Burlington instructed his friend. Wally went out in front to a slight down slope of the main tee a few yards and began hitting shots. They were not solid, though they weren't fat either. He started to reprimand himself. He seemed disgusted with the flight of the balls, which were now all surprisingly thin. Joe was pleased and this seemed to puzzle Wally, too. "Why are they thin now?"

"Just keep swinging as if you were in the Pathfinder."

Joe stepped back and whispered to me, "Wally isn't aware of the process his mind-body system has to go through to learn a balanced angle of attack. His feel conditioned him to find the golf ball at a very shallow angle, and the only place he probably felt secure was with a short iron on a fluffy lie. Actually, a fat shot and a thin one are similar even though they feel like the opposite. It's all a matter of arc and angle. Now that he has a lot of angle, he's still not gotten proficient at letting the club release downward in balance with the surface of the ground. You see, Geoff, Wally is blinded again by the result not being what he wants it to be. He wants to skip the step of learning the delivery and, if I let him, he'll never get it."

Wally was frustrated by now at the thinness of the impact, but Burlington insisted he keep matching the foam. After about ten minutes, Joe told him, "OK, Wally, I think you're ready for the delivery." Wally gave Joe a look that said 'why did you let me hit so many shots thin?'

"Wally, you needed to ingrain a little feel of the new angle," Burlington said, answering Wally's unvoiced question. "Patience, my boy! OK, let's see how you handle the delivery. You have basically two choices. Let's try one. Picture and feel the swing. Remember, the handle is you. See if once you get over the foam, you slow down the handle and let the club whiz on by down and through the impact. Just let it fly by. Accelerate to a slowdown." That was similar to what I needed to do with my driver, I told myself.

Wally asked, "You really mean I shouldn't try to accelerate?"

"That's right! In your downswing, picture and feel as though you accelerate over the foam to a slowdown."

"That sounds crazy, Joseph!"

"Just trust me."

Wally got back into the Pathfinder and, at first, hit the foam swinging down into the impact. He shook his head in disgust at his performance.

"Just keep at it," Joe encouraged.

Wally kept swinging and before long, he got it. "Unbelievable! That's the feeling I was looking for!" Wally's shots were right on now, and it was obvious he had increased his club head speed dramatically. Now he was grinning—he finally had the visualization and the feeling. The shots took off at incredible speeds and there was no way Wally was going to hit them fat with that much angle and speed. Now he started to punch shots and the club was coming to an abrupt stop just after the impact. He was having a ball.

"Move down to the front of the practice tee and try it from a downhill lie again, Wall." Wally smiled again; Joe was pushing his awareness further. If Wally could strike it solid from this downhill lie, surely he would have enough angle from a flat lie.

He started swinging and at first made contact with the ground a little early, but then the slope took over and his feet and legs drove downward and forward, the angle increased, and *wham*, he smashed it off a downhill lie with a three wood. It flew low, for sure, but the contact was solid. Burlington was having fun with him now and Wally just cracked up. He started walking forward after the swing like Gary Player.

I found the strategy fascinating: Having a golfer do what he doesn't want to do so that he could become aware of it, then reverse engines and see if he can feel the difference. It's amazing to see the body's intelligence when we allow it to learn through a fresh point of view and nothing is wrong or right. It just *is*! I was getting my money's worth now.

Kay was oblivious to it all. She was relaxing in the fresh air and sunshine. Cell phone at her side and book open on her lap, she was paying no attention to the golfing. Otter was asleep at her feet, with his huge head resting partially on her shoe, but she didn't seem to mind.

Joe stopped Wally to wind up his lesson. Quietly he told Wally that he was still concerned about how Wally had responded to what had occurred earlier.

"What do you mean, Joe?" Wally's expression was interested but questioning.

"When things went to the other extreme a few minutes ago, you began to get frustrated again. Something inside you was unwilling to give time for the process to take place. If I weren't here with you, I believe you would have abandoned a good adjustment before you had enough swings to synchronize it. Look, Wally, you have terrific talent, but I'm concerned that you sabotage change with your negative judgments about the results. You make assumptions about the value of the adjustment too soon. It causes discouragement, and there's no way to build confidence from there, right? That's the only thing that may trip you up, and I think it would serve you well to take a look at it."

Wally seemed to take these comments to heart. "You're right, I was frustrated. I'll really try to catch myself next time."

"Good," said Joe, "because it would be criminal if you didn't. With your talent, there's no reason you can't play scratch golf all the time." Wally seemed pleased with that possibility. "Is there anything else?"

"No, I don't think so; just work on this for now. I think you can have fun with it." Then Joe paused with one hand in the air as if trying to remember something. "How's the Auggie Doggie going?"

Wally smiled. "I did it on the first tee at Indianwood and got a few looks from my playing partners, but hit a great drive with a slight draw." Wally grinned as he pulled each foot backward across the grass making scuff marks like a dog claiming his territory. He remarked as he did it, "Auggie...Doggie."

The new approach was one thing, but this new golf lingo was beyond me.

23

FREDDIE: CURING THE SHANKS

Burlington came over to me when he finished up with Wally. "We have one more and then we can take a break." Joe told me Freddie had just flown in from New York for a sort of emergency lesson. Freddie had been a student for over 25 years and would come down about every other year for a tune up. But this time he was going to play a tournament and had a bad case of the shanks, especially with the wedge.

Freddie was one of his favorite students, Joe said. In addition to Freddie's talent, Joe liked his humble attitude. Burlington explained, "Freddie has more talent than he would lead you to believe, or for that matter, than he believes."

I was glad I wasn't giving this lesson. I had experienced so much difficulty getting students out of the dreaded shanks! It always seemed so psychological. I watched as Freddie approached; he saw Wally and Kay and greeted them first, fellow long-time alumni of the Joe Burlington School. Freddie was a tall, strong man. His long wavy salt-and-pepper hair curled up from under of his pulled-down cap. When he reached us, Freddie gave Joe a hug and asked how things were going; Joe introduced us. Before I knew it Freddie had pulled out a wedge and began swinging. I could tell he had a good swing.

After a few crisp shots, there it was. He shanked it to the right, almost a lateral. He shook it off and made a few more swings; the ball flew nicely to the target and then again, a shank to the right. Joe stopped him and walked in close. Fred's head was down. I could tell the shanks had taken the wind out of his sails. He didn't get excited, just seemed inwardly dejected. It always surprises me how a good player like this can get this far off with his contact. But there it was in living color. Joe said not to worry, that it was "simple, really."

He told Fred, "This time, at address place the club where the shank of the club is, here." Joe pointed to a spot on the far side of the ball. Fred gave Joe a puzzled look, much like Wally had done when Joe instructed him to place the ball forward when he was hitting it fat. But Freddie did as instructed and obviously trusted Joe. As the club swung down, it struck the ball right in the center of the club face. Freddie cracked a little smile.

Then Joe continued, "This time place the club all the way over here,"—a good four inches past the ball—"and try to hit the ball off the toe at impact." Fred looked a little miffed, but followed the instruction. He swung back from the far side of the ball and the club arrived at impact on the toe, as instructed.

Fred looked back and asked, "Where do you come up with this stuff, Joe?"

"What stuff?"

"To get rid of a shank, you need to line the club up on the shank."

"There's a method to it and believe it or not, logic too. Just not the logic you would think. You thought your shank was a result of an open club face from an inside path, right? Because you saw the ball fly way to the right."

Fred chuckled and nodded. "Mind reader," he muttered.

"So you tried to close the face more and the path traveled farther out, just adding to the problem. Freddie, it was easy to delude yourself about the face angle and path. Actually your path was outside and the club face was closed even though the ball flew to the right. The inside shank was not your shank. Your swing, although very athletic, was slightly out of balance regarding the path near impact. It was a blind spot for you. I'm sure you weren't feeling it.

"So the adjustment was to allow your athleticism to work out the improved path by forcing you to feel the path from over here." He pointed to the spot on the far side of the ball. "It really required you to change your path for the better if you were to even remotely find the ball on the face at impact. Did you notice that you've been setting up with the club face toward the toe at address and forward in your stance?"

"Now that you mention it, yes, a little."

"That's typical of a shanker and only exacerbates the problem. Your brain, on a subconscious level, then created an even greater path imbalance from way out here and still found the ball on the face, for a short while anyway." Joe pointed to a spot where the path would come from way outside the line of play. "You were actually accommodating the problem, not solving it. And it only takes a few swings to get back on track. Now as you go through this exercise, attempt to feel your whole hand path, especially near the impact zone."

"I can, Joe—it feels as though my hands are very near my side before impacting the ball, and after too. Very different from before."

"Great. You're waking up and dissolving the blind spot."

Freddie continued to practice and didn't even come close to the shank. He said he felt liberated and no longer tentative with a wedge in hand.

"Lastly, curl it to the end, like this." Joe's wrist looked odd at the end of his swing, still curled. He never let his wrist flex forward; it remained curled to the end. "Like Gary Player, Fred." Joe walked back a few feet from Fred, turned to me and elaborated. "Player has more talent than you can imagine. He's as entertaining a man as any who has ever swung a club, too. The things he does with a club and ball are an art form. And he's the king of positive attitude! My friend Allan knows him up close and personal, and he proclaims that when it comes to Gary, what you see is what you get."

Swing path from beyond the
ball on the backswing to
develop an inside approach.

FT

Then Joe was back to Freddie, who had been adjusting his swing with his new path.

"Curling to the end is so weird, Joe. I don't know if I can do that."

"It's just an exercise and with that goal, I doubt you'll ever shank it again, especially if you stay in the phone boot." Fred shook his head and smiled.

"I'll do it!" Freddie tried it and the shot was super solid with a little draw on it. "Feels weird, but the impact is phenomenous!" Like Wally, Freddie had a little Burlingtonism in his lingo, too.

"Freddie, that's it! You can stay and practice, but really, you have it now; have fun at the tournament." Joe and Freddie gave each other a friendly hug.

Joe turned to me. "I need a break, Geoff. Let's go get something good to eat." I couldn't have agreed more. I was famished.

Otter followed us around the corner. Joe gave him a bowl of fresh water and tied him to a big pine so he could enjoy another snooze in the shade. Joe and I got into his truck and set off to the Farmer's Market truck stop to get some lunch.

24
PERSONALITY TYPES

We found a booth and sat down. Burlington said he wasn't that hungry and after glancing at the menu said he was just going to have a bowl of soup. I was ravenous, so I ordered a turkey sandwich with my soup. While we waited, I brought up a subject that had been on my mind as we drove. "I noticed, as I watched you work with your students, that you teach everybody differently."

"Yes, in a sense I do. I can never predict how a lesson is going to go. Oh, I have my program, but I never know how the student will respond. It's totally up to them—how their experiences and their perceptions shape things. Of course, we're all headed in the same direction and hope to end up in the same place, but you as a teacher always need to consider the talent, experience, and personality types that you're working with. That makes it a different route every time.

"Remember when I spoke to you about perception? That's the whole key to getting right to the heart of change. You need to know how a student processes things, how he or she sees things. Get a feel for it right at your first meeting. Find out how students perceive themselves. Find out if their self-perception is accurate. You can discern some things right away and then you can choose a tactic that will get them going in the right direction quickly. I can discern personality types fairly quickly. Knowing a student's personality type is the key to relating to them. You can determine whether a student needs to change or whether their personality serves them well. It's exactly what makes teaching interesting and never boring for me. You can learn a lot from the myriad of personalities, even though some students may need to adopt a new one to get the most out of their golf game."

Our food arrived. The soup smelled wonderful and was obviously homemade.

"Could you give me an example?" I asked.

"I'll tell you what I've found to be the most challenging. Let's say you have a type-A personality businesswoman. Let's call her Misty. Misty is very competitive; her job requires that quality for her to be successful. Maybe she has to fight the good ol' boy culture every day. She arrives for a golf lesson and naturally enters it with a confrontational attitude. Misty knows that learning the facts, competing against herself, pushing herself, being driven, and basically having a bottom line mentality is what she needs to succeed. On top of this, Misty is a perfectionist-realist, which is an oxymoron in itself, right? She doesn't like fiction or any type of fantasy. Misty will tell you she lives in the real world. She bundles all these personality traits up into a package she calls success.

"Misty enters the lesson with the illusion that those are positive qualities because they made her successful in an unfair, highly competitive business arena. What she doesn't realize is those 'reality' qualities may not work well in learning to swing a golf club or play the game well. In fact, they become a stumbling block. Since she hasn't acquired any skills with a golf club yet, she will probably swing without perfect contact a lot of the time, right? She lacks optimism. Therefore, when she begins to make her usual bottom-line judgments, she will probably tell herself this is very hard—another stumbling block. Remember, from the belief comes the action!

"Well, Misty is so focused on the results that she misses the process. Throughout her practice, she moves in the direction opposite to awareness. She gets farther from her goal rather than closer because of her mind's conditioning and perception. Getting the picture?" he asked. "Now here's the kicker—*knowledge versus trust!*"

"We're back to the knowledge versus trust conflict again!" I interjected.

"That's right," Joe agreed. "That's why I called her Misty: Mistrust! The one trait that will allow her to see her potential the fastest, she has not developed, nor does she have an interest in developing it. She has no trust! In her business life, Misty has learned not to trust, and since she spends most of her day in this environment, it's ingrained very deeply. So if you begin the lesson by telling her something about trust based on feeling, you're likely to lose her. She just wants to know how to do it and see results! If she finds out how, then she can do it—or at least at this point, believes she can.

"Misty will tell you she just doesn't feel any faith or trust, but the beginning of the development of trust is not a feeling, it's a decision. She must commit herself to acting on faith and trusting. That's the beginning of it. The decision is the key to opening the door. Misty must first believe and trust that you are leading her to the best place, and then believe she can get there on her own after a little coaching from you."

Burlington had raised his voice a bit. He had obviously had a lot of experience with this type of personality. "Don't get me wrong, Geoff, type-A men are just as challenging. It's confusing because again what makes them successful in other arenas is of no value in learning golf. These are not easy traits for an instructor to work with. I have to admit, it is frustrating for me when I think of the barriers these bottom-liners erect for themselves, and then assume there is something wrong with your teaching method. The only thing they don't look at is their own trust level—at themselves. Sometimes during these lessons, I think to myself, 'just take a look, will you?' "

Burlington paused to eat his soup. "I'll tell you about another strong personality I especially remember. Matt used to fly down from New York once in a while to see me. Just to give you an idea of where he was when we started, he used to say things like 'what's good about it?' when I said good morning to him. Very demanding, arrogant, aggressive type. Liked to throw things around.

"He came to me because he figured he didn't have a swing. I didn't buy this, but it was a challenge even to get him to show me what he had. And as I'm sure you've heard from your students, he said he was fine until he had a ball to hit. I explained that this meant the problem was actually how he felt about his swing—he was so negative. He essentially demanded that I tell him what to do to fix it.

"I explained that there was actually nothing I could do until he took a long hard look at his own attitude and asked himself some important questions. He didn't think that had anything to do with it and had no patience for that line of inquiry. He demanded—lots of demands, our Matt—that I get to the point and look at his swing.

"So I cut to the chase and told him he had internal problems that were manifesting in his golf swing."

I could imagine how well that went over.

"This type of hyper-aggressive personality is actually pretty common, so I keep a big mirror around. I pulled it out of the workshop and asked Matt to take a good look in the mirror and tell me what he saw. He refused, he blustered, he threatened to leave, but instead stormed back to the practice tee and started whacking balls and complaining about his shot and complaining about the lesson. I just let him blow off steam. When he'd had enough and packed up his things, I reminded him to settle up for the lesson at the pro shop. I knew he wasn't really going to leave.

"Matt confronted me. He didn't think he should have to pay since he figured I hadn't given him anything."

I knew that by now I'd have been screaming at this guy.

"So I laid it out for him. I described his own behavior back to him. He'd begun by disturbing my previous lesson with his loud self-complaints and diminishing any positive energy at the practice tee. He'd behaved as if his negative attitude were acceptable and become confrontational when I'd refused to subsidize that belief.

"I also told him I'd be happy to accept the challenge of guiding him to a better place, but that he wasn't ready, as demonstrated by his refusal to tell me what he saw in the mirror. I explained that the reason he complained out loud so everyone could hear was that deep down he was deeply insecure. His damaged ego wanted people to think he was better than his swing revealed and that his time was worth more than anyone else's. I told him it wasn't just his swing he didn't like, but himself. And because he didn't like himself, it was impossible for him to have any compassion for himself or anyone else, never mind play better golf. Because golf required humility and appreciation, and his attitude just didn't fit. That got his attention."

I would think so.

"I told him he needed to leave his familiar zone of conditioned misery. Getting to a healthy place by finding out why he was so unhappy with his game would be uncomfortable but I assured him it would provide him with endless appreciation and enjoyment.

"That, I told him, was my lesson for that day. If he wasn't going to examine himself, and begin at the beginning by fundamentally changing his approach, there was nothing more I could do for him. As you know, Geoff, I don't 'fix problems.' He didn't know what to say. I said that the universe is a big place."

I wondered where he was going with this one!

"It's my opinion that we all need to become aware of how we fit into it. We need to be mindful of our significance—and our insignificance. Balancing behavior between those points is necessary to develop a well-balanced perspective, not only in golf but in life itself.[9]

"I let Matt think about all that for a while. I explained that I had to remain true to myself and my way of teaching, and so could not just give him the quick fix he sought. I pointed out that many golfers had gone through the attitude adjustment I was asking him to undertake—and that they had been pleased with the results. I told him he had a real chance here, because so many golfers never recognize their problem and therefore can do nothing to solve it."

"So what did he do?" I figured the guy had to have been either ready to blow his top or deeply embarrassed at this point.

"First, I think I'll get some dessert—how about you?"

"I thought you weren't hungry."

"Dessert has nothing to do with hunger." He smirked mischievously.

Joe tried to get the attention of our waitress. He caught her eye and she brought over the menu again so we could order some dessert. Joe was silent as he perused the options.

"To his credit, Matt actually took what I said to heart. He actually started to laugh!"

"Really?" That's not how I imagined it playing out.

"Yes. I told him a man named Charles Swindoll said, 'I am convinced that life is 10% what happens to me and 90% how I react to it...we are in charge of our attitudes.' Swindoll's got a lot to say about attitude, Geoff; look him up.

"We all have to deal with things that don't go the way we think they should. Matt and his golf are an example. How we respond is critical. The Buddhists have a way of dealing with conflict that to me is the most effective way to solve a problem."

"Which is?"

"They imagine being shot by an arrow. What's the first thing you'd do if you were shot by an arrow? Would you wonder who shot it or where it came from? Would you notice the smoothness of the shaft or the beauty of the feathers? Would you ask why you had been shot?"

"I'd pull the thing out as fast as I could!"

"Exactly, Geoff," he acknowledged. "You pull it out. That's the most effective way to deal with the arrows coming at us in life. In golf, often when we have problems, it's because we're shooting arrows at ourselves. We begin asking questions about why we got into the situation we're in. We reprimand ourselves for not being smarter or we feel sorry for ourselves. We do anything except pull out the arrow, which is the only right action. If we plan on playing this game for the long term, we must make an effort not to shoot ourselves, and if we do, we need to pull those arrows out immediately."

I'd been shooting some arrows of my own. In fact, I'd been my own worst enemy at times. The waitress returned and Joe ordered a slice of apple pie. My own hunger had abated with the soup and sandwich, but I decided to have something sweet to chase it down, and ordered blueberry pie.

"My role is to give my students what they need, which is not always what they desire. Matt needed to integrate a completely new way of looking at things and at himself, and to see how his attitude fit into change. Arrogance is a sign of weakness," Burlington continued, "loud weakness, acting-out weakness. What makes learning and playing golf more like life than any other sport is that no matter how skilled you become, this game will teach you humility. So often folks misconstrue humility. I believe humility is the true sign of strength, yet somehow our culture equates it with weakness. Arrogance masks itself as strength.

"Swindoll's thoughts on attitude hit home for Matt. I literally watched a look of peace come over his face. He thanked me for the lesson."

Joe's story made me determined not to point fingers elsewhere about what was happening to me. I vowed to myself to look in the mirror every day and make a choice to have a positive attitude. It was time to begin living and teaching with this strategy and attitude as my basis for life.

"How did you know Matt wasn't going to leave when you were at the mirror?"

"I just had a feeling, Geoff. I took that chance and frankly didn't care if Matt left. I couldn't abandon my principles just to keep him happy. I've had students leave before and that's their right. If they're not ready to change and accept responsibility, then we're just wasting our time anyway.

"You see, he really wanted to be helped, but he didn't know what he needed or how to ask for it. Relinquishing control is a big step for a student, especially people like Misty and Matt. Without that release, we would have gotten nowhere. It's not my favorite type of lesson, but one I have to give sometimes. But when someone needs a reality check, it takes a lot out of me, Geoff. I would much rather have helped Matt elevate his swing awareness, but that would have been a waste of time without him first changing the way he perceives things. You know, when you change the way you look at things, the things you look at change."[10]

I knew I would have handled the situation rather differently. I would have either kicked Matt off the tee or pleaded with him to try this or that, hoping something would work.

Our dessert arrived and the waitress refilled our coffee. "One thing that's absolutely critical with students like Misty and Matt is to stay calm. It goes back to what I said about being at peace. If you're secure in who you are and what you're doing, you will not respond in an aggressive or defensive way." I looked at the table. I knew this was something I needed to work on, and I knew he knew it too. "Matt has to own his aggressive behavior, not me. When he thought back on it, he might not have liked what he said or the way he said it. If he thought about my response, he wouldn't have seen a reflection of his tone of voice, but something very different. Maybe he realized that the reality check was truly in his own best interest.

"You must always remember that you're still in a student-teacher relationship even if you agree to disagree. I must admit, I work on this daily. It's still one of my biggest hurdles. It's important to keep in mind that so often, 'the eye sees not itself.' Those lessons are the most challenging! Matt's view of himself didn't coincide with how reasonable compassionate people view him."

"Anything else you can tell me about dealing with this kind of personality, Joe?"

"You have to start by not engaging in their game. You must get them to trust in you and then in themselves, Geoff. They must believe that you care. You have to listen and observe them very closely. They need to feel safe with you, not vulnerable. The coaching is very delicate in purpose but strong in boundaries. I have found I just have to be creative to get them out of their own way, with positive mind-talk and right-brain exercises."

"Tell me how..."

"You must set strict ground rules during the lesson. Don't let them get away with even one statement of disbelief. Never let them cross that barrier with statements like 'I can't do this or that' or 'this is hard.' Make them verbally cancel their negativity. Literally make them say 'cancel' to whatever negativities they throw down. This personality type tries to control; in their minds, that's how they succeed. They don't realize that the formula for success in golf is very different. Letting go is control, but they are conditioned to hold on, as though it were control both in the mind and on the club. To succeed in golf, these folks have to be willing to surrender, and that can be uncomfortable. It places them in unfamiliar territory, feeling very vulnerable.

"Most of the time, I've found that they'll try to get you to teach the way they like to learn. If you fall for that, you're no longer teaching. Never, I repeat, never, let them control the lesson with that brand of success! It must be process, process, process!"

Burlington made sense. I had run into students like this myself and found them very frustrating. I would be dissatisfied with my teaching and the negativity was contagious in both directions. These students didn't improve, and I would be left with a sour taste and an empty feeling when the lesson was over.

Joe continued to emphasize his point. "People with this type of personality are usually your most difficult cases. Remember the cure-is-too-painful story? Their greatest challenge is what is most painful: relinquishing control. Ask them, for just that hour, to adopt an attitude that will serve them better. If they're not willing to do that, I'm afraid you cannot help them, because surrender is paramount for this personality type. You can lead a horse to water...." he trailed off and dug into his pie. Mine was delicious—I had almost finished it while he was speaking.

"Sometimes you find that people like Matt have been emotionally injured in their past. Somehow you need to get them to feel safe with you. For example, if you tell them that following their lesson, they can return to their old ways of perceiving and doing, but just not in golf learning, and not with you, it may help. Their golf identities must be different than their identities in business, for instance. You may be able to get them to relive some of the moments in their past that were real positive times of learning and growth. Or, give them a picture of your past, your own failings, and how changing your attitude was the key to beginning your success. Tell them how you found your way.

"Ultimately, however, they need to realize that these personality traits, although possibly useful in the business world and maybe in golf competition, are real barriers to developing their feel for a golf swing, complicating things and making the process slower and more difficult. Once they make the decision, you need to set them up for success. Give them physical tasks that relate to their current state of awareness."

"What do you mean?" I inquired, polishing off the last bite of my dessert.

"If you were learning to play the violin you would not be asked to attempt a Bach partita the first week, right? It would be unachievable and would just put you off. 'Trying hard' would be your modus operandi. You would never see or hear your authentic musical awareness. Don't get me wrong, I love Bach, but if you were a beginner and you were to try some of his solo pieces, you'd find your fingers jammed together!

"Now Mozart, on the other hand, falls into your fingers like soft butter. I have always believed that Mozart better appreciated the limitations of the fingers and hands on the fingerboard of the average fiddle player and composed accordingly.

"So if you were teaching the violin, you could get your students to listen to the sound as they pluck a string. Feel the vibration, then play an easy scale. Their ears and brains would be getting familiar with the tones, and once they developed a finer sense of hearing, you could help them become aware of their fingers pressing a string to the board, each place for a certain tone. Eventually they could begin using the bow, first feeling it slide across the string at the best angle, with just the right friction for the volume you choose. Then you would move on to a simple tune.

"This type of progression is easy for them to pick up. So it goes in sports. Give your students challenging but achievable tasks and be ready to move forward to the next awareness level. They can develop some beliefs based on that beginning success pattern. You must set them up for success. Let them crawl, and then walk, before running. In golf that would be akin to putting and chipping the ball. Or if you begin with a longer club like I do, do everything in super slow motion.

"You need to support their decision to trust with appropriate tasks. They have to realize that this is not hocus-pocus. Try visualization exercises, or you may need to lighten up the lesson with some humor. To put them into the moment, you need to use your whole arsenal to help them to believe and develop. Getting students like this to believe and then to let go of their bottom-line personality will be your greatest challenge. These golfers have to learn the process to be able to stand on their own two feet when they are alone."

Joe stopped short, seeming to sense it was time to go, though I'd never seen him wear a watch. "This waitress needs to make a living and we've hogged this table long enough." Joe went to his pocket, but this time I was the one waving him off.

As we drove back to the golf center, Joe asked me, "Would you like to see a fun lesson? Don't you think we could use one about now?"

"Of course," I responded eagerly.

"Well, tomorrow morning I have a lesson with a young boy who has had some instruction before. As I understand it, he hasn't progressed the way his parents thought he should. I chose to work with him because it can be very fulfilling to see the transformation in a young person. He won my lesson lottery for his age group."

"I look forward to it, Joe. What time do we begin tomorrow?"

"Nine o'clock sharp."

"Sounds good to me." We parked and shook hands. I walked to my car with my mind filled with new thoughts and perspectives. I wrote down two more nuggets that Joe had nonchalantly voiced during our conversation when he described the strategy to helping Matt get out of his own way. The points were based on perspective, as I'd come to realize practically everything is: If you change the way you look at things, the things you look at change; and, The eye sees not itself. Matt had only seen outward at first.

No wonder Joe was so misunderstood. Throughout my career, I had attended many teaching pro workshops, yet never had I heard such insightful descriptions of how people perceive, learn, and perform. It occurred to me that the only way to get this is through experience, dedication, and being an exceptionally open learner. This stuff was wrought from the dirt, no other way. I felt privileged to receive the knowledge.

Golf was so much more than a game. Sure, it required developing the skill in swinging the club and playing, but it also required the development of humility and appreciation. All life lessons. Just watching how Joe Burlington approached each lesson brought that to life for me. How was I ever going to repay him for this?

332

25

TOMMY: THE KID'S ALRIGHT

I rose early, got down to Lou's Diner in just a few minutes, and ordered my usual. It was a perfect morning. I perused the *Sentinel*, but didn't see much of interest except that the Panthers were playing the Islanders at home again at the end of the week. Maybe Tim and I could catch another game.

I drove over to the golf center and went around the back, where I parked under the pine trees across the road. I could see Joe getting off his fairway tractor. It looked as though he had cut our hitting area, preparing for the day's practice and lessons. Not far away was a youngster making practice swings. It looked as though the boy's mother was watching from the bench behind the hitting area, which was littered with pine cones. It was warm this morning and looked like it was going to be a clear day.

I got to the practice area at the same time as Joe. He made the introductions all around and Tommy's mom told us a little of his golf history. Tommy was a beginner. His dad, whom she described as a fine golfer, thought it would be a good idea to get Tom started with professional lessons. He had taken some at a resort while the family was on vacation. Tommy's mother, Barbara, related that the lessons started out well, but soon became very complicated. Tommy's progress seemed to be slowing down, and after just two days, he was frustrated. He was not normally that way, she told us.

Barbara had gotten into a conversation with a fellow at the resort's practice tee; he knew of Joe and recommended that she not miss the opportunity to have her son work with him, so she entered Tommy in the draw.

Tommy continued swinging during this conversation and didn't hear the story. When Joe called him over, Tommy's ears seemed to prick up like a puppy's and he trotted over. He was slender but seemed sinewy and strong for his age. His dark brown hair complemented his tan. He was polite and respectful; his manner reminded me of Opie from Mayberry RFD. The kid seemed optimistic, too. Joe crouched to face him and asked how he was doing. Tommy had a soft voice, still high-pitched. He was obviously relaxed. Joe demonstrated again that he was able to establish a rapport with whomever he was with in short order.

"Let's get started, Tommy," Joe said. "Show me your swing."

Tommy went over to the practice tee and began by getting his grip in order, then he tried to aim toward the flag nearby. He set up to the ball, arched his back, and stuck out his rear end. A mean look came over his face as he stared down the ball. He took a mighty lash for someone his size and missed the ball completely.

"Try it again," Joe said good-naturedly.

Tommy went through the routine again and this time tipped the ball to the left. His face began to turn a light shade of red. Joe moved in closer to him and spoke very softly. I couldn't hear what he was saying, but Tommy's face relaxed.

Joe then gently took Tommy's left hand and turned it palm up, appearing to draw a pattern with his finger on Tommy's palm and fingers. He seemed to be showing him pressure points on his thumb and thumb pad along with the heal pad of his left hand. Next, Joe closed Tommy's last three fingers around the end of the grip. He then cradled the boy's hand in his own. Somehow it seemed a perfect match, as though Joe's hand was the perfect glove for Tommy's. You could tell Tommy was feeling secure by his new expression.

Next, Burlington took Tommy's right hand and placed it against the left with the life line against his left thumb and his fingers wrapped around the grip with most of his right hand above the grip. Joe was obviously taking great care with how Tommy placed his hands. I noticed this ritual in every lesson. When Joe finished the adjustment, Tommy's hands seemed like they melded together perfectly. The club appeared to be a part of his anatomy. Then Joe took hold of the shaft of the club below the grip and pulled it back and forth, as he looked at Tommy.

Joe asked Tommy to release much of the pressure with which he was holding the club, but not to let it slip—to hold just tight enough that he could move the shaft. Then Joe lifted the club up and down, back and forth, and rotated the shaft so the club faced the sky and then the ground. Everything they did together to change the club face direction matched what their hands did. Tommy's wrists now seemed very flexible.

When Joe felt the pressure was just right, he asked Tommy to move the club in the same manner alone. The boy did. He flexed his wrists and turned his hands in every direction. His flexibility rivaled Gumby's. This new grip gave him the maximum leverage and control over the club and the potential to generate the most speed with the flexibility and rotation. Joe then asked Tommy to put the club down and rest it on his leg and then pick it up and regrip it the way Joe had shown him. Tommy followed his request exactly and looked to Joe for approval. Joe nodded and Tommy rewarded him with a smile, beaming with confidence with his new grip on the club.

Before Joe let him go, he took another wood club from the bag, lined up about five balls, and got on his knees. Joe began swinging, hitting one after the other. Each ball sailed right over the target.

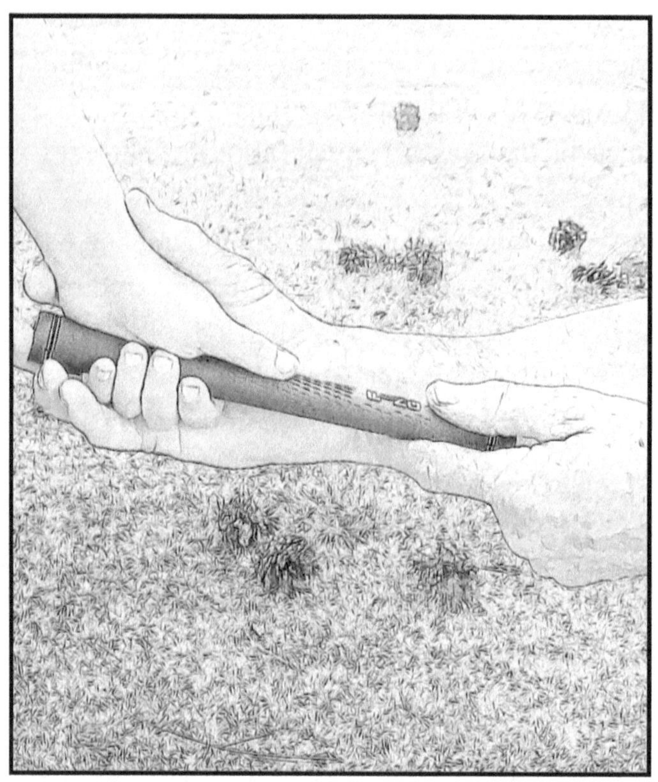

Joe's hand naturally forms a cradle for
Tommy's left-hand grip to be sound.

TC3

Tommy was fascinated. "How did you do that, Mr. Burlington?"

Joe smiled and said, "It's really not hard, Tommy. Now you do it."

Tommy took the club again and adjusted his grip just right, but you could see he was anxious. He began swinging and made good contact with two of the balls as he walked through each shot without stopping to stick out his rear or follow any of the swing rules he had been taught before. After this first set, there was a huge grin on the boy's face.

"Would you like to try again, Tommy?"

"Yeah," he said.

Tommy regripped, being careful about the new placement of his hands. Joe lined up the balls and Tommy went after them.

"This time see if you can copy me," Joe said. Burlington swung his arms very rhythmically and super fluid. Tommy started fast at first, but then Joe reminded him to pay attention to his speed. "Watch closely, Tommy."

Tommy's whole body, with his free swinging limbs, became more blended and more rhythmic. He also looked fluid-like. That beautiful circular path pattern was emerging again like clockwork. Maybe the path can be a function of the flow? Burlington went over to his bag and pulled out his famous foam Pathfinder and had Tommy swing the club through it without touching. After a couple of hits to the foam, Tommy's coordination with club in hand improved. It took only thirty seconds for him to swing the club smoothly through the corridor without touching either side. He seemed to be getting familiar with the boundaries. The circular pattern was again becoming ingrained.

Joe then placed some more balls some five feet away from the props in a line so Tommy could keep swinging while moving forward, hitting one after the other. This time Tommy swung very rhythmically. As he walked through, he struck several of the shots perfectly solid toward the target. I looked back at his mother and there was a startled look on her face. Her boy was hitting golf shots she hadn't thought possible without months of lessons! And it was a swing that was beautifully formed in its shape and speed.

Burlington walked over to Tommy's golf bag and picked out a wedge. Then he stood out in front of him. I thought that was awfully brave with this club in this lad's hands, but Joe seemed to know what he was doing. "Swing the club slow enough for me to catch the ball. Make a full swing but only with enough energy to get the ball to me," he instructed.

Tommy responded naturally. His swing became ever so gentle. Then Joe moved over to Tommy's right, about ten yards in front of him. He coached, "Continue to aim at the flag but make a swing so the ball can fly over here to me." Tommy swing's path took on a shape that still resembled a good approach path. Burlington then moved way to the left and said, "Keep aiming toward the flag, but feel the swing go toward me as it makes contact." The swing went around to the left, and then Joe moved directly in line with the flag. "Now swing so that the ball will fly into my hand here." He raised his hand and Tommy's club struck the ball softly with his wedge into Burlington's outstretched hand.

Joe began moving out about ten paces at a time. Tommy kept swinging and remarkably, the balls were going in the same direction. Joe was about thirty-five yards away from the boy now and he called to him, "Take your five wood, Tommy, and sail the ball over my head." Tommy went for his wood club and quickly set up five balls on the tees and began swinging, paying close attention to where he wanted the balls to fly. One after the other, they went sailing in a parabolic arch right over Burlington's head. It was incredible! How beautiful and simple this lesson was! And all Burlington did was get Tommy out of his own way.

The boy obviously trusted Joe now. Once his hands were well placed and the pressure was right, all Burlington did was get him to feel the speed and direction the club was going by getting him to focus on where he wanted the ball to go. He didn't need to let go of the target; it wasn't an obstacle to Tommy. It was attractive to him. And Joe didn't bog him down with instructions about how to do it. Joe came back in to speak to him. He dropped to one knee and put his arm around Tommy's shoulder while they had a short conversation. The kid turned and faced his mother. He was beaming, and Mrs. Tommy seemed happily flabbergasted. I just shook my head at how simple it had all been. Joe got up and came over to us while Tommy resumed practicing. Joe quietly discussed with Barbara what Tommy could do to continue improving on his own.

"That was neat, wasn't it?"

"Very," Tommy's mother said.

"You see, it doesn't take much to get youngsters like Tommy going in the right direction. Most of the time all they really need is to get their hands well placed on the club and establish sound patterns of speed and path with a target."

Joe looked back at me, winked, and whispered, "He doesn't need another target. Tommy's body sets up just like a cat ready to pounce—he's very athletic—especially without all the pre-swing positions and rules he seemed to be tangled up with before. Tommy's focus needs to be on his rhythm and where he wants the shot to go."

Joe turned to include me, "Geoff, in golf development, all you need to do is ask good questions." He looked back at Tommy. "Can you feel the shape of your swing, Tommy?"

The boy smiled and answered, "Yeah, it feels like going from a merry-go-round to a Ferris wheel." Tommy was relating perfectly to his experience in watching the rides at the carnival.

Joe beamed, "Exactly." He turned back to me. "You can ask questions like how fast do you want to go, is it rhythmic, can you feel the path, and where's the flag? Tommy's athleticism will work out any wrinkles as he practices focusing on those fundamentals. It really is that simple."

I believed him. I had seen with my own eyes the magic that can occur when someone is not distracted—when he returns to being athletic and begins to trust. These principles seem so simple, but somehow in my teaching I had forgotten them. I realized that kids, and everyone for that matter, do not need to have so many things to do. I was also beginning to realize that the problem with adults did not lie just in their athleticism, but also with their ability to trust.

A perfectly balanced swing path and club face ready to rip it.

TC3

Tommy's lesson was another example of the trust versus knowledge conflict, the thread that wove its way through every lesson Joe gave. Then, of course, there was Burlington's physics program. He was a master of asking the best questions when it came to the physics of the swing—that was the second part of his expertise, and exactly why his lessons seemed magical. The questions always dealt with the club: what direction it was traveling, what speed it was going, and when. This lesson really let me see the program work.

Tommy and his mother left on cloud nine. When Barbara tried to arrange another lesson, Joe told her it wouldn't be necessary. He suggested they wait a little while and let Tommy absorb this one and really learn it well.

Burlington and I sat on the bench. I could see he was tired this morning—he looked drained. He'd given a lot of lessons in the past few days.

"That kid had the perfect attitude, didn't he, Geoff? He readily let go of all the concepts he'd been working on and trusted quickly. That was the reason everything went so smoothly. He trusted within minutes and after that, it was just a matter of asking the right physics questions."

I was inwardly proud that I had realized what had happened before Burlington had explained it to me. I was getting it. I was beginning to think in a different way and look with a different perspective. With this new vision, I thought back on the lesson. It *was* possible that path can be a function of flow; that idea was like an epiphany for me.

I asked about the way Joe worked with Tommy's hands on the grip at the beginning. He answered without hesitation. "It's important that Tommy realize the critical nature of his hand position and pressure for his golf swing at this point in his golf development. It's an aspect of swing development that's so overlooked. Hopefully, we've made an indelible impression on him. After all, when hands are well placed and pressure is optimum for speed and awareness, it can make the whole action of the swing sound and simple. When teaching the physics of the club, there is no more telling aspect than how a golfer places his hands. That will determine whether the patterns of the swing and club face are in or out of balance. Pay close attention and notice your students' hands before you get into adjusting any other part of their swing.

"That's the only lesson I have today, so let's call it a day. Tomorrow I'm very busy in the morning. We need to verti-cut the green and trim the hedge first thing. If you come down early, you could practice, but the treat is on the course. I have a playing lesson in the afternoon with a very interesting pupil, Geoff. He has a personality totally different from what we've been discussing, but just as challenging. I would say his personality is complex, so it should be a good lesson to observe," he said as he walked me to my car.

I was exhilarated by all I had observed. These lessons were unpredictable. I'd thought I knew about the complexities of the golf swing, but that was the simple part. The real challenge was getting the students to get out of their ruts and their useless habits, and the challenge was inversely proportionate to their willingness to change their attitude if necessary. What was becoming very clear was that Burlington's methodology was entirely based on the student's trust in him first, and then trusting in themselves and the process. Even before the golf swing comes to issue, there should be an evaluation and adjustment of the student's perception and attitude.

As I was driving, I thought of the Swindoll quote Burlington had mentioned: The beautiful thing is we have a choice each and every moment, each and every day, what attitude we adopt. I thought of Claire, of how she seemed to live by that philosophy. Always ready every day with a positive and realistic attitude. Somehow I wished I could let her know that the way she perceived our relationship and how she lived her life were beginning to make sense to me now. In that moment realized I needed to pen a few lines to her.

I arrived at my place and ran upstairs to my room. I found a pad of paper in the nightstand, sat down on my bed, and began to write. I just let my feelings pour out. But mid-thought I realized I had to go: I'd arranged to meet Tim and Jake.

I put the letter aside on the night table; I would finish it later in the evening. Then I freshened up, and in few minutes was on my way to Pompano. I didn't want to be late for the guys.

26
BACK TO POMPANO

With only a few minutes to get to Pompano to meet Tim and Jake, I stepped on the gas. When I arrived at the first tee they were waiting.

We shook hands and I walked to the back tee with my driver. I teed my ball and took a couple of practice swings. Feeling uncharacteristically calm and confident, I looked down the fairway and lashed my tee shot with a slight draw down the right side. I smiled at Tim and Jake as I walked to their tee a good twenty yards ahead. Jake teed off next. He looked a little nervous and was muttering to himself while he made his practice swings. Tim told him to be quiet and swing. He proceeded to sail the ball down the center of the fairway. Tim was last up. He made his usual Snead waggle and kick start and struck the ball solidly down the middle.

We walked onward, our Sunday bags slung over our shoulders. We reached Jake's ball first. He pulled out a mid-iron and faded it into the right greenside bunker. He shook his head, called himself stupid and slammed his club into the ground. "I do that all the time, Geoff. You think that was bad, now you get to see my sand game." I knew exactly how he felt, but also found myself thinking that his reaction wouldn't help him play better or more enjoyable golf. When we reached Tim's ball, he looked at me and asked, "What do you think?"

"A medium punch eight should do the job." He pulled out his eight iron, took a couple of practice swings, walked in, and just as before, with no hesitation, looked toward the target, waggled, kick started, and swung. He struck the ball crisply and it landed some thirty feet from the hole. Tim was a confident golfer, steady and smooth. He believed in his swing and used it. I felt good that he respected my experience as a golf pro and had relied on my suggestion.

Here were two close friends with fairly equal golf talent, but one seemed to trust and enjoy and the other was cynical about his performance. I noticed that Tim was smiling as he strode to my ball down the right side of the fairway just in the rough. I had a three-quarter pitching wedge, which I punched low under the crosswind blowing from the west, landing it a few feet to the right of the pin. It was gratifying to play the shot I was capable of. Burlington's magic was working. I felt authentic as a teacher and a player.

As we approached the green, Jake took his sand wedge into the bunker, muttering again. I went over to inspect the situation. His ball lay in a footprint. He complained about the lie as he entered the bunker. After a couple of practice swings, he proceeded to skull the wedge shot across the green all the way to the fence bordering the little Pompano airport. He cursed as he walked to his ball. Before Jake even reached his ball, Tim played his putt to within a couple of inches. They didn't play by honors or who was away; they hit when ready. That was fine with me—it made for a fast pace of play. Jake picked up and waved at me to finish since he was done.

We all played the next couple of holes hitting the fairways and greens. No birdies, but easy pars. As we played, Jake kind of went off on his own, appearing disgusted as he walked to his ball, even though he had some good shots. I was a little uncomfortable. I've always found it difficult to play with a too-serious golfer. The other golfers are afraid to even say 'good shot' because someone like Jake would 'correct' them and say it wasn't. But now, I saw my former self in Jake, too. I needed to apologize to a lot of folks for acting this way.

We came to a long par three. Jake landed his tee shot in the front bunker. Tim and I hit the green. As we walked down the path toward the green, Jake asked, "Could you give me some help out of the bunker? I haven't a clue how to get out consistently."

"Sure, Jake." I jumped at the opportunity to help. "Before we begin, I have to have your word that you won't judge the technique or the result before it has been well tested."

"What do you mean?"

"I mean it could take a little time for your mind-body system to coordinate and integrate a different swing pattern. You need to adopt an open, non-judgmental attitude."

"But I'm not judgmental."

"OK, just do me the favor of not drawing any conclusions before you give it a fair trial period."

"OK, OK, I will."

"Are you sure?"

"Yes, just tell me what to do."

At that point I felt like Joe, setting the ground rules for his lessons with students like Jake. "How do you usually get out of the sand?"

"I don't," he said with a smile. "Really. I've had so many lessons that I don't know what to do now. But I've been taught by everyone to put the ball back a little, and aim for a spot a couple of inches behind the ball, then I open the club face and my stance, and swing the club a little out-to-in and try to cut the ball out of the bunker. What do you think?"

"I think you're in for trouble."

"Why?"

"First off, this technique has very little margin for error and too many things to do. If you don't strike the sand just right, you could easily find yourself in a big mess. The shot you're trying for is really best suited for a downhill or buried lie."

"What would you suggest, then?"

"If you have a normal lie, I would suggest you attempt to make a sweeping hook swing to get the ball out." Jake looked at me as though I were crazy. What I'd said contradicted the typical style of the pros. At once I knew how Joe must feel most of the time.

"Could you fill me in a little more?" he asked skeptically.

"You've been attempting to strike the shot with a sharp angle to spin the ball out of the bunker. I favor lobbing it out with a full swing that doesn't require so much precision. Also, I never aim for a spot. My wedge splashes a rather general swath of sand before, beneath, and after the ball naturally. You need to get a feel for the speed, length, and depth of the club passing through the sand. You don't have to be so precise. I would rather use the sand to absorb the club's energy and release the energy of the club with a long shallow splash. Go ahead, try it."

Jake walked down into the bunker. The shot was medium in length and needed to get up in the air to clear the lip. "Go ahead," I encouraged him, "close your stance too, so you can swing in a circular pattern." Jake continued to shake his head, not believing it could work. He made a practice swing. It was still too vertical for the technique. "Pretend you have a driver in your hand. That bunker swing is the closest swing to the driver."

"What?"

"It's the closest swing path and angle to a driver release."

The short game shots, especially the bunker, were an aspect of the game I had never lost. When I was growing up, I had learned to get out of the bunker with a nine iron. I was forced to hit soft shots by adding loft in my release and sweeping the ball out in a lobbing fashion. Finally, Jake gave it a try, exclaiming that he had nothing to lose since he hadn't had any consistency in years. Fear and tension had been his M.O. in the bunker. He closed his stance and took a long swing like a drive and skulled the shot again. "That doesn't work!" he yelled.

I shook my head. "In one swing you're gonna tell me whether it works or not? You're breaking our agreement. Try again. This time ground the club and sweep the sand back in a nice circular pattern."

"But touching the sand is against the rules."

"Not today."

"OK, but I still don't understand."

"Grounding the club will give you a better feel for the depth and texture of the sand. Eventually we'll play by the rules, but for now, just do it." I had raised my voice unintentionally and made a conscious effort to cool it. Golfers like Jake frustrated me, debating when they couldn't achieve even minor success with their own technique.

Then Joe came to mind; this was my lesson, too. Teaching is always learning twice. I reminded myself to be patient so that I could help Jake even though he resisted my strategy. I also knew I needed to be firm. I had to be the leader.

"For the next five minutes you need to let go of what you think you know and just learn as though you were a curious five year old, Jake."

He put his head down and checked himself. "OK, just show me, then."

I got down in the bunker, threw three balls down, and made three driver-type swings with my wedge in slow motion, lifting each ball out with the sand softly onto the putting surface. I turned around and looked at him.

He was smiling. "That's so much motion—I don't know if I can do that."

I returned his smile. "Jake, you have nothing to lose. What you've been doing is not working. Why not try something totally different?" I looked over to Tim, who had a grin on his face and had come over from the other side of the green to watch. After a moment's hesitation, Jake agreed he had nothing to lose in trying something new. I laid out three more balls in a row and asked him to swing without stopping. "Just walk through them and keep swinging."

He surrendered and did as I suggested. He struck the first ball too cleanly and it flew too far onto the back of the green. But the last two floated out like Trevino's butterflies with 'soar' feet. I threw some more balls down to Jake and he made more long swings, sweeping the sand under the ball. Each one rode out of the bunker on a cushion of sand. With this technique Jake was using the sand to his advantage. A grin began to creep over his face as he realized there were alternatives to what he had been taught. He lobbed the balls out with very little spin. The look on his face had changed to curiosity and joy. He was elated. So was I. But I wasn't finished yet. "This time, let go with your right hand after impact."

"Are you kidding?"

"No, try it."

Jake shook his head incredulously but tried it. He swung the club and let go with his right hand, soon remarking, "That one was the smoothest through the sand," as the sand and the ball flew beautifully onto the green. He tried several more shots, releasing his right hand and finishing with only his left hand on the club. His swing and his consistency were uncanny. He lofted the balls with perfect energy for the distance of the shot. "OK, I admit it works, but why would I do that?"

"It can really free up your swing and allow you to purify your hand and wrist action. According to Joe Burlington it could be the future of the golf swing."

As I observed Jake at that moment, I noticed him turn away from me slightly and glance out over the course; he clearly had a bias against Joe. Based on what Tim had intimated, Jake couldn't handle Joe's demand for an attitude adjustment during his lesson. But Jake was soon present again and remarked, "I always believed the sand shot was an explosion. I thought it required brute strength, but I can see your technique requires touch."

"Exactly. It requires light hand pressure and a smooth rhythm. Toss a couple more balls down in the bunker and try to really hook them out and let go."

Jake seemed liberated once he felt free to make his normal swing path and make a swing with a hooking feel in the release through the sand. I left Jake in the bunker to practice while Tim waited patiently for me to finish putting. Jake picked up the balls from the green and followed us to the next tee.

Luckily it was near dark and no one was playing behind us. We all hit good tee shots and then all hit the green. Tim and I headed down the fairway together. Jake was just ahead of us, practicing his hook release with his left hand. When we reached the green, Jake picked his ball up and tossed it into the bunker. As Jake was practicing, Tim and I hit good putts, but didn't make them. Across the green, Jake was making long, slow lob swings, sweeping the sand and balls out of the bunker easily. It was satisfying to witness his success.

Tim turned to me, "I really have confidence in my long game, but my short game is another story. Do you think there's a big difference between the two?"

"It depends on your purpose. To take a line from Joe Burlington, it's all connected, but in your long game, driving for instance, your purpose is usually to create as much energy as you can in the club head to energize the ball accurately. In the short game you're usually trying to take energy off the ball, especially with your wedge shots around these high mounded hard Bermuda greens."

"I don't get it. You can take energy off the ball?"

"In a sense you can."

"Could you show me the technique?"

"Sure. I developed one that's right down Joe's alley. I mean, you'll think it's radical."

"I'm open to it, Geoff; my short game could use it. Most of the time, I hit shots that are rolling to the hole, but when I can't run it there, I'm at the mercy of the greens."

"Tim, really it's simple. Remember the hockey game the other night, when you told me about the similarity between the slap shot and Joe's curl release?"

"Of course, that's his timing release for high energy."

"Right. If high energy is to let the club circle, rotate, and time the curl downward, can you guess what would create lower energy?" Tim looked at me, still puzzled. "Simply do the opposite! Reverse the face."

"What?"

"That's right, reverse the face. Shut it going back, then open it and lay it back going through." Tim looked at me as though I were from outer space.

"You've been hanging around Joe Burlington too long!" he laughed. "That's radical!"

"Here, let me show you." I took Tim over to the other side of the green. We both dropped several balls onto the grass. I took out my sand wedge and showed him the reverse face. "This is limited to fairly short wedge shots, but it works wonderfully when you need to stop the ball. It's especially good in long grass around the green."

The reverse face, shut and delofted back and opening with loft through impact.

GB

"You mean you can spin the ball in long grass, too?"

"Definitely. If you get good at rotating the face in reverse right at impact, you'll stop the ball very well."

"Let me see you do it again." I took my wedge, shut the face going back, and as I neared impact, reversed it open. The ball flew softly onto the green and came to an abrupt stop. "Wow. I'd never have thought of that, Geoff. Let me try."

I retrieved the balls from the green and tossed them to him. "Be sure to close it going back so you can really open it as you strike the ball. It's the action at impact that does the trick." Tim did it beautifully. His ball came to an abrupt stop. "Now try it over here." I took him to the other side of the green where the grass was long. "Pretend the pin is right here. I pointed to a spot only eight feet onto the green. Tim made a mini-swing and reversed the face perfectly. The ball hopped over the long grass and stopped quickly again. Tim smiled broadly. He had just learned a shot he didn't even know existed. I knew it would be very useful on these hard greens when he had a short-sided shot. I was happy to have shown him.

"Geoff, what about short putting? Do you have any tricks there?" he asked with a smirk and a wink. "I suffer a little shake once in a while. I know it's mental, but I haven't been able to overcome it."

"Actually, yes, there is an easy strategy for that and it works most of the time."

"Tell me."

"When you get ready to hit the putt," I explained, "first aim it off line, purposely."

"Really! What does that do?"

"It gets your brain to see the correct path of the ball into the hole."

"Is that it?"

"Well, no. Next look toward the hole as you putt and feel the energy."

"You mean not look at the ball?"

"That's right. Look where you would like the ball to go, not at the ball." I tossed a few balls near the hole and asked Tim to try it.

"This seems so weird. You're morphing into Joe Burlington!"

"Thank you."

Tim was a good student. He tried it and couldn't believe he made almost every putt without looking at the ball. And as he looked toward the hole the energy on the ball was excellent. "I can't believe this, Geoff—my stroke is beginning to feel smooth, like when I was young and my nerves were fresh. I never would have come up with this; I always thought I should concentrate harder with my eye on the ball."

"Yes, I know, and you watch the putter move and you try hard to hit is square and so on." Tim nodded in agreement. "But when your confidence wanes in putting, or anything for that matter, you need to know where to place your concentration so as not to interfere with your potential. The ball and club on a putt became a distraction to you so I just removed the distraction by having you place your attention on the target. Simple, right?"

"I can't argue with that." Tim putted a few more and made almost all of them from three to five feet away. He was amazed at how he could hit the putts solid and square without looking or concentrating on impacting the ball squarely. I was really pleased it worked so well for him, especially because he was the one who introduced me to Joe and made me feel welcome here.

Jake was still swinging away in the bunker. He would walk out and retrieve the balls to try again. Both guys seemed happy. I couldn't believe how good it felt to teach them my technique in a Burlington manner. I felt authentic. When we reached the final tee, and I was busy basking in my success, I hooked it wildly into the left rough. I chuckled to myself. It was the first fairway I'd missed, but I didn't care, and neither did the game of golf. I should still be able to hit the green from there.

Tim and Jake made solid, carefree swings. Their balls landed near each other on the fairway. As we walked I took a left turn and told them I'd meet them on the green. My ball was down a hill, one of the few in South Florida. They couldn't see me from the fairway. I reached my ball and had a blind shot. I was a good 190 yards from the green. The grass was long and I knew I had a flier. I just guessed where the flag was and fired away with a six iron. The ball flew high and arched in a draw pattern onto the green. I assumed it was good by Tim's and Jake's reaction—they clapped as they saw the ball land just a few yards from the hole. I walked back up the hill to join them on their way to the green.

We were satisfied. Jake had his new bunker swing, and Tim had his reverse face spinning the soft wedge shot from grass, as well as the concept of putting while looking at the hole. It was getting pretty dark now, so we finished up and headed to the grill.

The air inside was scented with freshly fried fish and chips, one of my favorites. We found a table in the back of the grill room. Tim and Jake greeted our waitress and in an instant a pitcher of Irish Red was on our table with three frosted mugs. Jake and I ordered the fish and chips. Tim ordered his usual, hot corned beef and cabbage. Jake spoke up as soon as the waitress left. "Well Geoff, I really appreciate the help you gave me today. I had no idea there was such a way to hit a sand shot."

I nodded, "No problem. But I'm concerned about another aspect of your play. We can discuss it sometime."

"No, tell me now. I want to know anything you think would help me with my game."

"Well, Jake, it really doesn't have anything to do with the way you swing the club."

He looked at me curiously. "What does it have to do with?"

"I may be over-stepping my bounds here."

"No, go on. I want to know what you think."

"Well, I am concerned that you're emotionally fragile on the course."

"What do you mean?"

"I mean that you seem totally connected to the good or bad result. That makes you extremely vulnerable to a bad attitude." I paused, wanting to put this in such a way that he would receive it, not reject it. "When you started today, you seemed pissed off. We were kind of walking on eggshells around you, like the other day in the skins game. Nobody is comfortable in that environment. You're robbing your playing partners of their enjoyment and freedom on the course, and you simply don't have that right. Nobody can even give you a compliment for a half-decent shot without you letting them know it wasn't what you wanted or that it wasn't perfect." I kept going. "Actually, I'm a little surprised they haven't abandoned you by now." There, I'd said it. Not politically correct, but correct.

Jake turned a little red and began to rationalize his behavior, just as I would have in the past. "Well, if you hit shots around the green like I do, you'd act that way too."

I paused a minute to think about that. The new authentic me had to admit the truth. "Maybe a week ago, but not anymore. I know exactly how you feel, Jake, and I can tell you from experience you'll never get the most out of your game or your time on the course with that attitude." I could sense that Jake was getting a little irked at me, but I didn't relent. I needed to make the point clear and not retreat. It was his option to accept it or reject it.

I looked at him and continued. "You have a choice about how you respond to your play, good and bad. I guarantee, if you take a look, you'll make the right choice for yourself. You need to disconnect your attitude from your performance."

Tim sat nodding in agreement. He had been waiting a long time for someone to have this talk with Jake, but Jake was so volatile that his friends were afraid to tell him. His behavior was really a form of abuse, and we should never let anyone get away with it.

"Something you could do when you get home is to Google Charles Swindoll and 'attitude.' It's easy to find. Make his ideas your gospel; you'll be amazed at how powerful it will be. It certainly helped me a lot."

Jake took a deep breath. He defensive expression had faded as be began to surrender his tightly clenched old attitude.

I had taken the same chance Joe would have, and it was paying off. I was being true to what I knew was essential for Jake to sustain his move toward better golf and better living. He hadn't thought he needed to change his attitude, only his technique.

Jake blurted out, "OK, I'll do it." We were quiet for a second.

Tim seemed surprised and pleased. He broke the silence. "Teaching seems to come naturally to you, Geoff. I like your creativity and simplicity. For you to get through to this bonehead," he grinned, "that's an accomplishment!"

"Thanks, Tim." Jake was smiling at the truth Tim had just declared. Just like that, things lightened up. Jake had let go of his seriousness. We traded golf stories through the rest of dinner. I had just enjoyed a good day playing, teaching, and now eating and drinking with them, talking golf and life. Jake insisted on paying for our dinner and Tim picked up the beer tab. I tried to contribute, but they would have none of it.

I was exhausted and would need a sound sleep to be ready for my next Burlington lesson. The guys had to go to work the next day. We said our goodbyes and were off. I took the scenic route home. I had the car moving at a snail's pace, taking in the beautiful scene all around, the ocean on my left and the old oaks hovering over the road from both sides. The realization that Joe's magic was working was fulfilling and enriching. I could be at ease when I played, and when I taught.

27
ROBERT:
I HATE MY SWING

I awakened to the sound of the wind howling. Salt air filled the room because I'd left the windows open all night. I shut them, then dressed and headed to Lou's for breakfast.

After breakfast I drove to the golf center. The temperature was crisp; there were a few clouds in the sky and lots of wind. Joe had really piqued my curiosity the day before. I arrived with great anticipation and optimism. I wanted to tell Joe about the short game lessons I'd given on the course yesterday. Answers to many of my questions had sifted into place and the bad mood I had carried to Florida was no more than a distant dream.

Robert arrived early for his lesson. Joe had told me what he knew about Robert. He was a serious golfer and had been a low handicapper most of his life. However, he had fallen on bad times golf-wise. After introductions, Burlington asked Robert how it was going.

"Well, life is OK, but my golf game sucks," he chuckled with resignation. Robert gave us a short history of how he had gotten to this point. "I played college golf and then went into the golf business after college. My dad was an excellent player. We've owned and operated golf courses for forty years. But now that I have time to play great courses, I'm very disappointed in my game. My swing feels loose and weak. That's the most discouraging thing, besides the inconsistency—the weakness. I feel like there's no compression in my swing. Everything collapses. The harder I try, the worse I get!" Robert waited for Burlington to react, but Joe was quiet, practically expressionless. When Burlington nodded, Robert continued his complaints.

"I just don't like the way I swing the club. It's very discouraging. I know I lay the club off, and then have a huge loop to get the path in order to find the ball at all. My swing path is way off and I've tried all kinds of ways to fix it, with no success. In fact, a senior golf pro told me recently that it's just the way it goes when a golfer gets older. What it comes down to is, I hate my swing!" Still no response from Joe.

Robert pointedly asked Joe if he thought he could help. There was a long pause. Now that I was familiar with Joe's response time, I didn't get antsy, but I could tell Robert was a little uncomfortable. A few more seconds ticked by before Burlington asked, "Do you believe him, Robert?"

"Believe who?"

"The pro who told you that's just the way it is."

"I don't know. After these past few rounds, I think I'm beginning to."

"Well, then let me see you make a few swings," Burlington said.

Robert obliged and, with a six iron, began hitting shots. The man was obviously athletic, but his swing path was complex. The club started back very straight for a long time, circled around late, and then looped incredibly. As he changed directions, he swooned downward to correct the imbalance. It seemed almost a magic trick the way Robert was able to find the ball and flight it toward the target. He hit a few good shots, but before long, he got frustrated. His shots began to fade and were simply not solid, just as he had told us. Although Robert was frustrated, he seemed satisfied that he had shown Joe exactly what he was talking about.

"Do you see what I mean?" Robert asked, his face twisted. "Do you think you can help me?"

Burlington looked at him and nodded. "I believe so, if you're willing. But the first part of the solution is for you to begin liking your swing. I mean the way you feel physically and emotionally. Even before you hit the ball."

"What?"

"You have a very negative image and feeling about your swing, right?"

"Yeah…"

"And you have identified what you don't like about it?"

"Yes," Robert responded.

"So we need to see why you haven't made the changes. That's why you're here, right? What we need to do first is fundamentally change the image you have of your swing."

"What do we change it to?"

"We change it to something you like, something physically and emotionally appealing to you. When you can trust it, hitting good shots will likely generate a good feeling about your swing. So let's address the feeling you dislike the most. I bet you can tell me which it is."

"Yeah, I want to get rid of the looseness and weakness, and the path too."

"And what is strong, from your perspective?" Joe asked.

Robert paused. Then, "I really don't know." All he seemed to know was that he didn't like what he had.

Burlington pressed him. "If you know what you don't like, then you must have an idea about what you do like or would like."

Robert thought about it for a moment. "I think I need to get my swing to feel as though it tightens up as I swing."

"You mean like a coil?"

"Yes, that's it! I want my backswing to feel like a spring tightening. Like this!" Robert torqued his shoulders and made a swing back.

Joe asked, "Tell me, if your swing felt tight, do you think it would be powerful?"

"Yes."

"Robert, your problem isn't typical. Most folks we see need to loosen up, but you and your swing are a totally different animal." Robert nodded in agreement. "If you felt wound up, do you think that would be better for you psychologically?"

"Yes, absolutely."

"There's one very important thing to do, though, if you want to get this feeling and still have awareness for the club face."

Robert was leaning toward Joe as though he was going to extract the words by force, like a dentist, but Joe didn't seem to mind the proximity. He instructed him, "Take the handle with your left hand and swing it behind you like this." He demonstrated. "That way, you'll tie the backswing pretty tight, which will pull the torso tight, which is the opposite of loose and wobbly. But, more importantly, you will still have club face awareness when you focus on swinging behind you in this manner. And the club face pattern will be fundamentally sound. However, you must do it with your lead hand. Only then will you have club face balance."

I thought about the handle arc from previous lessons; this seemed to be the same thing. Robert looked a little perplexed, so Burlington explained further. "I don't tell people too often what they don't want, but in your case, I need to make an exception. Never try to get the feeling by turning your shoulders independent of swinging the club behind you with your lead hand. Let me give you a little hint about building the simplest fundamental backswing path. The curvature of the swing always occurs when your hands are below your waist and the vertical action always occurs behind you. And one other thing: When it comes to power in the golf shot, it really is a function of the sequential action during the downswing, not the backswing. But I will leave it at that for now. To get you on solid psychological ground we will get rid of your loose feeling of weakness first."

Robert began to swing the handle of the club behind him. It was easy to see the plane and path matching and balancing his physique and the design of the club perfectly. Of course, this was slow motion. The loop and swoon dissolved instantly, too. I wondered if things would change back when Robert picked up speed. Robert looked at Joe and asked, "So, it's like this, but won't I get it too flat?"

Joe shook his head. "Everybody thinks that. But actually it can create exactly the opposite—the more you swing the club behind you early on an arc, the better chance it has to go up vertically behind you later, which would not be flat. And the club will not be laid off—exactly the opposite of what you thought, right?"

The handle getting behind on the backswing.

GB

"Yep."

"Your club was actually low and laid off precisely because you swung the club in too straight a line going back for too long. You thought that swinging in a longer, straighter 'extension,' as they say, would make your swing more upright but the opposite occurred. The club had to go around at some point, right? When the swing path curves around too late, often the weight and momentum of the club flatten the swing, shut the face, and lay off the shaft. And usually this happens for a golfer who has been taught to turn his shoulders as a dominant swing thought on the backswing."

Joe's instruction demonstrated the depth of knowledge. I, like Robert, had thought the opposite would occur. Typically, the way golfers have been trained to think about the golf swing is unhealthy. We really don't know the causes and effects. We have oversimplified the swing and thought that if a golfer swings straighter back, his swing should be upright. Wrong!

Robert's club had to be tremendously rerouted because of it. Joe continued, "I really don't want to continue explaining in this way, Robert, because it won't serve you. I just want you to be able to drop the notion that swinging in a straight line is good for your swing path. The straight line is minimal in a sound orbit, but you have really over-exaggerated it under the false impression that it would have a positive effect on the plane and path of your swing."

Robert still appeared to doubt this; it's hard to give up beliefs that have been embedded for years. Joe saw this, looked Robert straight in the eye, and said, "You know, your best effort got you to this point, Robert. So if I were you, I would begin changing the way I look at, think, and speak about my swing." Joe somehow said all this in utter seriousness, yet with a touch of a grin on his face.

Joe had again taken the puzzle out of a golfer's swing. The way Robert got there seemed paradoxical—until Burlington had explained it. I never thought swinging in a straight line would ultimately make a swing flat—I thought it would surely be vertical. But it could turn into what Robert had as likely as it could be too vertical. Although it seemed the former, laid off and flat was more likely.

Robert was now nodding in agreement with Burlington, finally hooked. Robert began to make more swings. I was glad to see that the complex route of his path seemed permanently dissolved in just a few minutes. It had morphed into a classic swing: a simple circular motion and then, almost without noticing, he would shift downward and forward to support the release of the club head energy into the ball. It was a perfectly synchronized action with little physical or mental effort. Robert practically cracked up at how simple it was once Joe had clarified the swing path principle.

Burlington's skill as a coach shone. Each lesson was different and yet every student ended up in a similar place: more aware of the club's action. In every lesson a wayward golfer grew into feeling secure in the environment Burlington created for them. The atmosphere was friendly, yet there was genuine awareness building all the time. Burlington would challenge them without intimidating them. He simply removed the blocks that we all seem to construct unknowingly, and then when the path of awareness is laid out, it's easy to see what to do. I needed to learn how to build this type of environment with my own students. But I didn't yet know how. With Joe Burlington, it just seemed to happen as a matter of course.

Robert was exclaiming his excitement about hitting shots he hadn't hit in years. "I feel like now I can synchronize my shift into the impact, too!" Robert was grinning from ear to ear when

Burlington asked for a time check. I wondered why it mattered this time. Robert looked at his watch. "We've been going about a half hour; do you have to go?"

"No, I was just thinking, you've been here about thirty minutes. Do you think you just received something you didn't have before, or did you just discover something good you've always had, but that's been buried by some false concepts that provided interference rather than awareness?" He smiled. "You see, Robert, if you didn't already have it, I couldn't have put it into you in thirty minutes."

Robert absorbed this. "Yeah, I guess I must have had it. I just didn't know how to tap into it."

"Right," Joe smiled, "you've got it, it's all yours, and it's always available because it comes from within you. Everyone has it! My job is to simply wake you up and lead you to discover your own potential. Now, show me your backswing."

Robert swung the club in a perfect orbit behind him. The club face was slightly open and now the shaft crossed the line. "Good," said Burlington. "Now show me your downswing." Robert shifted downward and forward naturally and the club followed perfectly into the slot. He delivered the club through the impact zone with virtually no resistance. "Great," said Joe. "You're on your way."

Joe was a master at handling different folks and their swing idiosyncrasies. When Robert's lesson ended, Joe filled me in on what was next, but I wanted to know what he considered to be the best path pattern—how the club head travels from beginning to end. "What is the best pattern a golfer can swing, Joe?"

He didn't hesitate. "The club takes on an orbit from behind the ball. If a golfer has well-placed hands and is postured athletically for their particular build, the club will take a course that goes back, around, and up. And it can be completely controlled by the lead hand and arm. That's my preference. It's the simplest pattern that's effective and repeatable. When done this way it's virtually impossible to see the curve in the swing. The average golfer misconstrues this as a straight back pattern, but in reality it's only straight for a short time. If you have to build a swing from the backswing, then suffice to say, back, around, and up. Often golfers will say they just swing it straight back, but again, that's what they may perceive, but we know the club is behind them and in the air."

Feeling versus physics. His philosophy was crystal clear, but I still wanted to see it. "Could you show me?"

As you know, I'm not a fan of developing a swing this way, but I guess you should know for yourself." He stood up to show me the sections of the differing directions the hands travel during the backswing.

"Thanks, Joe. I really needed to see it to understand."

"We've got one more lesson, Geoff, then I have some other things to do. My next student is a good player. I've worked with him little by little for a long time. He should have been here by now. Let's go for a walk with Otter; it shouldn't be long till Bryan arrives.

When we finished walking the dog, Bryan had arrived. Joe introduced me but Bryan wasn't listening, he was apologizing for being late. He had taken I-95 and there had been an accident, trapping him in traffic. Bryan also wanted to videotape the lesson, so he was setting up the camera and all.

Burlington just nodded and motioned for him to go ahead. While Bryan was getting organized, Joe began with a casual question. "What's been happening, Bry?"

The lead hand, arm, and club swing path
sequence of direction: 1, back; 2, around;
and 3, up.

GB

"Oh, I've been playing fairly well, Joe, but I have a few
questions that've been bugging me. I'm hoping you can help clear
them up." He went straight to the heart of the matter. "You know
that for years now I've been following your program of flow, path,
and timing."

"Yes," Burlington nodded.

"But my confusion lies in the fact that when I feel I really have
it, it doesn't last, at least not long enough. Could you tell me why,
if I follow the program, I can't always retain what I've learned or
stay on the same level?"

Joe considered the question and after his usual pause, responded. "Bry, as frustrating as this may seem, there is a principle that you must learn to accept."

Bry looked intrigued.

Joe continued. "It's a principle of nature, and golf is no exception. There is impermanence in all things."

"But what can I do about it?" Bryan asked respectfully with a hint of impatience.

"You can do nothing about the principle, but if you think about it, you have been taught to respond in kind to the dynamics of golf and life at any particular moment. You see, the program you've learned takes this principle into consideration. The program only gives you a strategy." Joe continued. "Every moment in our lives is flux."

"But Joe, with all due respect, I felt a couple of weeks ago that I had it!" Bryan proclaimed. "I was so sure about it."

"I'm sorry, Bryan; you never own awareness, it's only on loan to you. We all only pass through the awareness balance, although at times we feel as though we own it. Every aspect of your golf game is a discovery process and continues as long as you work on your swing action and play the game. Learn this principle and you will surely reduce your frustration. You have learned to balance out your swing action through the flow, path, and timing cycle. It deals first with the club and then with your feel. It is imperative that you practice with change in mind. Expect change as the only 'always' you can count on. In fact, embrace it. That's the attitude that will allow you to enjoy the journey more and continue to grow."

Then Joe suggested that Bryan hit a few shots, just to see where he was. Bryan pulled out a mid-iron and began swinging. He had a long, flowing swing and made beautiful contact, which had high energy on the impact. The ball flew very straight, too.

He continued to hit a few shots, all very consistent and pretty close to the same results. "Seems to be in good balance today, Bry," Joe told him.

"Yes, it feels pretty good, but I have a question."

"Shoot."

"I've been fiddling around with the idea of feeling connected. I mean, my swing feels firmer, and I feel like I have more control." Joe just nodded. "Anyway, sometimes when I really go for this feeling, I feel a little too mechanical and stiff with my body and the swing. What do you think?"

"I think you should feel whatever you feel. Feel will give you more control. Remember, you're just sensing. It's not fundamental. In fact, it will change day to day."

Bryan rephrased his query. "Well, let me put it this way, Joe. Would you teach someone to feel that in their swing?"

Joe looked surprised and a little dismayed. He replied adamantly. "I really don't teach anyone by my feel. They simply learn to feel based on the accurate physics of their club's action. You're describing your feel for the path or arc through which your hands travel. Being a lanky, flexible supple swinger, 'connected' feels good to you. That's fine. That description is foreign to me, although I understand it. You see, most of the folks I work with have too much tension in their bodies. They're not like you," Burlington said with a wink. "In fact, they would, in most cases, need to feel disconnected—to steal your phrase—to improve their flow and get rid of the physical tightness. However, if being on the prescribed hand arc gives you this feeling, that's fine. Remember, work on the club's action and then describe the feeling."

Again, Joe's program had answered another problem so often associated with golf teaching. There is no way to teach an individual's perception. Rather, Burlington describes the physics and lets his students freely describe what it feels like to them. "The answer to your inconsistency is to balance out your program. At times, you need to work on flow, other times path, and still others on timing. You can't develop a consistent action without balance in your practice. So no one is always going to play the same. The only things you can count on are being ready, accepting and embracing change, and learning to enjoy discovery every day."

"I guess you're right, Joe, but it's so frustrating that things are always changing."

"Then you really need to look at that attitude—that's what needs work, not your swing. There's no fundamental to the way a golfer swings except for his club action. Go to a tour event and watch the swings of the best golfers in the world. Notice how their bodies move during the swing. There is just no way to model them. They're all different. If you try to model them, you'll become confused. In fact, you'll discover their bodies achieve similar results differently. The only close similarity in all these swings is the club's action near the impact zone. Everything else is up for grabs."

"But what about your program?"

"Yes, my program. It says nothing about those things. The only principle in my program is the dynamic action of the club. When you develop a pattern of rhythm, and then a pattern of path and ultimately a pattern of timing, then voila! You have a swing. That's how you arrive with a sound swing."

"But Joe, your swing looks like a classic swing. I like it."

"Thanks, Bry, but I didn't arrive at this point by modeling different body parts and positions on other classic swings. I arrived at it by deftly developing those club patterns. It's a swing, a reliable swing, and my mind knows it." He added that last nugget with perfect timing and effect. Bryan understood. He shook his head and smiled. Always stick to the pattern of the club and accept the flux in golf—and life too.

Bryan shifted gears and asked Joe another question regarding the path pattern and the effect of working solely with the hands. "Joe, you've taught me to pay close attention to my hands for feedback about my swing; can the hand focus get me into trouble like the focus on the shoulders turning can shut the face and flatten the swing too much for some players?"

"Absolutely. If you're not aware of the pattern the hands travel throughout the swing, and you focus on them, you can often create a swing arc that gets very narrow and a club face that's very open. That, in turn, could cause you to lose the natural sequence that occurs from the arc and building momentum in your swing. Even the best focus can send your swing out of balance if you're not aware of the patterns."

"Can you show me what you mean, Joe?"

Without hesitation Burlington pulled a Pathfinder from his bag and placed it on the ground. He bent it into a pattern in which the length was like a virtual wall boundary for the inside path. Then he turned the back curve like an L in the air about five inches above the ground, similar to the configuration he had made for Wally.

"Place your club at the front of the foam and aim according to its direction. Now swing the club under the foam going back in your typical circular pattern and over it toward the impact, without touching the foam," Burlington instructed.

Bryan did just as Joe said. "Wow! That feels wider than I've been swinging, and narrower on the downswing."

"Exactly! You have a great arc for building momentum going back. And then what did you feel going down over the foam?"

"I felt a pretty good shift in my feet and legs to get over it going down."

"That's what I like to hear, Bry; now you're more aware of the club and you're feeling how it influences your whole body. It naturally created a lot of action throughout your body, especially, as you say, in your feet and legs. Now you can modify the degree of it if you wish, but that's essentially the best way I know to get the best arc and angle to strike the ball with high energy toward the target."

"What about the curl? Can that move ever cause a problem?"

"As I just described, Bry, any singular focus could potentially throw off the balance of the whole."

"Even the curl? How so?"

"Well, if you concentrate on the curl too much it could reduce the angle of the club too much as it approaches impact, or vice versa: if you work on angle too much it can reduce the curl. They need to be balanced and worked on in a balanced way."

I was fascinated by this method of creating a balanced swing action. In the past, I would have been all over Bryan to focus on his shoulder turn, his hips, and then his feet and legs, and by the time we finished he probably wouldn't have been able to make contact. I realized this was the power of Joe Burlington's philosophy: If the club is OK, the swing is OK. He didn't have to go into all the effects of sound club action; the whole body's action was the effect. After Burlington and Bryan reviewed the lesson, Bryan went to his wallet. I gave them a little space. As I walked a few yards away, I felt positive energy in my stomach. Dammit, I was getting it! I shook my fist in triumph.

As Bryan hit a few more shots, he told me that he'd gotten a deeper insight into the power of the program and felt he was no longer missing out on the total picture of the path and how to create it.

As Joe turned to go, I fell into step with him. "Geoff, I need to help Bob finish repacking and sealing the lift cylinders on the loader. He'll be here shortly. Feel free to practice!" He strode to his workshop.

I decided to take a stroll around the property to contemplate all I had observed and what was going on in my head. As I turned, I was surprised to see Otter come trotting after me. I guess I'd been adopted. I thought about the day and how pleased I was to be watching Joe's knowledge at work. I also felt good that I was beginning to anticipate how Joe might respond to certain questions. I no longer felt like a complete novice.

After our walk, I left Otter at the pro shop and headed back to the house before dark. I remembered I had leftovers in the fridge and heated them up for supper. I sat down in an easy chair in front of the picture window looking out over the turquoise ocean lightly splashing on the shore. I'd found a worn book by Lee Wulff on fly fishing for Atlantic salmon in Newfoundland. What a sportsman! But a few chapters in, I fell pleasantly asleep.

28

WOO: CAN HE TRUST THE TWIRL?

I'd gotten up early again. This was to be my last day with Joe and I needed to take the time this morning to find him a gift. I took my usual walk down to Lou's to have breakfast. I had been filling Lou in about Joe's lessons since I arrived. I thought it was curious that he had the impression that Joe played golf only as a hobby.

I told Lou of my problem: Joe wouldn't take money, so I needed to find him a gift. Luckily, Lou knew exactly where to go. "Go around the corner just north of Commercial on Federal Highway. There's a fly shop there on the east side of the road. See Dave. He'll have the perfect gift."

I followed Lou's directions and was there in a few minutes. The guy inside was just getting ready to open when I arrived. He waved at me to hang on while he retrieved the key to unlock the door.

"Good morning! Lou sent me down—he told me you could fix me up."

"What do you need?"

"I need a gift for a friend."

"Fly fisherman?"

"Yes, a damn good one."

"Is he from around here?"

"Yes, it's Joe Burlington, the golf pro."

A smile lit up Dave's face. "I know him, and I know exactly what he'd like."

By this time I was accustomed to the fact that practically everyone I met knew Joe in some way or another. "Great!"

"How much do you want to spend?"

"Whatever," I replied.

"Well, I have a very special bonefish rod in the back. It would make a great gift. It even comes with a cedar case." Dave went back and returned with the rod in hand. He began to lift it up and pull it down as if he were casting. "This has really nice action. Joe will love it."

"I'll take it." Dave rang it up and I was off.

I arrived at the golf center in the early afternoon as instructed. Burlington was giving one swing lesson and then a playing lesson after lunch. I checked in at the pro shop and found out he had another maintenance problem besides the work he'd planned to do in the morning. No matter how much Joe seemed to get ahead of the problems at the golf center, there was always some emergency to take care of. He seemed to take it all in stride, though, just accepting it and moving forward on his journey with such grace. I knew I wouldn't be able to respond the same way.

As I peered toward the barn, I could see him walking back and forth from inside the gate to outside near the loader. Bob was there, too. Maybe they hadn't finished the seals from yesterday. I decided to hang out near the pro shop until his lesson arrived. I bought a bucket of balls to warm up before we went out on the course and went over to the practice tee.

I began to hit shots, just feeling the rhythm and direction of my swing, without getting bogged down in the old intricacies I used to employ to get ready. I just felt my swing instead of burying it with concepts. It felt fluid. And I felt like a carefree kid. I didn't know if I would be playing during Joe's lesson on the course, but I wanted to be ready if called upon. I finished the bucket and decided to walk down to the barn. I found Joe and Bob sitting down at their table sipping cold water. They both looked satisfied, as though they had finished a job well done.

Joe introduced Bob and me and then glanced at the clock. "Eddie better get here soon or he'll miss his lesson. We're real tight for time today." He was remembering his playing lesson for the afternoon. Joe and I left Bob in the shop and went around the corner, where he would be conducting the lesson.

Joe looked out toward the main tee. He spied his student coming toward us. Joe looked at my watch and said, "Right on time; you'll love this guy." His nickname is Eddie Woo. He's a commercial pilot, flies for American Airlines. He's peculiar, but a real good guy. He's the type of person who has everything in order. Disorder makes him feel insecure. I imagine that if you went into his closet, all his clothes would be color coded," he laughed. "A great trait for a pilot, but very challenging for developing a golf swing.

"It seems his playing partners have gotten into this interesting habit: His name changes according to how well he's playing. A few months ago he was Ed Woods, playing out of his mind, but recently he has dropped two letters, to Eddie Woo. He had heard that I would be teaching this week and called me just yesterday morning to ask if he could get in a few minutes. He wants to get something straight about his contact. I figured it would be useful for you to see, because his problem is control—and not just control of his golf swing either. He only feels secure when he's in control. He deals in absolutes. He needs to know everything. You know what trouble that can cause when you're trying to develop a golf swing. So here we are again with trust."

Woo approached. "Lama!" he called out. Joe introduced me. Woo shook my hand and went right to his bag. He obviously was not one for small talk. He looked at Joe and said, "I know you don't have much time, and believe it or not I'm close now. I just need to know: How do I strike it square all the time?"

Joe looked back at me and winked. The impermanence principle rose instantly to my mind. I smiled back. We were on the same wavelength now.

Woo demanded, "I need a technique, Lama."

"I have given you one, Woo."

"No Lama, I know you are holding something back. There has got to be a way to hit it square all the time!"

Joe shook his head and chuckled. "Have you worked on the curl?"

"Yes, I love the curl, but what happens after that?"

"In your case, Woo, I would keep rotating."

"Rotating what?"

"Your left hand, wrist, and forearm."

"That seems so out of control."

Joe probed further. "Have you done the 'let go' exercise?"

"Yes, a little. Lama, you are skirting the issue. You hit it square all the time; I know you're doing something I can't figure out." Woo's rapid statements were almost comical. I wondered how Joe would help this guy. I knew that what he was asking for was virtually impossible, but Joe responded with ease.

"Woo, none of us hit it square all of the time. You want absolutes, and there are no absolutes. The golf swing is like life, especially at impact. Everything is an approximation. It's quantum, Woo—the uncertainty principle." As a pilot, Woo knew all about Heisenberg. "You can set up the conditions for striking the ball squarely more often, but there are no absolutes. Until you accept that, I'm afraid you will never end your search for the proper technique. For you to strike it more squarely, you simply need to set up the dynamic environment for release, through our flow and path constants." Burlington always returned to that principle. "Remember how you got consistent in the first place."

Woo shook his head in reluctant semi-agreement.

Joe walked in closer to Woo and said, "I know your problem."

"What are you waiting for? Tell me," Woo demanded like a kid about to get his way.

"Woo, I've given you several keys to balance your swing, right?" Woo gave one quick nod. "The problem is you constantly look in the wrong place for your keys. The answer to your problem lies in the dynamics of your swing, not the various positions you superimpose on it. You've reminded me of a story the real Dalai Lama tells. Let's say you arrive home from a long trip. You've been to ten cities in three days and you're tired. You pull into your garage, get out of your car, and head into the kitchen. But you realize you forgot to get the mail. You turn around, keys in hand, and head to the mailbox. It's stuffed. You slide the key ring around your pinky so you can pull out the wad of mail with both hands. You pull everything out then head back into the house. As you open the door from the garage and step into your kitchen with your hands full, your keys slip from your pinky down into a plant pot. You sort the mail and unpack. When you're finished, you take a nap.

"You awaken still groggy from jet lag, but now you're hungry. You need to go out and get something to eat. You head to the kitchen to get your keys. They are nowhere to be found. The last time you remember having them was when you put them on your pinky at the mailbox. So you search around the mailbox. You look through the flowerbed and run your fingers through the grass. You really look hard but still can't find them. You give up and get your spares.

"The moral to the story? No matter how thoroughly you search outside by the mailbox, you are never gonna find your keys there because they're inside in the plant pot! You must look *inside* to find them." Joe had made it clear earlier in the week that awareness is always an inside job.

Woo looked at Joe with half a smile. He shook his head and chuckled with comprehension. Just like the trout fisherman: You can't catch fish where they're not.

Joe continued. "In my opinion, the answer to your problem is to learn to look in a place that has the possibility of balancing out your swing. It's in the motion, the pace, the timing, the dynamics. And there are no guarantees. Woo, you've been looking in the wrong place for your swing keys!" Joe said with a smile.

"Woo," he continued, "I have described the action before and after impact."

"You mean the curl and twirl." Woo had framed Joe's release of the club head as a spiraling, twirling, whirling action.

Joe smiled. "Yes."

"I can feel and see the before and the after, but what about the middle, the impact?"

"Well, in my opinion, you have to let the middle go. Don't concentrate on the impact, just the before and after; let the angels beat their wings in your favor for the middle. Let the impact go, mentally. I guarantee something good will happen if you do."

I could tell Woo had a hard time accepting Joe's dynamic impact philosophy. At no time during his swing did he want to lose control, or at least his impression of control. He wanted a concrete method that described every muscle and joint action to get the impact. But by now I knew that wasn't going to get him anywhere.

"You mean as the club face approaches the ball, you don't aim it into the ball for a square impact?" he asked

"No, not at all. The club head just passes through square. "If you have the club's two reference points, the before and the after, and you don't interfere, square is the result of those references."

"That's a lot of action. It feels like I have no control when my club spins like that." Woo shook his head, obviously having a difficult time getting comfortable with the concept of dynamism, with the idea that square was the result of fluid action. He wanted to position the club and his body step by step, as though the release was a solid structure.

"Trust me," Joe said. "Solid impact comes from a fluid swing."

Woo with his key before and after impact.

EW2

Woo, like many golfers, thought he had to control the club with a keen eye on the ball and pressure in the hands to make sure he struck it square. He thought he had to impact the ball with tension and pressure to secure squareness. To Joe, control was dynamic: action, lightness, rotation, letting go, energy. Those were the keys.

"Give it a try Woo; forget about being conscious of making square contact and see if you can picture the before and after. Let the club rotate like crazy with this reference before and this one after."

By his practice swings, I could tell Woo was adept at the curl trigger before impact; his problem seemed to be after that. "Lighten your hand pressure so you have a chance," Joe told him.

Woo had continued to clench the club tight for control. "I can't lighten my pressure—how will I control the club?"

Joe seemed to be getting a little impatient. He took Eddie aside and had him make several swings through a Pathfinder so he could concentrate totally on the spiraling action of the club head. They returned and Joe set up several balls. "Just lighten it up and let it go, will you?"

"OK, here goes, but..." Woo made a swing. The club dug deep into the ground before contact. Disgust was instantly pasted on Woo's face.

Joe didn't give Eddie an opening to criticize the fat shot before he interjected, "Good, you did it, just not in balance." Woo had rotated the club like crazy. "Give it another shot." Woo made another swing. It was thin. He had rotated the club again without an acceptable result. "Good," Joe said again. I could see that Woo thought Joe was off base with his compliments. But I noticed Joe never even looked at the ball flight. He focused on Woo's hand action near impact, and it *was* action.

Next, Joe lined up several balls so Woo could continue with no time between swings. I knew the strategy: Don't give him time to doubt, question, or think, only to concentrate on the purpose. Joe was a master at shutting down judgments.

This time Woo curved the ball well to the left. "Good," Joe complimented again. Woo appeared confused, but Joe didn't care about the results, only the action. Woo still hadn't hit one shot solid toward his target, but he kept making swings. Joe encouraged him. "Curl it to the end. Let go with your right hand, finish in the boot." Woo smiled; he knew what Joe was talking about, and complied.

Joe's enthusiasm was infectious, and Woo was no longer trying to perform with a result in mind. He was into the process, feeling his new left-hand, wrist, and forearm action.

Curling to the end with the let-go exercise.

EW2

And then *wham*—a screamer. The ball took off like a rocket, and square as a bear. Woo looked at Joe in disbelief. "I hardly swung! I twirled fast, but I didn't swing fast." Joe smiled at Woo, knowing he was just beginning to scratch the surface of an effortless, powerful release.

Joe next positioned a line of balls ten feet long. Eddie kept whirling the release and the balls flew consistently straight and far. "It's not how hard I swing, it's the twirl!"

"Whatever you say, Woo."

Woo stood there shaking his head. Joe had let him find his way and now he was describing accurately how to strike the ball square and solid. Joe admired the strength and balance of the swing and the ball's flight, then eased back toward me and whispered with an Irish accent, "Isn't she lovely."

That was the strength of his method. And I knew his students could feel his strength and conviction when he taught—it helped them morph into their best authentic selves.

Woo grinned as he let himself go. His release was approaching that of a tour player. He had begun to accept the truth of approximation. He kept practicing, smiling and shaking his head each time he hit the ball. Joe wandered over to pat Otter, who had also witnessed the lesson but without a surprised look on his face. Woo asked me, "How does he do it? He gets me going every time. I need to stick with this; I need to commit to my keys. This is exactly what I needed."

Woo went over and handed Joe a Benji. Joe smiled and said, "Go partner up with Bill, Mr. Woods. You two should be able to take on John and Kate now."

The lesson was one of the best I'd witnessed—and all in about fifteen minutes. Eddie was a skeptic, but Joe didn't give his doubts a chance. He was like a Gatling gun with his instruction. Once he got Woo going, the rapid-fire positive remarks reinforced everything. As Woo was leaving us on his incredible high. Joe, like Columbo, added one more nugget. "Someday, Woo, when we have more time, we will reverse the engines at impact, like one of your landings."

"How so?"

"I will teach you to see yourself from every angle, every point of view—God's view." Woo just shook his head, smiling, and seemed satisfied with today's dose. He waved Joe off good naturedly. I was curious about that comment, but Joe just looked at me with a wink and a smile and said, "Lucky again. Now let's get going."

29

JOHN: THE POWER OF VISUALIZATION

I threw my clubs into the back of the truck, climbed in, and we were off. As we drove north on the turnpike, Joe told me about his next student. "The man I'm going to be working with, John, is a real good-hearted person—very compassionate and non-judgmental—but his confidence is very shaky. He's been asking me to play a round with him for the longest time. His difficulty is taking his best swing and play to the course. I hope you can get something out of this experience, Geoff."

It was a fifteen-minute drive to the course. We parked in the back near the practice range. Joe was a classic trunk slammer—he seemed to have an aversion to locker rooms and clubhouses. We changed our shoes on the tailgate of his truck.

Burlington's friend John was warming up on the practice tee a few yards away. He noticed us and waved for us to put our clubs on the golf cart parked behind him. As I watched John at the end of his warm up, he was striping it directly to his target with a driver. Joe asked me to wait while he greeted John. I realized Joe wasn't going to warm up. They spoke for a few seconds and then approached; Joe introduced us. John shook my hand gently and smiled. He was a diminutive middle-aged guy in good physical shape. His wavy hair had a hint of silver and receded a little under his cap.

John trotted to his cart and hopped in. Burlington took his clubs from my cart and placed them on John's. I would be riding along with them separately to observe. We drove over to the first tee. Burlington took out his driver and put his ball on a wooden peg at the championship markers. After a couple of practice swings, he drove the ball beautifully on a medium trajectory a long way down the middle. So ready and true to form right out of the box. Joe swung as though where the ball ended up was no big deal.

John also made some practice swings. They looked good to me—smooth and with fine shape. John chattered to Burlington while he was swinging, bringing Joe up to date on mutual friends. Both were refreshingly casual. But then their chat stopped and John began what turned out to be a long routine. His face became serious. I could see he had tensed up. He circled the ball tightly as though he was going to ambush it or catch it off guard. He got into his setup, looked down the fairway, and made one last waggle of adjustment.

Just then, a man drove a mower down the far side of the fairway a good distance off. This caused John to halt his routine. He had to start the whole thing again. Burlington waited patiently. John set up to the ball and took careful aim, but then stopped at the ready point again—this time because Burlington said, "Let 'er rip."

If it continued this way, we were never going to get off the first tee! After the third time through the routine, you could hear a pin drop. All of nature seemed to suspend itself for a moment so John could make his swing. Finally he did so, but with an action that did not remotely resemble his practice swing. The ball sailed way to the right. It caught a tree and dropped into the water hazard. John was into his pocket for a mulligan and looked very distressed.

Joe stopped him with a wave. John seemed utterly drained by the emotional energy expended on swinging the driver on the first tee. And this was only the first hole! Here was a golfer who knew what he wanted in a golf swing, but something always happened to interfere. Fear and tension nearly paralyzed him; even his breathing seemed difficult.

John walked slowly off the tee and joined Burlington in the cart. We all just sat there as Burlington began to interview him. "How long has this been going on, John?"

"A long time. Did you see that? I felt like it wasn't even me in my own body."

"I noticed," said Burlington.

"What can I do about it? Is there any hope?"

"There's always hope, big guy, but you're experiencing one of the toughest problems in golf. All golfers face it from time to time. Fear, I mean. John, let me ask you a few questions." There was that trademark pause. "Right before you swing, what are you thinking about?"

"Well, I have lots of thoughts, and then I go blank."

"Give me a concrete example."

"I think about swinging on a good path. I think about closing the face because I would like to draw the ball, and I figure if I get into a routine, I can be more consistent."

"Anything else?"

"Well, I try to swing with a good sense a rhythm."

"Is that all?"

"To be honest, I think of so many things at different times in my sequence that it would be hard for me to list them all."

"OK. Let's begin at the beginning, John. Let me give you a formula a fine musician gives his students." He took out a pad and pen and wrote:

Performance = Your Potential – Your interference

Joe then explained the formula to John using the same musical analogy he'd used to describe it to me. "What this means is, if you have a particular potential, like you see in your practice swing, and if you don't get in your own way either physically or psychologically, your potential and your performance should match each other. Does that make sense?"

"It makes perfect sense, Joe. But how do I go about doing it?"

"Well, first off, we need to clear up the interference."

"I thought that's what my routine would do."

"And you've probably seen it work from time to time. But you can't sustain it, because that's still not confidence—that intangible feeling and belief deep down that everything is OK and is going to work out well, an expectation of success. I've told you before, from the belief comes the action. The belief really does the performing, not your conscious effort. What's happening is that your mind is smart enough to know that the purpose of your routine is to get through the performance. Isn't that precisely the purpose of your routine—to stop the negative self-talk from interfering?" John nodded in agreement. "I believe your doubting mind is a clever fellow. It's as quiet as a mouse until you enter your actual swing with a ball on the first tee of the golf course. It's silent during the practice swing and on the practice tee. But just because it's silent doesn't mean it's not there. Just now it surely let you know that it's within you during your swing with a ball."

John nodded sadly and smiled in agreement.

"Your negative self has an attitude. When your negative self, harbored in your subconscious, figures out that you're playing a trick on it, it's insulted," Burlington said with a smirk. "It doesn't like to be shut out of your modus operandi so it plays a trick back on you. It lies in wait until after your routine is finished and then comes crashing out. You can execute your routine perfectly and try to convince yourself consciously that the simple plodding—step one, step two, etcetera, etcetera—will enable you to cha-cha-cha on the course. But your negative self-belief still has time to show up. Routine is a short-lived fix and can never replace genuine confidence and belief. You need to obliterate the doubt with confidence. It's a daily thing. I think you need to keep working on your belief system, John."

"So I shouldn't use a routine at all?"

"Not to replace confidence. You need to develop genuine confidence. That's the rock to build your game on. It's connected to the belief that you can successfully deliver the club time and again. It's the belief in a successful impact!"

Again, a truth I'd never heard, explained in one sentence.

"How do I do that?" John asked.

"There are many strategies."

As I sat in the cart and listened to this conversation, I noticed one thing this student had going for him, even though he was in a bad state golf-wise: a humble and open attitude. He was disappointed, but not angry or pointing fingers at himself or anyone else. He wanted to begin to solve his problems and was open to suggestions.

"Joe, we've known each other for a long time and I still can't understand why I don't get into the groove and have that confidence. After working with you, I'm OK for a while, then everything seems to go to pieces."

After a short pause during which Joe seemed to contemplate his friend's predicament, he began. "Let's begin with just two strategies that we can couple together to get you out of this funk. The important thing to know is you have to maintain your confidence daily."

"I can't wait," John said with just a trace of sarcasm.

"OK, to begin with, we'll attempt to elevate your confidence through visualization exercises. Go back up to the first tee and with your practice swing, picture the ball's perfect flight. Don't leave until you feel the ball would have flown where you wanted it to go."

John went up to the tee, driver in hand, and made several swings. He appeared satisfied, then began to put a ball on a tee. Joe stopped him in his tracks.

"What are you doing?"

"I'm going to hit one."

"No! Just put a tee in the ground, make a swing, and *visualize* where it goes."

"You mean don't hit a ball?"

"That's right."

I could see John was a little taken aback. "Let me understand you: You do not want me to hit a ball."

"Correct." Joe said.

John made another swing and Joe asked him to visualize where it ended up. He said, "OK, I got it."

As we drove down the fairway to the imaginary ball, I asked Joe, "I thought you needed to let go of the target to get to it."

Joe shook his head and smiled. "Only when the target is the obstacle. You need to find out if the target is attractive and positive, or negative. If it's not a negative and it's not interference, then you use it to your student's advantage. Visualizing the complete flight of the ball to the target could create the best swing too. Every case is different, Geoff; you need to find out what the interference is or what the best mental focus is for each individual." He turned to John. "Now where did you picture your invisible ball ending up, John?"

"I thought it would be back here in the right rough."

"OK, let's go there." We drove to where John said he pictured it landing. Joe asked him, "What club would you use from here?"

"I would swing a six iron since we're at about 160 yards," John offered.

"OK, make some swings. When you get the feeling you want to hit the shot, go ahead and make the swing."

"Without a ball again?"

"That's right," Burlington confirmed. John looked puzzled, but he trusted Joe. He did it again.

"Where did it go when you made that swing?"

"A little short and right again."

"Are you noticing a difference in the feeling of a practice swing and the actual swing?"

"Yes, and I can't figure it out. Why are they so different?"

"Interference, mister," Joe said with humor. "Don't worry, because before the day is out, you may be pleasantly surprised." We drove over to Joe's ball. He looked at the flag, pulled a club from his bag, and punched the ball under the wind directly toward the hole. He indicated it had landed about ten feet from the cup. Burlington smiled. "Lucky again."

Meanwhile John was approaching his third shot. He took a wedge. He was only about fifteen yards from the hole, but had to go over a bunker. He made a few preliminary swings first. The club went deep into the turf near where the impact would have been. John shook his head in disbelief and smiled. He walked into the bunker with his sand wedge to get the imaginary ball out. He made several more swings and then took one last one. This time, he walked near the hole with his putter and swung a few times before his final swing. He looked into the hole and grinned as he walked off the green.

Joe walked up to his putt and stroked it into the hole, completely nonchalant, as though he didn't even read the putt. "Is that all the time you take? You didn't even line it up." I asked him.

"Oh, I did, as I was walking. I didn't see a need to look any further, and, of course, I also got lucky!"

This was interesting. I would bet he hadn't played in a long time and yet he birdied the first hole and thought nothing of it. Right out of the box, he was ready to play. He jumped into the cart and we drove to the next hole, a long par four into the wind again. He had John go first, if you want to call it that—still no ball. John took a few swings and then one last one. He looked down the fairway. Joe asked him, "How was that one?"

"A little better," John replied, "but still to the right. More solid though."

"Good, John—you're beginning to let go."

"I can feel it both inside of me and out." He turned to look Joe in the face and said, "This is very strange, but I like it!"

Burlington got up, took one practice swing, and *wham!* He smashed it down the right side of the fairway.

"Nice shot," I said.

"Thank you," he said. "Almost."

This went on for the next few holes. Joe was basically driving down the fairways and onto the greens. When he missed one, he would just grin, and when he hit what I thought was a perfect shot, he invariably said, "Almost." Meanwhile, John was visualizing every shot and beginning to walk down the fairways and onto the greens in regulation. It was intriguing to watch. I considered that this guy had just paid about a hundred bucks to play this beautifully manicured course and, since the first hole, he hadn't hit a ball.

We came to the tenth hole, a long par four, into the wind again. It seemed that all the holes were into the wind, even though they were going in different directions. John got up first and made his practice swings. Just before he put the peg in the ground to hit his virtual ball, Burlington put a real ball on the tee for him.

"Now you want me to hit one?"

"That's right, John," Joe laughed good-naturedly.

John took a couple more practice swings and *wham!* He sailed one down the fairway a good distance. I couldn't help noticing that instead of looking sapped of energy and wilted, John looked energized. He was beaming and I laughed. It was a joyful golf shot!

John had made no conscious physical changes to his swing, yet through visualizing, in little more than an hour on the course, club in hand, his swing with the ball had completely changed— and matched his practice swing. It was a 'wow' moment for both of us.

Joe was happy too. He got up and hit a big hook into the left water. "Boy, that was a surprise!" he told us. "Concentration. I was so into your success, John, that I got complacent with my own. Oh well...." He teed up another ball and slammed it down the fairway. He said that was it, not an 'almost.'

For the last nine holes, John made all his swings with a ball. He hit them solidly and very much toward the target. I figured he was playing to his potential. I was amazed at the transformation. We finished the round and drove into the shade behind the eighteenth green.

"How do you feel, John?" Burlington asked solicitously.

"Like, let's go play again," John answered. "I can't believe how well I played those last nine holes—five pars and three birdies and one bogey! And I hit all the fairways and greens! I can't remember ever playing this way with such a feeling of confidence! The ball would go where I pictured and my swing would perform just as I'd practiced. I'm so excited, Joe. Thank you so much!"

"John, you had the potential all along. I didn't do anything to your swing. It just emerged when you lifted the bricks of disbelief."

"That's right! I feel a ton of weight has been lifted off my back. I feel light as a feather and energized." John did a happy dance to prove his point.

"Isn't it amazing, the power of visualization? It goes to show you that no matter how much stock you put into perfecting your swing and knowing your technique, it will rarely surface without you feeding your confidence, your trust, and your positive belief that things are going to work out. You must obliterate the doubt, and this is one way to smash it out of your system. It all has to happen in tandem. So can you go to the bank with what you've done here today?"

"Definitely. You've made a believer out of me! I can see that visualization of success and preparing for it by feeling and trusting are the missing tools for playing the game. It seems that combining that with the feeling of the swing is what I needed, more than knowledge of the golf swing," John said.

"You're obviously physically capable of making the swing you want, John. You could feel it in your practice swing, right? But in that instant between practice routine and the actual swing, what was happening? Just going back to the practice tee and not addressing what's happening between your practice swing and your actual swing is not dealing with it. If you keep doing the same things, expecting the results to change, well, that's a little insane. You've spent umpteen years practicing your technique. You needed to spend more time developing your positive belief instead.

"I'll tell you what, let's pretend you never get to practice again." John and I both looked at him with questioning eyes. He laughed again. "I mean working on your swing, fellas. You can't practice that, but you can play every day. Therefore, to practice now means to play. You would need to rely not on your swing technique, but rather on your belief, positive pictures, and your own feeling. You have enough experience in golf to do that. You have enough swing feel. It may surprise you how often you hit good shots that match your practice swings when you believe. Isn't it more fun this way, too?" Burlington smiled and winked, but soon became serious.

"Have you heard the tale of the American POW who was held in solitary confinement for seven years in a tiny underground cell? And the only way he could keep from going crazy was to find something to occupy his mind day in and day out."

"Yeah," I said. "I think it made the email rounds a few years ago." John nodded as well.

"Right. It's been retold in a couple of books too. The story goes that this POW had played golf, but he'd never broken eighty. So he decided to play golf in his head. He figured it would be the perfect activity to take up time and keep his mind off the hopelessness of his situation. Taking about four hours per round, he would mentally play golf on his home track just as if he were physically on the course.

"Many times he played thirty-six holes. He would take his time, imagining every step he took, from tees to greens, even to the point of tying his shoes. He would visualize everything, the hills, the slopes, the sky, the trees, the blades of grass, and especially the swings he made and the shots he hit. It was an incredible experiment in visualization! They say that when the POW was finally released at the end of the war, one of the first things he did when he got home was play a round of golf on his home course. The first round he played, he shot seventy-four, his personal best! Remember, he hadn't physically picked up a club in more than seven years!" Burlington's face lit up from telling this story.

"No one's been able to verify that this story is true, but legends exist because they provide valuable lessons. We just can't underestimate the power of the mind. This man's visualization was so deep and was sustained for so long that his belief system accepted what he created in his mind as reality. When he returned home, it came to pass—the laws of attraction, like a self-fulfilling prophecy! We can all learn from that.

"Of course I'm not suggesting that you go seven years picturing your swing before you play. But maybe you need to do a daily visualizing practice for a few minutes in conjunction with your physical swing practice. When you address the belief system, you can attain your full potential and it emerges like the sun rising over the water every day. The beauty of it is that we can access it through visualization, which comes easy to most of us. We can do it anywhere, at any time. You just got a little dose of it. Kind of neat, eh? From belief comes action."

John was smiling and nodding. He had just seen his potential emerge on those last nine holes and he was eager to go again. As for me, it was proof positive that I needed to adopt a program that involved elevating the belief system along with fundamental swing-feel therapy for my students. I had to find a way to obliterate the negative and to teach my students methods that would help dissolve their fear of failure.

If I'd been instructing John, I know I would have begun adjusting his swing right from the beginning on the first tee. That would have created confusion from the start and it would have turned out to be a bum day for both of us. Now I had a good idea of how to go about getting a swing that seemed to transform instantly from practice to actual. When we had said goodbye, John couldn't hide his enthusiasm to get out on the course to play more holes—a much different scenario than I could have imagined had I been teaching him with my old methods!

30
REFLECTING ON
MY FUTURE

Burlington needed to get back to the golf center, but I wanted to know more about strategies for developing confidence. So as we got going on the highway, I asked Joe about it.

"It's difficult for people to understand because a belief doesn't have to be based in logic," he explained. "But those who lack confidence need to begin somewhere. If they have no positive experience, they can't get confidence from their past, right?"

"Right. I'd always questioned why I lose my confidence. It never seemed to be sustainable."

"Yes, that's the most common problem, Geoff. It seems unsustainable because we fail to do preventive maintenance on it, the way we do with our swings or, for that matter, our houses and cars, our health, our relationships or anything else."

Instantly a chord was struck deep in me. Claire. I was taken aback for just a second; had he read my mind again? Did he know I had neglect in me?

But he continued. "It's like taking care of a garden. You can have the best plants in the world, but if don't take care of them, if you don't water them and you let weeds grow, the weeds flourish and your plants are choked out. It's the same with your confidence. All I'm saying is confidence and trust are like any relationship. You need to make a commitment to keep taking care of it. You need to nurture it with visualization, positive mind-talk, sound physical practice, and on-course practice therapies. You need them all.

"We tend to pass over the trust because trust seems so intangible. But we know it's there because it reveals itself on the course every time we swing. We need to do thorough preventive maintenance in our minds."

I pushed thoughts of Claire away and asked, "How much time do you spend each day visualizing success?"

"Picturing success in every situation is my method," he told me.

"Then how often do you use mind-talk to build your belief?"

"I have to work on it daily. Tell yourself a hundred or a thousand times a day for, let's say, a month that your golf swing is great and you're a great golfer. Even if you're not, you will begin to remove doubt. You see, the belief system can change without a physical demonstration of change. You will believe the thing to be true even though your action may not support it yet. 'Act as if.' The belief can precede the experience and then the action has a chance to improve and be sustained. At least with this approach, you won't be in your own way before you begin your practice— that is, when practice is appropriate.

"Then, of course, once you believe, you need to execute the due diligence to support the belief. That's basically the sequence you must incorporate when you start from a negative experience, Geoff. It's exactly how you can pry yourself from a rut. So often we spend time believing that things are not going to work out and then we're surprised when they don't. The starting point is not the physical practice, but rather the mind practice. That gives the physical an opportunity to follow suit."

I could see myself—and I guessed that pretty much all golfers could see themselves—doing things just the way Burlington had described. Every time I had problems in my play, I would just go and hit dozens of balls without addressing my confidence. In fact, I would practice to not get worse and embarrass myself. I could see clearly how backwards, mentally, that type of practicing was. I had never felt ready because even though I practiced hard, I never developed confidence and trust in myself. I had never spent time obliterating the negative and building the positive in my mind. Even if my swing was perfect, I couldn't perform at my best because I only played with half my resources—a body, but no mind, no confidence. If you played football that way, it would be like having five men against eleven.

I was lost in my thoughts as we neared the golf center. It was getting toward dusk, the sun slowly sinking into the horizon. "Geoff, let's go down to the shop. There's one more thing I want to discuss with you. It's the main ingredient for success or fulfillment—my master key. It's what makes life easy and teaching most effective." I nodded eagerly for him to continue. "There's one last quality you must acquire, if you don't already possess it, or should I say, have not let it emerge. One more thing you must do."

I'd been here for days and he's bringing this up now? We went into the shop. He turned on the lights, retrieved the coffee from the morning, and heated it in the microwave. I removed some of his tools from the table to make room and wiped it clean with a shop towel. He poured the hot coffee into fresh cups and we took our seats. He took a slug of coffee and with an uncharacteristically serious look on his face began speaking very slowly and deliberately.

"The final quality you must have is an *agape* love in all your relationships and a special love for yourself, too."

What, I wondered, is *agape* love?

Joe continued, "Everything else worthwhile will come from that. You must care for yourself, and that does not mean being selfish. You could have all the knowledge, all the strategies you have learned this week, and all the experience in the world, but without love, you will never be able to share it the way it needs to be shared. You will not evolve and grow into being your best self without it. This kind of love is essential for you to become a complete coach. You need to be willing to take a good honest look at yourself daily, based on love, and adjust if you need to.

"You know, Geoff, it may be important that you develop *agape* love first, before you resume coaching. You must implement all the strategies you've learned this week, and by being self-caring you can help others help themselves. But it is this *agape* love, where the purpose is supporting another person's quest to be their best, that is central in the end."

I was a bit shocked at his choice of a subject. When I caught up, I realized Burlington was talking about the type of care that serves our needs and then naturally others. I thought I kind of understood that; I felt I had that.

"This caring nourishes your students and you in a whole different way, Geoff." Then again, maybe it was all too deep for me. Burlington picked up on my discomfort. "It feels awkward because it's not the norm to address this aspect of teaching or coaching. But it ought to be. If I didn't love myself, I could not care for you, and the lessons you learned from me would be tainted. They would be filled with how I do things rather than how you need to go about them. *Agape* love allows you, as a teacher, to focus on the student, not on you. How could I help you, or for that matter why would I want to, if I didn't care for you? What I'm getting at is that it's impossible to care for others before you care for yourself," he declared.

I gave him the nod to continue. "This *agape* love is an integral part of communication and a healthy quality in any relationship—especially a teacher-student relationship. This quality will allow you to really enjoy the differences in each of your students and to endure as an instructor. It will create openness in your teaching so you'll be fearless. You'll never be blinded by your success or experience. Forgive me, Geoff, but I feel a need to emphasize this point. It is crucial, so it needs to be indelibly imprinted on your mind, if our time and experiences together are to last."

"OK," I agreed, as I was beginning to get the point.

"You must have real self-caring to teach. It's a simple principle. When you care for yourself, I mean deeply appreciate all your gifts, when you feel real warmth, then you can be at peace. When you're at peace, you have clarity. Then it becomes easy to clearly see the path your students need to take to elevate their awareness and reach their own potentials. A student can feel this caring and begin to trust you and let down their guard so that everything is exposed. Then there's no mask and you get exactly what you see."

He surprised me by pulling a leftover donut from the bag on the table and handing it across to me. It was the last one. I took it, but held it, thinking it belonged to Otter, who didn't care two woofs if it had my fingerprints on it. Burlington resumed his reflection.

"My mother-in-law was that way, Geoff. She was a woman with a deep faith, strength, and endurance. She lived a very simple life, especially after her husband died. She was also a great teacher, teaching by example. She did things in a manner that never imposed anything of herself on anyone. I would say that she lived in a state of grace. You see, a person who is self-caring loves who they are. Their words always come from a good place. These are the people you can trust and they're the people you can learn from the most. They have no need for pretense because they're very secure in who they are and what their purpose is in life." Burlington's voice took on a serene tone when he spoke of his mother-in-law. How unusual, I thought, for a man to admire his mother-in-law so openly. She must have been an amazing woman.

"In the few years I knew my wife's mother," he continued, "I came to understand and love her in a very special way. I had the utmost admiration for her. She was a very spiritual person, too. She said her peace came from a deep faith and from a deep sense of God's love for her. But you see, Geoff, she couldn't have lived the way she did and been the way she was without it being inside her. Everything she did was an outgrowth of what was inside her. She had a deep self-love, true self-caring, and it permeated everything she did. It follows that if you are at peace with yourself, then you will have clarity and really be able to help others, or at least give them an accurate perspective on things."

"So that's how teaching and love go together? You seem to have a totally different perspective on things, Joe, right down to the last drop," I said as I finished my coffee.

"Thank you. The beauty and elegance is in the simplicity of it all, my friend."

I realized that as much as I wanted to, I couldn't copy what I saw in Joe Burlington. I needed to become my best self from within and maybe then I would become the teacher I wanted to be. Better yet, the person I aspired to be.

But Joe wasn't finished. "This love must permeate every fiber of what you teach, Geoff, and it must always be in your communication. You cannot exhibit this quality without it being authentic. It cannot be faked. You cannot buy it, you just must *be* it.

"I have developed strong feelings about communication and the direction it's going in our culture. They say we communicate better now than ever before. But it is very superficial. Take e-mail and text messages. They're instant, but often like Morse code—not complete and rarely with any emotion. We have high-speed communication, but it has become less and less soulful. We have gotten so far away from communicating on a deep level. We rarely take time to find out what's really happening in the lives of those we deal with. We hardly write good letters anymore or take the time to really put something down that comes from our hearts. Letters are becoming a lost art form." I felt the weight of my cell phone in my pocket and thought about how I used it.

"Students of golf have become that way too with the new technological advances. That was my point earlier about the direction instruction has gone—more information, but less ability to play and enjoy by feeling. As a teacher, it's important for you to find out your students' thoughts and feelings. You need to know what's going through their minds because those things manifest themselves in their swings. If you see the inside clearly, then you have a good shot at adjusting the physics.

"That's why, when you asked me about the most important aspect of teaching, I knew right away what it was to me: listen and observe. Pay attention and do it in a loving way," he advised. "Your best teaching must come from the heart. You must love the discovery actions of your subject. You need to love your students and communicate that to them. It really helps the process.

"That reminds me, Geoff. I have something I'd like you to read."

"Of course," I said.

"It's a letter from the Civil War era. I think it might get my point across better than anything I could say."

He went to his standup toolbox and rummaged through an upper drawer. "Here it is." He pulled out a creased sheet of paper. "This letter was written at the beginning of the Civil War. It's an unbelievable communication from the heart. I copied it down from that Civil War series on PBS a few years ago.[11] It was written by a soldier from Smithfield, Rhode Island, a major in the second Rhode Island Volunteers. He was on the front lines at the first battle of Bull Run in Virginia. His name was Sullivan Ballou. He handed the page to me. "Wait, let me get my instrument and I'll play a tune to go with it." He got his fiddle from a cupboard and pulled it from its case. As he chinned the violin and adjusted his bow, he said, "This way you'll get the full effect."

This was getting a little too far out for me, but by now, I was kind of used to it. There we were, two grown men in a workshop, Burlington playing the fiddle and me reading a letter written over 150 years ago. And this was a lesson in teaching golf. If the other pros could see me now, they'd think we both were crazy. But by now I trusted Joe and knew better than to doubt his judgment. If he thought this would help me get more in touch, I was willing to go along.

He began to play and I put on my reading glasses and began to read aloud. His fiddle had a deep tone and the sound echoed off the walls and concrete floor of the barn. Burlington played softly, beautifully, and slowly at first. The music was exquisite, but seemed very sad. As I read I could tell the letter obviously came right from the bottom of the soldier's heart, yet my own heart was not in it; I was uncomfortable.

Joe stopped playing. "You're not listening to yourself read. You're going to miss the meaning. Slow down; hear yourself. Speak softly from your heart, Geoff."

So I started over, much slower, and the words began to take on new meaning. It felt as if this soldier was right there with us. I could feel my throat begin to tighten. There was so much love in this letter, and regret, too. This soldier knew he would never lay eyes on his wife and children again. It made me think of Claire.

I could picture Sullivan Ballou trying to write under the dim light of a candle on a dark, muggy summer evening. He had managed to pour all he was feeling into this letter. My voice began to crack as I continued to read. I couldn't remember ever feeling this way while I read something.

July the 14th, 1861, Washington, D.C.

Dear Sarah,

The indications are very strong that we shall move in a few days, perhaps tomorrow. And lest I should not be able to write you again I feel compelled to write a few lines that may fall under your eye when I am no more.

I have no misgivings about or lack of confidence in the cause in which I am engaged, and my courage does not halt or falter. I know how American civilization now leans upon the triumph of the government. And how great a debt we owe to those who went before us through the blood and suffering of the revolution. And I am willing, perfectly willing, to lay down all my joys in this life to help maintain this government and to pay that debt.

Sarah, my love for you is deathless; it seems to bind me with mighty cables that nothing but omnipotence can break and yet my love of country comes over me like a strong wind and bears me irresistibly with all those chains to the battlefield. The memories of all the blissful moments I have enjoyed with you come crowding over me and I feel most deeply grateful to God and you, that I have enjoyed them for so long, and how hard it is for me to give them up and burn to ashes the hopes, the future years when, God willing, we might still have lived and loved together, and see our boys grown up to honorable manhood around us.

If I do not return, my dear Sarah, never forget how much I loved you, nor that when my last breath escapes me on the battlefield, it will whisper your name.

Forgive my many faults and the many pains I have caused you. How thoughtless, how foolish I have sometimes been. But oh, Sarah, if the dead can come back to this earth and flit unseen around those they love, I shall always be with you on the brightest day and the darkest night always, always, and when the soft breeze spans your cheek it shall be my breath, or cool air your throbbing temple it shall be my spirit passing by.

Sarah, do not mourn me dead, think I am gone, and wait for me, for we shall meet again.

Joe stopped playing a few seconds after I finished reading the letter. We sat quietly for a few moments.

I now knew what I had to do to reach Claire. I would finish the letter I had started. The music and the letter had captured me. It was as if Joe had planned it all along. I didn't know what to say. Of course, Burlington was perfectly content to say nothing. I took a deep breath, "That was beautiful."

"Thank you."

"How long have you been playing?"

"I've been studying for years, but I'm just now learning to play music," he replied.

"What do you mean?"

"I mean with feeling from within, from the heart. Exactly how you will learn to teach golf, Geoff, if you open yourself up. How would it feel if you could get that deep during a golf lesson?"

"I don't know. It would probably take a lot out of me."

"Yes, but it would give you the feeling that your time was well spent, and the student would feel that way too. They would really know you cared. That's very important. And it only takes a few minutes to do...."

"However, I don't love my students the way Sullivan Ballou loved his wife..."

"Of course not, but you want badly for them to know you care. It's the depth that counts, right?"

"Yes, it is, but it's still just a golf lesson."

"Ah, that is where we differ. Yes, it is a golf lesson. But it is also your life and their lives and we need to get the most out of every moment. For the lesson to be memorable and lasting, the experience needs to be deep."

"How do I achieve that?"

"Well, look at what we just did. Will you ever forget this moment, you reading and me playing? You need to be creative and figure it out for yourself. The feeling you got inside, if I read you right, was very deep. You need to find your way," he said quietly.

"No, I won't forget this time..." I was choking up, to my great surprise.

Joe continued. "There were a lot of different types of love in that letter—the love of spouse, children, and country. It's timeless, isn't it? All you need to do is figure it out." Then Joe slapped his knee, breaking the solemnness, and said, "Well, that's it. You have the strategies, the confidence in yourself, and everything you need until we meet again. That is, unless you have more questions for me?"

Of course I had more questions, but I was speechless and just let out a big sigh. He noticed my pause but didn't say anything. I was really affected, but felt drained, physically and emotionally.

This lesson was exactly what I needed, the last piece of the puzzle. I felt I could go on and help myself and progress on solid fundamental ground. More, I felt ready for life, ready for life with Claire.

If she would only give me a second chance.

As he was putting his fiddle back into its case, Joe said, "You know, it's late. You want to get something to eat?"

"I don't want to intrude."

"No intrusion; I'm alone tonight. I know a place in Deerfield that has great seafood."

"Sure, I'd love that, but I feel a little grungy. Do I have time to take a shower?"

"Of course. I need to get cleaned up too. Let's meet there at 7:30. The place is called the Whale's Rib."

"I'll find it on my GPS." "Great. We can talk about anything else you may have on your mind over supper."

31
DINNER

I felt privleged to be having dinner with Joe. As I drove north, the sun was setting out my left window in a kaleidoscope of soft colors. Purples, yellows, and pinks were strewn across the scattered clouds on the horizon. I was beginning to appreciate all that was going on around me in a new way. In the past, such a sunset would have escaped me.

The restaurant was a hole in the wall. Some may have called it rustic; to me it seemed more worn out, like the hotel in Flamingo. Old nets and fishing gear were hung to the walls. The lighting was dim and the patrons were working-class locals, for sure. It was noisy and crowded. Joe had beaten me there. He had snared a booth toward the back. I wormed my way through the tight tables to his corner. Joe had already ordered himself an Irish Red. He caught the waitress's eye and a beer landed in front of me almost instantly as I took my seat opposite Joe. It was good, full-bodied beer with a nice head in a frosted mug.

"How did you know?" I asked.

"Just guessed," Burlington said.

"My dad used to brew beer just like this. It always brings back memories." We lifted our glasses together over the thickly varnished table.

Joe made a toast. "Cheers," he said, "and a long and healthy life."

"What a day we had. I can't tell you how satisfying..."

"Yes, it was great," he said. "I forgot how much fun golf can be, and John's great breakthrough makes it all worthwhile, eh?"

The waitress returned to our table to take our order. I hadn't even looked at the menu, so I looked at Joe for suggestions. He took the cue. "How about some fresh cod and chips and a little salad?"

"I guess you want the special, Joe?" the waitress asked with a wry smile. "It seems to me you'll never get out of this cod rut."

"Yeah, well, when I find something good, I stick with it. I prefer to call it a good groove." The waitress smiled, shook her head and was off.

I collected my thoughts about all Joe's lessons before I spoke. The thought that kept ringing in my mind was how quickly he developed a rapport with his students. I wanted to know how I could do that. Besides the level of trust he established in each lesson, this whole business of being able to see oneself while swinging intrigued me. I had been taught that the one reason to have a swing coach was because you *couldn't* see yourself. So I asked Joe about the 'seeing oneself' trick. "How does it work? I mean, how can it be taught?"

He took a swallow of beer before he began. "It goes back to what I've been getting at since our first day together and, for that matter, what I tried to do at that seminar. We all need to evaluate ourselves continuously to really keep evolving and progressing, right?" His voice hushed and it was hard to hear him in the noisy room. I leaned into the center of the table. I needed to hear and understand every word.

"The beginning of the lesson for a teacher of this method is silence. The teacher must have the wisdom not to superimpose his beliefs on the students. He must let them make the trip to awareness, only showing them the openings. Let them decide whether they want to enter a new and different place within themselves. At this point, the only activity of the teacher is to get to know the students. Students will pick up on this and begin to feel safe. That is the beginning of trust; letting go can follow. Even defensive students will be disarmed and the teacher will have no masks to sort through. It really makes the experience rewarding for all.

"You, my friend, must become an expert at listening and hearing. It is the listening that allows me to make good choices. You should say nothing at first. Allow students to learn to listen to themselves, which is ultimately the goal, right? You could begin by mirroring back to them exactly what they said to you so they can hear for themselves what they have said. This way they usually won't become defensive, which is to everyone's advantage.

"The spaces between the notes are an integral part of music," he said. "In conversation, the spaces between your remarks are as important as the words themselves. That's what I call absorption time—time for the transformation within the student to take place." He lifted his beer again.

"Remember when you asked me for a roadmap?[12] An sage once said, throw away the map; teach in a manner that allows enough freedom, creativity, and awareness for the students' sense of direction to become needle sharp. That way, when they really get going, they can travel without a map. They will never be lost. That's another reason why golf should never be reduced to analysis alone. In fact, that's why I so strongly object to video. It's so easy to misuse, and it lends itself to reducing the necessity of the students to develop their feel keenly. The lessons need to embody the actions of the students and their responses. And time is essential for it all to take place."

I felt like a bobble-head doll, nodding in agreement. But I returned to my original question. "How do you teach someone to see themselves?" Burlington swallowed the last of his brew. With a satisfied look on his face, he took a big breath and exhaled. Only then did he begin to speak.

"Let me tell you of an experiment I tried with a young student of mine. He's a good illustration of learning to see yourself as you swing. One summer long ago, young Al came down from Canada to work with me. He was a great student, a total pleasure to be with. We did everything together. We worked, we played, we practiced, we ate. To tell you the truth, I don't remember a moment during his stay that was not just right. He became a good friend of my wife, too." Joe paused while the waitress set down heaping plates of food.

"One day we were working on his swing path. I had described all kinds of ways for him to improve, but he still struggled. He was having trouble translating what I was saying into swing improvement. And he was hard to read because he wanted my advice to work so badly that he wouldn't tell me what he couldn't understand. But this day he finally blurted out, 'I just can't see it!' I was a little shocked, but really it was exactly the feedback I needed to help him move forward. A light clicked on.

"I told him to wait a minute while I ran down to the barn. I soon returned to the tee with the old Ford loader and asked Al to get into the bucket. With no hesitation he hopped in and knelt down. I slowly lifted him about fifteen feet in the air. Then I engaged the parking brake and got down. I grabbed my driver and attached an orange streamer to create a four-foot trail behind the club as it swung. I set up to the target and began swinging directly beneath him." Joe paused to let me absorb the picture.

I looked up at Al during my swing and saw understanding come to his face. He could now clearly see not only the orbit of the club travel but also the relationship of the swing path, the target, the ball, and me. Changing his point of view had shown what words and other demonstrations had failed to make clear.

"For Al to see things differently, I'd needed to make an indelible impression in a different way. Next I asked him to close his eyes and see if he could picture the pattern. And he could. When I brought Al back down from the loader bucket, he picked up his driver, anxious to show me what he'd learned from his new perspective. He'd gotten it! Next, I asked him to close his eyes again and hit a shot, feeling his swing form the picture he had in his mind. I needed him to elevate his reliance on his proprioceptors rather than his physical eye." Joe gave me one of his winks to remind me of the keystone science behind his method.

"I wanted Al to truly sense what was going on out of his sight and at a speed his physical eye couldn't pick up. I knew if he could use his sense of feel, his mind's eye first, he would have three tools to work with to elevate his awareness for his swing pattern. There was no way he could go wrong with that much redundancy. We all have beautiful awareness backup systems operating all the time, and they can be forced into action by shutting down the physical eye. Proprioception is inextricably linked to feel. It is an amazing tool to develop in any athletic endeavor. The proprioceptors are what send feedback to the brain, so we must find strategies that put them into action."

"You mean, muscle memory?"

"That's right."

I switched the dialogue back to Al. "Did it stay with him for the long haul?"

"It did. He began making swings at first with just fair contact. I would reinforce his feel development by asking him to continue feeling the swing and picturing it with his eyes closed. His brain accepted his ability to swing using his proprioception as the sole awareness tool. And Al marveled at the incredible accuracy of his swing feel for tee shots."

"Did you do anything else with Al?"

"I asked him to open his eyes and pretend they were closed when making a swing. He thought that was strange! It was a whole different mindset. Changing his point of view did the trick. Since then, Al has been able to picture his swing as though he were directly above himself.

"We practiced seeing from every viewpoint. I would move all around and ask, 'Can you see yourself now?' Finally he had all the views clearly in his head, and what an advantage he has had since! Video could never take the place of this technique. Video can be helpful, if used judiciously, but most often it's not. What could be better than having your own video going on inside your head whenever you want it? Now, Al could see from inside what was going on outside." Joe caught the waitress's eye with a small wave.

"So a golfer needs to be able to see himself. We always have this view available to us, we just need to access it, and you as an instructor need to use your creativity to show your students how to do that. We can all have twenty-twenty inner vision, in golf and in life, but we need to know how to focus our sight," he declared. The waitress set down another pair of beers.

Just then a dark-haired woman passed very close to our table. I lost my focus for a second and from nowhere Claire came to mind, catching me off guard. I was so ready now to turn my sights to her! Now that I was looking at us from the outside, I desperately wanted to get back in. I was visualizing us together on the beach outside the Pedersens' when Joe cleared his throat, probably noticing that I was somewhere else.

Burlington chuckled as he reminisced about his time with Al. "I would wait for Al to respond and he would wait for me, so we had these sort of silent standoffs. Then we would both burst out laughing. I wanted him to realize it was all in him, the change, I mean. And my purpose in teaching him, as with you or anyone else, is for me to become obsolete. Change most often needs to take place over time. Perfectionists, for example, in this culture don't really allow time for change and tend to view learning as an event rather than a process." I could see myself again as a young perfectionist and understood that that was a handicap and not something to be proud of.

"That idea tends to place a lot of pressure on them and they end up frustrated. They act as though the process is something they shouldn't have to deal with. Of course, that's a fatal flaw because it sets them up to give up. Then they come back for another lesson, and then give up again, and the cycle never ends. A waste of valuable time! Remember the point I was getting at during the seminar in New Orleans?"

"Yeah, Joe, those guys were such jerks," I said.

"That's not what I'm talking about. I really don't hold it against them. Their real problem was their unwillingness to be open. Those folks refused to let new ideas in or accept any point of view but their own. They've been taught to follow a set of rules that form a solid belief structure in their minds. Those beliefs are the foundation for the way they perceive things. This naturally tends to limit growth. Creativity is stifled and there can be no progress. This gap between perception and reality is obscured by unwillingness to take another look. My approach doesn't fit into that belief system, which limits the parameters of their life experiences and what they will accept as truth. So their teaching is sadly compromised by these rules."

"Doesn't it make you angry," I whispered. "How can their closed attitudes not affect you?"

But Joe got onto another tangent, not paying attention to my response. "There is plasticity to the wiring in the brain, though. It's a rather new discovery in neuroscience. It opposes the 'can't teach an old dog new tricks' mentality: You can if the dog is willing! Willingness allows that plasticity to come alive. Our minds can blaze new trails down the neurological ski slope at virtually any time in our lives. You can build a new belief system. That makes life exciting, doesn't it? And new experiences allow new pathways to form in our brains, allowing us to constantly evolve for the better. This doesn't only happen in golf, it happens in life too, don't you agree?" I nodded. "Anyway, that's what I think."

"I still don't get how you can be so detached from the way you were treated in New Orleans. They didn't give you a chance to even introduce your ways..."

He waved his hands, "Geoff, it's no use getting caught up in that. But you're right, detachment requires a lot of practice." He added, "I don't take myself too seriously. I'm constantly laughing at myself; there's so much to learn and most of it is about ourselves!" He paused to chuckle. "Only when we step outside ourselves can we have some inkling of what's really going on. This is why I attempt each day to start with a beginner's mind. I understand professional dancers do it all the time when they begin rehearsing a new piece. They begin by first learning to walk again, the most fundamental way to begin. They're able to learn something from that starting point every day, often something that in the past escaped their attention—all because they begin from the beginning. It only takes a few minutes.

"Think about it, Geoff, and you'll understand why I was met with such resistance at the seminar. My remarks were so contrary to what that audience had perceived as traditional and acceptable. I was probably viewed as a golf heretic. They were uncomfortable with what I said because of their fear, and their reaction was typical of anyone feeling this way—very insecure. They discredited and labeled me. But I'm used to it; it really didn't bother me, except for the disappointment I felt for them."

Through the night we drank another beer accompanied by more of the all-you-can-eat battered cod. The dinner was delicious; Joe had made a good choice. And our conversation had covered a lot of ground. But it was now getting late and the room had gone quiet. There were only a couple of diners left and the wait staff had begun cleaning up.

I made a commitment to myself. I was determined that I would begin each day anew. Joe called the waitress over to see if it was too late for some coffee. She smiled and insisted the staff would be cleaning up for some time yet. "Have whatever you want Joe," she told him. "I know how you feel about our apple crisp." I glanced at Joe and could see he was succumbing. We had caught the warm aroma when the waitress had delivered a piece to a nearby table.

So over coffee and pie our conversation began anew. "Joe, what do you think about these world-class players who insist that they don't want to rely on timing?"

"I believe they're operating under the false impression that timing is something bad—some sort of complicated recovery system that only comes into play when the swing shape or speed gets out of whack. Timing is actually critical in a golf swing, just as it is in life itself. It's as critical a fundamental as there is, as you can imagine from the very precise hand and wrist action I've taught you, the cup and curl, and so on. No, in my opinion underestimating the value of timing is a grave error. This could really mislead the novice golfer attempting to improve the club face and angle awareness in the impact zone," he told me with a sorry shake of his head.

"I just don't understand how these great golfers can be so far off the facts as explained by you. Why don't more of them come around to your way of thinking?" I must have looked visibly confused. It seemed to me that Burlington's program should be as popular as it was successful, and I didn't understand why it wasn't.

"We could go on and on about their perceptions, but when something has been drummed into your head so firmly, it's difficult to change. Let's leave it at that. What I have imparted to you these few days is diametrically opposed to many of their views."

There was a pause in the conversation. I hesitated, because my next thought had taken me by surprise. But I jumped in. "Would you mind if I asked you for some advice, not on golf, but on a personal level? About my relationship, or lack thereof, with my former fiancée?" As usual, he said nothing at first, which allowed me to open the floodgates. I told him how he had opened my eyes not only in golf, but about life in general. I poured out descriptions of the great times Claire and I had enjoyed together, and then our recent troubles. I told him how I wanted to rekindle the relationship. I told him of my phone messages to Claire and my fear that she was spent of our relationship and that there was nothing left in her tank. I explained to him how my not being ready to make a decision had appeared as a lack of commitment. And on and on. When I finished, the moment was awkward until he broke his silence.

"Do you have a photo?"

"Of course." I went into my wallet, pulled out the picture, and handed it to him. It wasn't typical, almost a profile. She wasn't exactly smiling either, but it was my favorite. It showed her in a pensive mood. Joe studied the picture. He remained silent, apparently digesting my story. He seemed to be looking into the picture, not just at it. My mind began its insecure dance, wondering if I'd overstepped my bounds. I sat there inwardly reprimanding myself for taking such a bold step.

"Has she responded to your messages?"

"Not so far, no. That's what concerns me. No returned calls, no nothin'." I looked at him. "Who am I kidding? It's over."

"I don't know Geoff; it's hard to say. But she may surprise you. Looking at this picture, I feel an energy—it's unmistakable. It rings loud and clear for those who can sense it. From your description of Claire, I would say she is in touch. That's about all I can tell you." I was frustrated and uncomfortable just talking about it.

So I changed the subject and with ease he went with me. "Joe, something you said has struck a chord in me since the seminar. What did you mean when you told the pro, 'one should be careful how one defines success.' How do you define success?"

"In my mind, Geoff, the Lama had it right. Actually, philosophers have been practicing success down through the ages, just not this culture's brand of it." He paused as usual, looked down at the table, and slowly defined it in a manner that a five-year-old could understand. "It's simple, really. Success only has to do with relationships. It's very tightly woven there. To be successful, all you need to do is reduce suffering and increase joy, in every encounter.[13] Think about it: It's what we've been working on this whole time, because it all boils down to this. All you can be is your best self, and from day to day, be better than your previous self. That is your competition. That is all you can really control. After that, you have to let the chips fall where they may. Be true to yourself and, like Baryshnikov used to say, just be better than your previous self."

Joe's voice intruded into my thoughts. "Listen." He drank down the last drop of decaf. "It's getting late; let's meet again tomorrow morning for a few minutes and you can give Otter a proper farewell. I do have a few maintenance things to do, but why don't you come over for a bit before you head to the airport."

We got up from the table slowly and stretched. We had been there a long time. I took care of the bill. Joe thanked me and we walked out to our cars. As I opened the car door, I called over. "Joe, one more thing; I almost forgot." I took the cedar box from the front seat and handed it to him. "Here, this is for you."

"What's this?"

"It's a life box," I kidded. "You have given me new life." It was pretty dark where we were standing, so we moved under one of the parking lot lights.

As he opened the box a smile came over his face and he shook his head. "You needn't have done this, Geoff."

"I know, but I felt like it."

"An original Orvis bamboo fly rod. Nice!" I hoped this gave him some understanding of my appreciation. He unraveled the cloth case and one by one put the four pieces of the rod together. He took the rod in his left hand and lifted it as though he were going to cast. He beamed appreciation. "This is perfect, Geoff. Thank you."

"I knew you would put it to good use and appreciate it."

"That I will, laddie."

"Besides, it makes up for the rod I damaged on our fishing trip."

"It's better than that one." Joe seemed elated at the gift and that made me happy, too.

I told him I would indeed come by for a few minutes in the morning.

32

MY LAST NIGHT

I reflected on what had happened today and, for that matter, the past few days—especially this evening. Change was happening inside me. I could feel it bubbling up. It was a little unsettling, but it was positive. Joe Burlington was my example. Just being himself, never trying. As I had been told I would, I was learning naturally without really being aware of it. It felt unforced.

I drove along the A1A, the two-lane road built in the early 1940s that runs adjacent to the ocean along the whole east coast. The speed limit is very low and you can really appreciate the view of the ocean. I drove a little north and found a beautiful untouched stretch of beach with no condos or homes. I parked on the side of the road and made my way through the dunes to the water. I felt a need to stop for a moment, soak it all in, and count my blessings. Being in the midst of nature at its best only enhanced the deep sense of everything fitting into place.

I began to walk. It was dark and the moon was almost full. A few of the bright stars hanging in the sky still shone faintly. A glorious night! The ocean was calm and the splash of the waves touching my feet was in perfect rhythm. The tide was going out. I could feel a gentle breeze on my face coming off the ocean, and I experienced a special calmness, an assuredness that I didn't recall feeling very often, except when I was very young.

I wondered what Joe was thinking when he extracted tangible meaning from Claire's photo. She wasn't into surprises. No, this time his instincts were a bit off track. Even so, I wanted to believe, and my imagination leapt to dreams of making love with Claire on this very beach. And to the many good things I had absorbed these past few days. I was feeling them very deeply. I would have a whole new set of tools to work with when I left this place. I walked on and on along the shore, realizing this visit with Joe Burlington was no accident.

I was feeling that intangible confidence he'd spoken about. I thought about all the different situations I'd observed and been a part of from the beginning: the maintenance, mower repairs, and irrigation fixes; the fly fishing; the golf without a ball; and all the different ways Burlington had taught his students—and me. I still wondered how he could have so many interests and yet apparently be highly skilled in all of them.

I felt energized in a different way, as if I could move steadily forward and not ever run out of gas—like a steady barge on a river, or a freighter on the ocean. This new confidence was different. I used to be like a speedboat that ran fast—and then ran out of gas. Confidence would wane and I'd be running on fumes, then I'd stop altogether. This new slow and steady move in the right direction gave me the assurance that this growing feeling was not just a temporary success. I felt I could improve and sustain it, as though I had the strategies that would support me through whatever situation might arise. I knew then that I'd never have chronic golf problems again.

I returned to my car and headed back to my place. I had certainly gotten a lot more than I ever dreamed possible. Maybe I could come back too—that was in the back of my mind; perhaps another trip in a few months. Maybe even with Claire. My newfound confidence extended to her. I thought maybe if I could speak with her face to face, I could win her back.

I began to think through the next few hours and everything I needed to do before I left. Maybe I would leave one last message for Claire, hoping she wouldn't just press 'delete.' I needed to clean up at the B&B, but there wasn't really much to do, as I'd used little more than my bed and the kitchen. I'd pack my bags tonight so I could meet with Joe and say goodbye to Otter first thing. After that, I would go to the airport straight away. It was back to the cold; winter was still in full gear at home. I dreaded it, mostly because I would have to wait weeks to put this new program to use. That's life. But thank God I had a program now so I could look forward to this season. I just hoped somehow I could use the interim time to show Claire I was ready for commitment.

As I approached the Pedersens' I noticed a light on in my room. I was sure I'd turned them all off and locked the door before I left. I pulled into the drive and went to the front door. It was unlocked. I began to feel nervous. I went back to the car and got an iron from my golf bag, just in case. I walked into the house, trying to adjust my eyes to the darkened room. It didn't seem as though anything was out of place. I made a pass through the whole downstairs. Nothing.

I began to cautiously tiptoe up the stairs with my heart in my throat and my club over my shoulder, cocked and ready. I moved down the hall, and as I peered through the half-open door to my room, I saw that my reading light was dimly shining.

And then shock, relief, and finally disbelief poured over me. I lowered my club and breathed. Still in her jacket, Claire sat on the side of the bed reading the unfinished letter I had left on the small bedside table.

I froze again. I didn't know what to do. I wanted to know what was going through her mind. How did she feel about my letter?

She sensed someone and turned. She looked beautiful. I still didn't move. I saw a tear rolling slowly down her cheek. Involuntarily I moved into clear view and she took a startled breath; I had scared her for an instant.

She let go of the letter and ran to me. Without a word, she clenched me in a hug. Our bodies melded together as I returned her embrace. The emotions were overwhelming. I tried to tell her what the letter meant; she looked up at me and gently placed her finger over my lips. She didn't need an explanation. We released. She wiped the tears away and said, "I've missed you, love." I was still unable to speak clearly. I just shook my head, but realized she knew the depth of my feelings. A flash of Joe passed through my mind. How did he know she would know?

After coming back to reality, I asked Clair if she wanted a glass of wine, coffee, or anything. "Wine," she nodded.

"Good. I have a couple of nice bottles of red downstairs for gifts to take back home. I'll be right back."

"No, you go downstairs. I need a few minutes to freshen up. I'll be down shortly."

I literally leapt down the stairs to the kitchen. I found glasses in the cupboard, uncorked one of the cabernets, and poured the deep red wine. I went into the living room with only the lights from the kitchen filtering through, placed the glasses on the coffee table and sat on the love seat, wondering and waiting. I took a deep breath. I was consumed by the thoughts firing through my mind. 'Take it easy,' I counseled myself.

I took a slow sip of wine, letting my taste buds absorb the flavor, hoping the wine would take effect and calm me down. But I didn't know if I should be calm. If I was going to be excited this is the excitement I preferred. The wine was full bodied and dry, just as Claire liked. A few more minutes passed, then I heard the creek of the old staircase. In the darkness I could just make out her outline as she stepped down the stairs barefoot in a lace-trimmed black slip, cut just above the knees. She came over and gave me a soft kiss. I handed her the glass and we toasted. I was still in the clouds.

"Geoff, I'm sure you know that coming down here goes against all my professional training. But something strong told me to come and I followed my intuition." She paused, smiled, then moved closer and caressed my unshaven cheek. "I can't tell you how many times my mind questioned this trip. But then I thought, sometimes in life, things aren't black and white. As much as I loved you, I really didn't understand you fully." I sat there silent. She continued, "Then I began listening closely to your messages. I realized that in making this trip you had made the right choice for yourself. Ultimately it may be the best choice for us as well. It's difficult to know. You know I rarely make exceptions. But now, you are my one big exception."

At that moment I felt total contentment welling up in me. It was something in a relationship that I don't think I had felt much, if ever, in my life. I felt known. When I thought about it, most of my friends didn't really know me. My siblings didn't know me, my parents really didn't know me. I knew they loved me, but they didn't *know* me. But now Claire did, and so did Joe Burlington. What else could I hope for? That was more than my share, a blessing of abundance. I felt I knew her too. I knew every curve in her face, her beautiful face, her voluptuous body, her loving heart, her pragmatic mind, and her strong sense of justice in this world.

She continued to explain her reentry into my life. "I didn't mean to barge in on you but when you left those messages about the changes taking place in you, good memories came rushing back. My feelings were so strong I knew I needed to come. I called the Pedersens and went and picked up a key. My plan was to surprise you." She looked sideways at me with a little curve of a smile.

"That you did."

"And then when I was about to closet my jacket, I saw your letter to me. I realized in an instant I had made the right decision. I could just feel a change in you. Whatever was happening to you was beginning to reveal itself, and it was a good change. I could tell it was authentic."

"You know, you sound like Joe."

"Really? I want to meet him."

"You will, tomorrow. I need to make one more trip over."

"Geoff, before, I was looking at our relationship as though you were the only one who needed to change, but in truth, we both needed some transforming. I think you found the right help in your guy." I nodded in agreement. We both took a deep breath and a long sip of wine.

I looked into her eyes and said, "I'm so glad you came. I didn't know if you would be willing to try for us again." She looked at me with consoling eyes and reached over and touched my shoulder to reassure me.

It was very late now. I motioned for us to go upstairs. I took a few minutes to take a quick shower while she readied the room and opened the windows to let in some fresh ocean air. When I returned, she had lit a candle and turned out the lights and there was soft easy listening on the clock radio. She was waiting for me in bed. I slid in next to her and realized I had forgotten how soft her skin was.

Before dawn I awakened to the sound of the waves slapping in rhythm against the dunes. I quietly went downstairs and made coffee. I came back to bed and lay there just enjoying my coffee and watching Claire sleep. It was a beautiful and peaceful sight. I felt content all over again.

Claire was a slow riser, but the smell of coffee always got her going. She yawned, stretched her arms, and opened her eyes. I kissed her good morning softly. "Have some coffee," I pointed to the cup I had placed on the table next to her. She loved her first cup of coffee.

After she'd taken a few sips, I looked at the clock and said, "I don't mean to rush you, but we haven't much time if we're gonna have breakfast and meet Joe before we catch our flight. She smiled back at me and didn't seem to register the time constraints the flight posed on our morning. "How about while you get dressed, I get everything closed up and packed in the car. We'll go down to Lou's, have breakfast, and I can tell you all about Joe Burlington."

Claire was able to get into high gear after that first cup of coffee. It was only a few minutes later—record time!—when she came down the stairs with her overnight bag and a suitcase. I couldn't imagine why she'd brought so much luggage. "Ready?"

She nodded. We locked up and took a brisk stroll down to Lou's. As we approached, the familiar smell of coffee, freshly baked bread and bacon filled the air.

We entered the diner and Lou greeted the two of us. He had a hard time hiding his surprise as a smile spread over his whole face. He came out from behind the counter to greet us. Claire gave him a hug and I shook his hand and gave him a half-hug. I could tell he was happy that Claire was with me. Seeing us together seemed to make his day. We took a booth in the back and ordered our usual. We were both in a state of mind not unlike that of a couple after the first night of their honeymoon.

"Tell me about your guy."

"What guy?" I smiled mischievously.

"Come on, Geoff," she said with playful eyes, "Joe!"

"OK, OK. Where shall I begin? You already know about the summit and what happened in New Orleans." She nodded. "And how I came to find him here in South Florida. So let me begin with the day I arrived at his golf center. You know how sometimes you can be overwhelmed by celebrities that seem larger than life? I mean, their persona. They have the looks, all the attributes, and the manner that go with being important in our culture. Well, Joe is *not* that guy! He is, at first, totally underwhelming. At least that's the first impression I got. He seems to be a regular guy who happens to be pretty good at teaching golf, but as you spend time with him, you realize your first impression was extremely shallow." I began to tell her about my adventure.

Claire sat captivated. "I could tell something was going on with you..."

I stopped her. "Claire, you were right all along. I needed to change. I knew it, I just didn't know how to go about it. I needed someone besides you to help me. I needed more than golf lessons, and guess what? I got more than golf lessons. I want to tell you everything but it's such a blur it's hard to describe."

"I can only describe Joe's golf center as a hole-in-the-wall range; it's here in Pompano Beach. To be honest, if you'd taken a look at the place you would have questioned it too. When I arrived something told me to get the hell out of there, but another voice followed and told me to stay. I listened; what did I have to lose?" I began to tell her of each day, describing everything that happened as it passed through my mind, as best I could remember. But mostly she wanted to know about Burlington and how he was able to get through to me.

"Actually, he didn't get through to me at all." She looked puzzled. "But he did show me how to get through to myself." She smiled and chuckled. "Claire, I don't know if I can adequately describe to you, or for that matter to anyone, what has happened to me these past few days—what it feels like to experience the gradual changes taking place within me. During this journey I believe I have moved toward some measure of enlightenment within myself, us, my golf game—in truth, life itself. The awareness I'm experiencing now isn't what I thought I was looking for or what I expected. But I like it. And now I know exactly what I need, and what's more, how to nurture it. Burlington made that infinitely clear. He shared things with me that I simply couldn't put into words."

"How so?"

"I can feel that elusive confidence that seemed so distant before and never lasted. I notice things in a different way." Her eyes livened as she seemed to picture what I was saying. I thought of Burlington and his technique; I still had a hard time categorizing him and it. He simply did not fit into any category. He wasn't a golf pro per se, he wasn't a guru, he wasn't like anyone I had experienced before. And now I was a totally different person. How could I explain all this to Claire? I just said, "Now I find myself coming from a wholly different perspective."

"Tell me more."

I paused, took a slug from my coffee cup, and tried to think of what to tell her next. "Well, for one, he predicted that you might surprise me."

She shook her head. "How would he know that? I decided to come here just yesterday; I didn't even know if I would go through with it until I fastened my seatbelt on the plane!"

"I only showed him a picture of you and described our relationship just last night. I don't know how he knew, he just did." We both just stared at each other in amazement for a moment before I continued.

"Let me tell you about his golf lessons. When he gives a lesson, there's none of the new technology that I use, no video, position models, and the like. His approach has no relation to the modern mechanistic golf world we know. When he begins a lesson, his first order of business is not about golf at all. He begins by finding out about his student's personality and experience. He establishes a rapport. Then he inquires about their golf problems from their perspective. Claire, it was nothing like how I used to conduct lessons! It's just him and his experience relating to a student—everything coming from within them and then within him.

"And he has a way with language. Words take on different meanings when arranged in his manner of speaking, and they seem to be exactly what his students need. He always seems to know what to say. It was like magic. Or...not magic, it was more mystical than magical. That's the word, he was like a mystic."

"A mystic?" Claire leaned in, intrigued.

"He has a timeless, mystical knowledge. I felt everything he did was done through an intuitive source deep within him and beyond reason." I had a flash of insight. Now realizing even more what Joe was about, I leaned in to tell Claire. "That's why, at first, his behavior and language seemed so strange and cryptic. He just comes from a totally different source than I was accustomed to. And there's no separation between how he lives life and teaches or plays golf. There is cohesion and connectedness. He relates golf and life to physics, believe it or not, in particular the aspect of that science that tells us all things are connected."

It was all pouring out of me now like water over a dam—I couldn't stop the flow. "And he made a big point about perspective, too, that attitude plays the major role in life and it doesn't matter what you do or where you are. Joe believes that what matters is who you are with and how you relate!

Relationships are key, and I saw him demonstrating that a special love needs to permeate all encounters. He kept reminding me to recognize the holistic nature in all things." Poor Claire couldn't get a word in.

"To make his point about the physics of the golf swing he used a foam Pathfinder he designed and a tee as a pointer in a special glove. His philosophy for developing a swing was completely foreign to me. He kept emphasizing, 'Don't teach the individual parts; the whole creates the parts.'" Claire's eyes encouraged me to explain more. "You develop the whole swing, and then the parts of a swing—the body's action—are a result of the student picturing, feeling, and knowing the complete action of the club. This way he can make it simple and not conflict anyone. Claire, he has turned the learning process upside down, or should I say right side up. He says there needs to be a paradigm shift. But he didn't just shift the paradigm, he flipped it.

"Do you know how I know that what he teaches is the truth? Because everyone got it, and no one was confused! Claire, I received an indelible imprint in my mind. Right now as I am telling you, as we sit here, I see even more clearly the purpose of everything that happened during the week." I shook my head and chuckled, looking downward and now smiling inside. "Anyway, after a few hours I was getting hooked. His message was clear. And it's a good message, Claire, it has a heart."

I reached across the table for her hand. "I want badly to live what he preached—no, he never preached, he expressed, laid it all out there and gave everyone a choice. I liked the freedom in his message." Her eyes showed me we had really connected on a different level this time.

I let go of her hand, took one last sip of my lukewarm coffee, and said, "We better go. We need to get there soon. No telling what he will be into." She drank down her last sip of coffee. I paid the bill, tipped the waitress, and we bid Lou farewell.

I drove faster than normal. We arrived at the golf center in record time. We parked and walked up the ramp into the clubhouse. Jimmy greeted us with a smile and winked at me when he saw Claire. "Want me to call Joe on the squawk box?"

"No, that's quite all right, we'll just head down there if that's OK."

Jimmy nodded. "Sure!"

We walked behind the main tee to the barn. Otter was there under his pine tree snoozing away. He raised his head as we approached, gazed up at us, and gave us a pitiful brown-eyed look. Claire bent down to scratch him under his chin and around his ears. He lifted his paw when she stood. I couldn't tell if he was thanking her or asking for more. We walked over to the open doors of the barn and I called for Joe. There was no way he could hear me with the compressor bellowing. The air-hose was stretched a good twenty feet across the floor onto the other side of the shop. I followed it to a pair of moccasins sticking out from under the Kubota carry-all. I chuckled to myself and thought, well, she's gonna get the whole enchilada.

The compressor shut down and the place fell silent. "Joe?"

From down under we heard "Geoff, good, good, I'm glad you came. Could you hand me the grease gun on the table? Use a towel to pick it up." Claire stood in the doorway with a puzzled smile. I went over to the table with a shop towel and got the grease gun for him. I handed it down to his outstretched hand. I still couldn't see his face. "Thank you. I'll be done in a second."

Claire still hadn't followed me in. I knew what was going through her mind. Leaves had blown in from the yard. Everything was about, there were tools laid out on the tables and floor. She was beginning to get my drift about the place, just as I had a week or so ago. Two more minutes passed, then Joe crawled out from under the machine. He was a bit dirty and sweat was dripping from his brow. "Good morning," he said as he wiped his hands. We were facing away from Claire and he hadn't noticed her yet.

"I have someone who would like to meet you." We turned and as he caught sight of Claire a smile spread over his face. Claire came in. I was proud of the way she looked. She was wearing a dark green golf shirt that complemented her Irish brown eyes. She extended her hand to Joe. "Good morning, Mr. Burlington."

He didn't seem surprised. "You must be Claire."

"Yes." She beamed as warmth radiated from him, as it had a week ago.

He nodded. "Yes, very, very nice to meet you. So you got his message. I'm glad. It seems you two are on the same page now."

She smiled and said, "Yes."

"That's good, real good. I have had a wonderful week with your man. He has rejuvenated me." I was pleasantly surprised by his description of our week. I thought I was the one who was rejuvenated.

"Really?" she said.

Then Joe remarked, "I understand you're heading back to the cold north today."

"Ah no, not really," she said. "That was Geoff's original plan but..."

I interrupted. "Honey, actually, really, he's right, and we don't have much time if we're gonna make our flight."

Claire looked at me with an impish grin. "I have one more surprise. We don't have a flight today."

"But the tickets..."

"Geoff darling, I've arranged it all. I had my friend Sandy set us up on Silver Seas Cruises for a week in the Caribbean. We do have a lot of catching up to do, don't you think?"

"Of course, of course." Joe nodded in agreement.

I looked at Claire. "You *are* full of surprises! It's all arranged, then?" She nodded. "OK, I'm there," I shrugged. Then I turned to Joe. "I don't know what to say except thank you."

As he looked at me, his eyes radiated deep warmth and connectedness. "Geoff, remember, it was always in there." He pointed to my heart. "I just helped you draw it out. You have all it takes. Now go and do what you were born to do." He looked at Claire. "You've got a good man here; he really loves you."

"I know," she said.

"Take good care of each other, it's well worth the effort." His words and the fact that we had to leave caused my eyes to well up. I leaned into him and gave him a farewell shake with my right hand and a goodbye hug with my left. He returned the hug and patted me on the back as he whispered "Geoff, you have your wings; carry on."

Joe walked us out the gate. Claire reached up to give him a kiss on the cheek and whispered, "Thank you."

Both of us were reluctant to leave. We walked away hand in hand, then paused for just a moment to glance back. Joe was kneeling down stroking Otter's chest. He looked out toward us to give one last wave. It struck me at that moment that Joe had given us the keys to our future. We turned and walked away together...into the next moment of our lives.

NOTES

1 Fritjof Capra, *The Tao of Physics* (Shambhala Publications, 1975).

2 Serendip. "Proprioception: How and Why?" by Shannon Lee, 2008. http://serendip.brynmawr.edu/exchange/node/1699.

3 "Proprioception: How and Why?"

4 S.J. Anthony Demello, *One Minute Wisdom* (Doubleday Dell Publishing Group, 1986).

5 Betty Edwards, *Drawing on the Artist Within* (Simon and Schuster, 1986).

6

I whispered, 'I am too young,'
And then, 'I am old enough';
Wherefore I threw a penny
To find out if I might love.
'Go and love, go and love, young man,
If the lady be young and fair.'
Ah, penny, brown penny, brown penny,
I am looped in the loops of her hair.

O love is the crooked thing,
There is nobody wise enough
To find out all that is in it,
For he would be thinking of love
Till the stars had run away
And the shadows had eaten the moon.
Ah, penny, brown penny, brown penny,
One cannot begin too soon.

7 Barry Green with W. Timothy Gallwey, *The Inner Game of Music* (Doubleday, 1986).

8 Demello, *One Minute Wisdom*.

9 Ahrandati Roy, *The God of Small Things* (Random House, 1997).

10 Wayne Dyer, *The Power of Intention* (Hay House, 2010).

11 Ken Burns, *The Civil War*, Episode 1, "The Cause" (PBS, 1990).

[12] Tom Morris, *True Success* (GP Putnam's Sons, 1994).

[13] His Holiness the Dalai Lama and Howard C. Cutler, *The Art of Happiness: A Handbook for Living* (Riverhead Books, 1998).

PHOTOS AND SKETCHES

GB   Gary Battersby

TC2   Tom Christensen, Jr.

TC3   Thomas Christensen III

KT   Kate Tappert

FT   Freddie Tichner

EW   Elliott Wexelman

JW   Jennifer Wood

EW2   Ed Wortzman

Order more copies of

The Golf Mystic

Email completed form to garobattersby@gmail.com,
or mail to 3909 Indian River Dr., Cocoa, FL 32927

Name ____

Address ____

City ___________________________________ State/Province ___________

Zip/Postal Code ___________________ Phone ____________________

Email ____

Ship to (if different from above):

Name ____

Address ____

City ___________________________________ State/Province ____________

Zip/Postal Code ___________________ Phone ____________________

Quantity ordered _________ × $24.95* = ____________________

*plus applicable taxes. Books ship free the same day orders are
received and typically arrive within 2 to 5 days.

Credit Card type: Visa _________ MasterCard _________

Credit Card # ___________________________________ Expiry ____________

Name on card ____

Signature ____

Order more copies of

The Golf Mystic

Email completed form to garobattersby@gmail.com,
or mail to 3909 Indian River Dr., Cocoa, FL 32927

Name ____

Address ____

City ________________________________ State/Province ___________

Zip/Postal Code _________________ Phone ____________________

Email ____

Ship to (if different from above):

Name ____

Address ____

City ________________________________ State/Province ___________

Zip/Postal Code _________________ Phone ____________________

Quantity ordered ________ × $24.95* = ____________________

*plus applicable taxes. Books ship free the same day orders are
received and typically arrive within 2 to 5 days.

Credit Card type: Visa ________ MasterCard ________

Credit Card # ____________________________________ Expiry ___________

Name on card ____

Signature ____

SHORT THINGS

STORIES INSPIRED BY JOHN W. CAMPBELL'S CLASSIC NOVELLA, "WHO GOES THERE?"

ALAN DEAN FOSTER

KRISTINE KATHRYN RUSCH

PAMELA SARGENT

CHELSEA QUINN YARBRO

DARRELL SCHWEITZER

ALLEN M. STEELE

KEVIN J. ANDERSON

NINA KIRIKI HOFFMAN

MARK MCLAUGHLIN

G. D. FALKSEN

ALLEN COLE

PAUL DI FILIPPO

JOHN GREGORY BETANCOURT

THE EXPANDED "THING" UNIVERSE

Frozen Hell, by John W. Campbell, Jr.
Who Goes There? by John W. Campbell, Jr.

FORTHCOMING

Mars Is Hell, by John W. Campbell, Jr. and John Gregory Betancourt
The Things from Another World, by John Gregory Betancourt

SHORT THINGS

STORIES INSPIRED BY JOHN W. CAMPBELL'S CLASSIC NOVELLA, "WHO GOES THERE?"

ART EDITOR
EVELYN KRIETE

EDITOR
JOHN GREGORY BETANCOURT

COVER BY
DAN BRERETON

INTERIOR ILLUSTRATIONS BY
MARC HEMPEL, ALLEN KOSZOWSKI,
RAIKY VIRNICID, AND MARK WHEATLEY

WILDSIDE PRESS

CONTENTS

INTRODUCTION

JOHN GREGORY BETANCOURT

You hold in your hands a curious volume, one that was never intended but just sort of happened on its own. It's as if the universe wanted this book to appear.

Let me back up. In 2018, a set of partial manuscripts by John W. Campbell, Jr. surfaced in the archives of Harvard University. Discovered by scholar Alec Nevala-Lee, these works—which had titles like "Pandora" and "Frozen Hell"—turned out to be early, alternate, incomplete drafts of Campbell's classic story, *Who Goes There?* (one of the most acclaimed science fiction stories of all time, filmed first by Howard Hawks as *The Thing from Another World*, then as *The Thing* by John Carpenter, and again as *The Thing* (though this third version is more of a prequel than a remake). And if all goes well, another remake will happen sometime in the next few years.

I manage the Campbell literary properties for the family, and I saw immediately that there were some great possibilities here. When I assembled all the partials into a single cohesive story, *Frozen Hell* turned out to be 45 pages longer than *Who Goes There?* with most of the new material at the beginning. With this amazing new work in hand, I decided the best way to to publish it properly was tp raise the money to do so through Kickstarter.

And that's where *Things* (if you'll pardon the pun) got interesting.

The *Frozen Hell* Kickstarter project took on a life of its own, ultimately garnering $155,000 in pledges to support it. Along the way, we began looking for stretch goals. It started with a single original Thing story (to be written by me). And as we blew past stretch goal after stretch goal, we kept adding stories. And adding stories. And adding stories.

Finally there were enough that I decided to publish them as a book, too. Here are 13 *original* stories featuring the Thing. Writers were allowed to use their imaginations to do whatever they wanted with this iconic monster. Continue the original story? Sure! Venture into space? Of course! Uncover new Things in other lands and times? Definitely!

These stories—with one exception, my own "Nature of the Beast"—are not officially part of the Thing canon, but they are a lot of fun, and I'm sure you will enjoy them thoroughly.

And watch for *more* new Thing novels and stories coming soon!

LEFTOVERS

ALAN DEAN FOSTER

The thing was dead. Fried, carbonized, reduced to a blackened stain. Even the oily smoke that had comprised the only residue was gone, dispersed by the Antarctic wind.

Macready, Barclay, and Norris stood in the tool shed and gazed thoughtfully at what the thing had left behind.

Despite the ragged entrance and broken door that left the interior open to the outside, it was one hundred and twenty degrees Fahrenheit within the storage facility. Hot and humid enough that all three of the survivors began to sweat despite the icy wind outside. Had the shack remained closed up, the heat would soon have suffocated them. Apparently for the thing, the altered climate had been just right.

The shed was filled with piles of material that had been scavenged from the base's supplies: bits and strips of metal, aluminum and titanium fasteners, cannibalized power tools, engine parts, batteries that had been warped and fused together in inexplicable configurations that resembled sculpture more than power sources, bulbs and tubes fashioned from carefully blown glass, and all of it linked together by glistening torons that looked as if they had been excreted rather than braided.

Resting in the center of it all was an alien mechanism composed of crystal, salvaged metal, and metallic glass. It stood next to and partially enveloped a solid block of stone that glowed with an inner blue fire. Approaching with caution, the three survivors studied it warily. As they drew closer it was apparent that the radiant block was the source of the extraordinary warmth that was heating, or to their minds overheating, the shack. Macready leaned toward the block, then straightened and glanced back toward the ruined doorway. Outside, a katabatic wind was rising. Inside and despite the gaping portal, it was downright tropic.

Barclay pursed his lips. "I've seen that blue color before." In response to his companions guarded reactions he hastened to add, "Not in person. In pictures." He turned back to the incandescent block of stone. "It looks exactly like the glow at the center of a functioning nuclear reactor."

"Sure, why not?" Macready grunted. "Give a thing some scrap, some rock, a little time, and hey presto, out comes your ordinary everyday portable nuclear reactor." He pushed his open palms toward the steady, intense blue light. "I wonder if can do hot dogs?"

"We know one thing it doesn't do," murmured Barclay. "It doesn't emit killing radiation. The thing was tough, but it was killable. Not likely it would knowingly subject itself to a radiation overdose. Of course, we have no way of knowing what its physical tolerance for radiation was. I feel like I'm in Aladdin's cave. The alien version, anyway." His gaze narrowed, and he nodded toward the far side of the shed. "I wonder what that is?"

Edging around the luminous stone block and its inexplicable font of heat, the trio found themselves contemplating a collage of metal, glass, and leather that appeared stuck to the ceiling. Though a small part near the center of the agglomeration looked as if it was on fire, no warmth emanated from it. A rat's nest of leather straps and buckles hung downward from the tangle. To Macready it most nearly resembled a demented artist's interpretation of a dead cephalopod. Or a leather-and-metal jellyfish.

Reaching up, Norris grasped one of the dangling straps and tugged. The leather straightened out but the device, if that's what it was, didn't budge.

"Pull harder," Barclay advised.

Norris stepped away. "_You_ pull harder. Let's see if it pulls back."

"That doesn't make sense." Barclay sounded confident. "If the thing wanted to booby-trap this place it could have done so with something less obvious." Moving underneath the apparatus, he examined the underside carefully.

Watching from a distance, Macready added, "If the thing wanted to booby-trap the shed we'd be dead already."

Barclay replied while continuing his inspection. "That's for sure. No, like the heater block, this must have been put together for some advantage." Reaching up, he grasped a strap and pulled. This had no more effect than had Norris's effort. Gritting his teeth and this time using both hands, he pulled on two of the hanging straps simultaneously and leaned back, putting his weight into the effort.

The device detached from the ceiling. Or more accurately, it was pulled downward. It strained in Barclay's grasp, trying to rise. Studying the ceiling, Macready could see a burn mark where the apparatus had rested. The roofing material was scorched but had not caught fire.

Barclay was already securing one strap after another around his body. When he finally ran out of buckles and clips and other attachments he looked like an early twentieth century urban junkman about to start on his morning rounds.

"How's it feel?" Norris asked him. "For something made for an alien body."

"Unnaturally light." Barclay shifted his shoulders against the mass resting on his shoulders and upper back. "Like it doesn't weigh anything, really."

"Not necessarily made to fit an alien body." Macready was peering hard at the now swathed Barclay. "All those straps and ties are of different length. There's enough slack to accommodate any body. Including a human one."

"I don't see any buttons, switches, or any other kind of control." Norris was frowning as he scrutinized the device. "What d'you think it's it supposed to do?"

Barclay twisted to his right, then to his left. Nothing. Experimentally, he gave a little jump. Rising into the air, he had to duck to avoid bumping his head on the ceiling. Macready blinked. Though it looked as if Barclay was traveling in slow motion, in actuality he had traversed the length of the shed so quickly that the crossing had fooled his companions' optics. It was a singular kind of blur, not unlike the effect that makes rapidly-spinning helicopter blades appear to move slowly.

No sound had come from the device. The air within the shed had not been disturbed. Yet Barclay had effortlessly navigated the room to land on his feet on the opposite side.

Norris shook his head in quiet amazement. "Interesting propulsion system. No evidence of ejecta, no noise, no heat. Some kind of anti-gravity?"

"You read too many stories," Macready snapped.

Unperturbed, Norris stared over at him. "You got a better explanation?"

Macready shook his head. "High-energy physics aren't my field."

"Let's try it outside—see what it can do if I give a really good push." Barclay took a step forward.

Carefully, Macready moved to block his path. "Why? Why outside?"

Taken aback, Barclay blinked at him. "Not much room in here." He frowned at his associate. "You look weird. What's up?"

"I may look weird," Macready replied, "but I'm not acting weird." He held his ground.

"You think I'm acting weird?" Barclay's voice was rising. "Because I want to see what advanced alien technology can do?" Seeing that the third member of their little group was now also eying him uncertainly, Barclay turned his attention to the other man. "You think I'm acting weird, Norris?" He tugged gently on one of the fastening straps. "Even if we only get to share in a portion of this discovery, we'll be famous. Also set for life. Tell me that doesn't interest you."

"Sure it interests me." Moving slowly, deliberately, and without taking his eyes off his companion, Norris reached down to pick a large hammer off the floor. "If I have a life to be set for."

Barclay was now genuinely upset. "What the hell's wrong with you? And you, Macready? All I want to do is try out this backpack a little more. Don't tell me you think…you're not implying…." He took a step backward, eyes darting rapidly between the two men. "You're losing it, both of you!"

Moving casually while careful to keep himself between Barclay and the open doorway, Macready removed one of several ice axes from where they hung on a nearby wall storage rack.

"You're the one who compared—or maybe recognized—the blue glow from the block as being like that in a nuclear reactor. You're the one who said, without any proof, that it didn't emit killing radiation. You're the one who explained why the device that's now on your back and the shed weren't likely to be booby-trapped. When Norris couldn't move detach it from the ceiling, you're the one who advised him to pull harder on a strap, and when he declined, you stepped right in, got it down, and onto your back. And <u>you</u> got it to work."

Patently nervous now, Barclay retreated another step. "Either of you two could have worked it. <u>Could</u> work it." Twisting, he reached for a strap. "Here, dammit, I'll take it off. Try it yourself, Macready. What did you think I was going to do, anyway?"

Raising the business end of the ice axe, Macready held it across his chest. "Take a bigger hop, you said. Where? To McMurdo Base? Maybe to New York?" He nodded at the apparatus. "We don't know what that thing is capable of. Maybe you do?" He took a step forward.

Barclay's reply was a mixture of fear and anger. "Crazy! You've both gone crazy! I'm not a thing—the thing. Get out of my way, goddamn it! Let's go back to the lab and I'll prove it to you!"

"Sure," Norris muttered. "Anything to get outside, where you can jump freely. One jump and you're out of here." He looked over at Macready, who was also advancing. "He almost made it, too."

"Insane, both of you!" Barclay yelled. Whereupon he promptly leaped, aiming for the busted portal.

Macready had been expecting it. Swinging the ice axe, he caught several of the leather straps—and promptly found himself lifted off the ground and being carried effortlessly toward the open doorway.

"Norris—before he gets outside!"

The big man was already in motion. Just as Barclay was about to exit the doorway, Norris heaved the heavy hammer. His accuracy was commendable. The hammer slammed into the side of Barclay's head with a dull thunk. Barclay's eyes glazed over, and he drifted sideways, slamming into the shed wall. As he slid downward, a frantic Macready freed his axe. One swing of the titanium tool pierced Barclay's skull. Blood spurted; staining the floor, the alien apparatus, and Macready's boots. Breathing hard, his heart racing, he stood with hands on knees beside the now motionless Barclay, waiting for him to writhe, to change, to transform.

"There's a torch on the workbench!" he gasped. "Get it, fire it up!" They would have to incinerate this latest and final manifestation of the thing before it could get away. One thing Macready was certain of: it wasn't going to get its pseudopods on him.

"I'm on it!" Norris shouted back. But he didn't rush for the workbench. Instead, he stayed where he was, pondering Macready.

Mac never saw the talon that penetrated his neck from back to front. Dropping the ice axe, he grabbed at his throat with both hands. Fountaining bodily fluids, he fell forward, to land atop the falsely accused and already dead Barclay. Choking on his own blood he bled out very quickly.

Behind him, Norris collapsed. As he folded onto the floor his torso split open like an overripe tomato. Emerging from the shell of the dead human, the mass of eyes and tentacles and protoplasm that was the thing's natural form oozed forward to examine first Barclay's corpse, then Macready's. Outside, the rising wind was howling now.

Emerging from millions of years of stasis, it had been forced into an extremely rapid learning curve. But its kind were clever and adept. Before ultimate death and destruction, it had just barely succeeded in learning how to cope with the primitive but lethal bipeds. Initially, it had reacted out of fear and a straightforward need to survive. Time to think, to analyze, to consider alternate methods of defense and survival had been in short supply. It had hoped to escape this very day by utilizing the transport device it had painstakingly constructed. Instead, it had been compelled to defend itself one more time.

Yet the confrontation had yielded invaluable information. As it slid various parts of itself into the lift device it knew it could now transport itself with confidence into the middle of one of the bipeds' swarming metropolitan throngs. It knew now, at last, how best to assemble and assimilate its primeval antagonists. While they were infinitely superior in numbers that it was by itself unlikely to overcome, the recent confrontation had effectively demonstrated that such forthright conflict was not only unnecessary but actually counterproductive.

With a little persuasion and the right wordings here and there, the thing was confident that the resident indigenous species was perfectly capable of self-extermination provided it was abetted by merely the slightest of verbal proddings from something like its own highly adaptable self....

THE MISSION, AT T-PRIME

KRISTINE KATHRYN RUSCH

Fifty ships ringed the planet they called T-Prime. God knows what the creatures called it. No one wanted to get close enough to find out.

Kessa stood on the bridge of her ship, hands clasped behind her back. She studied the holographic images before her.

They weren't that detailed. On a mission like this, she had learned, it was best not to see too clearly.

What she did see—in the real time imagery—was a thriving planetscape on two large continents, both far enough from the equator to thrive despite the hot sun. She half imagined teaming blue masses below, their round orange eyes taking in everything—miniature suns absorbing rather than giving off.

She had no idea how anything could live on a planet filled with telepathic shapeshifters, or what kind of culture they would build.

Again, she didn't want to find out.

Her palms were wet, and she wiped them on the side of her pants. She normally wasn't nervous. She had been given this job because she was calmer than almost any other captain in this cobbled-together mess of ships, dubbed Earth's Defenders by those who had stayed behind.

Because she was normally "emotionally muted," as the psych evals called her, most of her team was as well. Unlike other bridges in the EDF, this one was never filled with raucous laughter or panicked voices. All five members of her main bridge crew (as well as the five who formed the secondary crew) got the job done, efficiently and quietly, before returning to their quarters or going to the handful of public areas on deck three for private time.

Emotionally muted, and uncharacteristically nervous. She almost pinged her commander to tell them that *America's Pride* wasn't up to the job, but she didn't. It was too late. Back before it was too late, she thought her team could get the job done.

And maybe they could.

Maybe she was the only one who couldn't live with the results.

The ships surrounding T-Prime all bore names like *America's Pride*, only with different countries or unions in the title. The European Union was represented, along with the Pan-African Conference, and every organization in between. The smallest of Earth's 200 countries had sent representatives to work alongside the largest.

Finally, the event that had unified the Earth—at least for the moment—had been repeated discoveries of aliens encased in ice all over the planet. After the first discovery over 150 years ago, humans had fought back effectively, mostly by never thawing the creatures out, and eventually jettisoning their ice-packed bodies into space—outside of the solar system.

But it was clear, as the ice caps melted and the Earth warmed, that these creatures—dubbed "The Things" after the term used by that 1930s Antarctic crew—had scattered themselves all over the planet. That they hadn't accidentally stumbled outside their ships and froze nearly to death, but that they had deliberately planted themselves on Earth, to be found at roughly the same time.

No one knew why that was, but world leaders decided—with the concurrence of almost every scientific mind on the planet—that this had been some kind of odd invasion force, and that these Things had to be stopped.

Didn't matter—as some argued—that the plan the Things concocted was millions of years old, and that at the time, humans didn't even exist. Earth had been a primitive place, ripe for colonization. They could have been refugees, accidental survivors of some major interstellar catastrophe or anything else.

But those arguments hadn't held sway, and so Kessa found herself here, light years away from her home—one she would never see again, one that had probably moved on from this major endeavor, thinking it was safe from invaders that had maybe moved on themselves.

She took several deep calming breaths, quietly, so that her crew wouldn't see how nervous she was.

They all had their heads down, working their own holographic screens, making certain that everything was in order.

She checked the telemetry flowing from the other ships, seeing nothing out of the ordinary.

"Reston," she said, "any changes on T-Prime?"

She had asked Reston to monitor the planet, because it had bothered her from the moment they arrived in this solar system, that no one responded to the arrival of such a massive group of ships.

If the Things were truly hostile space-faring invaders, why hadn't they defended their own planet?

"No changes," Reston said. He looked at her over his shoulder. He was a short thin man whom she relied on for any kind of tricky work. His brain worked along a similar line to hers.

They'd already discussed the strangeness of this assignment, late one night after everyone else cleared out of the fifteen-seat area that was labeled as a "bar" by the ship's specs.

Higher-ups had planned the mission. Everything had taken years. Years upon years upon years, as different ships tracked the Things, monitored different regions of space for the strange ships that resembled early 20th century submarines and ran on some version of power that the unsophisticated Antarctic researchers had thought was magnetic. It wasn't. It had been something else, something she didn't entirely understand, and it had a signature that someone discovered and could follow.

Then there was the discovery of another cache of those ships—abandoned, fortunately—near an exploded moon. EDF had spent a few years retrieving information off those ships, figuring out where the ships had been heading, where they had come from, and what their mission was.

That was when the paranoia grew in the EDF, the belief that these Things were actually trying to supplant humanity, and would try to use humanity's resources, including the human bodies themselves, to expand around the globe.

It all rang false to her, and to Reston too. They didn't discuss it with the rest of the crew, because they had been assigned a mission, along with forty-nine other ships, and they were told, in no uncertain terms, that if they didn't follow the mission, the ship—and its crew—would be destroyed.

She had never faced orders like that before, and until she received the details of the mission, she didn't understand it.

She understood it now.

The look he gave her was a helpless *this makes no sense* look. But it did make sense, if the plans the EDF had found were accurate.

She had also read about the attacks on Earth itself. Scary, near-misses. It was almost impossible to defeat a being that was telepathic, smart, and shifted shape. The very idea of it made her skin crawl.

Like this mission. She clenched her fists, then released them, not sure exactly how to move forward.

The idea came from procedures used in the barbaric 19th and 20th centuries to execute criminals. A squad of men—and they were always men—stood in a line and, on command, shot at a tied-up blindfolded criminal, one who had been judged guilty and who deserved to die.

She had made a feeble protest about this mission: she had said that there had been no real proceeding here, no real determination. Just a guess and a lot of fear.

And that was when she had received the warning. *America's Pride* was already heading to T-Prime; she knew the mission; and if she wanted to divulge it to anyone or to protest it, then she and her crew would die.

Their communications array had already been partially destroyed. Not even removed; destroyed. She could only communicate with the other EDF ships around T-Prime. She couldn't communicate with anyone on the planet if she wanted to.

Nor could she send messages back home.

She and her crew had to do that long before they received details of the mission, and she had chosen not to. She was "emotionally muted" after all, and because of that, really didn't have enough friends and close family to worry about.

It was odd that she was worrying about her colleagues now. Before, she might have considered a job like this something they all had to get through, not something that might cause them sleepless nights in their future.

She bent over the holograms, thinking maybe she would get an up-close scan of the planet's surface. Maybe pick one of the well-lit areas, one that clearly had a lot of tech, and see exactly what a Thing community looked like.

Her hand hovered over the virtual controls for just one moment, and then she brought her hand back. If she did that, her rather limited imagination would have something to play with.

She didn't dare give it fuel. She didn't want to regret what she was required to do.

There's no way out of this, is there? Reston asked, just the night before.

No, she had said softly.

What if we're wrong? he asked. *What if they're harmless?*

There was no evidence that the Things were harmless. Every time humanity had encountered one, humanity had won…just barely. And the cost in human life had been great. It was also twenty or more humans to one original Thing entity.

They weren't harmless.

But she didn't say that.

She knew what he meant. He was asking about the life on the planet before. What if the Things that had come to Earth millions of years ago were outliers. What if the Things that had abandoned those ships were part of that outlier fleet?

What then?

"Um, Captain?" Reston said, a wobble in his voice. He was looking at his screens, and his face had turned a weird shade of gray. "You might want to see this."

"No time," she said.

Because as he spoke, she had gotten a timing packet from headquarters. The ships—all fifty of them—would release a small weapon all at the same time.

Some of the weapons were live. They would hit the planet's surface, and send several different kinds of death into the ecosystem. From gas that destroyed the environment that the Things thrived in to flame that would burn off the gas (and everything in its path) to actual bombs that would drill their way into the planet's core and, if all went as the models said it would, would blow the entire planet into tiny pieces.

By then, the ships would already be at the edge of the solar system. That was why the planet-destroying bombs were last, so that the ships had time to escape the destructive force of an exploding planet.

Her hands were shaking now. Imagine if she wasn't emotionally muted. Imagine if she had the full range of human emotions at her command. She wasn't sure if she'd be standing. She was taking part in the destruction of an entire race—and maybe many other races.

An entire planet, and everything that was part of it.

She took one ragged breath, and reminded herself: three different kinds of active weapons, all of them destructive, spread across thirty ships. And three different kinds of *inactive* weapons, none of them destructive, spread across twenty ships.

No one would know which weapon delivered what blow. The members of the EDF firing squad could, if they so choose, believe that they had nothing to do with the destruction to come.

The countdown began on her holographic panel.

"Ready weapons team," she said, her hand near the weapons release command. If no one had the balls to do this, then she would.

Even though, when it came down to it, she didn't believe in this decision. She regretted standing here, regretted being part of this mission, regretted ever volunteering for the EDF.

"Ready," said Dunster and Kinner in unison. She had assigned two team members for the exact same reason there were twenty ships with inactive weapons. Because she wanted each of her team members to have the ability to lie to themselves, to believe they actually had no part of this gigantic mess.

She watched the timer, ticking down, and then she said in her most forceful voice, "Fire."

Not *fire at will* which was what she was supposed to say. But *fire*, so they fired at *her* will, so that, if their weapons were active, *she* was responsible and no one else.

Her heart pounded against her chest, and she felt lightheaded. She watched as the weapons—dots on her holographic screen—dove toward T-Prime, and then penetrated the atmosphere.

"Bunder," she said to her pilot, "take us to the return coordinates."

Her voice remained calm, even though her entire system was alive with adrenalin. She wanted to look closer at that planet, to see what happened when the gas spread, to watch—

And then the atmosphere ignited, just like it was supposed to. Planet-wide—red and blue and filled with flame that they could actually see from space.

Her crew froze for a moment, staring at their screens, all of them knowing what that horrid fire meant.

Nothing could live through that. Nothing.

And the ship wasn't moving.

"Bunder," she said again.

He moved this time, hand floating over his virtual screen, seemingly as calm as she was pretending to be.

The ship moved, finally. They had more than an hour to get to the rendezvous coordinates.

She hoped those were far enough away.

She let out another breath, then shut off all live images from the planet. She would watch the telemetry from a distance. Hell, she might not even watch that.

It would be pretty damn clear when a planet in this solar system exploded.

She needed to think about something else, to *focus* on something else.

"All right, Reston," she said, proud of herself for that even tone in her voice. Proud that she could hold it together in the face what they all had done. "What were you going to say?"

He shook his head. He looked even sicker than he had earlier.

"It doesn't matter," he said.

"Tell me anyway," she said.

He scanned the bridge. Everyone was watching him, rather than looking at the horrors on their screens. Rather than letting what they had been a part of sink into their consciousness.

"You asked me to dig," he said.

"I did," she said. She had asked him to look at the data, see if there was anything in it that seemed a bit off. "But you're right. It no longer matters."

He nodded, then closed his eyes. One finger on his left hand moved, ever so slightly, and she received a notification on her virtual screen.

He had sent her something anyway.

She had the will power to look away from the planet, the will power to ignore what they were doing, but she couldn't quite ignore this.

She opened the file. It didn't make sense at first. She tapped the images that he had sent, watched as shapes shifted, and tiny blobs of blue liquid—like blood—replicated and injected themselves through environmental suits.

All that protection the teams had worn when they had gone into the abandoned ships: that protection hadn't worked.

This entire mission wasn't something dreamed up by human military leaders. The Things themselves were behind it.

Her knees buckled, but she managed to catch herself before she fell.

Reston was watching her. That strange color in his face—was that because he was as appalled as she was or was he one of them?

"Why?" she asked, and he shrugged.

Such a human motion, but something so easily adopted.

She could think of a dozen reasons why, though. They could be destroying other enemies, using human ships to do so, sparking an interstellar war.

Or they could be destroying their own kind, the ones in their world who *didn't* want to attack other species.

Or they could simply be screwing with the already guilt-laden captains, making them doubt whether or not this mission was the correct one.

As if she hadn't had doubts already.

She closed her eyes, took a deep calming breath, remembered that she was emotionally muted. Events like this shouldn't bother her.

But they did.

Oh, they did.

"Bunder," she said. "Return to our earlier coordinates."

"Captain," he said. "We'll be too close."

They would. And it didn't matter.

Because they should see what they had done, up close and personal. They should watch as an entire planet died—just before they died as well.

She saw no other choice. Not because she couldn't handle the emotions of all of this. Not because she was afraid it would bother her for the rest of her days.

But because she already doubted Reston, and the information she saw. And, she would wager, every other captain saw the same information at the same time.

She would give them a clue how to handle it.

She would show them the future.

Finally—belatedly—she agreed with the generals.

The only way to deal with the Things was to destroy everything they touched.

Not because they were shape-shifters or even because they were telepaths. But because they sowed the seeds of doubt into every action.

And there was only one way to remove any doubt.

She felt calmer than she had in days.

She clasped her hands behind her back, stared at the holographic screen in front of her, and watched a planet die.

She didn't even brace herself for what was going to come next.

She didn't have to.

For the first time since she had joined this mission, she finally felt like she was doing the right thing.

HIS TWO WARS

PAMELA SARGENT

Norris opened the door to find McReady standing on the front stoop, towering over him. The big man dropped his duffle bag, grabbed Norris's hand with a firm grip, and shook it.

"Great to see you again, Vance," McReady said with a heartiness that seemed forced.

"Come on in," Norris said as he stepped back. Abby had taken McReady's phone call that morning after his arrival at Hickam Field. The soldier who had dropped him off was already pulling away in his jeep. McReady picked up the duffel and stooped as he came through the doorway. He looked much the same, with the same broad shoulders and bronze hair, but the red beard that had covered his face during their mission in Antarctica was gone.

"Whew," McReady muttered, wiping his face with the back of his big hand. "Kind of a warm day. But I guess you must be used to it by now."

"It'll be cooler outside." Norris had not paid much attention to the weather except to note that it was slightly warmer than expected for Honolulu in early December. "And what brings you to Hawaii?"

"Heading for Manila. Seems MacArthur and his boys can use a meteorologist there. So I figured I might as well stop over for a few days."

"Mac's here," Norris called out to his wife as he led his visitor toward the lanai. Abby followed them outside from the kitchen, carrying a tray with two glasses and two bottles of beer. She glanced toward McReady as he set down his bag. He looked up and gazed back at her with slightly narrowed eyes. Norris was suddenly certain that Abby had secretly talked Mac into visiting them here on his way to the Philippines. She might have written to him or sent him a telegram. Given that he hadn't spotted any long-distance charges on their telephone bill, she might have placed a call to him from her desk at the newspaper.

They both thought he was crazy. Maybe he was, Norris thought. He couldn't even look at the red blossoms on the ohia lehua trees near the house without recalling the red eyes of that creature, the Thing that still haunted him. The damned Thing was still out there, somewhere. He could sense it hiding in the life around him. Up in the trees near the lanai, a myna bird screeched, as if in warning, and another myna cried out in response. The hills below the house were thick with the greenery of plants that might easily camouflage alien invaders.

"Good to see you both again," McReady said as he sat down in a wicker chair and stretched out his long legs, then glanced at the glasses and beer bottles. "You're not joining us?" he said to Abby.

"Can't," she replied. "Promised my editor I'd check in with him this afternoon but I'll be back in plenty of time to join you two for dinner."

"You two pick the place. Dinner's on me. Drinks, too."

"I'll look forward to it, especially since I won't have to cook, and I think I've found the perfect date for you."

McReady frowned. "Another Wellesley girl?" Back in Boston, Abby had set him up on a couple of blind dates with former classmates of hers that hadn't gone too well.

Abby shook her head. "A nurse at Tripler General. Interviewed her a month ago for a story about the hospital and I think you'll like her. See you later." She waved her fingers at them before retreating through the open door to the living room.

Norris heard the front door slam shut. "So Abby's still working," McReady said as he poured himself a beer. Norris could guess at what he wasn't saying, that Abby wouldn't be writing for the Honolulu *Star-Bulletin* if Norris was able to hold up his end, not that they needed the money from her job given what came in from her trust fund. She held on to the job, he couldn't help thinking, largely because it was preferable to spending long days at home with a brooding, shell-shocked husband. "And what have you been up to these days?"

"Tutoring. Basic science and some physics."

McReady frowned.

"A couple of local high school kids," Norris continued. "One of them has a rich dad who wants to make sure he's ready for Yale next year but the other boy shows some real promise."

McReady's ruddy face softened. He was feeling sorry for Norris now, and Norris didn't welcome his sympathy. McReady had stayed with him and Abby in Boston just after their return from Antarctica, when they had been given some much-needed leave time, and Norris had welcomed the other man's company. They had spent their afternoons taking long walks and sitting in on lectures at M.I.T. and their evenings at Boston Bruins games or making the rounds of the nearby bars. They never talked about their time in Antarctica, their battle against that shape-changing alien Thing, the comrades they had lost there, or the report that McReady, with input from the rest of the survivors, had written before it was finally classified and filed away.

McReady had left Boston after a month and a half to visit his parents in New Jersey, promising to visit again soon once he found out where his next assignment would be. Not long after that, Abby discovered she was pregnant and quit her job writing for the Boston *Herald*'s society pages to prepare for the birth of their first child.

And it was then that the Thing had started haunting Norris again. He would wake in the middle of the night, feeling it near him, knowing that if he moved even an inch he would feel the slimy grip of an alien tentacle. Whenever the winter wind howled outside, muffling the sound of the traffic in Boston's streets, he was back at the base in Antarctica, thinking he was again hearing Blair's hysterical gibberings from the shack where the biologist had imprisoned himself before the alien had taken over his body and erased Blair altogether. Lying next to Abby as she slept, Norris would suddenly recoil, imagining that a drop of blood from the Thing had somehow infected him and that something alien now gestated inside his wife's body.

In her sixth month, Abby had fallen on their icy front steps and had lost the baby afterwards. He remembered sitting with her in the hospital as she wept and grieved over their loss and confessed to him that the doctor had told her there was probably no chance for another child. All he could feel was relief at knowing nothing alien could ever grow inside her again.

He didn't remember much about the months after that. There was a vague memory of another visit from McReady, dim recollections of overheard mutterings about battle fatigue and nervous breakdowns, his angry refusal to submit to sessions with a psychoanalyst, and of being discharged from the Expeditionary Force team not long after that. He had been assured no dishonor or stigma would be attached to his discharge, which would officially be labeled an "indefinite leave." Even so, he had felt ashamed, unfit, less than a man somehow. It was Abby's idea to move to Honolulu, where she had a cousin who could get her a job there as a reporter. Maybe she had also been thinking that life in such a tropical paradise might finally heal him.

"…to the Philippines at the wrong time," McReady was saying. Norris forced his attention back to the other man. "The Japs aren't going to tolerate that oil embargo forever. They'll have to make a move sooner or later."

"Let's hope it's later." Or never, he thought. Abby had been saying much the same thing lately. They might soon be at war, according to some of her colleagues at the newspaper.

Norris poured beer into a glass as McReady lit a cigarette. A movement near him caught his eye as a house finch alighted on the railing near him and then flew away.

Norris repressed a shiver. The sight of any bird, even a tiny one like that finch, made him uneasy, reminding him of the albatross he had shot down in Antarctica. Occasionally while walking on one of the nearby beaches, he had seen an albatross circling overhead and thought of how easily they might have lost their battle against the alien. The Thing might not even have needed the antigravity device it had been putting together in order to conquer the world, or any of the alien technology Norris had hoped to study before the rest of the team had decided that mankind wasn't yet ready to be trusted with such knowledge. It might instead have hitched a ride on that big white bird, swallowed the albatross and taken on its form or infected it with one tiny stray drop of blood. Maybe just a molecule would have been sufficient to transform an albatross into a Thing that could threaten all of Earth.

They had been able to win one battle. They had defeated the monster and the alien technology lay hidden under the Antarctic ice. Now he wondered if they had actually won that war.

The front doorbell rang. Norris stood up. "Don't know who that could be," he said, wondering who would be dropping by. Apart from his two students and their families and a couple of Abby's coworkers, he hadn't made that many acquaintances here.

He went to the door and opened it.

Jonathan Nishimoto was outside, clutching a pulp magazine. He was small, with closely cropped black hair, a sixteen-year-old boy who looked no older than twelve. Norris remembered what it had been like for him at that age, when he had been smaller than all of the boys in his class.

"I forgot to bring this back before," the boy said, holding out the magazine, which bore a cover depicting a frightened man and a swath of starry sky above what looked like a telescope. "What a great story."

"Which one?" Norris asked. He hadn't read much pulp fiction during the last couple of years, although he picked up the occasional magazine mostly out of habit. Once the stories had been an escape for him; now they seemed pallid next to what he had experienced.

"'Nightfall,'" Jonathan said as he handed the magazine to him. Norris glanced at the title, printed in red capital letters on the cover, but didn't recognize the author's name. "It's about a planet where there's no night, only daytime, so nobody ever sees the stars, they don't even know there are any stars except for their own sun, but..." The boy fell silent. "Read it yet?"

Norris shook his head.

"Then I better not give away the ending."

"Come on outside and meet an old friend of mine." Norris dropped the magazine on the coffee table and led Jonathan toward the lanai. "He just got here from the States this afternoon." McReady looked up as they stepped outside. "Mac, meet Jonny Nishimoto. He's the boy I was telling you about, the one who'll be a darned good scientist one of these days." Jonathan lowered his head, as if embarrassed. "Jonny, this is Mac McReady."

McReady tensed, stared at the boy for a few long seconds, and then managed a half-smile. "Hello," he muttered.

"Hi," Jonathan said in a small voice.

"Can I get you a soda?" Norris asked.

"No, thanks." Jonathan turned toward him. "I have to get back home," he went on. "Promised Dad I'd help him weed our garden." He nodded in McReady's direction. "Nice to meet you, Mr. McReady." He glanced at Norris. "Thanks for letting me borrow your *Astounding*, Mr. Norris."

"Any time." Jonny always brought any borrowed magazines back in pristine condition. He was as meticulous in caring for them as his father was with their garden and his mother in maintaining their house, a small and spare but well-maintained wooden structure supported by large beams of teak.

McReady's eyes narrowed as the boy left the lanai. He gulped down more beer. "Maybe you shouldn't be tutoring that kid," he said at last. "You never know. The Japs might—"

"Jonny's as American as you are, Mac. His grandparents came here before …" He caught himself just in time. "Before the turn of the century," he finished. Before my grandfather got off the boat in New York, he had almost said. Norris had never told Mac about his immigrant grandfather or the father who had decided, probably correctly, that his son would do better in the new country with the name of Vance Norris instead of Vincente Naroni.

Jonny was, Norris thought, a hell of a lot more human than Blair had been at the end. He could look into Jonny's almond-shaped eyes and see a fellow human being gazing back at him, a boy not unlike the one Norris had once been.

* * * *

Norris listened as McReady talked about his future plans. Back in Washington that summer, there had been a change involving American policy toward the Philippines. If the Japanese were going to attack, those islands were probably where they would strike first. For some time, it had been generally accepted that there was little chance of defending the Philippines, with the Japanese holding Formosa and also in control of Indochina. But with a large concentration of American aircraft now based in the Philippines and General MacArthur having been busy building up the Filipino and U.S. forces, defending the islands was now feasible.

There was a good chance Mac would be in the middle of a war once he landed in Manila but he did not seem disturbed by that prospect. Maybe he was thinking that nothing could be worse than what they had already gone through in Antarctica.

"You're still in the reserves, aren't you?" McReady said. Norris nodded. "But you might not get called up."

"Think I can't handle that?"

"That wasn't what I was thinking. I'm worried about you, Vance, and not because I think you're a shirker or a coward. You proved you weren't, back in that frozen hell."

Norris shook his head. "At first I couldn't stop thinking that we didn't kill it all, end it for good. I kept thinking of ways some bit of it might have escaped us."

McReady looked away for a moment. Norris thought he glimpsed an uneasy, almost fearful look on the other man's face, as if he was thinking the same thing. "We got it all. I'm damned sure of that. If there was any chance, if I thought we hadn't—"

"—you would have burned out even more of the place and none of us would have left the station alive," Norris finished. "I know that. It doesn't help. I can't help wondering if that was the only one of their ships, if there isn't another one hidden somewhere, in Antarctica or maybe somewhere else."

"You're just spooking yourself, Vance."

"It's a possibility."

"Okay, it's possible. Maybe there's another Thing buried out there some-where. Maybe there's another alien ship on its way here right now that we haven't detected. But until we have hard evidence for something like that, I'm not going to sit around worrying about it."

That was what any rational man would do, Norris thought. That was how somebody like Mac, who had surely been as terrified as the rest of them while confronting the alien, would behave.

"And if anything like that shows up again,' McReady continued, "it'll be facing the deadliest species alive—Man. Now show me where I can park this duffel and then maybe we can take a tour of the neighborhood."

"Abby has the car."

"Doesn't matter. We—I can use some exercise."

* * * *

They left McReady's bag in the small room where Abby did her sew-ing and had set up a cot for their guest, then went for a walk. The narrow road from Norris's house led down a hill to a roadside stand where a few lo-cal farmers had pineapples, mangos, and lychees for sale and two boys were selling glasses of fresh tangerine juice. The farmers were Japanese and, like many of the people in the region, had fruit trees and gardens in the narrow plots next to their houses. McReady bought a glass of juice from one of the kids and complimented the adults on their produce, sounding a bit too expan-sive in his praise.

They left the fruit stand and walked on. To the west, they could glimpse the armada anchored at Pearl Harbor, but McReady kept on talking about the weather, the greenery around them, how tasty the tangerine juice was—any-thing, Norris supposed, that would distract them from brooding about more serious matters. Such efforts were useless. He was already thinking about the coming war that seemed inevitable. Maybe slapping an oil embargo on the Japs and freezing their assets would finally push them over the edge. He won-dered if war could still be avoided, how many opportunities for negotiation and understanding President Roosevelt and his Cabinet might have missed. The Japanese could be as merciless as their soldiers had been in China or they could also be as peaceful and industrious as the farmers selling their fruit and Jonny Nishimoto dreaming of becoming a scientist.

He could guess what McReady would think about such musings, that they were as useless and delusionary as hoping that one could make peace with something as alien as the Thing.

Norris tensed at that thought. Only a few nights ago, he had dreamed he was standing over the Thing again as it lay in its block of frozen ice. The ice had suddenly disappeared and Norris watched, unable to move, staring helplessly at the writhing blue worms on the creature's head. The alien glared at him with its angry red eyes and then abruptly took on the form of Commander Garry, who had led the Antarctic team. The Thing that had been Garry lifted its hand, and it came to Norris that the alien was trying to tell him something, that infecting and taking on the form of the commander and Blair and the others was not an attempt to conquer Earth, but instead a desperate attempt to communicate. If he waited, he might even be able to sense the Thing's thoughts, its plea for help in surviving in a frozen alien environment, on a world that lacked the familiar light of a blue sun.

"Vance." A big hand clutched his shoulder. "Are you all right?" Norris shook off the tendrils of the dream. "Something wrong?"

Norris shook his head.

"You just suddenly stopped walking and got this funny look on your face." McReady peered at him. "Sure you're okay?"

"I'm fine."

They walked on. Norris was thinking of the debriefings they had undergone after their return from Antarctica. The last debriefing had been more like an inquisition, with queries from various bureaucrats representing the War and Navy Departments that were more like accusations of incompetence and bad judgment than questions. They had destroyed an alien artifact before it could yield any of its secrets. They had wiped out an alien life form before being able to determine whether it was hostile or simply acting in its own defense. Norris began to wonder if they were going to be summarily discharged, court-martialed, or secretly consigned to a long stretch in Leavenworth. By the time the interrogation reached its end, McReady's frown had turned into a scowl and his heavy brows were drawn together over eyes narrowed in anger.

"Got anything else to ask us?" McReady said in a low voice. The Assistant Secretary of War, a small, balding man, shook his head. "Now I can't tell you for sure if that creature, that Thing, came here intending to take us over, or only because it got curious about our world, or just ended up landing here by accident, but that doesn't really matter. Whether it was acting in self-defense or out of pure malice doesn't matter, either. We know it had a technology far in advance of ours and that, if it wasn't stopped, it could have infected and taken over and wiped out the entire human race." He paused. "The only safe assumption to make was that it was either the Thing or us, that any species that managed to develop that level of technology, that could whip up an antigravity device using whatever happened to be at hand, that could make it across the galaxy to another planet, was going to arrive at the same conclusion once it encountered us—that it was either their species or ours. Them or us." McReady managed a crooked smile. "I can't even say for sure whether that Thing was even thinking consciously along those lines or just acting on blind instinct, but that doesn't matter, either. When it started taking over, when we found out it was a damned shape-changer, we did what we had to do. We knew we couldn't even trust each other until we eradicated every trace of that creature."

The Assistant Secretary of War scowled. "Even if we grant you that much," he began, "you needn't have destroyed the alien's equipment and deprived us of any opportunity to learn from it."

"Permission to speak frankly, sir," McReady muttered in a sarcastic tone. "Don't be an idiot." He showed his teeth. "If you'd crash-landed on an alien world, what would have been your priority? If you were a scout, which that Thing might well have been, you'd want to find a way to let the rest of your team know where you were. If you'd landed somewhere by accident, if you'd gone off course somehow and ended up God knows where, you'd be fixing to send out a signal. Whatever else that contraption it managed to build could do, I'm willing to bet some sort of communications device was part of it. The alien would have tried to get the word out."

"After twenty million years?" A gray-haired rear admiral from the Navy Department had spoken. "Didn't you determine that the alien vessel had landed here about that long ago?"

"Maybe it didn't realize it had been under ice for that long." McReady folded his arms. "And maybe a civilization that can cross space can stick around for twenty million years or longer. I hope I'm wrong about that, hope they're long gone, along with whatever hellish world spawned them, but you never know." He paused. "Right now our only defense against a Thing like that is to lie low and hope another one never finds its way back to our world again, destroy any evidence that it was ever here, make certain that it couldn't send out any kind of signal and that we wouldn't accidentally send out one ourselves on the device it was putting together. Whatever we might have learned from its technology, any discoveries we might have made, wouldn't be worth the risk."

The meeting had ended with their interrogators muttering among themselves before announcing their decision. The surviving members of their team would be granted a long leave before being assigned to other duties. Their report would be labeled top secret and anybody revealing what had happened in Antarctica to anyone outside that room would face the harshest of penalties. Not that anyone was likely to reveal any secrets, Norris had thought, given that anybody else hearing such a tale would find it unbelievable and consider its narrator nuts.

"What now?" McReady asked, startling him back into the present. "Sure you're okay?"

"I'm fine," Norris replied, keeping his eyes down. He was avoiding any glance at the shrubs and trees on either side of the road, fearing that all he would see there were fleeting hallucinatory glimpses of the writhing tentacles and repulsive red eyes of the Thing.

* * * *

Abby arrived at the house just before sunset after calling to say that she would pick up Mac's date for the evening on her way home. The date, Noelani Wieland, who wore a red silk dress, turned out to be a tall and shapely young woman with long black hair who bore a marked resemblance to Dorothy Lamour. At the sight of her, McReady brightened and quickly ushered her to the lanai, where the two sat down next to each other on the wicker love seat.

"Promised Abby and Vance our night out would be on me," McReady said as he lit Noelani's cigarette. "But I could use some recommendations about where to go."

"Depends on what you're looking for," Noelani murmured in a husky voice. "If you like living dangerously, just head for the bars on Hotel Street near the docks, but I don't think I'd recommend that to any respectable guy." McReady grinned, clearly happy that she didn't sound much like a Wellesley girl. "If you're looking for the swankiest place around, nothing beats the Royal Hawaiian, but it'll cost you. If you want a good steak and drinks and a dance band on the patio, there's Kemoo Farm outside the city. The soldiers at Schofield like to hang out there, but it's a long drive." Noelani seemed very familiar with the island's night life.

"You and Abby decide," McReady said, "and I don't mind spending money for a good time, so if it's the Royal Hawaiian—"

Noelani's face lit up. "We'll have to dress up for that," Abby said.

McReady grinned. "Then it's a good thing I packed my dinner jacket."

That was Mac, Norris thought, always prepared for anything. Abby glanced at him as he thought guiltily of how long it had been since he had taken her out.

* * * *

The dance floor overlooking the beach outside the pink façade of the Royal Hawaiian Hotel was already crowded with dancing couples by the time they arrived. Noelani had recommended that they dine at a Chinese restaurant along the way that had good food and strong drinks at about half the price they would have paid at the Royal Hawaiian. While they ate, Mac entertained them with tales of inventive pranks he had devised as a student at M.I.T. and Norris refrained from pointing out that his old friend had a talent for exaggerating his exploits. They had all agreed that the food was the best any of them had eaten in a while, and even Norris felt his spirits lifting as they left the restaurant.

Norris slipped a bellhop a few dollars to park his sedan, the least he could do since Mac was paying for everything else, then walked toward the dance floor, his arm around Abby's shoulders. McReady, with Noelani clinging to his right arm, was still steady on his feet even after enjoying three drinks at the restaurant. A waiter approached them as they sat down at an umbrella-covered table near the dance floor.

McReady murmured an order to the waiter, who nodded and left them. On the dance floor, Norris spotted a few men in the dress uniforms of Army and Navy officers, although they were outnumbered by those in tails or white jackets. The band was playing "Dancing in the Dark" and he found himself reaching for Abby's hand. She leaned toward him and smiled and he was at peace for the first time in a while. Below them, the incoming waves, illuminated by floodlights, lapped at the edge of the beach.

The waiter returned with four glasses and a bottle of wine in a silver ice bucket. McReady handed a bill to the waiter, waved him away, and poured the wine for them.

"To good times," Mac said as he lifted his glass, "and better days ahead." His glass clinked against Noelani's before he downed the wine in one gulp, stood up, and bowed. "And may I have this dance?"

Noelani laughed as she got to her feet. "Of course." The band segued into "In the Mood" as McReady ushered Noelani to the dance floor. For such a big man, Mac was surprisingly light on his feet. He drew Noelani toward him, then swung her out as she twirled under his arm. They moved into a jitterbug, Noelani following his lead, a Polynesian princess dancing with a Scottish warrior.

Abby reached for his hand and held it. Norris suddenly wanted to pull her to him, press his face against her soft brown hair, and unburden himself of his fears. *I had to battle a monster*, he would tell her, *an ungodly Thing, the stuff of nightmares. We were sure we defeated it but it was still after me, I kept seeing it, sensing it out there somewhere, that's how I became the way I am now, the way I've been ever since I came back, but It's over now, it has to be, I can put it behind me. Abby—*

"Vance, what is it?" Her grip tightened and he realized he had said her name aloud.

He shook his head. "Nothing." Abby had never asked him about his experiences in Antarctica. All she had ever said after he had been home for a few days, reluctant to talk about anything, plagued by insomnia, unable to resume their normal routines, was that she was glad he was home, that if he ever needed to unburden himself she would be there for him, and that she loved him. He wondered if he was worthy of her compassion.

"Come on, let's dance." She tugged at his hand and smiled. He couldn't remember the last time they had danced together. Abby glanced toward the dancing couples as Mac dipped Noelani toward the floor, then caught her in one arm.

He stood up and drew her toward him, willing himself to embrace the peace he had felt earlier.

* * * *

On the way home, Norris stopped to drop Noelani off at the small house she shared with her mother and sister. While he and Abby waited in the car, McReady lingered with Noelani in the shadows outside the front door, apparently deep in conversation.

"Looks like Mac's falling in love," Abby murmured.

"If you want to call it love," he replied. She poked him in the arm and then laughed. The door to the house opened to outline the silhouette of a couple locked in an embrace. The two quickly moved apart and the door closed.

Norris got out of the car as McReady approached and waited as he climbed into the back seat. "Thanks for our night out, Mac," Abby said as Norris slipped behind the wheel. "We had a wonderful time."

"Thanks for introducing me to Noelani." McReady paused. "Asked her if she'd care to show me around the island tomorrow afternoon. That is if I can borrow your car."

"Of course," Abby said. "I've got tomorrow off."

They passed the rest of the ride home in silent contentment. Mac passed up their offer of a nightcap and Norris was ready to go to bed, feeling relaxed enough to hope that there would be no bad dreams for him that night.

* * * *

The bedroom was still dark when Norris woke up. Abby's even breathing told him that she was still asleep.

He tried to remember what he had been dreaming. An unseen presence had been following him but he could not bring himself to turn and see what it was. Now that he was awake, he realized that someone else—something else—was in the room with them.

He kept his eyes closed. If he didn't open them, if Abby didn't wake up, if he kept perfectly still, nothing would happen. Something was moving closer to him, hovering over the bed, drowning out Abby's soft inhalations with loud, heavy breaths. He heard the Thing move away and then realized it was on the other side of the bed, preparing to swallow his wife.

He cried out, screaming himself out of the nightmare. "You won't!" he shouted. "Not Abby! You can't!" A wordless cry escaped him as he sat up. "I won't let you!"

"Vance!" Abby clutched at his arm. "What is it?"

"Get away!"

She threw her arms around him, trying to restrain him. "It's all right," she whispered. "It's just a bad dream, it's all right, you're safe."

The door to the bedroom opened and a light went on overhead. McReady stood in the doorway. "What's going on?" he asked.

The bare-chested man in pajama bottoms was not McReady, not any more. He hadn't come to Hawaii just to visit an old friend, but because he knew the Thing was still out there. Mac had come here on the trail of the alien and now it had swallowed him and taken on his form.

"Vance," McReady called out. There was a red glow in the big man's eyes, the suggestion of blue tendrils in his reddish hair. Norris pushed Abby away, leaped from the bed, and lunged at McReady, who knocked him aside. He hit the wall and was suddenly lying on his back, pinned to the floor by two strong hands.

"Vance!" Norris struggled for breath. "Hang on." Norris gulped more air, then took a deep breath. He was fully awake now, outside his dream, and saw concern in the other man's eyes.

Only Mac was there, with nothing else inside him.

McReady loosened his grip and Norris sat up. They were both silent for a while. Abby watched them from the bed, her arms crossed over her chest.

"Bad dream," Norris muttered at last.

"Figured as much," McReady replied in a steady voice. "Maybe we had too much to drink last night. Think we could use some coffee." That was Mac, forming a likely hypothesis, getting the situation under control, and then finding a quick solution to the problem. Norris looked away as the other man helped him to his feet.

* * * *

Abby and McReady were out on the lanai, with breakfast, a bowl of fruit, and the coffee pot on the table, when Norris finally came out to join them. He had washed up and dressed as slowly as possible, reluctant to face them after his outburst. McReady was wearing khaki pants and a loud Hawaiian shirt while Abby had put on a white linen blouse and light blue slacks. They both looked ready for a day of taking it easy. They would be calm, pretending that his display of panic and fear was only a momentary lapse.

The greenery around them looked bluer in the early morning light. A couple of myna birds in the trees behind Mac were already cawing loudly. Abby handed them both plates of eggs and bacon, their usual Sunday breakfast. "So when are you supposed to pick up Noelani?" she said to McReady.

"Told her I'd call first. Don't want to wake her up too early." Both of them went on chattering about their plans for the day in cheerful, brittle voices as Norris picked at his food. Abby was probably already thinking about how to distract him once Mac was on his way to meet Noelani.

In the distance, Norris heard intermittent cracks that might have been gunfire. Maybe the soldiers at Hickam Field were drilling again, although the sounds were louder than usual. The cracking sounds deepened into louder booms and then, just over the trees, he glimpsed small puffs of grey smoke against the clear blue sky.

Mac slapped his plate down and jumped to his feet, then looked west. "Sounds like anti-aircraft fire to me."

Norris stood up as more clouds of smoke appeared. Abby ran from the lanai into the living room. He hurried after her as she turned on the radio.

A singing choir broke off in the middle of a hymn. "This is not a drill," an announcer's voice called out from the radio. "We're being attacked. This is not a drill."

Mac came up behind Abby. "It's started," the big man said.

The cracks and booms were growing louder. "Pearl Harbor is under attack," the announcer continued. "This is not a drill."

Abby grabbed Norris by the arm. "I have to get to the office," she said.

"The hell you do," he replied.

"Vance, I'm a reporter."

"Not a war correspondent."

"I have to cover this story."

He grabbed her by the shoulders and shook her. "And get yourself killed?"

She pulled away from him and darted past Mac to the lanai. Norris followed her outside just in time to hear an explosion from somewhere on the green hillside. The house shook as a second explosion, closer this time, tore through the air. Smoke rose from a neighborhood farther down the hill as a plane rose above the trees. Even from this distance, Norris could see the bright orange circle of the Rising Sun on one wing of the low-flying plane.

Abby ran back inside. A hand clapped down on Norris's shoulder. "Take cover," Mac muttered as he pulled him inside the house.

Abby sank onto the sofa. Norris went to her, sat down, and reached for her hand. The wall behind the radio trembled at the sound of another explosion. McReady paced the room, frowning and looking uncharacteristically agitated. He would be thinking what Norris had already concluded, that the ships in Pearl Harbor and the planes at Hickam Field were sitting ducks.

Norris said, "We might not be safe here." He felt again as though something was watching him from behind, something alien, and forced himself to ignore that feeling.

McReady stopped pacing. Another deafening blast shook the house and he crouched, as if trying to shield himself. Norris could hear another plane overhead but the sound of its engine was muffled. He let go of Abby, stood up, and moved slowly toward the lanai. As he looked outside, he saw flames leap from one of the wooden houses farther up the hillside to the shingled roof next to it.

The Japanese neighborhood where Jonny Nishimoto and his family lived was on fire.

Norris turned. "Mac, come with me. Somebody may need our help. Abby…"

"I'm coming with you," she interrupted. "I'm probably not any safer here than out there."

There was no time to argue with her. He went to the front door, opened it to see their still undamaged sedan parked outside the house, and ran down the short pathway to the car. He opened the door on the driver's side and guided Abby into the back seat as McReady got in on the other side.

The car lurched as he gunned the motor. The sound of gunfire to the west was louder and more constant. He sped up the road and swerved around a crater that was still smoking. Several adults on foot herding children were fleeing from a row of burning dwellings toward the nearby school.

"Japs," McReady muttered behind him. "They're all Japs." The big man's voice sounded unlike him, low and raspy and distinctly hostile. "How do we know they aren't aiding the enemy?"

Norris kept his eyes on the road, ignoring McReady. He braked as a woman ran across the road toward the car and recognized Jonny's mother.

"Mr. Norris!" she cried, waving her arms. Her usually confined black hair was loose around her shoulders and her eyes were wide with panic. He opened the door and got out of the car. "My husband and Jonathan, they're…" She pointed toward her house, where smoke was billowing from a side window. "They haven't come out."

He turned and raced toward the house. "Jonny!" he called out, hoping that the boy and his father were near the open front door. Footsteps pounded behind him. "Jonny!" As he skidded to a stop near a small flower garden, a big hand gripped his shoulder and spun him around.

"Vance."

He looked up at McReady's face. Mac's pale eyes were wild with fury, his face contorted into a grimace. Norris had seen that expression before, in Antarctica.

"Vance," McReady continued, "leave it alone, there's nothing you can do."

Norris pulled away. Mac's face hardened as he gazed past Norris at the burning house. "Leave it alone," Mac said, "the fire'll kill it." He was back in Antarctica, Norris realized, fighting the Thing once more.

"Hiro!" Mrs. Nishimoto screamed. Abby held the weeping woman, trying to restrain her. A few people on their way to take shelter at the school watched from the road.

Mac suddenly swung at him. Norris blocked him with one arm and punched him in the gut with the other. The big man crumpled to the ground. Lucky punch, Norris thought, and ran to the door, smelling smoke inside the house. He stumbled inside, coughing as he struggled to breathe.

"Jonny," he called out, unable to see anything in the darkness.

Somebody whimpered and then gasped. He could barely see through watery eyes stinging from the smoke. A man lay on the floor, arms out, legs pinned under what looked like a long, thick beam. Norris drew closer and saw someone smaller crouching near the trapped man.

"Dad's stuck." Norris recognized Jonny's voice. "I tried to move it but I can't."

"Are you all right?" Norris asked.

"Yes, but—"

"Then get out of here."

"But Dad—"

Norris bent down and grabbed the beam, straining against its weight. "Help me lift this." The boy gripped one corner of the beam but failed to budge it. Tears streamed down Norris's face as he managed to lift the beam just a few inches. Hanging on, he said, "Now let go and pull your dad toward you, fast." He was straining now, holding the beam up with all his strength, as Jonny dragged his father a few inches across the floor. He lost his grip then and the beam crashed to the floor, barely missing Mr. Nishimoto's extended arm.

The smoke was thicker now. Norris thought he heard a moan. He staggered toward Jonny and his father. The other man shook his head as Norris slowly pulled him to his feet, wondering how badly injured he was. With Jonny holding up his father on the right, they shuffled toward the door.

A flaming strip of wood dropped in front of them, sparks flying. Norris inhaled smoke and gasped for air. Mr. Nishimoto let out a moan and Norris struggled to hang on to him.

A large indistinct shape appeared in the doorway. Norris was suddenly lying on the floor, his head throbbing. "Jonny," he called out but heard no response. He slapped the floor with one hand, feeling how hot it was, unable to see anything through the smoke. He blinked away more tears, barely able to keep his eyes open.

Arms lifted him up. "I've got you." That was Mac's voice. The smoke and darkness disappeared and Norris abruptly found himself lying on softer ground. A breeze cooled his face. He opened his mouth and gulped air.

"The kid's okay," Mac said. "His dad, too, but I think he might have a broken leg." A sharp whistling sound interrupted him and Norris heard an explosion farther down the hill. "Now we better get out of here."

* * * *

With the Nishimotos crowded into their car, Abby drove them all to the nearby school, where the principal was offering shelter. A nurse, a young Japanese-American woman, set Mr. Nishimoto's broken leg in a splint and patched up Jonny's burns and scrapes while the rest of them rested on tatami mats in the school's gymnasium.

Others seeking refuge gradually trickled into the large room and Norris soon saw that Abby, Mac, and he were the only white people there. Mac, sitting on a mat next to him, didn't say a word about that or anything else. He had not spoken during the drive, either. Norris wanted to tell his friend that dragging him to safety had more than made up for anything the big man had said or done earlier, but kept silent.

The people around them talked of what they had seen that morning, some in Japanese and others in English. Bombs had fallen all over the city. The local drugstore and a few stores next to it were now only charred ruins. One woman had seen the bodies of a couple of children lying in the road not far from a roadside farmers' stand. Over at Hickam Field, firemen and other volunteers were bringing injured soldiers and sailors to the station hospital and to Tripler General. At least one battleship had been sunk and maybe the whole fleet was lost. Soon a couple of Army officers showed up to announce that Hawaii was now under martial law and a mandatory blackout would begin that evening.

They were at war.

* * * *

The day after the attack, Norris and Abby, along with McReady, were allowed to return to their house, still standing with no damage that he could see apart from a couple of broken windows. By then they had all heard the grim statistics. More than two thousand dead, most of them Navy personnel, although civilians were also among the casualties. The *Arizona* and the *Oklahoma* had been sunk, and other ships had suffered severe damage, while most of the military aircraft at Wheeler and Hickam Fields had been destroyed. A gruff Navy officer ordered McReady to report to Hickam Field, although it didn't seem that he would be going to the Philippines any time soon. Anyone who might be out at night, as Abby often was when getting home late from her office, would need a curfew pass, and there would be limits on what she could publish in the Star-Bulletin.

Within a week, the Royal Hawaiian Hotel was sporting a barrier of barbed wire along its beach, gas masks had been issued to all civilians, and Norris was often out with a team of men conscripted to dig more holes for makeshift bomb shelters. Abby used much of her time at her newspaper desk making calls to the mainland for friends who wanted their families to know they were safe. Mrs. Nishimoto, along with a contingent of parents from Jonny's school, had approached Norris about replacing the current science teacher, who had already decided to enlist in the Army. He told them he would think about it and found himself welcoming the offer. He realized then that days had passed without nightmares, without feeling an unseen threat lurking nearby, without the fear that the Thing was still hunting him.

* * * *

McReady stopped by on Christmas afternoon with a present of Scotch hidden in his duffel. Abby shook her head at this unexpected gift of holiday cheer. A ban on alcohol was already in effect, along with rationing, so Norris did not ask how Mac had acquired a bottle of liquor.

"Noelani wanted to be here, too," Mac said as they sat in the living room with small glasses of Scotch, "but with all the patients at the hospital, she's on double shifts." He shrugged. "I'll head over there later before curfew. Have to firm up our plans before I find out what the powers that be might have in mind for me now." He paused and looked down. "You're still on to be our witnesses, aren't you?"

"Of course," Abby said.

"Good thing Noelani's mother's taken a shine to me and doesn't mind having me for a son-in-law."

Abby finished her drink and stood up. "All we have for Christmas dinner is sandwiches, I'm afraid," she said. "Then I'll have to head over to the office and put the final touches on my holiday story before the censors do their editing." She headed toward the kitchen while Norris led his friend to the lanai.

"Peace on Earth," McReady muttered as he sat down, shaking his head. "I doubt MacArthur can hold Manila." He was silent for a while. "Don't know what got into me before."

"You don't need to explain." They both had another enemy to fight now. Maybe, like the Thing and whatever hellish evolution had produced that alien species, human beings also had their own unconscious need for an enemy to fight.

Norris looked up as an albatross circled overhead. The large white bird dipped its wings and then flew west toward the bright red sun.

THE

CHELSEA QUINN YARBRO

"Who, or what, was that?" Astrogator Calculator Carstairs asked as she watched what looked like a four-foot-in-diameter lawn-bowl roll by, The's compressed sides shining as if made of platinum or some other valuable metal. She had been assigned to the bridge when she first came aboard, and she was trying to become acquainted with the rest of the bridge crew. This was only her second assignment to a fully integrated Worm ship, and she had not yet seen the full panoply of space-going life in the Reconciliation territories; Humans were new to the Reconciliation, and to space travel by wormhole to points far beyond the solar system. Carstairs was excited and tingling with fear at once and this strange being seemed more like a machine than a life-form.

"That's The," said the Helmsman, the translator crackling the effort to convey what it had said, and with whom Carstairs worked. "You'll get used to The."

"What makes it roll?" Carstairs asked.

"According to The, gravity does," the Helmsman said. Appointment to any given space-going ship was based upon the similarity of gravity on the crew's home planet, and no matter what they might look like, all shared a narrow range of gravitational tolerance; to do otherwise would have risked severe health problems among the crew, and deep space travel was demanding enough without that.

The *Star Treader* was preparing to cast off from *Station 8, Quadrant 61,* out beyond the band of solar rubble that hung around the vast field of Terran planets, on the far side of the Ort Cloud

"You'd best pay attention to The," said the captain—at least that was what her translation unit provided by way of identifying the lawn-bowl—who was a multi-limbed creature who might have been a centaur if centaurs had started out as octopuses and crustaceans instead of horses and Humans. "We need The to find our way." One of his arms extruded from his body to emphasize what he was saying.

"So I've been told," Carstairs responded without having to admit that she could not understand the reason why she found The confusing. "In my crew manual."

"This is the first time that you've seen The?"

"Yes." It was galling to have to admit that she had only recently acquired bridge rank and on her first ship, she was limited to the Astrogator calculator, the ship's libraries, and all the rehearsal halls for information of who and what was aboard. This was the first time she had been summoned to the bridge to watch the vast amounts of supplies being loaded into the *Star Treader*. It was a formidable task, she admitted to herself, studying the Bridge Crew monitoring their various displays. They had to coordinate the stacking and boxing and sacking and bagging devoted to the optimal use of limited space on the vast ship. They also looked after the devices that would turn the basic proteins from numerous home planets into the local dishes that the every species in the crew depended upon.

"We all rely on Thes, every Worm-ship in the Reconciliation. You might want to bear that in mind," the captain recommended.

"Yes, Captain; I will." Carstairs knew from everyone on the bridge that she had not been on board the *Star Treader* for very long, that she was still under scrutiny.

"Your evaluation will be completed during this run," the captain reminded her, as if Carstairs needed reminding.

The had stopped rolling and was instead spinning in place; the not-quite-spherical being had no eyes that she could make out, yet it rolled flawlessly through the containers of supplies being put into supply cabinets that lined the walls of the bridge that were not taken up by huge screens and various navigational equipment; they were being loaded without any problems or hesitations as soon as the systems' check began. Chief G#aa kept a close eye on every one of his workers, occasionally making a sharp remark to those not working as diligently as the Chief expected them to.

A half-dozen young midshipbeings were sent off to assist in securing the holds.

"Prepare to begin loading last cargo," said the First Mate.

The emitted a sound that the translator interpreted as something like a purr.

Sachsmatk-tk, the Interior Communications Officer glanced in The's direction, and one of his-2's multitude of limbs working, his-2's massive thorax, a cartilagenous length of finger clusters and oleagenous skin glistening with effort to keep up with all the reports of loading coming into the bridge. The translation pod that hung over his-2's mouth at mid-chest, said to Carstairs, "The's observing you."

"The what?" Carstairs asked, becoming more confused.

"The is the's name, and The's pronoun," Sachsmatk-tk informed her.

"Just The?" She wondered how anyone could tell that this rolling, metallic-looking object as actually alive.

Sachsmatk-tk's translation pod crackled. "The's your superior. The is the Astrogation Unit, and we're lucky to have The."

"Why?" Carstairs could not keep from asking.

"The, like all of Thes, has a part of The's…brain that has a much more sensitive…well…sense of direction than any other space-going species we've encountered yet." Sachsmatk-tk said, and it was apparent to Carstairs that his-2 translation pod was having difficulty with the concepts. "Thes are the only species the Reconciliation has found with such abilities."

"That—excuse me—*The* does? The doesn't even have eyes."

"Not as such, no, but that ring around the slightly flattened central disk on either side of the is a locational organ that not only has a very acute sight function, it also gauges temperature and…angle. Similar to the clusters of hair on top of my back, only many times more developed." He-2 examined the implant on his-2 upper wrist. "The last of the supplies should be aboard shortly. Then we can prepare for cast-off in two standard time units. You won't be needed again until then."

As if to confirm this, a signal from the loading bay brayed through the speakers.

Carstairs consulted her coordinator, selecting the screen dedicated to her duties for the work period. "The shuttle is coming up. Give it ten ticks."

Sachsmatk-tk's translator pod made a sound that Carstairs equated to a load of metal utensils being dropped down a flight of stairs, which she knew, from her dealings with other Matk-tk-tks was similar to laughter. "You'll get used to this, Human, in time. Your species has not been space-going long, and you have not completely adjusted. We should know if you, as a single Human, can adapt to deep-space travel, by the time we're through with this voyage, or to suggest that you try to find something else you could do, rather than serve on a Worm-ship." He-2 entered a column of data onto the screen in front of him-2. "We will be departing in…let me see…two…no, three standard time-units. You'll need to be on hand for cast-off."

Feeling a bit defensive, Carstairs said, "I may be new to the Worm-group, but I can handle Matk-tk-tks like you, and Ouoanau, and Zijhree, and Hods, and even ** Tppm**, and most of the other limbed species—I just have never seen something that rolled like The does."

"Don't get your tdotks up; all of us had to learn to deal with very different species than the one we came into when we went into the Reconciliation. I needed three journey's to get used to you Humans having so many of your sensory organs in that bulbous extension on top of your torsos."

Carstairs nodded, and her translation pod expressed agreement in Sachsmatk-tk. "How many of you Matk-tk-tks will be on this ship?"

"Forty-four. I know there will be nineteen Humans, counting you. Not bad for a new member-species of the Reconciliation."

"How many Thes?" she asked before she could stop herself.

"Just the one," said Sachsmatk-tk. "More than one within a lightyear of each other, and Thes' perceptions tend to jam up."

"How?" Carstairs asked.

"No idea; my guess would be it's something vibrational," said Sachs-matk-tk replied. "Not much information about that."

"But aren't they the reason we can go through worm-holes and get where we need to be?"

"And when," Sachsmastk-tk. "Getting us to a part of space where we want to be, that is relatively easy, but to repeat arriving in the same place *when* we want to be there, and then get us back to this part of the galaxy in our own space and time, that's their talent. That's why all Worm-class ships have Thes."

"Oh," said Carstairs, which her translation pod, collared around her neck, turned into a sort of hum for Sachsmatk-tk. She decided she would use her information Access to learn more about Thes when her watch was done and she had time to concentrate on something other than astrogation, when there were fewer distractions. "Do you need me before then?"

"Not here." He-2 looked toward the captain. "The Astrogator Calculator would like the opportunity to rest for a while. Her watch is almost up, and you won't need her until cast-off. Want to let her have a little down-time? She looks like she needs it."

A whoop warned the crew of the Worm-559#V *Star Treader* that the final shuttle was approaching, and Sachsmatk-tk moved away to his-2 place to record the last of the crew coming aboard, while the Organization Crew got ready for the last round of supplies.

The continued to spin in place.

* * * *

Being a Bridge Officer, Carstairs had been allocated her own cabin on the Ninth Forward Unit of the ship, so that she would be near to the bridge itself. The room was one-and-a-half times her height wide, twice her height long, and one-and-a-third times her height tall; generous space for a Worm-ship. There was a cleaning unit that opened up from the wall opposite the door, which not only provided her cleaning facilities for her clothes and cabin, but for her body as well. In addition, the room had a display in the ceiling that revealed all that was happening outside the ship, as well as enabling Carstairs to access all the informational material available to the crew. She let herself in with a blink of her eyes, closed the door, and went to her bunk, dropping down onto it with a sense of gratitude for the rest mixed with a hint of bewilderment. Why should The be interested in her? What capacity did it have that made it possible for The to astrogate in time and space? What sense did The have to be able to astrogate a Worm ship, and how did it work? She tapped the information Access in her right forearm, and said "Thes" to the air, and waited for the Access to respond.

A dizzying array flashed on the ceiling over her bed, with a formidable mix of languages, images, and narration, a combination that was truly overwhelming.

Carstairs coughed, and said, "Purposes aboard Worm-class starships."

The display began to sort itself out, the chaos of the information resolving into clusters of potential topics, the one at the top if the clusters labeled *The, Humankind, and Astrogation,* in which Carstairs found this disquieting paragraph:

> Attempts to study Thes' remarkable sense of direction have thus far been inconclusive, but current theories include either a keen sense of direction or hearing or perhaps some combination of the two which enables Thes to perceive the nature of space/time in a way that may be unique to them.

Carstairs sighed and began to make her way through the first articles in the file, which described the first contact between Humans and the Reconciliation, and what the first treaties had proposed for the first century of interaction. It was filled with comments and descriptions that Carstairs had studied in school, and so she was tempted to skim over the information she thought she knew, but then made herself peruse more closely, for her ninth-level studies mentor had warned about being careful about things you thought you knew.

"Origins of Thes," Carstairs asked the ceiling.

"Unknown," came the answer, along with a flurry of citation.

"Reasons for Thes' astrogational talents?"

"Unknown."

"Do they have a home planet, or location?"

"Unknown."

"What benefits them and what does not?" Carstairs felt she was running out of questions.

"Unknown."

"What about reproduction?" Carstairs sighed. "Unknown as well. Never mind." She lay back and stared at the ceiling, hoping for some insight, which eluded her. The one question that stuck in her mind was why Thes had not been discussed during her training, since, as an astrogator, Carstairs was required to work with one?

About forty minutes later, she dimmed the display on the ceiling and reached for her English horn case, the one at the top of the shelf, above the oboe, the shawm, and the bassoon below it, and took the very old instrument out, pausing to inspect the double-reeds in the mouthpiece. The Humans aboard the *Star Treader,* as part of their duties as members of the ship, which required all species in the crew to practice a native art as well as attend to the duties of their official positions, had founded a chamber music group, and rehearsal was scheduled in little more than an hour. They were to present a concert in ten days. Tonight, it was to be the Kyses who would be the first to present what Carstairs' translator had called a folkdance. She slipped the mouthpiece between her lips and licked the reeds until they were softened, and then began to play, the plaintive voice of the English horn reflected her mood, and she continued to play with more engagement, searching for the music in the notes, concentrating on the melodic line like the sense of a conversation; music provided context for Carstairs in a way that few other things could, and just at present, she felt an intense dislocation that she had not experienced since childhood.

* * * *

A little while later, there was a signal from the door that someone wanted to be admitted. Carstairs reluctantly set her English horn aside and looked to the door display to see who it was. To her astonishment, The was waiting for the door to open.

A voice sounded in her translator, so mechanical and strange that she had trouble comprehending what was being said. "What is the source of those vibrations?"

"That," she said, pointing to the English horn, adding, "It makes the vibrations."

"What is it?" The asked.

Carstairs sighed again and signaled the door to open. "It's an antique musical instrument from Terra, my home planet," she explained as she sat up and did what she could to make The feel welcome, much as she would have done had she been back on Terra instead of bound for a worm-hole that would take her half way across the galaxy.

The rolled into the exact center of the chamber and stopped. "Tell me more," The said. "This sound is unknown to me."

"It is what is called a woodwind," she offered.

"What is a woodwind?" The asked.

Carstairs decided to begin with the basics. "This instrument is called an English horn, although it's neither English nor a horn; it's this bend here"— she pointed to the bend—"that gives it the name, which actually means the bent horn."

"How does it make sound?" The asked.

"I blow through this mouthpiece, getting the double reeds to vibrate, and then I use these stops to change the pitch." She could not decide if this was what The wanted to know, but she struggled on gamely. "It's had a long and positive history in Western music."

"Can you make it give sound now?"

"Certainly," Carstaris said, wanting to do whatever she could to learn more about The. "Just one note, or sever al?"

"One first, then several," The told her, moving near. "Do not rush production of the vibrations. I want to…appreciate them."

"All right." Carstairs set the double-reed mouthpiece in place on her upper and lower lip, and chose E as her note. The sound filled her room, more loudly than it had earlier.

"Now more," said The, rolling back and forth as if rocking, but if in delight or agony, Carstairs could not tell.

Carstairs thought about what to play, and settled on a passage from *The Nutcracker*, which was easy to play and easily understood for many species. At the conclusion of the excerpt, she took the reeds out of her mouth. "That's the sound."

"A fairly small range of vibrations," said The; whether this was positive or negative to The was undetermined.

"Most wind instruments are like that," Carstairs agreed. "That's part of why there are so many of them."

"How many?"

"Probably many hundreds," said Carstairs, "if you include the folk instruments, many thousands. They're very old in our species; only drums are older." She wondered how much of what she said made sense to The, and waited for more questions.

"What do you call the vibration variations?"

"Pitch," she said, and regretted it, for The was turning around slowly. She decided to try to elaborate. "The instrument has a range of vibrational increments, which musicians call pitch. In order to produce a pleasant sound, all the instruments have to agree on the…vibrational increments, or the results are not pleasing."

"Do all Humans hear pitch?" The increased The's slow spin, turning first to the left and then to the right.

"Most of them, but not all. Why?" This was an unexpected turn in The's inquiry, and Carstairs could not quite figure out what it was that The wanted to know. "There are Humans who have no perception of these vibrations, or very limited oens, and there are those who lose the capacity to hear…perceive them, through accident or age or disease."

The made a noise not unlike a minor explosion in an echoing room.

"Does that trouble you?" Carstairs asked after a long moment.

"It perturbs me," said The. "It confuses me. It stimulates my balance."

"Why?" She wondered if this was going too far, but reminded herself on the regulations about overly inquisitive inquiry.

"I have no words that can tell you, nor would I if I could," The answered, and abruptly left the room.

* * * *

Rehearsal went well enough, but Carstairs was strangely dissatisfied with her own playing, and could not keep her mind on the Bach transcription of keyboard music they were working on. She decided that The's visit to her quarters had something to do with it, but found herself annoyed that such an event could discompose her.

At the end of rehearsal, she returned to the bridge to take over for the Master Astrogator—a burley, bustard-like N'Bsao hybrid with four sets of eyes that protruded along what Carstairs supposed to be its spine—and to plot in the next eight standard time-units of the voyage before going for the last meal of the day. She did her calculations, coordinated them with the Star Treader's current speed and any potential drift, and was about to engage them when she had a moment of light-headedness, as if she had just lost her balance. She cancelled her calculations and started again from the beginning, telling herself that she was being overly cautious, but better to be sure than sorry, as her grandmother used to tell her. She worked steadily, taking time to analyze everything she did, and worked out any irregularity she found, knowing that she would be late to dinner, but her work would bear the scrutiny of anyone aboard.

* * * *

By the time she had entered her new calculations, she was exhausted and famished; she headed for the Humans' mess, trying to shake that uneasy sensation that lingered. For once she had the place almost to herself, and that pleased her; she did not yearn for Human company and conversation, not with this feeling of disquiet taking hold of her. Was there something wrong with the ship's gravitational field? she wondered as she dialed in her selection for the meal and waited for it to appear on the table. She was slightly groggy when her food arrived, but she determined to eat so that she could put an end to the way she was feeling. The food tasted slightly odd, but not unpleasant, and the basic protein slurry from which all Human food was made did occasionally try a new approach to a familiar dish.

It was almost a standard time unit later that she left the Human mess and returned to her quarters, her senses calmed somewhat and were more of what she was used to. On coming aboard, all the Humans were warned about potential reactions to the gravity and air circulation, and to report it to the Medical Crew if they became disruptive; she decided to chalk this up to such an event, and to report it to the Medical Crew if she had not improved in the morning. Entering her chambers, she took a while to bathe in the chemical solution that cleaned, moisturized, and kneaded her skin—a process that often offered her still more tranquility—but tonight that eluded her, and she felt consumed by twitches.

"Overtired," she said to the air, and resigned herself to fidgety sleep, telling herself that she should take the sleeping solution before getting into her bunk for the night, but in the end, gave it up as an over-reaction, then spent almost half the night in restless dozing.

* * * *

For the next day, Carstairs went about fulfilling her duties with dogged determination but relatively little enthusiasm, which she chalked up to a poor night's rest. Her calculations were meticulous, her rehearsal went with precision, and there was no repetition of the peculiar lapse in balance that had plagued her yesterday. Once again, she told herself, the load-in had been more gravitationally upsetting than she had realized, which accounted for the strange sensations. She entered a report to the Medical Crew and hoped that was the end of it.

She did not encounter The throughout the whole of the day, for The was not on the bridge when she was on duty—which she was told was not unusual for The—and when she went to her quarters, she slept peacefully.

* * * *

On the fourth day out, Carstairs was called early to fill in for the N'Bsao, who was observing some sort of religious ritual and could not operate the Astrogational Calculator, so Carstairs did not get to practice her English horn, an exercise that usually got her morning off pleasantly; she arrived on the bridge to find The rolling in a figure-eight pattern in the center of the astrogational equipment.

"It is necessary to correct course by two-point-four degrees upward and one-point-one degrees toward galactic center; I have the coordinates ready to present," The's translator announced.

The Helmsman—this morning it was the multi-finned and ridged Ksy who had been among the folkdancers the first night out; now it handled all the instruments with an array limbs—did a number of rapid calculations and the ship responded in a way that was impossible to detect, although the images on the display screens changed ever so slightly. "Course correction complete. Verify, Astrogator Calculator," the Ksy announced, and Carstairs responded promptly that her astrogation equipment confirmed the turn as executed.

The captain was not on the bridge at the moment, but was due shortly. The First Mate was handling the bridge with its usual pragmatic aplomb, using its highly developed sense of touch to maintain an awareness of the functioning of the various sectors of the *Star Treader*. It was always a pleasure to watch it work; it was embedded in a number of instruments, and functioned by shifting parts of its complex body.

The came to a halt near Carstairs, and made a sound like a clarinet with a faulty reed, then said, "That was well done."

"Thank you," Carstairs said automatically, puzzled by the compliment, if it was a compliment.

"You have a sense of the movement," The told her.

Carstairs tried to hide her surprise. "What do you mean by that?"

"That you understand the movement you measure," said The, as if this were obvious.

"Hey, Carstairs," the First Mate called out through the translator, sounding agrieved. "Keep your mind on your displays. We have to recalculate for drift in a few ticks."

"Right," she said promptly, and added to The, "Sorry. Got to tend to this."

"Naturally," said The, and rolled away.

"I think The likes you," said the Helmsman.

"Do you?" Carstairs said, feigning indifference.

"The pays attention to you," the Ksy added.

"That doesn't mean that The likes me, only that The is curious. The's more curious about the music I play than The is in me." Carstairs had an instant of alarm at the idea that something so alien as The might like her, for she had no idea of how that would manifest itself. She redoubled her calculations, wanting to be sure that she had performed the verification faultlessly.

"Still, The's perplexing, isn't The?" the Ksy remarked in a tone that the translator presented as cynical in delivery.

Carstairs did not dignify that possible slight with an answer; she continued to run her course calculations without further comment.

The First Mate settled down to analyze their speed in relation to the remote systems out in this spiral arm, and order on the bridge was restored.

The left the bridge without explaining anything about The's unusual behavior.

* * * *

Jule Lui, the Midship Coordinator among the Humans who served as their musical leader, stopped Carstairs in mid-passage on her oboe. "Your intonation is odd." They were in one of the practice rooms provided to the musicians, and Carstairs was working on her solo for their concert. "So what's the matter?"

Carstairs took her oboe from her mouth, looked at Lui, and shrugged. "I thought it was okay—not great, but okay."

"But where's that faint overtone coming from?" Lui asked patiently.

This question nonplused Carstairs. "What faint overtone?"

"That octave-and-five above your pitch," said Lui, whistling the note for demonstration. "Don't you hear it?"

Carstairs held back a sharp retort, and answered candidly, "No, I don't."

Lui frowned. "Well, I can, and I think it's intrusive. Is there something wrong with your reeds, or any other part of your mouthpiece?"

"Not that I know of," Carstairs said, trying not to leap to her own defense. "The reeds are vibrating properly."

"I find that hard to believe," said Lui. "You have perfect pitch, and that overtone ought to stick out like a white rat in a coal scuttle."

Carstairs knew that when Lui resorted to old-time expressions that he was attempting to keep his temper, so she thought about her response before she gave it. "Well, I still didn't hear it."

"Are you okay? Do you need to have an ear exam?"

"It's possible," she allowed; ears were associated with balance, and she had had those minor disruptions in balance.

After an exasperated silence, Lui said, "Tell you what—we'll knock off for now, and you can get checked out for hearing. And we'll meet again tomorrow and have another run at this."

Carstairs knew that Lui was being sensible; little as she liked the prospect, she was aware that it was a pragmatic approach. "All right. I'll get my ears tested, and I'll go over the oboe. And I'll play the English horn for a while to see if the overtone is present in that instrument, too; it might have to do with some resonance in the ship, and perhaps it varies from person to person." As an improvisation, this was skimpy, but it was better than nothing, Carstairs told herself as she stood up and reached for her instrument case.

"Let me know what you find out about your ears," Lui said as he went to the door.

"As soon as I have a report, so will you," she promised as she removed the mouthpiece from the oboe and put it in its own little compartment in the case, then wiped off the oboe with a cloth and set both in their own position in the case. All the while, she tried to keep her sudden worry at bay, but was not doing it very well. With a cough that was partly a sigh, she left the practice room and began the walk toward the medical suite that served Humans and the Broket population on the *Star Treader*—among them, the cephaloid centaur who captained the ship—doing her best to quiet the dismay that had awakened within her. What would happen to this assignment if she was not allowed to continue play in the musical consort? Would she have to leave the ship? The idea was as repulsive as it was frightening, and it dogged her thoughts all the way to the medical suite.

* * * *

Two of the audiological assessment machines went to work on Carstairs at once, sending all kinds of tones, pitches, and sounds to test what she could hear properly for a Human, at the end of which, the technician who supervised the testing informed her that there was no discernable reason for her failure to detect the sound that Lui had claimed he heard, a report that was relayed to Lui when Carstairs left the suite to return to her quarters.

"Maybe it has something to do with the air pressure," she said as she lay back in her bunk, determined to come up with an acceptable explanation for this most uncharacteristic lapse in her musicianship. The steady sound of her own voice lent her a little relief from the nameless vexations that had been marshaling within her.

She was almost dozing when the speaker in the ceiling informed her that she was needed on the bridge at once. Telling herself this was a welcome diversion, Carstairs got up, checked the room for any other messages, then hied herself to the bridge, doing her best not to worry about why the captain required her presence.

The captain met her just outside the bridge, his array of tentacles moving far more than usual. "Carstairs."

"Sir," she said and saluted.

"We're having a bit of a problem with your equipment. It's going to have to be sent down to tech. In the meantime, you'll have to use the backup Astrogator Calculator. It's a newer model, and we don't know how familiar you are with the most recent models."

Carstairs did her best not to bristle. "I did my training on the last decade of machines, and on three of the most up-to-date prototypes for new ones. I think I ought to be able to handle whatever you have aboard."

"I do hope so," the captain's translator said. "But just to be certain, I'd like you to come and start work on it as soon as it's up and running. I'll have the speaker summon you."

"Of course," said Carstairs, while she wondered why he had to summon her to discuss this rather than use the communicator on her arm, or the speakers in her cabin.

"The thing is," the captain went on cautiously, "the problem may have a more pragmatic origin."

"And that is—?"

"Security thinks it might be deliberate sabotage, a way to throw us off course in small increments, so it would be difficult to detect until we are a long way from where we want to be. I'm waiting for their official report." The captain's tentacles writhed with emotion.

"Is that likely?" Carstairs asked, appalled.

"Security seems to think it's possible."

"Then I suppose you have to be especially careful with the new Astrogator Calculator as well as the old." For a long moment, Carstairs felt a cold lump settle into her chest.

"Security is planning for that," said the captain.

"Good," Carstairs said before she realized she was speaking aloud, not silently thinking. To cover her embarrassment, she went on, "What does The think about this?"

"I don't know," the captain admitted, an expression settling over his malleable upper side that Carstairs took for a frown. "Why do you ask?"

"The seems very much in tune with Astrogators, and Astrogator Calculators, given how The works aboard the ship. and might know if this is sabotage or something more…ordinary." She closed her mouth so as not to be tempted to speak out-of-turn again.

"That's interesting," the captain said in a rumbling tone. "I'll check with Security and ask them. For now, I have to tell you that you do not speak of this to anyone."

"Yes, sir," said Carstairs.

"And for now, return to your quarters and stay there until I order you to the bridge. Do not mention that you have been here."

Carstairs was nonplussed. "Don't you want me to start now? I'm ready to do what I can to—"

"Not yet," he said, much to Carstair's mystification. "I want you aware of what we're searching for, so that you will not blurt out any irregularity you discover. For now, I want you discussing this potential trouble with no one but me. So back to your quarters for now. You may order your food from there, if you're still in the room when the mess begins." And with that, the captain made a gesture of dismissal, turned away, and returned to the bridge.

Carstairs stood quite still for almost six ticks, trying to decide what she thought about what had just happened, but when she admitted that she was baffled, she went down to her quarters and tried to ease her increasing apprehension by practicing her bassoon, taking a degree of comfort from it lugubrious tones.

* * * *

For the next few days, Carstairs spent many extra hours on the bridge trying to help the Security detail search for any sign's of sabotage, but when nothing could be found, she was given an extra day to work on her music, in appreciation of her efforts. With a surge of joy, Carstairs made up her mind to make the most of the opportunity, and set out to practice for the consort's coming recital.

So it was that Risshima Patma, the principal double-bass player, who was also the best soprano in the chamber consort, was in a practice room with Carstairs, working on the very old Mozart *Laudate Domino*, trying to deal with the very long breaths that the piece required of them both, and finding it difficult. They ended up making four false starts before deciding that they would need a different approach to the opening phrases.

Patma stopped in the middle of the *omnes gentes*, shaking her head. "I have to get a breath before the *laudate eius* and *omnes populi*." She was one of the Environmental Monitors, who dealt with everything from the air and gravity of the ship to the psychological state of the crew. "How do you manage your breath, Carstairs?"

Carstairs shrugged. "I have reeds to contend with, and I suspect that makes a difference."

"But you're doing better than I am," Patma declared, then shook her head. "That sounds as if I'm competing with you, but I'm not. I'm surprised that I'm having trouble with the breathing. This piece is a really demanding one, but I don't usually have to struggle with the phrasing." She gave a single laugh. "At least we're not doing the last of the work."

"At least," Carstairs agreed. "Let's take a break. I'm working myself up for no good reason. We'll go along to the Humans Canteen for a cup of something hot, and see what we can work out."

"I feel like that's giving up," Patma said. "But I do need a break."

"Fine with me," said Carstairs, setting her bassoon into its stand after removing the mouthpiece and putting it in a small cup of ordinary water. "I'll do the reserve on this room, so we can come back later."

"Thanks," said Patma, and held the door open for them both.

As they made their way along to the Humans Canteen, Carstairs decided to take a chance and asked Patma, "Have you run into The yet?"

"Not really; I've seen The once or twice, but that's about it." Patma slowed down a bit. "Why do you ask?"

"Well, something about my playing seems to have caught The's attention. I'm trying to figure out why, and what—if anything—it means."

Patma shook her head. "I can't help you there. The is the only individual aboard who does not come to us Environentals for evaluations."

"Why not?" Carstairs asked.

"I don't know." Patma frowned. "I can ask, if you like."

"Don't go out of your way, but if it comes up, go ahead."

They had reached the Canteen door, and as they went into the place where the Humans gathered—a room with chairs and couches and tables with a service area at the far end where food and drink could be had—and made for a pair of comfortable chairs next to the service area. The nine other Humans in the room paid them little notice beyond friendly waves, and that allowed Carstairs and Patma to have a little privacy. There were half-a-dozen Brokets at the other end of the room engaged in what looked to Carstairs like a complicated board game; they paid no attention to the Humans.

"Since you're asking about The," Patma said after claiming a large cup of spiced tea with milk, "is there anything that you want to know about Thes in general?"

"Not especially. I already read up on Thes; the most I learned is that there's very little known about them." Carstairs got up to claim her serving of chicken-flavored salad and a cup of Italian coffee. When she sat down again, she and Patma devoted themselves to struggling with the Mozart, and for the time being, The was forgotten.

* * * *

But two days later, the captain called Carstairs to his office, and said to her, "You've got to keep quiet about what I'm going to tell you. Swear to me that you'll do as I order. What I have to tell you must be in total confidence, with an official seal on it."

Carstairs held up her right hand. "I swear," she pledged as her thoughts filled with alarm.

The captain motioned to Carstairs to sit, and then said nothing; Carstairs' fears increased dramatically, but she remained silent.

Finally the captain did the Broket equivalent of a cough and his translator began. "We've been going over the calculations that you and the other Bridge

Crew members have been reviewing, and I'm seriously concerned that we're a long way off-course. Our Astrogators do not line up with our outside scanners. Therefore, I'm going to need you to work with the Helmsman to try to correct this. We're out of alignment with the worm-hole, and that is extremely dangerous."

"Can't you use The to work that out? Doesn't The have the best sense of direction of any species aboard? Isn't that why The is on the ship?—to keep things like this from happening?" Carstairs asked, the anxiety she had done her best to keep at bay returning in double force.

"No to the first, yes to the second and third." The captain struggled to rise from his hammock-like chair. "The trouble is, some of the Bridge Crew are worried that The may be the source of the drift, and that means, we may not be able to go into the worm-hole safely. I don't like to think what would happen to the *Star Treader* if that happened."

Carstairs nodded, trying to discover when she was supposed to do these new calculations with the Helmsman. "I gather this is urgent as well as secret?"

"True enough," said the captain in a lowered voice. "More urgent than I thought at first."

Carstairs thought this over, then asked, "Why me? I understand about the Helmsman, but you have four other Astrogator Calculators you could call upon; I'm new aboard, and the others aren't." She almost held her breath as she waited for the captain's answer.

"For one thing, you haven't had the opportunity to fully acculturate to this ship yet, which means most of your alliances are with other Humans, and the ones with other species are still developing. Unless one of your species is the cause of this—which I doubt—you are going to be more willing to report accurately what you discover. You can act with independence and implicit loyalty to the ship, which is why I've put so much in your hands."

Carstairs could not come up with a response; she nodded, hoping that was enough.

The captain took her silence with respect. "There are a few among the S'sve aboard who may be allied with a splinter group in their home-system, and Security has been watching them, but I can't imagine why they should want to put eight hundred twenty-nine living beings and sentient machines aboard at such risk. You Humans are new to the Reconciliation, and have no history of multi-species political or economic or religious or territorial disputes as many of the rest of us have. For the time being, I ask you to help me."

"Of course, sir," said Carstairs, not entirely certain how to take this distinction. "Tell me how you want me to handle myself."

The captain hesitated. "As much as you can, maintain your usual schedules of duties; you may continue rehearsing and playing, but then, I will arrange for Security to place a small Astrogator Calculator in your quarters in a locked cabinet, and I ask you to scan every Astrogational calculation from the bridge that will be routed to your machine, and make note of any irregularity when it occurs and how far off it is from the Helmsman's records. I will ask you to give me a daily tabulation of any and all abnormalities you might find, no matter how small."

"That's a tall order, sir," said Carstairs.

"Agreed, but you're the one it falls to," said the captain.

"When is Security going to install this Astrogator Calculator?"

"It should be in place by the time you go back to your quarters," the captain said, offering Carstairs a glowing skin-insert. "Here's your key. Touch the lock with your thumb and this will open and afterward lock it for you."

Carstairs felt the skin-insert settle in beneath the base of her thumb, wondering as it did if it would affect her playing. "Is there anything else, sir?"

"Begin your calculations tonight after mess, and say nothing to anyone about this."

"Yes, sir," Carstaris responded with a salute.

"Then go down to your quarters and await my signal. I'll want to discuss your findings with you in a day or so. Dismissed."

Carstairs repeated her salute and left the captain alone with his musing.

* * * *

The Astrogator Calculator was half the size of the one on the bridge but so densely packed with toggles and displays that it was harder to use than the one on the bridge. Carstairs had rarely had trouble with vision, but after five standard time units on the small Astrogator Calculator, her eyes were sore and she felt as if she had been working for double the length of time that she had. She sent a record of the work she had done to the captain, put the Astrogator Calculator on sleep mode, closed up and locked its cabinet, and returned it to the port in the wall where Security had concealed it, which was on the underside of Carstairs' bunk.

For a standard time unit, she lay in her bunk, resting uneasily as if the Astrogator Calculator was commanding her attention even in sleep mode, but as fatigue caught up with her, she continued to will herself to sleep. After no more than four standard time units, she wakened with a start, and could return to sleep, so she sat up and took out her shawm, a very ancient double-reed instrument with a very temperamental mouthpiece. She played on it for a considerable time, then, truly worn out at last, she put the centuries-old instrument back in its case and gave herself over to slumber.

* * * *

Patma and Lui were waiting for her when she went to rehearsal the following morning. "Let's try the Mozart again, shall we? The *Vespri Confessore*. The breathing is too critical to get it wrong," said Lui to the women.

"No argument," said Patma.

"Agreed," said Carstairs.

Lui stared up at the ceiling. "Too bad our chorus isn't available. We'll need to rehearse their part shortly."

"The chorus is on duty," said Patma. "Perhaps after mid-day, we can arrange something."

Since most of the instrumentalists did double-duty as chorus, without the full consort, it would be impossible to perform the piece lacking a full complement of nineteen, and they all knew it.

Lui made an impatient gesture. "Well, let's make the most of the time we have, shall we?"

Carstairs had already moistened the mouthpiece and assembled her bassoon, and so she said, "Ready when you are."

"Very funny," said Lui.

Carstairs did not know what old-time saying Lui was referring to, but she manage to offer a quick grin, knowing that whatever Lui intended, he expected his witticism to be appreciated. She drew up a chair, turned on the music stand and tapped on the page of notes she was to play.

Patma did the same with her music stand, making sure that the light level was strong enough to show the marks she had made on the score.

"Err on the side adagio," said Lui as he adjusted his music stand and picked up his violin. "From the top. On four."

The first run-through went awkwardly, with occasional mistakes or loss of breath, but over six more repeats, the work improved significantly, and as Lui and Carstairs set their instruments aside and Patma turned off her music stand, they all felt that they had made real progress.

"Do you have duty tonight?" Lui asked Carstairs as she packed up the bassoon.

"Sorry, yes," she answered, remembering the Astrogator Calculator in her cabin. "But I'm off until afternoon tomorrow. If the rest of us are free, I can give you two standard time units without interruption."

"That could work," said Patma. "I have a busy morning, too. I don't know about the rest of us."

"I'll send a memo to them and see if we can manage another rehearsal in the next two days, in the smaller rehearsal hall, so we can all get the feel of it. We're not yet up to snuff, but we're getting there." Lui had wiped off his violin and was settling it into its case. "I'll let you know what we all decide before breakfast."

"Thanks," said Carstairs, for the first time having difficulties about the mission the captain had assigned to her. She had sworn to assist him, but her commitment to the consort was older than her promise to the captain. Perhaps she would have to speak to him about this unanticipated conflict, but not until she was certain that one existed.

* * * *

As Patma and Carstairs were leaving the smaller rehearsal hall, without warning The came rolling toward them. "Humans," The said as he grew near.

"Hello, The," said Carstairs, feeling almost clumsy in The's presence.

Patma looked around as if seeking a way to leave. "I'm one of the Environmentalists," she said, giving up escape for the time being.

"The vibrations you produced are hard to comprehend," The said, its translator sounding alarmed with this statement. "I have not been able to process them."

"They're not intended to be processed," said Carstairs quietly. "It is intended to provide entertainment. The piece was over five hundred Terra years old."

"What is entertainment?" The inquired.

"Some kind of presentation that provides pleasure or amusement or insight or inspiration," Carstairs attempted to explain. "Like the dancing and recitations the other species aboard offer to the rest of us."

"I don't understand," said The.

"I'm sorry you don't. This work we're rehearsing has been entertaining and inspiring Humans for centuries." Carstairs said, and Patma nodded.

"That's not ancient as Thes reckon time," said The, and rolled on past them to the door, spun around once, then left them.

"What do you make of that?" Patma asked Carstairs once The was out of sight.

"I don't know. The befuddles me." She turned toward her quarters. "I think we're getting the hang of the work, at long last. I'm glad that Lui was able to postpone our performance. We'll have a better concert with the consort," she added, wanting to convince herself.

"Now you sound like Lui," Patma said, turning down the opposite corridor and waving as she went.

* * * *

On the fifthteenth morning out, the captain summoned Carstairs to his quarters, his face clouded with dismay. "Sit down, Astrogator Calculator," he said before she had saluted.

Surprised by this unexpected courtesy, Carstairs did. "What's happened, sir?" she asked.

The captain gave the equivalent of a sigh. "I've been going over your calculations and I'm not liking what I see." The translator could not provide the tone of his voice, but his posture and lack of extruding tentacles told Carstairs that he was deeply fretful. "It is not the quality of your calculations, but what they reveal," he added.

"I find that disquieting, sir," she said, trying to remain calm.

"If you're correct, the implications are…terrifying," the captain told her. "I cannot review what you've provided without trepidation."

"Nor can I, sir," she said, a mixture of relief and dejection going through her.

The captain said nothing more for several ticks, then exclaimed, "We're seriously off-course, if you're right."

"That's what it looks like to me," Carstairs admitted. "Have you talked to The about it?"

"Not yet. I don't want to make The think that there's something this bad happening if The can't fix it. But it troubles me that The has issued no warning about the course drift." The captain paused once more. 'The hasn't said anything about our course in the last four days; I don't know why, but when I saw your last report, I began to feel distressed."

"What can be the cause?" she asked, a tightness developing in her chest.

"And why wouldn't The report it?"

Three of the captain's extruded tentacles made a gesture of helplessness. "I've never known a The to behave like this. Humans are new to Worm-class ships, but if you were a problem, The would have reported it. There's an outbreak of fever among the Kyses, but the Medical Crew is addressing it, and I doubt that The can catch a disease from another species, let alone one that would interfere with The's sense of direction. We'll have to use second-rank Helmsmen for the time being, until the Kyses recover. I've been trying to think what else might have happened to The, and if it isn't The that's making this happen, then what else in the ship might be responsible for all this drift. Because it must be The or the ship that's keeping us off-course." He shifted in his hammock, his skin going from light mauve to dark blue, a sure sign of suffering. "I don't like to send for The, but I fear that I'm going to have to, and to ask The if there's any way we can get back on course."

In spite of her best intentions, Carstairs asked, "And if we can't correct course, what then?"

"I don't know," the captain said, and repeated, "I don't know." He withdrew all but one of his largest tentacles and said, "We have eighteen species aboard this ship—including you Humans—and every one of us are in danger." The captain changed color to a bilious green, and his array of eyes took on a distant look.

"That's what I was thinking," Carstairs said blankly, horrified at the possibilities that loomed in her mind.

The captain made a strange sound, one that Carstairs had never heard him utter before. Finally he went silent, and then his translator sputtered into life. "Perhaps the sentient monitors that run the ship are aware of this, but I do not have the coordinates to rectify the error on my own. We need The for that."

"But correcting the monitors is The's function, isn't it?" Carstairs felt the knot tighten in her chest again, stronger than before.

"It all comes back to The," the captain said heavily.

Cartstairs did her best to swallow her rising dread. "How can we find out about whatever is causing The not to do The's job?"

"Don't know," the captain said as if it were a mantra. "I'm deeply concerned."

Both Carstairs and the captain went silent, each of them caught up in hideous contemplation.

"I'll send a message to The," the captain said. "It won't be pleasant, but I need to address the problems before they get any worse."

"What about one of the Empathizers in the Environmental Staff?" Carstairs asked. "Can one of them find a way to determine what The is doing, and why The's doing it? That is, if The is doing anything?" This last afterthought was more pro forma than any real hope.

"It might be worth a try," the captain said dispiritedly.

Another hush settled over the two.

"I want you on the bridge in the afternoon, at your usual time," the captain said suddenly. "I'll speak with one of the Empathizers before then, and determine how this is to be handled."

"What about the crew?" Carstairs inquired cautiously. "Do they have to know what's going on?"

"If we can't get this dealt with without the situation getting out among the crew, then I'll have to inform everyone, but otherwise, we have to keep it secret, for the good of the entire ship." He faltered. "If morale breaks down, there is a risk of a breakdown in Reconciliation rules."

Carstairs blinked in astonishment. "Is that among your Reconciliation experience? A breakdown of Reconciliation rules?"

"Yes," said the captain. "It is. And the consequences were not at all congratulatory. It nearly ended my captaincy." With that, he made a motion with his one extruded tentacle and sank back in his hammock-chair, and did not watch Carstairs salute and leave his quarters.

* * * *

The Empathizer that Patma brought to Carstairs' quarters was a tall, soft-scaled creature, sloe-eyed and graceful as a willow. The Empathizer had to bend down its long neck in order to fit in the room. "I am S'sve," its translator announced as it found a place to sit on the floor.

"It's name is Ooo-thooo," Patma explained to Carstairs in a musical yodel.

"Ooo-thooo?" Carstairs asked, trying to duplicate the pitches precisely.

Patma said, "Flat the G a little."

Carstairs repeated the name with a quarter-tone flattened.

"Good enough," the S'sve translator siad. "I'm told you have some questions about The?"

"I don't know if you can answer them, or if you're ethically allowed to, but I've noticed The behaving...strangely. Ever since I came on board, it seems that I've drawn a lot of attention from The. Most of the time The has questions about the music we—" She broke off. "At least, the music I play. I don't know whether The likes it or dislikes it, but something about the music seems to affect The in an unusual way, to irritate or bother The, and I would like to know what the music does to The, so I can change my behavior and give The a chance to be able to deal with it, if that's possible." Carstairs ended on a slight sigh, knowing there was no turning back from this request, which she was making without first alerting the captain.

"An interesting problem, no doubt the reason for the anguish the captain is feeling," Ooo-thooo's translator warbled. "I will try to find the nexus of emotion that has created this situation."

"I would appreciate it if you would keep what you discover to yourself, and inform me alone," Carstairs told the S'sve.

"Patma let me know of your request, and so long as doing so does not violate any of my ethical requirements, I will give you my word to do as you ask," the translator wandered over three octaves of trills and cadenzas to provide Ooo-Thooo's response.

"That's good enough for me," said Carstairs, hoping fervently that it was.

The Empathizer tucked two sets of legs under it and leaned back a little, its breath whistling softly. "I believe I can do as you ask," it said nine tics later.

"Good enough," Carstairs repeated.

"I perceive that you are concerned for the safety of this ship and all who travel on her," the S'sve went on. "It is for that reason that I consent to this work; if you asked for personal gain or advantage, I would not have agreed to do this," the translator continued accompanied by quavers and whistles.

"Understood," said Carstairs.

Patma found a place on Carstairs' bunk to sit, and settled into it.

"I must concentrate," Ooo-thooo went on. "I ask you to be silent while I locate The and try to feel with The. Any abrupt movement or sound will interrupt my capacity to feel with The."

Carstairs pulled out the one chair provided for the room from its niche in the wall then sat down and waited, doing her best to stifle the rush of emotional strain that ran through her as she realized what a risk she was taking, asking an Empathizer to do its work without benefit of official order. She did her best to put her mind on something else, something that would not disrupt what the S've was doing, and chose rehearsing the Mozart piece in her head, breathing out the phrases that were so demanding.

Patma rested her head on the foot bolster at the end of the bunk and dozed.

A little more than a standard time unit later. Ooo-Yhooo let out a yelp that became a honk, opened its eyes on a gasp, the translator swearing ferociously. The Empathize rose to its feet and lurched around the small space in the center of the room, narrowly missing banging into Carstairs. When it came to a stop, the translator exclaimed, "The's insane!" And then fell over, panting in five-note mordants. After a short while, the S'sve got to its feet again and made an effort to communicate what it had felt from The. "That is what I felt. Madness, and a darkness of emotion that was obliterating all feeling but misery. I believe this shows a toxic reaction to your music."

Carstairs bit her lower lip; this was not what she had wanted to hear, but she made herself ask, "My music does that?"

"Human musical instruments do that to The. Thes do not have the…capacity to engage with the sounds your species regard as musical. There is a vibrational characteristic that to you is harmonious and enjoyable, but to The are like the screams of the tortured." Ooo-Thooo howled in sympathy to what its empathic meditation had revealed.

"That's awful," said Patma as if the words tasted dreadful.

"Why didn't The say anything?" Carstairs clenched her teeth as she waited to hear the answer.

"Because The is unable to assess what the music does to The."

Carstairs stared at the S've, her thoughts jumbled with shock and outrage at this turn of events. "You mean that it actually interferes with its direction function?"

"Among other things, yes," said Ooo-thoo in a mournful glissando.

Patma sat up, revulsion in her manner and her voice. "But other Humans have begun to serve aboard Worm-class ships, haven't they? There are Thes on all Worm-class ships,, but there's been no mention of problems."

"That may be true, but how many of you Humans have orchestras of any sizs on a Worm-class ship?"

"There must be something in the Access files that can inform you if yours is the first, and if it is, something will have to be done about it," the S've said in a wisp of a melody.

Carstairs consulted the Access files and glanced up at the ceiling above them, reading the answers presented. "There is a gamalon group on the *Time Tracker* but the other nine Human crews on Worm-class ships, have, for their entertainment component of service, chosen theatrical performances rather than musical ones." She sighed. "There are no other orchestras or consorts on any Worm-class ships."

Patma looked about in consternation. "But what can we do to…" Her voice trailed off.

Ooo-thooo considered all it had experienced in its empatheic investigation, and lamented, "I could find nothing that would reasonably resolve this impasse. You Humans cannot stay aboard without your entertainment duty fulfilled, and we cannot enter a worm-hole without The."

"Then we'll have to leave the ship," said Carstairs.

"But how will you get back to *Station 8, Quadrant 61?*" Patma asked, her voice shaking. "We're already off-course. We could end up drifting around in deep space for a long time, searching for the station."

Carstairs let her breath out slowly. "Well, we go, or all the ship gets lost in the worm-hole. I don't think we have much choice."

Ooo-thooo lowered its head and said on a single, dreary note, "I doubt that your absence will return The to sanity at this point."

"Do you mean that The's sense of direction will be permanently damaged?" Carstairs asked.

"Yes," said the S'sve. "I found no repair activity in The, no awareness of the distortion in The's directional perceptions."

"I have to inform the captain," said Carstairs, willing herself to get to her feet and take out the small Astrogator Calculator. "If you don't want to stay for what I have to tell him, you'd better leave now." This last was intended as a way to spare Patma and Ooo-thooo from any condemnation for the empathic meditation that Patma had arranged for Ooo-thooo to undertake with The.

Patma answered for them both. "We'll stay here. You may need some back-up."

Carstairs made no protest as she activated the small Astrogator Calculated and a signaled the captain on his esoteric link ro impart what she had discovered, ending with saying, "It seems to me that we Humans ought to remove from the *Star Treader* and hope that the evacuation craft can find its way back to *Station 8, Quadrant 61.* Maybe Tech Crew can find a way to fix The so that you can find your way back to the station, or go on to *Station 9* before the ship runs out of supplies, or—"

The captain cut her off. "That depends on where we actually have drifted, and what kind of distances we're talking about. For all I know, we may be beyond the Reconciliation."

This had already occurred to Carstairs, and she had already thought of a response."Is there a way to send a message back to *Station 8* about The?"

"I don't know," the captain said wearily.

"Do you want the Humans to evacuate?"

"I don't know," the captain repeated. "Not yet," he added.

"What about The? If The is not functioning, is there any way to work out a course correction that The is not part of?" Carstairs asked desperately, afraid that the entire crew the *Star Treader* was doomed to wander in the vastness of space forever.

The captain was fatalistically silent, then said for a third time, "I don't know," and broke the connection with Carstairs.

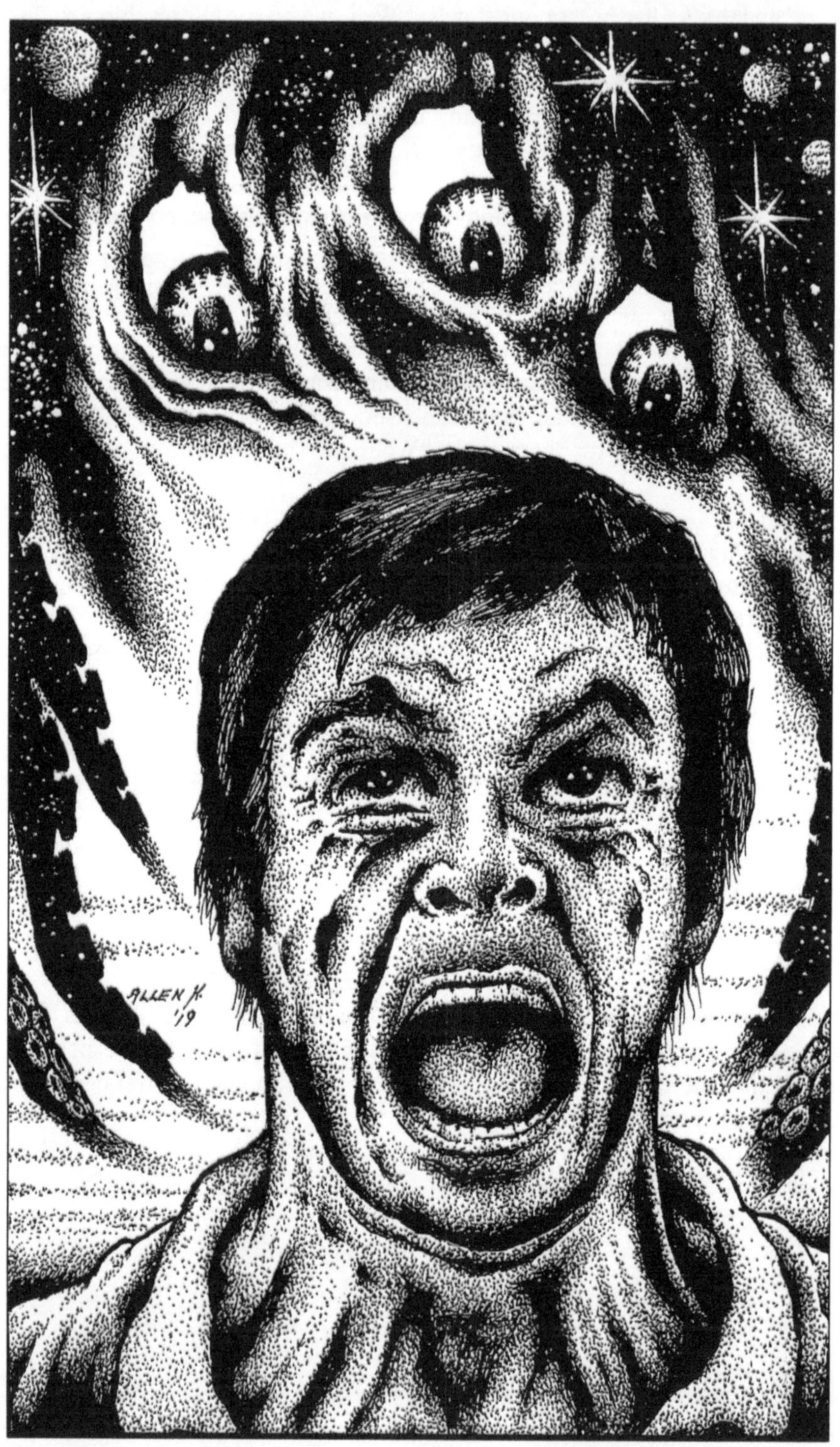

THE INTERROGATOR

DARRELL SCHWEITZER

My badge, from one of those agencies most people barely know exist, got me past the guards without difficulty. I was ushered into the bare, underground room, where he sat at the table. I sat down at the other side, opened my briefcase, and reviewed the files I had with me.

Sunlight filtered in fitfully from a slit of a window. From overhead you could hear fair sounds of traffic. We were supposedly under New York, near Central Park.

"Doctor Leonard Tremblay—"

He looked at me sharply and said, "You can't kill me! I am too valuable. I know too much about <u>them!</u> I will never be executed, regardless of what you think I have done."

One hell of a way to start an interview, as anyone might have said.

"You <u>need</u> what I know," he continued.

"I am not an executioner," I said.

I shuffled through the files, pulled out a couple of exceptionally gruesome photographs, and showed them to him. He had no reaction at all, no apparent empathy.

"Doctor Tremblay, you are accused of some very serious crimes."

At that he sat up straight, folded his hands on the table-top, and said almost cheerfully, "Guilty as charged. What are you going to do about it?"

I sighed. "As I said, I am not your executioner. I am not here to <u>do</u> anything about it, because of course once an action has been committed in the past, there is nothing to be <u>done</u> about it. It is only possible to do something about the present or the future. I am here to understand."

"That is very logical, but we humans sometimes go on more than just logic—"

I continued, controlling my impatience. I did not <u>like</u> this smug bastard, as the common idiom would describe him. I made a note of that.

"Doctor Tremblay, you were a member of the Secondary Magnetic Expedition to the Antarctic, were you not?"

"Not mentioned in the published account. One of the also-was-there-in-the-crowd types. Third lieutenant sub-deputy aide."

"This is not a matter to joke about."

"Assistant biologist."

I made a note. "You were Doctor Blair's colleague," I said.

"I had been his graduate student. He'd kept in touch after I got my degree. I was honored that he asked for me to come with him."

"I didn't ask you, 'How did you feel about Doctor Blair?' yet."

"Sorry. You must understand that we humans sometimes get ahead of ourselves."

"Is that an attempt at humor?"

"No, just bad taste."

I made a note.

"So, how did you feel about Doctor Blair?"

"I won't say I loved him, but I had deep respect for him. He was smart. He had the right instincts, even when that instinct was to trust no one, even me. In the end, as you doubtless know, he trusted no one and went off by himself and locked himself in the shed."

"I have read the report," I said. "I know that by the time they got back to the shed, Dr. Blair was long longer Dr. Blair."

"And you believe that?"

"I do not think the report is a work of fiction."

"Wasn't it just too convenient the way the alien tissue samples melted down into their component molecules and the strange gizmos they found in the shed turned back into junk—like fairy gold it was, you know, the gold that seems to be a great treasure, but the next time you look at them, they're just dead leaves? Like that. In the fairy tales. But you don't read fairy tales, do you? Just reports."

"I have not had the time to read fairy tales."

"But _we_ do. We find the time, at least when we're kids, when we are growing up. There's a time in our development when we are open to anything imaginative, when the boundaries between what is possible and what is not do not seem at all firm. Some of us even carry that into adulthood. It's called imagination. Creative people have it. But you, Mr.—you never did introduce yourself, did you? Make a note of that. It's what humans do. It sets the subject at ease—"

I detected that his heartbeat had increased, that he had begun to sweat. He was fidgeting. He pounded his fist on the table top. I assessed the threat level and determined that there was none. This was merely an emotional reaction.

"My name is Joseph Norton, Doctor Tremblay. Did that set you at ease?"

"Not particularly."

"Were you lying then, Doctor Tremblay?"

"Not particularly."

For a moment, he said nothing, just staring at me.

"I put forward to you, Joseph Norton, if that really is your name, if you even _have_ a name, that what was in that report, what I've told the others

before you, very much resembles the delusions of a madman, not a word of it
true, not even this what I tell you now. A liar paradox, in other words."

"I am aware of the liar paradox, Doctor Tremblay. 'All Cretans are liars.
I am a Cretan. Therefore I am lying about everything, even that Cretans are
liars and I am one of them.'"

"Maybe that should be 'cretins'."

"Please clarify."

"Attempt at humor. Failed. Make a note of it."

I made a note of it.

Then I pushed one of the particularly gory photographs across the table to
him. He picked it up and studied it for a while, then put it down again. "That
was McReady," he said. "Only it wasn't. Liar paradox again."

"You hunted down and killed five members of the expedition. In each
instance you tried to destroy their bodies with fire, acid, or both."

He tapped the photo with his finger. "Hell on the plumbing, to do that in
a bathtub."

"You committed murder."

"Let us say that McReady and the rest were not themselves. I destroyed
what they had become. It wasn't murder."

"I don't see the importance of this distinction."

"You wouldn't."

"Doctor Tremblay, I am going to be candid with you. Put my cards on the
table, as the saying goes—"

"You're learning our idiom fast—"

"What I wish to learn from you is how you were supposedly able to recognize that your colleagues had changed. I have read the report. You have
too, I am sure. It says that the extraterrestrial creature, if that is what it truly
was, had been completely destroyed before any of you left the Antarctic. All
of the dogs that were no longer dogs, the cows that were not cows, and the
men who were not men, up to and including the late, lamented Dr. Blair. So I
ask you to consider: Is it possible that everything you thought you perceived
afterwards was a delusion, the actions of a man in shock after the horrific
deaths of his companions?"

"You're asking me if I'm a raving paranoid?"

"Consider the possibility."

"Liar paradox. That is all I have to say about that. You figure it out. Take
as long as you need."

He sat with his head in his hands. It took several minutes for me to get
him to talk again. Then it was a long monologue. A tirade.

* * * *

"I don't think any of them came with us onto the steamer going home," he
said, beginning slowly. "What walked up the gangplank were humans. I am
sure of that. We had all been tested. We had destroyed the last fully developed

monster in Dr. Blair's shack. Everybody had been tested one more time. Yes, we were mourning our lost comrades, but we also felt like men coming back from a war. <u>We had survived.</u> We were going home. We would see our loved ones again and get on with our lives.

"On the voyage back, there was almost a party atmosphere, but with a tinge of desperation to it, as if everybody still had to prove he was human. Barclay on the banjo and singing dirty songs at all hours. Men playing cards and drinking beer and watching movies and doing all those stereotypical things rough, tough explorer types do in their leisure time to distract themselves from really thinking about what had happened.

"I stood on the deck as we headed North, watching the Antarctic continent receding behind the ship, thinking that we would never know all its secrets, that we shouldn't have ever gone there, that some things are better left the hell alone. Which is not the correct attitude of an inquiring scientific mind, I will admit, but that was how I felt.

"The auroras looked odd, somehow threatening. I was afraid again. For the next few days and nights I kept mostly to myself. If anybody asked, I said I was working on my data. A lot of guys were like that, actually. Real scientists. Maybe we had beaten a hasty retreat from Big Magnet, but we brought our papers, our data, which is what any scientist would rescue from a burning house.

"It was a week later, or more—the air had grown warm my then; we were somewhere in the Southern Temperate Zone—that Henry Gould knocked on my door, came into my cabin, and confided in me. You don't know Gould. Another one of those also-in-the-crowd types, an aviation mechanic's mate. But he came to me, and he was worried, and the next night Gould brought Dr. Copper—the physician—along, and we three confided in one another, compared notes, and concluded that all this enforced jollity, or even resumed diligence with scientific work just wasn't natural. It was <u>too normal.</u> You know the joke about how you don't want to be too normal because that's not normal and then people will <u>know.</u> Well, we knew. We hadn't figured it all out yet, but we knew that the real Barclay never played the banjo so obsessively or that Norris and Benning were not that good at cards. Somehow monsters had gotten onto the ship with us, and very likely mankind and the whole Earth was doomed.

"So the following evening, after most people had gone to bed, we invited Barclay down to my cabin with the promise of some very special booze, and Gould put a sack over his head and I smashed his skull with a crowbar. Then Dr. Copper served as lookout while we bundled Barclay up onto the deck and over the side.

"Well that, I assure you, put an end to far more than the banjo-playing. The party atmosphere was gone. The only conclusion had to be that Barclay had snapped from the strain after the fact—think of it as something like battle fatigue—and jumped to his death.

"The rest of the voyage was quiet. Everybody was trying to be watchful and compassionate and looking out for the first signs that his buddy might be about to crack. A lot of us did our scientific work, as best we could, usually not in our cabins, alone, but in the common mess room. The place had the atmosphere of a very grim school right before final exams.

"Acting Commander McReady wrote most of his report then, the one you have seen. He passed it around to the rest of us for comments and additions. I contributed a paragraph or two myself. All the while I could not get it out of my head that this was a report by a Thing for Things, in a world of Things.

"Then Doctor Copper really did commit suicide. He called me into his cabin. He explained what a <u>goddamned stupid</u> thing we had done disposing of Barclay like that, how, if the world of men ever had a chance to survive, we had just decreased it by several orders of magnitude. Why? Remember how all the dogs had become infected—taken over—because they had tasted Thing blood? Well, if Barclay had been a monster, and we'd just tossed him over the side, alive or dead, when the crabs and fishes or even oceanic bacteria had gotten finished with him, they too would be infected—would become Things, large or small, swimming, flying, or just drifting until they had reached every corner of the Earth and every level of the biosphere. If Things are to be destroyed, it must be with fire or with acid. They have to be <u>wiped out</u>, every cell of them, or it does no good.

"Doc Copper sobbed as he told me this. He was shaking. I actually held him in my arms as if he were a child. He said it was his fault, inasmuch as he had gone along with our plan or even originated it. I actually wasn't sure whose idea it had been.

"Then he told me that he had already taken poison, and before I could do anything for him, he dropped to the floor in convulsions and died, frothing at the mouth. But he did not melt or turn into anything else. He died human.

"Well, <u>that</u> put an even greater damper on the rest of the voyage, you may be certain. The rest was positively funereal. No celebrations as we crossed the Equator. <u>Some</u> of what happened got into the report. But not what he had said to me, of course, or what we had done. No, that was a secret. I don't suppose there is any point in keeping it now.

"I think I spent the rest of the trip home in my bunk. The report says 'nervous breakdown,' doesn't it? Not quite the case. I spent that time dreaming. The dreams came from outside my head, I am certain, as if I were a radio antenna picking up faint signals that were getting stronger and stronger. I dreamed of the white wastes of Antarctica, and what it was like to lie beneath its ice there for millennia waiting, vaguely sensing—as if in a dream—the evolution of the world outside. I dreamed too, from the perspective of Things, as they infiltrated themselves into every human society on the planet and gradually took over. I saw their black metal cities rise above the ruins of ours, like Mountains of Madness. I saw them soaring in metal ships like swarms of enormous bees, spreading out to the stars. I saw them touch our sun and make it bluer and hotter, burning off most native life from the Earth except for what they chose to keep in reserve—for study perhaps, or as food.

"And when we got to New York, I was examined first by psychiatrists, but I kept my secrets from them. I was brought in, like the rest of the survivors—if that is what they still were—to testify before some very, very secret committees.

"I kept on dreaming. It was as if my mind were no longer my own, as if I were becoming part of something larger, more grand than an individual human being. But at the same time I hated that and feared and fought it.

"But how can a man fight his own dreams? And for how long?

"I think you know the rest. I knew I had little time left. Once I was able to work my way free, I sought out Henry Gould—who had retired from exploring and was hiding in an apartment upstate—explained to him the conclusions I had reached through impeccable logic and what I had to do as a result of them, compared notes with him on our dreams, and then killed him and dissolved his body in acid in his bathtub. It had to be done, you see. That is all I can say about any of my actions. They had to be done. I had figured it all out, you see."

* * * *

After Dr. Tremblay had stopped speaking, there were a few minutes of strained silence. I shuffled papers. I took the gory photo back from him and put it in my briefcase. I made some more notes. He just sat there, motionless, like a machine that had been turned off.

"The most obvious conclusion I can come to," I said, "is that you, and some of your colleagues on the expedition, succumbed to a mysterious group psychosis. To any objective, rational person, your entire testimony does sound, you must admit, completely insane."

"But as you well know," he said, "in science the obvious answer is not always the right one. We have long since discarded Occam's Razor for Occam's Swiss Army Knife. There are multiple possibilities."

"You claims are also illogical. There are numerous gaps in your reasoning. You have not reached your conclusions through valid means."

"Call that an intuitive leap. And there were the dreams. I would not expect your kind to understand."

"Why did you kill Henry Gould? To silence him about the murder of Barclay?"

"No. I killed him because he sneezed."

I took more notes, then said softly, "I do not see where you are going with this."

"You don't? I had figured it all out, you see. You are trying to trick me, or torment me, or maybe both, by the question you <u>did not ask</u>. I think you don't want to ask it because you already know the answer and you know I know, and I know you know I know, and so everybody knows and it would be redundant to explain away the eight-hundred-pound gorilla in the room, which is, if all those expedition members were human when they boarded the ship, how did the alien creature, or some element of it, get off Antarctica? We thought we really had extinguished the last of the Things when we cornered what had been Blair and then cremated all those bodies, but, we overlooked one detail, didn't we? It was right in front of us. It was explained when McReady and the others did their clever thing with the electric wire which made a drop of Thing blood behave like an individual being and leap out of a test tube. If each cell of the Thing can function as an individual creature, and slowly absorb other organic material to gain size and strength, how could we ever hope to stop it? It didn't have to devour men or dogs or cows to take us over. All it had to do was scratch its dandruff or fart or sneeze. Particularly sneeze. That's the perfect way, the innocuous way that nobody thought of, to get a few cells airborne, after which they were just lying in wait patiently in our lungs or on our skin and clothing until we let our guard down, and then, slowly, stealthily, those cells call out to other cells—in dreams, perhaps—and come together, and whammo! They take over the planet. That is what I figured out. I should have noticed it earlier. About the time we put Barclay over the side, Gould was sneezing a lot. I should have noticed. It's well known that after about a month in the Antarctic, nobody sneezes, because everybody at the base has already caught everybody else's colds and developed immunity to those particular strains. On the ship, on the way back, we had not yet been exposed to anyone but our own colleagues. There were no stops in South American ports. No fooling around with beautiful Latin women. But there was Gould, sneezing away. After a while, I noticed that the others were sneezing a lot too. Particularly Substitute-Commander McReady, who had taken over after Commander Garry had proven to be one of them. Aa—choo! It aroused my suspicions, I tell you, but I was too distracted. My head was filled with dreams. I couldn't concentrate well enough. It took me a while to work out the implications. By then we were in New York, sneezing away. Gould was sneezing too damn much. Even when I killed him, he was still sneezing. Aa—choo!"

I closed my briefcase, placed it on the floor, and folded my hands on the table. I leaned forward.

"And tell me, Doctor Tremblay, when you killed Gould, did he melt into a shapeless blob?"

"By the time I had him the bathtub and was pouring acid on him, he certainly did. Hell on the plumbing."

"But not before then. Not when he was merely dead."

"How could I be sure he was dead, and not filled with alien monster cells that he had been sneezing all over the place?"

"Either you are telling the truth, Doctor Tremblay, and the Earth faces an extraordinary peril, or else you are completely insane and you are a danger to your fellow men unless you are locked up forever."

"You want to keep some of us around, as breeding stock, for food, or for study, don't you? Start with me. I am a particularly interesting specimen. I know you are fascinated. Aa—choo!"

At this point I deemed it a strategic necessity to deliberately provoke him. An emotional response can be like the light from a stellar explosion. You can read much data in the spectral lines.

I got up as if to leave. "My God," I said. "I don't believe a damned thing you have told me. You have no secrets, Tremblay. You haven't figured anything out. You are merely a sniveling, pathetic psychopath. You have murdered several men quite uselessly. None of this happened. There was no monster in Antarctica. You somehow spread the contagion of your madness there too, murdered several more of your colleagues, and deluded the rest. This is useless!"

"That's not a very professional attitude, if you want to cure me, doctor," he said. He sneezed at me.

"I never said I was a doctor. I am not here to cure you," I said.

Tremblay sneezed again, deliberately, as if to ridicule me, then laughed. He pointed his finger at me. "Of course you're not, because you can't. <u>You're one of them</u>. You're an imitation, not a human being. I could see through you all along. Maybe you've already taken over the planet and are just keeping a few of us humans around for study. You're trying to figure out what makes us human. Is that it? Your individual cells make up a kind of collective, but you can't comprehend what it is to be an individual, not in the human sense, not a complete being rather than a mass of protoplasm pretending to be a complete being. You still want what we have that you haven't got. Is that it? <u>Is that it?</u>"

I turned to him sharply and pointed back.

"I posit, Doctor Leonard Tremblay, celebrated individual that you claim to be, a completely different hypothesis. What if <u>you're</u> the liar? What if <u>you're</u> the extraterrestrial monster pretending to be a man? Huh? What about that?"

He screamed at me, with a howl you wouldn't think a human throat could make, and his face began to shift, but only within the range of what his facial muscles allowed. It was a vivid emotional display, eyes wide, frothing at the mouth, as he screamed and screamed. For a brief while he became articulate again and said, "Then I'll have to reveal my <u>true form</u> and sprout a few tentacles and claws, and hypnotize you with my three burning, red eyes while I break this table into bits and club you to death with it before I rip your head off and dissolve the rest of you in my drool." And he screamed some more, rising to his feet, attempting to lift the table, to tip it over, straining with all his strength while he raged at me in a white-hot fury of indescribable rage.

But he could not lift the table because it was affixed to the floor. He could not tear my head off because he had no tentacles or claws, and in the end he just dropped to the floor, helpless and sobbing, as I pressed the buzzer and two guards came and took him away.

* * * *

I must report that this session has been a failure. The experiment has yielded no results. The conclusion before us is that humans possess some quality that we, for all we perfectly mimic their physical forms and replicate their thought processes, cannot share. It as if there is another sense, beyond sight, hearing, taste, touch, smell, or even dreaming which enables them to somehow detect its absence in ourselves. I do not think they fully understand it themselves. They refer to it disparagingly as "madness" or "paranoia." It is a powerful weapon which we must add to our arsenal. Until then, we are not complete. Recommend further study.

In the meantime we dream of black cities rising, of the planet's sun changing color, and of our race, no longer the last survivors fleeing some unimaginable conflict deep in the universe twenty million years ago, but re-invigorated and renewed, soaring once more to the stars to conquer them.

"ACCORDING TO A RELIABLE SOURCE…"

ALLEN M. STEELE

ART BY MARC HEMPEL

A cold October rain was falling on the Hudson when the *Boliver* arrived in New York. From the front seat of his car, Scott watched the big Argentine freighter as it slowly came into port, hauled by tugboats the rest of the way to the dock. The longshoremen on the wharf were hunched over, hands in their pockets and the collars of their Navy-surplus pea coats turned up against the drizzle, as they waited for the ship to come in. It was the last light of day; along the waterfront, streetlights were beginning to come on.

Scott finished wiping his horn-rimmed glasses and put them on again, then turned to the younger man sitting beside him. "Look, if I'm right about this, we're going to have to work fast. It's not going to be what it's usually like when a ship comes in with some big-shot aboard. Even if any of the passengers want to talk to us, there's bound to be other guys running interference for them."

"Who are you talking about?" DeWitt was loading a film plate into the back of his Speed Graphics camera. "The cops? I thought you're pals with them, Scotty."

"I'm not worried about the cops. It's *those* guys." Scott nodded toward the line of Ford sedans parked nearby.

There were ten cars, coal-black and identical to one another. They'd shown up shortly after Scott and DeWitt did, traveling together as a convoy and parking bumper-to-bumper in the No Parking zone beside the dock. There were two men in the front seat of each vehicle, but so far only one man had climbed out, the passenger of the first car up front. He'd spoken briefly with the dock workers' foremen, who'd glanced at something the newcomer produced from inside his trench coat—probably a badge or another form of official I.D., Scott guessed—before nodding and turning away. Now the man in the trench coat stood near the longshoreman, umbrella open above his head.

"I'm guessing they're g-men," Scott said. "Here to pick up the survivors and take 'em someplace where nobody can talk to them."

"'Nobody' meaning us, right?" DeWitt slapped the film holder shut, then turned the camera around to check its flash bulb.

"Uh-huh. So it's not going to be like what we usually get, movie stars or ball players coming home from a vacation in Rio." As he spoke, Scott watched as the tugs pushed and pulled the *Boliver* the rest of the way in. Crewmen on the fore and aft decks were already tossing hawser lines down to the longshoremen. "Someone went to a lot of trouble to book passage for them on a freighter, not a liner," he went on. "They were trying to make sure these guys kept a low profile … and they might have succeeded if the *Classic* hadn't been tipped off."

"Who gave us the tip?"

"The brother of one of the guys who was in Antarctica. That's what Casey at City Desk told me."

"Well, it looks like we're the only paper in town to get it." DeWitt turned his head to glance back through the rear window, then peered further up the sidewalk along the row of wharf-side warehouses. "Y'know, if it's such a big story, why didn't they call the *Times*, too? Or even the *Daily News?*"

Scott didn't have an answer for that, and he'd wondered the same thing. Among the half-dozen newspapers published daily in New York City, the *Classic* ranked at the bottom. A tabloid specializing in street crime, celebrity gossip, and political scandals, it was the kind of paper principally read by those who wanted their news as grisly and salacious as they could get it. But a story like this … if it was true, then even the Gray Lady would put it on page one.

"I don't know," Scott said, "but a scoop is a scoop, so let's get something good for the bulldog." The freighter was motionless by now, the dock workers tying off the ropes. "You ready?" DeWitt nodded. "Okay, let's go."

As one, they threw open the car doors and jumped out. The man in the trench coat didn't notice them, but a police officer in a hooded rain poncho did. Turning away from the ship, he marched over to them and planted himself in their way. Even if the cop hadn't spotted DeWitt's camera, he couldn't have missed the yellow press tags both men wore in their hatbands.

"Not today, boys," he said, raising his hands. "Whoever you think you're going to meet, they don't want to talk to you."

"Really?" Scott asked. "All twenty-one of them? Because that's how many guys we hear made it out of Antarctica."

"Don't know how many there are, but that's not the point. No one's giving you an interview, and that's all there is to it."

The cop's attention was focused on Scott, which was good; it meant that he wasn't keeping an eye on DeWitt. And Scott knew how fast the young news photographer could be on his feet. DeWitt wasn't paying much attention to either him or the flatfoot. He watching the freighter; the gangway was being lowered, and although the passengers weren't yet in sight, it looked as if they'd be coming down any minute now. DeWitt wasn't going to wait for a waterfront cop to give him permission to do his job.

"C'mon, let them decide who they want to talk to." Ignoring DeWitt, Scott stepped a little closer to the cop. He already had a ten-spot folded and hidden within the half-closed fingers of his left hand. "Take your wife out to dinner and a movie tonight," he whispered, letting his hand brush against the palm of the cop's gloved right hand. "I hear the new Marx Brothers flick is pretty good."

"The old lady hates Groucho," the cop said quietly, but he made the ten-dollar bill disappear. "Okay … one picture, one question, and then you're outta here. Savvy?"

"Got it."

The cop nodded. "Wait here 'til they come down," he murmured just loud for both newspapermen to hear. "When they do. I'm gonna bend down to tie my shoes. That's your cue. I'll play dumb for a minute or so, but when I come up behind you and tell you to get lost, you get lost. No argument. Understand?"

"Sure thing, friend."

"I'm not your friend," the cop muttered, glaring at him, and Scott refrained from making the smart-aleck comeback that hovered on his lips. There weren't many New York cops who'd turn down a bribe, but it didn't mean they had to be proud of it. The Depression was over, or so it was said, but no one Scott knew was rolling in money. So the cop would take the juice, and in return he'd screw up just a little and let a couple of newshounds get by him.

Up on the ship's forward deck, just visible in the fading light, shadowed men were beginning to gather at the railing. As they appeared, Scott heard car doors opening and slamming shut. He looked around to see more men emerging from the row of parked sedans. All wore dark raincoats, their hats pulled low against the rain; if they weren't feds, Scott would have to ask if they had any Girl Scout cookies for sale. The g-men opened umbrellas and raised them above their heads as they moved toward the foot of the gangway ladder to meet the passengers as they came down.

The cop looked down at his feet, apparently noticed that his shoes were untied, and squatted down to do something about it. Scott nudged DeWitt, then both newsmen quietly stepped around the kneeling police officer. None of the feds noticed them. DeWitt had enough sense to keep his camera low until he was ready to use it, and Scott likewise kept his note pad and fountain pen clasped in his hands and out of sight in his coat pocket. Silently, pretending to be invisible, they came up behind the g-men, making sure they did nothing that would attract notice.

Scott watched as the *Bolivar's* passengers began walking down the ramp. None of them seemed to notice the weather; several were even bare-headed, and as they descended the gangway they looked about as wonderingly if the Hudson River waterfront and the luminescent Manhattan skyline belonged to another planet. Compared to Antarctica, a rainy October evening in New York must have seemed like Miami Beach. Yet no one smiled. In fact, it seemed to Scott as if he was seeing something again that he'd often seen when he was young reporter in France during the Great War, on the faces of American and British infantrymen coming back from the trenches of the front: a certain look of horror, the way men's eyes become when they've beheld something no man should ever behold.

Something had happened to them at the South Pole. Something awful.

The first ones had just reached the bottom of the gangway when, from the corner of his eye, Scott saw the nearest g-man look his way. The FBI agent, or whoever he was, studied Scott for a moment, then noticed DeWitt and his bulky rig. Once again, Scott wished that someone would hurry up and invent a camera you could hide in your coat pocket. The g-man tapped another fed on the shoulder, then cocked a thumb toward the two newshounds. Scott couldn't hear what they were whispering to each other, nor did he need to. In another second or so, he and Scott would be tossed out of there before either of them got a chance to do their jobs. So it was now or never.

"C'mon," he said to DeWitt, "follow me." And then they moved in, finding a hole amid the wall of umbrellas and darting through it before anyone could stop them. The feds were caught by surprise, some even stepping out of their way. Scott managed to reach the gangway in time to plant himself in front of the first guy to disembark from the *Boliver*, whom the reporter took to be the group's leader.

He was a big man, almost six and half feet tall, looking tough enough to wrestle polar bears or whatever the hell they got down at the South Pole. A face bronzed by a cold sun and even colder wind, framed by red hair and a coarse beard that had grown as long as a hermit's, turned toward Scott. He said nothing, but his cool grey eyes spoke a silent question: *yeah, so what do you want to know?*

"Scott from the *New York Classic*." Scott had his note pad and pen out now, ready to jot down notes. "What happened down there? We hear a lot of guys were killed … fifteen, sixteen, something like that."

"We had thirty-seven men at Big Magnet and lost sixteen." The giant stopped walking; he looked straight at Scott, his voice deep and matter-of-fact. "That includes Garry, our commander."

"And you are …?"

"McReady. Second-in-command, expedition meteorologist." As he spoke, there was an abrupt pop just behind Scott, followed by a burst of light that made McReady wince. DeWitt had just snapped a picture; Scott hoped he was fast enough to reload the camera and get another shot before the feds confiscated his rig.

"That's almost half the people who were in your expedition," Scott said, and McReady nodded. "So how did they die? Was there some sort of—?"

"Okay, that's enough." The FBI agent who'd spotted him and DeWitt just a second ago had come up beside him. "G'wan, beat it," he growled, laying a hand on the reporter's arm to pull him away.

"Was there an accident?" Although Scott ignored the g-man, he was careful not to physically resist him or do anything else that could give the feds sufficient cause to put him and DeWitt under arrest. "Was there a fire or a—?"

"A fire. Yeah, sure, there was a fire." McReady spoke without conviction. One look at his eyes and Scott knew he was lying, and McReady knew that he knew.

"There's going to be an official statement made to the press." The g-man was pulling him away. "We'll let the *Classic* know when these men are ready to speak. Until then … *stop him, damn it!*"

Another pop and flash told Scott that DeWitt had managed to get that second shot. The commotion that followed, along with the curse snarled by the photographer, also told him that there would be no more. Before the FBI agent at Scott's elbow could haul him away, though, McReady stepped closer to the reporter.

"It's good to meet you, mister," the big meteorologist said, thrusting out his hand. "I hope we get to talk again soon."

Surprised, Scott clasped McReady's hand. It was big and sinewy and strong enough to crunch walnuts, and there was a small slip of paper concealed within the palm, just the same way Scott himself had slipped a ten-dollar bill to the cop. Scott let the note slip into his own palm, and McReady's left eyelid fluttered in a sort of half-wink, then they let themselves be pulled apart by the feds.

Scott tucked the note into his coat pocket and didn't touch it again. Back at the edge of the crowd, bookended by two g-men and the no-longer-cooperative waterfront cop, he silently observed the men from Antarctica as they were loaded, two or three at a time, into the row of sedans. Once they were all in the cars, engines were started, headlights came on, and the cars began to move away from the dock, windshield wipers slapping away the rain. Scott watched them go, then he and DeWitt returned to Scott's car.

"Get some good pics?" Scott asked the photographer once they were in the front seat of the Packard again.

"I'll know once I'm in the darkroom." DeWitt reached into the back seat for the leather bag he used for carrying his gear. Out came a chamois lens cloth that he used to dry his camera. "Sorry you didn't get in more questions. The feds really didn't want you to talk to that guy, do they?"

"No, they didn't." Scott found the note McReady slipped him and opened it. A single word had been written on it: *Metrolite*. He smiled, understanding its meaning. "But I'll be speaking with him again anyway.

$$* \quad * \quad * \quad *$$

The Metrolite Hotel was located in midtown Manhattan, on Broadway a few blocks from Central Park. It wasn't as classy as the Waldorf or the Chelsea but neither was it a dump, and since it was also offered residential rooms for long-term guests, it was a good, low-key place for the government to park the expedition survivors while they investigated the matter at hand.

McReady must have known in advance where he and his people would be staying, which was why he'd written the hotel's name on a slip of paper and covertly handed it to the first reporter he met. That was Scott assumed, at least. Someone had managed to tip off the *Classic* and only the *Classic*, and it was a good bet that McReady was at the bottom of it.

DeWitt wouldn't be needed for the interview and he'd only be in the way, so Scott dropped him off at the *Classic* before driving crosstown to the Metrolite. He parked in the garage next door, but before he headed over to the hotel he stepped behind the car and opened the trunk. Inside were a couple of dark blue garment bags, the kind used by people who wore uniforms at work. Scott chose the one marked in chalk with a small letter "W" and took it with him.

He avoided coming in through the front door. The lobby was doubtless being staked out by g-men, and it was all too likely that they'd recognize him from the waterfront. Instead, he walked through the alley behind the hotel until he located the door used for kitchen deliveries. A few people in the kitchen looked up as he walked through, but no one paid much attention. Even though they wouldn't recognize his face, since he was carrying a garment bag and acted like he had every right to be there, they probably figured that he was a newly-hired staff member on his way in for his shift.

Which was exactly the impression Scott wanted to cast. He'd pulled this sort of gag before, when he wanted to get interviews from people who were holed up in hotels or hospitals. It was sleazy and unethical, but it got results. The other garment bag in his car contained a hospital orderly's uniform; the one he'd taken from his trunk held the sort of white tuxedo jacket, high-collar dress shirt, black trousers, and bow tie worn by a typical room service waiter. Scott changed clothes in a janitorial closet where he could stash his street clothes until he was ready to leave. He searched the bulletin board on the service corridor wall outside the kitchen until he located a clipboard holding a roster, several pages long, that listed the last names of hotel guests and their room numbers. From this, he learned that McReady was in Room 1207.

Scott loitered in the corridor, smoking a cigarette and pretending to be on break, until the kitchen's double-doors swung open and a cook pushed out that which he'd been waiting for: a room service cart with some guest's dinner to be delivered to their room. The receipt beside the covered platter stated that it was supposed to be taken to someone named Cooley, A., on the eighth floor. Well, A. Cooley was going to have to wait a little longer for his steak and potato. Shoving the receipt in his pocket, Scott wheeled the cart to the automatic service elevator and pushed the button marked 12.

On the way up, Scott removed his glasses and tucked them in his shirt pocket. He couldn't see very well without them, but he'd learned a while ago that, when he wasn't wearing them, no one except his wife and kids easily recognized him. And since he'd been wearing his hat as well when he and De-Witt had been down on the waterfront, it was unlikely that even an FBI agent would realize that a room service waiter looked an awful lot like an annoying reporter he'd seen earlier tonight. Or so he hoped. If this didn't work, he hoped there was someone at the *Classic* who'd come over to the court house and post bail for him.

But it worked. There was a g-man posted on the twelfth floor, but he was watching the guest elevators, not the service lift. He barely noticed Scott as he came around a corner and continued down the hall. The two men exchanged a silent nod, and Scott tried not to smile as he pushed the cart past him. For the agent's sake, he hoped that J. Edgar Hoover didn't find out that one of his men could be fooled so easily.

Luckily, the numbers on the doors were large enough that Scott could read them without his glasses. Just around another corner, he located 1207. He knocked on the door, and on his second try he heard its latch being unlocked. Then the door swung open and there stood McReady, looking both annoyed and slightly confused.

"I didn't order—"

"Shh!" Scott raised a finger to his lips, then whispered, "I'm from the *Classic* ... remember me?" McReady's eyes widened, and Scott hastily glanced back the way he'd come, making sure that the FBI agent hadn't followed him. "Hurry up and let me in."

"Yeah, sure." McReady hastily stepped aside and watched as Scott pushed the cart inside. "If that's dinner, then it's going to go to waste," he said as he closed the door. "Not hungry."

"Eat it anyway. It's going to look funny if you ordered a steak and didn't touch it." Then Scott noticed the bottle of Scotch on bureau, an empty glass beside it. It appeared that McReady had ordered room service already, only he was taking dinner in liquid form.

"Yeah, well ... if you've seen what I've seen, you'd have trouble with your appetite, too." McReady grimaced as he picked up the bottle and poured another couple of fingers of whisky. "Anyway, looks like my message got through to my brother and he called your paper."

Putting on his glasses again, Scott sat down on the bed. It was a small room with just one chair, and McReady had already claimed it. "All I know is what my editor told me ... something happened to an American scientific expedition to Antarctica, a lot of people lost their lives, and the ones who didn't were aboard an Argentine freighter called the *Boliver* that was on its way to New York. Aside from what little you were able to tell me before the feds hustled me out of there, that's all we got."

"That's because I didn't tell my brother much about it either. He lives in Queens. While the *Boliver* was at sea, I had the wireless operator send him a ship-to-shore telegram." A wry smile. "Back when we were kids, we worked out a secret code that only the two of us know. I told him to get hold of a newspaper here in the city and tell them to meet the ship at the dock. I figured that, if a reporter showed up, I could pass a message along if I could just get close enough to hand him a piece of paper."

"Well, it worked. I'm here." Scott hesitated. "Just one question … why did your brother contact the *Classic*? Let's be honest, it's not the biggest paper in town."

"I dunno." McReady shrugged. "I don't read the papers, he does. I guess he likes the *Classic,* period."

That sounded like as good of an answer as any. At the very least, it explained why he was sitting here instead of a reporter from the *Times.* "All right then," Scott said as he pulled out his note pad and turned to a fresh page, "let's get started. I guess the obvious first question is, how on Earth did you lose sixteen members of your expedition?"

McReady said nothing for a few moments. He picked up his glass, rocked back his head, and killed the shot he'd just poured in one gulp. Then he picked up the bottle again and, taking a seat in the room's only chair, poured another drink of whiskey without offering any to his visitor. Scott waited patiently. He was familiar with this sort of behavior: it comes when a source wants to spill his guts to a reporter, but doesn't know where to begin.

Unexpectedly, a smile appeared on McReady's weathered face, the sort of smile that's ironic and without humor. "'How on Earth?'" he asked, repeating what Scott just said. "Funny you should put it that way …"

* * * *

The feds caught him on the way back to the service elevator. It wasn't a total surprise. Scott had a premonition that they were onto him. Upon leaving McReady's room, while pushing the room service cart back the way he came, Scott passed the guest elevators and noticed that the g-man who'd been there a couple of hours ago was now absent. The hair on the back of his neck rose when he saw this, and in hindsight he should've abandoned the cart, doubled back to the emergency exit, and scurried down the fire escape to the alley. But he didn't, and so when he came around the corner, the feds were waiting for him.

Scott dropped the pretense the moment they nabbed him. In situations like this, the worst things a reporter can do are run away, resist arrest, or continue pretending to be whomever they'd been trying to pass themselves off as being. But easy surrender didn't stop the two g-men waiting for him from gloating.

"What did you do," asked the FBI agent whom Scott had seen earlier, "stick around for dinner? Shouldn't have stayed so long, pal … that's what got my attention." He lifted the dinner tray cover, glanced at the untouched steak. "Waste of a good t-bone," he muttered in disgust. "Now *that's* criminal!"

The feds put the cuffs on Scott and led him back down the hall, past McReady's room to 1701, where they'd set up a base of operations. It turned out that the FBI had rented out the hotel's entire seventeenth floor, with every room either occupied by a surviving member of the Secondary Pole Expedition or otherwise left vacant. It was not a comforting notion to realize that, if the feds wanted to put the thumbscrews to him, they could do so with impunity; Scott doubted that any of McReady's fellow explorers would come to his rescue.

No, the best thing to do now was to cooperate, and hope that the feds would decide in the end that he was more of a nuisance than a menace.

There was already a senior FBI agent in the room, a fellow whom the other two respectfully addressed as Agent Marquette. Before they left again, presumably to resume guard duty by the elevators—this time, their chief told them to keep an eye on the service lift as well—Marquette didn't take any chances with Scott trying to make a break for it. Instead, he unfastened the handcuff bracelet on the reporter's left wrist, then refastened it to the radiator beside the window. He then searched Scott's tux jacket until he found what he was looking for, his note pad. Ignoring Scott's protests, Marquette lay down on one of the twin beds, propped his back against the headboard and put his feet up, then opened the little black pad and proceeded to study the notes from Scott's interview with McReady.

When he was through, Marquette closed the pad and tossed it on the bedside table. He folded his hands together on his belly and quietly regarded Scott for a minute or so, saying nothing. Scott responded in the same manner. The two men carried on a little staring contest, and it was Marquette who spoke first.

"So, Mr. Scott … what should we do with you?"

"If you were smart, you'd let me go. I haven't broken any laws."

Marquette nodded. "You're right. There's not much we can charge you with except maybe misdemeanor trespassing, and impersonating a waiter is so trivial that I wouldn't waste a judge and jury's time with it. So, yeah, I'm inclined to take the cuffs off and let you go."

"Glad to hear it." The radiator was warmer than Scott liked, even on a cold and rainy night like this. His left wrist was getting hot and he was beginning to sweat.

"First, though, we're going to have a little chat. Namely, about what Mr. McReady has just told you and whether any of it belongs in that newspaper of yours."

"Of course it does. The people has a right to know—"

"No, sir … no, they don't." Marquette shook his head. "When it comes to matters where public safety is at risk, that so-called right to know takes a back seat."

"If the public is at risk, then why shouldn't they know?" Scott jabbed a finger at the note pad. "You've read what McReady told me. That … that *thing* he and his people found down there, the way it wiped out nearby half of their expedition … don't you think it poses a significant public risk? Particularly when it's something no one has ever seen until now?"

"I've read your notes, and I've already interviewed Mr. McReady and other members of his party. And there's nothing mysterious about it. A monster didn't kill all those people, Mr. Scott … a man did."

Scott stared at him. For a moment, he was unable to speak. "What?"

"You heard me. A man, not a thing from another world. Dr. Connant, to be precise."

It took a few seconds for Scott to recall exactly whom Marquette was talking about. Connant, the expedition physicist. The first person at the Antarctic base nicknamed Big Magnet who was killed and … *duplicated*, for lack of a better word … by the creature they'd discovered near the buried wreckage of an alien spacecraft.

"You've got the story mixed up, Mr. Marquette," he said, "Connant killed some of the others, sure, but he wasn't a man any more by then. He was the thing … one of the things … that assumed human form and then went about murdering anyone at the base they caught alone. Those victims were then duplicated themselves, since the thing was capable of splitting off part of its body and reproducing itself as a replica of its victim."

Marquette casually folded his arms together. "That's what you were told, sure, but do you realize how absolutely paranoid that is? A creature that kills someone, then imitates him so perfectly that it even *sounds* like the original? And then goes about killing and duplicating everyone else, even the sled dogs?"

"It wasn't just Connant." Straining against his handcuffs, Scott reached over to the bedside table, snatched up his pad, and flipped it open to the pages where he'd written the notes from his interview with McReady. "Commander Garry …Dr. Blair, the biologist … Kinner, the cook—"

"Yes, I know … they were all killed, allegedly first by the creature, and then again by the other expedition members when that blood test Dr. Copper developed exposed their true identities. And after they were killed, their bodies were burned out on the ice together with any organic remains they left behind, such as their bloodstained clothes. They shot the dogs, too, and even an albatross someone spotted circling the base."

"And you think McReady made all that up?"

"On his own?" Marquette shook his head. "No. I think he had help, all right … the worst case of mass psychosis anyone has ever seen."

"Aw, c'mon!" The newspaperman was incredulous. "You can't seriously believe all twenty-one of those men lost their minds, do you?"

"Why not?" The FBI agent shrugged nonchalantly. "It's happened before. Look what happened in Salem, Massachusetts, a few hundred years ago. Those men were isolated from the rest of humanity, living in close quarters at the edge of the world, in the harshest environment know to—"

"Sounds to me like you're hunting for rationalizations."

"And it sounds to me like *you're* hunting for a story that'll sell a lot of papers," Marquette no longer sounded as smug as he'd been. "But that's as irresponsible as shouting 'fire' in a crowded theater. If you write that story, Mr. Scott, and the *Classic* prints it, every nut case who reads it is going to come away believing that anyone they don't like ... wife, husbands, children, co-workers, even their elected public officials ... are actually monsters from outer space pretending to be human. You and the *Classic* will cause a panic, and more lives will be lost."

"That's not going to happen." But even as he said this, Scott realized that he wasn't persuaded by his own words.

"You don't think so?" Marquette shook his head. "I'm sorry, Mr. Scott, but I disagree. And I'm warning you right now, if the *Classic* runs that story the way you heard it from McReady, Director Hoover will take steps to make sure your paper is shut down and you personally are discredited. And don't think for a second that he can't or won't do that."

Scott said nothing for a moment. He'd been on the crime beat long enough to know that the FBI didn't make empty threats, particularly when it came to stories they want to have spiked. And reporters who lost their jobs at the *Classic* didn't usually find themselves working for the *Wall Street Journal* as their next career move. He'd be lucky to find himself handling classified ads at the *Daily News*.

"Okay, all right," he said, "so what do you want me to write instead? That Connant or Garry or someone else lost his mind, and that was enough to the other fellows over the edge?"

"No," Marquette said, shaking his head again. "Those men had families. Their loved ones don't need to know that truth if they don't need to. What you're going to say is that there was a fire. It started in the base kitchen as a grease fire that Kinner or someone else accidentally caused while working on dinner, and it swept through Big Magnet and killed sixteen men before the others got it under control."

"And what if those guys ... McReady, Norris, Copper, or any of the other survivors ... comes back later and reveals the truth?"

"They won't. Our people spoke to them while they were still aboard the *Boliver*. Everyone agreed to the cover story except McReady. He was the only hold-out, and now that we knows he's talked to you, I'm going to be have a little chat with him, too." A brief, flickering smile. "I'm sure that Mr.

McReady will come around and support the cover story. If he knows what's good for him, this is the last time anyone will hear that tale of his."

Marquette then rose from his chair and, stepping closer to Scott, extended his hand, palm up. "Your notes, Mr. Scott … give them to me, please."

"Agent Marquette—"

"Mr. Scott, there is absolutely nothing you can say to me that will make me change my mind. And I'm not *asking* you, I'm *telling* you … hand over your notes, now."

Scott hesitated. Then, realizing that he was never going to leave this hotel room with the note pad still in his possession, he reluctantly held it out to Marquette. The g-man took the pad from him and slipped it into his coat pocket.

"Very good," he said, a little more pleasantly. "Now, listen … in about an hour or so, there's going to be a press conference downstairs in the hotel's main ballroom. Several members of the Navy and the scientific community will host it, during which they'll reveal the results of their preliminary investigation into the causes of the fire at Big Magnet. Since you've agreed to cooperate with us, I'll make sure that you're given a seat in the front row and that the first question goes to you."

Scott scowled. He wasn't satisfied with any of this, let alone the small favor he'd just been offered. Yet he knew that he didn't have much choice. It went without saying that, if his first question didn't have to do with a kitchen fire, things would go badly for him. So he said nothing and quietly nodded his head.

"Very good," Marquette said. "I think that covers everything. You can go now."

The FBI agent took a keyring from his pocket, found the one that unlocked the cuffs Scott was wearing, and used them to free the reporter from the radiator. Gently rubbing at his wrist, which felt as if it had been slowly broiled, Scott stood up from his chair. He headed for the door, with Marquette falling in behind him.

Scott was just about to lay his hand on the doorknob when another thought occurred to him. He stopped and thought about it for a moment, then he turned to Marquette again. "Say, there's just one thing I'd like to know … off the record, that is."

"So long as it's off the record …" Marquette didn't look as if he was very pleased to have the reporter pose a question to him, or at least not before the dog and pony show they were about to have in the ballroom downstairs.

"Well, if I remember correctly, McReady said that he, Dr. Copper, and Van Wall travelled across the ice to where they detected a magnetic anomaly about eighty miles southwest of the South Magnetic Pole. That's where they found what seemed to be an enormous craft … a space ship … buried about a hundred feet beneath the ice, and that it had apparently been there for millions of years."

"That's what Mr. McReady told me, too." Marquette was impatient to leave the room and get rid of this nosey reporter.

"Uh-huh. And when they tried to excavate it by planting thermite charges around the vessel, the charge reacted with something volatile like a fuel-tank, the explosion destroyed the ship."

"That's the story." Marquette's eyes became flinty and cold. "Scott, don't you go reporting this…"

"I won't, but there's just one more thing." Scott was doing his best to refrain from smiling, but he wasn't able to do so. "McReady said that, after they discovered the thing … or monster, or alien, or whatever you want to call it … and excavated it from the ice pack where it had fallen upon escaping from the ship, they discovered something else. Three more bodies, apparently no longer living but intact all the same, buried in the ice much like the first one. Do you remember that, Mr. Marquette?"

The FBI agent didn't reply. Instead, he continued to silently regard the reporter, not saying a word but carefully listening to everything Marquette had to say.

"So—" Scott didn't like the expression on Marquette's face, but there was no way to back down now "—if there are three more of those things down there, and they're like the one McReady and the other guys found and brought back to Big Magnet, then…"

He let his voice trail off, giving Marquette a chance to finish the thought for him. The FBI agent didn't speak for a minute or so. Instead, he looked away from Scott, gazing at nothing in particular as if trying to formulate an answer to Scott's unasked question.

"Since you're asking me about something we know to be untrue," Marquette said at last, "then your question is entirely hypothetical. And the FBI doesn't deal with hypothetical issues."

"But—"

"That will be all, Mr. Scott." Stepping around the reporter, Marquette opened the hotel room door. "And don't let me see that in your paper, all right?"

Scott didn't reply. Instead, he let Marquette escort him back down the hall to the elevator.

This story wasn't over. In fact, it was just getting started.

NEVER
CALL
FOR
HELP

COLD STORAGE

KEVIN J. ANDERSON

Being assigned to an ultra-secret government warehouse deep in the Nevada desert wasn't as exciting as it sounded, but nobody chose a civil service job for the excitement. That was exactly the way Malcolm Hobbs liked it.

The work was interesting and engaging, especially on days when a new object landed on his desk. After he passed through the guard gates and security fences and entered the small cinderblock Unusual Object Intake Office, Malcolm found a plastic-wrapped package waiting for him.

The sturdy government-issue desk was painted seafoam green, and he had his own rolling chair on the linoleum floor. A metal file cabinet stood like a sentinel with gray fireproof drawers locked with combination dials and marked with classification tags. He glanced at the Uncle Sam calendar hanging on the wall, May 1950. Before considering the new package, he X'ed out the previous day with a black marker, as if it had been redacted and locked away. For the sake of national security, Malcolm did his best to forget everything he had seen, but some things he could never forget. It all went with the job.

He regarded the rectangular package, about fifteen inches on a side, wrapped and wrapped in several layers of plastic with hazard stickers on each layer. A standard Unusual Object Intake Form, in triplicate, was attached with cellophane tape. The form listed serial numbers and a chain of custody, but—as usual—gave very little real or useful information about the item in question.

Up and down the chain of command, no one did the slightest bit more than they were authorized to do. Malcolm was just a small cog in a very large machine, and he was on his own to figure this out.

He sat in the swivel chair, pulled a new government-issue notebook from the side desk drawer, and opened to a clean page. He sharpened his pencil, then began to record his observations. Malcolm would fill many pages with a thorough description of the item, and the logbook would then be stored in the fireproof, floodproof, and atomic-bomb-proof drawers of his secure file cabinet. After he was finished, the object itself would be locked away inside the gigantic government warehouse complex, where it would remain safe.

Once he finished his external observations, he took a box cutter from his top desk drawer and sliced the packing tape to unwrap the first sheet of thick plastic, only to find another layer of equally thick plastic and more hazard stickers beneath.

The warnings made Malcolm uneasy, but he was a loyal civil servant, and the government was here to help him. They had assigned him this job, and he knew they would never expose him to undue risk.

After making a few more notes, he cut through to the third layer, sawed through the thickest layers of tape yet, and finally exposed the actual object inside—a bound journal, a scientific notebook that was burned at the edges, battered and crimped as if it had been dropped out of a low-flying bomber. The broken spine had been taped to hold together the charred and bent pages. The bitter tang of soot rose from the book.

Gingerly, Malcolm lifted the cover with a creak of exhausted binding. The front page, marked in clear, confident handwriting, identified the journal as from "Antarctic Research Station, 1939," written by someone named Blair.

"What did you get today, Buddy?" said a voice that was altogether too loud for the hushed confines of the small office cubicles. "I sure don't want to trade with ya, though. I got cattle mutilations. Those are always fun!"

Flinching, Malcolm looked up to see blustery Glenn Romero, his lone coworker in the intake office. Instinctively, he covered the journal with the flat of his hand. "None of your business, Glenn. This is classified. Eyes only."

"Sure, but I've got eyes." He poked a finger at his face as if he meant to gouge out his orbs. "Were you expecting some bug-eyed monster?"

"I was expecting you to respect boundaries." Malcolm leaned protectively over the journal. "I take my security clearance seriously."

"Of course you do, Buddy. Nobody ever confused you for a fun-loving guy, but you're all the company I have in this dungeon."

In previous years, the Unusual Object Intake Office had employed many more workers. During World War II, even before the testing of the atomic bomb down in Alamogordo, New Mexico, the giant desert warehouse had been used to store dangerous and important items, including weapons stolen from the Nazis—the Spear of Destiny, some Biblical ark, spell books, magical artifacts, and numerous technological prototypes. One entire wing of the warehouse held super-secret materials from the Manhattan Project, as well as the far more destructive and even more super-secret Brooklyn Project. During the War, Malcolm often received as many as five mysterious artifacts in a single week. The work was dizzying and exhausting, not at all what he'd expected when he'd taken his civil service exam.

After the end of the war, they had begun to catch up, until the Roswell Incident in 1947 threw everything into turmoil again, forcing the intake offices to bring in an army of extra staff, with desks crammed together, diligent clerks filling drawers with classified records, and entire file cabinets rolled out and locked away forever. Now, three years after Roswell, the world had settled into a relative calm and the Unusual Object Intake Office had only himself and Glenn Romano to work on the backlog.

He hated Glenn.

The man had no personal boundaries, asking pesky questions, always snooping into Malcolm's work under the guise of "friendship," but Malcolm didn't want to be friends. This was a top secret installation, and Malcolm didn't even know who his immediate supervisor was.

The intake office building was no larger than a bunker and as secure as a bomb shelter, with thick cinderblock walls, no windows. His desk and Glenn's were at opposite sides of the main room. The only human touch was a little kitchen area with a refrigerator and a hotplate. Employees were allowed to socialize there, which Malcolm avoided whenever possible.

In the middle of the cinderblock wall near his desk was a large red button, prominent but untouched. Stenciled letters admonished NEVER CALL FOR HELP. Both he and Glenn knew that the red button was to be used only in extreme circumstances and would result in the termination of their employment and the revocation of their security clearance.

Though Glenn Romano was extremely annoying, Malcolm doubted a personality conflict warranted pressing the red button.

"I've got this new intake. You're interrupting my work."

"Sure thing, Buddy." Glenn slapped the painted wall with the flat of his hand. "Maybe we can meet at the commissary after hours, have a beer, let your hair down?"

Self-consciously Malcolm touched the short and receding stubble on his head. He liked his hair just the way it was.

Finally, he couldn't control his annoyance any longer. "You took my sandwich from the Frigidaire yesterday! Ham and cheese, just the way I like it. I went without lunch because of you!"

Glenn snickered. "I didn't eat your sandwich."

"It wasn't there. I looked."

The other man kept grinning. "Aww, I was just pulling a prank on you. Lighten up! Look in the bottom drawer. I kept waiting for you to say something, but you spoiled the joke." Glenn strolled over to his own desk to enjoy his new photos of cattle mutilations.

Malcolm turned back to the burned journal, wondering what had happened to the 1939 Antarctic Expedition. He'd never heard about it, which didn't mean anything. That was the whole point of this government installation. The journal had remained here, wrapped and untouched in the intake office for more than a decade. He would read it, cover to cover.

Before starting, he went into the kitchen area, pulled open the heavy door of the Frigidaire, and looked at the empty shelves where he had placed his sandwich yesterday. Determined not to go hungry again, he had brought a fresh sandwich this morning, sliced ham, Swiss cheese, and bright yellow mustard on white bread, wrapped up in butcher paper. Malcolm pulled open the bottom drawer designed for fresh produce, which was never used because here in the Nevada desert fresh produce was as rare as a UFO sighting.

Yesterday's sandwich was exactly where Glenn had hidden it.

In frustration, Malcolm snatched up the wrapped package and went back to the desk. He would eat the sandwich while reading the mysterious journal. Munching on the cold ham and cheese, he paged through the damaged book, careful not to get mustard on the paper.

Blair was the expedition's biologist at the Antarctic station, serving with dozens of meteorologists, geologists, engineers, radio men, support crew. Malcolm read with widening eyes about the discovery of an enormous alien spacecraft buried deep within the ice. From the description, the ancient ship sounded vastly larger than the more recent flying saucer found near Roswell, New Mexico.

During excavations, the team had found a hideous blue creature with three red eyes, also frozen in ice outside the ship. The alien inhabitant was certainly dead, especially since one of the diggers had accidentally cleaved its head with an ice axe when they chopped it out of the ice. When they had used thermite bombs to clear more of the ice sheet, they unintentionally vaporized the entire alien vessel.

A shame, Malcolm thought, since the ship would surely have been brought back here to Nevada to be stored inside the warehouse.

"You've got to see this, Buddy!" Glenn stalked over from his desk holding up a manila folder. He pulled out glossy black-and-white photos of mangled cattle, their bodily organs strewn across fields in Montana. "It looks like a combination of Dr. Mengele and some insane barbecue chef."

"We've already processed all the Mengele records." Malcolm looked up from Blair's engrossing journal, but quickly averted his eyes. "Hey, I'm not supposed to see that! It's not my project."

"Sure, sure," Glenn said as he wandered back to his desk. "Thought you'd find it interesting."

Malcolm went back to reading, turning one page after another as Blair described how the supposedly dead alien had thawed from the block of ice and come alive again…but more than alive. As the research crew studied it, they found that the alien organism was somehow infectious, a cellular chameleon that was much more than the three-eyed blue monster they found in the ice. The "alien" itself had infected the expedition members like a plague, taking over and mimicking one man after another. Something as small as a cell could spread the inhuman presence like a virus.

Malcolm kept reading, amazed. With all those expedition members crowded in tiny huts, shoulder to shoulder with no privacy whatsoever, how could they possibly remain in quarantine for an entire Antarctic winter? There would be no stopping such an insidious extraterrestrial invasion.

He was suddenly reminded of how he and Glenn were sealed inside a cinderblock office building in the middle of the desert, forced to work under conditions that were far too close for comfort. Malcolm shook his head, tried to get his thoughts back on track.

The journal described how the monsters subsumed one member after another, while Blair himself, a suspected alien, had been locked away in his own hut, isolated from everyone else. He had written this account, thinking that he was the safe one, while the crew turned on one another both through genuine alien violence but also with all-too-human paranoia.

Blair had huddled in his shack day after day. As his account grew more erratic and less rational, Malcolm thought the biologist might be suffering from cabin fever, slowly going insane. Then the writing itself became illegible, no longer the clear and concise letters from the opening pages, following the neatly ruled lines in the scientific ledger. The writing degenerated into scrawls and, chillingly, into a different language entirely—undeniably alien symbols conveying a message that no human was ever meant to read.

Malcolm swallowed a mouthful of ham-and-cheese and wiped mustard from the corner of his lip.

According to Blair's account, the alien presence was amazingly infectious. One little germ could transform a man into an extraterrestrial monster. At least the bubonic plague had required rats and fleas, but this silent invasion passed from person to person through nothing more than a touch. It was terrifying.

Self-consciously, he wiped his hand on a napkin, then froze, looked down at his fingers, at the pages he had been touching. He swallowed hard.

If Blair was contaminated when he'd written this journal, how long would the germs endure? Many disease organisms could not survive in the open air and stopped being contagious after only a minute or two. But this thing from another world had been frozen under the Antarctic ice for thousands of years, and it had thrived as soon as it was exposed.

Malcolm tossed the rest of his sandwich into the wastebasket, no longer hungry. He scrubbed his hands on his slacks and hurried to the lavatory to wash his hands, again and again, with hot water and soap. Finally clean, he heaved a sigh of relief. Next time he would wear gloves.

* * * *

The following morning, Malcolm passed through the guard gate and thick vault door, eager to finish documenting Blair's journal so he could be done with the unsettling story. He would fill out the Unusual Object Report and lock away this case once and for all. Flying saucers and little green men were far more palatable than a shape-shifting alien plague.

He went straight to the kitchen area and opened the Frigidaire to verify that his uneaten sandwich was still there from yesterday. Good, he was set for lunch. Just to be cautious, he slid it into the bottom produce drawer, hiding it. Maybe Glenn wouldn't notice.

When he entered the main room, he caught Glenn at his desk hunched over the charred journal, reading intently. His face bore a lascivious expression like a man staring at a pornographic pamphlet.

Malcolm squawked, "What are you doing? That's a breach of security!"

The other man had the decency to look embarrassed before he laughed it off. "I won't report it if you won't."

"I just might!" Malcolm snapped. He would have done so if he knew exactly where to file a complaint. He glanced at the red button on the wall—NEVER CALL FOR HELP—and sighed in frustration. "You're not supposed to be looking at my cases."

"I'll show you mine if you show me yours."

"No!"

Glenn offered a disarming grin that did not work on Malcolm. "We're co-workers, Buddy. We both have the same top-level security clearance." Trying to change the subject, he pointed down at Blair's journal. "That's an amazing story! I've been pawing through the pages, trying to get more information. You think it's real? Pretty hard to believe!"

Malcolm crossed his arms over his chest. "Think of all the things we've cataloged and placed into storage. *Everything* here is real."

With his bare hands, Glenn flipped the pages again, then closed the cover of Blair's journal. "That story reminds me of hoof-and-mouth disease, which I've been researching for my report. That's the official government explanation for the cattle mutilations, you know. Hoof-and-mouth disease is so deadly that if one cow gets infected, you can't just cull and quarantine the animal. The only way to be sure is to take out the whole herd." He nodded as if agreeing with himself. "The whole herd.

"Now, of course that's not the real explanation for the cattle mutilations, but the government is incinerating every carcass, burning an entire ranch to the ground and blaming it on wildfires. The ranchers who first reported the mutilated cattle are also suffering convenient accidents."

Malcolm backed away. "You're not supposed to tell me that."

Glenn tapped his finger on the closed cover of Blair's journal. "That's probably what happened to the 1939 expedition, extreme measures to stop the infestation. I bet the whole camp was burned to the ice, no survivors, no bodies, nothing left to salvage. Newspapers back in the day must have reported a fierce winter storm wiping out the station, condolences to the brave scientists, et cetera, et cetera. You know what I'm talking about, Buddy. We've both written stories like that ourselves."

"That's above my pay grade!" Malcolm said. "My job is to document the unusual object, fill out a report, and place it into storage. And you'd be well advised to do your job."

"Whatever." Glenn stepped away from the desk, rubbed his fingers together, then wiped them on his pants before he went back to his cattle mutilations.

Today, Malcolm pulled on a pair of latex gloves and turned the fragile pages with care. He filled half a notebook with his impressions of what he'd read yesterday, determined to make his report as complete as possible. Once Blair's journal went into cold storage, he wanted no excuse for anyone to touch it again.

In the journal, the biologist speculated that the infection rate might progress at different rates, depending on the host. The alien cells could seize and subsume any organic matter, not just the expedition members themselves, but also the cows at the research station, the sled dogs used for transport across the ice. Blair feared that a wandering gull might be infected, copied, and fly off to spread the alien infestation to the mainland.

The second time through, Malcolm read the speculations with increasing interest as well as skepticism. Since Blair had been quarantined and isolated in his shack, he was away from the rest of the camp. Therefore, how had he known the things he described as the camp fell apart around him?

Unless the alien cells that were taking over his body had some sort of connection with the others. Telepathy? An alien biological network? Maybe as he became more and more inhuman, Blair in his quarantine shack did know everything the other aliens knew.

Or maybe he was just a man losing his mind due to the isolation and the howling Antarctic wind.

Yes, that was the best explanation. Considering Malcolm's experience here in the government storage complex, though, mundane explanations rarely turned out to be true.

* * * *

That night back in his assigned employee barracks on site, Malcolm locked the flimsy plywood door then barricaded it with the single chair from his dinette table. He didn't want to talk to anyone, didn't want to go to sleep, but he couldn't stay awake.

He lay on his hard bunk, wide-eyed and listening to muted sounds through the thin walls. In the adjacent room, Glenn had a record player and was not shy about sharing his music. He played platter after platter, Nat King Cole, Bing Crosby, Guy Lombardo, the Andrews Sisters. Tonight, the music was at least comforting, and it was *human*. And Glenn himself was human, even though Malcolm didn't want his company.

He was hungry and queasy. That day, he had been so disturbed and distracted that he'd forgotten to eat his sandwich, so he left it in the refrigerator for the next day. Maybe he would have his appetite back then. His head throbbed. His ears had a ringing in them, possibly from the music next door.

Though still edgy, he finally dozed off, but the nightmares that came to him were far from comforting—vile dreams of monsters and spaceships. The cold emptiness of the universe was Earth's only real protection against all the terrors out there. Though he didn't dream in words or distinct images in his

fugue state of sleep, Malcolm was overwhelmed by a surging loneliness replaced by intense anger, a need for conquest, a hunger to take over the world.

When he woke at dawn, those strange thoughts persisted, as did the head-
ache, worse than an extreme hangover. He sat alone in the commissary and
drank his morning coffee, shaking and confused. For some reason, his body
was sluggish and hard to control, but the alien thoughts disturbed him more
than anything.

Malcolm Hobbs was a civil servant, a quiet man; some might even call
him meek. He had no delusions of grandeur. In fact, he had very few aspira-
tions at all, and he was proud of it. He was comfortable with his role as a tiny
cog in a big machine. He was not an emperor. If he took over the world, what
would he do with it?

Thus, these thoughts clearly were not his own. They originated from outside his personality. Something alien.

He rubbed his hands together and washed them again furiously with soap
and water. Was that sufficient? But if soap and water could kill an alien invasion, then surely the Antarctic research station would never have fallen.

What if the thing was inside him now? What if some alien cells had
survived on the pages of Blair's journal? What if they had worked their way
through his fingertips, penetrated his bloodstream, then swirled through his
body, changing him cell by cell, organ by organ. Would he even know?

And what could the thing possibly want with him? He was isolated in the
bleakest desert in the United States, a place as barren and isolated as savage
Antarctica.

The answer dropped on him like a meteor falling from above. This government storage complex was no minor meteorological station. The top secret government warehouses held the most amazing artifacts, extraterrestrial
technologies, powerful objects considered too dangerous for anyone but the
U.S. government.

What if the thing wanted the Roswell spacecraft?

If the aliens spread among the workers here, they would have access to all
the technology and resources they needed—not only to fly home, but to take
over the Earth, even destroy it a dozen times over!

According to Blair, the alien organism could easily transfer from host to
host without being noticed—not just human to human, but the sled dogs, the
cows, everything in the research station had been infected. The alien cells
could take over any organic substance.

What if an infected person got out of this installation? Even if the "human" were killed, the alien cells could jump to a desert rat or a tortoise, a
rattlesnake, a beetle. The Nevada desert wasn't nearly as lifeless as it looked.
What if the thing got loose?

Malcolm rushed off. He couldn't get through the guard gates, sally ports,
and heavy vault doors quickly enough. He needed to get to his desk so he

could seal away Blair's journal, along with its fully completed unusual object information form, forever!

He hoped he wasn't too late.

* * * *

Malcolm nearly collapsed with relief when he saw the journal still there in the middle of his desk. He had to finish the paperwork so the unusual object could be placed under even higher security deep in the warehouses, where Malcom need not worry about contamination.

He pulled on rubber gloves, then donned a second pair for extra security. The bland scientific journal looked so innocuous, like the lab reports he had written in college chemistry class, but he knew it contained a ticking biological bomb. The ringing in his head was so loud he couldn't concentrate.

He found the original layers of thick industrial plastic and wrapped the journal as tightly as he could, taping and retaping, scribbling *Danger! Hazardous Material! Danger!* in bold black marker. When that was done, he stuffed the bulky package into a lead-lined Top Secret courier packet. On the tag he wrote *Dangerous Material. Do Not Open.*

With shaking hands, he fumbled with the combination lock on the top drawer of his armored file cabinet. Due to his blurred vision, he had to try three times before he finally got the combination settings right. Malcolm stuffed the object inside the drawer, wedged it between thick manila folders about other mysterious artifacts he had worked on. When he slammed the drawer and spun the combo lock, at last he let out a sigh. He swept a hand across his forehead, smearing away beads of perspiration, and swallowed hard. His mouth tasted funny. He wondered if he was coming down with the flu.

Glenn barged in, whistling. He paused to give Malcolm a long suspicious look. "You okay, Buddy? You look like you went on a bender last night."

"I'm fine. It's all taken care of." Inside his head, he heard what sounded like faint and distant fire alarms ringing. He didn't want to talk to Glenn, couldn't stand to be around the man.

What if his office mate was infected? Glenn had smeared his sweaty hands across the pages, maybe contaminating himself. What would he do if Glenn was secretly an alien?

What if Malcolm himself was an alien?

He slapped a palm against his temple as if to jar his brain loose.

"Whoa, careful there, Buddy!" Glenn cried. "Don't hurt yourself."

Malcolm ran to the kitchenette just to get away. His stomach felt queasy, his body was shaking, and with a start he realized that he hadn't eaten since the day before. He had been so engrossed in filling out the report and documenting the terrifying journal that he had left his ham sandwich hidden in the drawer. Maybe that was all, low blood sugar, malnutrition...

Unreasonably ravenous, Malcolm pulled open the Frigidaire, ready to wolf down the sandwich right there. He just needed to eat.

But when he pulled open the produce drawer, he saw that the butcher paper wrapped around the bread had burst open, the paper tape split apart. The top slice of exposed white bread was pulsing and writhing. Startled, Malcolm recoiled.

Exposed to the light and the warmer air, the sandwich twisted, awake now. The neatly cut bread flapped open like the lips around a toothless mouth. The slices of ham churned and became alive.

Malcolm sucked in a breath to scream, realizing that the alien cells could invade anything organic…like ham, cheese, even mustard!

Before his eyes, the slices of ham grew needlelike fangs. The sandwich became a rabid, chomping monster. Long, thin tentacles flashed out, whips filled with mustard-colored blood.

Malcolm screamed and kicked the refrigerator door shut as the sandwich thing tried to escape from the drawer. The heavy door sealed and locked.

His heart pounding, his pulse racing, Malcolm staggered back. He heard a thump from inside the Frigidaire as the unearthly thing hammered inside its cold prison. He turned and ran.

He was isolated here in the office complex. Malcolm bolted to the main room, gasping for breath and trying to form words. He had screamed in the kitchenette, but now he saw Glenn patiently working at his desk, undisturbed, studying his cattle-mutilation photos as if enjoying them for breakfast.

"There's something weird in the refrigerator. It's trying to take over the world!"

The other man turned to him, and his eyes were strange. "You're acting a little odd, Buddy."

"Odd? The odd thing is in the produce drawer!"

Glenn rose to his feet, letting his swivel office chair turn slowly like a planet in a dying orbit. "Maybe you need a rest. You're not yourself."

"Nothing is the same!" Malcolm screamed.

Glenn took a step closer, consoling. "This is awfully strange behavior."

From the kitchenette behind him, Malcolm could hear the louder thumping and then a crash. The sandwich thing had burst through the seal and the lock, tearing open the refrigerator door. "Can't you hear that? It's escaping!"

"Come here, Buddy." Glenn's expression was unusual, as if he couldn't quite control his face.

Malcolm froze. "You're not acting normal, Glenn. I think you're—"

"Everything's fine, Buddy." Glenn reached out, but as he extended his arm, it kept growing. His fingers elongated into twisted tentacles. His hands split, and his chest swelled, reshaping itself to sprout a third arm that popped through the buttons of his shirt. All the appendages reached toward Malcolm, bursting with claws and suckers. One of Glenn's hands sported three red eyes.

Malcolm squirmed away as the Glenn-thing closed in. The sandwich monstrosity shambled out of the kitchenette, no longer resembling bread, deli meat, cheese, and mustard. It grew in bulk as if absorbing material from the air, and more tentacles lashed out as it approached Malcolm from the opposite direction.

Glenn's face melted, and his mouth dropped open, filled with fangs, yet still moaning in a quiet voice. "It's all right."

Pressed against the cinderblock wall, Malcolm expected to be torn to pieces as the monster grasped him, but the disfigured tentacle hand simply patted his shoulder. "It's all right."

Malcolm looked down to watch his own arm elongating as if the bones themselves had become thorns, as if the cartilage added extra inches. His fingers twitched and twisted with minds of their own, and one sprouted a bright red eye that peered back at his face.

Malcolm couldn't stop screaming.

The sandwich thing thumped into the room, joining them. Glenn's body split in half, sprouting fangs and claws in all the wrong places.

Malcolm's own throat was changing, his neck stretching. His corrupted vocal cords altered his scream into an inhuman roar.

But he saw the red button on the adjacent cinderblock wall. It wouldn't normally have been within reach, but his arms were freakishly longer now. They flopped about, but he could still control them…somewhat.

NEVER CALL FOR HELP.

Malcolm didn't care about losing his job or his security clearance. If there had ever been a time to push the red button this was it.

The Glenn-thing tried to stop him as it realized what he intended to do. The ham-and-cheese monster lunged, but not in time.

Malcolm hit the big red scary button.

A recorded woman's voice spoke calmly from the ceiling speakers, "Thank you for initiating the extreme decontamination protocol. Please stand by."

Alarm sirens went off along with rotating magenta danger lights, flooding the intake office with storm of racket and light. Ignited flame jets dropped down through the ceiling panels, bursting into bright orange fire at the same time as acid nozzles gushed a flood of caustic liquid.

As Malcolm saw a last burst of bright heat and searing chemical pain, he realized he was looking through a dozen additional alien eyes, all of which mercifully went dark in an instant.

* * * *

Being assigned to an ultra-secret government warehouse deep in the Nevada desert wasn't as exciting as it sounded, but nobody chose a civil service job for the excitement. That was exactly the way Dennis McGann liked it.

He was proud to have his top secret security clearance and glad to serve his country. This wasn't necessarily the most glamorous job assignment, but it would be interesting, no doubt about that.

Dennis was a new hire brought into the Unusual Object Intake Office. He and his new partner, a man named Wilson, had the office all to themselves, each with a sturdy government-issue desk and his own file cabinet. The office had plenty of elbow room, even a kitchenette with a new-model Frigidaire refrigerator. The cinderblock walls had a fresh coat of white paint.

"Nice digs," he said to Wilson. The other man just grunted and took a seat in a swivel office chair at his desk.

Dennis was pleased to see he already had a project waiting for him on his desk, a bulky lead-lined classified courier envelope. It contained a rectangular package, wrapped in layers upon layers of plastic. Someone had handwritten on the package label *Dangerous Material. Do Not Open*—obviously meant for someone at a lower pay grade.

Dennis had been brought in to document unusual objects, study them, and write reports. He intended to do a good job. He cut the layers of plastic and began unwrapping.

"Best get to work," he said aloud, receiving only a grunt from his office partner. Dennis opened the package.

GOOD AS DEAD

NINA KIRIKI HOFFMAN

When Lilian's husband came home to Norfolk, Virginia, from his scientific Antarctic expedition after seven months away, he brought his dirty laundry with him.

Lilian rushed to the store and bought Arthur's favorite food when she got the telegram saying his ship had come into port: big baking potatoes and fresh butter. The butcher sold her two steaks. Back home, she set the table with the good china and silver her parents had given her and Arthur when they had married two years earlier. She straightened up the living room, where she'd been doing mending for people in the neighborhood for extra money in the evenings, and she mopped the floor.

By the time he got home, the potatoes were almost ready.

"Oh, Arthur," she said in despairing tones as she unpacked his duffle in their bedroom. The stench wafting up from the furs and garments was enough to paralyze a parrot. Their wire-haired terrier, Asta, was as interested in the duffle as she often was in the manure the ice-cart and milk-cart horses left on the street. "Shoo," Lilian whispered to the dog, afraid Asta might roll in the filthy fur jacket Lilian had pulled from the duffle.

"Oh, Lilian!" Arthur grabbed her, hugged her, and swung her around in a foxtrot step. He had been able to wash on the steamer ship on the way home, and he smelled like coconut castile soap. "Isn't life grand?"

"Well, it's grand to have you home again," she said, "but I'm not so sure about your clothes."

"We washed our underwear at Big Magnet, but the outer garments—"

"They had no laundries on the ship?"

Humming "Life Is Just a Bowl of Cherries," he danced her out of the bedroom and into their living room, with its gramophone, cabinet radio, and fireplace. They had bought a house with a big living room just so they could dance. She laughed as her body remembered how well they matched tempo. They had met in a taxi dance hall. He had spent all his dance tickets on her that first night. He came back every Friday night until the night he brought the ring with him, and then she didn't ever taxi dance again.

They took three turns around the living room. He stopped, his arms still around her. "I had other things to do on the trip home," he said, and then let go of her. He lost his smile, and his gaze went past her into memory. Then he shook his head. "Good to have that behind me."

"What happened?"

He focused on her again, and his expression softened. He hugged her tight, then kissed her. "Honey, I can't tell you how glad I am to be home."

* * * *

"Do I smell something burning?" Arthur asked.

Lilian tightened her arms around him. He was so tense, not relaxed as he used to be when they danced. "Probably." She released him and went through the swinging door into the kitchen. She opened the oven and smoke poured out. "Oh no!" The bakers were charred. She hadn't started the steaks yet; Arthur always did the grilling.

He laughed. "We can go out," he said. "I'd love to take my best girl to a swanky place for dinner. Our rations down there were pretty darned basic. I've been dreaming of lemon meringue pie for months."

Lilian heaved a sigh and pulled the potatoes out of the stove with a big fork. She put them on a crockery plate near the sink. She'd cut them up later to see if anything could be salvaged. She put the steaks back in the ice box to keep. Good thing Asta hadn't gotten to them while she and Arthur were dancing.

"Asta," she said, suddenly.

Asta barked from the bedroom.

"Oh, no." Lilian rushed back to the bedroom to discover her fears had been realized: Asta was rolling around ecstatically on the stinking fur jacket from Arthur's duffle. "Bad dog!" Lilian cried, dragging the jacket out from under a wriggling Asta. "Can't we throw this horrible thing away?"

"That jacket saved my life. It was cold enough there to freeze flesh in a minute or two, honey. Sixty below zero. We spent a lot of time inside."

"Thank you, Jacket, for saving my husband's life," she said to the jacket. "For now, you're going in the storage shed." She stuffed it back into the duffle and hauled the whole thing out on the back porch, then put it in the shed with the washtub and washboard. She'd start the soak tomorrow.

She'd probably have to give the dog a bath, too, but the smell was much less pungent with the offending garment removed.

* * * *

She dabbed some Woolworth's perfume at her wrists and behind her ears, and put on lip paint. They walked to Granby Street in the cool April night and went to Arthur's favorite diner for supper. Arthur groaned with pleasure as he ate the meatloaf special, followed by his favorite lemon meringue pie. Later, in a night club with live music, when he had his arms around her on the dance floor, Lilian relaxed and leaned into him. He was warm, strong, and solid, and he smelled so male. She'd missed him so much.

They got home after midnight. "Asta? Do you want to go out?" she called as they entered the house.

The dog didn't bark.

Arthur laughed and pulled her toward the bedroom.

"Just a minute." She wriggled out of his embrace and went to close all the curtains. "Mrs. Milligan next door, I swear, Arthur, I've caught her in our yard peering in through the windows. Anytime, day or night. She's a menace to the neighborhood."

"A menace?" Arthur said, and laughed. "That old biddy? What menacing could she possibly do?"

"She makes up stories and tells them to all the meanest, most gossipy people on the block. And then—" Why had she brought this up? Lilian groaned. It had taken her three weeks to shrug off the story Mrs. Milligan had spread about Lilian having a man visiting her at night.

"Let's give her something to talk about," Arthur said, and tugged her to the bedroom, then unbuttoned her dress. She squealed and rushed to close the curtains before her dress slid off her.

"I've been dreaming of this," Arthur murmured as he stripped and followed her into bed.

"I have, too," she whispered.

* * * *

Later in the night, he woke screaming and thrashing. He pushed her away so hard she tumbled off the bed onto the floor. "You're one of them!" he screamed.

Her heart pounded. She had been sound asleep, and the shock of waking and being shoved out from under warm covers into cool air, the impact—she couldn't remember where she was or whom she was with. She lay on the floor, the cool night air reviving her, and tried to piece things together.

Arthur still thrashed in the bed. "Get away from me! Don't touch me! You're one of them!"

Shivering, Lilian wrapped her negligee around her. She'd heard one shouldn't wake a sleeper having a nightmare, but Arthur wasn't making sense, and he was in such distress. She turned back the covers as he fought with phantoms. "Arthur," she whispered, then louder, "Arthur!"

"Stay back! You've gotten the commander and the others, but you won't get me!" he screamed so loudly she was afraid Mrs. Milligan would hear.

"Arthur." She spoke sternly. "Wake up this instant." She took the glass of water she kept by the bed and poured it on his chest.

He jerked awake. "What?" he asked, and breathed as if he'd just run a race.

"You were having the most dreadful dream," she said. "What on Earth happened down there?"

"Lily," he said, and sobbed. He held out his arms, and she went into them. He hugged her so tightly her ribs creaked. "I thought I'd never see you again," he whispered into her hair. "We were all ready to die to save the world from—from—" His arms tightened, then relaxed. "But now…"

"You're home," she murmured, stroking his back.

* * * *

She got up early the next morning and put on her negligee, house coat, and slippers so she could boil water for coffee and check the chicken coop for eggs. "Asta," she called, because the dog always needed to be let out first thing; it was part of their routine. Asta wasn't waiting by the back door, and she should have been; Lilian hadn't let her out the night before. "Asta?"

The dog came out of the living room, shaking her head, then barked.

"Did you have an accident? You bad dog!"

Asta scratched at the back door and Lilian let her out into the yard. Lilian looked in the living room for a puddle or a poop, but found nothing. She grabbed the egg basket and followed Asta outside. Her hens had been laying well. Today she wouldn't have any extra eggs to sell to Mr. Elliott next door; she'd need them for Arthur.

Mr. Elliott was at the back gate, waiting. He was a much better neighbor than Mrs. Milligan. Gray-haired and stooped with age, he was a retired railroad man who lived simply, and was quick to help if Lilian needed someone to fix a misbehaving oven or a loose shingle. She gathered the eggs in her basket and walked over to tell him the news. "I'm afraid you'll have to find someone else with chickens. My husband's home."

"Is that who it is?"

"What did Mrs. Milligan tell you?"

Mr. Elliott smiled. "I don't ever believe her, but she's always entertaining."

"Would you care to hear what she's told me about you?"

His eyes sparkled. "What could be interesting about an old dog like me?"

"Honey?" Arthur, in his threadbare flannel robe, walked barefoot out the back door into the chilly morning.

"Arthur, this is our neighbor to the left, Mr. Elliott. Mr. Elliott, my husband, Arthur Vane. He's just come back from a trip to the bottom of the world!"

"Elliott," said Arthur, offering his hand. They shook hands. "We've met."

"Yes, of course," said Mr. Elliott.

"I've got fresh eggs, and I bought a loaf of bread at the bakery yesterday," said Lilian. "Excuse us, Mr. Elliott." She turned to go inside. Arthur followed her after a few murmurs to Mr. Elliott. "Asta!"

The dog rushed in ahead of her, and she poured some kibble for Asta in a bowl, then made coffee, toasted bread, and fried the eggs. Arthur sat and watched as she prepared him a plate. "You're a sight for sore eyes," he said, smiling.

"Thanks." She set the plate down in front of him and made one for herself. "I've got to get to work in half an hour. Will you be staying home today?"

"There's a debriefing at the naval base," he said. "We'll be studying all the data we collected for the next six months, at least."

"All right." She ate quickly and made him a sandwich to take to work. "Tell me all about it later."

* * * *

When she got home after her shift in the secretarial pool at the Ford Factory, Arthur wasn't back yet. On the back porch, she filled the wash tub with water and soap flakes and dumped Arthur's horrid fur jacket in to soak overnight, then snapped Asta's leash on and took the dog for a stroll.

The dog was behaving strangely. She didn't stop and sniff at every tree trunk, fence post, bush, and mailbox as she usually did, but walked head up, looking back and forth at everything around them.

The bulldog from the Petersons' house down the street was running loose. Asta and the dog had a growling relationship with each other that had never escalated to an outright fight. Today, the bulldog came up and growled at Asta, and Asta lowered her head. The other dog approached, and Asta nudged it with her shoulder. It yipped and ran.

Lilian frowned.

Mrs. Milligan was sitting on her front porch next door, and called out as they went by. She was thin, with a hawk nose, and hair so black it must come from a bottle. It crowned her head in a thick, braided coronet. She wore a sapphire blue gown, dark stockings, and polished black shoes, and she sat up straight, as though her righteousness gave her power. The knitting needles in her hands clacked away at something gray.

Lilian thought about ignoring her, but that was always a bad idea. She opened the white picket gate and walked up to the porch with Asta.

"Your husband's home?" Mrs. Milligan asked.

"Yes, ma'am." _How I hate you_, Lilian thought.

Asta stared up at Mrs. Milligan.

"It must be nice after such a long absence."

"Yes, ma'am." _I wish you had a husband who would beat you every time you told a lie. And every time you tell the truth._

"What will you do with your other man now?" Mrs. Milligan's smile showed her small, pearly teeth.

"Why, nothing, ma'am." _It was never any of your business in the first place._ "Is that all you have to say to me, ma'am?"

"For now."

"Good day, ma'am." Lilian tugged on Asta's leash, and the dog finally turned around.

GOOD AS DEAD, BY NINA KIRIKI HOFFMAN | 107

"How I wish she were dead," Lilian whispered to Asta after they'd rounded a corner. The dog looked up at her with bright eyes.

* * * *

Lilian and Arthur listened to "It's Dance Time" on the radio after supper, and tried all the fancy steps they used to dance. Arthur smelled of cigarette smoke and sweat. She held him close. He was still the best dancer she'd ever known.

She woke when his nightmares started, and eased out of the bed before he could shove her out this time. She took a blanket from the linen cupboard, went to the living room, and curled up on the couch.

Asta climbed up with her. She rested her hand on the dog's wiry fur. Asta's back was warm against her thigh.

In her dream, the dog spoke to her.

"I don't mean you any harm," said Asta in a warm voice that reminded Lilian of her mother's. "We worked too swiftly before. We had no strategy. Sometimes that's effective, but now it's time to put our second plan in place. We need…a friend. Will you be my friend, Lily?"

"We've always been friends, ever since you were a puppy," Lilian said. "But I never heard you talk before."

"I'm not talking now," said Asta, cocking her head to one side and then the other, the way she always did when she was considering something.

"Aren't you?" Lilian asked.

"Not out loud."

"Oh."

Asta licked her hand with a warm, wet tongue. "Be my friend, Lily." It was true: the voice didn't come out of Asta's mouth, but was somehow in Lilian's head.

"All right," said Lilian.

* * * *

She had a crick in her neck from sleeping sideways on the couch. It was Saturday, Lilian's wash day, since she worked at the Ford Factory on Mondays. Arthur slept late; he had the weekend off. After a solitary breakfast, Lilian heated pots of water on the stove and set up the wash tub and the mangle on the back porch. Today she had piles of clothes to wash—most of what Arthur had brought back with him, and all her own undergarments and her two work dresses. And that horrid jacket. After its long soak, it wasn't so terrible, only bedraggled. She didn't run it through the mangle, but she scrubbed it on the washboard so fiercely it shed some fur. She hung it on the end of the line farthest from the house.

When she turned around, Mrs. Milligan stood there.

Lilian startled. "Oh! You gave me quite a turn!"

Mrs. Milligan wore a scarlet dress today. It was starched and looked scratchy. She was taller than Lilian by a head, and seemed to enjoy looking down her nose at Lilian and everyone else. Mrs. Milligan said, "Your husband has been away so long. Perhaps he'd like to know what you did while he was out of town. I wonder if I feel like talking with him today."

"You don't," said Lilian. She had never seen Arthur in a rage, but he'd told her stories about fights he'd been in when he was younger. He'd been a boxer in college, and he'd gotten into trouble with the law a few times for street brawls.

If Mrs. Milligan told her about Peter, she'd be as good as dead.

"I wonder," Mrs. Milligan said, drawing out the syllables.

"What do you want?"

"I'll bring my wash over here, shall I?"

Lilian stared at Mrs. Milligan and ground her teeth.

"I'll come back for it when it's clean. I'll hang it on my own line when you're done. Unless you'd like to come over and do it for me."

Lilian lowered her gaze and stared at her roughened red hands against the washboard. Her head hurt. Probably from clenching her teeth so hard.

Asta barked. She darted toward Mrs. Milligan and growled.

"Leash your dog," Mrs. Milligan muttered, and backed out of the yard. She returned and dropped a basket of laundry over the gate.

Asta barked once at Lilian and raced to the fence. She stood watching Mrs. Milligan walk next door.

Lilian finished her own wash and hung it to dry on the line, then tackled Mrs. Milligan's. If only she had a box of the itching powder her little brother Paul used to torment her with, or a supply of frogs, or poisonous spiders. How she hated the woman's power.

* * * *

When she brought the basket of clean, wet clothes to Mrs. Milligan's front porch, the woman was nowhere to be found. Lilian knocked on the door, softly at first, then louder, but no one came. Muttering, Lilian went around back and hung Mrs. Milligan's clothes on the line herself. There must be something she could do to stop the woman ordering her around, but she wasn't sure what. She wished she could talk to Arthur about it, but that was the problem. Too long an absence made the heart grow fonder, and then weary of waiting. She had been so lonely.

She went home and made Arthur a late breakfast/lunch, and then they went to Ocean View Beach. Asta didn't answer her call when they left the house. Maybe she was sleeping. She would be sorry she missed the beach. She loved trotting along the water's edge, sniffing for new and disgusting things to roll in.

Chesapeake Bay was calm under the cool spring sky, and the beach stretched out in both directions, stirred by footsteps, empty of people. "Can you tell me what happened?" she asked Arthur as they walked along the water's edge. "The nightmares?"

He didn't speak for a while, staring out at the water and away from her. At last he said, "We discovered something amazing. I can't tell you much more about it—it's classified. It was exciting at first, though. And then…it killed half of us."

She gripped his hand. "Oh, Arthur."

"Killed half of us and made us all suspect each other. Broke our trust. We destroyed it, but—"

They walked a while without speaking.

"Where have you been spending the night? I woke up and you weren't there," he said presently.

"When those dreadful dreams take you, you punch. You pushed me off the bed. I didn't know whether to wake you, so last night, I didn't. I spent the rest of the night on the living room couch."

He turned and pulled her into his arms, resting his chin on the top of her head. "Oh, Lily. I'm so sorry. I wouldn't hurt you for the world."

"I know." She hugged him back, her cheek against his chest. What if half her friends had died? She thought of the other girls in the typing pool, and the couples she and Arthur sometimes went to clubs with or played cards with, the girls at the taxi dance club, and her childhood best friend Clara. She knew some of Arthur's colleagues from summer barbecues and Christmas parties. When he and the other men got to talking about their work, she and the other wives fled. She had liked most of the men, even if they talked about natural forces and numbers too much. "I'm sorry you lost your friends," she said into his shirt.

His arms tightened around her, then dropped to his sides. He took her hand and they walked again. "I guess we were in a war and didn't know it."

* * * *

She took all the laundry off the line and folded it when they got home, separating out the pile to be ironed. Then she glanced over the hedge and saw Mrs. Milligan's wash still on the line. Spiteful beast.

Asta scratched at the kitchen door while Lilian was making cornbread for supper. Lilian opened the door and the dog rushed in. She danced a little, then went to her food bowl and ate.

"Where have you been, you naughty dog?" Lilian asked.

Asta stared up at her with bright eyes, and dropped her jaw in a dog smile. Lilian knelt and hugged her. "Wherever it was, it doesn't smell horrid. Welcome home." The dog licked her cheek.

Someone knocked on the back door. She peeked around the edge of the curtain on the door's window and saw it was Mrs. Milligan again. Good lord, what could she want now? Lilian looked to see where Arthur was. He was in the living room, reading the paper, with the radio on low; Stan Kenton was reading the latest sports scores. She toed the doorstop away from the swinging door and let it flap closed, cutting off her view of her husband. Then she went to the kitchen door and opened it a crack. "What do you want?" she muttered to Mrs. Milligan.

The woman stared at her face.

"What is it? I have to make supper."

"I came to make peace," said Mrs. Milligan. She stooped to pet Asta, who smiled at her and shook all over with delight when Mrs. Milligan scratched behind her ears.

"What?" Lilian looked at her dog, who routinely growled and barked at Mrs. Milligan. Sometimes Lilian gave Asta dog biscuits to encourage her.

"I won't be threatening you anymore, my dear. I hope we can be friends." Mrs. Milligan held out a hand. Lilian stared at it, and then finally shook it, though she suspected this was a trick.

Mrs. Milligan's hand was warm, her clasp gentle. "Thank you for cleaning my clothes," she said.

"Sure." Lilian wiped her hands on her apron. "Excuse me."

"Of course." The woman turned and walked down the back porch steps. Lilian closed and locked the door behind her, then turned on the gas stove so she could heat a pan she could fry hash in.

"Well, Asta, that was strange, wasn't it? Why do you like her now?"

Asta barked, turned around three times, and lay by the stove, resting her muzzle on her front paws.

* * * *

That night, after she and Arthur had made love, she slid out from under the covers and pulled on her nightgown.

"Don't go, honey. You don't know how much I've missed hanging onto you in the dark."

She hesitated, then slipped back into bed and into his embrace. His arms were cabled with muscle, his chest padded with musky fur. He rolled onto his back so she lay half on top of him. She laid her head on his chest and listened to his heart. His breathing was quiet as he held her. She relaxed into sleep.

She woke to a storm. "Get off me, you vampire, you monster! You got the others, but you won't get me!" Arthur shoved her away from him and she rolled off the bed onto the floor again. Her head thunked against the wooden floor boards. She landed badly, barking her elbows. She lay on the floor and cried silently while he fought with the covers and screamed. She crept from the room.

In the bathroom, she studied her elbows and painted Mercurochrome on the bleeding scratches. She took an aspirin for her aching head, then retreated to the living room couch again, curling up with Asta.

* * * *

Asta was in her dream again. "You don't have to worry about Mrs. Milligan anymore. She's a changed person."

"All right." Lilian stroked along Asta's jaw and scratched behind her ears. "Does anyone really change?"

"Oh, yes," said Asta. "I've changed, too."

"Yes, you have." Asta didn't pull on her leash as much, jerking Lilian's arms nearly out of the socket when she saw a squirrel or a bird. She was much more well-behaved on their walks, not even barking at other dogs or cats but just brushing against them, and she hadn't chewed up a couch cushion or a shoe in two days.

Arthur had changed. Everyone had changed but Lilian.

"Arthur can change again," Asta said.

"His nightmares frighten me."

"I'll make them go away."

* * * *

Sunday morning, Lilian and Arthur met in the kitchen. His eyes had dark shadows under them, and his shoulders sagged. "Did I hurt you?" he asked.

She held up an elbow to show him the red stain from the Mercurochrome. "Only a little. It wasn't you, it was the floor."

"The floor!" he cried, and pulled her into his arms.

"Come on, honey," she said after a moment. "I've got to get ready for church. Are you coming?"

He shook his head. "I didn't sleep well last night."

"Go back to bed. Maybe the nightmares won't bother you in the daylight."

He kissed her and went back to bed.

* * * *

Some of Lilian's friends from the secretarial pool invited her out after church. She went, figuring Arthur could use extra time to sleep.

Over pastries at the tea room, Mary McReady said, "How's Arthur? Mac came back so—so strange."

"Did he tell you what they discovered? Arthur has terrible nightmares," Lilian said.

"Mac's staying mum," said Mary. "Classified."

"Arthur said a lot of men died."

Mary's gaze sharpened. "That's more than Mac's said. No wonder he's been so gloomy. Between bouts of excitement."

"Excitement?" Lilian said.

"They made some major discoveries down there. Mac won't say a word beyond that."

"Arthur yells in his sleep, but it's about vampires and monsters."

Mary touched Lilian's hand. One of the other women spoke about a recent film she'd seen, and they let the subject drop.

* * * *

The house was silent when she let herself in. "Asta? Arthur?" she called.

The dog barked from the bedroom and came racing out to greet her. "Who's a good dog? Who's a good dog?" Lilian knelt to rub the dog's ears. Asta yipped and danced around her. "That's right! It's you! Where's Daddy?"

Asta ran to the kitchen and Lilian followed. Asta barked at her empty food bowl. "Arthur didn't feed you? Poor thing, you must be starving!" She filled the bowl, then looked in the cupboard for ingredients for supper. "Arthur?" she called. She went to the bedroom door and looked in. Her husband was covered with a sheet and blankets; even his face was hidden.

"I don't feel well," he said from under the sheet. "I need to rest a while longer."

"Oh, dear!" She stepped over the threshold. Should she take his temperature? Feel his forehead? Bring him aspirin and water?

"Don't come any closer. I don't want you to catch this," he said, muffled.

"Is there anything I can get you?"

"Not now. I'll let you know when I feel better. Could you close the door?"

She went out, closing the door gently.

She put together supper, not sure whether he would eat.

Later, he came out of the bedroom wearing only his skivvies, looking tired, pale, and rumpled. She had made a pot of chili, and it was still warm on the stove. He gave her his half smile, the one she'd fallen in love with, then came over and kissed the top of her head. "Hey," he said. "Everything will be all right now."

She put her hand on his forehead. No temperature. "How's your appetite?"

"Just dandy. Is that chili I smell?"

She dished up a bowl for him and sat with him while he ate. Afterward, they danced. He had lost the tension that had tightened his shoulders, and he was an even dreamier dancer than he'd been before. Every step was in perfect unison, and just when she was thinking he might dip her, he did. As though he could read her mind.

He held her tight after they made love. "You don't have to leave tonight. I promise," he said.

She sighed, not sure whether to believe him. Then she snuggled close.

He was right. The nightmares were gone.

THE HORROR ON THE SUPERYACHT

MARK MCLAUGHLIN

"Okay, we're here!" Warren Piedmont said, lifting the latch of the passenger door. "Be sure to put on your gloves. Models, you go first. Each of you, please grab an equipment case on your way out."

Capheen was the first to step out of the silver luxury helicopter, onto the frozen surface of Antarctica. Or rather, the *slushy* surface—it wasn't as frozen as she'd thought it would be.

"Shouldn't it be a lot colder than this?" she shouted into the vehicle. In addition to a black-leather equipment case, she also carried a lumpy leopard-print purse, slung over her left shoulder.

"Of course!" replied Piermont. "Why do you think we're here?"

The rest of the models—Dilektibl, Anemone, and Tymebomb—followed Capheen. Piedmont helped Quentin, the photographer, to carry out the remaining cases.

The group walked toward the burnt remains of the nameless camp. Behind them, the helicopter rose into the air. Everyone stopped to watch it fly off.

"Oh!" Capheen cried. "He *is* coming back, isn't he?"

Piedmont laughed. "Certainly! Do you really think he'd abandon us here?"

"How long is he going to be gone?" said Dilektibl with a worried pout.

"Like, I hope he doesn't forget about us!" whined Tymebomb.

Piedmont scanned the group and sighed with exasperation—the models were staring at him with worried frowns. He flashed what he hoped would be construed as a reassuring smile. "I promise you, we're going to be fine! Let's take a moment to go over the game plan one more time, okay?"

The models and the photographer all nodded. Dilektibl was curvaceous and red-haired, while Anemone was tall and slender, with blue-green dreadlocks and no eyebrows. Tymebomb was a lean, muscular young man with a thick shock of silver hair. Capheen was the most exotic member of the group. Her face, arms and cleavage were tattooed yellow and black in a tiger-stripe pattern. Quentin Slay, the photographer, was a chubby young man with a thick blond beard.

The models wore stylish snowsuits, gloves and boots in various fluorescent colors, as well as full makeup, foundation and all. The makeup was to be expected, since they were the top beauty icons of Sceptir Fashions, one of the world's most prestigious lifestyle brands, founded by world-famous designer Emil Sceptir. The team looked expectantly toward Piedmont, marketing expert and supervisor for the project.

"As you all should *already know…*"—Piedmont turned to Capheen for a moment as he said those words—"we're here for the big 'Save Antarctica' photo shoot. People need to see that this whole continent is starting to thaw out! So, we're going to shoot pics here at this old research base. Later, I'll call the pilot with a special transceiver and he'll take us back to our nice big yacht." He turned to the photographer. "Quentin, could you start setting up over there, in front of the biggest building? Everybody else, please help him with the equipment."

Capheen kicked at the slush with a hot-pink boot. "I always thought Antarctica was frozen solid. I guess I don't get how this whole 'global warming' deal works."

"Why did you agree to be part of this campaign?" Piedmont said.

"For the publicity—and the money, of course."

"Well, you were right earlier: Antarctica *is* supposed to be a lot colder. It used to have seasonal thaws, but never like this. Right now, this part of the continent is as warm as a late-winter day in the Midwest, with spring just around the corner. Ice is melting faster than ever around the coastline, and as a result, beaches worldwide are being covered by rising water."

Capheen nodded. "Okay, I get what you're saying … but how is a photo shoot going to fix anything?"

"We're building public awareness. Sceptir Fashions is involved with a lot of high-profile causes. It makes us look like we care for the Earth. And I suppose we do! It's the only planet we've got." He smiled warmly at Capheen.

Suddenly, a high-pitched *yip* sounded from within the model's purse. The smile faded from Piedmont's lips. "*Tell me* you didn't bring that animal of yours with you," he said.

"I didn't bring that animal of mine with me," Capheen said with a defiant shrug. She reached into her purse and pulled out a black chihuahua. "He was having a nice cozy nap in there. Guess he woke up!" Once the dog saw the light of day, he squirmed out of her grasp and began to scamper across the slush.

"Now, don't get mad," Capheen said. "I thought it would be cute for him to be the first chihuahua to visit Antarctica! I was going to keep him in my purse, but since it's not so cold, he can run around and get some exercise."

Piedmont rolled his eyes. "Let's go join the others."

Quentin was already shooting the individual models as they posed among the burnt ruins, taking care not to smear ashes on their snowsuits.

"How did these buildings burn up in the middle of Antarctica?" the photographer said. "It doesn't make any sense."

"When we came up with this project," Piedmont said, "we spent weeks flying around in the helicopter, trying to find a locale in this crazy slush that was even remotely interesting. It was a miracle we found this place. We know it was a research base, because … well, what *else* has ever been built in Antarctica? A shopping mall?"

Anemone shook her head sadly. "So much destruction in the middle of nowhere…. How *creepy.*"

"It's a mystery, that's for sure," the supervisor said. "It must've been some kind of secret project. It has to be from a long time ago, back when America had one president."

Tymebomb tilted his head to one side. "There used to be *just one* president? Like, how can one person do a mega-job like that? Even the three we have *now* doesn't seem like enough."

Dilektibl, who had been wandering by herself, rejoined the group. "I've been looking around," she said. "I noticed something kind of weird."

Anemone looked around nervously. "*Everything* here is kind of weird. What did you notice?"

"It's hard to explain," Dilektibl said, "Looking at the scorched areas, I don't think everything was burned *at once*. Some spots look more faded … older. It's like they set fires here and there, and somebody came back much later and burned it up some more."

Anemone's eyes grew wide with fear. "Maybe there was some kind of disease here. I hope we're safe!"

"If you folks don't like hanging around this place, we'd all better hurry up," Piedmont said, nodding toward Quentin.

"Capheen, I haven't shot any pics of you yet," the photographer said. "Stand over by those beams. Stare into the distance, like you're worried about the planet."

The tiger-tattooed model hurried into position. "Hey, does anyone see Yippy? He's around here somewhere," she said.

"Like, you brought that stupid rat-dog?" Tymebomb said, shaking his head. "I hope he freezes to death. Once he starts yapping, he won't shut up!"

"So why isn't he yapping now?" Anemone said. "Quentin already has plenty of shots of me. I'll look around for Yippy."

Anemone looked for half an hour, but couldn't find the dog. Capheen and Dilektibl took over the search, since Quentin wanted to get some shots of Anemone and Tymebomb together.

Piedmont walked toward Capheen, to scold her about bringing the chihuahua, but then noticed that she'd started to cry. Clearly she already felt bad enough. He decided to join the search for Yippy. The photo shoot was nearing completion, so their top priority was finding that stupid dog.

Suddenly he saw a quick movement out of the corner of his eye. He walked toward it and saw a small, wagging tail, protruding from under some scorched boards. He lifted one of the boards and saw Yippy—chewing furiously on the partially burned, decayed remains of a frozen sled-dog. Like the surrounding slush, the sled-dog was thawing. The dead tissue was horribly freezer-burnt from countless years of freezing, thawing, and refreezing. And yet the hungry chihuahua was gnawing on it as though it were sirloin steak.

Piedmont saw that the chihuahua was feasting on the sled-dog's bowels. Looking closer, he saw dead intestinal worms in the rotten, fleshy mix.

"Yippy, you are revolting!" He picked up the dog and pulled it away from the corpse. He tucked the chihuahua under one arm and pushed the burnt boards back on top of the dead sled-dog. He then carried the dog back to the others.

Tymebomb was the first to see him. "Look! Like, he found the rat-dog!"

"My *baby!*" shouted Capheen. She rushed toward Piedmont and pulled the dog into her arms.

"Capheen, don't let it—" But, Piedmont didn't utter his warning quickly enough.

The chihuahua began to lick the model's face.

"*Peeeuuw!*" the model cried, laughing. "Yippy, you need a mint! What in the world have you been *eating?*"

* * * *

Once their work was finished, the helicopter returned to take the team back to *Her Highness*—the Sceptir superyacht, cruising off the coast. It was a truly massive vessel, with a spacious helipad that allowed the helicopter to come and go with ease.

Once they were aboard the superyacht, Capheen let everyone know that she would shampoo Yippy, since he had somehow "picked up an awful stink!" Piedmont had decided not to tell her about the chihuahua's gruesome meal under the boards.

While Piedmont and Quentin were talking about the day's results, Tymebomb came up to them, all smiles. "Wow! Like, that was a real adventure!" he said. He swept an arm toward the female models, who were fawning over Yippy. "We're going to our rooms to take showers, and later, we're gonna meet up in my room for drinks. I make a killer Manhattan! You guys want to join us?"

Piedmont shook his head. "I appreciate the invite, but I'm way too tired."

"Same here," Quentin said. "I'm going to sleep like a log tonight."

"Like, that's funny!" Tymebomb said. "Logs don't need sleep!"

The next day, they all met mid-morning on the sun deck for brunch. Piedmont was the first one to show up, followed by Quentin. The superyacht's buffet was laid out full English breakfast-style, including black pudding and fried tomatoes, along with an elaborate Bloody Mary bar.

"What a spread!" Quentin said. "But, I'm more of a dinner person. I can't even *imagine* eating that much so early in the day."

"Yeah, I'm not a big brunch person, either," Piedmont said. "I'm sure our models won't be eating much. You know how models are! Dilektibl might have a plateful, but I'll be surprised if any of the others even nibble on a slice of toast."

Both men prepared small plates of food and sat at the table. A few minutes later, Capheen, Dilektibl, Anemone, and Tymebomb showed up, walking together in a tight, silent group. Piedmont was surprised to see that none of them had bothered to apply any makeup or hair products. He also noticed, they seemed to have unusually *intense* looks in their eyes. Maybe they were hungover.

The models moved to the buffet and loaded their plates ridiculously high—mostly with meat dishes. They sat down at the table, and without saying a single word to ether Piedmont or Quentin, began to devour their food ravenously. Never before had the supervisor seen anyone eat with such bestial hunger.

"Are you folks okay?" Piedmont asked. "You're really wolfing down that grub!"

Tymebomb glanced toward them, his mouth filled with blood pudding. He simply nodded before returning to his overloaded plate.

A young blonde crew member walked onto the sun deck. "Good morning, everybody! I'm Jessica," she said with a perky smile. "Sorry I wasn't here to meet you." She moved closer to Capheen. "I wanted to tell you, I saw Yippy running around down below. I tried to see if I could catch the him, but he was too fast for me. Could you please try to keep him in your room? I wouldn't want the little cutie to get hurt!"

"Don't mind the dog," Tymebob said.

"Yes, it just wants to look around," Capheen said.

"'It'?" Quentin echoed.

Capheen stared at him without a word, an oddly blank look on her face.

"You called Yippy 'it,'" the photographer said. "You always call your dog 'he.'" He pointed to Tymebomb. "And *you* call Yippy the 'rat-dog.'"

"What are you trying to tell us?" Dilektibl asked, chewing ferociously on a fat sausage.

"You are observant, Quentin. But you should mind your own business," Anemone said, matter-of-factly.

"In what area of the vessel did you see Yippy?" Capheen said to Jessica.

"Like I said: down below," the blonde said. "Near the crew members' rooms."

"Good," the striped model said.

"Hey, none of you have made yourself a Bloody Mary yet!" said Jessica. She walked over to the Bloody Mary bar and began to prepare cocktails for the group.

"We do not want any…." Capheen said, but clearly there was uncertainty in her voice. "We do not … want…."

"Come on now!" Jessica said with a laugh. "My goodness! Who are you and what have you done with Capheen?" She laughed again, louder this time. "You've been onboard plenty of times before. I know my girl Capheen and she hasn't refused a drink in her entire life!"

Jessica brought a Bloody Mary to the striped model. It was an exceptionally large cocktail, garnished with a celery stalk and a slice of dill pickle, as well as green olives and chunks of bacon on a skewer.

"I really should *not*…" Capheen said, just before she took the glass and chugged down the savory beverage.

"I want one, too!" Tymebomb yelled.

"So do I!" Anemone shouted.

Dilektibl slapped her palms against the table repeatedly. "Me! Me, too!"

Jessica returned to the bar and made more drinks as quickly as she could. The models left the table and swarmed around Jessica, eager to receive their drinks as soon as they were prepared.

Piedmont watched as the models swilled down the Bloody Marys. He had seen them drunk before, but this was something else altogether. The models were squealing and grunting like pigs! He had no idea what was going on with them.

Piedmont finished his meal and left the table. Quentin followed close behind. They did not bother to say goodbye, and the others did not acknowledge their departure.

Once they'd reached the deck below, the photographer said, "What is *up* with them? They're acting so weird this morning."

"*Something's* going on, that's for sure," Piedmont said. "They had drinks last night, and now they're having way more. And they weren't wearing make-up! That's the first time I've ever seen any of our models without makeup."

Quention looked out toward Antarctica. Even as he watched, a massive chunk of ice fell from the edge of the continent into the ocean. "Look at it! The place is thawing out right in front of us," he said. "Even the *air* is warm, and it's still early. We could be wearing swimwear right now, as far as the temperature is concerned." On the coast, another huge chunk tumbled into the water.

"Maybe that's the problem," Piedmont said. "Our models are tired of seeing so much slush and snow. It's so sad and dreary. They're party-people and they aren't having any fun. They're stressed out!"

"I have an idea," Quentin said. "Let's do a shoot on the sun deck this morning, while they're still tipsy. We'll bring 'em more shots. Models partying as Antarctica melts! They can wear their best swimwear. I'll get the coastline in the picture behind them. Those would be fabulous pictures. They'd really capture how warm the weather has become down here."

"I'm not sure if we'd be able to use those pictures," Piedmont said. "The head-honchos might think they're too frivolous."

Quentin shrugged. "So what if they do? Even if we can't use the shots, at least everybody had fun at the shoot."

Piedmont grinned and nodded. "I like how you think! I'll tell the models to get into their swimwear. And you—go get your camera! You'll need help setting up, so feel free to ask some crew members. See you up on the sun deck!"

* * * *

Within an hour, the brunch furnishings had been cleared away from the sun deck and Quentin's equipment was set up, thanks to Jessica and two cabin boys. The models had returned from their rooms, wearing their best swimwear. Capheen wore a leopard-print one-piece, and Dilektibl's scarlet bikini was lightly trimmed with black lace. Anemone's bikini featured cyan and navy-blue stripes, while Tymebomb kept it simple in a silver swim-thong.

Jessica found some beach balls and soon the photo shoot was underway. "I wish I knew where all the other crew members were," she said to Piedmont. "Half of them are nowhere to be seen."

"Now that you mention it," the supervisor said, "I haven't seen little Yippy this morning, either. Though I recall, you said you'd seen him down below."

"Yes, but only for a few seconds," Jessica said.

"I want this to be a festive shoot," Piedmont said, "so could you prepare a couple trays of tequila shots? Make sure there's plenty of salt and lime wedges."

Jessica smiled, nodded, and hurried off to see to the task.

Piedmont walked back to the photo shoot. The models were tossing beach balls back and forth, but it was clear that their buzz from the brunch Bloody Marys was quickly wearing off.

"People! Don't tell me you're done for the day!" Piedmont said. "Let's see some energy!"

"How long are we going to be trapped on this boat?" Capheen said. It occurred to Piedmont that somewhere along the way, she had become the spokesperson for the models.

"You *do* work for Sceptir Fashions," Piedmont replied. "Is there some other place you'd rather be?"

"We want to be around people," she said. "Lots and lots of *people*. Millions! You are right: we work for Sceptir Fashions. We need to leave this place and go to Sceptir headquarters in New York City."

"I don't think I've ever seen you this *forceful* before," Piedmont said. He noticed Jessica and a cabin boy approaching with trays of shots. "Ah, here we are! I told Jessica to bring more refreshments. I think this trip has been stressful for everyone. A whole continent covered with slush is pretty depressing … enough to fray anybody's nerves. Here's some more joy-juice to lift our spirits."

He noticed that as the tequila drew closer, the models' eyes grew wider and they began to lick their lips, like thirsty beasts. They sure were craving the booze this morning!

Once again, the models guzzled down the alcohol, every drop, in record time.

"More!" Tymebomb cried. "Bring us more!"

"They'll bring more, no worries!" Piedmont said. "In the meantime, start tossing those beach balls! Laugh, dance, have some fun! The sooner we get some great shots, the sooner we'll head for New York!"

The models began to hoot and squeal with gusto. The sounds they made as they partied hardly seemed human. "Yes! Off to New York!" Capheen cried. Quentin began shooting, jumping back and forth among the models to capture the best images.

"Make sure Antarctica's in the background whenever possible!" Piedmon called to the photographer.

"No problem!" Quentin replied. "It's a big continent! I can't miss it!"

Piedmont heard sounds from the far end of the sun desk. He turned and saw several crew members silently approaching—led by Yippy, who walked slowly and deliberately. Capheen saw the chihuahua, but did not rush to pick up her pet. In fact, Piedmont noticed that she actually *nodded* in a sudden, jerky way toward the dog. Was it his imagination, or did the animal *nod back?* The crew members seemed to have oddly intense looks in their eyes, like the models.

"Jessica!" Piedmont yelled. "It looks like we have more guests. Double that last order of tequila. Or better yet, triple it!"

A moment after Piedmont uttered those words, he began to wonder if he was doing the right thing. He was beginning to feel unnerved … perhaps even frightened. The current situation was simply unnatural. The models just weren't themselves anymore—and neither were those crew members who'd joined the party. He decided he should keep his distance from the party, in case things got ugly.

He couldn't figure out what was happening, but one factor did seem to connect the odd goings-on. It was as though everybody who'd come into con- tact with Yippy had changed … after the chihuahua had eaten that decayed meat. On Antarctica, he had held the dog for a short time, but he'd been wear- ing gloves.

Did the chihuahua have some sort of mad-cow disease? Mad-*dog* dis- ease? *Rabies?* Maybe it was something else altogether … some condition that humans could contract.

The crew members began to suck down the tequila, while the models drank their shots two at a time. He saw Quentin have some shots, as well as

Jessica and the cabin boys. He did not dare to have any tequila himself. He needed to stay sober so he could monitor this bizarre situation. He felt that it would soon take a turn for the worse.

He didn't have to wait long.

The models stripped off their skimpy swimwear. The drunken crew members also shed their clothes.

"Whoa, steady now!" Jessica shouted. "I'm seeing *waaay* too much skin! I know it's a party, but let's keep it rated PG, okay?"

"Yeah, I don't take X-rated pics!" Quentin said.

Suddenly, squirming clusters of tentacles shot out of the naked bodies of the models and the crew members. The slick tentacles wrapped around Jessica and the cabin boys. Dilektibl made sure that Quentin received an extra-special hug. Tentacles shot out of Yippy's body as he jumped into the hideous fracas.

"Get your ass over here, Warren!" Capheen cried, laughing uproariously. Her eyes blazed as red as fire—and there were three of them now.

"Yeah, come join us!" Tymebomb called. "Don't let this pretty lady have *all* the fun!" He drove two wriggling tentacles down Jessica's throat.

"It's a party, honey, and you're invited!" Anemone winked at the supervisor, just before wagging an impossibly long blue-white tongue at him.

Piedmont turned and ran until he reached a stairway to a lower level. As he'd watched the grotesque bacchanalia, something had *clicked* in his mind. Now that he had the facts, after seeing them *firsthand*, things were starting to make sense.

Obviously, that scientific base in Antarctica had been taken over by some horrible creature … something alien and monstrously aggressive. It took over other life-forms, infected and *converted* them. People had tried to burn the monsters to death—maybe more than once, based on what Dilektibl had said she'd seen. Yippy had eaten some meat from a sled-dog that had been infected, long ago. The meat must have infected the chihuahua.

He gasped as he remembered Capheen's words: "We want to be around people. Lots and lots of *people*."

He kept running down stairways until he found himself standing near the prow of the superyacht. He looked around but couldn't figure out where to go next. Should be go down into the lower levels and hide? Or, maybe he could find the helicopter pilot. Then they could fly off and—

Suddenly he remembered, to his despair, that the pilot had been one of the crew members following Yippy. Piedmont had no idea how to fly the vehicle by himself.

A new thought came to mind. Maybe he could escape in the tender. The tender was a smaller boat, housed in an internal dock, that was used whenever travel between the superyacht and a dock was necessary.

He had used the tender before on two previous photo shoots, both in Hawaii. He'd even been instructed on how to drive it. The boat had contained food, water, and medical supplies. There was also a communications system, so that crew members operating the tender could stay in touch with both the superyacht and its destination.

Clearly some sort of evil intelligence was behind the transformations—an intelligence that had access to the knowledge of its victims. Once a victim was converted, the new creature became part of a sort of team, bent on world conquest. The team had probably already figured out that the captain of the superyacht would need to be converted. So, trying to find the captain wouldn't do him any good.

But, many members of that monstrous team were now drunk. Distracted. Perhaps they had not yet realized that he could use the tender to escape.

Piedmont found a door leading down to the level where the tender was kept. He descended the stairs quickly and quietly, listening to make sure no one else was nearby. After a while, he could discern the faint but unmistakable scent of marijuana smoke. As he drew closer to the tender, he could hear that was the vessel was occupied. Once he'd reach the level of the dock, he slipped into the darkness under the metal stairs.

On the tender, two young male crew members were being assaulted by a trio of tentacled, humanoid creatures with blazing red eyes. The two men had obviously popped into the tender to share a joint, only to fall victim to the invading monstrosities.

Piedmont tried to think what he could possibly do to save the men, but it was far too late for heroics. All he could do was wait in the shadows. Maybe after the crew members were converted, the attackers and victims alike would depart and he'd be able to use the tender.

It appeared that the creatures were able to sprout body parts with relative ease. They had covered the men's mouths with flat, flipperlike appendages to muffle the screams. One of them had grown a small, crooked arm ending in a pincer to hold the wrist of one of the men.

Piedmont watched in horror as the creatures slid clusters of sinuous tentacles into their victims. The men writhed in excruciating pain at first, but as time passed, it became hideously clear that the humans were *adjusting* to the ordeal. At one point, the pincer relaxed its grip on the victim, who did nothing to fight back.

As Piedmont waited for the completion of the grotesque acts taking place in the tender, he looked around to see if he could spot any possible weapons, in case one was needed. He noticed, in a hallway to his left, a door marked SECURITY. The metal door was halfway open and the lights were on in the room. That had to be where those two crew members worked.

The creatures seemed to be fully absorbed in their actions. So, he decided to take a chance. Maybe there were weapons in that room. He dropped to his belly and moved, as slowly as possible, out of his hiding place. He crept down the hall and before long, he was able to crawl into the Security room.

Once inside, he stood up and looked around. The walls of the room were covered with security monitors, showing various areas of the superyacht. He was dismayed to see that creatures were attacking the remaining crew members throughout the vessel. He searched the room but could not find any weapons. But then, firepower probably wouldn't be a high priority aboard a private superyacht in the fashion industry. In a drawer, he found a cigarette lighter, so he took that. It wasn't much, but it was better than nothing.

On one screen, Piedmont noticed a curious sight: walking along outside the executive conference room, he saw a handsome, silver-haired gentleman in a black silk robe. The old man smiled as though he didn't have a care in the world....

Piedmont looked more closely and suddenly recognized the old man. He was designer Emil Sceptir, owner of the superyacht and of course, the entire company. He had given Piedmont a warm handshake on his first day, years ago. He recalled that the old fellow had told him, "I'm sure you'll do a fabulous job. If you ever decide to switch jobs, you can always be one of our models. You're very handsome."

Piedmont glanced outside the door. The tender was now empty. Creatures and victims alike had moved on. Of course, now the victims were creatures, too.

He hurried out of the Security room—and up the stairs. He wanted to escape in the tender, but he couldn't possibly do it without trying to bring Emil Sceptir with him. The route to the executive conference room was pretty much straight up some stairways, without too much rambling. With luck, he'd be able to run up and find that kind old man without encountering any of the creatures.

Once he'd reached the top of the stairs, he stepped cautiously out onto the deck. Fortunately, there was no one else to be seen in that area. All he needed to do now was take another stairway to reach the upper level.

Suddenly, Tymebomb staggered out of a side corridor. He had sprouted several smaller arms of various lengths, and each held a different bottle. He'd also grown several thick-lipped, misshapen mouths—all the better to drink with.

"There you are!" Tymebomb roared. "Why'd you take off? Don't you like me, buddy?"

Piedmont looked at the bottles—rum, cognac, high-proof grain alcohol. "You're quite the party monster. Those are some powerful refreshments you've got there."

The model poured more liquor into his mouths, splashing booze all over his body. He reached toward the supervisor with his longest tentacles. "Don't be shy! Let me give you a back rub!"

Piedmont noticed a newspaper sticking out of a nearby trash canister. He grabbed the paper, set it on fire with the lighter he'd found, and threw the flaming mess onto Tymebomb. The flammable fluids covering the model burst into blue flame.

Tymebob squealed like a wounded hog. He lurched from side to side, beating at the fire with his tentacles and extra arms. But he hadn't let go of the bottles, so all he managed to do was cover himself with broken glass and more alcohol.

Piedmont pulled a fire extinguisher out of its wall bracket. He hit the living nightmare over the head with the metal cylinder, and then used it to shove the creature away from him. As Tymebomb staggered off, Piedmont used the extinguisher once more to push him over the rail. The flaming horror screeched with rage all the way down to the ocean.

The supervisor rushed back to the stairway that led to the executive conference room. At the base of the stairs, he looked up—and saw Emil Sceptir coming down.

"Thank God!" Piedmont called, smiling. "You're still okay!"

Sceptir returned the smile. "Well, of course I'm okay! Why *wouldn't* I be okay?" When he reached the lower level, he looked closely at the supervisor. "You're Warren Piedmont, aren't you? We're certainly having a noisy day. I keep hearing the strangest hubbub, coming from here, there, and everywhere. Must be some kind of party!"

"Actually, we're right in the middle of a crisis situation. You obviously don't know about it. When did you come aboard?"

Sceptir laughed. "I've been here since the trip began! But I've kept to my cabin, since I wanted to catch up on some work. Jessica has been taking care of me. Wonderful young lady! Now please, tell me about this crisis you mentioned."

"You wouldn't believe what's going on. It's so horrible!" Piedmont said. "We just need to get in the tender and *go*, sir. Right now, before it's too late!"

"Please, calm down. Nothing can be *that* bad." The old man laid a hand gently on Piedmont's arm. "You're simply under a lot of stress, that's all. You know what you need? A pet! Pets always bring out the best in us. Our inner gentleness and serenity. Why, just last night I was playing with the cutest little chihuahua, and now I feel much better!"

So saying, Sceptir opened his black robe and embraced his screaming employee with writhing tentacles.

APOLLYON

G. D. FALKSEN

On the plain below the monastery, the laborers struggled knee-deep in mud and oil, digging new wells and cutting channels to coax the thick black liquid from the earth. It seeped out naturally all across the island, but the oil that came unbidden was never enough for the alchemists. So the men had to dig, and pile, and haul the stuff until now the whole of the rocky shore was stained by it.

Markos wrinkled his nose as he watched the scene from a window. He knew the stench of rock oil so well that he had almost forgotten what it was like to smell clean air. Even the salt air of the Black Sea was drowned out. Eight months they had been trapped on the island, exiled at the command of the Emperor until the work could finally be finished. Absolute isolation for absolute secrecy, that had been the decree.

He was drawn from his musing by angry voices from across the room.

"You must not rush things, General," began old Theodoros. The gray-haired alchemist wagged one boney finger at the stern-faced General Andronikos. "This sort of work is complicated, it takes time...."

"Time!" snapped Andronikos. His cheeks were red with anger behind the thick black beard that covered his chin. "Time is a luxury that we do not have, old man! When this damned venture began, you swore to me that you would require three months to perfect the formula. It has been almost a year."

"General, please—"

Andronikos flicked a hand at Theodoros to dismiss him. The general's anger often outstripped his patience for the complexities of alchemy. He turned to Markos.

"What do you say, boy? How much longer until the liquid fire is ready?"

Markos looked away from the window, bristling at the general's dismissive words. At twenty-three he was half the age of Andronikos, but hardly a boy.

"As my master says, it is a matter of time, my lord," Markos replied, his tone obedient and humble. He was angry, not stupid. "We have tested so many different formulae, it is inevitable that we will get it right soon."

"How hard can it be to pump naphtha through a siphon?" Andronikos demanded.

Markos grimaced. Very hard, in fact. The weapon's pump mechanism was proving even more difficult than the formula itself. But there was no reason to alert Andronikos, who would only rage all the more at yet another setback.

"Respectfully, my lord, it is one matter to spray oil at an enemy's ship. It is another to make that oil stick, or to ignite upon contact with water, or even to fly far enough that one's own fleet is not threatened. As it stands now, we are half as likely to drench our own ships...."

"Then correct the problem," Andronikos snarled. "I have promised the Emperor liquid fire, and you two are expected to deliver it."

"Yes, General," Theodoros began timidly. "We are aware of the urgency."

Andronikos turned his back on them and gazed outside, across the dark rolling sea. Markos sighed. There was a speech coming, one that he had heard dozens of times already. Behind Andronikos's back, he mouthed the words as the general spoke them. It was the same every single time.

"For centuries," Andronikos said, "liquid fire has protected the Empire against its enemies, from the Saracens to the Rus. But in our darkest hour, the secret was lost and when the Latins betrayed us, our navy was helpless against them. That must never happen again. We are beset on all sides by enemies. Even now, the Turks swarm across Anatolia. Should they reach the Bosporus, liquid fire may be the only thing that stands between them and Constantinople." Andronikos turned back to them with a dark look in his eyes. "So I ask again, when will it be ready?"

Markos and Theodoros looked at one another. Neither wanted to be the one to speak. As they both hemmed and hawed around the fringes of an answer, there came a distant shouting from the oil fields. Markos went to the window and looked out. There was some commotion among the laborers at the far side of the island.

"What is that noise?" Andronikos demanded.

It was an opening for escape, and Markos gladly took it.

"I know not, my lord, but I will investigate at once."

* * * *

Markos hurried from the monastery, eager to be away from the oppressive place. The monks had abandoned it a two hundred years ago, and Markos didn't blame them. It was squat and shadowy, and it had smelled of oil even before the workers started digging the wells. Now, it was unbearable, and seepage had contaminated the cellar with equal parts oil and water.

Most of the laborers were still at their work, hauling the oil out of the ground for Markos and Theodoros to use. A few of them had come from the mainland with Andronikos's soldiers, but most were the fishermen who lived on the island, pressed into service in exchange for food and water and the promise of future pay.

Fishermen. There were no longer any fish for them to catch. After months of runoff from the wells, the local wildlife had quit the shallows, and Andronikos had ordered all of the fishing boats burned to preserve security. The only way on or off the island was the supply galley that arrived twice a month with food. So the fishermen had become diggers, trading their nets for shovels and fish for naphtha.

A brisk wind struck Markos as he crossed the field. In the distance, he saw a familiar figure running in his direction: a young woman with long dark hair and a wide mouth that seemed always eager to smile.

"Helena!" Markos called, waving both hands to get her attention.

There came the smile, so broad and genuine that it almost hid the sunken hollows of Helena's cheeks. Food was rationed, and the soldiers always had their fill before the villagers.

"Markos!"

Helena sprinted to Markos's side and grabbed his hand in both of hers. She looked around quickly to be sure that no one was watching them, and stole a kiss from him. Markos blushed. For four months they had been together, and still he was giddy every time she looked at him.

"Helena, I…"

But Helena had no time for sweet murmurings. She gripped Markos's hand and pulled him along after her. "Come, you must see this! Thomas has found something!"

Markos laughed and stumbled as he tried to keep up.

"What has your fool of a brother done now?"

"He's not a fool!" Helena protested. "You must not call him a fool! And besides, he has found a fallen star!"

"A…what?"

"A fallen star. I know it must be one, because it is as bright and silver as any of the ones in the sky."

"I do not understand," Markos said.

"Come, you'll see."

Markos followed Helena to the far end of the oil field, where a new well was being dug. A few diggers stood around, their mouths open in wonder. They were pointing and murmuring to each other in nervous tones. As Markos approached the well, he saw why. At the bottom of the hole rested a large, silver shape, like half of a dome swallowed up by the rock. It looked like it had been encased in rock, until some ancient disturbance had broken open a fissure above it, revealing it to the soil and waiting to be unearthed by the hands of men.

Markos just stood and stared for a little while, his mouth agape like the diggers.

"So? What do you think?" Helena asked breathlessly.

"I don't know what to think," Markos confessed.

Helena's gangly brother Thomas crawled out of the pit, wiping dirt from his hands.

"Ah, Markos!" he exclaimed. "Look what I have found! I'm going to be rich!"

Helena scoffed at her brother. "The general won't allow you to keep it, you know. And what are you going to do? Pull a boulder out of the ground and roll it across the sea to Constantinople? Who is going to buy it from you?"

"Bah!" Thomas dismissed her words with a wave. "It's not a boulder, it's a room!"

Markos stared at him, and then glanced at the dome. "What?"

"Look, you can see the door."

Thomas pointed to where some of the men were straining to force open part of the silver wall with picks and shovels. The metal creaked and groaned, until finally a door sprang open with a tremendous clang. Two of the workers lost their footing and were flung into the dirt. Cursing like a sailor, Thomas scrambled down into the pit to help them.

"Stay here," Markos said to Helena.

Helena gave him a look. "You know that I won't."

Markos sighed. "I know."

They descended a wooden ladder and joined Thomas at the doorway. The air that drifted out from inside the dome was stale and peculiar, half the odor of a cold cellar and half the stench of heated metal, though how the two could coexist was beyond Markos.

Now at the threshold of his prize, Thomas became hesitant. "What do you suppose is in there?" he asked.

"You didn't wonder that before you opened it?" Helena asked her brother.

"Well, I…"

Markos ran his fingertips along the edge of the doorway. It was perfectly smooth. Impossibly smooth, in fact. It was hard as well, harder than silver had a right to be. The banging of the picks and shovels had left no mark at all. Mighty was the smith who had forged this.

As the siblings argued behind him, Markos went through the doorway. Inside was a small, cramped chamber, dimly lit by the light from outside. Markos suddenly wished that he had a lamp, but the workers were careful not to bring any fire onto the oil fields. Still, it was bright enough for his purpose.

The chamber was perhaps the size of a small boat, or an especially large carriage. Just inside the door, Markos saw a kind of table wedged against the wall, and something resembling a chair in front of it. The table and the nearest wall were covered in flat, glossy tiles colored pitch black. Most of them were badly cracked. In a small depression at the side of the table, Markos saw a pile of strange waxy paper. It was covered in markings that might have been language, but certainly wasn't Greek.

Some instinct of self-preservation told him not to touch anything.

The only other object in the chamber was a tall sheet of glass built into a metal frame. Markos could half see his reflection as he approached, but there was something else behind it: a dark shape nestled inside the container. It was hard to make out any details. The inside of the glass was covered in frost, which distorted his view. Markos reached out his hand and held it near the surface. The glass felt cold to the touch, like a church window on a winter's night.

"What is this place?" Helena whispered, as she joined Markos. She gasped in wonder, expressing Markos's own sentiments with excitement rather than apprehension. "Did the monks build this?"

"I do not think so," Markos said.

He took Helena's arm and drew back from the glass. Everything in the chamber was strange, but it slowly dawned on him just what this last curiosity might be.

"We should leave."

"Why?" Helena asked.

Markos pointed at the glass. "That is a sarcophagus, and this is a tomb. I am certain of it."

Thomas pushed past them, holding a pick in his hand. "A crystal coffin in a silver tomb? Someone rich is buried here! Like a pharaoh of Egypt!"

"Thomas, wait—" Markos exclaimed.

Thomas did not listen. The light of greed danced in his eyes. He jammed the point of his pick into the edge of the sarcophagus's lid and started pulling with all his might.

"Thomas!" Helena shouted at him, angry and disgusted. "Grave-robbing? Do you have no shame?"

"I am not going to be a fisherman all my life!" Thomas retorted.

With a few loud grunts and a strong pull, Thomas yanked the pick backward and the sarcophagus snapped open. A draft of cold air rushed out and stung Markos's nose and cheeks. He brushed his face, and heard Helena gasp in fright. Thomas made a similar noise, more of a gurgle than a gasp. The pick hit the ground with a loud clang.

"What is it…?" Markos asked, rubbing his eyes.

No one answered, and no one had to. With the lid open, the figure inside was clear to see. Markos had expected a corpse, but the corpse of a man. The thing that reclined against the back of the sarcophagus was nothing of God's Creation. The figure was short and squat, with four gangly arms and fingers shaped more like the tentacles of an octopus than the digits of a hand. It was blue in color, with flesh that better resembled the viscus body of a sea beast than anything that walked the earth. Three red eyes set in its head gazed blankly into the distance, and in place of hair its hideous form was covered in oddly curving protrusions that put Markos in mind of worms burrowing into the soil.

"What is that?" Helena asked.

Markos had no reply to give her.

Thomas slowly leaned in and peered at the monstrous cadaver. "That…
It is a statue, isn't it?"

Again, Markos could not find his words. He just shook his head.

"It must be a statue," Thomas continued, trying to convince himself as
much as the other two. "Those eyes are rubies, yes? And the body is some
kind of stone. It must be."

"I don't think so, Thomas," Helena said. Her voice sounded hoarse.

Finally, Markos forced himself to speak. "Out. We have to get out."

He grabbed for Helena and Thomas, and pulled them out of the chamber
with feverish urgency. Some instinctive part of his brain told him to flee, and
he obeyed. Panic seemed the most reasonable response to such a sight. Once
he was in the sunlight again, the fear ebbed a little. Markos leaned against the
earthen wall and rubbed his face with one hand, while Thomas collapsed to
his knees, mumbling again and again that the thing in the sarcophagus must
be a statue.

"That was not a statue," Markos whispered.

Helena held onto Markos's arm and cast a hesitant look back toward the
chamber. "It was not," she agreed. "What are we to do?"

Markos thought about it for a little while. He was half tempted to bury the
thing again, to leave it forgotten under piles of soil and rock. He was equally
tempted to drag the thing out into the light and examine it in detail. As much
as it horrified him, his curiosity was driven wild by the sight of something
so impossible. Such a creature could not have been made by God, and yet it
existed.

Still, that decision was not his to make. There was a strict hierarchy on
the island, and he knew better than to violate it.

"We tell the general," Markos said, "and the general will call Father Cyril, and hopefully one of them will have an explanation."

* * * *

Andronikos was where Markos had left him, still ranting to poor Theodoros about the preservation of the Empire and the unacceptability of further
delays. Old Theodoros dithered like always, mumbling excuses that failed
to address to very real restrictions and setbacks the research faced. Better to
hem and haw about water in the oil, than to admit that they were attempting
the impossible: to recreate a formula known only in legend, with barely any
hint of where to begin. Any one of the dozen compounds they had already
devised might actually be the sought-after mixture, and yet they had no measure to evaluate it with other than Andronikos's outlandish expectations.

But no matter. There was a more pressing issue. At first, Andronikos
and Theodoros both listened to Markos's report with skepticism. Only after
Markos insisted, did Andronikos summon Father Cyril, and together the four
of them went to the pit to see the truth of Markos's "mad ravings." Theodoros

grumbled all the way, and Andronikos, though silent, did nothing to hide his displeasure.

Markos led them to the chamber. His heart began pounding as he stepped through the low doorway. His hands trembled. He was a reasonable man and prided himself on keeping his wits, but there was something deeply unnerving about the figure in the glass sarcophagus. It was surely nothing of this earth, and its very unnaturalness made Markos sick and dizzy.

"So," Andronikos murmured, "you spoke true, boy." He cleared his throat like he wanted to be sick, but had too much dignity to give in and do it.

"Mother of God…" Cyril whispered, crossing himself as he saw the body. Markos, Andronikos, and Theodoros followed his example. The priest peered at the body and shook his head slowly. "This is… This… What is it?"

Andronikos grunted. "That is the question I would put to you, priest. You are a man of God. How can this *thing* exist? Do not tell me that this abomination crawled through the Garden of Eden, or that Noah brought two of it upon the Ark."

Cyril reached out to touch the body, but then he shuddered and drew back his hand. He crossed himself again. "'And I looked, and behold a pale horse: and his name that sat on him was Death, and Hell followed with him.'"

Cyril's voice quaked with fear, the same thing felt by the rest of them. Markos clutched his hands to keep from shivering. The chill that had enveloped the sarcophagus before was now completely gone, replaced by the lingering warmth of autumn. Even the frost on the body was melting, and droplets of water trickled to the floor.

"Does the Apocalypse mention a blue horse?" Markos muttered, seeking humor in blasphemy, and finding a little comfort in it.

"What was that?" Andronikos asked.

"Nothing, my lord."

Father Cyril set his face firmly, and clutched at the heavy cross around his neck. He turned back to Markos and the others.

"We all know what this is," he said. "There is no point in pretending otherwise. This creature is not of God's earth. It is an abomination, a fallen angel cast from Heaven. 'They were ruled by a king, the angel of the bottomless pit, whose name in Hebrew is Abaddon, and in Greek Apollyon, the Destroyer.'"

"A devil, then," Andronikos mused. He scratched at his bearded chin and grimaced. "I never believed I would see such a thing in my life." He paused. "Why doesn't it move? Is it dead? Can a fallen angel die?"

Cyril shook his head. "No, certainly not." However sure his pronouncement, the priest did seem unsure about the other half of the question. "It… slumbers, of course. Banished from Heaven and flung into the earth, it waits for some evil purpose to awaken."

The four men all considered his words, and as one they took a step back from the body.

"What are we to do?" Markos asked. "Should we…um…" He cast around for the most probably means of killing a devil. "Burn it?"

"Surely not!" Cyril exclaimed. He quickly silenced himself, and cast a nervous look at the sarcophagus, fearful that his loud voice might stir Apollyon from its slumber. "Anything we do to it might awaken it."

Andronikos grabbed Cyril by the arm. "Then what exactly are we to do?"

For the moment, Father Cyril had no answer. He looked at Theodoros for help, but Theodoros had no answer either.

"Perhaps we should just bury it and hope that it stays asleep," Markos suggested.

The three older men answered him with more or less identical looks of patronizing distain.

"Shut up, boy," Andronikos said. He turned back to Cyril. "Well?"

Cyril clasped his hands and exhaled. "There is only one thing to do. We must exorcise it. I will perform an exorcism and banish the creature to Hell."

"Have you ever exorcised a demon before?" Andronikos asked.

"I have never even seen a demon before," Cyril confessed, "but I know how it is done. I will pray that the Lord give me strength to cast out this evil."

Andronikos nodded. "Good. Get to it."

"What? Now?" Cyril sputtered. "It is almost sundown!"

"I will have some lamps brought, and you can exorcise it over night." Andronikos leaned over and looked Cyril in the eyes. "I do not care how it is done, but I want that thing gone! Exorcise it, burn it, bury it, it makes no difference to me. But I will not spend two nights on the same island as that monstrosity!"

Markos said nothing, but he agreed with Andronikos's words. The only thing he questioned was the methodology. Surely, it would be better to just cover the silver chamber with heaps of rock and dirt until nothing could possibly climb out again, devil or otherwise. It wasn't that he doubted the power of exorcism, he simply refused to believe that it could possibly work.

* * * *

That evening, Father Cyril went into the chamber alone to perform the exorcism. A few of Andronikos's soldiers stood guard at the top of the pit to ensure he was left undisturbed, and they eyed each other nervously, as the sunlight faded. Several of the workers lingered near the pit, trying to catch a glimpse of what was happening, though in the end this proved impossible. There was no way to observe the exorcism without venturing into the pit itself, and Andronikos had forbidden anything that might distract Cyril.

Markos, still harboring misgivings, stole away from the others and looked for Helena. He found her by the shore, watching the sun setting over the Black Sea. She glanced at him as he approached, and flashed a smile.

"So that is that, I suppose," she mused. "Our brave priest will banish that horror back to Hell, and life will return to normal."

Markos put his arms around Helena and gazed at the sea with her. "So it seems. By tomorrow, it will be as though your brother never dug up that tomb. Imagine: the strangest episode of my life over and done with in half a day."

Helena laughed. "You sound disappointed."

"Nothing of the sort, my love," Markos replied. "I'll admit, that horrible thing intrigues me, but it is a monstrous curiosity. I know better than to indulge it, just as I know better than to put my hand in a fire. To be honest, I wish that thing had never been unearthed in the first place. I fear it will haunt my dreams tonight."

"Mine too," Helena said. Silence drifted between them, growing with the lengthening shadows. After a little while, Helena touched Markos's cheek and looked into his eyes. "Markos… When all of this is done, and you return to Constantinople…."

"Yes?"

"You are going to take me with you, aren't you?" Helena sounded hesitant and uncertain, like she feared giving voice to the question would somehow make it impossible.

Markos held her tighter and kissed her temple. "Of course, my love. As I promised, when I leave here you will come with me as my wife."

"Good," Helena murmured, resting her head against Markos's chest. "I do not think I could bear to life the rest of my life on this island, and certainly not without you."

Markos smiled at her. "I do not wish to live in a world without you, Helena. You bring me a kind of joy I didn't know could exist. It is as simple as that."

Helena chuckled softly, and seemed pleased. They stood together for a little while, watching the darkness creep across the sea.

* * * *

Markos slept fitfully that night. At first his dreams were of Helena, and of the life they would have in Greece once they could finally leave the accursed island. But quickly, they turned from his future happiness to visions of the demon in the silver tomb. He saw its hideous blue face, writhing with worms that were its own flesh. Its red eyes stared blankly ahead, frozen as if in death, but still they bored through him, gazing into his very soul. Cyril's words echoed in Markos's slumbering mind:

A king, the angel of the bottomless pit.

Hour after hour, he tossed and turned, only half sleeping yet unable to wake. When the morning light finally roused him, he found himself drenched in cold sweat. Markos cursed loudly as he crawled from his bed. This was going to be a bad day. He could feel it.

Despite his doubts about the exorcism, he went straight to the pit to see the results. His skepticism did not invalidate the power of the divine. When he arrived, he found a whole crowd of people standing at the edge, waiting for Cyril to emerge. The soldiers kept the onlookers back. It wouldn't do to disturb a holy man in the middle of casting out demons.

Two of the soldiers were well known to Markos: Ioannis and Georgios, who were often tasked with helping the alchemists test new formulae for the liquid fire. Markos joined them and exchanged uneasy greetings. Having spoken, all three of them looked back into the pit nervously. The tension in the crowd was almost physically uncomfortable, and that was just what had grown from rumor and speculation. None of the frightened on-lookers had even seen the devil in the tomb. Perhaps that was worse. Markos was haunted by what he knew it looked like, but the soldiers and the workers were free to imagine all manner of horrors even worse than the corpse in the glass coffin.

"Any word from Father Cyril?" Markos asked.

"Nothing," Georgios said. "No one has been in or out except that girl of yours."

"Helena?"

Georgios nodded. "Brought Father Cyril some breakfast, oh 'bout an hour ago. Said he was sat there on his knees praying. Didn't even notice her."

Ioannis glanced toward the back of the crowd and pointed. Markos looked and saw Helena waiting there, leaning against a dead tree as she watched the pit. The sight of her soothed Markos's nerves, and for a little while banished the troubling thoughts that had invaded his dreams.

"Ask me," Ioannis added, "I think she just wanted to sneak a peek at the exorcism."

"Can you blame her?" asked Georgios. "None of us have even seen one done before. I've half a mind to go take a look myself!"

"Don't you dare." Ioannis jabbed a finger at his comrade. "Stick to your post. I have no wish to get into trouble on account of your curiosity."

Markos quickly excused himself before the two soldiers could start bickering over who was more likely to get who into trouble. He stole away to the back of the crowd and sidled up to Helena.

"So, has Father Cyril made any progress?" he asked knowingly.

Helena grinned at him, but she shrugged at the question. "Who knows? He didn't notice his breakfast when I brought it. I hope that's a good sign."

"Better than if he got up and started eating."

"I'm sure he can pray and eat at the same time," Helena said with mock seriousness. "Our priest is very talented."

Markos snorted. "I wonder what is taking so long. I would have expected him to be finished by now."

Helena gave Markos an irreverent smirk. "Perhaps he is wrestling with the Devil."

"Mm." Markos's reply was noncommittal. He was still unnerved by what he had seen the previous day and by the dreams that had followed, and he felt ashamed of it.

"You are handling this very well," he noted. "Aren't you afraid of that monster?"

"If it were alive, yes," Helena replied. "But it was dead, and I have seen dead things before."

"Those tentacles and that flesh…" Markos was speaking more to himself than to Helena. The particulars of the creature's physiology had been especially pronounced in the dream.

Helena shivered, but she refused to show fear, and as she so often did, tossed it away with a flippant comment.

"I am a fisherman's daughter, Markos. I *have* seen the dreaded octopus before."

Markos scoffed at the analogy. "I wish it were just an octopus, or some beast of the sea. But that thing is not of our world…."

His words trailed off as Father Cyril emerged from the tomb, with his hands raised in triumph. Markos and Helena pushed their way forward to the edge of the pit, to hear the priest's pronouncement.

"It is done!" Cyril declared. "The demon is vanquished! There is nothing more to fear!"

The workers began to murmur with excitement, pleased at being saved from an evil that had only appeared the day before and none of them had seen. The soldiers were more stoic in their expressions, and they remained silent. At the edge of the pit, General Andronikos gazed down at Cyril with folded arms and a cautious expression.

"Well done, Father," he called. "Tell me: what has become of the fiend? Should we burn its body now?"

Father Cyril looked astonished at the question. He motioned to the tomb and said, "There is no need, General. It is gone, banished back to Hell. Come and see for yourself."

Andronikos nodded. After some consideration, he climbed down the ladder and approached the tomb, one hand resting on the hilt of his sword. Markos, for his part, felt his heart grow calmer at the news. The devil gone? He had to see it for himself.

Markos followed Andronikos and Cyril into the tomb. It was silent and still. The sarcophagus that had interred the monstrosity was completely empty. Markos stared at it for a while, dumbfounded. The devil had simply vanished into thin air. The exorcism had worked.

"Incredible…" he gasped.

Andronikos's response was more practical and less overawed. "Good. The men can return to work."

"Of course." Father Cyril looked especially pleased with himself. Pride was a sin, but under the circumstances he could be forgiven for indulging it.

"What should we do with the tomb?" Andronikos asked. "Bury it?"

"Probably the best course of—" Markos began.

"No, I would advise against that," Cyril quickly interjected. "The demon is banished, but there may still be a touch of evil that lingers here. If we rebury this place now, it will bring misfortune upon the venture. Perhaps this is why there have been so many setbacks. In a day or two, I will return and cleanse this place of whatever evil remains. But for now, I fear that I am far too weary after my struggle with the beast."

Markos began to protest, to point out that the delays were caused by the sheer complexity of the task, not by some lingering demonic aura haunting the island. He was cut off by Andronikos.

"That would seem to make sense," the general agreed. "I will trust your judgment in these matters. Whatever must be done to speed the work along, will be done."

As he spoke, Andronikos looked at Markos, without any pretense of subtlety. Markos gritted his teeth to keep from saying something foolish. He was glad that Cyril had dispatched whatever foul fiend had inhabited the tomb, but the exorcism was not going to make the tedious process of alchemy go any faster. Of course, Andronikos would fly into a rage if Markos said it aloud.

"With your permission, my lord, I will return to Theodoros and resume my work," he said.

Andronikos nodded. "Good. Get to it, boy. And tell Theodoros, the two of you had better start producing some results!" Having dismissed Markos, he looked back at the sarcophagus and addressed Father Cyril. "And you are certain that…thing…will not return? It will not conjure itself up from the depths of Hell some night?"

"Certainly not, my lord," Cyril assured him. "Exorcism springs from the power of God, not man. No devil is strong enough to withstand it." There was a pause. "Although…"

"Although?"

Cyril smiled. "Perhaps, just to be safe, you might wish to join me in the chapel for prayer tonight."

"If I must," Andronikos grunted. "I have never been much of a man for prayer. I find the concerns of this world more pressing."

Markos didn't care to remain behind to hear them discuss the respective merits of prayer and the sword. Besides, he had work to do. Though Andronikos hid his fear well, he had been as frightened by the demon as Markos. That kind of fear would not sit well with an old soldier like Andronikos. Any more delays, and he would start venting his nerves upon Markos and Theodoros.

Helena was waiting for him at the top of the pit. They stole away from the crowd, and lingered near the edge of the hill. They were still in plain sight if anyone cared to look at them, so Markos was careful to keep his behavior appropriate. Helena was not his wife yet, and he would best remember that.

"Well?" Helena asked breathlessly.

"The devil is gone," Markos assured her.

Helena exhaled in a gush of relief. "Thank the Lord. That thing haunted my nightmares last night."

"Mine too," Markos said. "Half the time it felt like the devil was there with me, hovering above me in the dark. I'm glad there will be no more of that tonight."

"Markos," Helena murmured, brushing his hand with her fingers. It was subtle. No one would notice, but it conveyed the tenderness it needed to.

"Yes?"

"Will I see you tonight?"

Markos frowned sadly. "I don't think so. Andronikos wants results. He was berating us about the delays yesterday. After *that*," Markos nodded toward the tomb, "I've no doubt he will wish to be finished and off the island as soon as can be. I fear he'll be a harsh task-master. I need to at least make some progress before I can go sneaking out at night."

"I could always sneak in," Helena suggested. Her eyes twinkled at the idea.

"Sneak into the monastery?" Markos nearly laughed aloud at the idea. "The soldiers would catch you in a moment." He took Helena's hands, and turned so that no one in the crowd could see it. "No, my love, I fear there is no choice but for me to lock myself away with Theodoros until the work is done. I want to be off of this island as soon as can be, and with you at my side."

"Mmm, then I suppose you are going to be as impatient as the general," Helena said.

"Yes, but for very different things," Markos replied. "Once we have the formula, Andronikos can return to Constantinople in triumph and have his audience with the Emperor, whereas I just want an audience with you in a home of our own."

The two of them traded a smile and gazed into each other's eyes, and Markos felt certain that all would finally be well.

* * * *

He spent the day and the night in the workshop, barely sleeping or eating. It helped distract him from his memories of the devil in the pit. The beast might be gone, but the image of it lingered in Markos's mind. He imagined every shadow stalking him in the candlelight. Every hint of movement he saw from the corner of his eye was transformed in his mind into a suggestion of the hideous creature.

Theodoros was not particularly understanding of Markos's feverish pace of work. He grumbled when he retired to bed with Markos still awake, and did so again when rose to find Markos already mixing fresh chemicals. Half the time, Markos didn't even bother listening to what the old man was saying. He just wanted the work to finally be done so he could get away from the island that stank of oil and harbored the corpses of fallen angels.

Markos skipped lunch on second day, the better to keep an eye on the experiments. He had a pot of naphtha on the table in front of him, and was agonizing over the exact measurements of the chemicals being mixed in. Liquid fire had to burn even when drenched with water, stick fast to its target, and spray far enough to threaten only the enemy. So many mixtures could do any of them, or even all to a degree, but none so far had met Andronikos's demands.

He yawned and stretched his neck as he heard the door open. A glance told him that Theodoros had returned. The old man had gone to dine with Father Cyril, and likely to enjoy the company of someone more sensible than his frantic apprentice.

"How is Father Cyril?" Markos asked, still focused on his work.

There was no immediate reply, but he heard Theodoros close the door. The alchemist crossed the room with a soft shuffling noise. Markos thought nothing of it.

"If it had been me wrestling with the devil, I'd be a wreck even now," Markos continued.

He didn't mention that he still was a wreck himself, still haunted by just the sight of the fiend in the glass box. He turned in his chair to say more, and froze. The devil in the sarcophagus stood behind him, right where Theodoros had been. Right where Theodoros was. Markos saw the last vestiges of Theodoros melting away and reshaping into the demon Apollyon, like clay molded by a potter.

Theodoros was the devil and the devil was Theodoros. It stood there, with blue quivering flesh and burning red eyes, and four hands that were not hands, outstretched to catch him. If he had not turned, he would be even now caught in its grasp.

Markos screamed and bolted from the chair. His heart pounded inside his chest, threatening to burst in its frenzy of terror. His eyes grew wide and he stared dumbly at the monster facing him, approaching him.

Do something, he screamed to himself. *Do something or you will die!*

One tentacled hand caught his arm and pulled him in. The others grabbed for other parts of him: a shoulder, a leg, his throat. Markos thrashed and pulled away before the thing could strangle him. His hand found a knife on the table, and suddenly Markos forgot everything in the world but that single weapon and the thing in front of him.

The tentacle hand finally got a grip on his neck as Markos grabbed the knife. He wanted to panic, and knew that to panic would be his death. The devil would choke him until he was too weak to fight back. It would crush the life from him and pull his soul into the abyss! Well, if he was to be dragged to Hell, he would give a good account of himself along the way.

Markos drove the knife into the demon's eyes. He stabbed again and again, all the while writhing and fighting against the hands that were not hands and the fingers that were not fingers. Within moments, the three red eyes were eyes no longer. The devil seemed not to have expected such fanatical resistance. It let out a hideous shriek, like nothing born upon the earth, and pulled away. Markos slashed at the tentacle around his throat and forced it off. Next, he hacked at the hand grasping his arm until it finally released him.

The devil scurried backward, shrieking and shaking its head. A noxious green fluid tricked out from the gashes across its face. The creature paused in the middle of the room and turned in all directions, as if listening for Markos. At each hint of noise, it lashed out with one of its horrid limbs, in case its victim had approached close enough to attack again.

Markos shuddered and struggled not to lose his mind. The most sensible thing he could do, he reasoned, was to laugh, and scream, and jump out of the window. Suddenly nothing in God's Creation made any sense. The devil had been banished, yet here it was. It had occupied Theodoros's form, but now Theodoros was nowhere to be seen, not even his lifeless body. Could the creature even be killed? If a priest's exorcism was useless against it, what could Markos do with a knife?

His gaze fell on the pot of naphtha. It was still incomplete, far from liquid fire, and that was assuming the current formula was even close to correct. Still, oil was oil. Markos grabbed the pot and flung it at the devil. The contents splattered all over it, and the devil snapped its head toward Markos. It snarled and chortled, and then it sniffed the air. It was hard to gauge any sentiment on its contorted face, but its posture stiffened. It understood what had happened.

Markos grabbed a candle and tossed it into the pool of oil at the devil's feet. The naphtha ignited instantly, and the creature burst into flame. It wailed horribly and thrashed around, fumbling for a means of escape. As it stumbled toward Markos, he grabbed his chair and beat it back desperately.

The fire was quick and powerful, and in due course the devil collapsed into a heap. Its body melted into a kind of thick fluid, but this burned just as well as solid flesh. Eventually, there was nothing left but a stain of char across the stone floor.

Markos collapsed onto the ground and vomited. His chest kept heaving even after his stomach had emptied itself, until at last his body was too exhausted to continue. Markos curled into a ball and lay there, quaking less with fear than with an utter inability to understand his own existence. His mind turned circles upon itself trying to understand what he had just seen, and coming up with nothing. Nothing in the world made sense any more, and that prospect seemed better than any possible explanation a rational mind could conjure.

* * * *

Markos did not know how long he lay there. He vomited again at some point and didn't remember it. At last, he uncurled himself and rolled onto his back. He gazed at the ceiling and reminded himself that this was not a dream. This was the world, and he was alive in it.

"Get up," he whispered. "Get up. Get up. Get up."

On the fourth recitation, he managed to sit. On the seventh, he forced himself to his feet. The air smelled disgusting, a mix of charred flesh and charred something else entirely. The thing that had once been Theodoros was gone, burned into an unidentifiable heap of ash. But was that the end of it? Could devils be killed so easily with fire?

Markos clutched his head and fought the urge to wail in despair. He felt like he was going mad. Cyril had banished the demon, and yet the demon had returned. And poor Theodoros! Had that thing been the old man all along, possessed by the unholy, flesh twisted into such a monstrous form? Or had the thing that returned merely worn Theodoros's face as a disguise?

Stop. Don't panic. What must be done?

Father Cyril. The priest would know what to do.

Markos looked down at the knife in his hand. It was covered in a sickening yellow-green fluid that couldn't possibly be blood. Markos wiped it clean on a rag, and then threw the rag into the fire in disgust. Was the devil gone, or had its spirit broken free with the destruction of Theodoros's body? Might it possess another hapless person? Might it attack Markos again on his way to Father Cyril's chamber?

Fire at least would destroy the form of the possessed. Markos filled some flasks with naphtha and tucked them into his leather bag. He approached the door, and had to spend another minute forcing himself to open it. Each time he reached for the handle, he had a vision of the devil and his hand pulled back as if stung.

Markos shook his head. No, he would not be a coward. People were in danger. Helena was in danger. He couldn't let the others end up like poor Theodoros.

The hallway was deserted. Markos quickly hid the knife inside his bag and hurried toward the cloister, where the soldiers were housed. Father Cyril was there too, in a set of rooms next to the chapel.

As Markos reached the end of the hallway, a figure in a hood and cloak darted in front of him, hurrying in the opposite direction. Markos threw out his hand to catch the person before they could collide, and without thinking, he also reached for his bag and the knife inside it.

Thankfully, there was no call for it. Helena stopped short and pulled back her hood, her eyes wide with surprise at the sight of him.

"Markos!" she exclaimed, her voice barely above a whisper.

"Helena? What are you doing here?"

Helena looked bewildered at the question. "I came to see you. I thought you would be in your workshop." She reached up and touched his face. "My God, Markos, have you slept? You look terrible!"

Markos caught Helena's hand and pulled it away from his face. After the near-death struggle with the devil, he shuddered at the thought of being touched, even by her.

"I have been working," he explained. "But what about you? What are you doing here?" Markos looked into the cloister and saw soldiers on guard. They had probably seen her. "You could get into a lot of trouble if Andronikos finds you!"

Helena laughed. "No, it is fine, Markos. Thomas and I came to see Father Cyril. Thomas has been having nightmares, so we thought he should unburden himself with confession. And I..." Helena grinned at Markos as her delicate fingers played with the folds of his tunic. "I thought perhaps I would go and see you."

Markos sighed in despair. If the devil truly was on the loose, the monastery was the last place Helena should be.

"You shouldn't have come, Helena! It isn't safe!"

"What? Why not?"

"Because the devil is not banished," Markos replied. "It is *here*!"

Helena turned pale and drew back. "What...?"

They were interrupted by the arrival of Ioannis and Georgios, and a third soldier called Simon.

"You! Girl! What are you doing here?" Ioannis snapped at Helena. "You were supposed to remain in the chapel until your brother is finished with confession."

"Oh, I, um..." Helena stammered. She blushed modestly and cast a shy glance at Markos. "I simply wanted to say hello to Markos."

Simon snickered. "Yeah, I'm sure you did." He gave Markos a knowing nudge. "I like a good 'hello' now and then."

Markos looked Simon dead in the eyes and said, "The devil is loose in the monastery. It just attacked me in the workshop."

"W-what?" Simon stammered.

Ioannis and Georgios traded looks and began asking questions that Markos didn't have time to answer. He pushed past them and hurried across the cloister toward the chapel. Helena raced after him, with the soldiers close behind her. It was probably the exhaustion as much as fear, but Markos was frantic. He could think of nothing but reaching Cyril. The priest would have to know how to banish the demon forever. The alternative was unthinkable.

The chapel was empty, and the door to Cyril's private chamber was closed. Markos tried it and found it latched. He banged on the door with his fist and shouted Father Cyril's name.

"What are you doing?" Georgios demanded. "Father Cyril is at prayer!"

"It doesn't matter! This is more important!" Markos snapped. He banged on the door again. "Father Cyril! I must speak with you!"

Ioannis caught his arm. "Markos, what do you mean 'the devil is loose in the monastery'?"

"Just that," Markos said, still pounding his fist on the door.

From the other side of the door, he heard Cyril shout angrily, "Yes! Yes! I am coming!"

The door opened and the priest stuck his head out, looking furious at the disturbance.

"I am at prayer…" Cyril began.

Markos did not let him finish. He force the door open and pushed past Cyril. The priest sputtered and shouted for Markos to leave, and Markos clasped his hands in penance for the intrusion.

"Father, you have to perform another exorcism," he said.

"What?"

"The devil was not banished like we thought. It just attacked me in the workshop. It had possessed Theodoros, and…" Markos paused and looked around the room. It was sparse, like everything in the monastery. "Where is Thomas?"

"Thomas?" Father Cyril gave Markos a curious look. "Why would he be here?"

That was odd, Markos thought. Hadn't Thomas gone to confession?

"Oh, because he came for confession," Cyril said, as if just then realizing what Markos meant. "We finished a few minutes ago and I sent him away. Now, if you will please leave me in peace, I have my own prayers to complete."

He began pushing Markos toward the door, shooing him and the others out.

Helena took Markos by the arm. "We should go. We can look for Thomas."

"No! No!" Markos shoved everyone away from him and forced his way to the center of the room. "Father Cyril, the devil is still on the island. You must exorcise it again!"

Father Cyril looked at Markos sternly. "That is ridiculous, Markos. Look, Theodoros told me you have not been sleeping. Your thoughts are playing tricks on you. Go back to your room and rest, and stop all of this foolishness."

"No, you don't understand," Markos insisted. "Theodoros, he… He was possessed. He attacked me. The demon attacked me pretending to be Theodoros!"

There was a long, uncomfortable pause, and Markos realized what he had just said. He was suddenly conscious at the three soldiers standing close to him. They were all exchanging looks. Georgios put his hand on the hilt of his sword.

"Markos, what have you done?"

Markos pulled away from them and drew back, trying to find the words to explain.

"It was not Theodoros, it was the devil!" he insisted. "Blue flesh, blood-red eyes, claws and tentacles… I had to kill it with fire. I didn't have any choice!"

The soldiers drew their swords, and Markos knew that it was all over. They thought he was insane and he had murdered Theodoros. He looked at Helena, silently pleading for her to understand. Helena just shook her head, a distant look in her eyes.

"Come quietly, Markos," Ioannis said. "If you killed Theodoros, the general will want you alive. Don't make this difficult."

Markos looked at Father Cyril. The priest fell to his knees and began to pray, beseeching the Almighty for the preservation of Markos's soul. It confirmed what the soldiers already thought.

Markos kept backing away until there was no more room left. The soldiers continued to advance, moving cautiously in case Markos threw all sense to the wind and attacked them too. Ioannis was right: with Theodoros dead, Andronikos needed him alive to finish the formula, but he had no illusions about what would happen to him once the work was finished. He could spend the rest of his days mixing chemicals in a prison cell.

He passed Cyril's bed and pressed against the wall, hemmed into the corner.

Cyril glanced up from his prayer and his eyes widened. "Don't just stand there gawking, grab him!" he shouted at the soldiers. "Get him away from there! He is dangerous!"

Markos tensed and put up his hands, ready for a fight he couldn't possibly win. As he did, he turned and saw a shape on the floor behind the bed, concealed from the rest of the room. It was Thomas, but only part of him. Thomas's body was missing from the waist down, along with half of one arm. The division was clean and precise, like flesh and bone had simply melted away into nothing. No tearing, no cutting, just gone.

"Oh God!" Markos screamed. His body convulsed at the sight. Ioannis grabbed him, and Markos did not put up a fight. Instead, he just pointed at the corpse.

"What are…?" Ioannis looked. "Oh God!" he echoed in horror.

Georgios joined them and recoiled as he saw the body. Simon fell to his knees and was sick.

Ioannis released Markos and slowly knelt by Thomas's remains. "I don't understand. What has happened to him? What killed him?"

"The devil in the pit," Markos said.

"Where is the rest of him?"

Markos had no answer. "Destroyed, with hellfire perhaps?"

"But if he was killed here…" Ioannis said.

They both looked toward Father Cyril. Now it was the priest's turn to back away, retreating toward the door.

"No you don't!" Ioannis shouted.

The soldier pushed Markos aside and charged at Cyril. The priest turned to flee, but Ioannis caught him by the shoulder and pulled him back. Cyril turned, and suddenly he was no longer Cyril. Markos felt a dizzy sickness fill his head as he watched Cyril's face melt away and transform into the devil's writhing blue flesh and burning red eyes. Cyril's whole body followed, lashing out with tentacles and claws, snarling in desperation.

Ioannis howled in pain as he was struck, but he was a good soldier and he knew his business. He grabbed the thing that had been Cyril and stabbed it again and again with his sword. Georgios and Simon rushed to help him, and together they hacked the demon to pieces, until it lay in a sickening heap on the floor. The soldiers stumbled away, gasping for air.

Simon sat on the bed and put his face in his hands. "Lord preserve us, we have killed a priest!" he cried.

"I think it was the devil that did the killing," Markos said, approaching the body cautiously. "That thing was no longer Father Cyril."

"That is what happened with Theodoros?" Ioannis asked.

Markos nodded. "The very same."

"Do you think the devil traveled from Theodoros to Cyril?" Georgios asked nervously.

"Maybe." Markos wasn't actually sure, but suddenly he was being regarded as the expert on the matter. "Or maybe Cyril was possessed during the exorcism, and he conjured an entirely new devil up from Hell to possess Theodoros."

Simon looked up, ashen-faced. "If that's the case, who is to say it is only the two devils? Anyone could be possessed. Any one of us!"

"My God, you are right," Georgios agreed. He drew his sword and held it out to keep the others back. "Any one of you could be possessed! Perhaps all of you!"

Helena looked at him sternly. "Don't be stupid. And put that thing away before you hurt yourself." She looked at Markos. "We must all be fine. If any of us were possessed, why didn't they help Cyril?"

"Ah, she makes a good point," Ioannis agreed. "Still, what about the others? What about the garrison and the workers?"

Simon whimpered softly, and muttered what the rest of them were thinking: "How can we know who among them is possessed?"

Markos shrugged helplessly. "The only man who could have answered that was Cyril."

He looked at the hideous corpse on the ground and grimaced. So much for seeking a priest's advice. They were now adrift in a world of fallen angels and the darkest of unholy things, and he had no idea how to combat this evil.

Suddenly, there was another matter to concern him. As he looked upon the body, Markos saw its severed hand twitch. For a moment, he was certain it was his imagination taunting him. How could a limb, even a demonic one, move once it had been separated from its body? And yet, it did indeed move.

As Markos watched, the hand clenched and wriggled its fingers, and then began to crawl away as though its body were still attached and struggling to flee.

"Look!" Markos shouted, pointing at the hand.

Ioannis stared dumbfounded, mumbling an oath. Georgios cursed, Helena gasped, and Simon was sick again. Markos ran to the hand and kicked it away before it could escape under the bed. In that time, Ioannis came to his senses, and stabbed the thing with his sword. He lifted it into the light, and the thing continued to squirm.

"This is not possible," he said, staring transfixed at the horror at the end of his blade. "Not possible at all."

Markos grabbed the blade from him and flung the hand into the hearth fire. The appendage squirmed all the more as it burned away. A piercing shriek issued from the dying flesh, though it had no mouth with which to scream. Finally, it succumbed and stopped moving, as the cozy fire rendered it to ash.

"Did that just happen?" Ioannis asked.

Markos handed his sword back to him. "It did. There is no question now. We must burn the devil's body, every last piece of it."

"I don't understand," Simon moaned. "How can that be possible? How can a severed hand move?"

"It was controlled by the devil that possessed Father Cyril's body," Markos said. It was the only explanation he could think of.

Georgios shook his head in disbelief. "Impossible. Why would the demon go into the hand? Perhaps you were seeing things. I didn't see it move. Did you?" he asked Helena, who gave him no reply but a cold stare.

"Maybe there are many demons," Simon offered, picking himself up from the floor. "Legion, like in the Bible. One demon for every limb, for every portion of the body. Cut off the hand, the demon in the hand tries to escape...."

Simon was rambling, but in the chaos of his words, Markos found the germ of an idea.

"Maybe indeed," he said. He raised a finger as an idea blossomed in his head. "And if that is so, then that is how we can tell that someone is possessed!"

"What?" Georgios exclaimed. "You're talking nonsense."

"You mean cut off a hand and see if the devil in the hand tries to escape?" Ioannis asked. He exhaled and stared at the fire. "That is a steep price for confirmation."

"Maybe not a whole hand," Markos agreed.

Ioannis shook his head in disbelief. "Just a finger?" he chided. "No Markos, this will not work. We cannot be chopping limbs off our comrades in the hope that one of them is possessed!"

Markos scratched his head. There was more of an idea lurking in there, waiting to be coaxed out. Not hands, not fingers, then what?

"Blood," he cried, as the idea came to him. "What if there are devils lurking in the victim's blood? If we could bleed one out, it would be trapped, and it would try to escape."

Ioannis made a face. "I won't lie and pretend it's a good plan, but I suppose I would rather try that before I start cutting my fingers off."

Georgios scoffed at the idea. "And I suppose you expect us to bleed ourselves dry while you stand there and watch, eh? How do we know you're not possessed too? You might be running us in circles to keep us distracted."

"Hey, just a moment!" Ioannis exclaimed. "Markos is the one who warned us about the demon in the first place."

"Exactly! The perfect way to draw suspicion away from him!"

Markos threw up his hands. "Stop! Please!" More calmly, he said, "I will go first. I don't know if it will work, but as Ioannis says, I would rather try this before cutting off fingers and toes."

He took out his knife and cleaned it again, holding it to a candle flame for a while to be sure that every last trace of the devil had burned away. Then he cut a small gash in his forearm, and allowed his blood to drip onto a metal plate from Cyril's table. He bandaged his arm as the others gathered around.

Markos pondered what to do next. Should he stab the blood? Would that threaten a devil lurking there? Not that he believed there were any devils in his own body, but he needed a method they could use for everyone on the island, and this way he proved that he was treating himself no differently than the rest of them.

"Well? What now?" Ioannis asked.

"Um." Markos frowned. He picked up the plate and held one of the candles close to it, until the heat upon the blood was unmistakable. As he expected, nothing happened.

Georgios scoffed. "A lot of good that did."

Helena sighed and touched Markos's hand. "Markos, please stop hurting yourself. This isn't going to do any good. Maybe if we pray, we can force the devils to reveal themselves."

There was a pause, and then Ioannis pushed up his sleeve. "No, I'm willing to try this. It's better than any idea I have."

"You cannot be serious!" Georgios said.

"I'd rather shed some blood than lose a hand," Ioannis said. "I have bled in battle before. This is nothing."

Markos nodded. He dumped the plateful of blood into the fire and cleaned both it and the knife. Best to leave no trace after each person was tested. He cut Ioannis's forearm, and the soldier bled onto the plate just as he had done. Markos held a flame to the blood as before, and the result was the same. Nothing.

"This is stupid," Georgios declared, as Markos cleaned the plate and the blade again. "If you will excuse me, I'm going to report what has happened to the general, and hopefully he will know what to do. It's obvious that you don't!"

The parting comment was for Markos, and the barb in Georgios's words made Markos frown, ashamed at his failure. In truth, he had no way of knowing whether this would work at all.

"No," Ioannis said firmly, grabbing Georgios by the shoulder.

"What did you say?"

"None of us have an answer to this, but at least Markos is trying to find one. If you wish to be so rude about it, you can go next."

Georgios pushed Ioannis away. "I am not going to dignify this madness! We need leadership and prayer, not bloodletting!"

Ioannis took the knife from Markos and held it up to Georgios's face.

"You are going next, Georgios. Do it yourself, or I'll do it for you. And you won't like it if I do it."

"Well, what about Simon? What about the girl?" Georgios protested.

"They'll go after you," Ioannis said. "Now get cutting."

Georgios grumbled some more, but he pulled back his sleeve and made the cut. After bleeding onto the plate, he drew back and folded his arms angrily.

Markos took the plate and held the candle to the blood. At first, it was as before: nothing worth noting. The blood grew hot, but it was only blood. Suddenly, the pool of blood began to wriggle of its own accord. Small tendrils reached out, lashing at the candle, only to pull away again, fearful of the heat. Markos tilted the plate to force the blood to pool next to the flame. Instead, the liquid defied all sense of reason, and began to crawl away from the candle, up the metal incline.

"Do you see that?" Markos shouted.

"I do!" Ioannis replied. The soldier turned toward Georgios, only to find that Georgios was already halfway to the door. "No you don't!"

Ioannis and Simon rushed Georgios before he could flee the room. They grabbed for him, but by now the demon that had possessed Georgios had given up all pretense. Human flesh erupted in a torrent of blue wriggling tentacles and hooked claws. Red eyes bubbled out of Georgios's forehead as his body twisted and reshaped into the unholy form. He struggled, but as with Cyril, the soldiers knew their business. They had swords and armor, and they hacked the devil that had been Georgios to pieces.

Dumbfounded, Markos barely had the sense to throw the living blood into the fire before it could crawl its way off the plate. As the second demon's corpse fell to the ground, Simon rushed to Markos's side.

"Test me! Test me!" he cried frantically. "I don't want to become one of those things!"

Ioannis slumped against the wall, breathing hard from the fight. "I don't think it works that way. If you were possessed, you'd know it. Georgios was doing everything he could to dissuade us. I should have seen it."

"He said I was mad and stupid for suggesting we do a mad and stupid thing," Markos replied. "I would be more suspicious if he'd said anything else."

He tested Simon's blood, and like his and Ioannis's, it proved to be ordinary. That was good. So far, only one of them had been possessed, and the test was proven to work. Markos turned to Helena, but she was nowhere to be seen.

"Helena?" he asked aloud, rushing to the door. Helena was gone, and the chapel was empty.

Ioannis and Simon joined him at the doorway.

"You don't think…?" Ioannis began.

Markos's heart sank, and his stomach grew sick. "Why else would she leave?" he asked.

"But how? When?"

The muscles in Markos's face tightened. "You said she brought Father Cyril breakfast that morning?"

"Yes."

"There is your answer." Markos closed the door and secured it. He wanted to rush after Helena, to beg her for proof that his worst suspicions were not true. That was foolish, and he didn't intend to be foolish now. "I am going after her. When I return, test me again."

"But you're not possessed," Simon protested.

"When I return, test me again," Markos repeated. "If anyone is ever separated from the group, they must be tested again. We don't know how the possession happens. Out of sight invites danger."

Ioannis nodded. "Agreed." He motioned to Simon. "We'll burn the bodies and start checking the rest of the garrison. I hope this thing hasn't spread far."

"One person at a time," Markos said. "Never let yourselves be outnumbered."

"What about General Andronikos?" Simon asked. "Shouldn't we warn him?"

Ioannis gave his comrade a grave look. "The general went to prayer with Father Cyril right after the exorcism. We must assume he is possessed as well."

"Surely not!" Simon protested.

"Surely he is," Markos said grimly. "The general, Father Cyril, and Theodoros are the three most important people on the island. They were all compromised, there is no doubt." A thought came to him and he muttered a curse. "If Theodoros and I finally managed to perfect the formula, Andronikos would shortly find himself in a private audience with the Emperor. What a triumph it would be for the forces of Hell to place an agent of their wickedness upon the throne of Rome."

Simon crossed himself. "God preserve us!"

"So," Markos continued, "you must treat everyone like they are possessed until you know that they are not. Even me when I return, understood?"

"Understood." Ioannis clapped a hand on Markos's arm. "Good luck. I hope you don't die."

"Me too," Markos said.

He picked up Georgios's sword, which had been abandoned in the fight. Clutching his bag close to him, Markos steeled his nerves and went out into the cloister. He ducked out of sight before the other soldiers could notice him carrying a weapon around. No good would come of alerting any of them now, even those who were not possessed. As Markos crept along the wall, he caught sight of a figure in Helena's hood and cloak ahead of him, moments before it darted into one of the adjoining corridors. Markos stopped himself from calling her name, and hurried in silence to the doorway.

There was another glimpse of the figure as it ducked into the stairway leading down to the cellars. It was Helena. She paused just long enough to see him and for him to see her. She knew that he was following her, and she was leading him along intentionally.

In his heart, Markos knew the truth. Helena was possessed and she was leading him into a trap, and yet he couldn't stay away. He grabbed a torch from a wall sconce and descended into the cellar. Again, he was given just enough time to spot Helena, before she vanished into the shadows to his left. Markos grimaced. He was meant to follow her, to run along from glimpse to glimpse until he was cornered somewhere.

Well, he was having none of that. If the devil wanted to corner him so badly, it could do so on his terms. Markos turned to the right and hurried through the dimly lit cellar into a store room that he knew well. It had once contained wine, but now the barrels were filled with oil, some for storage and others containing the results of failed formulae. It was familiar ground, and that gave Markos some very small measure of comfort.

He placed his back against the far wall of the room and waited. Minutes dragged past, and Markos soon lost track of the time. There was nothing but him and the stench of oil, the flickering shadows, and the beating of his heart. Had he been mistaken? What if it really was Helena? Perhaps she had lured him there to comfort her in secret, or to relay some news she didn't trust the others knowing? Had he made a mistake?

Helena appeared in the doorway, her face marked by that familiar, too-wide smile. Markos had always delighted in seeing it before. It did not delight him now.

"Clever Markos," Helena said, slowly approaching him. "Knowing a trap when one is set for you."

She stopped in the middle of the room, as the figures of Andronikos and two of the garrison soldiers entered behind her. One of the soldiers closed the door and secured it behind them, in case Markos had any illusions about escape.

"Not so clever," Andronikos noted. "He avoids one trap, only to corner himself here." He grinned, and even in human form it was horrible to see. "I know your mind, boy. You thought it would only be her."

"Yes," Markos confessed, tightening his grip on the sword. He certainly hadn't expected to face four of them. One alone would be challenge enough. Markos began to panic.

Helena frowned at him, sad and sympathetic. "Poor Markos. Just close your eyes and it will all be over soon. I promise, I do not wish to hurt you. But with Theodoros dead, you must become one of us."

"So I can finish the formula," Markos said. "So that Andronikos can meet the Emperor. So that you can do *this* to him!" Markos waved his sword at the four of them.

"Yes," Helena answered. "Your Emperor, your Patriarch, every high and mighty lord of your Roman Empire will become one of me."

"Why?" Markos cried. "Why are you doing this to us?"

The laugh that issued from Helena chilled him to the bone, and was made all the worse as it was echoed exactly by Andronikos and the soldiers.

"Because I must get off of this pathetic planet. I have been conscious for two of its days, and already I despise it."

"I don't understand," Markos said. "The earth is not a planet. It is the earth."

Andronikos scoffed at him. The general advanced a pace, and the soldiers went with him. Markos raised his torch and sword menacingly. He was little threat to them, and likely they all knew it, but he wouldn't allow them to take him without returning some injury. And they seemed to sense his certainty as well, for Andronikos hesitated, and so did the soldiers. Their courage seemed to have faded, and along with it their obedience to their commander. Markos snickered at this realization. It seemed the demons all feared death, and none wished to be sacrificed for the sake of the others.

"I have neither the time, the patience, nor the wish to explain the vastness of the cosmos to you, boy," the general said. "It would be a wasted effort, like explaining mathematics to an ant."

Markos bristled at Andronikos's dismissal. The insult was nothing compared to the fear he felt, but even so it made him angry and that strengthened his resolve.

Helena gave Andronikos an irritated glare, and then just as quickly offered Markos a gentle smile.

"Your planet is one of many," she explained, "just like mine. There is no divine vastness in the sky, like you imagine, nor devils in the depths of the earth. Simply space: darkness unending, punctuated here and there with spots of light, and worlds revolving around them. Worlds like yours and worlds like mine, although the difference between my planet and this place would be like Constantinople compared to a hovel. Put simply, I am trapped here and I wish to leave. That is all."

"Then leave!" Markos snarled. "We want nothing to do with you!"

Helena sighed. "If only it were so easy. Had I the means of building a spacecraft, I would depart this wretched place at once, but you don't even have the basic materials for me to use."

"What?"

"You Romans believe that you are the greatest civilization on your entire planet, and you cannot even *fly*!" Helena laughed. "You have no *computers*, no *rocketry*, no *electricity*. You have nothing for me to use."

Markos felt his head spin. Helena spoke in plain Greek, but phrases she used felt out of place, like she had to jumble together concepts to explain things beyond Markos's knowledge. Thinking machines? Flying towers? Captured lightning? Each explanation made less sense than ignorance.

"You want an explanation?" Helena asked. "It is this. I will replace your Emperor, your Patriarch, your priesthood and your nobles with myself. Through them, I will transform your entire society into a vehicle of technological progress. I will drag your species into modernity, so that within my lifetime you can build me a vessel that will free me from this place!"

She gazed at Markos, and Markos shuddered to see Helena's eyes looking into his. "I only want to go home," Helena pleaded. "Is that truly so wicked of me?"

Even though he knew better, Markos felt his heart soften. His ears heard Helena's gentle voice, and the genuine sorrow lurking there. She was lost in this hellish place, and she needed him to help her escape.

It was almost enough to distract Markos as one of the soldiers crept toward him from the side. Almost, but not quite. Markos snapped out of the trance and quickly pointed his sword at the soldier. The thing had already begun to change, its fingers extending into long tentacles ribbed with barbs and claws. But again, at the sight of the sword and the torch, it hesitated.

"We tried it your way," Andronikos said to Helena. "Now we do it my way." He pointed at Markos and advanced cautiously, mirrored by the soldiers step-by-step as they formed a semi-circle in front of him. "Close your eyes, boy, and die without a struggle. You will not like how death comes if you resist."

Markos glared back defiantly. "I will take one of you with me, at least. Maybe more. Which of you wishes to die first?"

There came that hesitation again, but this time Andronikos shrugged it away and motioned the soldiers forward again.

"I will take my chances."

Markos felt the fear of death well up inside of him. He wanted to scream, to cry, to beg, to plead for his life. His instinct was to think that he didn't want to die. But as that thought passed through his mind, he suddenly realized that he no longer cared. Living or dying didn't matter now. All that mattered was stopping this evil before it could hurt more people. It had to be stopped here on the island, and if that meant his death, Markos would pay that price.

He threw the torch onto the ground at Andronikos's feet. The general scrambled backward as if afraid. The soldiers froze too, and Helena drew back from the rest of them.

"What are you doing...?" Andronikos began.

In truth, Markos hadn't come there with a plan, but now one blossomed to life in his mind. Fire. Oil. A closed door and a stone room. He ran to the nearest barrel of naphtha and forced it open with his sword. Andronikos was shouting for him to stop, as if the general knew the contents of Markos's mind as soon as Markos did. It was a curious notion that Markos had no time to ponder. As Andronikos and the soldiers rushed at him, Markos tipped the barrel over and a wave of thick, foul oil spilled out to meet them.

Andronikos scrambled back to keep clear of the thick black liquid. One soldier slipped and fell to his knees, though as he fell his entire form shifted into the monstrous blue creature. It caught itself with its tentacles and tried to rise, moments before the oil reached the torch and the whole pool ignited.

The air was filled with heat and smoke, and the horrible high-pitched wail of the demons as they burned. Both soldiers were caught before they could run, and writhed in the flames as they died. Andronikos abandoned all pretense as he fled from the wall of fire, transforming into his demon body and shrieking in fear. Across the room, Helena ran to the door and forced it open, disappearing into the cellar. Markos knew he couldn't reach her, but at least he could keep Andronikos from escaping too.

Markos ran to the next barrel and broke it open. The thing that had been Andronikos advanced on him, lashing with its tentacles. Claws tore Markos's flesh, and he scrambled away, bleeding and gasping amid the smoke. As Andronikos came at him again, Markos reached into his bag and flung the bottles of naphtha at the devil. Andronikos seemed almost to smile at him, as its tentacles swatted the bottles away one at a time. They tumbled to the ground and there was the audible sound of glass cracking. The contents seeped out all around Andronikos, mingling with the oil from the barrels, and together they created an unbroken chain.

Torch to oil to devil.

The wall of fire reached Andronikos in a violent rush, faster than the devil could react. There was barely time for its blood-red eyes to fix on Markos with an almost human expression of hatred. He was supposed to die in that room. The devil was supposed to live.

The fire engulfed Andronikos.

Markos grabbed his sword and ran for the door, barely ahead of the fire. It clawed at him from behind, threatening to overtake him if he slowed for a single moment. Markos reached the cellar, and slammed the door shut. Choking and gasping for air, he slid down onto the floor, unable to stand any longer.

Keep moving.

Markos began to crawl for the stairs, all the while willing himself to get up even though his body refused to obey. It was all too much, but if he stopped there, he would surely die. There was no knowing how far the fire would spread in the stone building, but the cellar would soon be choked with smoke.

He reached the top of the stairs and collapsed. Unconsciousness took him soon after.

* * * *

Markos woke in the chapel, surrounded by soldiers. He sat up with a fearful gasp and put up his fists. The soldiers looked at him like he was crazy, but one did reach for a sword. Ioannis came into view and motioned for the man to put away his weapon.

"You're safe, Markos," Ioannis said. "You are among friends."

Markos looked around fearfully. "All of these people? They're not possessed?"

Ioannis shook his head. "We have tested every one of them. Two devils, both dead now. The rest are men."

"Test me!" Markos demanded, offering his arm.

Ioannis looked confused. "Do you think you're possessed?"

"No, I know I am not," Markos said.

"Then why…?"

"Because you don't know it! That's the rule: everyone is tested whenever they rejoin the group. No exceptions."

Ioannis nodded. He gathered a knife, a basin, and a candle, and performed the test. Even though Markos was certain he remained himself, he felt a pang of uncertainty as he waited for the blood to either boil or react. If he was possessed, would he even know?

He breathed a sigh as his blood remained still.

"See? I knew you were yourself," Ioannis said.

"Did you, though?" Markos asked. It was a joke, or at least both of them chose to take it as one. They chuckled together, and found it better than admitting whatever doubts they had harbored.

Ioannis motioned to the cloister. "There was a fire raging in one of the storerooms when we found you. What happened?"

"Andronikos, Helena, two more soldiers," Markos said. "All devils."

"Dead?"

"Helena escaped," Markos replied. He frowned and looked down at the floor. It wasn't Helena. He had to remember that it wasn't Helena.

"I will get some men and go looking for her."

"No." Markos shook his head. "Finish the garrison and move on to the villagers. I will find Helena."

"Should we test you a third time when you come back?"

"Yes." Markos didn't voice his certainty that he wasn't coming back. Instead, he laid a hand on Ioannis's arm and said, "The supply ship is due here in a day or two. We must have this contained before it arrives."

"Agreed."

"When you see its sails on the horizon, test everyone again before it docks. Everyone."

"You truly believe that's necessary?" Ioannis asked.

"When I was in the cellar, the devils spoke of possessing the Emperor and the Patriarch. We cannot risk them escaping this island."

Ioannis thought of something and frowned, suddenly even more worried than before. "What should we say to the crew? We've lost several men, including our commander, our priest, and the alchemist. The imperial court will want answers, and I don't think they are going to believe stories of demonic possession. I don't want to escape all of this, only to be executed for murder."

"Say there was an accident. The oil caught fire and the dead died trying to put it out. It's a better way to be remembered than what happened."

"Better than the truth, I suppose," Ioannis agreed, sighing heavily.

* * * *

Markos said his farewells to the soldiers before leaving the chapel. He didn't let on, but he did not expect to escape his next encounter alive. A part of him was at peace with that.

He took his borrowed sword, a lamp, and a bucket from Father Cyril's room. He needed more oil, and after the fire in the storeroom, there was precious little of it left. The soldiers watched him cautiously. None of them could understand why he was going alone, risking his life and inviting suspicion upon his return. Well, that was fine. He didn't plan on returning.

On the way to the demon pit, Markos filled the bucket with oil from one of the wells. The tomb that had held the demon needed to be destroyed. It was a single-minded task he could focus on, which freed him from the weight of everything else that had happened that day.

Helena was inside the tomb when he arrived. She sat on the floor, an expression of abject resignation on her face. And it was still her face that the devil wore, though the hellish form began to creep through in other places. Her hands had become the strange tentacle-fingered appendages, and they held a pile of the curious waxy paper Markos had seen stacked by the table when the tomb was first opened. He had thought little of them then, but it seemed they were of significance to the devil.

Helena looked up as Markos entered and set the bucket down on the floor. She laughed. It was still Helena's laugh, but it was bitter and dejected. Markos's heart twitched at the sound. He wanted to rush to her and comfort her, even though it was not Helena sitting there.

"You survived," she said.

"I did."

"I assume the others are dead."

"They are," Markos replied.

"And now you have come to kill me." It was a statement, not a question, and strangely, it was spoken with acceptance rather than fear.

"I don't want to kill you," Markos confessed.

Helena grinned. It was angry and cruel. "Oh no? Or do you mean to say, you don't want to kill me while I am *wearing her face*?" The devil laughed again. "I could simply transform into myself, make it easy for you. You'll have no qualms about killing me then."

"I never wanted to kill anyone," Markos said.

"But you did when you had to," Helena mused. "You have learned something about yourself."

"I have learned a great deal." Markos turned his eyes heavenward. "I've learned that there are things up there that I cannot imagine, and that I will probably never understand. You spoke of other worlds...."

"More numerous than the stars in the sky," Helena said.

"And I will never see them. I have devoted my life to understanding the mysteries of Creation, and you have revealed to me the inescapable fact that most of them will forever remain beyond my grasp. And I would be at peace with that if Helena was still alive. Now that she is gone, I have nothing. You have shattered my world and left me with *nothing*!"

The devil scoffed at him. "You knew her for less than one of your planet's years. Don't pretend it was more profound than it really was."

"I loved her!" Markos shouted. "She was good and kind and clever, and she deserved better than this! Better than to be transformed into your puppet!" Markos felt his cheeks grow wet with tears. "Why did you kill her? She had done nothing to you!"

"Expediency," Helena replied softly.

"Andronikos, I can understand. Father Cyril, I can understand. Theodoros, even me! But why *her*? What use could her death possibly be to you?"

Helena sighed and leaned back against the wall, staring off into the distance.

"I was on a transport vessel passing through your star system. There was a malfunction and we became trapped in your planet's gravity. The ship had only one working escape pod, and I took it." Her tone became hard and determined. "I did what I had to do to survive." The hardness died away in a bitter laugh and she said, "It seems it was a wasted effort. The pod launched too late. It couldn't escape the gravity well. But I didn't know that. Once aboard, I followed procedure and put myself into cold sleep. The next thing I knew, I was here."

Again, she spoke in proper Greek but the words and phrases she used were confusing to Markos, hinting at even more secret knowledge that would forever remain beyond his reach.

"I expected to be rescued by my own kind. The first face I would see once I had thawed would be familiar, blue, three-eyed. *Normal*." Helena scowled.

"Instead, I awoke to the sight of a grotesque, two-eyed monster with spongey pale flesh, kneeling in front of me and wailing in a hideous unnatural voice."

"Father Cyril," Markos said.

Helena nodded. "What was I to do? I confess, my mind was not entirely together at the time. Freezing and reviving every cell in one's body does take a toll, even being adapted for it. I killed him, and I ate him, and then I made a copy of myself in his image."

It took Markos a few moments to grasp what she had said.

"Copy? That was never Father Cyril?"

"It was never any of them. They were all me, and yet not me. Cells of my cells, arranged in perfect mimicry."

"Then why Helena?" Markos demanded.

The devil shrugged. "I had just finished making the Me-Cyril, when I realized that I couldn't copy that form too. There couldn't be two Cyrils walking around. Your species is clever enough to notice a thing like that. And then who should enter, but your dear friend. Pretending to bring the priest food, but really she was curious, and that curiosity killed her. I ate her and I became her." She grinned and spread her arms dramatically. "In a way, 'tis like she never died."

"You are a monster!" Markos shouted.

"Are you a monster for eating a cow or a goat, and wearing its skin?" Helena asked. The question sounded sincere, though it was cruel and no doubt calculated to offend. "It doesn't matter anyway. All my labors have been for nothing."

The dejected tone in her voice gave Markos pause. "What do you mean?"

Helena threw the handful of waxy paper at Markos. The sheets scattered across the floor of the tomb, their words as meaningless as when first Markos had seen them.

"Status reports," Helena said. "The pod was very diligent. Every year it reported on my vitals, the state of the systems, and the surrounding environment." She picked up one sheet and pointed to it. "Oh, look. Still buried under dirt and rock."

Helena allowed the paper to slip from her fingers. "They said the pods were made to last, but I never understood just what that meant. The reports only stopped when the main systems finally shut down after five thousand years."

"Five…thousand?" Markos was certain he had misheard.

"Five thousand. And that is only as long as the computers lasted. Main power died. Reserve power died. I would have died too, if the cold sleep chamber hadn't remained sealed. To put it frankly, I have absolutely no idea how long I have lain here. Thousands of years? Hundreds of thousands? *Millions*?"

Helena's voice was distorted with uncertainty, tinged with madness at the very contemplation of such a thing. She rose to her feet and fixed Markos with a furious glare. Her eyes glinted, and green began to fade into stark blood red.

"Answer me!" she screamed. "How long have I been trapped on this planet? Does my civilization even *exist* anymore?"

She collapsed to her knees and her whole body sagged from the weight of despair.

"Am I the last of my kind?"

Markos had no answer.

Helena's face darkened with impotent rage. "I should take my revenge on you. I should stride across your world like a scourge, consuming every last living thing that draws breath, until there is nothing left alive here but me! Untold billions of me, exactly me, perfect copies of me! And that way…" Her voice choked. "And that way I will no longer be alone."

Silence filled the tomb, and slowly Helena forced her expression to grow hard and cold again. "Forgive my outburst. Your kind are sentimental. Something happens when you copy a creature cell by cell, neuron by neuron. Fragments of the original seep through. It seems that this fragment is terrified of being abandoned."

"How can you be so callous about murder?" Markos snarled. "My heart would feel for your plight, but you have killed and eaten innocent people! You wanted to enslave us! You fear being the last of your kind? And yet in the next breath you speak of slaughtering every last person on earth! How am I to have sympathy for that?"

Helena looked down at her hands, which remained caught between the forms of human and devil. "There is no sympathy to be had. It is an illusion, a fantasy in a cold and uncaring cosmos." She looked up at him, her expression suddenly calm, serene even. "You came to kill me."

"I did," Markos admitted.

Helena thought for a bit and then nodded. "I think I am ready to die."

Markos tightened his grip on the sword. He still didn't trust the devil. It obviously knew his mind, knew his soft heart. All of this might be a plot to put him off guard.

"I have all of your Helena's memories," the devil said. "They are very strange. She imagined that there is an immaterial world waiting beyond this one."

"She did," Markos agreed.

"My people have traveled to the furthest reaches of space, but we have found no evidence of any such world." Helena looked at Markos and asked, "Do you believe it exists?"

Markos emptied the bucket of oil across the floor of the tomb, and picked up the lamp.

"I suppose we will find out together," he said.

THE MONSTER AT WORLD'S END

ALLEN COLE

Deception Bay, Antarctica
Latitude: -62° 58' 22.19"
Longitude: -60° 38' 59.99" W
20XX A.D.—The Cusp of Winter
Temperature: -50 (F) -45 (C

* * * *

I must escape.
Escape what?
Escape this place.
I must get out.
Out of what?
Out of here.
Where is here?
I'm not sure.
Confused.
Head swimming.
I think they shot me with drugs.
They? Who are They?
I don't know. Beasts of some kind.
Things.
They have two legs like us. Two arms like us. Hands with five digits. Faces, lips, eyes, ears. Mouths that make sounds.
Word sounds?
Possibly… Yes, I think so.
The sounds are loud. Angry.
Who are they angry at?
Me.
They push close. Shout in my face. Wave objects at me. Objects that can harm.

Threats, then. But why are they threatening you?

I don't know. Last cycle they wheeled a Thing into the place where they keep me.

It was naked. Female, unlike the others who were white males. Dark hair. Dark skin.

She didn't move. She didn't breathe. Her eyes were closed. Her throat had been cut and there was blood everywhere. So much blood that I knew she had to be dead.

They shouted at me. The smallest Thing, whose face and head were hairless, brandished a sharp object and screamed at me.

Screamed?

Yes, and jabbed at my eyes.

I tried to turn, but another Thing—taller and hairy—held my head and shouted encouragement at the other. At least I think it was encouragement. The sound he made was like this: "Dewit! Dewit!"

Each time the small one jabbed the blade point came closer to my eyes. Closer. And closer.

Suddenly, I realized the blade was my own knife. It had been a gift from Kaarla. Black anodized with intricate engravings.

Where did the Thing get it? I'd lost the knife several cycles back when they were chasing me. I guess he found it.

The hairless Thing waved the knife before my face.

Malice eyes.

Grinning. Like the rictus grin on the corpse.

And the hairy Thing shouted, "Dewit! Dewit! Deewit! Dewit!"

Then I saw the light change in the small Thing's eyes.

I thought: *This time he will blind me.*

I managed to jerk my head aside. The blade missed my eyes but slashed my forehead. Blood sheeted. Blinding me. I tried to wipe it away, but the manacles stopped me.

The hairy Thing keened.

I shook blood from my eyes, spattering them. They jumped back. Sounds of disgust. Scrubbing away my blood like I was diseased.

They came at me. Angrier. Strong hands caught my head. The hairy Thing again. The small one approached, brandishing the blade.

Close. So close. Breath foul with hate.

I thought—this time he is going to cut out my eyes.

Fear and anger gave me strength. I pushed my head closer despite the resistance of the hairy Thing's strong hands.

Readied my teeth.

They are long and sharp.

Thinking: *I will bite this Thing, if I can. I will rip off his face, if I can. Kill him, if I can.*

Unbidden, my talons arced out. When he saw them the Thing's eyes fear-flashed.

Stepped back.

Eyes narrowing.

I saw decision in those eyes.

Hate in those eyes.

He would strike first.

A step forward—knife raised.

A shout.

A sound like: "Stawp!"

The small one turned. With a start, the hairy one released his grip. The shout came from the third Thing. A forgotten presence. The third Thing was taller than the others. Narrow face. Eyes pale. Commanding eyes.

Motioning them away. Made sounds like, "Kuum heer." The voice was low. Compelling.

They joined the tall Thing by the door. Quarreling. My tormentors shouted at the third Thing. He seemed to argue back, but kept his voice calm. Measured. Authoritative.

The leader?

Yes. I'm sure of it.

The shouting stopped. But not the anger. Snorts of disgust. Murderous looks at me.

But for the moment, the crisis had passed.

The Things shrugged on thick red parkas. Shoved their legs into insulated red trousers.

The tall Thing escorted the others from the room, letting in the cold wind.

I shivered.

Will I ever be warm again?

The door shut against the wind with difficulty. The lock clicked in place.

I sagged against my bonds. Alone with the dead Thing. Blood and gore and rictus grin.

Sightless eyes…

Accusing?

Yes, accusing.

Was she blaming me for her death? For cutting her throat?

I don't know. Probably.

Do the Things think you killed her? Is that why they are angry?

Yes. It must be so.

Did you?

Kill her?

No.

Well… Possibly.

My memory is…

But the knife… I'd lost the knife… so how could I have killed her?

Hard to remember.

My mind was awhirl from the drugs I'd been shot with. The last moment of clarity was just before the green-tipped dart struck. Then time collapsed into itself until I was unsure when or where I was.

The Things caught me not far from my base camp. It was a foolish error. A stupidity likely to have cost me my life and doomed our mission.

I had been carrying away some accumulated trash. I'd be in the open ten minutes tops. Bury the trash and dash back into the shelter for a little breakfast.

Then they were upon me. Hunters popping out of nowhere. Electronic eyes lighting up. Proximity alarms squealing, in a mechanical display of victory.

I dodged and there was a Pop! Pop! Pop! as they fired their dart guns.

I ran. Digging in with my ice striders. I am strong and tall with long legs that carried me faster than their tracks. But I couldn't shake them. No matter how hard I tried. No matter the tricks I played or the traps I laid. They kept coming with the never-wavering confidence of machines.

They chased me for several cycles. Hunters on tracks that raced across the ice and snow. Two sky vehicles that followed wherever I ran.

Wherever I went, the hunters were on my heels, alerting the Things piloting the flying machines. No matter how well I hid myself their sensors managed to find me.

Even so, I ran and kept running. Legs numb. Heart hammering. Clouds of labored breath streaming behind me. Heralding my presence wherever I fled.

With each cycle I grew weaker. The intense cold burning calories I couldn't afford to waste.

And then the dart struck and it was over.

Thinking back on it—reliving the ordeal—I finally fell asleep.

Hanging in my bonds, it was a troubled sleep.

Sudden cold brought me back. Cold and the sound of wind howling down from the mountains. The wind's freezing breath finding gaps around the window and door, chilling me to the very bone.

Door?

What was happening with the door?

Were they coming back?

I heard the lock click. Raised my head to see, but my eyelids were glued together with dried blood.

The door opened.

A blast of freezing air.

It slammed shut.

I heard someone approaching.

Pounding heart.

Sweat soaked palms.

It was a Thing.

The Thing came close. A sweet smell, quite unlike the foul, unwashed odors of my tormentors.

A light voice. A gentle voice.

Do I detect sympathy?

I tried to open my eyes.

Useless.

Slumped in my bonds.

Dispirited.

Emptied of all hope.

The Thing moved away. I heard it bustle about. Cabinet doors opening and closing.

Then… Was that running water?

Mouth desert dry. Tongue swollen. Parched throat closing over. I made a sound. I didn't mean to. It was the first sound I had made since I was captured.

The sound of running water pulled it from me unbidden. My desperate thirst overruled my pride. The sound I made was a croaked plea.

The footsteps came near. I sensed a presence. Then a warm, wet cloth closed over my face.

The Thing wiped the blood away. Slowly my eyes came open. At first, I saw nothing but the out of focus wet cloth and I gripped it in my teeth and desperately sucked it dry. The cloth pulled against my teeth. Gently. The Thing made an imploring sound and I released the cloth.

Now I could see the new Thing. Like the corpse, she was a dark skinned and female. She was about the size of my small tormentor. Except slender. Limbs graceful. Black curly hair falling in waves to slim shoulders. Heart-shaped face. Large dark eyes.

Unconsciously, I made the croaking sound again.

Pity turned to understanding. The new Thing turned away and went to a sink. Turned a lever and water streamed. She filled a vessel and brought it to me.

Held it out.

I tried to reach, but the manacles restrained me.

Another groan.

My desire for water was agony.

She nodded understanding and lifted the vessel to my lips.

Drinking.

Gulping.

Choking.

Water, precious water, spilling down my chin. I sucked the vessel dry compelling yet another unbidden groan of frustration. The vessel was repeatedly refilled. I drank all I could hold, swelling up, flooding my cells until I finally had enough.

The Thing wiped wetness from my face. Made a sound. A questioning sound. Then motioned—hand to open mouth.

Meaning dawned.

Was I hungry?

I nodded. Desperate. Please! Trying to convey just how hungry I was. The last time I had eaten was well before I left the safety of home.

A long time ago.

Impossible to know exactly how long in a place where sunlight is endless for many revolutions of the planet the Things called Earth. Followed by night as dark as uttermost space for many revolutions more.

The Thing moved to the corner, opening a small cupboard door and rummaged inside.

With a shock, I realized the corpse was gone. I had slept through the drama of opening and closing doors, freezing blasts of wind, Things moving about, throwing vicious glares. Threatening noises.

Exhaustion had shut away the world as if I had died. For a crazy moment I wondered if I had.

The small Thing rattled implements. I smelled cooking odors. It returned with a tray. On it was a vessel brimming with a dark brown liquid. It smelled delicious. Saliva flooded my mouth.

Soup?

What kind of soup? I don't care, just give me that soup.

A spoon carried a portion to my lips. Gratefully, I accepted it. The soup was sweet and nourishing, coating my tongue and warming my belly. She spooned up more and I eagerly took it in. So fast that it dribbled down my chin.

She laughed. It was the first time I had heard one of them laugh. It was a pleasant sound.

She paused to wipe my chin, then made a sound. A word.

"Chklette," she said "Gud chkelette,yas?"

A definite question. But what was she asking?

"Gud?"

Did I want more? Is that what she was asking?

I nodded and opened my mouth. It must have been the right answer because she fed me more and didn't stop until the spoon clicked against an empty bowl.

She patted my lips clean with a cloth and stepped away. I felt a sudden desire to speak. To thank her.

I said, "Gud."

Her eyes widened. Did she understand me? Had I made the proper Thing sound?

Emboldened, I said "Chkelette gud. Yas?"

She laughed. Then opened her mouth to speak, but before she could there was a sudden rumbling and the floor lurched.

Plaster and dust fell.

Cupboard doors crashed open.

A sound like an explosion.

Then another. Closer. More violent. The floor bucked under us. The small Thing fell against me. I tried to catch her—to help—but the manacles restrained me. Her body was soft. Trembling with fear. She was so close I was able to stroke her head. Whisper comforting words.

A sudden start as frightening awareness sank in. She gasped, pushing away from me.

Eyes wild and fearful.

I shook my head, wanting to say, "No, no. I won't hurt you." Waving my hands. Manacles clattering. But my voice and the clatter only seemed to make her more afraid.

She backed away.

Hesitated. Then calm returned. I saw a smile, realizing Things can smile too. Before, I had only seen anger. Hate. And the corpse's grin.

Another explosion shook the building. Followed by more rumbling and lurching—cupboard doors slamming shut. Soon we were covered in plaster and dust.

The small Thing made an angry sound. But not at me. She glared at the door, muttering under her breath. Face taking on stubborn look. Angry resolve.

Resolve to do what?

I wish I knew. Was it possible we shared similar worries?

Interesting.

She pulled on a parka and went to the door. Opened it, struggled to hold it against the buffeting wind. Then she slipped out and was gone.

The lock clicked into place and I heard footsteps hurrying away.

I was alone in my prison again.

Despair gnawing back to the surface. A nasty little animal with small, sharp teeth. Weary, I leaned against my bonds.

My heart jumped.

What was this?

Did the bonds gave way?

Once again, I leaned forward.

Testing.

A definite slackening.

Breath quickening, I pushed harder. Behind me a groan of complaining metal.

Bear down. Push and push and push… bolts screeching in their sockets. Push more. Harder. Sockets tearing.

I wrenched with all my strength and I ripped free.

Falling face first. Somehow I caught myself just in time. Hands and wrists taking the sudden shock of weight.

I allowed myself to sink to the floor. I had been on my feet for a long time now.

Rested a moment. Heart a joyous race.

Fear returned.

Had they heard the tearing metal? Were they coming? The small hairless Thing will kill me if he finds me like this.

I listened. No sounds but wind beating against the walls of my prison.

I rose to my knees and I turned to see what I had accomplished. To my delight, the bolts holding the chains had been ripped from the wall. Wind knifed through a large hole where the chains had been connected. And I realized that the explosions and the combination of my weight and the Thing's had done the job.

On my feet, I inspected the hole. It was about the size of my head. I gripped the edges and pulled with both hands. It resisted at first, then gave way.

Not large enough, and the edges were sharp, cutting my fingers. I found rags by the skink and wrapped my hands.

I gathered all my strength and pulled.

A frighteningly loud shriek, and then icy wind blasted through the enlarged gap. Now my shoulders would fit through. I poked my head out, wind biting my nose and cheeks.

The way was clear for my escape.

But the chains?

What about the chains?

And the manacles?

I pulled at them. No use. I searched the room for a key. Heart trip hammering. The Things might return at any minute.

Nothing.

Very well. The chains and manacles must remain for now. Ripped up rags made ideal pads for the manacles. Gripping with both hands, I experimentally swung the chains.

An excellent weapon.

I found a thick musty blanket in a corner. It was double thick, padded and insulated. Rummaging in a drawer near the sink, I found a large sharp blade with a wooden handle.

Another weapon.

First, I used it to make a holes in the padded blanket. Worked my head through. Much better. I was warmer now.

I wanted to rush out before I was discovered, but I steeled myself. To stay free, to stay alive, I needed supplies. Without high calorie food I would soon exhaust myself. Then it would be a race between capture or death on the ice.

The room was a jumble of castoffs. I found a few tools that looked useful, including a heavy hammer and chisel. Better still, I found packets and cans with pictures of what appeared to be food. Also, two large insulated flasks. I filled them with steaming hot water from the tap.

In the corner, I found a old sled with heavy tarps and ropes to lash them in place. Now I had the means to transport an increasingly heavy burden.

Then, wonder of all wonders, I came upon my ice striders tossed in a corner.

Problem: how to fit all this through the hole? I tried to enlarge it. Pulling with all my strength. The screech of tearing metal frightened me. If they heard, they would come. If they came, I was dead.

I lifted the chains. Swung them experimentally. I would kill some of them first.

But that satisfaction was false and only lasted a foolish bloodlust moment. I had to guard myself against selfish emotions. If I die, all of us were threatened.

A loud explosion rocked the prison.

Then another—*Boom!*

And another—*Boom!*

Then a whole series of explosions: *Boom! Boom! Boomboomboomboomboom!*

Fighting to keep my feet I struggled with the metal siding. Ripping and tearing. The ear-piercing sounds covered by the explosions.

Finally, I was done.

Now there was room enough for the sled. Shouldering the chains, I grasped the harness and stepped out to face the wind. It whipped at my makeshift coat. Icy fingers stabbed the flesh beneath. From experience, I knew it was many degrees below the freezing point of water.

I looked around. There was only ice and snow. In the distance I saw a long, low building. It was crouched at the edge of a bay, whose wind-whipped waters were blanketed with floating chunks of ice.

The bay was empty except for an enormous, startling green iceberg. It was like a work of art, framed by towering mountains covered with thick ice. I had seen many bergs during my sojourn here. All shimmering with glorious colors. Green and gold and blue and white so pure that it was difficult to believe one's own eyes.

I scanned the area. Not a single Thing in sight.

To get a better look I eased closer to the edge of the shack that had been my prison. I nearly fell over a metal object protruding from the ground. It was painted a bright red. Presumably to keep dimwits like me from stumbling over it.

I looked closer. The object appeared to be the end of a large pipe with a heavy metal cap. There was an aperture in the cap. I leaned close to sniff at it.

Familiar.

A fuel of some kind.

Then it came to me. It smelled like the exhaust of one of the flying machines. Aviation fuel? Sniffed again. Yes, I was sure of it.

There was a small shed next to the pipe. I opened it, hoping to find something useful. But the only Thing inside, other than gauges and switches, was a large wrench. It looked like it was meant for the fitting on top of the pipe. I had no use for it, or anything else, so I shut the door.

Looking down the hill, I saw two of the flying machines parked in an enclosure with open double doors.

Still feeling brain-fogged, I toyed with the notion of trying to disable the machines, but gave it up when I realized just how foolhardy that idea was.

I gave my head a violent shake.

Damned drugs.

I crept to the edge of the shack for a better look. Nothing but the iceberg. There was an acrid smell on the wind. It was the distinctive odor of an enormous colony of flightless birds. I'd investigated the colony before the Things arrived. The birds were tubby little creatures about as high as my knee. They were black and white and had stubby wings. They looked clumsy when waddling about on two legs.

The birds tended nests made of piled rocks. Usually one or two large eggs rested in the nest, which the birds warmed with their bodies. I had witnessed fuzzy babies cracking through their egg shells with the help of their parents. Those birds, so clumsy on land, were amazing acrobats in the sea, scooping up food they would later regurgitate into the gullets of their ever-hungry young. They defecated a pink liquid, which covered the breeding grounds. That was what I smelled when I emerged from my prison.

I heard their distinctive cheeping. Thousands of birds calling for their mates and young among an immense crowd of what appeared to be identical birds. How did they ever find one another? Looking closer, I could see tens of thousands of little figures hopping around in a vast colony near the base of a mountain of ice. After six winters in this place the little animals still charmed me. During my visits they paid no attention as I moved among them. Sensing that I was no threat.

They had never seen my like before, so how could I possibly be a threat? So unlike the Things who had also never seen my kind before, but immediately feared me.

To them I was so fearful that they spent days in the biting cold hunting me with their machines until they finally ran me to ground and shot me with a dart gun. Then hauled me to their base and locked me in chains. I wondered what they had planned for me, beyond torment.

A deafening roar hammered my ears as another explosion rocked the earth. I clung to the side of the shack for support.

And then an enormous mass of ice ripped away from the mountain and crashed down with a force so tremendous it nearly knocked me off my feet.

Only the oversize ice striders kept me upright.

Then more ice broke free. A gathering avalanche poured down the mountainside and to my horror, the avalanche obliterated the entire colony of birds, before spilling into the sea.

A moment later the door of the building burst open and a group of Things raced out. They were bundled against the cold in thick red parkas and trousers. They seemed excited. Waving their arms and shouting.

At first I thought they'd discovered my escape.

I shrugged off the harness and got ready to run. Losing the supplies would be devastating. But they were so close I'd never be able to outrun them while hauling the sled.

Then it came to me: They weren't shouting in anger.

But in glee.

I wondered what manner of beings these creatures were who found joy murdering tens of thousands of helpless little birds and their nestlings.

Looking up at the area the thick ice had covered, I saw bare black rock. Now, instead of bird droppings I smelled another familiar stench.

Oil?

Yes, that was it.

Oil.

Black liquid poured down the mountainside, fouling everything in its path until it streamed into the pristine waters of the bay.

Already bodies of dead fish were floating to the surface and washing ashore. A big black mass of a creature struggled to the beach. It collapsed, gasping for breath. Its flippers moving weakly as it tried to drag itself from the foul water.

I'd seen its like before—beautiful animals with glistening brown fur and large dreamy black eyes.

One of the Things walked out to it, carrying a long black object.

Realization: It was the one I had come to think of as My Thing. The gentle female with black skin. She took a small box from her parka, sorted it through it, then withdrew what looked like one of the darts I'd been shot with. She loaded it into what I now recognized as a dart gun.

The creature on the beach moaned, flippers barely moving. My Thing straightened. Took careful aim. A long hesitation. Then she pulled the trigger and there was a sharp report.

The creature jumped.

I saw a slender dart with red stabilizers hanging from its throat. Another sharp report. Another dart piercing its body.

For a short time, the creature moaned. Flippers moving as if it thought it was swimming.

Then it gave a long sigh and fell still.

My Thing lowered the dart gun and walked slowly back to the others. Their excited jabbering continued. They had talked during the entire incident.

Only pausing at the sound of the shot. Some of them glanced at the scene, then continued on as nothing had happened. Totally indifferent.

Shouldering the harness, I slowly retreated to the other side of the shed. Then I set off, taking care to keep the shed between me and the Things.

Soon, I came to a place where there was no cover. I'd be exposed for a hundred meters or more.

Leaning forward I caught a glimpse of the Things. Still talking excitedly. The small, hairless tormentor was among them. I saw him pass a flask to his hairy friend, who drank greedily and passed it back.

Standing apart from the others, I spotted My Thing. She seemed isolated from the others both in attitude and skin color. I wondered if she was the only female among them? If so, she was isolated by gender as well.

Then it came to me that the others might blame her for my escape, even though it was the explosions that had freed me. If so, I was sorry for that. It seemed a cruel way to repay a kindness. A rare commodity in this frozen wilderness.

Once again, there was nothing to be done about it.

I crouched there—waiting in the freezing wind. First my ears and nose, then my fingers and toes grew numb.

After a time, the Things went inside. My Thing was last—hesitating for a long moment. Turning to look at the oil-befouled corpse on the beach. Then the great heaps of oil-fouled ice and rock where the colony of birds had been.

Her head slowly turned to look in my direction. There was a pause—as if she sensed my presence.

I crouched lower, expecting a cry of alarm.

Then she seemed to shake off whatever had captured her attention and went inside. The door shut behind her.

I jumped to my feet. Shouldering the harness, I threw my weight from side to side, breaking the runners free of the ice. Then I dashed for the cover of a jumble of boulders.

A moment later I was safe from view. I paused for breath and to calm my racing heart. Then I started off again. Burning kilometers with a survivor's stride. Running a hundred paces. Walking fifty. Repeat. A hundred, then fifty. And so on.

I couldn't head directly home. It was vital that they didn't discover my base camp, where I have labored for six long winters and summers. It was well hidden and stocked with supplies and sophisticated tools and weapons. I would need them to complete my mission and file my long-overdue final report.

The wind was fiercer now. To my delight, dark storm clouds boiled on the horizon. A storm would delay any search. If so, I could take a more direct route home.

As I paced, I used the position of the sun to help guide me. The sun was nearing its lowest point just now. Soon, it would be winter when the blackest of black nights would descend on the land. Driven by gravity the winds would blast down the mountains onto the icy plains at speeds up to 300 kilometers an hour. The cold would deepen to an unimaginable hundred and thirty degrees below zero, or more.

In other colonies, flightless birds would huddle together for warmth. At regular intervals, the birds on the outside traded places with those closer in so every one of them would have a chance to live.

But this cycle the storm never came. I had been counting on it to delay the search. The luck that began with a gift of water and the soup the Thing called "Chklette" ended with my escape.

Just as I feared, the hue and cry began within a few scant hours. They pursued me relentlessly with their flying machines and powered ice sleds. Even more dangerous were their mechanical hunters. They were about waist high and were equipped with powerful laser guns and sophisticated sensing devices that seemed able to track me no matter how well I was hidden.

I eluded them for several cycles, going to ground whenever I caught sight of them.

Then one cycle I felt safe enough to breakfast on a soup made from a packet of nasty-smelling powder mixed with hot water, which I boiled in one of the flasks with a heating element. It was nothing like the delicious Chklette My Thing had fed me. Never mind the taste, my belly complained that what I had eaten was not enough, so when I trekked on I was paying poor attention to my surroundings.

That carelessness almost cost my life. As I moved around an ice cropping I almost fell over one of the hunters.

It appeared to be at rest. It was making little beeping sounds and it had a solar umbrella arrayed to recharge. Fortunately, it was also paying poor attention to its surroundings.

Very slowly, I shed the harness and lowered it to the ground. My intention was to abandon the sled before I was noticed and get quickly out of there.

Then one of my ice striders bumped against something. The scraping sound was so miniscule that at first I thought I was safe.

But the hunter caught the sound. In a scant millisecond the solar array furled and shot out of sight. At the same instant the turret whipped about and the muzzle of its laser gun came up.

Before it could fire, I lashed out with my chains. The desperate blow struck with such force that it bent the muzzle.

Still, the hunter tried to fire, but the effort failed. It tried again and again and there was a mad clicking noise with each attempt. Going, clickclickclick-chilc.

Seeing it helpless, my spirits soared. Then my temper blew. All that pent-up anger from so many hours of torment and hunger and thirst exploded.

The hunter had found me.

Too bad for the hunter.

I slashed at the machine. Over and over. Pummeling it with the heavy chains until it was nothing but a ruin of metal and exposed wiring that sparked feebly.

Finally, there was a shower of sparks and the hunter was still.

I was so exhausted I dropped to my knees.

Then I started laughing.

Within seconds the laughter became uncontrollable. I laughed until my ribs ached and I was bent over gasping for breath.

Then I wept.

Tears streaming.

Gobs of snot.

Choking on my own hysteria.

On my own despair.

On my own desolate loneliness.

Finally, I rested my head on my knees. Gradually, I gathered my strength. Grabbed two big handfuls of snow and scrubbed my face clean.

Took a deep breath and then rummaged in the sled until I found the hammer and chisel. I sat there on the sled and started hammering at the links. So desperate to be free that for a long moment of near insanity I didn't care if they found me.

I hammered away. Sitting there in plain view while the flying machines traced a relentless pattern that came close, but somehow kept missing me.

Finally, I was free.

I stood up with only the manacles on my wrists. I dropped the chains, then strode away on my ice walkers, leaving the sled behind, carrying only a small bundle of supplies.

Time passed.

The relentless hunt continued.

Hunger gnawed at my belly.

It became impossible to quench my thirst, or make more soup. I didn't dare stop long enough to thaw out a flask full of snow, so I had to make do with hasty scoops stuffed into my mouth. Eking out so little water that it was hardly worth an ice-burned tongue.

I found my base camp with little time to spare.

First, came the roar of the snow cats.

Then. The whop, whop of flying machines.

Proximity alarms blared from the hunters closing in from all sides.

I was traversing a broad beach blanketed with black rocks. The beach was warm from volcanic activity. Steam rose in thick clouds that obscured me. I'd chosen the area partly because of this, and partly because of the strange magnetic field that my instruments had detected. The field served to blind my pursuer's devices. The area also offered a rare luxury: a grotto with a pool of water hot enough to bathe.

Suddenly, a flying machine popped into view and headed my way.

Even so, I was sure they hadn't spotted me yet and I made a mad dash for the grotto, diving into the water just in time. Vanishing in the delicious steam as the machine roared overhead.

I held my breath until my lungs were ready to burst, then surfaced just long enough for a breath.

The sky was empty, but the proximity alarms of the hunters sounded all around me and I heard the voices of Things coming from a snow cat that had stopped on the beach.

I went under again.

Waiting.

Waiting.

Lungs burning.

But still I waited.

When I could stand it no longer, I was forced to surface. The sounds of the hunt were still all around me and down I went again.

The hiding game went on for an hour or so, until finally I surfaced to be greeted with nothing but the sound of the wind and the waves crashing against the beach.

I crawled out, limp from so much time in the water. The skin of my hands and fingers so wrinkled it made me smile.

I slipped out of the padded blanket and then my clothes and spread them out over warm boulders. With the sun blazing through a cloudless sky I knew they'd soon dry.

Nothing stays wet very long in this strange but beautiful land the Things named Antarctica. Moisture evaporates instantly. Even the snowflakes seem dry. At so many degrees below the freezing point of water the flakes won't melt. You just brush them from your shoulders like dust. The snow on the ground just remains there. Piling up, snowstorm after snowstorm until it is as impenetrable as ice and many kilometers thick.

Enjoying a rare moment of leisure out of the cold, I checked for injuries. My torso was a mass of bruises from the beatings the small, hairless Thing had administered while his bigger companion held me. Other than several scrapes and ribs more prominent than usual from being denied food for so long, I seemed to be in decent shape.

The cut on my forehead wasn't infected. No surprise there. Infections are rare in this land where it is too cold for most bacteria to survive. Another good sign: my skin had a healthy sheen, black as the volcanic rocks on the beach.

When my clothes were dry enough I pulled them on. Then donned the padded blanket, which was still uncomfortably damp. With luck, I'd be wearing it for the last time.

I set off and soon I spotted the towering pile of enormous white bones that marked my destination. I lost sight of them for a moment as I moved through a warren of boulders.

When I emerged, the beach was in full view. The bones were the skeletal remains of hundreds of gigantic beasts that were scattered about with no thought, much less care.

When I first found the place, I thought I was hallucinating. It was if I had stepped into a child's nightmare. A cruel tale told by a bored creche nurse to bully her little charges into an early nesting time.

Once I got over my initial shock, I realized I was looking at the remains of enormous mammals. Their bleached pelvises towered over me. On all sides were huge backbones, shoulder bones, and spinal columns many meters long. And there were rib cages big enough to stand up and walk around in.

At first I was puzzled by the absence of leg, or arm bones. There were so many of the beasts that their absence was mysterious. Did whatever creature that preyed on them particularly favor legs, eating them bones and all?

Which made me wonder about the size of their predators. I shuddered at the thought.

It turned out to be a foolish one. Not far from that graveyard of giants, I came upon a wind-battered building. It had the look of a long abandoned facility of some sort. Although in this land nothing ever truly rusts or is reduced to ruins. Looking inside, it soon became apparent that the facility had been built by small, but no less deadly, predators.

Things had built this place.

Things had killed all those animals on the beach.

The building proved to be an old factory where Things had processed the giants. Gutting them and stripping them of fat and flesh until there was nothing left but morsels for birds to pick at until only sun-bleached bones remained.

With the instruments at my base camp it took little extrapolation to realize just how staggering the slaughter must have been. The appetite for those poor creatures was such that surely their very existence as a species must have been threatened.

But that was in the early days of my mission. When my heart was full of hope and I saw promise, despite the warnings of my mission mates that were trickling in from all over the globe.

Later I saw several of the giant animals surface in the bay. They were magnificent creatures. My marine listening devices recorded the songs they sang to each other and I soon came to realize they were animals of great wisdom and intelligence.

After a little more investigation, and consulting with my mission mates I learned just how few had survived during the days of that great slaughter. Since then their numbers have grown smaller with each passing cycle. For a time, my mission mates reported similar findings in non-Thing life all over the globe.

The appetite of the Things was so voracious that only a favored few creatures seemed to thrive.

We found that everywhere they go the Things excrete so much waste and burn so much fuel that it is overwhelming the rivers, the oceans, the mountains and the plains and the deserts and the very air they breathe.

Still, my mission mates and I held to our hopes.

I suppose it is the nature of our kind to cling to such ephemeral hopes. It has been so long since our own world was turned to cosmic dust we can't imagine that all sentients don't treasure the planets they are fortunate to inhabit.

Otherwise, how could we have clung so long to the singular goal of finding the one place where we could end our search and settle peacefully among the native inhabitants?

It had been our dream that Earth was such a place.

To begin with there had been twelve of us. We were spread strategically across the planet. We had all been specifically educated and trained for the mission.

Over the centuries, many missions had been launched. For one reason or another they had all failed. Each failure had been a costly blow that ended in many deaths and the squandering of precious supplies.

Our leaders said by cruel necessity this mission would be the last. No one seemed to have the heart to continue. Much less risk the precious supplies these missions required. Great age had taken its toll on our ships, equipment and hydroponic farms. Even the seeds we'd carried away when we fled the orphaned exoplanet that destroyed our world were failing to germinate.

Soon, our storerooms will be empty.

Our species doomed.

When my mission mates and I began we were brimming with energy and optimism. Our initial reports sang Earth's praises. We were told that with each report the spirits of our families and friends rose to giddy heights.

Unfortunately, the doomsayers among us have been growing in power. They have urged us to just take the planet and be damned to the sentient overlords. But such a thing is against our nature. And has always been so. I feared if we chose that path it would be at the cost of our very souls.

My mission mates were of the same mind and we worked diligently, repeatedly risking our lives for the good of the cause. Then reality sank in. As perfect a world as this planetary body must seem, its sentient overseers appear to be intent on destroying it.

Even so, for a time we thought this frozen continent to the south might offer a solution. It is of no use to the Things. Yet with our technology, we could live here and flourish.

We could exchange vast knowledge they are centuries from achieving in return for permission to peacefully settle here. To make a home in a place other than uttermost space where it seems we are doomed to wander until there are no more of us.

That was to be the conclusion of our final report.

A report now long overdue.

Then my mission mates began vanishing.

One by one their regular communications stopped. Operative after operative lapsed into a silence that I knew must have been forced.

Kaarla was the last.

In her final communication, she feared she'd been discovered and was being hunted.

She said they were close.

So very close.

But she said she'd located a better place for a base camp safe from prying eyes.

In her last message Kaarla said: "We are the last best hope of the people, brother mine. Be on guard. And stay safe."

Then I heard no more.

Nothing but the static of stars like our own that vanished from the universe long ago.

Her loss shook me to the core. Kaarla and I had been lovers once—back during the latter days of our training.

Our love was fierce.

Beyond mere passion.

It burned brighter than any Starfall celebration. Then, as quickly as it had enveloped us, it flamed out. But unlike most failed love affairs we were neither angry or felt betrayed.

Instead, we became fast friends.

Actually, it was more than mere friendship. We bonded together like twins. Each feeling the emotional ups-and-downs of the other no matter how far apart we were.

It was an uncanny connection. Almost telepathic.

I didn't need the absence of her regular communications to know in my heart that she was gone.

One sleep period, a searing—almost unbearable pain—brought me out of a deep sleep.

I shot up from my cot gasping for breath.

Then another wave of pain struck.

And another.

And once more.

So terrible I fell to the floor.

I remained there for a long time, dragging in precious air. Then the pain vanished, leaving me feeling empty and drained.

It was then that I knew my sister was gone from me forever.

My lover, my friend, my sister and the last of my mission mates was dead. Even worse, I realized everything now rested on my shoulders.

Then they found me.

Hunted me relentlessly.

Until I was brought to ground.

Later, when looking into the eyes of the small, hairy Thing I came to believe I was seeing pure evil. When his companion in evil gripped my head for the blinding I thought all Things must be like this.

They all must be evil.

How else to explain it?

But after meeting the female Thing I regained a modicum of hope. I retained it, despite the disaster that killed the colony of birds. It became stronger still when I witnessed her act of mercy when she ended the pain of that poor struggling creature on the beach.

We shall see how that all plays out in the end.

When the long winter's night comes, I will investigate one more time. Until then I will rest here. Regain my strength and formulate a plan. And then I will decide if these Things are worth saving.

There was no one to welcome me home when I finally reached my base camp. It was a shelter made of special thermal material, arranged in a jumble of boulders. A holo device provided camouflage so cunning that even if a Thing were standing right next to the entrance he wouldn't be able to see that anything was amiss.

The moment I entered the warmth of the heaters enveloped me. I dropped my gear. Threw off my makeshift coat and fell into my cot without bothering to undress.

I just pulled a thermal blanket over me and slept.

Hours passed before I reentered the world. I was awakened with a start. Heart racing. The chill of evaporating fear sweat. The whop, whop, whop sound of a flying machine hovering overhead.

Had they found me?

What was that?

There!

Tracks grinding against stone.

The beep, beep, beep of electronic sniffing just beyond the camouflaged entrance.

A desperate clumsy search for a weapon.

Finally!

Fingers closing on a gun.

I backed into a corner—weapon aimed at the door.

Ready to fire.

To escape I had to get a jump start.

I'd shoot through the door, then charge straight out, catching them unawares.

A spray of automatic fire, then run for it.

With luck they wouldn't catch me.

But if they did...

If they did...

At that moment I determined to take my own life before I'd let myself fall into their hands again.

Then, just as I decided to fire and rush the door, the sniffing ended. And the sound of the flying ship moved away.

I collapsed in relief.

So close.

So very close.

I pulled myself together. Washed under a clever little showering device with soothing hot water that lasted for seven minutes on extra hot. Fifteen if lukewarm.

I chose the extra hot.

I pulled on clean clothes and heated a container of my favorite stew. I ate it out of the pot and washed it down with a mug of high calorie brew.

My first order of business was to get rid of the blasted manacles. They were a constant reminder of my captivity. A little file from my dental emergency kit did the trick. Then I settled down to wait for the endless dark of winter.

Two cycles later, food, sleep and restlessness led me to change my mind.

And there was another factor.

The blood tests I ran in my little lab revealed that the drug they'd shot me with was meant for animals much larger than myself. No wonder my brain had been so clouded. My thinking so jagged.

It was remarkable I was even alive.

Now that my mind was clear, I realized that although winter's darkness might be safer, I needed light to learn what was really going on. What was their true goal.

Oil?

Unlikely.

It was too simple an answer. And with time running out for my people, I needed the answer fast.

Kaarla and the others had reported a plentitude of oil in places easier and cheaper to exploit than this wilderness where the ground is locked in ice many kilometers deep. And where the elements made travel and movement impossible during the long winter's night.

It had to be more than just oil.

I prepared carefully. Filling my knapsack with the barest essentials so it wouldn't slow me down if I had to run.

Actually, it wasn't a matter of "if," but "when."

With all their resources it was only a matter of time before I was discovered. Then they'd be on me like a fury.

I armed myself with two weapons. Three, if I counted the knife I wore in a belted sheath. It was a poor replacement for the one Kaarla had given me. The foolish thought came to me that I could hunt down the hairless Thing and take it back. I surprised myself with the joy I felt imagining how good it would feel to kill him.

That was quite unlike me. But I suppose that is what happens when you are in the company of Things too long. Thoughts of murder and destruction become ordinary.

Balancing the sheathed knife was a fazergun with adjustable focus. It could be dialed to take out a single target, or multiple targets if they weren't too far apart. It was light weight, fit easily into my hand and could only be fired by its owner.

For long range I carried a Lazzerus rifle. It was under 60 centimeters long, was fitted with a powerful scope, and fired rounds with adjustable explosive power.

One setting meant death for one.

Another, the deaths of many.

I had another weapon that could only stun. But I had neither room in my pack or compassion in my heart to carry it.

When I felt rested enough to proceed, I set out for my enemies' base camp. I took a roundabout route and approached from the far side of the main building.

To my surprise, none of the hunters were patrolling for me. Better still— the alarms and traps the Things had set were so simple I easily bypassed them.

I approached along a narrow beach that ran past a jagged cliff face that rose out of the sea a hundred meters or so from their base.

The silence was eerie. Nothing but the booming surf. What was I missing? Then as I crept around a bend I saw the damage the explosions had wrought and realized that what I was missing were the sounds and smells of the normally busy colony of wingless birds.

There was nothing left of the million or more breeding pairs that had once made the place their home but mounds of oil-fouled rubble.

The oil had stopped flowing and in the middle of the field I saw four poles with red flags speared into the ground marking an area about four meters square.

I checked for spy cameras, spotted two hidden on either side of the beach. Soon, I determined that they were inoperable. Their batteries were dead— drained by the stress of intense cold. A storm had swept out of the sea not many hours before and with the wind chill factor the temperatures would have dropped to 130 degrees below zero.

It was balmy today. The wind light. Temperature about twenty degrees below zero.

Birds were out in force. Hundreds of them wheeling in the sky, or squabbling amongst themselves in their cliff-side nests. There were easily a score or more species of birds who dwelled there, ranging in size from tiny creatures that could fit in the palm of my hand, to their larger cousins with wingspans of two meters or more.

I'd noted previously that each species favored certain areas on the cliff face to build their nests. Each group took possession of a specific strata and never encroached on the others.

Staying alive is difficult in this harsh climate—so perilous—that the birds chose peaceful coexistence over inter-species warfare.

Which is exactly the sort of arrangement my kind wanted with the Things.

The question in my mind was whether the damage the Things were causing was so vast that in a few short years the planet will become uninhabitable for any species.

If that's what happens my own people are doomed. Because Earth is the last best place within reach. If we are denied a place here, we face a long and torturous death with the wails of starving children the last sounds we heard.

A great horn blared. The blast was so sudden, so loud, that I feared I'd been discovered.

I dropped to the ground so quickly I banged my chin against the ice. Even so, I had the presence of mind to unsling my rifle. Cautiously, I raised my head, scanning the area through the rifle scope.

I settled on the building first. The only sign of activity was steam rising from an exhaust stack.

The horn sounded again.

This time I was ready, and I traced the sound to a strange ship anchored in the bay. It was a surprising sight. The last time I'd seen a ship was when the Things had arrived at winter's end. That ship had been sleek, as if meant for luxurious travel. This one had seen better times. Crates of equipment were stacked on the deck. A large crane was fixed to the bow. I wondered what the Things were up to.

There was another blast of the horn, and this time it was answered. A long, loud blast emanated from the building.

A moment later the front door opened and red clad Things emerged. I could clearly see My Thing among them. She was on the edge of the group.

I centered the scope on her face. She looked troubled. Even a little frightened. I saw her flinch and push away from the group.

Moving my scope, I spotted the pair she'd stepped away from with such alacrity. And there were my old companions in torment: the small hairless Thing and his taller companion. They appeared to be mocking her. My Thing grew angry. I saw her shake a finger at them, but they only laughed more.

The Thing I took as the leader spoke to them. I couldn't hear the sounds he made but I was fairly certain he was admonishing them. Even so, I could tell he wasn't putting much effort in it. They nodded, but when he turned away I saw them roll their eyes.

The hairless one wagged his tongue at My Thing. For some reason I took it as an obscene gesture. My Thing turned away and tried to ignore them.

The group walked toward the beach. In the bay, I saw several small boats being lowered from the strange ship. They were crowded with equipment and

Things clad in white cold weather gear. The boats sped for shore and a few moments later they landed.

Two of the visitors approached the shore party, while the others unloaded the boats.

One of the visitors wore red epaulets on his shoulders. He extended a hand to the land group's leader. They clasped hands and a lively discussion ensued. The acted like friends. The leader of the land group called out to the hairless one and his companion. They trotted up, carrying knapsacks stuffed with equipment.

After a few words were exchanged, they all moved over to the oily rubble, fastidiously picking their way through the worst of it until they reached the red flags.

Soon the knapsacks were unpacked, a clear sheet of plastic spread on the ground, and the hairless Thing scooped up a shovelful of rocks and dumped them on the plastic sheet. Meanwhile his companion hooked up the visitor's leader to a device consisting of earphones, a black box and a long, red-tipped wand.

The visitor gave the leader of the land group a questioning look. He appeared to laugh, then made a deep, flourishing bow, then waved his hand as if to say, "Proceed."

The visitor shrugged and passed the wand over the rocks. Immediately the black box lit up with madly winking lights. Even at a distance I could hear clicking noises.

The visitor was so surprised he took a step back. Through the scope I saw nervous laughter. Then he passed the wand over the rocks again. Once again the box lit up and it went cliclclickclickclick.

For some reason this caused a great deal of excitement and back slapping. The visitor fished out what I took as a com unit because he immediately began speaking into it. His excitement was such that I could hear him shout something that sounded like, "Phantaztik!"

A few minutes later the two groups trooped into the building. The last one was My Thing. I saw her look back at the red flags, then give a sad shake of her head.

As I watched her, I felt an odd sensation. A prickling at the back of my neck. It wasn't unpleasant. Just a gentle sort of probing.

Then My Thing's head suddenly came up. Her eyes cut to where I was hidden. Something stirred inside me. It was almost like those odd moments of near telepathy that I once shared with Kaarla.

My heart wrenched.

I missed Kaarla so.

Finally, My Thing shook her head. The feeling vanished and she stepped through the doorway. A moment the door closed.

I waited for a long time, making sure they were settled. Then, just as the cold was making my wait almost unbearable, I heard the raucous sounds of celebration coming from the building. To my delight, it sounded like they'd be busy for at least several hours.

I crept from cover and carefully made my way to the red flags. I studied the rocks spread out on the plastic sheet. There was nothing obvious to cause such joy. I pawed though the rocks until I had a nice sample. Then, just to make certain, I scanned the area with an instrument and recorded a rough estimate of the scope of their find.

Burning with curiosity, I hurried home. I was hungry, so I put something on to heat while I cleaned the samples, then slid then into the analyser. The answer came not long after I finished my meal.

Unfortunately, my instincts had been right.

It wasn't about oil. It was about a substance with 92 protons and 92 electrons. It was definitely radioactive, although mildly so.

Very well, what the Things had discovered was a rare element that was undoubtedly valuable. But was it valuable enough to mine in a place with such a hostile climate? To find out I had to chance another trip to their base camp.

Also, I was troubled by the position My Thing had found herself in. From the way the hairless one behaved, I sensed she was in danger.

Then I thought, but what if she was?

What did that have to do with me, much less the overriding importance of my mission?

Whatever the situation, it was my duty to just shrug it off. Ignore it.

Still.

Still.

I repacked with even greater care. Stripping the weight down to the barest necessities so I could add a few more measuring instruments.

The celebration was still going on full blast when I returned. Voices were louder. Music blared. Meanwhile, a group of Things from the ship were unloading several small boats. I watched for a long time to get some clue of their purpose.

They were unpacking crates right on the shoreline. Lining them up and using crowbars to rip them open. I wondered why they were performing the work here, instead of loading the crates on power sleds and hauling them to the building, out of the elements.

To my horror their purpose soon became clear.

Each crate contained one of the hunters. When the visiting Things were done I counted at least two dozen. Even more disturbing, the moment their tracks hit the ground the hunters came to life.

Motors firing up.

Red eyes blinking to life.

And then, one by one they set off toward a long low, metal building. Two workmen stood at the open door of the shack, checking off each hunter as it made its way inside.

I was so shaken by this development I sank to the ground, not feeling the intense cold. With that many hunters my capture was practically guaranteed.

The glittering eyes of the hairless Thing jumped into my mind. Threatening me with my own knife. Jabbing at my eyes, while his companion held my head in a vise-like grip chanting, "Dewit! Dewit! Deewit! Dewit!"

I remained there for a long time.

Gathering my nerve.

Renewing my purpose.

Steeling myself for what I had to do next.

By the time I had recovered the beach was empty. The boats had returned to the ship, carrying broken up crates.

I approached the flags with care. My weapons at ready. I kept my eye on the building's entrance while I worked, taking readings and running preliminary calculations.

Determined to kill any Thing unlucky enough interrupt me.

I worked quickly. I had to get this information back to my base camp for my final report. My final recommendation.

Now, for the rest of it.

I found a back door to the building.

It was unlocked.

The sounds of celebration poured out when I opened the door. I waited, stretching my senses to their fullest. All the noise came from the front of the building where the Things were gathered.

There was no one about as I crept through the hallways, peeking in rooms as I went.

As I approached one door I heard footsteps coming down the hall. Quickly I ducked into the darkness inside. The footsteps continued, but sounded a little odd. Faltering. Someone was stumbling about, bumping into walls. The footsteps paused outside the door. Then there was a horrible retching sound. Someone sputtering. A long silence followed.

The Thing moved away. I peeked outside and saw a disgusting mess on the floor.

Thing vomit.

The sight and smell made me nauseous. What nasty creatures these Things were.

As I turned away, I nearly knocked over some sort of free-standing object. I steadied it, making sure it was upright, and stepped away.

When I shined a pinlight on the object I nearly jumped out of my skin. And I found myself gaping at one of our kind.

It was so realistic I almost blurted a greeting. Widening the beam, it was obviously a replica.

A replica that had my face.

There were red marks on the "body" that at first, made no sense. Then I realized they were marking my major organs.

Killing targets?

No doubt about it.

The only way they could have gleaned this information was by physically examining one, or several of us.

A sob caught in my throat, imagining the agony my mission mates must have suffered.

And Kaarla. My dear sister of the mind.

For long seconds I could barely breathe.

I flashed the light around the room. On the walls were a series of large photographs. They were grainy, and blurred. They were pictures of me on the run. The Things must have snapped them while they were hunting me.

On one wall was a large map of the surrounding area, with tiny flags marking various locations. They had been charting sightings of me. Soon it became apparent that they were closing in on my home.

A large red circle took in the beach of giant bones and the volcanic area.

It was only a matter of time before they narrowed that circle and cornered me. And with those new hunters the time I had left was frighteningly short.

This had to end soon or I was done for.

More determined than ever, I moved on.

I came to another room where there was an immense diorama of the bay and the land surrounding it.

The whole center of the diorama was a replica of a vast mining enterprise. Nothing was left to the imagination. From the gigantic black crater that encompassed the landscape, to the giant machines that dug the pits. As well as the smaller ones that would crush the rock, and process the radioactive ore.

The mine ran all the way down to the bay, where miniature freighters waited for small boats heaped with ore.

A vision of the avalanche that destroyed the colony of flightless birds flashed into my mind. Then the image of the poor oil-befouled creature My Thing had put out of its misery, while the other Things watched, amused, or just indifferent.

I recorded images of the diorama and considered what to do next. I quickly decided I had all that I needed. It was time to return to my base camp and make my final report.

If I could remain free long enough to transmit it, that is.

I retraced my steps. In the background I could hear that the celebration had reached a crescendo.

The noise was so loud I nearly missed a voice coming from a nearby room. It was a familiar voice and had a desperate pleading sound to it. A frightened sound.

It came from a closed door with light streaming through the gap in the threshold.

Drawing my side weapon, I moved closer to the door. Placed an ear against it. The voice was more distinct.

It was My Thing.

Then I heard other voices. The mocking tones of the hairless Thing. Then the voice of his companion.

Chanting, "Dewit. Dewit. Dewit"

Cautiously I cracked open the door.

Through the gap I saw the frightened face of My Thing. The hairless one had her pushed onto a bed.

He held a knife to her throat.

My knife.

Then everything became frighteningly clear.

This how the other female Thing had died.

A death they had blamed on me.

I pushed the door wide and stepped in, kicking it closed behind me.

A frozen tableaux.

My Thing sprawled on the bed, clothing ripped and in disarray.

The hairless Thing bent over her, knife pressed against her throat so hard a trickle of blood ran down to her torn blouse.

The tall, hairy Thing, an audience of one.

Delighting in the fear and torment.

Calling out "Dewit. Dewit. Dewit."

I made the same sound their leader had made when I had been their captive.

I croaked, "Stawp!"

They whirled. Eyes registering shock when they saw me. I know how I seemed to them—a living incarnation of their worst nightmares.

I was taller.

Much taller.

And big.

Much bigger.

I was so angry I knew my eyes burned as yellow and hot as the sun. In anger, the lips of my kind instinctively draw back, displaying long, sharp fangs. And just as instinctively our talons arc out, blood red against black skin.

In my wrath, they have never in their lives seen a monster such as me.

I took a step forward and there was a sudden foul odor as the hairless one's bladder gave way.

The other held up both hands.

Puny shields against my burning hate.

Another step, and the foul odor increased as his bladder followed suit.

I laughed, taking evil pleasure in their fear.

Then I shot them both.

First the hairless one.

Then his friend.

My Thing came upright, pulling her torn blouse together.

For a moment I feared she saw me as a monster as well. I made an effort to make myself less threatening. Talons vanishing. Fangs covered by my lips. I hunched down, trying to appear smaller. Like one does with a frightened child.

I wanted to tell her, "No. Please. Don't be afraid. It's only me."

But I hadn't the words.

I started to turn.

I'd have to run.

She was so frightened she'd surely raise the alarm and I'd have scant minutes to escape.

And then she rushed to me, throwing her arms around me and burying her face in my chest. Weeping, and mumbling a stream of words I had no hope of understanding.

I stood there awkwardly. My hands dangling fools at my side. Finally, my arms closed around her. I stroked her hair. Whispered words meant to calm her.

Gradually her heartbeat slowed, and she pushed against me. But gently so.

I released her, and she took a step back. She looked in my face. Our eyes met and although we couldn't speak a word of each other's language, we suddenly understood.

I felt that familiar tingle in my mind. She shivered and rubbed her arms and I knew that she felt it too.

Kaarla had the exact same shiver and goose bumps on her arms when we were together. As did I.

Then, coming down the hallway I heard approaching voices.

Panic welled.

I had to get out of here.

Run.

I had to run.

I wrested Kaarla's knife from the hairless Thing's dead hands and shoved it into my belt.

Then I gripped the doorknob, ready to fling it open. I would kill as many as I could, then escape in the confusion.

But then My Thing placed a hand on mine. I looked down at her. She shook her head, then placed a finger against her lips.

Silence.

She wanted silence.

I nodded, and she reached over and shut off the light. Then ever so quietly, she locked the door.

A moment later the footsteps stopped just outside. The doorknob turned slightly as someone tried to open it, then found it locked.

A moment later someone called out in a low voice. I looked at My Thing and again she shook her head again. Finger pressed firmly against her lips.

Then another Thing called out.

This time My Thing answered, but in a low, sleepy voice as if she'd been awakened.

A tap at the door. Someone entreating. Pleading.

My Thing replied in a voice full of irritation. The kind I used when I was sleepy child, whining for my creche nurse to go away and let me sleep.

After a long tense moment, the footsteps and voices retreated down the hall.

I looked at the bodies sprawled on the floor, then at My Thing. I made motions—what should I do? I pantomimed tying her up, so no blame would fall on her.

A violent shake of her head. She tugged hard on my sleeve. Pointed at herself, then me. And then outside.

I was incredulous.

Pantomimed question: *You want to go with me?*

She nodded: Yes. Pantomiming: *Hurry. We must hurry.*

I shook my head. Made motions: *Impossible. Too dangerous.*

She grabbed both my hands in hers and stared into my eyes. Looking long and deep. There was a tingling at the back of my spine. A whirl of images flooded my brain. It was like being with Kaarla again—the sister of my mind.

It came to me that My Thing might face imprisonment or even death if she stayed behind. She trusted no one here. They all either meant her harm or were indifferent to her fate.

After a long moment, I relented. I nodded. Then urged her to make haste.

She jammed a few belongings into a pack, pulled on cold weather gear, then grabbed a pair of ice striders and motioned—*Let's go.*

We had no trouble getting out of the building. The Things had been too consumed with their revelries to be bothered to set a watch.

When we were safely outside, I looked around. It was bright and sunny. The skies a clear blue. The air was crisp and had a quality to it that I've never experienced before. Especially after a lifetime of breathing recycled shipboard air.

How to say it? Well it was delicious. Food for the lungs and the brain.

A sudden burst of energy.

My mind buzzed with ideas and plans.

The Things would come for us soon. And they would come with a fury. Doubly so, because now they would not just be hunting me, but My Thing as well.

I looked down the hill to the shed where they kept the hunters. Just beyond was the shelter that housed the flying machines.

I remembered a game we played where the ultimate challenge was to pin a minor game piece in front of a more important one. If your opponent moved the minor piece, the important one was doomed. But, if she didn't, the game was over. Leaving no choice but to sacrifice the important piece and hope for a miracle recovery.

Motioning for My Thing to follow I ran to the shed where I had been imprisoned.

I found the pipe I'd nearly tripped over. I turned to the shed and then groaned when I saw that some clever Thing had thought to secure the door with a heavy lock.

I grasped the lock and pulled.

It didn't give.

I tried again. Pulling with all my strength, which is considerable.

It started give way and there was frighteningly loud screech of metal as the screws holding the lock in place started give away.

Then stopped.

They would go no further.

A tap on the shoulder and I turned to see My Thing holding a long metal bar.

She motioned me aside, jammed the tip of the bar between the lock and the door of the shed and gave a mighty heave.

A loud SCREECH! and the lock fell to the ground.

We both looked around to see if anyone had heard us.

Nothing besides the sounds of the party.

I grabbed the wrench, fit it to the aperture, and heaved. It stuck for a moment, then came free. The smell of aviation fuel grew stronger and I heard bubbling deep within.

Turning to the shed, I examined the gauges and dials. I saw what appeared to be writing on a metal plate, with red pictographs showing what I took to be operational directions.

I sighed. This was hopeless, By the time I deciphered the directions we'd be in chains, or dead.

My Thing pushed me side. She looked at directions, glanced at the pictographs, then spun several dials.

She motioned for me to move away.

I took two steps back.

My Thing wriggled her fingers.

More.

Two more steps.

A snort of impatience, then more finger waggling.

I almost laughed. It was a nervous reaction that drew glares from My Thing. Clearly, this was a female who had no use for slow-witted beings.

I got well back and she pulled down a lever, jumping away as she did so.

A geyser of fuel burst from the pipe.

My Thing scrambled to where I was and we both ran for shelter as the aviation fuel shot out of the pipe.

We watched from cover as the fuel pooled around the pipe. Clouds of steam rose from the frozen ground.

Soon a river of fuel was running down the hill, flooding the area where the hunters were kept. Then rolling on to envelop the place where they housed the flying machines.

When the whole area was saturated with steaming fuel, I hoisted the Lazzerus rifle to my shoulder.

Dialed in the most explosive force.

And fired.

A sheet of flame erupted that was so intense we were momentarily blinded.

Soon as my vision cleared, I grabbed My Thing and started running.

We ran as fast as we could. Ice striders ripping up frozen ground. With my long legs I would soon outpace her, so I grabbed a hand and pulled her along. She came willingly. Pumping her legs as fast as she could to keep from being dragged along the ground.

And then there was an explosion so great it hurled us into the air.

I landed on my back. So stunned I didn't move for long seconds. A faint voice penetrated the ringing in my ears.

A tug at my sleeve.

I opened my eyes to find My Thing kneeling over me. She urged me to look and I sat up to see what we had done.

The homes of the flying machines and the hunters were fully engaged. Flames shooting up. Black clouds of smoke rising to the sky.

My hearing cleared, and I heard shouts. My Thing was pointing, and I turned to see Things pouring out of the building.

Hysterical confusion reigned for long minutes, then the leaders of the two groups got their underlings organized to start fighting the fires.

A moment later, there was an explosion, and one side of their quarters burst into flame. Now they concentrated on that fire, letting the others burn. It was either that or face the most severe environment on the planet without food or shelter.

Every bone in my body ached. I fell back when I tried to rise. My Thing didn't seem to have been affected as much and helped me to my feet.

We set off for my base camp. Slowly at first. Then, as my muscles warmed up, and the aches and pain diminished, we moved faster.

Behind us we heard shouts, and then another explosion.

We slowed, husbanding our strength.

They wouldn't be coming after us soon.

As we made our way, I ran over my preliminary findings. I would confirm them when we reached home, but even a cursory look at my device's screen staggered the imagination.

The proposed mining site contained at least thirty-five thousand metric tons of Element 92.

Ripping it from the earth would create an environmental nightmare. Just one more nightmare to add to the Things' crimes against their own planet.

Tens of thousands of square kilometers of landscape ripped apart.

Whole mountains leveled to get at the ore.

The waters of the bay despoiled for a thousand years or more.

Sea life and birds dead and dying by the millions.

And the only pristine continent on the globe would be destroyed forever.

In my heart—no, not just my heart, but my entire being—I knew the Things would continue their destructive practices until the entire Earth was unfit for life of any sort.

Me and my kind have been star wanderers for many centuries now. And never in all that time have we come upon such monsters.

As we trudged across the ice I glanced over at My Thing.

She smiled at me. Teeth sparkling in the sunlight. Her ebony features so bright and gleaming that it was as if she were saying grace.

And I thought, *I don't even know her name.*

* * * *

"We're not all monsters," Eva said.

I said, "So far, you seem to be in the minority."

She sighed and lapsed into silence, contemplating the iceberg floating serenely in the otherwise empty bay. In the sunlight it shone a deep emerald green, so compelling you could stare at for hours, your mind awhirl with dreamy thoughts and images.

We sat on a large couch we had rescued from the blackened ruins of the place the Things had called home. They left in a hurry after I burned them out.

A translator rested between us. Little green lights winking when she spoke. Red lights for me. Theoretically, the sounds emanating from it perfectly imitated the tonal nuances of whoever was speaking.

To me, her voice was gentle and sweet. I don't know how mine seemed to her. At least she didn't flinch when I spoke.

She said, "What do you call yourselves? Your species, I mean. If that's the correct terminology to use for beings from another planet. Another star system."

I frowned. "Call ourselves?"

She grimaced. "Don't do that," she said. "It's scary when you make that face. Your whole forehead comes forward and your lips curl up in the opposite directions."

"What's so scary about that?" I asked.

"Well," she said, looking embarrassed, "Your teeth are really long and sharp. And your jaw juts forward like…well… I don't know… It's just scary."

She ducked her head. "I'm sorry," she said. "That's not very professional of me. My only excuse is that I'm just not used to it yet."

Then she looked up at me. "What about me? I must look scary to you sometimes. Tell me the truth. Am I ugly?"

It was probably rude of me, but I couldn't help laughing. The red lights winking like mad, trying to interpret the uninterpretable.

"One question at a time," I said.

"Answer number one, we call ourselves The People. For that's what we are—people."

She nodded, and I went on. "Answer number two: no, I don't find you ugly. Your body is well formed. Your skin a healthy black. Your features nicely proportioned. Your eyes are clear and full of intelligence. And your teeth, although rather small, are pearly white."

I paused, then added. "I'd suppose you'd be considered rather beautiful in the eyes of your own…people."

She laughed at my little joke. It was a peasant sound. The little green lights winked rhythmically. Visual music.

Then I asked a question that had troubled me since we fled together. "Why did you come with me, Eva? You could have blamed the deaths on me. After all, I was the one who killed them."

She hesitated, getting her thoughts in order. She'd probably been asking herself the same question since we'd set the entire facility ablaze and fled.

Finally, she said, "At first it was partly out of panic. Hank and Jerry were going to rape me and kill me. Just like they did Shawntelle. They planned to blame you. They boasted about it. Thought it was a big joke.

"We were the only women in the group, you know. Also we're both black. Lesser human beings in their view, and probably most of the others. Although they'd never admit it."

I almost asked how someone could be a "lesser being," but guessed that question was much too complicated a subject for the moment.

She said, "But the real reason is that I am a biologist. As a scientist I grabbed at the opportunity to study a life form from an entirely different world. To learn if Darwinian evolution is a universal phenomenon. If life develops similarly throughout the cosmos."

I chuckled. "We have a saying—'Curiosity slew the reek.'" The translator beeped. Stumped by the word. I said, "A reek is a little animal about so…" I spread my hands, trying to indicate size and looks.

She laughed and grabbed my hands, pulling them back together. "We have the same saying," she said. "'Curiosity killed the cat.'"

Then she looked at our clasped hands. It was the first time we had touched. After a moment, she gently pulled hers back.

"That's always been my problem," she said. "Curiosity. It's landed me in trouble more times than I care to admit. Curiosity is what led me to this place and my current predicament."

"I don't understand," I said.

"Jobs for female scientists are hard to come by," she said. "Doubly so for black female scientists. So when the opportunity to join this expedition arose, I jumped at it. Not just for the money, but for the chance to study the wildlife at the bottom of the Earth.

"When I got here, I immediately fell in love. I've never known a place of such beauty. The birds and animals are incredible. The way they cling to life in the most difficult and dangerous climate on the planet. It really made me appreciate what all forms of life will endure just to stay alive."

"And the land itself boggles the mind. Here in Antarctica all directions are North. And every year consists of a single day, divided into six months of summer when the sun never sets. And six months of winter when the sun never rises."

"But it was a mining expedition," I said. "It had nothing to do with science. Much less a scientific study."

"Well, Shawntelle and I didn't know that," she said heatedly. "They fooled us with pretty words about their noble intentions to save the planet. Also, there was a mixture of nationalities: American, British, Russian, German and Chinese. Making its purpose seem international. That appeared to add dignity to the effort.

"What Shawntelle and I didn't realize is that we were the only scientists among the group. The others were miners and engineers and people whose only interest is business.

"We were their façade. A carefully constructed and publicized façade to hide the fact that their intent was to violate international law.

"They were betting that their discoveries would be so enormous, so valuable, that greed would overcome complaints by anyone except the most extreme environmentalists. And everyone mocks them, anyway."

"What did you do when you found out what they were really up to?" I asked.

"We hit the roof," Eva said.

The translator went crazy at that. Lights blinking red and green. It has trouble with idioms.

Eva got it before I had to explain. She wiped the air with an open hand. As if scrubbing the words away.

"We were really, really angry," she said. "We made our views known in no uncertain terms. Art—the leader of the expedition—tried to calm us down. To 'see reason,' as he put it. He swore a percentage of the profits would go toward environmental concerns."

I snorted. "There is no way mere money could fix the damage."

"Well, we knew that," Evan said scornfully. "We refused to go along. We said we were going to report it. But when we tried to use the radio, they stopped us. Put a lock on the door of the communication center and forbid anyone but authorized personnel to enter."

"Did you try to circumvent Art?" I asked. "Find a way to communicate another way."

"We certainly did," Eva said. "Shawntelle stole a satellite phone from the supply room. She was going to report it the other day, but then she went missing. Art said she must have been lost in a white out and made a big a deal about sending out search parties. Then they… They…"

Eva fell silent. Her face pale. Eyes brimming as she remembered.

"It was horrible," she said. "Horrible. They said… They said…" She looked at me. "They said you had killed her."

"The first time I saw your friend," I said, "was when they wheeled her corpse into the room."

"That's what I figured," she said. "Shawntelle was no fool. She wouldn't have wandered from the barracks during a white out.

"Besides, some of the others warned us to shut up. They said they'd heard Art tell Hank and Jerry to talk to us. To put the fear of God into us."

The translator rebelled at that, but I had no trouble guessing the meaning.

"Hank and Jerry were Art's enforcers," Eva continued. "They were like his private cops to keep order. We all knew they were nothing but crazy thugs. That they were drunks who never bathed or did a lick of work, other than strong arm people who were foolish enough to publicly disagree with Art. They were always trying to catch Shawntelle and me alone. And made snide sexual comments and gestures when the thought no one was listening.

"Apparently, the theft of the satellite phone was discovered. There were cameras. Hidden cameras we didn't know about. We flipped a coin to see who would steal the phone. We were like little schoolgirls, giggling over being so…so…"

Eva choked up and couldn't go on. Her eyes brimmed, threatening to over flow.

I remained silent. Realizing one comforting word or touch would unleash a torrent of weeping. If she were like Kaarla, instead of thanking me, she'd feel resentful. So I waited while she gathered herself, taking deep breaths. Then she smiled her thanks at me, and continued.

"I suspect that when they went to talk to Shawntelle—on Art's orders— the situation got out of hand. Power went to their booze-addled heads and they raped and killed her. I'm sure Art knew what really happened. But he was afraid of them. You could tell. He always deferred to Hank and Jerry. No matter what they said or did, or how much they drank. So they concocted a story and blamed you."

"Murder, I might have been guilty of," I said. "But never rape. It isn't just that I'm not inclined to commit such an awful crime. But it would be a biological impossibility. How to put this… I don't have the necessary equipment."

"I realized that," Eva said. "Although I didn't know they were hunting you until just before your capture. When I saw the pictures, and learned about the strange beings that had been discovered in other parts of the globe, I knew we were talking about sentient beings from another world. And then I saw you when they brought in your unconscious body.

"Right after that Art blamed Shawntelle's murder and rape on you. I knew then he was lying. This time I didn't say a word. I was afraid the same thing would happen to me. But I'm a terrible liar. I must not have covered it up very well. Hank and Jerry started acting even weirder around me. Giving me creepy looks.

"Then, the other day… During the party…" She shook her head at the memory. "If you hadn't shown up I would have been next."

I thought about that a minute. Considered her position. I said, "I'm sure you panicked when you insisted on coming with me. Figuring that Art would get someone else to kill you. Or do it himself. It was the only way to continue the cover up."

Eva nodded. "I didn't panic," she said. "I'm not the kind to panic. But in the heat of the moment it seemed the best thing to do."

"The problem," I said, "is that now that you are here with me there may be no going back. What of your friends? Your family?"

She looked at her feet. "I have few friends. And as for family…" She shrugged. "Mine are all dead. The last of them were killed one summer in Chicago during a murder spree."

Eva's head came up, realizing what she'd said. "But that doesn't mean all of us are like that," she said. "We're not all murderers. Monsters."

I said, "My entire experience with your kind is one of murder and acts of monstrosity. The attacks on you and Shawntelle are just the latest examples. Such as the colony of flightless birds—"

"Penguins," she said. "They're called penguins."

I nodded. "Penguins… Then the bones of the giant animals dumped in that mass graveyard on the beach—"

"Whales," she said. "A shameful tragedy. And I'll admit that although most countries have banned the practice, whale hunting still goes on."

I shuddered. "I know how they hunt," I said. "They'll go to any extreme to capture and kill their prey."

Eva patted my hand. "I'm so sorry," she said. "I can't imagine how terrible it was for you."

I waved it away. I wasn't looking for sympathy. There were more important matters at stake than reliving threats to my own worthless hide.

I said, "My mission mates reported a host of similar crimes against nature. Then they were hunted down and killed without sense or reason. None of them harmed any of your kind. Or threatened to do so."

"They are afraid of you," she said. "There is nothing more dangerous on the face of the Earth than a frightened human being.

"As for the rest—your other accusations—those depredations are the fault of a greedy, deliberately ignorant few who have seized power over the rest of us."

I looked at her for a long time. Then I asked, "But who gave them that power in the first place? And who allows them to retain that power now?"

She hung her head. And in a voice so low the translator strained to deliver the words, she said, "We did."

Then her head came up and she looked me full in the face, dark eyes flashing.

Defiant.

And she said, "We did, damn it! And it's true, we keep repeating that error time and time again. Even though it is painfully obvious what is happening to our world. Air so polluted it is unhealthy to breathe. Water so poisoned that our own children are getting sick and dying. Devastating storms and fires…"

Her voice trailed off. She drew a deep breath. Then she pointed at the startling blue sky. With winter near, the sun was low on the horizon. And I could plainly see an enormous pale yellow halo directly overhead. It seemed to vibrate and I could see darkness just beyond. As if I were looking at outer space.

"That is a hole in the sky," she said. "A hole created by us. And we're leaking atmosphere like crazy. Not long ago it was starting to heal, then we resumed doing the greedy practices we had all agreed had to stop."

I nodded and settled back. "There it is, then," I said. "The answer to your own question. The crimes against nature committed by your fellow beings are monstrous.

"So they must be monsters.

She leaned forward, face desperate, eye pleading, "But don't you see, we're all so afraid."

Once again she grasped my hands. "Just like you are afraid. You told me yourself your people are on their last legs. Without Earth as your new home you are all doomed. And so you are terrified. Understandably so.

"So terrified that your leaders are seriously considering that the only answer is euthanasia. Wiping out the entire human race to save yourselves."

"And your planet," I said. "As well as all the other life forms who dwell on Earth." A great sadness settled on me. I sighed, then added, "Your kind won't be missed, you know.

"If the other life forms on this planet could applaud, the sound would be beyond deafening."

Eva squeezed my hands harder. I was surprised at the strength of such a tiny being.

She said, "If you do this, you'll become just like what you are accusing us of being.

"Monsters."

Her words struck me like a physical blow. She was right. At this moment our leaders were weighing the fate of the human race.

If we attacked there would no warning. Although we could win any war, without surprise on our side we would suffer so many losses it would unconscionable. Bring our numbers so low our very existence would be in doubt.

I said, "It's not up to me. I have no control over their decision."

"Please don't wash your hands of it," she begged. "Speak for us. And let me speak. All I ask is a chance.

"I know I'm a nobody, but at least try to convince them to hear me out. And I'll speak to others. People more important than I am. And in turn, they know even more important people."

I felt confused. Helpless. I sighed, and she released my hands.

And I thought, what was the use?

Then I recalled another time when I was confused, helpless and devoid of hope. Then an act of kindness restored that hope with a gift of clear, cold water.

I reconsidered. Thought of the many hours Eva and I had spent together. She was a remarkable woman. Kind and gentle and incredibly intelligent.

Surely, she wasn't unique. A human anomaly. Surely, there were others. Possibly many others.

Would my people listen?

I don't know.

Should they listen?

I don't know that either.

I looked out at the pristine waters of Deception Bay. As my eyes took in the shimmering emerald green iceberg, I saw a little penguin in a comic waddle to the edge. Once there it dived into the bay and literally flew through the water.

"So graceful," Evan murmured. "And beautiful. How could something that looks so funny be so beautiful?"

As I watched there was a whooshing sound, and a geyser of water shot into the sky. Painting glorious rainbows.

Then I saw the waters gently part.

An enormous gray shape surfaced.

A whale.

Magnificent and in its own way as graceful as the little flightless bird.

"Beauty comes in all sizes, does it not?" Eva said in a low voice.

As the whale glided through the water, I imagined it was observing me from through one great eye.

"She looks so wise," Eva murmured.

"Infinitely so," I replied.

"It's as if she held the secrets of everything—past, present and future," Eva said.

I felt a tingling sensation, as if the whale was trying to speak to me. I strained all my faculties trying to catch what she was saying. Then she spouted water and went under, her tail slapping the surface of the bay, as if in farewell.

Eva said, "Could you feel it?" She tapped her head. "Up here, did you feel it?"

"Yes," I said.

"I think she was trying to talk to you," Eva said.

"You mean to us," I said.

Eva shook her head. "No, to you. She was speaking to you."

"What did she say?" I asked.

"You know," Eva insisted. "You know."

I sighed. "She said, 'Welcome, brother.'"

And at that moment I knew what the future would hold.

AUTHOR'S NOTE

This story way inspired by Angus Erskine, Richard Rowlett, Peter Harrison, and Sabina and Dennis Mense who helped us appreciate the beauty of the seventh continent and the fortitude of our fellow lifeforms who dwell there during our expedition to Antarctica in the summer of 1989.

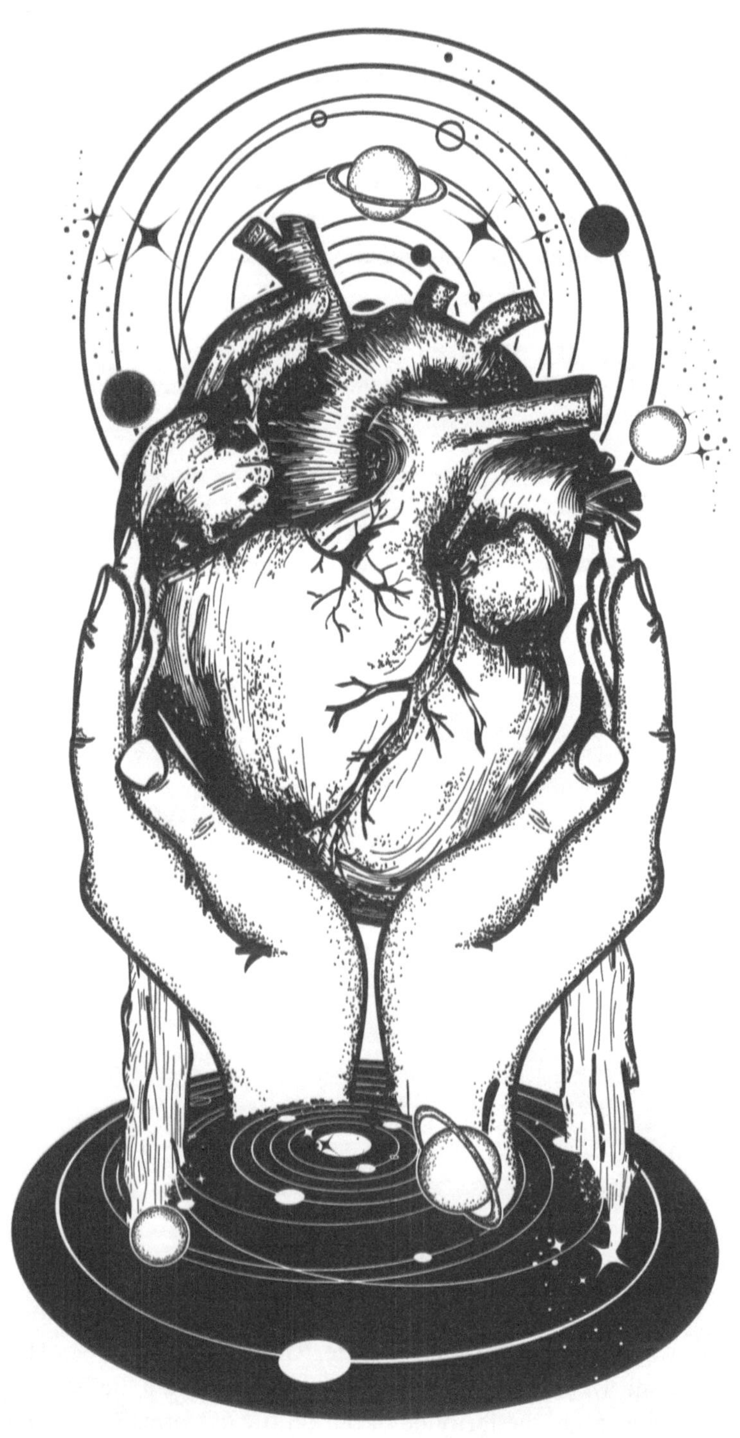

THINGMAKER

PAUL DI FILIPPO

On the late afternoon of December 7, 1941, Senator Harry Truman arrived at the secret government establishment dubbed "Thingmaker" in a discreet Nash 600 sky-sled that appeared to be a standard Washington, DC, taxicab. Behind the wheel of the floating vehicle sat a youthful fellow with dark wavy hair and a long oval face featuring an aquiline nose above full lips. Looking back over his shoulder at his passenger, the driver received a positive nod. He maneuvered the controls of the sky-sled in response, so as to cause it to sink slowly onto its undercarriage bumpers as they made contact with the pavement.

The building before which the car settled, an innocuous and shabby warehouse-type structure with its windows boarded up, stood in the shadow of the Nehi Bottling Plant at 1923 New York Avenue in the Ivy City district of the nation's capital, a zone devoted to light manufacturing, gas stations, railyards, junkyards, and other rough utilitarian structures of modern civilization. Today, a Sunday, the famous soda pop enterprise was dormant, and there was little traffic, vehicular or pedestrian. The day was sunny, and in fact a high temperature of ninety degrees had been recorded, now dwindling as the evening approached.

The driver emerged from the Nash. Out on the street, he proved to be only in his smooth-cheeked mid-adolescence, despite affectations to maturity. Although dressed informally—colorfully printed cotton sports shirt, gabardine slacks, rubber-soled tennis shoes—he still carried himself with a military alertness. Abetting this impresion was a pistol tucked into his trousers waistband at the small of his back. He keenly sized up the sparse traffic, being sure to look overhead as well, for other sky-sleds, then spoke to his passenger in a voice that bore a hint of Texas twang.

"It's all jake, Senator. Climb on out."

Harry Truman levered himself out of the curbside door. The well-known politician today wore a lightweight tweed suit. At the age of fifty-seven, his hair had noticeably thinned from its youthful richness. His trademark round wire-rimmed spectacles caught a glint from the sinking sun. Perspiration dotted his brow.

The driver had joined Truman on the sidewalk. "Where's the door?"

"Around back," said the Senator, indicating an alley between the warehouse and the adjacent building.

The driver regarded the passage suspiciously.

"I'll go first."

Truman chuckled. "One would imagine you were scouting in the ruins of Berlin, Audie."

"Yeah, well, maybe I was too young to get into that scrape. It was over before it hardly began. Had to haul myself out here to the War Office just to find some action. Then what job do they give me? Babysitting a politician. No offense, sir, but that's just how I see it."

"Your description, while unflattering, is mostly accurate."

"'Preciate your understanding, sir. Anyhow, I stalked a lot of critters back home in Farmersville, and if I didn't shoot them before they saw me, we didn't eat that night. So I always figure that it's a good thing if you can see your opponent before they can see you."

Truman seemed thoughtful when he said, "Assuming one can always recognize friend from foe."

Audie registered a bit of puzzlement at that remark, but did not follow it up. Instead, he moved to the mouth of the alley, which was well lit by the fading daylight and offered no places of concealment, save for a couple of dented galvanized trash cans behind which perhaps a Munchkin from *The Wizard of Oz* might be able to crouch. After making great show of his inspection, he beckoned Truman to follow. The pair quickly traversed the brick corridor with its assorted litter: the wrapper from a Chicken Dinner candybar; a takeout menu from the famous China Clipper restaurant; an empty bottle of Lucky Tiger hair tonic, and one of Ancient Age whiskey.

At the end of the alley a board fence, separated from the rear of the building by a few feet, allowed them to turn left. On this far side of the warehouse, they encountered the door: a rusting iron facade with a padlock and chain that seemed immovably soldered to the entrance by time.

"You sure this is the right door?" Audie asked.

Truman said nothing, but instead merely knocked in a complex pattern.

A door-sized section of the brick wall, adjacent to the fake door, pivoted outward. A Marine with a rifle awaited them. Senator Truman showed the soldier an identification card, and the visitors were allowed entrance. The wall swung silently shut behind them.

The interior of the warehouse belied its exterior, comprised entirely of modern textures under bright overhead lights—at least in this large anteroom, which featured crisp checkerboard linoleum floors, a steelcase desk, and three futuristic looking wooden Eames chairs.

Behind the desk sat a young dark-haired woman, more striking than beautiful, in the uniform of a WAC—complete with a large Webley Mk VI .455 calibre revolver in a well-oiled holster. Her somewhat haughty features failed to completely mask a warm and concerned soul. A nametag on the breast of her uniform read COL. K. SUMMERSBY. She smiled at the newcomers—a contrast to the unrelentingly stern visage of the Marine—and Audie made sure to beam back. When she spoke, she revealed British origins.

"Welcome, Senator."

"You're looking lovely, as usual, Kay. Life with Ike must be agreeing with you."

"Oh, he's a tad mardy, griping at how peaceful the world is these days. Old soldiers, you know. But he's basically a dear. Still, I shouldn't detain you with household talk. You're here to see Doctor Delbrück, I assume. He's expecting you."

"Yes. And if Doctor Luria could spare some time to accompany us as well, I'd be grateful."

"I'll see if he's available."

Using the intercom on her desk, Summersby received confirmation from both Delbrück and Luria that they would soon be present to receive the visitors. An inner door to the rest of the mysterious warehouse beckoned, but a second stern Marine kept vigil by it, not offering admittance.

After a minute or so the door swung open into the anteroom, and two men strode through. Any observer could discern by their labcoats and savant's demeanors that they were scientists of some stature.

Truman took the time to introduce his companion, producing a smile of pleasure from the boy.

"Doctor Delbrück, this is my chauffeur and all-round general factotum, Audie Murphy."

Delbrück proved to be a skinny fellow in his mid-thirties with a wry and puckish face and a wing of dark hair sloping across his forehead. His German accent layered his impeccable English.

"I'm very pleased to meet such an accomplished youngster. Call me Max."

"Aw, shucks, I ain't so much, nor so young!"

"And this is Doctor Luria."

His black hair trimmed short and adhering to a high line above his wide forehead, Luria resembled a continental movie star, such as the newcomer Rossano Brazzi. And in fact, his speech showed Mediterranean origins.

"*Ciao, ragazzo*! Any friend of the Senator's is a friend of Salvador's."

The introductions over, Truman was quick to assert the urgency and importance of his visit.

"Gentlemen, as head of the Senate Committee on Wolf-Rayet Technology, I'm here to make one final inspection tour before we render our decision on the continuation of your project."

Delbrück and Luria straightened their shoulders and looked hopeful but wary. The German scientist said, "We will show you everything again, of course, and answer any questions in full. You already have all our written reports and records."

"Your forthcomingness is admirable, professors. But I should warn you that the votes are trending against your research."

An excitable Luria responded intemperately. "*Madonna mia!* What is the problem, Senator? Are you and your comrades blind to the potential benefits of our discoveries? Have you not seen how vital and important the other technologies from the Garry Expedition has become? Why, atomic power and anti-gravity have revolutionized our world in just three short years, ever since those heroic explorers returned with the goods from the South Pole. And they allowed the Allies to put a quick end to the Axis powers, shortening a war that surely would have killed millions. But even those life-saving innovations are trivial in comparison to what we offer here!"

Truman nodded somberly to acknowledge the truth of Luria's protest. "Yes, the United States monopoly on anti-gravity and the neutron-beryllium power sphere, shared with her partners, did bring those bastards Hitler and Tojo and *il Duce* up short. Pardon the aspersions on your native lands, gents, I know where your true sympathies lie. But no matter how revolutionary, those gadgets were just that—gadgets. What you two are working on is the stuff of life itself."

"And thus its greater potential for good!"

"I don't deny that, Doctor Luria. But it's a double-edged sword. The potential for harm, should the technology ever escape your built-in restraints, is immense. You know the men of the Garry Expedition suffered great losses and barely avoided total annihilation."

An impatient and curious Audie interjected a question. "What're you talking about, Chief? I know Commander Garry lost some of his crew and all their dogs during a brutal storm in 1938. But you can't rightly associate a faraway force of nature like that with something going on right here in Washington—can you?"

The three men looked at each other significantly, and then Delbrück said, "Is the boy cleared to receive the true story?"

Truman looked fondly at the lad. "He's one hundred percent loyal to his country, and smart enough to keep his mouth shut. He's bound to hear a lot as my aide-de-camp. So I'll take responsibility for his silence."

"Very well, then." Delbrück assumed a lecture-hall mien. "*Herr* Murphy, the reality of what transpired at the South Pole is otherwise than you and the general public have been led to believe. The official story explains that the Garry Expedition uncovered an alien spaceship, and retrieved from the wreck the technologies of antigravity and atomic power, all before the ship was destroyed by a foolish misuse of a thermite heat source. This is a conflation and omission of the real events. What those men took from the crashed interstellar vessel was not any kind of technology, but rather a frozen alien corpse. Or so Doctors Blair and Copper assumed. But the corpse came alive, and proved savage and lethal, exhibiting strange abilities of mimicry derived from a destructive possession of its victims. This 'thing from another world,' if I may so call it, was just on the point of either escaping to civilization or exterminating the humans—or both—when it was finally defeated by the bravery of the men and an ingenious tactic. They eradicated all contagious traces of its body, then turned their attention to the aftermath of its secret doings, when it had been sequestered in a hut. Secretly roaming the base, it had replicated from local parts both the antigravity mechanism and the neutron-beryllium power source before it died, as well as a simulation of its native environment in an outbuilding of the camp—a simulation that revealed its preference for the light of a blue-white star. These stars are classified as Wolf-Rayet types, and so we have adopted that general term to distinguish the alien technology."

Audie absorbed the radical revelations with his quick intelligence, then asked, "Well, what's the secret third technology that's you're hiding here? The Chief said something about 'life itself.'"

Luria gave the answer to that question. "The thing was a creature composed of infinitely malleable protoplasm—what we call totipotent cells. If it managed to insinuate the smallest traces of itself into a living creature, its alien protoplasm would rapidly replicate and replace all the original material of a being, while retaining both surface and cellular appearances. To all eyeball and instrumental tests, the creature reproduced itself as a perfect duplicate of the subject. But in reality, the victim would be a scion of the alien, an heir in disguise. In a way, just as green algae can fission into daughter cells, so the thing would have reproduced itself on the coattails of its victims, while wiping out the integrity and identity of the original host."

His eyes big as saucers, Audie said, "Jeepers, it's a good thing they wiped out all traces of that monster." When the scientists said nothing, the boy's eyes narrowed. "Or did they?"

Senator Truman chimed in. "Bright boy! Yes, the Garry Expedition felt sure that they had neutralized every iota of the thing. If they hadn't been certain, they would never have risked coming home and infecting us. And upon their return, all the experts did in fact deem them clean. And they were. But the monster survived, back in the Antarctic, in a most unlikely host. What the men had not reckoned with was the presence of polar microorganisms, bacteria living just beneath the snows. Drops of blood from the slaughter of the infected dogs penetrated the snow and infected these microrganisms. The thing from another planet could do nothing in these primitive vessels, but it remained alive. It was Doctors Delbrück and Luria here—two of our most brilliant biologists—who theorized this might be so. And the next expedition to the South Pole brought back core samples that proved their theory correct."

"Are you saying that you've got living bits of this monster here in bacterial form?"

Luria smiled proudly. "Much more than that, *ragazzo*! But we waste the Senator's valuable time in talking. Let us conduct the necessary tour, so that he might return to his committee with a positive report, and save our project that offers so much possibility of alleviating mankind's ancient sufferings."

With a nod to the stony-faced Marine, the two scientists led the way through the inner door, which swung shut tightly behind them.

The party found itself in a corridor whose walls, floor and ceiling appeared to be all stainless steel, apparently formed into shape from a single plate, with but a lone double-welded seam running down the middle of the ceiling. The metal chute conveyed the sense of travelling through some industrial network of pipes.

"Nothing permeable, no means of even the smallest particle escaping," said Delbrück. "We have complete confidence in the harmlessness of our charge, but even so, we take these incredible precautions."

Ahead a massive door like that of a bank's vault intervened. It had to be unlatched by the spinning of a wheel, and was able to be dogged shut from either side.

"A kind of airlock between the subject and the outer world. There are several more."

True to the scientist's word, the group passed through additional airlocks. The final one opened onto a view of a large room that constituted the bulk of the warehouse's cubic center.

This inner sanctorum was sharply illuminated. Again, all vertical and horizontal surfaces were bright metal, as if in a lounge built for robots. Central to the room, various pipes and tubing and effectuators ran into and out of a large glass sphere, big as a cottage. The sphere in its cradle featured a platform around its equator. Banks of instruments, attended by a handful of technicians, occupied much of this platform. Various apparatuses protruded into the sphere, through tightly gasketed openings.

Several more Marines, their rifles held ready for action, were stationed around the lab.

But these details were not what would immediately draw the eye of any observer. It was the incredible contents of the sphere that commanded all rapt gazes.

Inside the glass bubble, a mass of ivory protoplasm like a gigantic tapioca or blancmange, not quite enough to fill the entire enclosed space, roiled and churned as if agitated by propellors. But no such mechanism existed: the thing twisted and seethed, bubbled and pullulated under its own quasi-muscular impulses.

The quartet of newcomers crossed the gleaming stainless steel floor to the platform that surrounded the sphere, climbing the four steps that led to the banks of instruments. The technicians looked up briefly from monitoring their gauges and dials and uttered brief greetings, before returning to their vigilance.

Having seen this alien spectacle before, Truman was not completely taken aback, although even his face registered glimmers of a requisite awe. But Audie experienced a vertiginous sense of confronting the unthinkable. Drawn to the surface of the glass sphere like a rabbit sucked into a snake's ocular orbit, he was unprepared for a sudden unexpected change in the undifferentiated convulsing mass.

The protoplasm closest to Audie's face sprouted a cluster of three malevolent red eyes and a beak-like orifice surrounded by writhing blue worms!

Audie jumped away and instinctively reached behind his back for his gun. The Marines all snapped alert, pointing their rifles at the boy. Luckily, Truman intervened swiftly, catching Audie's arm in mid-reach and repositioning it away from his weapon.

The lad wiped the spontaneous freshet of sweat from his brow and said, "Holy cats! I ain't never been so shaken by anything as I was by that! Not even coming on a nest of rattlers in my bare feet! But you don't gotta worry. I don't aim to take no potshots at that creature—so long as you got it pent up safe like that."

Delbrück and Luria actually seemed proud of their captive monster, and amused at Audie's dissipated fright. The former said, "The enclosure is indeed escape-proof. But more than that, the monster is now harmless."

"How's that? You mean it can't take over a person no more?"

"No," Luria said, "it can't. For one very good reason. We have rendered its predatory genes docile. Max and I, along with invaluable help from our peers Thomas Morgan, Edward Tatum and George Beadle, have discovered how to shut off the expression, if you will, of its virulence. Oh, it might smother you with its sheer bulk, if it fell atop you. But its former ability to conquer by ingestion and replication is banished. But its new harmlessness is far from all we have achieved. Much more to the point, we have discovered how to control and shape expression within these totipotent cells."

"I don't rightly understand."

"A demonstration will convey our achievement more clearly than words."

Delbrück turned to one of the technicians. "Joe, initiate the Leghorn Sequence, please."

Inside the glass ball, a mechanical arm, tipped with a hypodermic needle, descended from above. All eyes were drawn to the needle, and Audie noticed a hitherto-unseen feature of the spherical cage. A glass box protruded both inside and outside the sphere. The inner mouth of the box was open to the protoplasm, while the outside face of the box was sealed with a door. Another instance of an airlock.

The needle plunged into the white gelatinous blob. Instantly, as if in utter obedience, the thing budded off a piece of itself, and spat the disconnected segment into the box. An inner door slid down, capping the little chute. Luria walked to the airlock and, opening it, removed the segregated bit, about as large as a brick, with a pair of forceps.

"Joe, the torch, please."

The technician clicked alight a small propane torch and played the flame over the detached mass.

"Are you aiming to kill that piece of the critter?"

Delbrück smiled. "Not precisely. This sample is already inert."

A very familiar aroma began to permeate the room.

"Is that—is that *chicken*?"

"Good nose, *ragazzo*." Joe ceased flaming the sample, and Luria waved it in the air to cool it. "Anyone care for a taste? No? Too bad. But it is past my lunch."

Luria plucked off a piece of the alien-sourced meat and popped it into his mouth. Delbrück did the same. "We have all enjoyed several such meals, without suffering any consequences other than a full stomach. All risked only after extensive animal testing, of course. We now have much better indicators of alien possession than the primitive immunity blood tests rigged up by Doctor Copper during the Antarctica crisis. And we affirm with absolute certainty that the monster's flesh is one-hundred-percent non-invasive."

Looking humble, pleased and serious all at once, Luria added, "Senator Truman, Mister Murphy—you have just witnessed an end to human hunger and starvation on this planet. With this artificial meat, endlessly replenishable and infinitely variable, we have conquered want and privation."

"What's this here jello-mold critter feed on?"

"Anything organic. Grass clippings, seaweed, even sewage. All turned into healthy edible products."

Audie gagged a bit at that last named contribution to the thing's diet, before recovering his aplomb. "Well, I guess what goes around's gotta come around."

Luria and Delbrück focused on Senator Truman now. "Senator, don't you agree that this achievement alone is sufficient justification to continue our project?"

Truman cupped his chin mediatatively. "I know there's over two billion people on the planet, and that's a lot of mouths to feed. Not that I see the population numbers going much higher than that anytime in the next century or so. But we've got this smart fella Norman Borlaug working on the problem, and he thinks he's got it licked by conventional means. So why do we need to invest in all this far-out technology, even with minimal risk? And besides, you've got the extra barrier of convincing folks to eat this foreign stuff. Once they know they'll be chowing down on converted roadkill and dead plow horses, say, you've got a major public-relations and marketing problem on your hands."

Delbrück sighed and looked to his partner, who nodded affirmatively. "All right, Senator, we are not quite ready with this development yet, but we feel we need to bring it center-stage to convince you of how invaluable this new Wolf-Rayet technology is. Mary, please initiate the Valentine Sequence."

A female technician worked the controls that sent another needle jabbing into the protoplasm to deliver its cargo of instructive tailored enzymes and proteins and chromosonal fragments. As before, the captive thing responded by forming its totipotent cells into a specialized unit, which it deposited into the transfer chute.

Luria had donned a pair of surgeon's gloves. He reached into the glass box and removed the output of the thing.

There in the biologist's cupped latex hands quivered a human heart, tinted with the natural colors of humanity. It beat for half a minute, disgorging residual tank fluids from its arteries, before it shivered to a halt.

Audie whistled in awe. "You gents got yourselves an all-purpose thingmaker there!"

Delbrück's gaze was both dreamy and practical, even a shade messianic. "Healthy, functional, a universal match for any blood type, and nonantigenic. If we had the surgical procedures perfected for transplantation—and studies such as Carrel and Lindbergh's *The Culture of Organs* are already leading the way—and if all operating rooms were equipped with a small-scale version of this tank, organ failures would become an archaic abomination of the brutal past. New kidneys, lungs, livers—all on demand."

Luria chimed in. "Not only internal organs, but limbs as well! New arms and legs that might not even need to be surgically attached, but which might attach themselves upon command!"

Truman at first was speechless. But, recovering his wits, he said, "Doctor Delbrück, Doctor Luria—I am a Baptist because I think that sect gives the common man the shortest and most direct approach to God. But I'll be goddamned if I can figure out what the Good Lord would think of this unholy idea of inserting monster parts into a person. Maybe the deity would approve, maybe not. He's already allowed his creations to perform some amazing feats that would have counted as blasphemy in other eras. But I do think you've just raised more obstacles to approval of your project—and big ones—instead of removing some."

The two scientists were plainly marshalling their further arguments in favor of the revolutionary technology when a new development precluded all talk.

The boom of a huge explosion sounded from the rear of the warehouse, shaking and rattling the inner chamber. The Marines instantly responded with practiced moves, taking up defensive positions with their rifles aimed at the only entrance.

Audie leaped in front of Truman, his gun in his hand.

"Get down, Senator! This ain't no playtime!"

The scientists and technicians activated controls that dropped a heavy metallic curtain around the thingmaker tank. Then they crouched as best they could behind the control kiosks on the platform.

The wait seemed to last forever, although it was only half a minute or so, but then came a second explosion at the inner door, sending acrid smoke and flying debris into the lab.

Gunfire rattled from both sides of the engagement. Flat on the decking, Truman practically felt Audie's booming pistol in action. Again, time stretched during the battle. Then the gunfire ceased—and Audie fell atop the Senator!

A Marine approached the platform. "It's over now. Are you folks all okay?"

"No!" Truman said. "We have a man down!"

He levered Audie's body off, and kneeled to investigate.

The boy was still alive, but suffering from a large deep chest wound.

Truman heard the protective curtain rattling upward, and Delbrück shouting, "The Patch Sequence!"

Luria dropped down beside the stricken lad. Somehow he found the courage and bravado to grin at Truman. "Allow me to introduce myself. The most famous never-matriculated undergraduate of the University of Turin medical school." He began ripping away Audie's shirt.

Delbrück raced over with his hands full of protoplasm. He tossed it to Luria, who slapped it down on Audie's chest like a mustard plaster.

The totipotent cells went straight to work, integrating themselves and rebuilding the shattered bones, flesh and organs, becoming human in color, shape and texture. In almost no time at all, Audie was sitting up, a slightly dazed yet competent and cogent look on his face. He placed a hand tentatively on his breastbone, regarding the invisible repairs with quiet astonishment.

"Jeepers! Sure hope this don't mean all my kids are gonna have three red eyes and blue catfish whiskers!"

In a few moments the thingmaker had produced a half-dozen more all-purpose patches, carried in spare Erlenmeyer flasks. Thus equipped for instant first aid, the two scientists, Truman and Audie followed the Marines on a path back out to the reception area. They paused first to examine the bodies of the fallen attackers. Contrary to any expectations that the invaders might have been uniformed soldiers of a hostile nation, they appeared to be native Americans of a certain type, that class known as the "gangster" or "underworld" figure: hard-nosed mugs in flashy suits, armed with tommyguns.

Once attaining the reception area, they discovered a scene of chaos. The outer door had been blown away. The lone Marine on guard had been mercilessly cut to pieces, too far gone for even thingmaker fixes.

Across Summersby's desk sprawled another gangster, facedown, this one unarmed and dressed with more panache.

A Marine flipped the body over.

Truman exclaimed, "I know this yegg from when he testified to Congress! It's Bugsy Siegel!"

At the sound of his name, the mobster opened his eyes, took in his audience, and spoke in a grating whisper. "Truman, you bastard… Cut off my radium-atomite sales to Mussolini… Knew you had something big going on here… Figured you owed me a share…"

Siegel lapsed back into unconsciousness. Truman said, "Get him fixed up. The US government is going to want to hold this pissant responsible for all this mess."

Audie shouted from where he was squatting behind the desk. "It's Miss Summersby! She's still breathing!"

In a brief time both Summersby and Siegel were once more hale and hearty. Her trig uniform all in disarray, Summersby got to her feet, still instinctively clutching her huge Webley revolver. Siegel glared at her with traces of reluctant approbation at her courage.

"Thought the bitch was dead on the floor, but she took me out when my back was turned."

Summersby holstered her sidearm. "One does not go skeet shooting every week since age twelve for nothing, nor endure the Blitz as an ambulance driver without mustering some resilience."

The exterior phone line proved to be intact, and soon the warehouse was flooded with troops and police and high-level politicos. Everything got sorted out with speed and precision.

After Siegel had been led away and all the corpses removed, Truman turned to Luria and Delbrück.

"Professors, this is no longer a safe or secret site for your project. I suggest we get you set up in a more secluded place. We have a facility in Los Alamos, New Mexico, that we're not using for anything. I think it would be just right for Project Thingmaker."

Audie piped up. "Much as I like working with you, Chief, I might ask to be assigned to help these guys. After all, I gotta pay back my pound of flesh, don't I?"

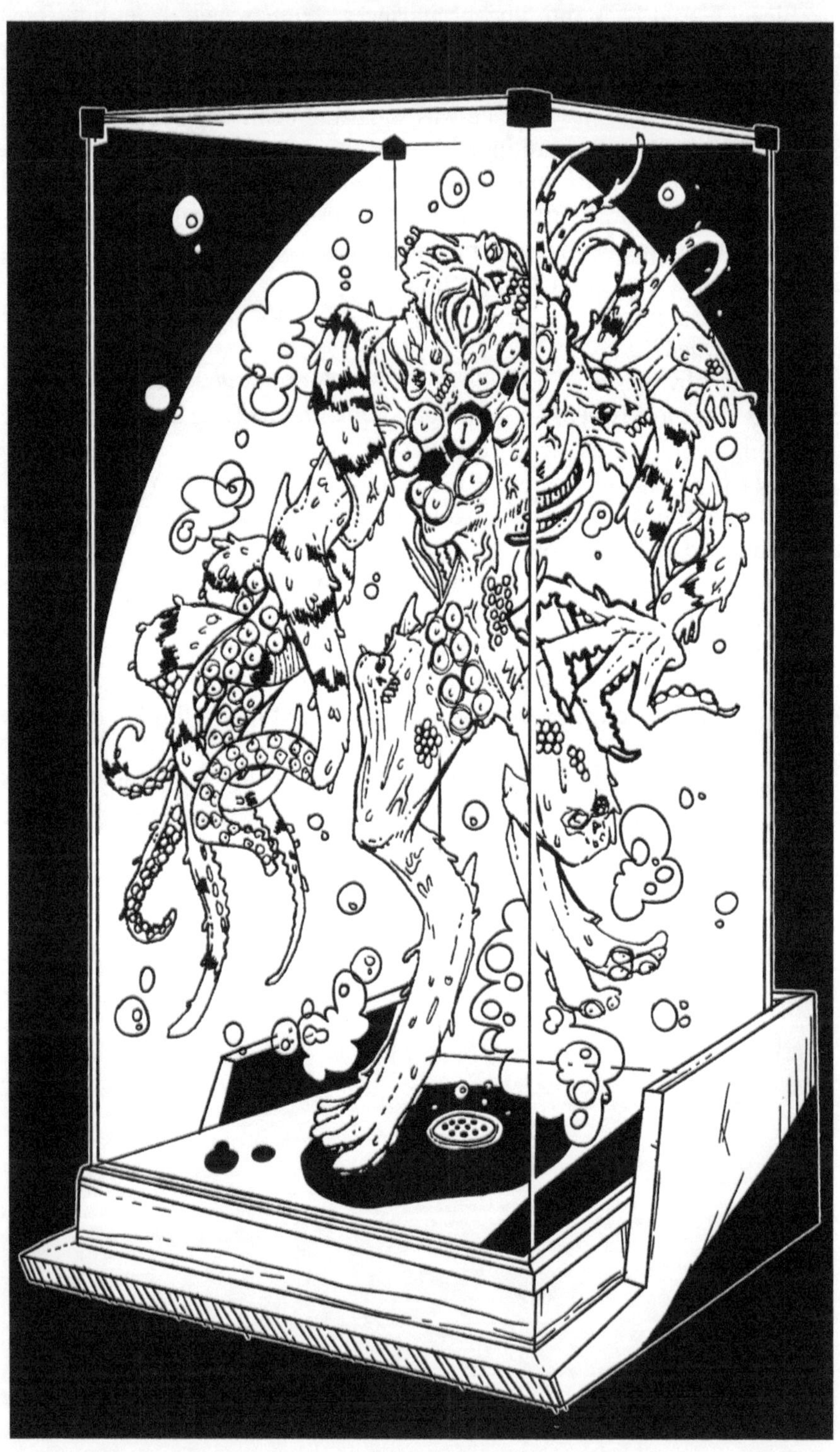

THE NATURE OF THE BEAST

JOHN GREGORY BETANCOURT

The Thing in the glass cage paced, as it had done every day for the last month, flowing from form to form as it did. Tentacles, claws, fingers—a vaguely human face giving way to bluish, sheeplike fur—shimmering scales to feathers to prickly, gray-green skin—and on to other, even stranger forms.

This process was something out of my worst nightmare, yet I could not look away. It was my job: observe and record—and try to establish contract.

I checked the camera mounted on the table before me. The red light glowed steadily; still recording. The analysts at home base, who would watch after my shift when I hand-delivered the recording on a secure thumb drive, were going to love *this* session. I'd seen bits of at least two or three creatures we hadn't catalogued before.

Then faint whispers started in the back of my mind: *Open the door. Open the door. Open the—*

I slapped the red button on the control panel in front of me, and the steel floor of the cage delivered a jolt of electric current. The Thing yelped, spasmed, flipped onto its back, and writhed. The voice in my head shut up. I released the button, and the Thing withdrew to the far corner. Sulking, no doubt. There, it grew a very human-looking eye at the end of long, multi-jointed stem. The eye stared at us, not blinking. But then, it never blinked.

"You heard that?" Paul Jarman, my assistant, asked from behind me. He had a soft step; I hadn't realized he'd come into the observation room.

"Yeah." I shuddered as the Thing's eye-stalk pulled back into its body. A dozen additional limbs sprouted along its torso. Had it settled on a new form?

"Don't like it getting into our heads," he muttered. "Ought to kill it and be done."

"You know it's too valuable," I said. But secretly I agreed with him. "We have to get through to it. Find a way to communicate. To negotiate."

He snorted. "Only way to beat them is to kill them. Can't negotiate with something that wants to eat you." He studied the Thing. "Does it know we can't open the door?"

"Would it keep asking if it did?"

"Guess not." He dropped into the office chair next to mine, spun it in a circle, then stopped facing me. He held out a large white envelope.

I took it. "New orders?"

"New orders."

The envelope had DR. IAN GRAHAM written in black sharpie on the front. I slit the red security-tape with my thumbnail, then pulled out a single sheet of paper. Department of Home Defense, today's date, and all the other usual stuff. I tracked down to the instructions. *Assessment 38. Rewards and incentives.*

"They've got to be kidding," I said, as I skimmed our instructions. "I think they want us to train it!"

"Good dogs get treats?" Jarman snorted. "How do you train *that*?"

"It's too smart for training."

"More like too stubborn." He shrugged. "Refuses to bend an inch. Why keep trying to escape? Why refuse to make any effort to communicate?"

"Too smart or too stubborn—does it matter? It's the nature of the beast. You get the same result either way."

I glanced at the Thing, which had now settled on the form of a large, brown, armor-plated lizard with twelve legs and a pointy, thick-boned skull. Interesting. I hadn't seen this one before. I glanced at the camera—red light blinking, still recording—and leaned forward. What now?

Without warning, it charged straight at us, striking the wall head-on. *Bam!* It was clearly audible through the two-inch-thick glass. The Thing staggered, then backed up and charged again. *Bam!* And again. *Bam!* And again. *Bam!*

It wouldn't get through, of course. It had to know that. And yet it still kept trying. Why? Why not learn from its mistakes?

"Can I?" Jarman's hand hovered over the electric shock button.

I sighed. "Be my guest."

His finger stabbed down. The Thing howled, spasmed, withdrew to the far corner of its cell. There it hunkered down, grew three more eye-stalks, and regarded us. Again, no eyelids. Maybe it didn't like to blink.

I reread our instructions. *Protein in exchange for verbal interaction.*

Protein? What sort of protein? It had to mean meat. Maybe…a lab rat? If so, we'd be seeing incisors and long, naked tails in its transformations from now on.

If it cooperated. Which, of course, it wouldn't.

Clearing my throat, I read the memo aloud to Jarman, who snickered. He also knew it wouldn't work. I could see that.

"Ready?" I asked.

Jarman nodded and switched off the microphones.

I leaned forward and read the script aloud: "I know you can hear and understand me. This will be easier for all of us if you cooperate. As a sign of good will, if you adopt a human form to communicate with us, we will provide you with 8 ounces of protein in a form you can digest."

Silence. The three eyes stared. No change.

I continued: "If you do not cooperate, you will be punished. Take my advice, you will be much happier if you make an effort to meet us halfway."

Nothing.

I looked at Jarman. His index finger hovered over the shock button. When I nodded, he pushed it.

The Thing began to scream.

* * * *

So it continued, day after day, week after week, in four-hour shifts. Jarman and I relieved Dr. Chang at 10 A.M., and Dr. Rodriguez relieved us at 2 P.M. I didn't know the other teams. Since the Thing never slept, it had keepers on duty 24 hours a day. We had established a monotonous pattern of question-and-punishment, as we hammered at its will around the clock. Eventually it had to break.

I always paused to compare notes with both Dr. Chang and Dr. Rodriguez as we relieved each other. Neither of them had made any progress, either. Our sessions with the Thing were not so much variations on a theme—there were no variations—as a series of elaborate tortures imposed on another sentient creature. Each carefully worded script we read to it ended the same way: in screaming and pain.

"God, I hate that thing," Jarman told me on Day 72.

"Me, too."

"Think how many there would be if we hadn't captured it? Thousands!"

"More like thousands of trillions," I said idly. I'd done the math. "That's how we know we've got them under control. Everyone on the planet would be a Thing by now if we hadn't stopped our friend here. And probably every dog, cat, bird, and fish, too."

"If it gets loose—"

"It won't."

The whispers started in my head again: *Open the door. Open the door. Open the door—*

Jarman looked at me, eyebrows raised, and I nodded.

He pushed the red button, and he kept it pushed long after the voice had stopped.

"Die already," he muttered. "Die already and be done."

Killing the Thing would have ruined both our careers. I pulled his finger from the shock button.

"Not today. Not on our shift. Stay on mission."

I watched the Thing crawl to the far corner and curl up into a ball of writhing yellow worms. Another new form. It sprouted a pair of eyeballs and trained them on us.

If looks could kill…both Jarman and the Thing would be dead.

* * * *

The questioning dragged on.
Eight weeks.
Ten weeks.
Eleven.

* * * *

On day 79, I had just finished saying, "If you adopt a human form and speak with us, we will provide you with an extra ration of water," when Jarman grabbed my arm.

"Look!" he cried.

I glanced up from the page and gasped.

The Thing was gone. A naked man now stood in the glass cage, muscular arms folded across his well developed chest. His had short black hair, mud-brown eyes, and a strong chin. He appeared perhaps twenty-five years old. I noticed a puckered white scar on his right shoulder, another long scar along his left thigh, and a third on his abdomen where his appendix would have been. He was staring straight at us.

"Can you understand me?" I asked.

When it spoke, a faint Texas twang colored its voice, distant and tinny through the speaker.

"Of course, Dr. Graham."

I swallowed hard. "You know my name. How?"

"I have been studying you."

Jarman reached out and killed the microphones. He covered his mouth, as if the Thing might be reading lips, and said, "Don't you recognize him?"

He did look familiar, but... "Should I—?"

"That's *Varnas*, the guy it killed. Looks just like him! The photo's in his file—"

"Get it."

He ran from the room. He was back in a minute with a blue file folder, which he threw down on the table in front of me. *Staff Sergeant Vitas Varnas,* it said.

"See? That's him." He poked a finger at the photograph taped to the front.

Nodding, I said, "I believe you're right."

The Thing had been captured while absorbing an off-duty sergeant in New Jersey. Our analysts had decided it wanted to infiltrate the Picatinny Arsenal in Dover, where Varnas worked. Luckily, it had been discovered by sanitation workers in a parking garage in mid absorption. They trapped it in a steel dumpster until help could be found.

I looked closely at the Thing, then down at the picture. It *was* Varnas, down to the smallest detail. No doubt the real man had those same scars. If I hadn't seen the Thing in its other forms, I would have thought it *was* Varnas. It would have fooled his wife or mother.

Varnas—rather, the Thing that looked like Varnas—stepped to the edge of its cell and opened its mouth, saying something. I couldn't hear it with the microphones off. I wasn't sure I *wanted* to hear it.

I turned my back so it couldn't read my lips. Better safe than sorry.

"Call HQ," I told Jarman. "Tell them it's talking. This is out of our hands now."

"Right."

As he scrambled from the room to let our superiors know, I swiveled around to face the Thing again and flipped on the microphones. I didn't want to speak to it, but this was my job. I took a deep breath.

"You look like Staff Sergeant Varnas," I said. "Is that what we should call you?"

It shrugged. "If you wish. Is Dr. Rodriguez there?"

I glanced at my watch. "She's not due for another ten minutes. Why?"

"You will understand when Dr. Rodgriguez arrives," it said. "I have something to say to all of you."

"We do not have the authority to negotiate. You must wait for our superiors."

"There is plenty of time for them. I am not trying to negotiate with you, Dr. Graham."

At that moment, I heard Helen Rodriguez's voice. She was speaking urgently to Jarman in the hallway. Luckily she had arrived early today.

"We did it," I said, facing her as she strolled through the door. "We made contact."

Her steel-gray hair had been pulled back in its usual tight bun, and her white lab coat was spotless. She gave a curt nod.

"Well done," she said.

Rare praise, indeed. Normally she remained cooly remote with colleagues, treating us like so many lab rats. I often gave thanks to the gods of Homeland Security that I'd been paired with Jarman instead of her.

She joined me at the control table, taking in the creature that now looked like Sergeant Varnas. Her assistant, Juan Fox, trailed in with Jarman. Everyone stared at the Thing in its new human form. You could have heard a pin drop.

The Thing smiled. It was not a pleasant expression.

"Too smart or too stubborn to be trained," it said, settling its gaze on me. "You said that was our nature. You were wrong, Dr. Graham."

This could be a breakthrough—everything we had all been waiting for. But what did it mean? The breath caught in my throat.

I felt Rodriguez's hand on my shoulder. She leaned forward, too.

Raising my chin, I looked into the Thing's eyes. "Tell me, then—what *is* your nature?"

"Patience." I caught a hint of smug, alien superiority in its tone. "Time is *our* ally, not yours. Conversion is a game of numbers."

Then an alien voice filled my head with whispers: *Sleep... Sleep... Sleep...*

Automatically, I reached for the red button to shock it. But Dr. Rodriguez's hand on my shoulder grew hard and heavy, pushing me back down in my chair. Like a warm molasses, her arm began to melt and spread across my neck and chest and mouth. I tried to jerk away, but couldn't move, couldn't breathe—

Sleep... Sleep... Sleep...

Then I realized it was Rodriguez in my mind, not the Thing in the cage. A chill went through me. I couldn't move—couldn't breathe—

Like a puppeteer playing with a marionette, Dr. Rodriguez jerked my body backwards, over the chair and to the floor with inhuman strength. My head tilted; I glimpsed ceiling tiles before she loomed over me.

Her lab coat swung open, and as I watched, powerless to stop it, her torso split down the middle. Tentacles with fish-hook barbs reached toward me. They snagged my flesh, began pulling me toward her, *into* her. There came no pain. I floated far from myself, an observer rather than a participant.

No, no, no! This couldn't happen. I couldn't allow it. I struggled through the fog, like a heavy sleeper trying to rouse mid-dream.

"Paul!" I managed to gasp. My assistant had to do something—had to get help—

With the last of my strength, I kicked, tried to twist, almost wrenched an arm free. Somehow, I turned my face away from the Thing that had been disguised as Dr. Rodriguez.

"We don't need billions," Varnas was saying from what seemed an impossible distance. "Not at first. We only need the ones in charge of the herd."

My eyesight dimmed. I couldn't fight off sleep much longer. Far, far away, as though down a long, dark tunnel, I saw my assistant standing open-mouthed by the door.

Run! I tried to scream. No words came out. *Run, Paul! Run!*

Paul Jarman didn't move. He, too, must have been paralyzed by the siren song playing in his head.

He didn't begin to scream until the Thing that looked like Juan Fox reached for him with dozens of lashing white tentacles.

www.ingramcontent.com/pod-product-compliance
Lightning Source LLC
Chambersburg PA
CBHW020737020826
48980CB00018B/632/J